Nral/cc

D0316152

RUDYARD KIPLING

The Jungle Book

The Second Jungle Book

Kim

Published in 2010 by Prion
An imprint of the Carlton Publishing Group
20 Mortimer Street
London W1T 3JW

10 9 8 7 6 5 4 3 2 1

Design © Carlton Books Limited 2010
Illustrations © Carlton Books Limited 2010

All rights reserved. This book is sold subject to the
condition that it may not be reproduced, stored in a
retrieval system or transmitted in any form or by any
means, electronic, mechanical, photocopying, recording or
otherwise without the publisher's prior consent.

A CIP catalogue record for this book is available from the
British Library.

ISBN 978 1 85375 762 4

Printed in Thailand

RUDYARD KIPLING

The Jungle Book
The Second Jungle Book

Kim

PRION

Contents

Introduction

Rudyard Kipling has, since his death in 1936, been accused of being many things. Imperialist, militarist, racist and Nazi are some of the brickbats that have been hurled in his direction, but was he any of these things?

Imperialist? Kipling was born in Bombay, now Mumbai, in India in 1865. His father, John Lockwood Kipling and mother, Alice, had moved there from England the previous year when John, an artist, sculptor and pottery designer, had become Professor of Architectural Sculpture at the Sir Jamsetjee Jeejeebhoy School of Art and Industry. By the time baby Rudyard, whose Christian name was actually Joseph (his parents gave him the middle name of Rudyard in memory of their first meeting at Rudyard Lake in Staffordshire), was a year old his father was Dean of Sir JJ's. Rudyard's sister, Alice, arrived two years later and the family lived a comfortable, rather than opulent, colonial lifestyle.

Rudyard was fascinated by the Indian folk tales recited to him and his sister by the nanny and servant who looked after them. As the years passed, he came to think and speak in what he called "the vernacular idiom" and had to make a conscious effort to talk to his parents in proper English, a common problem for children like him, who spent so much time in the company of their Indian family servants. The colonial idyll came to an end for the children when Rudyard was six and they were packed off to England to be cared for in Southsea by a couple who specialised in "fostering" children for parents who were working abroad. Rudyard detested the time he spent in Southsea; the couple who were supposed to be looking after him neglected him cruelly. His sister, perhaps because their foster parents saw her as a potential match for their own son, was not treated so harshly.

Rudyard escaped purgatory in Southsea when Alice Kipling came home from India in 1877, taking charge of her children once more. The following year he was sent to the United Services College at Westward Ho! in Devon. The college was a boarding school specialising in preparing boys for military service and Kipling's book of short stories, *Stalky & Co*, was based on his experiences there.

It was not felt that Rudyard was either right for a military career or bright enough to win a university scholarship, therefore, as there was no way that his father could pay his son's way through university, he found himself aboard ship once more, approaching seventeen years of age and bound once again for Bombay. From Bombay he travelled by train to Lahore (now in Pakistan) where his father had been appointed Principal of the Mayo College of Art and Curator of the Lahore Museum. This is the "Wonder House" described in the early pages of Kim and the "Sahib with a white beard" was John Kipling. Many of Kipling's childhood memories, from the Zam-Zammah cannon that stood on display opposite the museum to the range of colourful characters Kim encounters, are brought together as Kim's story unfolds.

Kipling travelled widely throughout India while working for the Civil and Military Gazette in Lahore and later The Pioneer newspaper in Allahabad. He saw a great deal of the way the British Empire worked both in India and during subsequent travels in South Africa. In his upbringing, his education and his early working life –through all of his formative years – Kipling was a product of the Empire and, while he had grave reservations about the way the British imposed themselves on other nations, he was undoubtedly in favour of the Empire. An English patriot, Kipling was president of the Royal Society of St George, an organisation devoted to maintaining English values and traditions. In a speech to the Society in 1920, Kipling applauded how the British abroad could "establish and maintain reasonable security and peace among simple folk in very many parts of the world".

Militarist? Kipling did not come from a military background. He was the son of an artist, his father creating illustrations for several of Kipling's books; both of his grandfathers were Methodist ministers. Yet his life in India and his school in Devon, which produced a number of generals and admirals, showed him how the bonds of governance and commerce that held the Empire together were underpinned by Britain's military might. As a journalist, Kipling often wrote about military matters. When he left India he travelled home to England via Singapore, Hong Kong and Japan to San Francisco. He then journeyed all over America, writing articles to entertain the readers of The Pioneer, poking fun at American society, including their army and embryonic navy. In 1898 Kipling's reports of his experiences aboard ship on manoeuvres with the Royal Navy's Channel Squadron were published, praising the expertise and professionalism of the British seamen in the face of expanding German naval power.

In his fiction, too, he paid tribute to the gallantry of military men. Kipling maintained that his 1896 poem If, voted Britain's favourite poem in a BBC radio poll in 1995, was inspired by the exploits of Dr Leander Starr Jameson, who led a British raiding force against the Boers in South Africa in 1895. Kipling was also a friend of Lieutenant-General Robert Baden-Powell, who established the Boy Scouts movement in 1907. With the author's blessing, Baden-Powell borrowed a number of ideas from Kipling's work. The memory game played in Kim as part of Kim's espionage training became known as "Kim's Game" and is still popular with Scouts today. The most obvious influence Kipling had on Scouting is, of course, the names used by Cub Scout Pack (formerly known as Wolf Cubs) leaders, with Akela as the head of the Pack.

The final story in The Jungle Book, "Her Majesty's Servants" also demonstrates Kipling's respect for the loyalty, dedication, discipline and dignity inherent in the structure and traditions of the military hierarchy. Yet even in "Her Majesty's Servants", where animals in a military camp talk together about their jobs in battle, Kipling has them consider "why we have to fight at all", with the only answer being "Because we are told to." If this was intended as a question about the need for war, the need for young men (and animals) to die, it did not stop Kipling using his influence to help his son, Jack, gain a commission in the Irish Guards during the First World War. Sadly, Jack was killed at the Battle of Loos in 1915. Initially posted as missing, it was some time before Jack's death was confirmed. Kipling wrote the poem, My Boy Jack about a parent waiting for news of a lost son. He also wrote a regimental history of the Irish Guards and became involved with the War Graves Commission. His short story The Gardener is about a woman paying a visit to one of the cemeteries kept by the Commission. Militarist? For Kipling that went hand in hand with his patriotic support of the Empire, but it became a heavy burden.

Racist? Surely a man who had travelled the whole world and seen the deprivation suffered by the poorest of the poor; a man who had witnessed the worst excesses of colonialism and understood the barriers of class, creed and race that divide society, could not be deemed racist? Unfortunately, the figures of influence in the Victorian age were not as sensitive to what constitutes racism as we are today. Kipling was a friend of Sherlock Holmes' creator Arthur Conan Doyle, who also wrote The Lost World. In that novel Conan Doyle described one character as "a negro named Zambo, who is a black Hercules, as willing as any horse and about as intelligent". Were Conan Doyle writing today, hopefully he would be more prudent in his use of language. The same could certainly be said of Kipling. In one of the articles he wrote while travelling in the United States, Kipling begged his readers to "Now, let me draw breath and curse the negro waiter, and through him the negro in service generally… as complete a heavy-footed, uncomprehending, bungle-fisted fool as any mem-sahib in the East ever took into her establishment." That and subsequent comments in the same article were, by today's standards – by any standards – undeniably racist.

Yet Kipling had a deep understanding and respect for the religions and traditions of the native population in India. In Kim, the eponymous hero disguises himself as an Indian boy to travel the country, encountering characters from all walks of life. Some of these may be regarded as racial stereotypes but Kipling certainly demonstrates a profound knowledge of the beliefs and customs of the ordinary people. While he believed in what he saw as the benefits the British Empire had brought to India, he did not believe that the British should try to impose "… a code of ethics foreign to the climate and instincts of those races whose most cherished customs they outrage and whose gods they insult". That displays a sensitivity which would surely be absent from the character of a man who was intrinsically racist, but the evidence in his other writings remains. Kipling intended his American travelogues to be light-hearted fun and probably did not plan an intentionally racist diatribe, but flippant remarks are no less racist for their lack of forethought. Just as his support for the Empire and the military stemmed from the way he was influenced by the general attitudes of the period in which he lived, so too were the words he used and sentiments he expressed.

Nazi? While there is justification for the other charges laid against him, no one could seriously believe that Kipling was a Nazi. The main basis for the accusation was the fact that the covers of his books had been decorated with a swastika symbol, but the use of the motif had no connection with the Nazi movement.

The swastika is an ancient eastern symbol used for many thousands of years in India where a number of different religions, including Hinduism and Buddhism, adopted it as a kind of talisman. The word swastika comes from the translated Sanskrit word svastika, generally taken to mean "well being" or "good luck". Use of the swastika was not confined to the far east but, perhaps because it is merely an extension of a simple cross or because the shape can occur either by chance or design when tiles are being laid or in basket weaving, its use was widespread throughout the Nordic countries and Europe more than 2,000 years before the rise of Hitler's Nazis. As a heraldic symbol it is sometimes also known as a fylfot. The swastika is still used by religious orders around the world, but in Europe its association with the Nazis has tainted it forever.

In the twentieth century, prior to the appearance of the Nazis in the 1920s, the swastika emblem was still in common usage. Kipling's friend, Baden-Powell, even incorporated the swastika on a merit award for his Boy Scouts. The badge design was changed in 1935 when it became clear that the swastika had developed into a Nazi icon. Kipling had insisted some years before that new printings of his books should not carry the emblem. He was appalled by the emergence of the Nazis as a potent power in Europe. In May 1935, less than a year before his death, Kipling delivered a speech to the Royal Society of St George about the threat posed by the rise of the Nazi regime. Kipling's patriotism and the fact that he had lost his son in a previous conflict with Germany ensured that he could never in any way condone the Nazi warmongers.

The absurd Nazi slur is easy to dismiss, but the other criticisms levelled at Kipling can be only weakly defended against with the assertion that his attitudes were entirely in tune with most of his peers. Had he lived in a more enlightened age, Kipling would have cast an entirely different shadow and his critics would have had to concentrate on his work rather than his character traits. There, they would have had a tougher job. A master story-teller and inspirational poet, the youngest ever winner of the Nobel Prize in Literature and the first writer working in the English language to be so honoured, Kipling's most famous creations – The Jungle Book stories – are known the world over, not least because of the timeless Disney animated movie adaptation. Kim, the story of a young boy being nurtured as a government agent while travelling India on a religious quest, is seen by many as Kipling's masterpiece. It is reproduced in full in this volume, along with both Jungle Books, to be read and enjoyed just as Kipling intended.

The Jungle Books

Contents

Preface to Book I

The demands made by a work of this nature upon the generosity of specialists are very numerous, and the Editor would be wanting in all title to the generous treatment he has received were he not willing to make the fullest possible acknowledgment of his indebtedness.

His thanks are due in the first place to the scholarly and accomplished Bahadur Shah, baggage elephant 174 on the Indian Register, who, with his amiable sister Pudmini, most courteously supplied the history of "Toomai of the Elephants" and much of the information contained in "Servants of the Queen." The adventures of Mowgli were collected at various times and in various places from a multitude of informants, most of whom desire to preserve the strictest anonymity. Yet, at this distance, the Editor feels at liberty to thank a Hindu gentleman of the old rock, an esteemed resident of the upper slopes of Jakko, for his convincing if somewhat caustic estimate of the national characteristics of his caste – the Presbytes. Sahi, a savant of infinite research and industry, a member of the recently disbanded Seeonee Pack, and an artist well known at most of the local fairs of Southern India, where his muzzled dance with his master attracts the youth, beauty, and culture of many villages, has contributed most valuable data on people, manners, and customs. These have been freely drawn upon, in the stories of "Tiger-Tiger!", "Kaa's Hunting," and "Mowgli's Brothers". For the outlines of "Rikki-tikki-tavi" the Editor stands indebted to one of the leading herpetologists of Upper India, a fearless and independent investigator who, resolving "not to live but know," lately sacrificed his life through overapplication to the study of our Eastern Thanatophidia. A happy accident of travel enabled the Editor, when a passenger on the *Empress of India*, to be of some slight assistance to a fellow-voyager. How richly his poor services were repaid, readers of "The White Seal" may judge for themselves.

Book I

Mowgli's Brothers

Now Chil the Kite brings home the night
That Mang the Bat sets free –
The herds are shut in byre and hut
For loosed till dawn are we.
This is the hour of pride and power,
Talon and tush and claw.
Oh, hear the call! – Good hunting all
That keep the Jungle Law!

Night-Song in the Jungle

It was seven o'clock of a very warm evening in the Seeonee Hills when Father Wolf woke up from his day's rest, scratched himself, yawned, and spread out his paws one after the other to get rid of the sleepy feeling in their tips. Mother Wolf lay with her big grey nose dropped across her four tumbling, squealing cubs, and the moon shone into the mouth of the cave where they all lived. *"Augrh!"* said Father Wolf, "it is time to hunt again." And he was going to spring down hill when a little shadow with a bushy tail crossed the threshold and whined: "Good luck go with you, O Chief of the Wolves; and good luck and strong white teeth go with the noble children, that they may never forget the hungry in this world."

It was the jackal – Tabaqui the Dish-licker – and the wolves of India despise Tabaqui because he runs about making mischief, and telling tales, and eating rags and pieces of leather from the village rubbish-heaps. But they are afraid of him too, because Tabaqui, more than any one else in the jungle, is apt to go mad, and then he forgets that he was

19

ever afraid of any one, and runs through the forest biting everything in his way. Even the tiger runs and hides when little Tabaqui goes mad, for madness is the most disgraceful thing that can overtake a wild creature. We call it hydrophobia, but they call it *dewanee* – the madness – and run."

"Enter, then, and look," said Father Wolf, stiffly, "but there is no food here."

"For a wolf, no," said Tabaqui, "but for so mean a person as myself a dry bone is a good feast. Who are we, the *Gidur-log* [the Jackal-People], to pick and choose?" He scuttled to the back of the cave, where he found the bone of a buck with some meat on it, and sat cracking the end merrily.

"All thanks for this good meal," he said, licking his lips. "How beautiful are the noble children! How large are their eyes! And so young too! Indeed, indeed, I might have remembered that the children of kings are men from the beginning."

Now, Tabaqui knew as well as any one else that there is nothing so unlucky as to compliment children to their faces; and it pleased him to see Mother and Father Wolf look uncomfortable.

Tabaqui sat still, rejoicing in the mischief that he had made, and then he said spitefully:

"Shere Khan, the Big One, has shifted his hunting-grounds. He will hunt among these hills for the next moon, so he has told me."

Shere Khan was the tiger who lived near the Wainganga River, twenty miles away.

"He has no right!" Father Wolf began angrily. "By the Law of the Jungle he has no right to change his quarters without due warning. He will frighten every head of game within ten miles, and I – I have to kill for two, these days."

"His mother did not call him Lungri [the Lame One] for nothing," said Mother Wolf, quietly. "He has been lame in one foot from his birth. That is why he has only killed cattle. Now the villagers of the Wainganga are angry with him, and he has come here to make *our* villagers angry. They will scour the jungle for him when he is far away, and we and our children must run when the grass is set alight Indeed, we are very grateful to Shere Khan!"

"Shall I tell him of your gratitude?" said Tabaqui.

"Out!" snapped Father Wolf. "Out and hunt with thy master. Thou hast done harm enough for one night."

"I go," said Tabaqui, quietly. "Ye can hear Shere Khan below in the thickets. I might have saved myself the message."

Father Wolf listened, and below in the valley that ran down to a little river, he heard the dry, angry, snarly, singsong whine of a tiger who has caught nothing and does not care if all the jungle knows it.

"The fool!" said Father Wolf. "To begin a night's work with that noise! Does he think that our buck are like his fat Wainganga bullocks?"

"*Hsh*. It is neither bullock nor buck he hunts tonight," said Mother Wolf. "It is Man." The whine had changed to a sort of humming purr that seemed to come from every quarter of the compass. It was the noise that bewilders woodcutters and gipsies sleeping in the open, and makes them run sometimes into the very mouth of the tiger.

"Man!" said Father Wolf, showing all his white teeth. "*Faugh!* Are there not enough beetles and frogs in the tanks that he must eat Man, and on our ground too!"

The Law of the Jungle, which never orders anything without a reason, forbids every beast to eat Man except when he is killing to show his children how to kill, and then he must hunt outside the hunting-grounds of his pack or tribe. The real reason for this is that man-killing means, sooner or later, the arrival of white men on elephants, with guns, and hundreds of brown men with gongs and rockets and torches. Then everybody in the jungle suffers. The reason the beasts give among themselves is that Man is the weakest and most defenceless of all living things, and it is unsportsmanlike to touch him. They say too – and it is true – that man-eaters become mangy, and lose their teeth.

The purr grew louder, and ended in the full-throated *"Aaarh!"* of the tiger's charge.

Then there was a howl – an untigerish howl – from Shere Khan. "He has missed," said Mother Wolf. "What is it?"

Father Wolf ran out a few paces and heard Shere Khan muttering and mumbling savagely, as he tumbled about in the scrub.

"The fool has had no more sense than to jump at a woodcutters' camp-fire, and has burned his feet," said Father Wolf, with a grunt. "Tabaqui is with him."

"Something is coming up hill," said Mother Wolf, twitching one ear. "Get ready."

The bushes rustled a little in the thicket, and Father Wolf dropped with his haunches under him, ready for his leap. Then, if you had been watching, you would have seen the most wonderful thing in the world – the wolf checked in mid-spring. He made his bound before he saw what it was he was jumping at, and then he tried to stop himself. The result was that he shot up straight into the air for four or five feet, landing almost where he left ground.

"Man!" he snapped. "A man's cub. Look!"

Directly in front of him, holding on by a low branch, stood a naked brown baby who could just walk as soft and as dimpled a little atom as ever came to a wolf's cave at night. He looked up into Father Wolfs face, and laughed.

"Is that a man's cub?" said Mother Wolf. "I have never seen one. Bring it here."

A wolf accustomed to moving his own cubs can, if necessary, mouth an egg without breaking it, and though Father Wolf's jaws closed right on the child's back, not a tooth even scratched the skin, as he laid it down among the cubs.

"How little! How naked, and – how bold!" said Mother Wolf, softly. The baby was pushing his way between the cubs to get close to the warm hide. *"Ahai!* He is taking his meal with the others. And so this is a man's cub. Now, was there ever a wolf that could boast of a man's cub among her children?"

"I have heard now and again of such a thing, but never in our pack or in my time," said Father Wolf. "He is altogether without hair, and I could kill him with a touch of my foot. But see, he looks up and is not afraid."

The moonlight was blocked out of the mouth of the cave, for Shere Khan's great square head and shoulders were thrust into the entrance. Tabaqui, behind him, was squeaking: "My lord, my lord, it went in here!"

"Shere Khan does us great honour," said Father Wolf, but his eyes were very angry. "What does Shere Khan need?"

"My quarry. A man's cub went this way," said Shere Khan. "Its parents have run off. Give it to me."

Shere Khan had jumped at a woodcutters' camp-fire, as Father Wolf had said, and was furious from the pain of his burned feet. But Father Wolf knew that the mouth of the cave was too narrow for a tiger to come in by. Even where he was, Shere Khan's shoulders and fore paws were cramped for want of room, as a man's would be if he tried to fight in a barrel.

"The wolves are a free people," said Father Wolf. "They take orders from the head of the pack, and not from any striped cattle-killer. The man's cub is ours – to kill if we choose."

"Ye choose and ye do not choose! What talk is this of choosing? By the bull that I killed, am I to stand nosing into your dog's den for my fair dues? It is I, Shere Khan, who speak!"

The tiger's roar filled the cave with thunder. Mother Wolf shook herself clear of the cubs and sprang forward, her eyes, like two green moons in the darkness, facing the blazing eyes of Shere Khan.

"And it is I, Raksha [the Demon], who answer. The man's cub is mine, Lungri – mine to me! He shall not be killed. He shall live to run with the pack and to hunt with the pack; and in the end, look you, hunter of little naked cubs – frog-eater – fish-killer – he shall hunt *thee*! Now get hence, or by the sambur that I killed (*I* eat no starved cattle), back thou goest to thy mother, burned beast of the jungle, lamer than ever thou camest into the world! Go!"

Father Wolf looked on amazed. He had almost forgotten the days when he won Mother Wolf in fair fight from five other wolves, when she ran in the pack and was not called the Demon for compliment's sake. Shere Khan might have faced Father Wolf, but he could not stand up against Mother Wolf, for he knew that where he was she had all the advantage of the ground, and would fight to the death. So he backed out of the cave-mouth growling, and when he was clear he shouted:

"Each dog barks in his own yard! We will see what the pack will say to this fostering of man-cubs. The cub is mine, and to my teeth he will come in the end, O bush-tailed thieves!"

Mother Wolf threw herself down panting among the cubs, and Father Wolf said to her gravely:

The tiger's roar filled the cave with thunder.

"Shere Khan speaks this much truth. The cub must be shown to the pack. Wilt thou still keep him, Mother?"

"Keep him!" she gasped. "He came naked, by night, alone and very hungry; yet he was not afraid! Look, he has pushed one of my babes to one side already. And that lame butcher would have killed him and would have run off to the Waingunga while the villagers here hunted through all our lairs in revenge! Keep him? Assuredly I will keep him. Lie still, little frog. O thou Mowgli – for Mowgli the Frog I will call thee – the time will come when thou wilt hunt Shere Khan as he has hunted thee."

"But what will our pack say?" said Father Wolf.

The Law of the Jungle lays down very clearly that any wolf may, when he marries, withdraw from the pack he belongs to; but as soon as his cubs are old enough to stand on their feet he must bring them to the pack council, which is generally held once a month at full moon, in order that the other wolves may identify them. After that inspection the cubs are free to run where they please, and until they have killed their first buck no excuse is accepted if a grown wolf of the pack kills one of them. The punishment is death where the murderer can be found; and if you think for a minute you will see that this must be so.

Father Wolf waited till his cubs could run a little, and then on the night of the pack meeting took them and Mowgli and Mother Wolf to the Council Rock – a hilltop covered with stones and boulders where a hundred wolves could hide. Akela, the great grey Lone Wolf, who led all the pack by strength and cunning, lay out at full length on his rock, and below him sat forty or more wolves of every size and colour, from badger-coloured veterans who could handle a buck alone, to young black three-year-olds who thought they could. The Lone Wolf had led them for a year now. He had fallen twice into a wolf-trap in his youth, and once he had been beaten and left for dead; so he knew the manners and customs of men. There was very little talking at the rock. The cubs tumbled over each other in the centre of the circle where their mothers and fathers sat, and now and again a senior wolf would go quietly up to a cub, look at him carefully, and return to his place on noiseless feet. Sometimes a mother would push her cub far out into the moonlight, to be sure that he had not been overlooked. Akela, from his rock would cry: "Ye know the Law – ye know the Law. Look well,

25

O wolves!" And the anxious mothers would take up the call: "Look – look well, O wolves!"

At last – and Mother Wolf's neck-bristles lifted as the time came – Father Wolf pushed "Mowgli the Frog," as they called him, into the centre, where he sat laughing and playing with some pebbles that glistened in the moonlight.

Akela never raised his head from his paws, but went on with the monotonous cry: "Look well!" A muffled roar came up from behind the rocks – the voice of Shere Khan crying: "The cub is mine. Give him to me. What have the Free People to do with a man's cub?" Akela never even twitched his ears. All he said was: "Look well, O wolves! What have the Free People to do with the orders of any save the Free People? Look well!"

There was a chorus of deep growls, and a young wolf in his fourth year flung back Shere Khan's question to Akela: "What have the Free People to do with a man's cub?" Now the Law of the Jungle lays down that if there is any dispute as to the right of a cub to be accepted by the pack, he must be spoken for by at least two members of the pack who are not his father and mother.

"Who speaks for this cub?" said Akela. "Among the Free People who speaks?" There was no answer, and Mother Wolf got ready for what she knew would be her last fight, if things came to fighting.

Then the only other creature who is allowed at the pack council – Baloo, the sleepy brown bear who teaches the wolf cubs the Law of the Jungle: old Baloo, who can come and go where he pleases because he eats only nuts and roots and honey – rose up on his hind quarters and grunted.

"The man's cub – the man's cub?" he said. "*I* speak for the man's cub. There is no harm in a man's cub. I have no gift of words, but I speak the truth. Let him run with the pack, and be entered with the others. I myself will teach him."

"We need yet another," said Akela. "Baloo has spoken, and he is our teacher for the young cubs. Who speaks besides Baloo?"

A black shadow dropped down into the circle. It was Bagheera the Black Panther, inky black all over, but with the panther markings showing up in certain lights like the pattern of watered silk. Everybody knew Bagheera, and nobody cared to cross his path, for he was as cunning as Tabaqui, as bold as the wild buffalo, and as reckless as the wounded elephant. But he had a voice as soft as wild honey dripping from a tree, and a skin softer than down.

"O Akela, and ye the Free People," he purred, "I have no right in your assembly, but the Law of the Jungle says that if there is a doubt which is not a killing matter in regard to a new cub, the life of that cub may be bought at a price. And the Law does not say who may or may not pay that price. Am I right?"

"Good! Good!" said the young wolves, who are always hungry. "Listen to Bagheera. The cub can be bought for a price. It is the Law."

"Knowing that I have no right to speak here, I ask your leave."

"Speak then," cried twenty voices.

"To kill a naked cub is shame. Besides, he may make better sport for you when he is grown. Baloo has spoken in his behalf. Now to Baloo's word I will add one bull, and a fat one, newly killed, not half a mile from here, if ye will accept the man's cub according to the Law. Is it difficult?"

There was a clamour of scores of voices, saying: "What matter? He will die in the winter rains. He will scorch in the sun. What harm can a naked frog do us? Let him run with the pack. Where is the bull, Bagheera? Let him be accepted." And then came Akela's deep bay, crying: "Look well – look well, O wolves!"

Mowgli was still deeply interested in the pebbles, and he did not notice when the wolves came and looked at him one by one. At last they all went down the hill for the dead bull, and only Akela, Bagheera, Baloo, and Mowgli's own wolves were left. Shere Khan roared still in the night, for he was very angry that Mowgli had not been handed over to him.

"Aye, roar well," said Bagheera, under his whiskers, "for the time comes when this naked thing will make thee roar to another tune, or I know nothing of Man."

"It was well done," said Akela. "Men and their cubs are very wise. He may be a help in time."

"Truly, a help in time of need, for none can hope to lead the pack for ever," said Bagheera.

Akela said nothing. He was thinking of the time that comes to every leader of every pack when his strength goes from him and he gets feebler and feebler, till at last he is killed by the wolves and a new leader comes up – to be killed in his turn.

"Take him away," he said to Father Wolf, "and train him as befits one of the Free People."

And that is how Mowgli was entered into the Seeonee Wolf Pack for the price of a bull and on Baloo's good word.

Now you must be content to skip ten or eleven whole years, and only guess at all the wonderful life that Mowgli led among the wolves, because if it were written out it would fill ever so many books. He grew up with the cubs, though they, of course, were grown wolves almost before he was a child, and Father Wolf taught him his business, and the meaning of things in the jungle, till every rustle in the grass, every breath of the warm night air, every note of the owls above his head, every scratch of a bat's claws as it roosted for a while in a tree, and every splash of every little fish jumping in a pool, meant just as much to him as the work of his office means to a business man. When he was not learning he sat out in the sun and slept, and ate and went to sleep again; when he felt dirty or hot he swam in the forest pools; and when he wanted honey (Baloo told him that honey and nuts were just as pleasant to eat as raw meat) he climbed up for it, and that Bagheera showed him how to do. Bagheera would lie out on a branch and call: "Come along, Little Brother," and at first Mowgli would cling like the sloth, but afterwards he would fling himself through the branches almost as boldly as the grey ape. He took his place at the Council Rock, too, when the pack met, and there he discovered that if he stared hard at any wolf, the wolf would be forced to drop his eyes, and so he used to stare for fun. At other times he would pick the long thorns out of the pads of his friends, for wolves suffer terribly from thorns and burs in their coats. He would go down the hillside into the cultivated lands by night, and look very curiously at the villagers in their huts, but he had a mistrust of men because Bagheera showed him a square box with a drop-gate so cunningly hidden in the jungle that he nearly walked into it, and told him that it was a trap. He loved better than anything else to go with Bagheera into the dark warm heart of the forest, to sleep all through the drowsy day, and at night see how Bagheera did his killing.

Bagheera killed right and left as he felt hungry, and so did Mowgli – with one exception. As soon as he was old enough to understand things, Bagheera told him that he must never touch cattle because he had been bought into the pack at the price of a bull's life. "All the jungle is thine," said Bagheera, "and thou canst kill everything that thou art strong enough to kill; but for the sake of the bull that bought thee thou must never kill or eat any cattle young or old. That is the Law of the Jungle." Mowgli obeyed faithfully.

And he grew and grew strong as a boy must grow who does not know that he is learning any lessons, and who has nothing in the world to think of except things to eat.

Mother Wolf told him once or twice that Shere Khan was not a creature to be trusted, and that some day he must kill Shere Khan. But though a young wolf would have remembered that advice every hour, Mowgli forgot it because he was only a boy – though he would have called himself a wolf if he had been able to speak in any human tongue.

Shere Khan was always crossing his path in the jungle, for as Akela grew older and feebler the lame tiger had come to be great friends with the younger wolves of the pack, who followed him for scraps, a thing Akela would never have allowed if he had dared to push his authority to the proper bounds. Then Shere Khan would flatter them and wonder that such fine young hunters were content to be led by a dying wolf and a man's cub. "They tell me," Shere Khan would say, "that at council ye dare not look him between the eyes." And the young wolves would growl and bristle.

Bagheera, who had eyes and ears everywhere, knew something of this, and once or twice he told Mowgli in so many words that Shere Khan would kill him some day. And Mowgli would laugh and answer: "I have the pack and I have thee; and Baloo, though he is so lazy, might strike a blow or two for my sake. Why should I be afraid?"

It was one very warm day that a new notion came to Bagheera – born of something that he had heard. Perhaps Sahi the Porcupine had told him; but he said to Mowgli when they were deep in the jungle, as the boy lay with his head on Bagheera's beautiful black skin: "Little Brother, how often have I told thee that Shere Khan is thy enemy?"

"As many times as there are nuts on that palm," said Mowgli, who, naturally, could not count. "What of it? I am sleepy, Bagheera, and Shere Khan is all long tail and loud talk – like Mor the Peacock."

"But this is no time for sleeping. Baloo knows, it; I know it; the pack knows it; and even the foolish, foolish deer know. Tabaqui has told thee, too."

"Ho! Ho!" said Mowgli. "Tabaqui came to me not long ago with some rude talk that I was a naked man's cub and not fit to dig pig-nuts; but I caught Tabaqui by the tail and swung him twice against a palm-tree to teach him better manners."

"That was foolishness, for though Tabaqui is a mischief-maker, he would have told thee of something that concerned thee closely. Open those eyes, Little Brother. Shere Khan dare not kill thee in the jungle; but remember, Akela is very old, and soon the day comes when he cannot kill his buck, and then he will be leader no more. Many of the wolves that looked thee over when thou wast brought to the council first are old too, and the young wolves believe, as Shere Khan has taught them, that a man-cub has no place with the pack. In a little time thou wilt be a man."

"And what is a man that he should not run with his brothers?" said Mowgli. "I was born in the jungle. I have obeyed the Law of the Jungle, and there is no wolf of ours from whose paws I have not pulled a thorn. Surely they are my brothers!"

Bagheera stretched himself at full length and half shut his eyes. "Little Brother," said he, "feel under my jaw."

Mowgli put up his strong brown hand, and just under Bagheera's silky chin, where the giant rolling muscles were all hid by the glossy hair, he came upon a little bald spot.

"There is no one in the jungle that knows that I, Bagheera, carry that mark – the mark of the collar. And yet, Little Brother, I was born among men, and it was among men that my mother died – in the cages of the king's palace at Oodeypore. It was because of this that I paid the price for thee at the council when thou wast a little naked cub. Yes, I too was born among men. I had never seen the jungle. They fed me behind bars from an iron pan till one night I felt that I was Bagheera – the Panther – and no man's plaything, and I broke the silly lock with one blow of my paw and came away. And because I had learned the ways of men, I became more terrible in the jungle than Shere Khan. Is it not so?"

"Yes," said Mowgli, "all the jungle fears Bagheera – all except Mowgli."

"Oh, *thou* art a man's cub," said the black panther, very tenderly, "and even as I returned to my jungle, so thou must go back to men at last – to the men who are thy brothers – if thou art not killed in the council."

"But why – but why should any wish to kill me?" said Mowgli.

"Look at me," said Bagheera, and Mowgli looked at him steadily between the eyes. The big panther turned his head away in half a minute.

"*That* is why," he said, shifting his paw on the leaves. "Not even I can look thee between the eyes, and I was born among men, and I love thee, Little Brother. The others they hate thee because their eyes cannot meet thine; because thou art wise; because thou hast pulled out thorns from their feet – because thou art a man."

"I did not know these things," said Mowgli, sullenly, and he frowned under his heavy black eyebrows.

"What is the Law of the Jungle? Strike first and then give tongue. By thy very carelessness they know that thou art a man. But be wise. It is in my heart that when Akela misses his next kill – and at each hunt it costs him more to pin the buck – the pack will turn against him and against thee. They will hold a jungle council at the rock, and then – and then – I have it!" said Bagheera, leaping up. "Go thou down quickly to the men's huts in the valley, and take some of the Red Flower which they grow there, so that when the time comes thou mayest have even a stronger friend than I or Baloo or those of the pack that love thee. Get the Red Flower."

By Red Flower Bagheera meant fire, only no creature in the jungle will call fire by its proper name. Every beast lives in deadly fear of it, and invents a hundred ways of describing it.

"The Red Flower?" said Mowgli. "That grows outside their huts in the twilight. I will get some."

"There speaks the man's cub," said Bagheera, proudly. "Remember that it grows in little pots. Get one swiftly, and keep it by thee for time of need."

"Good!" said Mowgli. "I go. But art thou sure, O my Bagheera" – he

slipped his arm round the splendid neck, and looked deep into the big eyes
– "art thou sure that all this is Shere Khan's doing?"

"By the broken lock that freed me, I am sure, Little Brother."

"Then, by the bull that bought me, I will pay Shere Khan full tale for
this, and it may be a little over," said Mowgli, and he bounded away.

"That is a man. That is all a man," said Bagheera to himself, lying down
again. "Oh, Shere Khan, never was a blacker hunting than that frog-hunt
of thine ten years-ago!"

Mowgli was far and far through the forest, running hard, and his heart
was hot in him. He came to the cave as the evening mist rose, and drew
breath, and looked down the valley. The cubs were out, but Mother Wolf,
at the back of the cave, knew by his breathing that something was troubling
her frog.

"What is it, Son?" she said.

"Some bat's chatter of Shere Khan," he called back. "I hunt among the
ploughed fields tonight." And he plunged downward through the bushes,
to the stream at the bottom of the valley. There he checked, for he heard
the yell of the pack hunting, heard the bellow of a hunted sambur, and the
snort as the buck turned at bay. Then there were wicked, bitter howls from
the young wolves: "Akela! Akela! Let the Lone Wolf show his strength.
Room for the leader of the pack! Spring, Akela!"

The Lone Wolf must have sprung and missed his hold, for Mowgli heard
the snap of his teeth and then a yelp as the sambur knocked him over with
his fore foot.

He did not wait for anything more, but dashed on; and the yells grew
fainter behind him as he ran into the crop-lands where the villagers lived.

"Bagheera spoke truth," he panted, as he nestled down in some cattle-
fodder by the window of a hut. "Tomorrow is one day both for Akela and
for me."

Then he pressed his face close to the window and watched the fire on
the hearth. He saw the husbandman's wife get up and feed it in the night
with black lumps; and when the morning came and the mists were all white
and cold, he saw the man's child pick up a wicker pot plastered inside with
earth, fill it with lumps of red-hot charcoal, put it under his blanket, and
go out to tend the cows in the byre.

"Is that all?" said Mowgli. "If a cub can do it, there is nothing to fear." So he strode round the corner and met the boy, took the pot from his hand, and disappeared into the mist while the boy howled with fear.

"They are very like me," said Mowgli, blowing into the pot, as he had seen the woman do. "This thing will die if I do not give it things to eat." And he dropped twigs and dried bark on the red stuff. Half-way up the hill he met Bagheera with the morning dew shining like moonstones on his coat.

"Aleka has missed," said the panther. "They would have killed him last night, but they needed thee also. They were looking for thee on the hill."

"I was among the ploughed lands. I am ready. See!" Mowgli held up the fire-pot

"Good! Now, I have seen men thrust a dry branch into that stuff, and presently the Red Flower blossomed at the end of it. Art thou not afraid?"

"No. Why should I fear? I remember now – if it is not a dream – how, before I was a wolf, I lay beside the Red Flower, and it was warm and pleasant."

All that day Mowgli sat in the cave tending his fire-pot and dipping dry branches into it to see how they looked. He found a branch that satisfied him, and in the evening when Tabaqui came to the cave and told him rudely enough that he was wanted at the Council Rock, he laughed till Tabaqui ran away. Then Mowgli went to the council, still laughing.

Akela the Lone Wolf lay by the side of his rock as a sign that the leadership of the pack was open, and Shere Khan with his following of scrap-fed wolves walked to and fro openly being flattered. Bagheera lay close to Mowgli, and the fire-pot was between Mowgli's knees. When they were all gathered together, Shere Khan began to speak – a thing he would never have dared to do when Akela was in his prime.

"He has no right," whispered Bagheera. "Say so. He is a dog's son. He will be frightened."

Mowgli sprang to his feet. "Free People," he cried, "does Shere Khan lead the pack? What has a tiger to do with our leadership?"

"Seeing that the leadership is yet open, and being asked to speak – " Shere Khan began.

"By whom?" said Mowgli. "Are we *all* jackals, to fawn on this cattle-butcher? The leadership of the pack is with the pack alone."

There were yells of "Silence, thou man's cub!" "Let him speak. He has kept our Law." And at last the seniors of the pack thundered: "Let the Dead Wolf speak." When a leader of the pack has missed his kill, he is called the Dead Wolf as long as he lives, which is not long.

Akela raised his old head wearily:

"Free People, and ye too, jackals of Shere Khan, for twelve seasons I have led ye to and from the kill, and in all that time not one has been trapped or maimed. Now I have missed my kill. Ye know how that plot was made. Ye know how ye brought me up to an untried buck to make my weakness known. It was cleverly done. Your right is to kill me here on the Council Rock, now. Therefore, I ask, who comes to make an end of the Lone Wolf? For it is my right, by the Law of the Jungle, that ye come one by one."

There was a long hush, for no single wolf cared to fight Akela to the death. Then Shere Khan roared: *"Bah!* What have we to do with this toothless fool? He is doomed to die! It is the man-cub who has lived too long. Free People, he was my meat from the first. Give him to me. I am weary of this man-wolf folly. He has troubled the jungle for ten seasons. Give me the man-cub, or I will hunt here always, and not give you one bone. He is a man, a man's child, and from the marrow of my bones I hate him!"

Then more than half the pack yelled: "A man! A man! What has a man to do with us? Let him go to his own place."

"And turn all the people of the villages against us?" clamoured Shere Khan. "No! Give him to me. He is a man, and none of us can look him between the eyes."

Akela lifted his head again, and said: "He has eaten our food. He has slept with us. He has driven game for us. He has broken no word of the Law of the Jungle."

"Also, I paid for him with a bull when he was accepted. The worth of a bull is little, but Bagheera's honour is something that he will perhaps fight for," said Bagheera, in his gentlest voice.

"A bull paid ten years ago!" the pack snarled. "What do we care for bones ten years old?"

"Or for a pledge?" said Bagheera, his white teeth bared under his lip. "Well are ye called the Free People!"

"No man's cub can run with the people of the jungle," howled Shere Khan. "Give him to me!"

"He is our brother in all but blood," Akela went on, "and ye would kill him here! In truth, I have lived too long. Some of ye are eaters of cattle, and of others I have heard that, under Shere Khan's teaching, ye go by dark night and snatch children from the villager's doorstep. Therefore I know ye to be cowards, and it is to cowards I speak. It is certain that I must die, and my life is of no worth, or I would offer that in the man-cub's place. But for the sake of the honour of the pack – a little matter that by being without a leader ye have forgotten – I promise that if ye let the man-cub go to his own place, I will not, when my time comes to die, bare one tooth against ye. I will die without fighting. That will at least save the pack three lives. More I cannot do; but if ye will, I can save ye the shame that comes of killing a brother against whom there is no fault – a brother spoken for and bought into the pack according to the Law of the Jungle."

"He is a man – a man – a man!" snarled the pack. And most of the wolves began to gather round Shere Khan, whose tail was beginning to switch.

"Now the business is in thy hands," said Bagheera to Mowgli. "*We* can do no more except fight."

Mowgli stood upright, the fire-pot in his hands. Then he stretched out his arms, and yawned in the face of the council. But he was furious with rage and sorrow, for, wolf-like, the wolves had never told him how they hated him. "Listen you!" he cried. "There is no need for this dog's jabber. Ye have told me so often tonight that I am a man (and indeed I would have been a wolf with you to my life's end), that I feel your words are true. So I do not call ye my brothers any more, but *sag* [dogs], as a man should. What ye will do, and what ye will not do, is not yours to say. That matter is with *me*. And that we may see the matter more plainly, I, the man, have brought here a little of the Red Flower which ye, dogs, fear."

He flung the fire-pot on the ground, and some of the red coals lit a tuft of dried moss that flared up, as all the council drew back in terror before the leaping flames.

Shere Khan's ears lay flat back on his head … for the blazing branch was very near.

Mowgli thrust his dead branch into the fire till the twigs lit and crackled, and whirled it above his head among the cowering wolves.

"Thou art the master," said Bagheera, in an undertone. "Save Akela from the death. He was ever thy friend."

Akela, the grim old wolf who had never asked for mercy in his life, gave one piteous look at Mowgli as the boy stood all naked, his long black hair tossing over his shoulders in the light of the blazing branch that made the shadows jump and quiver.

"Good!" said Mowgli, staring round slowly. "I see that ye are dogs. I go from you to my own people – if they be my own people. The jungle is shut to me, and I must forget your talk and your companionship; but I will be more merciful than ye are. Because I was all but your brother in blood, I promise that when I am a man among men I will not betray ye to men as ye have betrayed me." He kicked the fire with his foot, and the sparks flew up. "There shall be no war between any of us in the pack. But here is a debt to pay before I go." He strode forward to where Shere Khan sat blinking stupidly at the flames, and caught him by the tuft on his chin. Bagheera followed in case of accidents. "Up, dog!" Mowgli cried. "Up, when a man speaks, or I will set that coat ablaze!"

Shere Khan's ears lay flat back on his head, and he shut his eyes, for the blazing branch was very near.

"This cattle-killer said he would kill me in the council because he had not killed me when I was a cub. Thus and thus, then, do we beat dogs when we are men. Stir a whisker, Lungri, and I ram the Red Flower down thy gullet!" He beat Shere Khan over the head with the branch, and the tiger whimpered and whined in an agony of fear.

"Pah! Singed jungle-cat – go now! But remember when next I come to the Council Rock, as a man should come, it will be with Shere Khan's hide on my head. For the rest, Akela goes free to live as he pleases. Ye will *not* kill him, because that is not my will. Nor do I think that ye will sit here any longer, lolling out your tongues as though ye were somebodies, instead of dogs whom I drive out – thus! Go!" The fire was burning furiously at the end of the branch, and Mowgli struck right and left round the circle, and the wolves ran howling with the sparks burning their fur. At last there were only Akela, Bagheera, and perhaps ten wolves that had taken

Mowgli's part. Then something began to hurt Mowgli inside him, as he had never been hurt in his life before, and he caught his breath and sobbed, and the tears ran down his face.

"What is it? What is it?" he said. "I do not wish to leave the jungle, and I do not know what this is. Am I dying, Bagheera?"

"No, Little Brother. That is only tears such as men use," said Bagheera. "Now I know thou art a man, and a man's cub no longer. The jungle is shut indeed to thee henceforward. Let them fall, Mowgli. They are only tears." So Mowgli sat and cried as though his heart would break; and he had never cried in all his life before.

"Now," he said, "I will go to men. But first I must say farewell to my mother." And he went to the cave where she lived with Father Wolf, and he cried on her coat, while the four cubs howled miserably.

"Ye will not forget me?" said Mowgli.

"Never while we can follow a trail," said the cubs. "Come to the foot of the hill when thou art a man, and we will talk to thee; and we will come into the croplands to play with thee by night."

"Come soon!" said Father Wolf. "Oh, wise little frog, come again soon, for we be old, thy mother and I."

"Come soon," said Mother Wolf, "little naked son of mine, for, listen, child of man, I loved thee more than ever I loved my cubs."

"I will surely come," said Mowgli, "and when I come it will be to lay out Shere Khan's hide upon the Council Rock. Do not forget me! Tell them in the jungle never to forget me!"

The dawn was beginning to break when Mowgli went down the hillside alone, to meet those mysterious things that are called men.

Hunting-Song of the Seeone Pack

As the dawn was breaking the sambur belled
    Once twice, and again!
And a doe leaped up and a doe leaped up
From the pond in the wood where the wild deer sup.
This I, scouting alone, beheld
    Once, twice, and again!

As the dawn was breaking the sambur belled
    Once, twice, and again!
And a wolf stole back and a wolf stole back
To carry the word to the waiting pack,
And we sought and we found and we bayed on his track.
    Once, twice, and again!

As the dawn was breaking the wolf pack yelled
    Once, twice, and again!
Feet in the jungle that leave no mark!
Eyes that can see in the dark – the dark!
Tongue – give tongue to it! Hark! O hark!
    Once, twice, and again!

Kaa's Hunting

His spots are the joy of the leopard: his horns are the buffalo's pride.
Be clean, for the strength of the hunter is known by the gloss of his hide.
If ye find that the bullock can toss you, or the heavy-browed sambur
    can gore,
Ye need not stop work to inform us: we knew it ten seasons before.
Oppress not the cubs of the stranger, but hail them as Sister and Brother,
For though they are little and fubsy, it may be the bear is their mother.
"There is none like to me!" says the cub in the pride of his earliest kill;
But the jungle is large and the cub he is small. Let him think and be still.
Maxims of Baloo

All that is told here happened some time before Mowgli was turned out of the Seeonee Wolf Pack, or revenged himself on Shere Khan the Tiger. It was in the days when Baloo was teaching him the Law of the Jungle. The big, serious, old brown bear was delighted to have so quick a pupil, for the young wolves will only learn as much of the Law of the Jungle as applies to their own pack and tribe, and run away as soon as they can repeat the Hunting-Verse: "Feet that make no noise; eyes that can see in the dark; ears that can hear the winds in their lairs, and sharp white teeth, all these things are the marks of our brothers except Tabaqui the Jackal and the hyena whom we hate." But Mowgli, as a man-cub, had to learn a great deal more than this. Sometimes Bagheera the Black Panther would come lounging through the jungle to see how his pet was getting on, and would purr with his head against a tree while Mowgli recited the day's lesson to Baloo. The boy could climb almost as well as he could

40

swim, and swim almost as well as he could run. So Baloo, the Teacher of the Law, taught him the Wood and Water Laws: how to tell a rotten branch from a sound one; how to speak politely to the wild bees when he came upon a hive of them fifty feet above ground; what to say to Mang the Bat when he disturbed him in the branches at mid-day; and how to warn the water-snakes in the pools before he splashed down among them. None of the Jungle-People like being disturbed, and all are very ready to fly at an intruder. Then, too, Mowgli was taught the Strangers' Hunting-Call, which must be repeated aloud till it is answered, whenever one of the Jungle-People hunts outside his own grounds. It means, translated: "Give me leave to hunt here because I am hungry"; and the answer is: "Hunt then for food, but not for pleasure."

All this will show you how much Mowgli had to learn by heart, and he grew very tired of saying the same thing over a hundred times. But, as Baloo said to Bagheera, one day when Mowgli had been cuffed and run off in a temper: "A man's cub is a man's cub, and he must learn *all* the Law of the Jungle."

"But think how small he is," said the black panther, who would have spoiled Mowgli if he had had his own way. "How can his little head carry all thy long talk?"

"Is there anything in the jungle too little to be killed? No. That is why I teach him these things, and that is why I hit him, very softly, when he forgets."

"Softly! What dost thou know of softness, old Iron-feet?" Bagheera grunted. "His face is all bruised today by thy – softness. *Ugh.*"

"Better he should be bruised from head to foot by me who loves him than that he should come to harm through ignorance," Baloo answered very earnestly. "I am now teaching him the Master Words of the jungle that shall protect him with the birds and the Snake-People, and all that hunt on four feet, except his own pack. He can now claim protection, if he will only remember the words, from all in the jungle. Is not that worth a little beating?"

"Well, look to it then that thou dost not kill the man-cub. He is no tree-trunk to sharpen thy blunt claws upon. But what are those Master Words? I am more likely to give help than to ask it" – Bagheera stretched out one paw and admired the steel-blue, ripping-chisel talons at the end of it – "still I should like to know."

"I will call Mowgli and he shall say them – if he will. Come, Little Brother!"

"My head is ringing like a bee-tree," said a sullen little voice over their heads, and Mowgli slid down a tree-trunk very angry and indignant, adding as he reached the ground: "I come for Bagheera and not for *thee*, fat old Baloo!"

"That is all one to me," said Baloo, though be was hurt and grieved. "Tell Bagheera, then, the Master Words of the jungle that I have taught thee this day."

"Master Words for which people?" said Mowgli, delighted to show off. "The jungle has many tongues. *I* know them all."

"A little thou knowest, but not much. See, O Bagheera, they never thank their teacher. Not one small wolfling has ever come back to thank old Baloo for his teachings. Say the word for the Hunting-People then – great scholar."

"We be of one blood, ye and I," said Mowgli, giving the words the bear accent which all the Hunting-People use.

"Good. Now for the birds."

Mowgli repeated, with the kite's whistle at the end of the sentence.

"Now for the Snake-People," said Bagheera.

The answer was a perfectly indescribable hiss, and Mowgli kicked up his feet behind, clapped his hands together to applaud himself, and jumped on to Bagheera's back, where he sat sideways, drumming with his heels on the glossy skin and making the worst faces he could think of at Baloo.

"There – there! That was worth a little bruise," said the brown bear tenderly. "Some day thou wilt remember me." Then he turned aside to tell Bagheera how he had begged the Master Words from Hathi the Wild Elephant, who knows all about these things, and how Hathi had taken Mowgli down to a pool to get the Snake Word from a water-snake, because Baloo could not pronounce it, and how Mowgli was now reasonably safe against all accidents in the jungle, because neither snake, bird, nor beast would hurt him.

"No one then is to be feared," Baloo wound up, patting his big furry stomach with pride.

"Except his own tribe," said Bagheera, under his breath; and then aloud to Mowgli: "Have a care for my ribs, little Brother! What is all this dancing up and down?"

Mowgli had been trying to make himself heard by pulling at Bagheera's shoulder fur and kicking hard. When the two listened to him he was shouting at the top of his voice: "And so I shall have a tribe of my own, and lead them through the branches all day long."

"What is this new folly, little dreamer of dreams?" said Bagheera.

"Yes, and throw branches and dirt at old Baloo," Mowgli went on. "They have promised me this. Ah!"

"*Whoof!*" Baloo's big paw scooped Mowgli off Bagheera's back, and as the boy lay between the big fore paws he could see the bear was angry.

"Mowgli," said Baloo, "thou hast been talking with the *Bandar-log* – the Monkey-People."

Mowgli looked at Bagheera to see if the panther was angry too, and Bagheera's eyes were as hard as jade-stones.

"Thou hast been with the Monkey-People – the grey apes – the people without a Law – the eaters of everything. That is great shame."

"When Baloo hurt my head," said Mowgli (he was still on his back), "I went away, and the grey apes came down from the trees and had pity on me. No one else cared." He snuffled a little.

"The pity of the Monkey-People!" Baloo snorted. "The stillness of the mountain stream! The cool of the summer sun! And then, man-cub?"

"And then, and then, they gave me nuts and pleasant things to eat, and they – they carried me in their arms up to the top of the trees and said I was their blood-brother except that I had no tail, and should be.their leader some day."

"They have *no* leader," said Bagheera. "They lie. They have always lied."

"They were very kind and bade me come again. Why have I never been taken among the Monkey-People? They stand on their feet as I do. They do not hit me with hard paws. They play all day. Let me get up! Bad Baloo, let me up! I will play with them again."

"Listen, man-cub," said the bear, and his voice rumbled like thunder on a hot night. "I have taught thee all the Law of the Jungle for all the peoples of the jungle – except the Monkey-Folk who live in the trees. They have no Law. They are outcaste. They have no speech of their own, but use the stolen words which they overhear when they listen, and peep, and wait up above in the branches. Their way is not our way. They are without leaders. They have no remembrance. They boast and chatter and pretend that they are a great people about to do great affairs in the jungle, but the falling of a nut turns their minds to laughter and all is forgotten. We of the jungle have no dealings with them. We do not drink where the monkeys drink; we do not go where the monkeys go; we do not hunt where they hunt; we do not die where they die. Hast thou ever heard me speak of the *Bandar-log* till today?"

"No," said Mowgli in a whisper, for the forest was very still now Baloo had finished.

"The Jungle-People put them out of their mouths and out of their mind. They are very many, evil, dirty, shameless, and they desire, if they have any fixed desire, to be noticed by the Jungle-People. But we do *not* notice them even when they throw nuts and filth on our heads."

He had hardly spoken when a shower of nuts and twigs spattered down through the branches; and they could hear coughings and howlings and angry jumpings high up in the air among the thin branches.

"The Monkey-People are forbidden," said Baloo, "forbidden to the Jungle-People. Remember."

"Forbidden," said Bagheera, "but I still think Baloo should have warned thee against them."

"I – I? How was I to guess he would play with such dirt? The Monkey-People! *Faugh!*"

A fresh shower came down on their heads and the two trotted away taking Mowgli with them. What Baloo had said about the monkeys was perfectly true. They belonged to the tree-tops, and as beasts very seldom look up, there was no occasion for the monkeys and the Jungle-People to cross each other's path. But whenever they found a sick wolf, or a wounded tiger, or bear, the monkeys would torment him, and would throw sticks and nuts at any beast for fun and in the hope of being noticed. Then they would howl and shriek senseless songs, and invite the Jungle-People to climb up their trees and fight them, or would start furious battles over nothing among themselves, and leave the dead monkeys where the Jungle-People could see them. They were always just going to have a leader, and laws and customs of their own, but they never did, because their memories would not hold over from day to day, and so they compromised things by making up a saying: "What the *Bandar-log* think now the jungle will think later," and that comforted them a great deal. None of the beasts could reach them, but on the other hand none of the beasts would notice them, and that was why they were so pleased when Mowgli came to play with them, and they heard how angry Baloo was.

They never meant to do any more – the *Bandar-log* never meant anything at all. But one of them invented what seemed to him a brilliant idea, and he told all the others that Mowgli would be a useful person to keep in the tribe, because he could weave sticks together for protection from the wind; so, if they caught him, they could make him teach them. Of course Mowgli, as a woodcutter's child, inherited all sorts of instincts, and used to make little huts of fallen branches without thinking how he came to do it, and the Monkey-People, watching in the trees, considered his play most wonder-ful. This time, they said, they were really going to have a leader and become the wisest people in the jungle – so wise that every one else would notice and envy them. Therefore they followed Baloo and Bagheera and Mowgli through the jungle very quietly till it was time for the mid-day nap, and Mowgli, who was very much ashamed of himself, slept between the panther and the bear, resolving to have no more to do with the Monkey-People.

The next thing he remembered was feeling hands on his legs and arms – hard, strong, little hands – and then a swash of branches in his face, and then he was staring down through the swaying boughs as Baloo woke the jungle with his deep cries and Bagheera bounded up the trunk with every tooth bared. The *Bandar-log* howled with triumph and scuffled away to the upper branches where Bagheera dared not follow, shouting: "He has noticed us! Bagheera has noticed us. All the Jungle-People admire us for our skill and our cunning." Then they began their flight; and the flight of the Monkey-People through tree-land is one of the things nobody can describe. They have their regular roads and cross-roads, up hills and down hills, all laid out from fifty to seventy or a hundred feet above ground, and by these they can travel even at night if necessary. Two of the strongest monkeys caught Mowgli under the arms and swung off with him through the tree-tops, twenty feet at a bound. Had they been alone they could have gone twice as fast, but the boy's weight held them back. Sick and giddy as Mowgli was he could not help enjoying the wild rush, though the glimpses of earth far down below frightened him, and the terrible check and jerk at the end of the swing over nothing but empty air brought his heart between his teeth. His escort would rush him up a tree till he felt the thinnest topmost branches crackle and bend under them, and then with a cough and a whoop would fling themselves into the air outwards and downwards, and bring up, hanging by their hands or their feet to the lower limbs of the next tree. Sometimes he could see for miles and miles across the still green jungle, as a man on the top of a mast can see for miles across the sea, and then the branches and leaves would lash him across the face, and he and his two guards would be almost down to earth again. So, bounding and crashing and whooping and yelling, the whole tribe of *Bandar-log* swept along the tree-roads with Mowgli their prisoner.

For a time he was afraid of being dropped. Then he grew angry but knew better than to struggle, and then he began to think. The first thing was to send back word to Baloo and Bagheera, for, at the pace the monkeys were going, he knew his friends would be left far behind. It was useless to look down, for he could only see the top-sides of the branches, so he stared upwards and saw, far away in the blue, Chil the Kite balancing and wheeling as he kept watch over the jungle waiting for things to die. Chil saw that the monkeys were carrying something, and dropped a few hundred yards to find out whether their load was good to eat. He whistled with surprise when he saw Mowgli being dragged up to a tree-top and heard him give the kite call for "We be of one blood, thou and I." The waves of the branches closed over the boy, but Chil balanced away to the next tree in time to see the little brown face come up again. "Mark my trail," Mowgli shouted. "Tell Baloo of the Seeonee Pack and Bagheera of the Council Rock."

"In whose name, Brother?" Chil had never seen Mowgli before, though of course he had heard of him.

"Mowgli the Frog. Man-cub they call me! Mark my trail!"

The last words were shrieked as he was being swung through the air, but Chil nodded and rose up till he looked no bigger than a speck of dust, and there he hung, watching with his telescope eyes the swaying of the tree-tops as Mowgli's escort whirled along.

"They never go far," he said with a chuckle. "They never do what they set out to do. Always pecking at new things are the *Bandar-log*. This time, if I have any eyesight, they have pecked down trouble for themselves, for Baloo is no fledgeling and Bagheera can, as I know, kill more than goats."

So he rocked on his wings, his feet gathered up under him, and waited.

Meantime, Baloo and Bagheera were furious with rage and grief. Bagheera climbed as he had never climbed before, but the thin branches broke beneath his weight, and he slipped down, his claws full of bark.

"Why didst thou not warn the man-cub?" he roared to poor Baloo, who had set off at a clumsy trot in the hope of overtaking the monkeys. "What was the use of half slaying him with blows if thou didst not warn him?"

"Haste! O haste! We – we may catch them yet!" Baloo panted.

"At that speed! It would not tire a wounded cow. Teacher of the Law – cub-beater – a mile of that rolling to and fro would burst thee open. Sit still and think! Make a plan. This is no time for chasing. They may drop him if we follow too close."

"*Arrula! Whoo!* They may have dropped him already, being tired of carrying him. Who can trust the *Bandar-log?* Put dead bats on my head! Give me black bones to eat! Roll me into the hives of the wild bees that I may be stung to death, and bury me with the hyena, for I am the most miserable of bears! *Arulala! Wahooa!* O Mowgli, Mowgli! Why did I not warn thee against the Monkey-Folk instead of breaking thy head? Now perhaps I may have knocked the day's lesson out of his mind, and he will be alone in the jungle without the Master Words."

Baloo clasped his paws over his ears and rolled to and fro moaning.

"At least he gave me all the words correctly a little time ago," said Bagheera, impatiently. "Baloo, thou hast neither memory nor respect. What would the jungle think if I, the Black Panther, curled myself up like Sahi the Porcupine, and howled?"

"What do I care what the jungle thinks? He may be dead by now."

"Unless and until they drop him from the branches in sport, or kill him out of idleness, I have no fear for the man-cub. He is wise and well-taught, and above all he has the eyes that make the Jungle-People afraid. But (and it is a great evil) he is in the power of the *Bandar-log*, and they, because they live in trees, have no fear of any of our people." Bagheera licked one fore paw thoughtfully.

"Fool that I am! Oh, fat, brown, root-digging fool that I am," said Baloo, uncoiling himself with a jerk, "it is true what Hathi the Wild Elephant says: *'To each his own fear.'* And they, the *Bandar-log*, fear Kaa the Rock Snake. He can climb as well as they can. He steals the young monkeys in the night. The whisper of his name makes their wicked tails cold. Let us go to Kaa."

"What will he do for us? He is not of our tribe, being footless – and with most evil eyes," said Bagheera.

"He is very old and very cunning. Above all, he is always hungry," said Baloo hopefully. "Promise him many goats."

"He sleeps for a full month after he has once eaten. He may be asleep now, and even were he awake, what if he would rather kill his own goats?" Bagheera, who did not know much about Kaa, was naturally suspicious.

"Then in that case, thou and I together, old hunter, might make him see reason." Here Baloo rubbed his faded brown shoulder against the panther, and they went off to look for Kaa the Rock Python.

They found him stretched out on a warm ledge in the afternoon sun, admiring his beautiful new coat, for he had been in retirement for the last ten days changing his skin, and now he was very splendid – darting his big blunt-nosed head along the ground, and twisting the thirty feet of his body into fantastic knots and curves, and licking his lips as he thought of his dinner to come.

"He has not eaten," said Baloo, with a grunt of relief, as soon as he saw the beautifully mottled brown and yellow jacket. "Be careful, Bagheera! He is always a little blind after he has changed his skin, and very quick to strike."

Kaa was not a poison-snake – in fact, he rather despised the poison-snakes as cowards – but his strength lay in his hug, and when he had once lapped his huge coils round anybody there was no more to be said. "Good hunting!" cried Baloo, sitting up on his haunches. Like all snakes of his breed Kaa was rather deaf, and did not hear the call at first. Then he curled up ready for any accident, his head lowered.

"Good hunting for us all," he answered. "Oho, Baloo, what dost thou do here? Good hunting, Bagheera. One of us at least needs food. Is there any news of game afoot? A doe now, or even a young buck? I am as empty as a dried well."

"We are hunting," said Baloo carelessly. He knew that you must not hurry Kaa. He is too big.

"Give me permission to come with you," said Kaa. "A blow more or less is nothing to thee, Bagheera or Baloo, but I – I have to wait and wait for days in a wood-path and climb half a night on the mere chance of a young ape. *Psshaw!* The branches are not what they were when I was young. Rotten twigs and dry boughs are they all."

"Maybe thy great weight has something to do with the matter," said Baloo.

"I am a fair length – a fair length," said Kaa, with a little pride. "But for all that, it is the fault of this new-grown timber. I came very near to falling on my last hunt – very near indeed – and the noise of my slipping, for my tail was not tight wrapped round the tree, waked the *Bandar-log*, and they called me most evil names."

"Footless, yellow earth-worm," said Bagheera under his whiskers, as though he were trying to remember something.

"*Sssss!* Have they ever called me *that?*" said Kaa.

"Something of that kind it was that they shouted to us last moon, but we never noticed them. They will say anything – even that thou hast lost all thy teeth, and wilt not face anything bigger than a kid, because (they are indeed shameless, these *Bandar-log*) – because thou art afraid of the he-goats' horns," Bagheera went on sweetly.

Now a snake, especially a wary old python like Kaa, very seldom shows that he is angry, but Baloo and Bagheera could see the big swallowing-muscles on either side of Kaa's throat ripple and bulge.

"The *Bandar-log* have shifted their grounds," he said quietly. "When I came up into the sun today I heard them whooping among the tree-tops."

"It – it is the *Bandar-log* that we follow now," said Baloo, but the words stuck in his throat, for that was the first time in his memory that one of the Jungle-People had owned to being interested in the doings of the monkeys.

"Beyond doubt then it is no small thing that takes two such hunters – leaders in their own jungle I am certain – on the trail of the *Bandar-log*," Kaa replied, courteously, as he swelled with curiosity.

"Indeed," Baloo began, "I am no more than the old and sometimes very foolish Teacher of the Law to the Seeonee wolf-cubs, and Bagheera here – "

"Is Bagheera," said the black panther, and his jaws shut with a snap, for he did not believe in being humble. "The trouble is this, Kaa. Those nut-stealers and pickers of palm leaves have stolen away our man-cub of whom thou hast perhaps heard."

"I heard some news from Sahi (his quills make him presumptuous) of a man-thing that was entered into a wolf pack, but I did not believe. Sahi is full of stories half heard and very badly told."

"But it is true. He is such a man-cub as never was," said Baloo. "The best and wisest and boldest of man-cubs – my own pupil, who shall make the name of Baloo famous through all the jungles. And besides, I – we – love him, Kaa."

"*Ts! Ts!*" said Kaa, weaving his head to and fro. "I also have known what love is. There are tales I could tell that – "

"That need a clear night when we are all well fed to praise properly," said Bagheera, quickly. "Our man-cub is in the hands of the *Bandar-log* now, and we know that of all the Jungle-People they fear Kaa alone."

"They fear me alone. They have good reason," said Kaa. "Chattering, foolish, vain – vain, foolish, and chattering are the monkeys. But a man-thing in their hands is in no good luck. They grow tired of the nuts they pick, and throw them down. They carry a branch half a day, meaning to do great things with it, and then they snap it in two. That man-thing is not to be envied. They called me also – yellow fish was it not?"

"Worm – worm – earth-worm," said Bagheera, "as well as other things which I cannot now say for shame."

"We must remind them to speak well of their master. *Aaa-sspl* We must help their wandering memories. Now, whither went they with the cub?"

"The jungle alone knows. Towards the sunset, I believe," said Baloo. "We had thought that thou wouldst know, Kaa."

"I? How? I take them when they come in my way, but I do not hunt the *Bandar-log*, or frogs – or green scum on a water-hole for that matter. Hsss!"

"Up, up! Up, up! Hillo! Illo! Illo, look up, Baloo of the Seeonee Wolf Pack!"

Baloo looked up to see where the voice came from, and there was Chil the Kite, sweeping down with the sun shining on the upturned flanges of his wings. It was near Chil's bedtime, but he had ranged all over the jungle looking for the bear and missed him in the thick foliage.

"What is it?" said Baloo.

"I have seen Mowgli among the *Bandar-log*. He bade me tell you. I watched. The *Bandar-log* have taken him beyond the river to the monkey city – to the Cold Lairs. They may stay there for a night, or ten nights, or an hour. I have told the bats to watch through the dark time. That is my message. Good hunting, all you below!"

"Full gorge and a deep sleep to you, Chil," cried Bagheera. "I will remember thee in my next kill, and put aside the head for thee alone – oh, best of kites!"

"It is nothing. It is nothing. The boy held the Master Word. I could have done no less," and Chil circled up again to his roost.

"He has not forgotten to use his tongue," said Baloo, with a chuckle of pride. "To think of one so young remembering the Master Word for the birds too while he was being pulled across trees!"

"It was most firmly driven into him," said Bagheera. "But I am proud of him, and now we must go to the Cold Lairs."

They all knew where that place was, but few of the Jungle-People ever went there, because what they called the Cold Lairs was an old deserted city, lost and buried in the jungle, and beasts seldom use a place that men have once used. The wild boar will, but the hunting-tribes do not. Besides, the monkeys lived there as much as they could be said to live anywhere, and no self-respecting animal would come within eye-shot of it except in times of drouth, when the half-ruined tanks and reservoirs held a little water.

"It is half a night's journey – at full speed," said Bagheera, and Baloo looked very serious. "I will go as fast as I can," he said, anxiously.

"We dare not wait for thee; Follow, Baloo. We must go on the quick-foot – Kaa and I."

"Feet or no feet, I can keep abreast of all thy four," said Kaa, shortly. Baloo made one effort to hurry, but had to sit down panting, and so they left him to come on later, while Bagheera hurried forward, at the quick panther-canter. Kaa said nothing, but, strive as Bagheera might, the huge rock python held level with him. When they came to a hill-stream, Bagheera gained, because he bounded across while Kaa swam, his head and two feet of his neck clearing the water, but on level ground Kaa made up the distance.

"By the broken lock that freed me," said Bagheera, when twilight had fallen, "thou art no slow goer!"

"I am hungry," said Kaa. "Besides, they called me speckled frog."

"Worm – earth-worm, and yellow to boot."

"All one. Let us go on," and Kaa seemed to pour himself along the ground, finding the shortest road with his steady eyes, and keeping to it.

In the Cold Lairs the Monkey-People were not thinking of Mowgli's friends at all. They had brought the boy to the Lost City, and were very pleased with themselves for the time. Mowgli had never seen an Indian city before, and though this was almost a heap of ruins it seemed very wonderful and splendid. Some king had built it long ago on a little hill. You could still trace the stone causeways that led up to the ruined gates where the last splinters of wood hung to the worn, rusted hinges. Trees had grown into and out of the walls; the battlements were tumbled down and decayed, and wild creepers hung out of the windows of the towers on the walls in bushy hanging clumps.

A great roofless palace crowned the hill, and the marble of the courtyards and the fountains was split, and stained with red and green, and the very cobblestones in the courtyard where the king's elephants used to live had been thrust up and apart by grasses and young trees. From the palace you could see the rows and rows of roofless houses that made up the city looking like empty honeycombs filled with blackness; the shapeless block of stone that had been an idol, in the square where four roads met; the pits and dimples at street-corners where the public wells once stood, and the shattered domes of temples with wild figs sprouting on their sides. The monkeys called the place their city, and pretended to despise the Jungle-People because they lived in the forest. And yet they never knew what the buildings were made for nor how to use them. They would sit in circles on the hall of the king's council chamber, and scratch for fleas and pretend to be men; or they would run in and out of the roofless houses and collect pieces of plaster and old bricks in a corner, and forget where they had hidden them, and fight and cry in scuffling crowds, and then break off to play up and down the terraces of the king's garden, where they would shake the rose-trees and the oranges in sport to see the fruit and flowers fall. They explored all the passages and dark tunnels in the palace and the hundreds of little dark rooms, but they never remembered what they had seen and what they had not, and so drifted about in ones and twos or crowds telling each other that they were doing as men did. They drank at the tanks and made the water all muddy, and then they fought over it, and then they would all rush together in mobs and shout: "There is no one in the jungle so wise and good and clever and strong and gentle as the *Bandar log*." Then all would begin again till they grew tired of the city and went back to the tree-tops, hoping the Jungle-People would notice them.

Mowgli, who had been trained under the Law of the Jungle, did not like or understand this kind of life. The monkeys dragged him into the Cold Lairs late in the afternoon, and instead of going to sleep, as Mowgli would have done after a long journey, they joined hands and danced about and sang their foolish songs. One of the monkeys made a speech and told his companions that Mowgli's capture marked a new thing in the history of the *Bandar-log*, for Mowgli was going to show them how to weave sticks and canes together as a protection against rain and cold. Mowgli picked up some creepers and began to work them in and out, and the monkeys tried to imitate; but in a very few minutes they lost interest and began to pull their friends' tails or jump up and down on all fours, coughing.

"I wish to eat," said Mowgli. "I am a stranger in this part of the jungle. Bring me food, or give me leave to hunt here."

Twenty or thirty monkeys bounded away to bring him nuts and wild pawpaws, but they fell to fighting on the road, and it was too much trouble to go back with what was left of the fruit. Mowgli was sore and angry as well as hungry, and he roamed through the empty city giving the Strangers' Hunting-Call from time to time, but no one answered him, and Mowgli felt that he had reached a very bad place indeed. "All that Baloo has said about the *Bandar-log* is true," he thought to himself. "They have no Law, no Hunting-Call, and no leaders – nothing but foolish words and little picking thievish hands. So if I am starved or killed here, it will be all my own fault. But I must try to return to my own jungle. Baloo will surely beat me, but that is better than chasing silly rose leaves with the *Bandar-log*."

No sooner had he walked to the city wall than the monkeys pulled him back, telling him that he did not know how happy he was, and pinching him to make him grateful. He set his teeth and said nothing, but went with the shouting monkeys to a terrace above the red sandstone reservoirs that were half-full of rain water. There was a ruined summer-house of white marble in the centre of the terrace, built for queens dead a hundred years ago. The domed roof had half fallen in and blocked up the underground passage from the palace by which the queens used to enter, but the walls were made of screens of marble tracery – beautiful milk-white fret-work, set with agates and cornelians and jasper and lapis lazuli – and as the moon came up behind the hill it shone through the open work, casting shadows on the ground like black velvet embroidery. Sore, sleepy, and hungry as he was, Mowgli could not help laughing when the *Bandar-log* began, twenty at a time, to tell him how great and wise and strong and gentle they were, and how foolish he was to wish to leave them. "We are great. We are free. We are wonderful. We are the most wonderful people in all the jungle! We all say so, and so it must be true," they shouted. "Now as you are a new listener and can carry our words back to the Jungle-People so that they may notice us in future, we will tell you all about our most excellent selves." Mowgli made no objection, and the monkeys gathered by hundreds and hundreds on the terrace to listen to their own speakers singing the praises of the *Bandar-log*, and whenever a speaker stopped for want of breath they would all shout together: "This is true; we all say so." Mowgli nodded and blinked, and said "Yes" when they asked him a question, and his head spun with the noise. "Tabaqui the Jackal must have bitten all these people,", he said to himself, "and now they have the madness. Certainly this is *dewanee*,

"There is only one here! Kill him! Kill."

the madness. Do they never go to sleep? Now there is a cloud coming to cover that moon. If it were only a big enough cloud I might try to run away in the darkness. But I am tired."

That same cloud was being watched by two good friends in the ruined ditch below the city wall, for Bagheera and Kaa, knowing well how dangerous the Monkey-People were in large numbers, did not wish to run any risks. The monkeys never fight unless they are a hundred to one, and few in the jungle care for those odds.

"I will go to the west wall," Kaa whispered, "and come down swiftly with the slope of the ground in my favour. They will not throw themselves upon *my* back in their hundreds, but – "

"I know it," said Bagheera. "Would that Baloo were here, but we must do what we can. When that cloud covers the moon I shall go to the terrace. They hold some sort of council there over the boy."

"Good hunting," said Kaa, grimly, and glided away to the west wall. That happened to be the least ruined of any, and the big snake was delayed a while before he could find a way up the stones. The cloud hid the moon, and as Mowgli wondered what would come next he heard Bagheera's light feet on the terrace. The black panther had raced up the slope almost without a sound and was striking – he knew better than to waste time in biting – right and left among the monkeys, who were seated round Mowgli in circles fifty and sixty deep. There was a howl of fright and rage, and then as Bagheera tripped on the rolling kicking bodies beneath him, a monkey shouted: "There is only one here! Kill him! Kill." A scuffling mass of monkeys, biting, scratching, tearing, and pulling, closed over Bagheera, while five or six laid hold of Mowgli, dragged him up the wall of the summer-house and pushed him through the hole of the broken dome. A man-trained boy would have been badly bruised, for the fall was a good fifteen feet, but Mowgli fell as Baloo had taught him to fall, and landed on his feet.

"Stay there," shouted the monkeys, "till we have killed thy friends, and later we will play with thee – if the Poison-People leave thee alive."

"We be of one blood, ye and I," said Mowgli, quickly giving the Snake's Call. He could hear rustling and hissing in the rubbish all round him and gave the call a second time, to make sure.

"Even ssso! Down hoods all!" said half a dozen low voices. (Every ruin in India becomes sooner or later a dwelling-place of snakes, and the old summer-house was alive with cobras.) "Stand still, Little Brother, for thy feet may do us harm."

Mowgli stood as quietly as he could, peering through the open work and listening to the furious din of the fight round the black panther – the yells and chatterings and scufflings, and Bagheera's deep, hoarse cough as he backed and bucked and twisted and plunged under the heaps of his enemies. For the first time since he was born, Bagheera was fighting for his life.

"Baloo must be at hand; Bagheera would not have come alone," Mowgli thought. And then he called aloud: "To the tank, Bagheera. Roll to the water-tanks. Roll and plunge! Get to the water!"

Bagheera heard, and the cry that told him Mowgli was safe gave him new courage. He worked his way desperately, inch by inch, straight for the reservoirs, halting in silence. Then from the ruined wall nearest the jungle rose up the rumbling war-shout of Baloo. The old bear had done his best, but he could not come before. "Bagheera," he shouted, "I am here. I climb! I haste! *Ahuwora!* The stones slip under my feet! Wait my coming, oh, most infamous *Bandar-log!*" He panted up the terrace only to disappear to the head in a wave of monkeys, but he threw himself squarely on his haunches, and, spreading out his fore paws, hugged as many as he could hold, and then began to hit with a regular *bat-bat-bat*, like the flipping strokes of a paddle-wheel. A crash and a splash told Mowgli that Bagheera had fought his way to the tank where the monkeys could not follow. The panther lay gasping for breath, his head just out of water, while the monkeys stood three deep on the red steps, dancing up and down with rage, ready to spring upon him from all sides if he came out to help Baloo. It was then that Bagheera lifted up his dripping chin, and in despair gave the Snake's Call for protection – "We be of one blood, ye and I" – for he believed that Kaa had turned tail at the last minute. Even Baloo, half smothered under the monkeys on the edge of the terrace, could not help chuckling as he heard the black panther asking for help.

Kaa had only just worked his way over the west wall, landing with a wrench that dislodged a coping-stone into the ditch. He had no intention of losing any advantage of the ground, and coiled and uncoiled himself once or twice, to be sure that every foot of his long body was in working order. All that while the fight with Baloo went on, and the monkeys yelled in the tank round Bagheera, and Mang the Bat, flying to and fro, carried the news of the great battle over the jungle, till even Hathi the Wild Elephant trumpeted, and, far away, scattered bands of the Monkey-Folk woke and came leaping along the tree-roads to help their comrades in the Cold Lairs, and the noise of the fight roused all the day-birds for miles round. Then Kaa came straight, quickly, and anxious to kill. The fighting strength of a python is in the driving blow of his head backed by all the strength and weight of his body. If you can imagine a lance, or a battering ram, or a hammer weighing nearly half a ton driven by a cool, quiet mind living in the handle of it, you can roughly imagine what Kaa was like when he fought. A python four or five feet long can knock a man down if he hits him fairly in the chest, and Kaa was thirty feet long, as you know. His first stroke was delivered into the heart of the crowd round Baloo – was sent home with shut mouth in silence, and there was no need of a second. The monkeys scattered with cries of "Kaa! It is Kaa! Run! Run!"

Generations of monkeys had been scared into good behaviour by the stories their elders told them of Kaa, the night-thief, who could slip along the branches as quietly as moss grows, and steal away the strongest monkey that ever lived; of old Kaa, who could make himself look so like a dead branch or a rotten stump that the wisest were deceived, till the branch caught them. Kaa was everything that the monkeys feared in the jungle, for none of them knew the limits of his power, none of them could look him in the face, and none had ever come alive out of his hug. And so they ran, stammering with terror, to the walls and the roofs of the houses, and Baloo drew a deep breath of relief. His fur was much thicker than Bagheera's, but he had suffered sorely in the fight. Then Kaa opened his mouth for the first time and spoke one long hissing word, and the far-away monkeys, hurrying to the defence of the Cold Lairs, stayed where they were, cowering, till the loaded branches bent and crackled under them. The monkeys on the walls and the empty houses stopped their cries, and in the stillness that fell upon the city Mowgli heard Bagheera shaking his wet sides as he came up from the tank. Then the clamour broke out again. The monkeys leaped higher up the walls; they clung round the necks of the big stone idols and shrieked as they skipped along the battlements, while Mowgli, dancing in the summer-house, put his eye to the screen-work and hooted owl-fashion between his front teeth, to show his derision and contempt.

"Get the man-cub out of that trap; I can do no more," Bagheera gasped. "Let us take the man-cub and go. They may attack again."

"They will not move till I order them. Stay you sssso!" Kaa hissed, and the city was silent once more. "I could not come before, Brother, but I *think* I heard thee call" – this was to Bagheera.

"I – I may have cried out in the battle," Bagheera answered. "Baloo, art thou hurt?"

"I am not sure that they did not pull me into a hundred little bearlings," said Baloo, gravely shaking one leg after the other. *Wow!* I am sore. Kaa, we owe thee, I think, our lives – Bagheera and I."

"No matter. Where is the manling?"

"Here, in a trap. I cannot climb out," cried Mowgli. The curve of the broken dome was above his head.

"Take him away. He dances like Mor the Peacock. He will crush our young," said the cobras inside.

"Hah!" said Kaa with a chuckle, "he has friends everywhere, this manling. Stand back, manling, and hide you, O Poison-People. I break down the wall."

Kaa looked carefully till he found a discoloured crack in the marble tracery showing a weak spot, made two or three light taps with his head to get the distance, and then, lifting up six feet of his body clear of the ground, sent home half a dozen full-power smashing blows, nose-first. The screen-work broke and fell away in a cloud of dust and rubbish, and Mowgli leaped through the opening and flung himself between Baloo and Bagheera – an arm round each big neck.

"Art thou hurt?" said Baloo, hugging him softly.

"I am sore, hungry, and not a little bruised, but, oh, they have handled ye grievously, my brothers! Ye bleed."

"Others also," said Bagheera, licking his lips and looking at the monkey-dead on the terrace and round the tank.

"It is nothing, it is nothing if thou art safe, oh, my pride of all little frogs!" whimpered Baloo.

"Of that we shall judge later," said Bagheera, in a dry voice that Mowgli did not at all like. "But here is Kaa to whom we owe the battle and thou owest thy life. Thank him according to our customs, Mowgli."

Mowgli turned and saw the great python's head swaying a foot above his own.

"So this is the manling," said Kaa. "Very soft is his skin, and he is not unlike the *Bandar-log.* Have a care, manling, that I do not mistake thee for a monkey some twilight when I have newly changed my coat."

"We be one blood, thou and I," Mowgli answered. "I take my life from thee tonight. My kill shall be thy kill if ever thou art hungry, O Kaa."

"All thanks, Little Brother," said Kaa, though his eyes twinkled. "And what may so bold a hunter kill? I ask that I may follow when next he goes abroad."

"I kill nothing – I am too little – but I drive goats towards such as can use them. When thou art empty come to me and see if I speak the truth. I have some skill in these" – be held out his hands – "and if ever thou art in a trap, I may pay the debt which I owe to thee, to Bagheera, and to Baloo, here. Good hunting to ye all, my masters."

"Well said," growled Baloo, for Mowgli had returned thanks very prettily. The python dropped his head lightly for a minute on Mowgli's shoulder. "A brave heart and a courteous tongue," said he. "They shall carry thee far through the jungle, manling. But now go hence quickly with thy friends. Go and sleep, for the moon sets, and what follows it is not well that thou shouldst see."

The moon was sinking behind the hills and the lines of trembling monkeys huddled together on the walls and battlements looked like ragged shaky fringes of things. Baloo went down to the tank for a drink and Bagheera began to put his fur in order, as Kaa glided out into the centre of the terrace and brought his jaws together with a ringing snap that drew all the monkeys' eyes upon him.

"The moon sets," he said. "Is there yet light enough to see?"

From the walls came a moan like the wind in the tree-tops: "We see, O Kaa."

"Good. Begins now the dance – the Dance of the Hunger of Kaa. Sit still and watch." He turned twice or thrice in a big circle, weaving his head from right to left. Then he began making loops and figures of eight with his body, and soft, oozy triangles that melted into squares and five-sided figures, and coiled mounds, never resting, never hurrying, and never stopping his low humming song. It grew darker and darker, till at last the dragging, shifting coils disappeared, but they could hear the rustle of the scales.

Baloo and Bagheera stood still as stone, growling in their throats, their neck-hair bristling, and Mowgli watched and wondered.

"*Bandar-log*," said the voice of Kaa at last, "can ye stir foot or hand without my order? Speak!"

"Without thy order we cannot stir foot or hand, O Kaa!"

"Good! Come all one pace nearer to me."

The lines of the monkeys swayed forward helplessly, and Baloo and Bagheera took one stiff step forward with them.

"Nearer!" hissed Kaa, and they all moved again.

Mowgli laid his hands on Baloo and Bagheera to get them away, and the two great beasts started as though they had been waked from a dream.

"Keep thy hand on my shoulder," Bagheera whispered. "Keep it there, or I must go back – must go back to Kaa. Aah!"

"It is only old Kaa making circles on the dust," said Mowgli. "Let us go." And the three slipped off through a gap in the walls to the jungle.

"*Whoof!*" said Baloo, when he stood under the still trees again. "Never more will I make an ally of Kaa," and he shook himself all over.

"He knows more than we," said Bagheera, trembling. "In a little time, had I stayed, I should have walked down his throat"

"Many will walk by that road before the moon rises again," said Baloo. "He will have good hunting – after his own fashion."

"But what was the meaning of it all?" said Mowgli, who did not know anything of a python's powers of fascination. "I saw no more than a big snake making foolish circles till the dark came. And his nose was all sore. Ho! Ho!"

"Mowgli," said Bagheera, angrily, "his nose was sore on *thy* account, as my ears and sides and paws, and Baloo's neck and shoulders are bitten on *thy* account. Neither Baloo nor Bagheera will be able to hunt with pleasure for many days."

"It is nothing," said Baloo. "We have the man-cub again."

"True, but he has cost us heavily in time which might have been spent in good hunting, in wounds, in hair – I am half plucked along my back – and last of all, in honour. For, remember, Mowgli, I, who am the Black Panther, was forced to call upon Kaa for protection, and Baloo and I were both made stupid as little birds by the Hunger-Dance. All this, man-cub, came of thy playing with the *Bandar-log*."

"True, it is true," said Mowgli, sorrowfully. "I am an evil man-cub, and my stomach is sad in me."

"*Mf!* What says the Law of the Jungle, Baloo?"

Baloo did not wish to bring Mowgli into any more trouble, but he could not tamper with the Law, so he mumbled; "Sorrow never stays punishment. But remember, Bagheera, he is very little."

"I will remember, but he has done mischief, and blows must be dealt now. Mowgli, hast thou anything to say?"

"Nothing. I did wrong. Baloo and thou art wounded. It is just."

Bagheera gave him half a dozen love-taps from a panther's point of view (they would hardly have waked one of his own cubs), but for a seven-year-old boy they amounted to as severe a beating as you could wish to avoid. When it was all over Mowgli sneezed, and picked himself up without a word.

"Now," said Bagheera, "jump on my back, Little Brother, and we will go home."

One of the beauties of Jungle Law is that punishment settles all scores. There is no nagging afterwards.

Mowgli laid his head down on Bagheera's back and slept so deeply that he never waked when he was put down in the home-cave.

Road-Song of the Bandar-log

Here we go in a flung festoon,
Half-way up to the jealous moon!
Don't you envy our pranceful bands?
Don't you wish you had extra hands?
Wouldn't you like if your tails were – *so* –
Curved in the shape of a cupid's bow?
    Now you're angry, but – never mind,
    Brother, thy tail hangs down behind!

Here we sit in a branchy row,
Thinking of beautiful things we know.
Dreaming of deeds that we mean to do,
All complete, in a minute or two –
Something noble and wise and good,
Done by merely wishing we could.
    We've forgotten, but – never mind,
    Brother, thy tail hangs down behind!

All the talk we ever have heard
Uttered by bat or beast or bird –
Hide or fin or scale or feather –
Jabber it quickly and all together!
Excellent! Wonderful! Once again!
Now we are talking just like men!
    Let's pretend we are – never mind,
    Brother, thy tail hangs down behind!
    This is the way of the monkey-kind.

Then join our leaping lines that scumfish through the pines,
That rocket by where, light and high, the wild grape swings.
By the rubbish in our wake, and the noble noise we make,
Be sure, be sure, we're going to do some splendid things!

"Tiger-Tiger!"

What of the hunting, hunter bold?
    Brother, the watch was long and cold.
What of the quarry ye went to kill?
    Brother, he crops in the jungle still.
Where is the power that made your pride?
    Brother, it ebbs from my flank and side.
Where is the haste that ye hurry by?
    Brother, I go to my lair to die.

When Mowgli left the wolfs cave after the fight with the pack at the Council Rock, he went down to the ploughed lands where the villagers lived, but he would not stop there because it was too near to the jungle, and he knew that he had made at least one bad enemy at the council. So he hurried on, keeping to the rough road that ran down the valley, and followed it at a steady jog-trot for nearly twenty miles, till he came to a country that he did not know. The valley opened out into a great plain dotted over with rocks and cut up with ravines. At one end stood a little village, and at the other the thick jungle came down in a sweep to the grazing-grounds, and stopped there as though it had been cut off with a hoe. All over the plain, cattle and buffaloes were grazing, and when the little boys in charge of the herds saw Mowgli they shouted and ran away, and the yellow pariah dogs that hang about every Indian village barked. Mowgli walked on, for he was feeling hungry, and when he came to the village gate he saw the big thornbush that was drawn up before the gate at twilight pushed to one side.

"*Umph!*" he said, for he had come across more than one such barricade in his night rambles after things to eat. "So men are afraid of the people of the jungle here also." He sat down by the gate, and when a man came out he stood up, opened his mouth, and pointed down it to show that he wanted food. The man stared, and ran back up the one street of the village shouting for the priest, who was a big, fat man dressed in white, with a red and yellow mark on his forehead. The priest came to the gate, and with him at least a hundred people, who stared and talked and shouted and pointed at Mowgli.

"They have no manners, these Men-Folk," said Mowgli to himself. "Only the grey ape would behave as they do." So he threw back his long hair and frowned at the crowd.

"What is there to be afraid of?" said the priest. "Look at the marks on his arms and legs. They are the bites of wolves. He is but a wolf-child run away from the jungle."

Of course, in playing together, the cubs had often nipped Mowgli harder than they intended, and there were white scars all over his arms and legs. But he would have been the last person in the world to call these bites, for he knew what real biting meant.

"*Arré! Arré!*" said two or three women together. "To be bitten by wolves, poor child! He is a handsome boy. He has eyes like red fire. By my honour, Messua, he is not unlike thy boy that was taken by the tiger."

"Let me look," said a woman with heavy copper rings on her wrists and ankles, and she peered at Mowgli under the palm of her hand. "Indeed he is not. He is thinner, but he has the very look of my boy."

The priest was a clever man, and he knew that Messua was wife to the richest villager in the place. So he looked up at the sky for a minute, and said solemnly: "What the jungle has taken the jungle has restored. Take the boy into thy house, my sister, and forget not to honour the priest who sees so far into the lives of men."

"By the bull that bought me," said Mowgli to himself, "but all this talking is like another looking over by the pack! Well, if I am a man, a man I must be."

The crowd parted as the woman beckoned Mowgli to her hut, where there was a red lacquered bedstead, a great earthen grain-chest with funny raised patterns on it, half a dozen copper cooking-pots, an image of a Hindu god in a little alcove, and on the wall a real looking-glass, such as they sell at the country fairs for eight cents.

She gave him a long drink of milk and some bread, and then she laid her hand on his head and looked into his eyes, for she thought perhaps that he might be her real son come back from the jungle where the tiger had taken him. So she said: "Nathoo, O Nathoo!" Mowgli did not show that he knew the name. "Dost thou not remember the day when I gave thee thy new shoes?" She touched his foot, and it was almost as hard as horn. "No," she said, sorrowfully, "those feet have never worn shoes, but thou art very like my Nathoo, and thou shalt be my son."

Mowgli was uneasy, because he had never been under a roof before; but as he looked at the thatch, he saw that he could tear it out any time if he wanted to get away, and that the window had no fastenings. "What is the good of a man," he said to himself at last, "if he does not understand man's talk? Now I am as silly and dumb as a man would be with us in the jungle. I must speak their talk."

He had not learned while he was with the wolves to imitate the challenge of bucks in the jungle and the grunt of the little wild pig for fun. So, as soon as Messua pronounced a word Mowgli would imitate it almost perfectly, and before dark he had learned the name of many things in the hut.

There was a difficulty at bed-time, because Mowgli would not sleep under anything that looked so like a panther-trap as that hut, and when they shut the door he went through the window. "Give him his will," said Messua's husband. "Remember he can never till now have slept on a bed. If he is indeed sent in the place of our son he will not run away."

So Mowgli stretched himself in some long clean grass at the edge of the field, but before he had closed his eyes a soft grey nose poked him under the chin.

"*Phew!*" said Grey Brother (he was the eldest of Mother Wolfs cubs). "This is a poor reward for following thee twenty miles. Thou smellest of wood-smoke and cattle – altogether like a man already. Wake, Little Brother; I bring news."

"Are all well in the jungle?" said Mowgli, hugging him.

"All except the wolves that were burned with the Red Flower. Now, listen. Shere Khan has gone away to hunt far off till his coat grows again, for he is badly singed. When he returns he swears that he will lay thy bones in the Wainganga."

"There are two words to that. I also have made a little promise. But news is always good. I am tired tonight – very tired with new things, Grey Brother – but bring me the news always."

"Thou wilt not forget that thou art a wolf? Men will not make thee forget?" said Grey Brother, anxiously.

"Never. I will always remember that I love thee and all in our cave, but also I will always remember that I have been cast out of the pack."

"And that thou mayest be cast out of another pack. Men are only men, Little Brother, and their talk is like the talk of frogs in a pond. When I come down here again, I will wait for thee in the bamboos at the edge of the grazing-ground."

For three months after that night Mowgli hardly ever left the village gate, he was so busy learning the ways and customs of men. First he had to wear a cloth round him, which annoyed him horribly; and then he had to learn about money, which he did not in the least understand, and about ploughing, of which he did not see the use. Then the little children in the village made him very angry. Luckily, the Law of the Jungle had taught him to keep his temper, for in the jungle, life and food depend on keeping your temper; but when they made fun of him because he would not play games or fly kites, or because he mispronounced some word, only the knowledge that it was unsportsmanlike to kill little naked cubs kept him from picking them up and breaking them in two. He did not know his own strength in the least. In the jungle he knew he was weak compared with the beasts, but in the village, people said that he was as strong as a bull. He certainly had no notion of what fear was, for when the village priest told him that the god in the temple would be angry with him if he ate the priest's mangoes, he picked up the image, brought it over to the priest's house, and asked the priest to make the god angry and he would be happy to fight him. It was a horrible scandal, but the priest hushed it up, and Messua's husband paid much good silver to comfort the god. And Mowgli had not the faintest idea of the difference that caste makes between man and man. When the potter's donkey slipped in the clay-pit, Mowgli hauled it out by the tail, and helped to stack the pots for their journey to the market at Khanhiwara. That was very shocking, too, for the potter is a low-caste man, and his donkey is worse. When the priest scolded him, Mowgli threatened to put him on the donkey, too, and the priest told Messua's husband that Mowgli had better be set to work as soon as possible; and the village head-man told Mowgli that he would have to go out with the buffaloes next day, and herd them while they grazed. No one was more pleased than Mowgli; and that night, because he had been appointed a servant of the village, as it were, he went off to a circle that met every evening on a masonry platform under a great fig-tree. It was the village club, and the head-man and the watchman and the barber, who knew all the gossip of the village, and old Buldeo, the village hunter, who had a Tower musket, met and smoked. The monkeys sat and talked in the upper branches, and there was a hole under the platform where a cobra lived, and he had his little platter of milk every night because he was sacred; and the old men sat around the tree and talked, and pulled at the big *huqas* (the water-pipes) till far into the night. They told wonderful tales of gods and men and ghosts; and Buldeo told even more wonderful ones of the ways of beasts in the jungle, till the eyes of the children sitting outside the circle bulged out of their heads. Most of the tales were about animals, for the jungle was always at their door. The deer and the wild pig grubbed up their crops, and now and again the tiger carried off a man at twilight, within sight of the village gates.

Mowgli, who naturally knew something about what they were talking of, had to cover his face not to show that he was laughing, while Buldeo, the Tower musket across his knees, climbed on from one wonderful story to another, and Mowgli's shoulders shook.

Buldeo was explaining how the tiger that had carried away Messua's son was a ghost-tiger, and his body was inhabited by the ghost of a wicked, old money-lender, who had died some years ago. "And I know that this is true," he said, "because Purun Dass always limped from the blow that he got in a riot when his account-books were burned, and the tiger that I speak of *he* limps, too, for the tracks of his pads are unequal."

"True, true, that must be the truth," said the greybeards nodding together.

"Are all these tales such cobwebs and moon-talk?" said Mowgli. "That tiger limps because he was born lame, as every one knows. To talk of the soul of a moneylender in a beast that never had the courage of a jackal is child's talk."

Buldeo was speechless with surprise for a moment, and the head-man stared.

"Oho! It is the jungle brat, is it?" said Buldeo. "If thou art so wise, better bring his hide to Khanhiwara, for the Government has set a hundred rupees on his life. Better still, talk not when thy elders speak."

Mowgli rose to go. "All the evening I have lain here listening," he called back, over his shoulder, "and, except once or twice, Buldeo has not said one word of truth concerning the jungle, which is at his very doors. How then shall I believe the tales of ghosts, and gods, and goblins which he says he has seen?"

"It is full time that boy went to herding," said the head-man, while Buldeo puffed and snorted at Mowgli's impertinence.

The custom of most Indian villages is for a few boys to take the cattle and buffaloes out to graze in the early morning, and bring them back at night; and the very cattle that would trample a white man to death allow themselves to be banged and bullied and shouted at by children that hardly come up to their noses. So long as the boys keep with the herds they are safe, for not even the tiger will charge a mob of cattle. But if they straggle to pick flowers or hunt lizards, they are sometimes carried off. Mowgli went through the village street in the dawn, sitting on the back of Rama, the great herd bull; and the slaty-blue buffaloes, with their long, backward-sweeping horns and savage eyes, rose out of their byres, one by one, and followed him, and Mowgli made it very clear to the children with him that he was the master. He beat the buffaloes with a long, polished bamboo, and told Kamya, one of the boys, to graze the cattle by themselves, while he went on with the buffaloes, and to be very careful not to stray away from the herd.

An Indian grazing-ground is all rocks, and scrubs, and tussocks, and little ravines, among which the herds scatter and disappear. The buffaloes generally keep to the pools and muddy places, where they lie wallowing or basking in the warm mud for hours. Mowgli drove them on to the edge of the plain where the Wainganga came out of the jungle; then he dropped from Rama's neck, trotted off to a bamboo clump, and found Grey Brother.

"Ah," said Grey Brother, "I have waited here very many days. What is the meaning of this cattle-herding work?"

"It is an order," said Mowgli. "I am a village herder for a while. What news of Shere Khan?"

"He has come back to this country, and has waited here a long time for thee. Now he has gone off again, for the game is scarce. But he means to kill thee."

"Very good," said Mowgli. "So long as he is away do thou or one of the four brothers sit on that rock, so that I can see thee as I come out of the village. When he comes back wait for me in the ravine by the *dhâk*-tree in the centre of the plain. We need not walk into Shere Khan's mouth."

Then Mowgli picked out a shady place, and lay down and slept while the buffaloes grazed round him. Herding in India is one of the laziest things in the world. The cattle move and crunch, and lie down, and move on again, and they do not even low. They only grunt, and the buffaloes very seldom say anything, but get down into the muddy pools one after another, and work their way into the mud till only their noses and staring china-blue eyes show above the surface, and then they lie like logs. The sun makes the rocks dance in the heat, and the herd-children hear one kite (never any more) whistling almost out of sight overhead, and they know that if they died, or a cow died, that kite would sweep down, and the next kite miles away would see him drop and follow, and the next, and the next, and almost before they were dead there would be a score of hungry kites come out of nowhere. Then they sleep and wake and sleep again, and weave little baskets of dried grass and put grasshoppers in them, or catch two praying mantises and make them fight, or string a necklace of red and black jungle-nuts, or watch a lizard basking on a rock, or a snake hunting a frog near the wallows. Then they sing long, long songs with odd native quavers at the end of them, and the day seems longer than most people's whole lives, and perhaps they make a mud castle with mud figures of men and horses and buffaloes, and put reeds into the men's hands, and pretend that they are kings and the figures are their armies, or that they are gods to be worshipped. Then evening comes and the children call, and the buffaloes lumber up out of the sticky mud with noises like gunshots going off one after the other, and they all string across the grey plain back to the twinkling village lights.

Day after day Mowgli would lead the buffaloes out to their wallows, and day after day he would see Grey Brother's back a mile and a half away across the plain (so he knew that Shere Khan had not come back), and day after day he would lie on the grass listening to the noises round him, and dreaming of old days in the jungle. If Shere Khan had made a false step with his lame paw up in the jungles by the Wainganga, Mowgli would have heard him in those long still mornings.

At last a day came when he did not see Grey Brother at the signal place, and he laughed and headed the buffaloes for the ravine by the *dhâk*-tree, which was all covered with golden-red flowers. There sat Grey Brother, every bristle on his back lifted.

"He has hidden for a month to throw thee off thy guard. He crossed the ranges last night with Tabaqui, hot-foot on thy trail," said the wolf, panting.

Mowgli frowned. "I am not afraid of Shere Khan, but Tabaqui is very cunning."

"Have no fear," said Grey Brother, licking his lips a little. "I met Tabaqui in the dawn. Now he is telling all his wisdom to the kites, but he told *me* everything before I broke his back. Shere Khan's plan is to wait for thee at the village gate this evening – for thee and for no one else. He is lying up now, in the big dry ravine of the Wainganga."

"Has he eaten today, or does he hunt empty?" said Mowgli, for the answer meant life and death to him.

"He killed at dawn – a pig – and he has drunk too. Remember, Shere Khan could never fast, even for the sake of revenge."

"Oh! Fool, fool! What a cub's cub it is! Eaten and drunk too, and he thinks that I shall wait till he has slept! Now, where does he lie up? If there were but ten of us we might pull him down as he lies. These buffaloes will not charge unless they wind him, and I cannot speak their language. Can we get behind his track so that they may smell it?"

"He swam far down the Wainganga to cut that off," said Grey Brother.

"Tabaqui told him that, I know. He would never have thought of it alone." Mowgli stood with his finger in his mouth, thinking. "The big ravine of the Wainganga. That opens out on the plain not half a mile from here. I can take the herd round through the jungle to the head of the ravine and then sweep down – but he would slink out at the foot. We must block that end. Grey Brother, canst thou cut the herd in two for me?"

"Not I, perhaps – but I have brought a wise helper." Grey Brother trotted off and dropped into a hole. Then there lifted up a huge grey head that Mowgli knew well, and the hot air was filled with the most desolate cry of all the jungle – the hunting-howl of a wolf at mid-day.

"Akela! Akela!" said Mowgli, clapping his hands. "I might have known that thou wouldst not forget me. We have a big work in hand. Cut the herd in two, Akela. Keep the cows and calves together, and the bulls and the plough-buffaloes by themselves."

The two wolves ran, ladies'-chain fashion, in and out of the herd, which snorted and threw up its head, and separated into two clumps. In one, the cow-buffaloes stood with their calves in the centre, and glared and pawed, ready, if a wolf would only stay still, to charge down and trample the life out of him. In the other, the bulls and the young bulls snorted and stamped, but though they looked more imposing they were much less dangerous, for they had no calves to protect. No six men could have divided the herd so neatly.

"What orders!" panted Akela. "They are trying to join again."

Mowgli slipped on to Rama's back. "Drive the bulls away to the left, Akela. Grey Brother, when we are gone, hold the cows together, and drive them into the foot of the ravine."

"How far?" said Grey Brother, panting and snapping.

"Till the sides are higher than Shere Khan can jump," shouted Mowgli. "Keep them there till we come down." The bulls swept off as Akela bayed, and Grey Brother stopped in front of the cows. They charged down on him, and he ran just before them to the foot of the ravine, as Akela drove the bulls far to the left.

"Well done! Another charge and they are fairly started. Careful, now – careful, Akela. A snap too much, and the bulls will charge. *Hujah!* This is wilder work than driving black-buck. Didst thou think these creatures could move so swiftly?" Mowgli called.

"I have – have hunted these too in my time," gasped Akela in the dust. "Shall I turn them into the jungle?"

"Aye! Turn. Swiftly turn them! Rama is mad with rage. Oh, if I could only tell him what I need of him today."

The bulls were turned, to the right this time, and crashed into the standing thicket. The other herd-children, watching with the cattle half a mile away, hurried to the village as fast as their legs could carry them, crying that the buffaloes had gone mad and run away. But Mowgli's plan was simple enough. All he wanted to do was to make a big circle uphill and get at the head of the ravine, and then take the bulls down it and catch Shere Khan between the bulls and the cows, for he knew that after a meal and a full drink Shere Khan would not be in any condition to fight or to clamber up the sides of the ravine. He was soothing the buffaloes now by voice, and Akela had dropped far to the rear, only whimpering once or twice to hurry the rear-guard. It was a long, long circle, for they did not wish to get too near the ravine and give Shere Khan warning. At last Mowgli rounded up the bewildered herd at the head of the ravine on a grassy patch that sloped steeply down to the ravine itself. From that height you could see across the tops of the trees down to the plain below; but what Mowgli looked at was the sides of the ravine, and he saw with a great deal of satisfaction that they ran nearly straight up and down, while the vines and creepers that hung over them would give no foothold to a tiger who wanted to get out.

"Let them breathe, Akela," he said, holding up his hand. "They have not winded him yet. Let them breathe. I must tell Shere Khan who comes. We have him in the trap."

He put his hands to his mouth and shouted down the ravine – it was almost like shouting down a tunnel – and the echoes jumped from rock to rock.

After a long time there came back the drawling, sleepy snarl of a full-fed tiger just wakened.

"Who calls?" said Shere Khan, and a splendid peacock fluttered up out of the ravine screeching.

"I, Mowgli. Cattle thief, it is time to come to the Council Rock! Down – hurry them down, Akela! Down, Rama, down!"

Shere Khan heard the thunder of their hoofs, picked himself up, and lumbered down the ravine, looking from side to side for some way of escape.

The herd paused for an instant at the edge of the slope, but Akela gave tongue in the full hunting yell, and they pitched over one after the other just as steamers shoot rapids, the sand and stones spurting up round them. Once started, there was no chance of stopping, and before they were fairly in the bed of the ravine Rama winded Shere Khan and bellowed.

"Ha! Ha!" said Mowgli, on his back. "Now thou knowest!" And the torrent of black horns, foaming muzzles, and staring eyes whirled down the ravine just as boulders go down in flood-time, the weaker buffaloes being shouldered out to the sides of the ravine where they tore through the creepers. They knew what the business was before them – the terrible charge of the buffalo herd against which no tiger can hope to stand. Shere Khan heard the thunder of their hoofs, picked himself up, and lumbered down the ravine, looking from side to side for some way of escape, but the walls of the ravine were straight and he had to hold on, heavy with his dinner and his drink, willing to do anything rather than fight. The herd splashed through the pool he had just left, bellowing till the narrow cut rang. Mowgli heard an answering bellow from the foot of the ravine, saw Shere Khan turn (the tiger knew if the worst came to the worst it was better to meet the bulls than the cows with their calves), and then Rama tripped, stumbled, and went on again over something soft, and, with the bulls at his heels, crashed full into the other herd, while the weaker buffaloes were lifted clean off their feet by the shock of the meeting. That charge carried both herds out into the plain, goring and stamping and snorting. Mowgli watched his time, and slipped off Rama's neck, laying about him right and left with his stick.

"Quick, Akela! Break them up. Scatter them, or they will be fighting one another. Drive them away, Akela. *Hai*, Rama! *Hai! hai! hai!* my children. Softly now, softly! It is all over."

Akela and Grey Brother ran to and fro nipping the buffaloes' legs, and though the herd wheeled once to charge up the ravine again, Mowgli managed to turn Rama, and the others followed him to the wallows.

Shere Khan needed no more trampling. He was dead, and the kites were coming for him already.

"Brothers, that was a dog's death," said Mowgli, feeling for the knife he always carried in a sheath round his neck now that he lived with men. "But he would never have shown fight. *Wallah!* His hide will look well on the Council Rock. We must get to work swiftly."

A boy trained among men would never have dreamed of skinning a ten-foot tiger alone, but Mowgli knew better than any one else how an animal's skin is fitted on, and how it can be taken off. But it was hard work, and Mowgli slashed and tore and grunted for an hour, while the wolves lolled out their tongues, or came forward and tugged as he ordered them. Presently a hand fell on his shoulder, and looking up he saw Buldeo with the Tower musket. The children had told the village about the buffalo stampede, and Buldeo went out angrily, only too anxious to correct Mowgli for not taking better care of the herd. The wolves dropped out of sight as soon as they saw the man coming.

"What is this folly?" said Buldeo, angrily. "To think that thou canst skin a tiger! Where did the buffaloes kill him? It is the Lame Tiger, too, and there is a hundred rupees on his head. Well, well, we will overlook thy letting the herd run off, and perhaps I will give thee one of the rupees of the reward when I have taken the skin to Khanhiwara." He fumbled in his waist-cloth for flint and steel, and stooped down to singe Shere Khan's whiskers. Most native hunters always singe a tiger's whiskers to prevent his ghost from haunting them.

"*Hum!*" said Mowgli, half to himself as he ripped back the skin of a fore paw. "So thou wilt take the hide to Khanhiwara for the reward, and perhaps give me one rupee? Now it is in my mind that I need the skin for my own use. *Heh!* Old man, take away that fire!"

"What talk is this to the chief hunter of the village? Thy luck and the stupidity of thy buffaloes have helped thee to this kill. The tiger has just fed, or he would have gone twenty miles by this time. Thou canst not even skin him properly, little beggar brat, and forsooth I, Buldeo, must be told not to singe his whiskers. Mowgli, I will not give thee one anna of the reward, but only a very big beating. Leave the carcass!"

"By the bull that bought me," said Mowgli, who was trying to get at the shoulder, "must I stay babbling to an old ape all noon? Here, Akela, this man plagues me."

Buldeo, who was still stooping over Shere Khan's head, found himself sprawling on the grass, with a grey wolf standing over him, while Mowgli went on skinning as though he were alone in all India.

"Ye-es," he said, between his teeth. "Thou art altogether right, Buldeo. Thou wilt never give me one anna of the reward. There is an old war between this lame tiger and myself – a very old war, and – I have won."

To do Buldeo justice, if he had been ten years younger he would have taken his chance with Akela had he met the wolf in the woods, but a wolf who obeyed the orders of this boy who had private wars with man-eating tigers was not a common animal. It was sorcery, magic of the worst kind, thought Buldeo, and he wondered whether the amulet round his neck would protect him. He lay as still as still, expecting every minute to see Mowgli turn into a tiger, too.

"Maharaj! Great King," he said at last, in a husky whisper.

"Yes," said Mowgli, without turning his head, chuckling a little.

"I am an old man. I did not know that thou wast anything more than a herdsboy. May I rise up and go away, or will thy servant tear me to pieces?"

"Go, and peace go with thee. Only, another time do not meddle with my game. Let him go, Akela."

Buldeo hobbled away to the village as fast as he could, looking back over his shoulder in case Mowgli should change into something terrible. When he got to the village he told a tale of magic and enchantment and sorcery that made the priest look very grave.

Mowgli went on with his work, but it was nearly twilight before he and the wolves had drawn the great gay skin clear of the body.

"Now we must hide this and take the buffaloes home! Help me to herd them, Akela."

The herd rounded up in the misty twilight, and when they got near the village Mowgli saw lights, and heard the conches and bells in the temple blowing and banging. Half the village seemed to be waiting for him by the gate. "That is because I have killed Shere Khan," he said to himself. But a shower of stones whistled about his ears, and the villagers shouted: "Sorcerer! Wolfs brat! Jungle-demon! Go away! Get hence quickly, or the priest will turn thee into a wolf again. Shoot, Buldeo, shoot!"

The old Tower musket went off with a bang, and a young buffalo bellowed in pain.

"More sorcery!" shouted the villagers. "He can turn bullets. Buldeo, that was *thy* buffalo."

"Now what is this?" said Mowgli, bewildered, as the stones flew thicker.

"They are not unlike the pack, these brothers of thine," said Akela, sitting down composedly. "It is in my head that, if bullets mean anything, they would cast thee out."

"Wolf! Wolfs cub! Go away!" shouted the priest, waving a sprig of the sacred *tulsi* plant

"Again? Last time it was because I was a man. This time it is because I am a wolf. Let us go, Akela."

A woman – it was Messua – ran across to the herd, and cried: "Oh, my son, my son! They say thou art a sorcerer who can turn himself into a beast at will. I do not believe, but go away or they will kill thee. Buldeo says thou art a wizard, but I know thou hast avenged Nathoo's death."

"Come back, Messua!" shouted the crowd. "Come back, or we will stone thee."

Mowgli laughed a little short ugly laugh, for a stone had hit him in the mouth. "Run back, Messua. This is one of the foolish tales they tell under the big tree at dusk. I have at least paid for thy son's life. Farewell, and run quickly, for I shall send the herd in more swiftly than their brickbats. I am no wizard, Messua. Farewell!"

"Now, once more, Akela," he cried. "Bring the herd in."

The buffaloes were anxious enough to get to the village. They hardly needed Akela's yell, but charged through the gate like a whirlwind, scattering the crowd right and left.

"Keep count!" shouted Mowgli, scornfully. "It may be that I have stolen one of them. Keep count, for I will do your herding no more. Fare you well, children of men, and thank Messua that I do not come in with my wolves and hunt you up and down your street."

He turned on his heel and walked away with the Lone Wolf, and as he looked up at the stars he felt happy. "No more sleeping in traps for me, Akela. Let us get Shere Khan's skin and go away. No, we will not hurt the village, for Messua was kind to me."

When the moon rose over the plain, making it look all milky, the horrified villagers saw Mowgli, with two wolves at his heels and a bundle on his head, trotting across at the steady wolf's trot that eats up the long miles like fire. Then they banged the temple bells and blew the conches louder than ever. And Messua cried, and Buldeo embroidered the story of his adventures in the jungle, till he ended by saying that Akela stood up on his hind legs and talked like a man.

The moon was just going down when Mowgli and the two wolves came to the hill of the Council Rock, and they stopped at Mother Wolfs cave.

"They have cast me out from the man pack, Mother," shouted Mowgli, "but I come with the hide of Shere Khan to keep my word." Mother Wolf walked stiffly from the cave with the cubs behind her, and her eyes glowed as she saw the skin.

"I told him on that day, when he crammed his head and shoulders into this cave, hunting for thy life, little frog – I told him that the hunter would be the hunted. It is well done."

"Little Brother, it is well done," said a deep voice in the thicket. "We were lonely in the jungle without thee," and Bagheera came running to Mowgli's bare feet. They clambered up the Council Rock together, and Mowgli spread the skin out on the flat stone where Akela used to sit, and pegged it down with four slivers of bamboo, and Akela lay down upon it, and called the old call to the council: "Look, look well, O wolves," exactly as he had called when Mowgli was first brought there.

Ever since Akela had been deposed, the pack had been without a leader, hunting and fighting at their own pleasure. But they answered the call from habit, and some of them were lame from the traps they had fallen into, and some limped from shot-wounds, and some were mangy from eating bad food, and many were missing. But they came to the Council Rock, all that were left of them, and saw Shere Khan's striped hide on the rock, and the huge claws dangling at the end of the empty dangling feet.

"Look well, O wolves. Have I kept my word?" said Mowgli. And the wolves bayed Yes, and one tattered wolf howled:

"Lead us again, O Akela. Lead us again, O man-cub, for we be sick of this lawlessness, and we would be the Free People once more."

"Nay," purred Bagheera, "that may not be. When ye are full-fed, the madness may come upon you again. Not for nothing are ye called the Free People. Ye fought for freedom, and it is yours. Eat it, O wolves."

"Man pack and wolf pack have cast me out," said Mowgli. "Now I will hunt alone in the jungle."

"And we will hunt with thee," said the four cubs.

So Mowgli went away and hunted with the four cubs in the jungle from that day on. But he was not always alone, because, years afterward, he became a man and married.

But that is a story for grown-ups.

Mowgli's Song

*That he sang at the Council Rock when he danced
on Shere Khan's hide*

The Song of Mowgli – I, Mowgli, am singing. Let the jungle listen to
the things I have done.

Shere Khan said he would kill – would kill! At the gates in the twilight
he would kill Mowgli the Frog!

He ate and he drank. Drink deep, Shere Khan, for when wilt thou drink
again? Sleep and dream of the kill.

I am alone on the grazing-grounds. Grey Brother, come to me! Come to
me, Lone Wolf, for there is big game afoot!

Bring up the great bull-buffaloes, the blue-skinned herd-bulls with the
angry eyes. Drive them to and fro as I order. Sleepest thou still, Shere
Khan? Wake, O wake! Here come I, and the bulls are behind.

Rama the king of the buffaloes stamped with his foot. Waters of the
Wainganga, whither went Shere Khan?

He is not Sahi to dig holes, nor Mor the Peacock that he should fly. He
is not Mang the Bat to hang in the branches. Little bamboos that
creak together, tell me where he ran?

Ow! He is there. *Ahoo!* He is there. Under the feet of Rama lies the
Lame One! Up, Shere Khan! Up and kill! Here is meat; break the
necks of the bulls!

Hsh! He is asleep. We will not wake him, for his strength is very great.
The kites have come down to see it. The black ants have come up to
know it. There is a great assembly in his honour.

Alala! I have no cloth to wrap me. The kites will see that I am naked. I
am ashamed to meet all these people.

Lend me thy coat, Shere Khan. Lend me thy gay striped coat that I may go to the Council Rock.

By the bull that bought me I made a promise – a little promise. Only thy coat is lacking before I keep my word.

With the knife, with the knife that men use, with the knife of the hunter, I will stoop down for my gift.

Waters of the Wainganga, Shere Khan gives me his coat for the love that he bears me. Pull, Grey Brother! Pull, Akela! Heavy is the hide of Shere Khan.

The man pack are angry. They throw stones and talk child's talk. My mouth is bleeding. Let me run away.

Through the night, through the hot night, run swiftly with me, my brothers. We will leave the lights of the village and go to the low moon.

Waters of the Wainganga the man pack have cast me out. I did them no harm, but they were afraid of me. Why?

Wolf pack, ye have cast me out too. The jungle is shut to me and the village gates are shut. Why?

As Mang flies between the beasts and birds so fly I between the village and the jungle. Why?

I dance on the hide of Shere Khan, but my heart is very heavy. My mouth is cut and wounded with the stones from the village, but my heart is very light, because I have come back to the jungle. Why?

These two things fight together in me as the snakes fight in the spring. The water comes out of my eyes, yet I laugh while it falls. Why?

I am two Mowglis, but the hide of Shere Khan is under my feet.

All the jungle knows that I have killed Shere Khan. Look, look well, O wolves!

Ahae! My heart is heavy with the things that I do not understand.

The White Seal

Oh! hush thee, my baby, the night is behind us,
    And black are the waters that sparkled so green.
The moon, o'er the combers, looks downwards to find us
    At rest in the hollows that rustle between.
Where billow meets billow, then soft be thy pillow,
    Oh, weary wee flipperling curl at thy ease!
The storm shall not wake thee, nor shark overtake thee,
    Asleep in the arms of the slow-swinging seas!

Seal Lullaby

All these things happened several years ago at a place called Novas-toshnah or North East Point on the island of St. Paul, away and away in the Bering Sea. Limmershin the Winter Wren told me the tale when he was blown on to the rigging of a steamer going to Japan, and I took him down into my cabin and warmed and fed him for a couple of days till he was fit to fly back to St. Paul again. Limmershin is a very quaint little bird, but he knows how to tell the truth.

Nobody comes to Novastoshnah except on business, and the only people who have regular business there are the seals. They come in the summer months by hundreds and hundreds of thousands out of the cold grey sea, for Novastoshnah Beach has the finest accommodation for seals of any place in all the world. Sea Catch knew that, and every spring would swim from whatever place he happened to be in – would swim like a torpedo-boat straight for Novastoshnah and spend a month fighting with his companions for a good place on the rocks, as close to the sea as possible. Sea Catch was fifteen years old, a huge grey fur-seal with almost a mane on his shoulders, and long, wicked dog-teeth. When he heaved himself up on his front flippers he stood more than four feet clear of the ground, and his weight, if any one had been bold enough to weigh him, was nearly seven hundred pounds. He was scarred all over with the marks of savage fights, but he was always ready for just one fight more. He would put his head on one side, as though he were afraid to look his enemy in the face; then he would shoot it out like lightning, and when the big teeth were firmly fixed on the other seal's neck, the other seal might get away if he could, but Sea Catch would not help him. Yet Sea Catch never chased a beaten seal, for that was against the Rules of the Beach. He only wanted room by the sea for his nursery, but as there were forty or fifty thousand other seals hunting for the same thing each spring, the whistling, bellowing, roaring, and blowing on the beach was something frightful. From a little hill called Hutchinson's Hill, you could look over three and a half miles of ground covered with fighting seals, and the surf was dotted all over with the heads of seals hurrying to land and begin their share of fighting. They fought in the breakers, they fought in the sand, and they fought on the smooth-worn basalt rocks of the nurseries, for they were just as stupid and unaccommodating as men. Their wives never came to the island until late in May or early in June, for they did not care to be torn to pieces; and the young two-, three-, and four-year-old seals who had not begun housekeeping went inland about half a mile through the ranks of the fighters and played about on the sand-dunes in droves and legions, and rubbed off every single green thing that grew. They were called the holluschickie – the bachelors – and there were perhaps two or three hundred thousand of them at Novastoshnah alone.

Sea Catch had just finished his forty-fifth fight one spring when Matkah, his soft, sleek, gentle-eyed wife, came up out of the sea, and he caught her by the scruff of the neck and dumped her down on his reservation, saying gruffly: "Late as usual. Where *have* you been?"

It was not the fashion for Sea Catch to eat anything during the four months he stayed on the beaches, and so his temper was generally bad. Matkah knew better than to answer back. She looked round and cooed: "How thoughtful of you. You've taken the old place again."

"I should think I had," said Sea Catch. "Look at me!"

He was scratched and bleeding in twenty places; one eye was almost out, and his sides were torn to ribbons.

"Oh, you men, you men!" Matkah said, fanning herself with her hind flipper. "Why can't you be sensible and settle your places quietly? You look as though you had been fighting with the killer whale."

"I haven't been doing anything *but* fight since the middle of May. The beach is disgracefully crowded this season. I've met at least a hundred seals from Lukannon Beach, house-hunting. Why can't people stay where they belong?"

"I've often thought we should be much happier if we hauled out at Otter Island instead of this crowded place," said Matkah.

"*Bah!* only the holluschickie go to Otter Island. If we went there they would say we were afraid. We must preserve appearances, my dear."

Sea Catch sank his head proudly between his fat shoulders and pretended to go to sleep for a few minutes, but all the time he was keeping a sharp lookout for a fight Now that all the seals and their wives were on the land you could hear their clamour miles out to sea above the loudest gales. At the lowest counting there were over a million seals on the beach – old seals, mother seals, tiny babies, and holluschickie, fighting, scuffling, bleating, crawling, and playing together – going down to the sea and coming up from it in gangs and regiments, lying over every foot of ground as far as the eye could reach, and skirmishing about in brigades through the fog. It is nearly always foggy at Novastoshnah, except when the sun comes out and makes everything look all pearly and rainbow-coloured for a little while.

Kotick, Matkah's baby, was born in the middle of that confusion, and he was all head and shoulders, with pale, watery blue eyes, as tiny seals must be, but there was something about his coat that made his mother look at him very closely.

"Sea Catch," she said, at last, "our baby's going to be white!"

"Empty clam-shells and dry sea-weed!" snorted Sea Catch. "There never has been such a thing in the world as a white seal."

"I can't help that," said Matkah. "There's going to be now." And she sang the low, crooning seal-song that all the mother seals sing to their babies:

You mustn't swim till you're six weeks old,
  Or your head will be sunk by your heels;
And summer gales and killer whales
  Are bad for baby seals.

Are bad for baby seals, dear rat,
  As bad as bad can be;
But splash and grow strong,
  And you can't be wrong,
Child of the open sea!

Of course the little fellow did not understand the words at first. He paddled and scrambled about by his mother's side and learned to scuffle out of the way when his father was fighting with another seal, and the two rolled and roared up and down the slippery rocks. Matkah used to go to sea to get things to eat, and the baby was only fed once in two days, but then he ate all he could and throve upon it. The first thing he did was to crawl inland, and there he met ten of thousands of babies of his own age, and they played together like puppies, went to sleep on the clean sand, and played again. The old people in the nurseries took no notice of them, and the holluschickie kept to their own grounds, and the babies had a beautiful playtime. When Matkah came back from her deep-sea fishing she would go straight to their playground and call as a sheep calls for a lamb, and wait until she heard Kotick bleat Then she would take the straightest of straight lines in his direction, striking out with her fore flippers and knocking the youngsters head over heels right and left. There were always a few hundred mothers hunting for their children through the playgrounds, and the babies were kept lively. But, as Matkah told Kotick: "So long as you don't lie in muddy water and get mange, or rub the hard sand into a cut or scratch, and so long as you never go swimming when there is a heavy sea, nothing will hurt you here."

Little seals can no more swim than little children, but they are unhappy till they learn. The first time that Kotick went down to the sea a wave carried him out beyond his depth, and his big head sank and his little hind flippers flew up exactly as his mother had told him in the song, and if the next wave had not thrown him back again he would have drowned. After that, he learned to lie in a beach-pool and let the wash of the waves just cover him and lift him up while he paddled, but he always kept his eye open for big waves that might hurt. He was two weeks learning to use his flippers, and all that while he floundered in and out of the water and coughed and grunted and crawled up the beach and took cat-naps on the sand and went back again, until at last he found that he truly belonged to the water. Then you can imagine the times that he had with his companions, ducking under the rollers; or coming in on top of a comber and landing with a swash and a splutter as the big wave went whirling far up the beach; or standing up on his tail and scratching his head as the old people did; or playing "I'm the King of the Castle" on slippery, weedy rocks that just stuck out of the wash. Now and then he would see a thin fin, like a big shark's fin, drifting along close to shore, and he knew that that was the killer whale, the grampus, who eats young seals when he can get them, and Kotick would head for the beach like an arrow, and the fin would jig off slowly, as if it were looking for nothing at all.

Late in October the seals began to leave St. Paul for the deep sea, by families and tribes, and there was no more fighting over the nurseries, and the holluschickie played anywhere they liked. "Next year," said Matkah to Kotick, "you will be a holluschickie, but this year you must learn how to catch fish."

They set out together across the Pacific, and Matkah showed Kotick how to sleep on his back with his flippers tucked down by his side and his little nose just out of the water. No cradle is so comfortable as the long, rocking swell of the Pacific. When Kotick felt his skin tingle all over, Matkah told him he was learning the "feel of the water," and that tingly, prickly feelings meant bad weather coming, and he must swim hard and get away. "In a little time," she said, "you'll know where to swim to, but just now we'll follow Sea Pig, for he is very wise." A school of porpoises was ducking and tearing through the water and little Kotick followed them as fast as he could. "How do you know where to go to?" he panted. The leader of the school rolled his white eye and ducked under: "My tail tingles, youngster," he said. "That means there's a gale behind me. Come along! When you're south of the Sticky Water [he meant the Equator] and your tail tingles, that means there's a gale in front of you and you must head north. Come along. The water feels bad here."

This was one of very many things that Kotick learned, and he was always learning. Matkah taught him to follow the cod and the halibut along the undersea banks and wrench the rockling out of his hole among the weeds; how to skirt the wrecks lying a hundred fathoms below water and dart like a rifle bullet in at one port-hole and out at another as the fishes ran; how to dance on the top of the waves when the lightning was racing all over the sky, and wave his flipper politely to the stumpy-tailed albatross and the man-of-war hawk as they went down the wind; how to jump three or four feet clear of the water like a dolphin, flippers close to the side and tail curved; to leave the flying-fish alone because they are all bony; to take the shoulder-piece out of a cod at full speed ten fathoms deep, and never to stop and look at a boat or a ship, but particularly a row-boat. At the end of six months what Kotick did not know about deep-sea fishing was not worth the knowing; and all that time he never set flipper on dry ground.

One day, however, as he was lying half asleep in the warm water some-where off the island of Juan Fernández, he felt faint and lazy all over, just as human people do when the spring is in their legs, and he remembered the good firm beaches of Novastoshnah seven thousand miles away; the games his companions played, the smell of the sea-weed, the seal-roar, and the fighting. That very minute he turned north, swimming steadily, and as he went on he met scores of his mates, all bound for the same place, and they said: "Greeting, Kotick! This year we are all holluschickie, and we can dance the Fire Dance in the breakers off Lukannon and play on the new grass. But where did you get that coat?"

Kotick's fur was almost pure white now, and though he felt very proud of it he only said: "Swim quickly! My bones are aching for the land." And so they all came to the beaches where they had been born and heard the old seals, their fathers, fighting in the rolling mist.

That night Kotick danced the Fire Dance with the yearling seals. The sea is full of fire on summer nights all the way down from Novastoshnah to Lukannon, and each seal leaves a wake like burning oil behind him and a flaming flash when he jumps, and the waves break in great phosphorescent streaks and swirls. Then they went inland to the holluschickie-grounds and rolled up and down in the new wild wheat and told stories of what they had done while they had been at sea. They talked about the Pacific as boys would talk about a wood that they had been nutting in, and if any one had understood them he could have gone away and made such a chart of that ocean as never was. The three- and four-year-old holluschickie romped down from Hutchinson's Hill crying: "Out of the way, youngsters! The sea is deep and you don't know all that's in it yet. Wait till you've rounded the Horn. Hi, you yearling, where did you get that white coat?"

"I didn't get it," said Kotick. "It grew." And just as he was going to roll the speaker over, a couple of black-haired men with flat red faces came from behind a sand-dune, and Kotick, who had never seen a man before, coughed and lowered his head. The holluschickie just bundled off a few yards and sat staring stupidly. The men were no less than Kerick Booterin, the chief of the seal-hunters on the island, and Patalamon, his son. They came from the little village not a half mile from the seal nurseries, and they were deciding what seals they would drive up to the killing-pens – for the seals were driven just like sheep – to be turned into sealskin jackets later on.

"Ho!" said Patalamon. "Look! There's a white seal!"

Kerick Booterin turned nearly white under his oil and smoke, for he was an Aleut, and Aleuts are not clean people. Then he began to mutter a prayer. "Don't touch him, Patalamon. There has never been a white seal since – since I was born. Perhaps it is old Zaharrof's ghost. He was lost last year in the big gale."

"I'm not going near him," said Patalamon. "He's unlucky. Do you really think he is old Zaharrof come back? I owe him for some gulls' eggs."

"Don't look at him," said Kerick. "Head off that drove of four-year-olds. The men ought to skin two hundred today, but it's the beginning of the season and they are new to the work. A hundred will do. Quick!"

Patalamon rattled a pair of seal's shoulder-bones in front of a herd of holluschickie and they stopped dead, puffing and blowing. Then he stepped near and the seals began to move, and Kerick headed them inland, and they never tried to get back to their companions. Hundreds and hundreds of thousands of seals watched them being driven, but they went on playing just the same. Kotick was the only one who asked questions, and none of his companions could tell him anything, except that the men always drove seals in that way for six weeks or two months of every year.

"I am going to follow," he said, and his eyes nearly popped out of his head as he shuffled along in the wake of the herd.

"The white seal is coming after us," cried Patalamon. "That's the first time a seal has ever come to the killing-grounds alone."

"*Hsh!* don't look behind you," said Kerick. "It *is* Zaharrof's ghost! I must speak to the priest about this."

The distance to the killing-ground was only half a mile, but it took an hour to cover, because if the seals went too fast Kerick knew that they would get heated and then their fur would come off in patches when they were skinned. So they went on very slowly, past Sea Lion's Neck, past Webster House, till they came to the Salt House just beyond the sight of the seals on the beach. Kotick followed, panting and wondering. He thought that he was at the world's end, but the roar of the seal-nurseries behind him sounded as loud as the roar of a train in a tunnel. Then Kerick sat down on the moss and pulled out a heavy pewter watch and let the drove cool off for thirty minutes, and Kotick could hear the fog-dew dripping off the brim of his cap. Then ten or twelve men, each with an iron-bound club three or four feet long, came up, and Kerick pointed out one or two of the drove that were bitten by their companions or too hot, and the men kicked those aside with their heavy boots made of the skin of a walrus' throat, and then Kerick said: "Let go!" And then the men clubbed the seals on the head as fast as they could. Ten minutes later little Kotick did not recognize his friends any more, for their skins were ripped off from the nose to the hind flippers, whipped off, and thrown down on the ground in a pile. That was enough for Kotick. He turned and galloped (a seal can gallop very swiftly for a short time) back to sea, his little new moustache bristling with horror. At Sea Lion's Neck, where the great sea lions sit on the edge of the surf, he flung himself flipper-overhead into the cool water and rocked there, gasping miserably. "What's here?" said a sea lion gruffly, for as a rule the sea lions keep themselves to themselves.

"*Scoochnie! Ochen Scoochnie!*" ["I'm lonesome, very lonesome!"] said Kotick. "They're killing *all* the holluschickie on *all* the beaches!"

The sea lion turned his head inshore. "Nonsense," he said, "your friends are making as much noise as ever. You must have seen old Kerick polishing off a drove. He's done that for thirty years."

"It's horrible," said Kotick, backing water as a wave went over him, and steadying himself with a screw-stroke of his flippers that brought him all standing within three inches of a jagged edge of rock.

"Well done for a yearling!" said the sea lion, who could appreciate good swimming. "I suppose it *is* rather awful from your way of looking at it, but if you seals will come here year after year, of course the men get to know of it, and unless you can find an island where no men ever come you will always be driven."

"Isn't there any such island?" began Kotick.

"I've followed the *poltoos* [the halibut] for twenty years, and I can't say I've found it yet. But look here – you seem to have a fondness for talking to your betters – suppose you go to Walrus Islet and talk to Sea Vitch. He may know something. Don't flounce off like that. It's a six-mile swim, and if I were you I should haul out and take a nap first, little one."

Kotick thought that that was good advice, so he swam round to his own beach, hauled out and slept for half an hour, twitching all over, as seals will. Then he headed straight for Walrus Islet, a little low sheet of rocky island almost due north-east from Novastoshnah, all ledges of rock and gulls' nests, where the walrus herded by themselves.

He landed close to old Sea Vitch – the big, ugly, bloated, pimpled, fat-necked, long-tusked walrus of the North Pacific, who has no manners except when he is asleep – as he was then – with his hind flippers half in and half out of the surf.

"Wake up!" barked Kotick, for the gulls were making a great noise.

"Hah! Ho! Hmph! What's that?" said Sea Vitch, and he struck the next walrus a blow with his tusks and waked him up, and the next struck the next and so on till they were all awake and staring in every direction but the right one.

"Hi! It's me," said Kotick, bobbing in the surf and looking like a little white slug.

"Well! May I be – skinned!" said Sea Vitch, and they all looked at Kotick as you can fancy a club full of drowsy old gentlemen would look at a little boy. Kotick did not care to hear any more about skinning just then; he had seen enough of it; so he called out: "Isn't there any place for seals to go where men don't ever come?"

"Go and find out," said Sea Vitch, shutting his eyes. "Run away. We're busy here."

Kotick made his dolphin-jump in the air and shouted as loud as he could: "Clam-eater! Clam-eater!" He knew that Sea Vitch never caught a fish in his life but always rooted for clams and sea-weeds, though he pretended to be a very terrible person. Naturally the chickies and the gooverooskies and the epatkas – the burgomaster gulls, and the kittiwakes, and the puffins who are always looking for a chance to be rude – took up the cry, and – so Lim-mershin told me – for nearly five minutes you could not have heard a gun fired on Walrus Islet. All the population was yelling and, screaming: "Clam-eater! *Stareek* [old man]!" while Sea Vitch rolled from side to side grunting and coughing.

"*Now* will you tell?" said Kotick, all out of breath.

"Go and ask Sea Cow," said Sea Vitch. "If he is living still he'll be able to tell you."

"How shall I know Sea Cow when I meet him?" said Kotick, sheering off.

"He's the only thing in the sea uglier than Sea Vitch," screamed a burgomaster gull, wheeling under Sea Vitch's nose. "Uglier, and with worse manners! *Stareek!*"

Kotick swam back to Novastoshnah, leaving the gulls to scream. There he found that no one sympathized with him in his little attempt to discover a quiet place for the seals. They told him that men had always driven the holluschickie – it was part of the day's work – and that if he did not like to see ugly things he should not have gone to the killing-grounds. But none of the other seals had seen the killing, and that made the difference between him and his friends. Besides, Kotick was a white seal.

"What you, must do," said old Sea Catch, after he had heard his son's adventures, "is to grow up and be a big seal like your father, and have a nursery on the beach, and then they will leave you alone. In another five years you ought to be able to fight for yourself." Even gentle Matkah, his mother, said: "You will never be able to stop the killing. Go and play in the sea, Kotick." And Kotick went off and danced the Fire Dance with a very heavy little heart.

That autumn he left the beach as soon as he could, and set off alone because of a notion in his bullet-head. He was going to find Sea Cow, if there was such a person in the sea, and he was going to find a quiet island with good firm beaches for seals to live on, where men could not get at them. So he explored and explored by himself from the North to the South Pacific, swimming as much as three hundred miles in a day and a night. He met with more adventures than can be told, and narrowly escaped being caught by the basking shark, and the spotted shark and the hammerhead, and he met all the untrustworthy ruffians that loaf up and down the seas, and the heavy polite fish, and the scarlet spotted scallops that are moored in one place for hundreds of years, and grow very proud of it; but he never met Sea Cow, and he never found an island that he could fancy. If the beach was good and hard, with a slope behind it for seals to play on, there was always the smoke of a whaler on the horizon, boiling down blubber, and Kotick knew what *that* meant. Or else he could see that seals had once visited the island and been killed off, and Kotick knew that where men had come once they would come again.

He picked up with an old stumpy-tailed albatross, who told him that Kerguelen Island was the very place for peace and quiet, and when Kotick went down there he was all but smashed to pieces against some wicked black cliffs in a heavy sleet storm with lightning and thunder. Yet as he pulled out against the gale he could see even there had once been a seal-nursery. And it was so in all the other islands that he visited.

Limmershin gave a long list of them, for he said that Kotick spent five seasons exploring, with a four months' rest each year at Novastoshnah, when the holluschickie used to make fun of him and his imaginary islands. He went to the Galápagos, a horrid dry place on the Equator, where he was nearly baked to death; he went to the Georgia Islands, the Orkneys, Emerald Island, Little Nightingale Island, Gough Island, Bouvet Island, the Crozets, and even to a little speck of an island south of the Cape of Good Hope. But everywhere the people of the sea told him the same things. Seals had come to those islands once upon a time, but men had killed them all off. Even when he swam thousands of miles out of the Pacific and got to a place called Cape Corientes (that was when he was coming back from Gough Island) he found a few hundred mangy seals on a rock and they told him that men came there too. That nearly broke his heart, and he headed round the Horn back to his own beaches; and on his way north he hauled out on an island full of green trees, where he found an old, old seal who was dying, and Kotick caught fish for him and told him all his failures. "Now," said Kotick, "I am going back to Novastoshnah, and if I am driven to the killing-pens with the holluschickie I shall not care."

The old seal said: "Try once more. I am the last of the Lost Rookery of Más Afuera, and in the days when men killed us by the hundred thousand there was a story on the beaches that some day a white seal would come out of the North and lead the Seal-People to a quiet place. I am old, and I shall never live to see that day, but others will. Try once more."

And Kotick curled up his moustache (it was a beauty) and said: "I am the only white seal that has ever been born on the beaches, and I am the only seal, black or white, who ever thought of looking for new islands."

This cheered him immensely, and when he came back to Novastoshnah that summer, Matkah, his mother, begged him to marry and settle down, for he was no longer a holluschick but a full-grown sea catch, with a curly white mane on his shoulders, as heavy, as big, and as fierce as his father. "Give me another season," he said. "Remember, Mother, it is always the seventh wave that goes farthest up the beach."

Curiously enough, there was another seal who thought that she would put off marrying till the next year, and Kotick danced the Fire Dance with her all down Lukannon Beach the night before he set off on his last exploration. This time he went westwards, because he had fallen on the trail of a great shoal of halibut, and he needed at least one hundred pounds of fish a day to keep him in good condition. He chased them till he was tired, and then he curled himself up and went to sleep on the hollows of the ground-swell that sets in to Copper Island. He knew the coast perfectly well, so about midnight, when he felt himself gently bumped on a weed bed, he said: "*Hm*, tide's running strong tonight," and turning over under water opened his eyes slowly and stretched. Then he jumped like a cat, for he saw huge things nosing about in the shoal-water and browsing on the heavy fringes of the weeds.

"By the Great Combers of Magellan!" he said, beneath his moustache. "Who in the deep sea are these people?"

They were like no walrus, sea lion, seal, bear, whale, shark, fish, squid, or scallop that Kotick had ever seen before. They were between twenty and thirty feet long, and they had no hind flippers, but a shovel-like tail that looked as if it had been whittled out of wet leather. Their heads were the most foolish-looking things you ever saw, and they balanced on the ends of their tails in deep water when they weren't grazing, bowing solemnly to each other and waving their front flippers as a fat man waves his arm.

"*Ahem!*" said Kotick. "Good sport, gentlemen?" The big things answered by bowing and waving their flippers like the Frog-Footman. When they began feeding again Kotick saw that their upper lip was split into two pieces that they could twitch apart about a foot and bring together again with a whole bushel of sea-weed between the splits. They tucked the stuff into their mouths and chumped solemnly.

"Messy style of feeding that," said Kotick. They bowed again, and Kotick began to lose his temper. "Very good," he said. "If you *do* happen to have an extra joint in your front flipper you needn't show off so. I see you bow gracefully, but I should like to know your names." The split lips moved and twitched, and the glassy green eyes stared, but they did not speak.

"Well!" said Kotick, "you're the only people I've ever met uglier than Sea Vitch – and with worse manners."

Then he remembered in a flash what the burgomaster gull had screamed to him when he was a little yearling at Walrus Islet, and he tumbled backwards in the water, for he knew that he had found Sea Cow at last! The sea cows went on schlooping and grazing and chumping in the weed, and Kotick asked them questions in every language that he had picked up in his travels; and the Sea-People talk nearly as many languages as human beings. But the sea cows did not answer, because Sea Cow cannot talk. He has only six bones in his neck where he ought to have seven, and they say under the sea that that prevents him from speaking even to his companions; but, as you know, he has an extra joint in his fore flipper, and by waving it up and down and about he makes what answers to a sort of clumsy telegraphic code.

By daylight Kotick's mane was standing on end and his temper was gone where the dead crabs go. Then the sea cows began to travel northwards very slowly, stopping to hold absurd bowing councils from time to time, and Kotick followed them, saying to himself: "People who are such idiots as these are would have been killed long ago if they hadn't found out some safe island; and what is good enough for the sea cow is good enough for the sea catch. All the same, I wish they'd hurry."

It was weary work for Kotick. The sea cows' herd never went more than forty or fifty miles a day, and stopped to feed at night, and kept close to the shore all the time, while Kotick swam round them, and over them, and under them, but he could not hurry them up one mile. As they went farther north they held a bowing council every few hours, and Kotick nearly bit off his moustache with impatience till he saw that they were following up a warm current of water, and then he respected them more. One night they sank through the shiny water – sank like stones – and for the first time since he had known them began to swim quickly. Kotick followed, and the pace astonished him, for he never dreamed that Sea Cow was anything of a swimmer. They headed for a cliff by the shore, a cliff that ran down into deep water, and plunged into a dark hole at the foot of it, twenty fathoms under the sea. It was a long, long swim, and Kotick badly wanted fresh air before he was out of the dark tunnel they led him through.

"My wig!" he said, when he rose, gasping and puffing, into open water at the farther end. "It was a long dive, but it was worth it."

The sea cows had separated and were browsing lazily along the edges of the finest beaches that Kotick had ever seen. There were long stretches of smooth-worn rock running for miles, exactly fitted to make seal-nurseries, and there were play-grounds of hard sand sloping inland behind them, and there were rollers for seals to dance in, and long grass to roll in, and sand-dunes to climb up and down, and best of all, Kotick knew by the feel of the water, which never deceives a sea catch, that no men had ever come there. The first thing he did was to assure himself that the fishing was good, and then he swam along the beaches and counted up the delightful low sandy islands half hidden in the beautiful rolling fog. Away to the northward, out to sea, ran a line of bars and shoals and rocks that would never let a ship come within six miles of the beach, and between the islands and the mainland was a stretch of deep water that ran up to the perpendicular cliffs, and somewhere below the cliffs was the mouth of the tunnel.

"It's Novastoshnah over again, but ten times better," said Kotick. "Sea Cow must be wiser than I thought. Men can't come down the cliffs, even if there were any men, and the shoals to seaward would knock a ship to splinters. If any place in the sea is safe, this is it." He began to think of the seal he had left behind him, but though he was in a hurry to go back to Novastoshnah, he thoroughly explored the new country, so that he would be able to answer all questions.

Then he dived and made sure of the mouth of the tunnel, and raced through to the southward. No one but a sea cow or a seal would have dreamed of there being such a place, and when he looked back at the cliffs even Kotick could hardly believe that he had been there.

He was ten days going home, though he was not swimming slowly, and when he hauled out just above Sea Lion's Neck the first person he met was the seal who had been waiting for him, and she saw by the look in his eyes that he had found his island at last.

But the holluschickie and Sea Catch, his father, and all the other seals, laughed at him when he told them what he had discovered, and a young seal about his own age said: "This is all very well, Kotick, but you can't come from no one knows where and order us off like this. Remember *we*'ve been fighting for our nurseries, and that's a thing you never did. You preferred prowling about in the sea." The other seals laughed at this, and the young seal began twisting his head from side to side. He had just married that year, and was making a great fuss about it.

"I've no nursery to fight for," said Kotick. "I only want to show you all a place where you will be safe. What's the use of fighting?"

"Oh, if you're trying to back out, of course I've no more to say," said the young seal, with an ugly chuckle.

"Will you come with me if I win?" said Kotick, and a green light came into his eye, for he was very angry at having to fight at all.

"Very good," said the young seal, carelessly. "*If* you win, I'll come." He had no time to change his mind, for Kotick's head was out and his teeth sank in the blubber of the young seal's neck. Then he threw himself back on his haunches and hauled his enemy down the beach, shook him, and knocked him over. Then Kotick roared to the seals: "I've done my best for you these five seasons past. I've found you the island where you'll be safe, but unless your heads are dragged off your silly necks you won't believe. I'm going to teach you now. Look out for yourselves!"

Limmershin told me that never in his life – and Limmershin sees ten thousand big seals fighting every year – never in all his life did he see anything like Kotick's charge into the nurseries. He flung himself at the biggest sea catch he could find, caught him by the throat, choked him and bumped him and banged him till he grunted for mercy, and then threw him aside and attacked the next. You see, Kotick had never fasted for four months as the big seals did every year, and his deep-sea swimming trips kept him in perfect condition, and, best of all, he had never fought before. His curly white mane stood up with rage, and his eyes flamed, and his big dog-teeth glistened, and he was splendid to look at. Old Sea Catch, his father, saw him tearing past, hauling the grizzled old seals about as though they had been halibut, and upsetting the young bachelors in all directions, and Sea Catch gave a roar and shouted: "He may be a fool, but he is the best fighter on the beaches! Don't tackle your father, my son! He's with you!"

Kotick roared in answer, and old Sea Catch waddled in with his moustache on end, blowing like a locomotive, while Matkah and the seal that was going to marry Kotick cowered down and admired their men-folk. It was a gorgeous fight, for the two fought as long as there was a seal that dared lift up his head, and when there were none they paraded grandly up and down the beach side by side, bellowing.

At night, just as the Northern Lights were winking and flashing through the fog, Kotick climbed a bare rock and looked down on the scattered nurseries and the torn and bleeding seals. "Now," he said, "I've taught you your lesson."

"My wig!" said old Sea Catch, boosting himself up stiffly, for he was fearfully mauled. "The killer whale himself could not have cut them up worse. Son, I'm proud of you, and what's more, *I'll* come with you to your island – if there is such a place."

"Hear you, fat pigs of the sea. Who comes with me to Sea Cow's tunnel? Answer, or I shall teach you again," roared Kotick.

"He may be a fool, but he is the best fighter on the beaches!"

There was a murmur like the ripple of the tide all up and down the beaches. "We will come," said thousands of tired voices. "We will follow Kotick the White Seal."

Then Kotick dropped his head between his shoulders and shut his eyes proudly. He was not a white seal any more, but red from head to tail. All the same he would have scorned to look at or touch one of his wounds.

A week later he and his army (nearly ten thousand holluschickie and old seals) went away north to Sea Cow's tunnel, Kotick leading them, and the seals that stayed at Novastoshnah called them idiots. But next spring when they all met off the fishing-banks of the Pacific, Kotick's seals told such tales of the new beaches beyond Sea Cow's tunnel that more and more seals left Novastoshnah. Of course it was not all done at once, for the seals are not very clever, and they need a long time to turn things over in their minds, but year after year more seals went away from Novastoshnah, and Lukannon, and the other nurseries, to the quiet, sheltered beaches where Kotick sits all the summer through, getting bigger and fatter and stronger each year, while the holluschickie play round him, in that sea where no man comes.

Lukannon

This is a sort of sad Seal National Anthem.

I met my mates in the morning (and, oh, but I am old!)
Where roaring on the ledges the summer ground-swell rolled.
I heard them lift the chorus that drowned the breakers' song –
The Beaches of Lukannon – two million voices strong.

The song of pleasant stations beside the salt lagoons,
The song of blowing squadrons that shuffled down the dunes –
The song of midnight dances that churned the swell to flame –
The Beaches of Lukannon – before the sealers came!

I met my mates in the morning (I'll never meet them more!).
They came and went in legions that darkened all the shore.
And o'er the foam-flecked offing as far as voice could reach
We hailed the landing-parties and we sang them up the beach.

The Beaches of Lukannon – the winter-wheat so tall,
The dripping, crinkled lichens, and the sea-fog drenching all!
The platforms of our playground, all shining smooth and worn!
The Beaches of Lukannon – the home where we were born!

I met my mates in the morning, a broken, scattered band,
Men shoot us in the water and club us on the land.
Men drive us to the Salt House like silly sheep and tame,
And still we sing Lukannon – before the sealers came.

Wheel down, wheel down to southward – oh, Gooverooska, go!
And tell the Deep Sea Viceroys the story of our woe.
Ere, empty as the shark's-egg the tempest flings ashore,
The Beaches of Lukannon shall know their sons no more!

"Rikki-Tikki-Tavi"

At the hole where he went in
Red-Eye called to Wrinkle-Skin.
Hear what little Red-Eye saith:
"Nag, come up and dance with death!"
Eye to eye and head to head
    (*Keep the measure, Nag*).
This shall end when one is dead
    (*At thy pleasure, Nag.*)
Turn for turn and twist for twist
    (*Run and hide thee, Nag*).
Hah! The hooded Death has missed!
    (*Woe betide thee, Nag!*)

This is the story of the great war that Rikki-tikki-tavi fought single-handed, through the bathrooms of the big bungalow in Segowlie cantonment. Darzee the Tailorbird helped him, and Chuchundra the Musk-rat, who never comes out into the middle of the floor, but always creeps round by the wall, gave him advice, but Rikki-tikki did the real fighting.

He was a mongoose, rather like a little cat in his fur and his tail, but quite like a weasel in his head and his habits. His eyes and the end of his restless nose were pink; he could scratch himself anywhere he pleased with any leg, front or back, that he chose to use; he could fluff up his tail till it looked like a bottle-brush, and his war-cry as he scuttled through the long grass was: *Rikk-tikk-tikki-tikki-tchk!*

One day, a high summer flood washed him out of the burrow where he lived with his father and mother, and carried him, kicking and clucking, down a roadside ditch. He found a little wisp of grass floating there, and clung to it till he lost his senses. When he revived, he was lying in the hot sun on the middle of a garden path, very draggled indeed, and a small boy was saying: "Here's a dead mongoose. Let's have a funeral."

"No," said his mother, "let's take him in and dry him. Perhaps he isn't really dead."

They took him into the house, and a big man picked him up between his finger and thumb and said he was not dead but half choked. So they wrapped him in cotton wool, and warmed him over a little fire, and he opened his eyes and sneezed.

"Now," said the big man (he was an Englishman who had just moved into the bungalow), "don't frighten him, and we'll see what he'll do."

It is the hardest thing in the world to frighten a mongoose, because he is eaten up from nose to tail with curiosity. The motto of all the mongoose family is "Run and find out," and Rikki-tikki was a true mongoose. He looked at the cotton-wool, decided that it was not good to eat, ran all round the table, sat up and put his fur in order, scratched himself, and jumped on the small boy's shoulder.

"Don't be frightened, Teddy," said his father. "That's his way of making friends."

"Ouch! He's tickling under my chin," said Teddy.

Rikki-tikki looked down between the boy's collar and neck, snuffed at his ear, and climbed down to the floor, where he sat rubbing his nose.

"Good gracious," said Teddy's mother, "and that's a wild creature! I suppose he's so tame because we've been kind to him."

"All mongooses are like that," said her husband. "If Teddy doesn't pick him up by the tail, or try to put him in a cage, he'll run in and out of the house all day long. Let's give him something to eat."

They gave him a little piece of raw meat. Rikki-tikki liked it immensely, and when it was finished he went out into the veranda and sat in the sunshine and fluffed up his fur to make it dry to the roots. Then he felt better.

"There are more things to find out about in this house," he said to himself, "than all my family could find out in all their lives. I shall certainly stay and find out."

He spent all that day roaming over the house. He nearly drowned himself in the bath-tubs, put his nose into the ink on a writing-table, and burnt it on the end of the big man's cigar, for he climbed up in the big man's lap to see how writing was done. At nightfall he ran into Teddy's nursery to watch how kerosene lamps were lighted, and when Teddy went to bed Rikki-tikki climbed up too. But he was a restless companion, because he had to get up and attend to every noise all through the night, and find out what made it. Teddy's mother and father came in, the last thing, to look at their boy, and Rikki-tikki was awake on the pillow. "I don't like that," said Teddy's mother. "He may bite the child." "He'll do no such thing," said the father. "Teddy's safer with that little beast than if he had a bloodhound to watch him. If a snake came into the nursery now – "

But Teddy's mother wouldn't think of anything so awful.

Early in the morning Rikki-tikki came to early breakfast in the veranda riding on Teddy's shoulder, and they gave him banana and some boiled egg; and he sat on all their laps one after the other, because every well-brought-up mongoose always hopes to be a house-mongoose some day and have rooms to run about in; and Rikki-tikki's mother (she used to live in the General's house at Segowlie) had carefully told Rikki what to do if ever he came across white men.

Then Rikki-tikki went out into the garden to see what was to be seen. It was a large garden, only half cultivated, with bushes, as big as summer-houses, of Marshal Niel roses, lime- and orange-trees, clumps of bamboos, and thickets of high grass. Rikki-tikki licked his lips. "This is a splendid hunting-ground," he said, and his tail grew bottle-brushy at the thought of it, and he scuttled up and down the garden, snuffing here and there till he heard very sorrowful voices in a thorn-bush. It was Darzee the Tailorbird and his wife. They had made a beautiful nest by pulling two big leaves together and stitching them up the edges with fibres, and had filled the hollow with cotton and downy fluff. The nest swayed to and fro, as they sat on the rim and cried.

"What is the matter?" asked Rikki-tikki.

"We are very miserable," said Darzee. "One of our babies fell out of the nest yesterday and Nag ate him."

"*H'm!*" said Rikki-tikki, "that is very sad – but I am a stranger here. Who is Nag?"

Darzee and his wife only cowered down in the nest without answering, for from the thick grass at the foot of the bush there came a low hiss – a horrid cold sound that made Rikki-tikki jump back two clear feet. Then inch by inch out of the grass rose up the head and spread hood of Nag, the big black cobra, and he was five feet long from tongue to tail. When he had lifted one-third of himself clear of the ground, he stayed balancing to and fro exactly as a dandelion-tuft balances in the wind, and he looked at Rikki-tikki with the wicked snake's eyes that never change their expression, whatever the snake may be thinking of.

"Who is Nag?" said he. "*I* am Nag. The great God Brahm put his mark upon all our people, when the first cobra spread his hood to keep the sun off Brahm as he slept. Look, and be afraid!"

He spread out his hood more than ever, and Rikki-tikki saw the spectacle-mark on the back of it that looks exactly like the eye part of a hook-and-eye fastening. He was afraid for the minute, but it is impossible for a mongoose to stay frightened for any length of time, and though Rikki-tikki had never met a live cobra before, his mother had fed him on dead ones, and he knew that all a grown mongoose's business in life was to fight and eat snakes. Nag knew that too and, at the bottom of his cold heart, he was afraid.

"Well," said Rikki-tikki, and his tail began to fluff up again, "marks or no marks, do you think it is right for you to eat fledgelings out of a nest?"

Nag was thinking to himself, and watching the least little movement in the grass behind Rikki-tikki. He knew that mongooses in the garden meant death sooner or later for him and his family, but he wanted to get Rikki-tikki off his guard. So he dropped his head a little, and put it on one side.

"Let us talk," he said. "You eat eggs. Why should not I eat birds?"

"Behind you! Look behind you!" sang Darzee.

Rikki-tikki knew better than to waste time in staring. He jumped up in the air as high as he could go, and just under him whizzed by the head of

Nagaina, Nag's wicked wife. She had crept up behind him as he was talking, to make an end of him, and he heard her savage hiss as the stroke missed. He came down almost across her back, and if he had been an old mongoose he would have known that then was the time to break her back with one bite, but he was afraid of the terrible lashing return-stroke of the cobra. He bit, indeed, but did not bite long enough, and he jumped clear of the whisking tail, leaving Nagaina torn and angry.

"Wicked, wicked Darzee!" said Nag, lashing up as high as he could reach towards the nest in the thorn-bush, but Darzee had built it out of reach of snakes, and it only swayed to and fro.

Rikki-tikki felt his eyes growing red and hot (when a mongoose's eyes grow red, he is angry), and he sat back on his tail and hind legs like a little kangaroo, and looked all round him, and chattered with rage. But Nag and Nagaina had disappeared into the grass. When a snake misses its stroke, it never says anything or gives any sign of what it means to do next. Rikki-tikki did not care to follow them, for he did not feel sure that he could manage two snakes at once. So he trotted off to the gravel path near the house, and sat down to think. It was a serious matter for him. If you read the old books of natural history, you will find they say that when the mongoose fights the snake and happens to get bitten, he runs off and eats some herb that cures him. That is not true. The victory is only a matter of quickness of eye and quickness of foot – snake's blow against mongoose's jump – and as no eye can follow the motion of a snake's head when it strikes, this makes things much more wonderful than any magic herb. Rikki-tikki knew he was a young mongoose, and it made him all the more pleased to think that he had managed to escape a blow from behind. It gave him confidence in himself, and when Teddy came running down the path, Rikki-tikki was ready to be petted. But just as Teddy was stooping, something wriggled a little in the dust, and a tiny voice said: "Be careful. I am Death." It was Karait, the dusty brown snakeling that lies for choice on the dusty earth, and his bite is as dangerous as the cobra's. But he is so small that nobody thinks of him, and so he does the more harm to people.

Rikki-tikki's eyes grew red again, and he danced up to Karait with the peculiar rocking, swaying motion that he had inherited from his family. It looks very funny, but it is so perfectly balanced a gait that you can fly off from it at any angle you please, and in dealing with snakes this is an advantage. If Rikki-tikki had only known, he was doing a much more dangerous thing than fighting Nag, for Karait is so small, and can turn so quickly, that unless Rikki bit him close to the back of the head, he would get the return-stroke in his eye or his lip. But Rikki did not know. His eyes were all red, and he rocked back and forth, looking for a good place to hold. Karait struck out, Rikki jumped sideways and tried to run in, but the wicked little dusty grey head lashed within a fraction of his shoulder, and he had to jump over the body, and the head followed his heels close.

Teddy shouted to the house: "Oh, look here! Our mongoose is killing a snake." And Rikki-tikki heard a scream from Teddy's mother. His father ran out with a stick, but by the time he came up, Karait had lunged out once too far, and Rikki-tikki had sprung, jumped on the snake's back, dropped his head far between his fore legs, bitten as high up the back as he could get hold, and rolled away. That bite paralysed Karait, and Rikki-tikki was just going to eat him up from the tail, after the custom of his family at dinner, when he remembered that a full meal makes a slow mongoose, and if he wanted all his strength and quickness ready, he must keep himself thin. He went away for a dust-bath under the castor-oil bushes, while Teddy's father beat the dead Karait. "What is the use of that?" thought Rikki-tikki. "I have settled it all." And then Teddy's mother picked him up from the dust and hugged him, crying that he had saved Teddy from death, and Teddy's father said that he was a providence, and Teddy looked on with big scared eyes. Rikki-tikki was rather amused at all the fuss, which, of course, he did not understand. Teddy's mother might just as well have petted Teddy for playing in the dust. Rikki was thoroughly enjoying himself.

That night at dinner, walking to and fro among the wine-glasses on the table, he might have stuffed himself three times over with nice things. But he remembered Nag and Nagaina, and though it was very pleasant to be patted and petted by Teddy's mother, and to sit on Teddy's shoulder, his eyes would get red from time to time, and he would go off into his long war-cry of *"Rikk-tikk-tikki-tikki-tchk!"*

Teddy carried him off to bed, and insisted on Rikki-tikki sleeping under his chin. Rikki-tikki was too well bred to bite or scratch, but as soon as

Teddy was asleep he went off for his nightly walk round the house, and in the dark he ran up against Chuchundra the Muskrat creeping round by the wall. Chuchundra is a brokenhearted little beast. He whimpers and cheeps all the night, trying to make up his mind to run into the middle of the room, but he never gets there.

"Don't kill me," said Chuchundra, almost weeping. "Rikki-tikki, don't kill me!"

"Do you think a snake-killer kills muskrats?" said Rikki-tikki scornfully.

"Those who kill snakes get killed by snakes," said Chuchundra, more sorrowfully than ever. "And how am I to be sure that Nag won't mistake me for you some dark night?"

"There's not the least danger," said Rikki-tikki, "but Nag is in the garden, and I know you don't go there."

"My cousin Chua the Rat told me – " said Chuchundra, and then he stopped.

"Told you what?"

"*Hsh!* Nag is everywhere, Rikki-tikki. You should have talked to Chua in the garden."

"I didn't – so you must tell me. Quick, Chuchundra, or I'll bite you!"

Chuchundra sat down and cried till the tears rolled off his whiskers. "I am a very poor man," he sobbed. "I never had spirit enough to run out into the middle of the room. *Hsh!* I mustn't tell you anything, Can't you *hear*, Rikki-tikki?"

Rikki-tikki listened. The house was as still as still, but he thought he could just catch the faintest *scratch-scratch* in the world – a noise as faint as that of a wasp walking on a window-pane – the dry scratch of a snake's scales on brickwork.

"That's Nag or Nagaina," he said to himself, "and he is crawling into the bath-room sluice. You're right, Chuchundra. I should have talked to Chua."

He stole off to Teddy's bathroom, but there was nothing there, and then to Teddy's mother's bathroom. At the bottom of the smooth plaster wall there was a brick pulled out to make a sluice for the bath-water, and as Rikki-tikki stole in by the masonry curb where the bath is put, he heard Nag and Nagaina whispering together outside in the moonlight.

"When the house is emptied of people," said Nagaina to her husband, *"he* will have to go away, and then the garden will be our own again. Go in quietly, and remember that the big man who killed Karait is the first one to bite. Then come out and tell me, and we will hunt for Rikki-tikki together."

"But are you sure that there is anything to be gained by killing the people?" said Nag.

"Everything. When there were no people in the bungalow, did we have any mongoose in the garden? So long as the bungalow is empty, we are king and queen of the garden. And remember that as soon as our eggs in the melon-bed hatch (as they may tomorrow), our children will need room and quiet."

"I had not thought of that," said Nag. "I will go, but there is no need that we should hunt for Rikki-tikki afterwards. I will kill the big man and his wife, and the child if I can, and come away quietly. Then the bungalow will be empty, and Rikki-tikki will go."

Rikki-tikki tingled all over with rage and hatred at this, and then Nag's head came through the sluice, and his five feet of cold body followed it. Angry as he was, Rikki-tikki was very frightened as he saw the size of the big cobra. Nag coiled himself up, raised his head, and looked into the bath-room in the dark, and Rikki could see his eyes glitter.

"Now, if I kill him here, Nagaina will know, and if I fight him on the open floor, the odds are in his favour. What am I to do?" said Rikki-tikki-tavi.

Nag waved to and fro, and then Rikki-tikki heard him drinking from the biggest water-jar that was used to fill the bath. "That is good," said the snake. "Now, when Karait was killed, the big man had a stick. He may have that stick still, but when he comes in to bathe in the morning he will not have a stick. I shall wait here till he comes. Nagaina – do you hear me? – I shall wait here in the cool till daytime."

There was no answer from outside, so Rikki-tikki knew Nagaina had gone away. Nag coiled himself down, coil by coil, round the bulge at the bottom of the water-jar, and Rikki-tikki stayed still as death. After an hour he began to move, muscle by muscle, towards the jar. Nag was asleep, and Rikki-tikki looked at his big back, wondering which would be the best place for a good hold. "If I don't break his back at the first jump," said

"And when I am once there, I must not let go."

Rikki, "he can still fight, and if he fights – O Rikki!" He looked at the thickness of the neck below the hood, but that was too much for him, and a bite near the tail would only make Nag savage.

"It must be the head," he said at last, "the head above the hood. And, when I am once there, I must not let go."

Then he jumped. The head was lying a little clear of the water-jar, under the curve of it, and, as his teeth met, Rikki braced his back against the bulge of the red earthenware to hold down the head. This gave him just one second's purchase, and he made the most of it. Then he was battered to and fro as a rat is shaken by a dog – to and fro on the floor, up and down, and round in great circles, but his eyes were red and he held on as the body cart-whipped over the floor, upsetting the tin dipper and the soap-dish and the flesh-brush, and banged against the tin side of the bath. As he held he closed his jaws tighter and tighter, for he made sure he would be banged to death, and, for the honour of his family, he preferred to be found with his teeth locked. He was dizzy, aching, and felt shaken to pieces when something went off like a thunderclap just behind him; a hot wind knocked him senseless and red fire singed his fur. The big man had been wakened by the noise, and had fired both barrels of a shot-gun into Nag just behind the hood.

Rikki-tikki held on with his eyes shut, for now he was quite sure he was dead, but the head did not move, and the big man picked him up and said: "It's the mongoose again, Alice. The little chap has saved *our* lives now." Then Teddy's mother came in with a very white face, and saw what was left of Nag, and Rikki-tikki dragged himself to Teddy's bedroom and spent half the rest of the night shaking himself tenderly to find out whether he really was broken into forty pieces, as he fancied.

When morning came he was very stiff, but well pleased with his doings. "Now I have Nagaina to settle with, and she will be worse than five Nags, and there's no knowing when the eggs she spoke of will hatch. Goodness! I must go and see Darzee," he said.

Without waiting for breakfast, Rikki-tikki ran to the thorn-bush where Darzee was singing a song of triumph at the top of his voice. The news of Nag's death was all over the garden, for the sweeper had thrown the body on the rubbish-heap.

"Oh, you stupid tuft of feathers!" said Rikki-tikki angrily. "Is this the time to sing?"

"Nag is dead – is dead – is dead!" sang Darzee. "The valiant Rikki-tikki caught him by the head and held fast. The big man brought the bang-stick, and Nag fell in two pieces! He will never eat my babies again."

"All that's true enough, but where's Nagaina?" said Rikki-tikki, looking carefully round him.

"Nagaina came to the bathroom sluice and called for Nag," Darzee went on, "and Nag came out on the end of a stick – the sweeper picked him up on the end of a stick and threw him upon the rubbish-heap. Let us sing about the great, the red-eyed Rikki-tikki!" And Darzee filled his throat and sang.

"If I could get up to your nest, I'd roll your babies out!" said Rikki-tikki. "You don't know when to do the right thing at the right time. You're safe enough in your nest there, but it's war for me down here. Stop singing a minute, Darzee."

"For the great, the beautiful Rikki-tikki's sake I will stop," said Darzee. "What is it, O killer of the terrible Nag?"

"Where is Nagaina, for the third time?"

"On the rubbish-heap by the stables, mourning for Nag. Great is Rikki-tikki with the white teeth."

"Bother my white teeth! Have you ever heard where she keeps her eggs?"

"In the melon-bed, on the end nearest the wall, where the sun strikes nearly all day. She hid them there weeks ago."

"And you never thought it worth while to tell me? The end nearest the wall, you said?"

"Rikki-tikki, you are not going to eat her eggs?"

"Not eat exactly – no. Darzee, if you have a grain of sense you will fly off to the stables and pretend that your wing is broken, and let Nagaina chase you away to this bush. I must get to the melon-bed, and if I went there now she'd see me."

Darzee was a feather-brained little fellow who could never hold more than one idea at a time in his head, and just because he knew that Nagaina's children were born in eggs like his own, he didn't think at first that it was fair to kill them. But his wife was a sensible bird, and she knew that cobra's eggs meant young cobras later on. So she flew off from the nest, and left Darzee to keep the babies warm, and continue his song about the death of Nag. Darzee was very like a man in some ways.

She fluttered in front of Nagaina by the rubbish-heap, and cried out: "Oh, my wing is broken! The boy in the house threw a stone at me and broke it." Then she fluttered more desperately than ever.

Nagaina lifted up her head and hissed: "You warned Rikki-tikki when I would have killed him. Indeed and truly, you've chosen a bad place to be lame in." And she moved towards Darzee's wife, slipping along over the dust.

"The boy broke it with a stone!" shrieked Darzee's wife.

"Well! It may be some consolation to you when you're dead to know that I shall settle accounts with the boy. My husband lies on the rubbish-heap this morning, but before night the boy in the house will lie very still. What is the use of running away? I am sure to catch you. Little fool, look at me!"

Darzee's wife knew better than to do *that*, for a bird who looks at a snake's eyes gets so frightened that she cannot move. Darzee's wife fluttered on, piping sorrowfully, and never leaving the ground, and Nagaina quickened her pace.

Rikki-tikki heard them going up the path from the stables, and he raced for the end of the melon-patch near the wall. There, in the warm litter above the melons, very cunningly hidden, he found twenty-five eggs, about the size of a bantam's eggs, but with whitish skins instead of shells.

"I was not a day too soon," he said, for he could see the baby cobras curled up inside the skin, and he knew that the minute they were hatched they could each kill a man or a mongoose. He bit off the tops of the eggs as fast as he could, taking care to crush the young cobras, and turned over the litter from time to time to see whether he had missed any. At last there were only three eggs left, and Rikki-tikki began to chuckle to himself, when he heard Darzee's wife screaming:

"Rikki-tikki, I led Nagaina towards the house, and she has gone into the veranda, and – oh, come quickly – she means killing!"

Rikki-tikki smashed two eggs, and tumbled backwards down the melon-bed with the third egg in his mouth, and scuttled to the veranda as hard as he could put foot to the ground. Teddy and his mother and father were there at early breakfast, but Rikki-tikki saw that they were not eating anything. They sat stone-still, and their faces were white, Nagaina was coiled up on the matting by Teddy's chair, within easy striking distance of Teddy's bare leg, and she was swaying to and fro, singing a song of triumph.

"Son of the big man that killed Nag," she hissed, "stay still I am not ready yet. Wait a little. Keep very still, all you three! If you move I strike, and if you do not move I strike. Oh, foolish people, who killed my Nag!"

Teddy's eyes were fixed on his father, and all his father could do was to whisper: "Sit still, Teddy. You mustn't move. Teddy, keep still."

Then Rikki-tikki came up and cried: "Turn round, Nagaina, turn and fight!"

"All in good time," said she, without moving her eyes. "I will settle my account with *you* presently. Look at your friends, Rikki-tikki They are still and white. They are afraid. They dare not move, and if you come a step nearer I strike."

"Look at your eggs," said Rikki-tiki, "in the melon-bed near the wall. Go and look, Nagaina!"

The big snake turned half round, and saw the egg on the veranda. "Ah-h! Give it to me," she said.

Rikki-tikki put his paws one on each side of the egg, and his eyes were blood-red. "What price for a snake's egg? For a young cobra? For a young king-cobra? For the last – the very last of the brood? The ants are eating all the others down by the melon-bed."

Nagaina spun clear round, forgetting everything for the sake of the one egg, and Rikki-tikki saw Teddy's father shoot out a big hand, catch Teddy by the shoulder, and drag him across the little table with the tea-cups, safe and out of reach of Nagaina.

"Tricked! Tricked! Tricked! *Rikk-tck-tck!*" chuckled Rikki-tikki. "The boy is safe, and it was I – I – I that caught Nag by the hood last night in the bathroom." Then he began to jump up and down, all four feet together, his head close to the floor. "He threw me to and fro, but he could not shake

115

me off. He was dead before the big man blew him in two. I did it! *Rikki-tikki-tck-tck!* Come then, Nagaina. Come and fight with me. You shall not be a widow long."

Nagaina saw that she had lost her chance of killing Teddy, and the egg lay between Rikki-tikki's paws. "Give me the egg, Rikki-tikki. Give me the last of my eggs, and I will go away and never come back," she said, lowering her hood.

"Yes, you will go away, and you will never come back, for you will go to the rubbish-heap with Nag. Fight, widow! The big man has gone for his gun! Fight!"

Rikki-tikki was bounding all round Nagaina, keeping just out of reach of her stroke, his little eyes like hot coals. Nagaina gathered herself together, and flung out at him. Rikki-tikki jumped up and backwards. Again and again and again she struck, and each time her head came with a whack on the matting of the veranda and she gathered herself together like a watch-spring. Then Rikki-tikki danced in a circle to get behind her, and Nagaina spun round to keep her head to his head, so that the rustle of her tail on the matting sounded like dry leaves blown along by the wind.

He had forgotten the egg. It still lay on the veranda, and Nagaina came nearer and nearer to it, till at last, while Riki-tikki was drawing breath, she caught it in her mouth, turned to the veranda steps, and flew like an arrow down the path, with Rikki-tikki behind her. When the cobra runs for her life, she goes like a whip-lash flicked across a horse's neck. Rikki-tikki knew that he must catch her, or all the trouble would begin again. She headed straight for the long grass by the thorn-bush, and as he was running Rikki-tikki heard Darzee still singing his foolish little song of triumph. But Darzee's wife was wiser. She flew off her nest as Nagaina came along, and flapped her wings about Nagaina's head. If Darzee had helped they might have turned her, but Nagaina only lowered her hood and went on. Still, the instant's delay brought Rikki-tikki up to her, and as she plunged into the rat-hole where she and Nag used to live, his little white teeth were clenched on her tail, and he went down with her – and very few mongooses, however wise and old they may be, care to follow a cobra into its hole. It was dark in the hole, and Riki-tikki never knew when it might open out and give Nagaina room to turn and strike at him.

He held on savagely, and stuck out his feet to act as brakes on the dark slope of the hot, moist earth. Then the grass by the mouth of the hole stopped waving, and Darzee said: "It is all over with Rikki-tikki! We must sing his death-song. Valiant Rikki-tikki is dead! For Nagaina will surely kill him underground."

So he sang a very mournful song that he made up on the spur of the minute, and just as he got to the most touching part the grass quivered again, and Rikki-tikki, covered with dirt, dragged himself out of the hole leg by leg, licking his whiskers. Darzee stopped with a little shout. Rikki-tikki shook some of the dust out of his fur and sneezed. "It is all over," he said. "The widow will never come out again." And the red ants that live between the grass stems heard him, and began to troop down one after another to see if he had spoken the truth.

Rikki-tikki curled himself up in the grass and slept where he was – slept and slept till it was late in the afternoon, for he had done a hard day's work.

"Now," he said, when he awoke, "I will go back to the house. Tell the coppersmith, Darzee, and he will tell the garden that Nagaina is dead."

The coppersmith is a bird who makes a noise exactly like the beating of a little hammer on a copper pot, and the reason he is always making it is because he is the town-crier to every Indian garden, and tells all the news to everybody who cares to listen. As Rikki-tikki went up the path, he heard his "attention" notes like a tiny dinner-gong, and then the steady *"Ding-dong-tock!* Nag is dead – *dong!* Nagaina is dead! *Ding-dong-tock!"* That set all the birds in the garden singing, and the frogs croaking, for Nag and Nagaina used to eat frogs as well as little birds.

When Rikki got to the house, Teddy and Teddy's mother (she looked very white still, for she had been fainting) and Teddy's father came out and almost cried over him. And that night he ate all that was given him till he could eat no more, and went to bed on Teddy's shoulder, where Teddy's mother saw him when she came to look late at night.

"He saved our lives and Teddy's life," she said to her husband. "Just think, he saved all our lives."

Rikki-tikki woke up with a jump, for the mongooses are light sleepers.

"Oh, it's you," said he. "What are you bothering for? All the cobras are dead, and if they weren't, I'm here."

Rikki-tikki had a right to be proud of himself. But he did not grow too proud, and he kept that garden as a mongoose should keep it, with tooth and jump and spring and bite, till never a cobra dared show its head inside the walls.

Darzee's Chant

Sung in Honour of Rikki-tikki-tavi

Singer and tailor am I –
    Doubled the joys that I know –
Proud of my lilt to the sky,
    Proud of the house that I sew.
Over and under, so weave I my music – so weave I the house
    that I sew.

Sing to your fledgelings again,
    Mother, O lift up your head!
Evil that plagued us is slain,
    Death in the garden lies dead.
Terror that hid in the roses is impotent – flung on the dung-hill
    and dead!

Who has delivered us, who?
    Tell me his nest and his name.
Rikki, the valiant, the true,
    Tikki, with eyeballs of flame –
Rikk-tikki-tikki, the ivory-fanged, the hunter with eyeballs of
    flame!

Give him the thanks of the birds,
    Bowing with tail-feathers spread,
Praise him with nightingale words –
    Nay, I will praise him instead.
Hear! I will sing you the praise of the bottle-tailed Rikki with eyeballs
    of red!

(Here Rikki-tikki interrupted, so the rest of the song is lost.)

Toomai of the Elephants

I will remember what I was. I am sick of rope and chain.
   I will remember my old strength and all my forest affairs.
I will not sell my back to man for a bundle of sugar-cane.
   I will go out to my own kind, and the wood-folk in their lairs.

I will go out until the day, until the morning break –
   Out to the winds' untainted kiss, the waters' clean caress –
I will forget my ankle-ring and snap my picket-stake.
   I will revisit my lost loves, and playmates masterless!

Kala Nag, which means Black Snake, had served the Indian Government in every way that an elephant could serve it for forty-seven years, and as he was fully twenty years old when he was caught, that makes him nearly seventy – a ripe age for an elephant. He remembered pushing, with a big leather pad on his forehead, at a gun stuck in deep mud, and that was before the Afghan War of 1842, and he had not then come to his full strength. His mother Radha Pyari – Radha the Darling – who had been caught in the same drive with Kala Nag, told him, before his little milk tusks had dropped out, that elephants who were afraid always got hurt. And Kala Nag knew that that advice was good, for the first time that he saw a shell burst he backed, screaming, into a stand of piled rifles, and the bayonets pricked him in all his softest places. So, before he was twenty-five, he gave up being afraid, and so he was the best-loved and the best-looked-after elephant in the service of the Government of India. He had carried tents, twelve hundred pounds' weight of tents, on the march in Upper India. He had been hoisted into a ship at the end of a steam-crane and taken for days across the water, and made to carry a mortar on his back in a strange and rocky country very far from India, and had seen the Emperor Theodore lying dead in Magdala, and had come back again in the steamer entitled, so the soldiers said, to the Abyssinian War medal. He had seen his fellow-elephants die of cold and epilepsy and starvation and sunstroke up at a place called Ali Masjid, ten years later, and afterwards he had been sent down thousands of miles south to haul and pile big baulks of teak in the timber-yards at Moulmein. There he had half killed an insubordinate young elephant who was shirking his fair share of work.

After that he was taken off timber-hauling, and employed, with a few score other elephants who were trained to the business, in helping to catch wild elephants among the Garo Hills. Elephants are very strictly preserved by the Indian Government. There is one whole department which does nothing else but hunt them, and catch them, and break them in, and send them up and down the country as they are needed for work. Kala Nag stood ten fair feet at the shoulders, and his tusks had been cut off short at five feet, and bound round the ends, to prevent them splitting, with bands of copper, but he could do more with those stumps than any untrained elephant could do with the real sharpened ones. When, after weeks and weeks of cautious driving of scattered elephants across the hills, the forty or fifty wild monsters were driven into the last stockade, and the big drop-gate, made of tree-trunks lashed together, jarred down behind them, Kala Nag, at the word of command, would go into that flaring, trumpeting pandemonium (generally at night, when the flicker of the torches made it difficult to judge distances), and, picking out the biggest and wildest tusker of the mob, would hammer him and hustle him into quiet while the men on the backs of the other elephants roped and tied the smaller ones. There was nothing in the way of fighting that Kala Nag, the old wise Black Snake, did not know, for he had stood up more than once in his time to the charge of the wounded tiger, and, curling up his soft trunk to be out of harm's way, had knocked the springing brute sideways in mid-air with a quick sickle-cut of his head, that he had invented all by himself; had knocked him over, and kneeled upon him with his huge knees till the life went out with a gasp and a howl, and there was only a fluffy striped thing on the ground for Kala Nag to pull by the tail.

"Yes," said Big Toomai, his driver, the son of Black Toomai who had taken him to Abyssinia, and grandson of Toomai of the Elephants who had seen him caught, "there is nothing that the Black Snake fears except me. He has seen three generations of us feed him and groom him, and he will live to see four."

"He is afraid of *me* also," said Little Toomai, standing up to his full height of four feet, with only one rag upon him. He was ten years old, the eldest son of Big Toomai, and, according to custom, he would take his father's place on Kala Nag's neck when he grew up, and would handle the heavy iron *ankus*, the elephant-goad, that had been worn smooth by his father, and his grandfather, and his great-grandfather. He knew what he was talking of, for he had been born under Kala Nag's shadow, had played with the end of his trunk before he could walk, had taken him down to water as soon as he could walk, and Kala Nag would no more have dreamed of disobeying his shrill little orders than he would have dreamed of killing him on that day when Big Toomai carried the little brown baby under Kala Nag's tusks, and told him to salute his master that was to be. "Yes," said Little Toomai, "he is afraid of *me*." And he took long strides up to Kala Nag, called him a fat old pig, and made him lift up his feet one after the other.

"*Wah!*" said Little Toomai, "thou art a big elephant." And he wagged his fluffy head, quoting his father. "The Government may pay for elephants, but they belong to us mahouts. When thou art old, Kala Nag, there will come some rich rajah, and he will buy thee from the Government, on account of thy size and thy manners, and then thou wilt have nothing to do but to carry gold earrings in thy ears, and a gold howdah on thy back, and a red cloth covered with gold on thy sides, and walk at the head of the processions of the king. Then I shall sit on thy neck, O Kala Nag, with a silver *ankus*, and men will run before us with golden sticks, crying: 'Room for the King's elephant!' That will be good, Kala Nag, but not so good as this hunting in the jungles."

"*Umph!*" said Big Toomai. "Thou art a boy, and as wild as a buffalo-calf. This running up and down among the hills is not the best Government

And he took long strides up to Kala Nag, called him a fat old pig,
and made him lift up his feet one after the other.

service. I am getting old, and I do not love wild elephants. Give me brick elephant-lines, one stall to each elephant, and big stumps to tie them to safely, and flat, broad roads to exercise upon, instead of this come-and-go camping. *Aha*, the Cawnpore barracks were good. There was a bazaar close by, and only three hours' work a day."

Little Toomai remembered the Cawnpore elephant-lines and said nothing. He very much preferred the camp life, and hated those broad, flat roads, with the daily grubbing for grass in the forage-reserve, and the long hours when there was nothing to do except to watch Kala Nag fidgeting in his pickets. What Little Toomai liked was to scramble up bridle-paths that only an elephant could take; the dip into the valley below; the glimpses of the wild elephants browsing miles away; the rush of the frightened pig and peacock under Kala Nag's feet; the blinding warm rains, when all the hills and valleys smoked; the beautiful misty mornings when nobody knew where he would camp that night; the steady, cautious drive of the wild elephants, and the mad rush and blaze and hullaballoo of the last night's drive, when the elephants poured into the stockade like boulders in a landslide, found that they could not get out, and flung themselves at the heavy posts only to be driven back by yells and flaring torches and volleys of blank cartridge. Even a little boy could be of use there, and Toomai was as useful as three boys. He would get his torch and wave it, and yell with the best. But the really good time came when the driving out began, and the keddah, that is, the stockade, looked like a picture of the end of the world, and men had to make signs to one another, because they could not hear themselves speak. Then Little Toomai would climb up to the top of one of the quivering stockade-posts, his sun-bleached brown hair flying loose all over his shoulders, and he looking like a goblin in the torch-light. And as soon as there was a lull you could hear his high-pitched yells of encouragement to Kala Nag, above the trumpeting and crashing, and snapping of ropes, and groans of the tethered elephants. *"Maîl, maíl, Kala Nag!* [Go on, go on, Black Snake!] *Dant do!* [Give him the tusk!] *Somalo! Somalo!* [Careful, careful!] *Maro! Mar!* [Hit him, hit him!] Mind the post! *Arré! Arré! Hai! Yai! Kya-a-ah!"* he would shout, and the big fight between Kala Nag and the wild elephant would sway to and fro across the keddah, and the old elephant-catchers would wipe the sweat out of their eyes, and find time to nod to Little Toomai wriggling with joy on the top of the posts.

He did more than wriggle. One night he slid down from the post and slipped in between the elephants, and threw up the loose end of a rope, which had dropped, to a driver who was trying to get a purchase on the leg of a kicking young calf (calves always give more trouble than full-grown animals). Kala Nag saw him, caught him in his trunk, and handed him up to Big Toomai, who slapped him then and there, and put him back on the post. Next morning he gave him a scolding, and said: "Are not good brick elephant-lines and a little tent-carrying enough, that thou must needs go elephant-catching on thy own account, little worthless? Now those foolish hunters, whose pay is less than my pay, have spoken to Petersen Sahib of the matter." Little Toomai was frightened. He did not know much of white men, but Petersen Sahib was the greatest white man in the world to him. He was the head of all the keddah operations – the man who caught all the elephants for the Government of India, and who knew more about the ways of elephants than any living man.

"What – what will happen?" said Little Toomai.

"Happen! The worst that can happen. Petersen Sahib is a madman; else why should he go hunting these wild devils? He may even require thee to be an elephant-catcher, to sleep anywhere in these fever-filled jungles, and at last to be trampled to death in the keddah. It is well that this nonsense ends safely. Next week the catching is over, and we of the plains are sent back to our stations. Then we will march on smooth roads, and forget all this hunting. But, Son, I am angry that thou shouldst meddle in the business that belongs to these dirty Assamese jungle-folk. Kala Nag will obey none but me, so I must go with him into the keddah, but he is only a fighting elephant, and he does not help to rope them. So I sit at my ease, as befits a mahout – not a mere hunter – a mahout, I say, and a man who gets a pension at the end of his service. Is the family of Toomai of the Elephants to be trodden underfoot in the dirt of a keddah? Bad one! Wicked one! Worthless son! Go and wash Kala Nag and attend to his ears, and see that there are no thorns in his feet, or else Petersen Sahib will surely catch thee and make thee a wild hunter – a follower of elephant's foot-tracks, a jungle-bear. *Bah!* Shame! Go!"

Little Toomai went off without saying a word, but he told Kala Nag all his grievances while he was examining his feet. "No matter," said Little Toomai, turning up the fringe of Kala Nag's huge right ear. "They have said my name to Petersen Sahib, and perhaps – and perhaps – and perhaps – who knows? *Hai!* That is a big thorn that I have pulled out!"

The next few days were spent in getting the elephants together, in walking the newly caught wild elephants up and down between a couple of tame ones, to prevent them giving too much trouble on the downward march to the plains, and in taking stock of the blankets and ropes and things that had been worn out or lost in the forest. Petersen Sahib came in on his clever she-elephant Pudmini. He had been paying off other camps among the hills, for the season was coming to an end, and there was a native clerk sitting at a table under a tree, to pay the drivers their wages. As each man was paid he went back to his elephant, and joined the line that stood ready to start. The catchers, and hunters, and beaters, the men of the regular keddah, who stayed in the jungle year in and year out, sat on the backs of the elephants that belonged to Petersen Sahib's permanent force, or leaned against the trees with their guns across their arms, and made fun of the drivers who were going away, and laughed when the newly caught elephants broke the line and ran about. Big Toomai went up to the clerk with Little Toomai behind him, and Machua Appa, the head-tracker, said in an undertone to a friend of his: "There goes one piece of good elephant-stuff at least. 'Tis a pity to send that young jungle-cock to moult in the plains."

Now Petersen Sahib had ears all over him, as a man must have who listens to the most silent of all living things – the wild elephant. He turned where he was lying all along on Pudmini's back, and said: "What is that? I did not know of a man among the plains-drivers who had wit enough to rope even a dead elephant."

This is not a man, but a boy. He went into the keddah at the last drive, and threw Barmao there the rope, when we were trying to get that young calf with the blotch on his shoulder away from his mother." Machua Appa pointed at Little Toomai, and Petersen Sahib looked, and Little Toomai bowed to the earth.

"He throw a rope? He is smaller than a picket-pin. Little one, what is thy name?" said Petersen Sahib. Little Toomai was too frightened to speak, but Kala Nag was behind him, and Toomai made a sign with his hand, and the elephant caught him up in his trunk and held him level with Pudmini's forehead, in front of the great Petersen Sahib. Then Little Toomai covered his face with his hands, for he was only a child, and except where elephants were concerned, he was just as bashful as a child could be.

"Oho!" said Petersen Sahib, smiling underneath his moustache, "and why didst thou teach thy elephant *that* trick? Was it to help thee steal green corn from the roofs of the houses when the ears are put out to dry?"

"Not green corn, Protector of the Poor – melons," said Little Toomai, and all the men sitting about broke into a roar of laughter. Most of them had taught their elephants that trick when they were boys. Little Toomai was hanging eight feet up in the air, and he wished very much that he were eight feet under ground.

"He is Toomai, my son, Sahib," said Big Toomai, scowling. "He is a very bad boy, and he will end in a gaol, Sahib."

"Of that I have my doubts," said Petersen Sahib. "A boy who can face a full keddah at his age does not end in gaols. See, little one, here are four annas to spend on sweetmeats because thou hast a little head under that great thatch of hair. In time thou mayest become a hunter too." Big Toomai scowled more than ever. "Remember, though, that keddahs are not good for children to play in," Petersen Sahib went on.

"Must I never go there, Sahib?" asked Little Toomai, with a big gasp.

"Yes." Petersen Sahib smiled again. "When thou hast seen the elephants dance. That is the proper time. Come to me when thou hast seen the elephants dance, and then I will let thee go into all the keddahs."

There was another roar of laughter, for that is an old joke among elephant-catchers, and it means just never. There are great cleared flat places hidden away in the forests that are called elephants' ball-rooms, but even these are only found by accident, and no man has ever seen the elephants dance. When a driver boasts of his skill and bravery the other drivers say: "And when didst *thou* see the elephants dance?"

Kala Nag put Little Toomai down, and he bowed to the earth again and went away with his father, and gave the silver four-anna piece to his mother, who was nursing his baby-brother, and they all were put up on Kala Nag's back, and the line of grunting, squealing elephants rolled down the hill-path to the plains. It was a very lively march on account of the new elephants, who gave trouble at every ford, and needed coaxing or beating every other minute.

Big Toomai prodded Kala Nag spitefully, for he was very angry, but Little Toomai was too happy to speak. Petersen Sahib had noticed him, and given him money, so he felt as a private soldier would feel if he had been called out of the ranks and praised by his commander-in-chief.

"What did Petersen Sahib mean by the elephant-dance?" he said, at last, softly to his mother.

Big Toomai heard him and grunted. "That thou shouldst never be one of these hill-buffaloes of trackers. *That* was what he meant. Oh you in front, what is blocking the way?"

An Assamese driver, two or three elephants ahead, turned round angrily, crying: "Bring up Kala Nag, and knock this youngster of mine into good behaviour. Why should Petersen Sahib have chosen *me* to go down with you donkeys of the rice-fields? Lay your beast alongside, Toomai, and let him prod with his tusks. By all the Gods of the Hills, these new elephants are possessed, or else they can smell their companions in the jungle."

Kala Nag hit the new elephant in the ribs and knocked the wind out of him, as Big Toomai said: "We have swept the hills of wild elephants at the last catch. It is only your carelessness in driving. Must I keep order along the whole line?"

"Hear him!" said the other driver. "*We* have swept the hills! Ho! Ho! You are very wise, you plains-people. Any one but a mud-head who never saw the jungle would know that *they* know that the drives are ended for the season. Therefore all the wild elephants tonight will – but why should I waste wisdom on a river-turtle?"

"What will they do?" Little Toomai called out.

"*Ohé*, little one. Art thou there? Well, I will tell thee, for thou hast a cool head. They will dance, and it behoves thy father, who has swept *all* the hills of *all* the elephants, to double-chain his pickets tonight."

"What talk is this?" said Big Toomai. "For forty years, father and son, we have tended elephants, and we have never heard such moonshine about dances."

"Yes, but a plains-man who lives in a hut knows only the four walls of his hut. Well, leave thy elephants unshackled tonight and see what comes. As for their dancing, I have seen the place where – *Bapree bap!* How many windings has the Dihang River? Here is another ford, and we must swim the calves. Stop still, you behind there."

And in this way, talking and wrangling and splashing through the rivers, they made their first march to a sort of receiving-camp for the new elephants. But they lost their tempers long before they got there.

Then the elephants were chained by their hind legs to their big stumps of pickets, and extra ropes were fitted to the new elephants, and the fodder was piled before them, and the hill-drivers went back to Petersen Sahib through the afternoon light, telling the plains-drivers to be extra careful that night, and laughing when the plains-drivers asked the reason.

Little Toomai attended to Kala Nag's supper, and as evening fell, wandered through the camp, unspeakably happy, in search of a tom-tom. When, an Indian child's heart is full, he does not run about and make a noise in an irregular fashion. He sits down to a sort of revel all by himself. And Little Toomai had been spoken to by Petersen Sahib! If he had not found what he wanted I believe he would have been ill. But the sweetmeat-seller in the camp lent him a little tom-tom – a drum beaten with the flat of the hand – and he sat down, cross-legged, before Kala Nag as the stars began to come out, the tom-tom in his lap, and he thumped and he thumped and he thumped, and the more he thought of the great honour that had been done to him, the more he thumped, all alone among the elephant-fodder. There was no tune and no words, but the thumping made him happy. The new elephants strained at their ropes, and squealed and trumpeted from time to time, and he could hear his mother in the camp hut putting his small brother to sleep with an old, old song about the great God Shiv, who once told all the animals what they should eat. It is a very soothing lullaby, and the first verse says:

Shiv, who poured the harvest and made the winds to blow,
Sitting at the doorways of a day of long ago,
Gave to each his portion, food and toil and fate,
From the king upon the *guddee* to the beggar at the gate.
  All things made he – Shiva the Preserver.

Mahadeo! Mahadeo! He made all –
Thorn for the camel, fodder for the kine,
And mother's heart for sleepy head, O little son of mine!

Little Toomai came in with a joyous *tunk-a-tunk* at the end of each verse, till he felt sleepy and stretched himself on the fodder at Kala Nag's side. At last the elephants began to lie down one after another as is their custom, till only Kala Nag at the right of the line was left standing up, and he rocked slowly from side to side, his ears put forward to listen to the night wind as it blew very slowly across the hills. The air was full of all the night noises that, taken together, make one big silence – the click of one bamboo-stem against the other, the rustle of something alive in the undergrowth, the scratch and squawk of a half-waked bird (birds are awake in the night much more often than we imagine), and the fall of water ever so far away. Little Toomai slept for some time, and when he waked it was brilliant moonlight, and Kala Nag was still standing up with his ears cocked. Little Toomai turned, rustling in the fodder, and watched the curve of his big back against half the stars in heaven, and while he watched he heard, so far away that it sounded no more than a pinhole of noise pricked through the stillness, the *"hoot-toot"* of a wild elephant. All the elephants in the lines jumped up as if they had been shot, and their grunts at last waked the sleeping mahouts, and they came out and drove in the picket-pegs with big mallets, and tightened this rope and knotted that till all was quiet. One new elephant had nearly grubbed up his picket, and Big Toomai took off Kala Nag's leg-chain and shackled that elephant fore foot to hind foot, but slipped a loop of grass-string round Kala Nag's leg, and told him to remember that he was tied fast. He knew that he and his father and his grandfather had done the very same thing hundreds of times before. Kala Nag did not answer to the order by gurgling, as he usually did. He stood still, looking out across the moonlight, his head a little raised and his ears spread like fans, up to the great folds of the Garo Hills.

"Tend to him if he grows restless in the night," said Big Toomai to Little Toomai, and he went into the hut and slept. Little Toomai was just going to sleep, too, when he heard the coir-string snap with a little *ting*, and Kala Nag rolled out of his pickets as slowly and as silently as a cloud rolls out of the mouth of a valley. Little Toomai pattered after him, barefooted, down the road in the moonlight, calling under his breath: "Kala Nag! Kala Nag! Take me with you, O Kala Nag!" The elephant turned, without a sound, took three strides back to the boy in the moonlight, put down his trunk, swung him up to his neck, and almost before Little Toomai had settled his knees, slipped into the forest.

There was one blast of furious trumpeting from the lines, and then the silence shut down on everything, and Kala Nag began to move. Sometimes a tuft of high grass washed along his sides as a wave washes along the sides of a ship, and sometimes a cluster of wild-pepper vines would scrape along his back, or a bamboo would creak where his shoulder touched it, but between those times he moved absolutely without any sound, drifting through the thick Garo Forest as though it had been smoke. He was going up hill, but though Little Toomai watched the stars in the rifts of the trees, he could not tell in what direction. Then Kala Nag reached the crest of the ascent and stopped for a minute, and Little Toomai could see the tops of the trees lying all speckled and furry under the moonlight for miles and miles, and the blue-white mist over the river in the hollow. Toomai leaned forward and looked, and he felt that the forest was awake below him – awake and alive and crowded. A big brown fruit-eating bat brushed past his ear; a porcupine's quills rattled in the thicket, and in the darkness between the tree-stems he heard a hog-bear digging hard in the moist warm earth, and snuffing as it digged. Then the branches closed over his head again, and Kala Nag began to go down into the valley – not quietly this time, but as a runaway gun goes down a steep bank – in one rush. The huge limbs moved as steadily as pistons, eight feet to each stride, and the wrinkled skin of the elbow-points rustled. The undergrowth on either side of him ripped with a noise like torn canvas, and the saplings that he heaved away right and left with his shoulders sprang back again, and banged him on the flank, and great trails of creepers, all matted together, hung from his tusks as he threw his head from side to side and ploughed out his pathway. Then Little Toomai laid himself down close to the great neck lest a swinging bough should sweep him to the ground, and he wished that he were back in the lines again. The grass began to get squashy, and Kala Nag's feet sucked and squelched as he put them down, and the night mist at the bottom of the valley chilled Little Toomai. There was a splash and a trample, and the rush of running water, and Kala Nag strode through the bed of a river, feeling his way at each step. Above the noise of the water, as it swirled round the elephant's legs, Little Toomai could hear more splashing and some trumpeting both up-stream and down – great grunts and angry snortings, and all the mist about him seemed to be full of rolling wavy shadows. *"Ai!"* he said, half aloud, his teeth chattering. "The Elephant-Folk are out tonight. It *is* the dance, then!"

Kala Nag swashed out of the water, blew his trunk clear, and began another climb, but this time he was not alone, and he had not to make his path. That was made already, six feet wide, in front of him, where the bent jungle-grass was trying to recover itself and stand up. Many elephants must have gone that way only a few minutes before. Little Toomai looked back, and behind him a great wild tusker, with his little pig's eyes glowing like hot coals, was just lifting himself out of the misty river. Then the trees closed up again, and they went on and up, with trumpetings and crashings, and the sound of breaking branches on every side of them. At last Kala Nag stood still between two tree-trunks at the very top of the hill. They were part of a circle of trees that grew round an irregular space of some three or four acres, and in all that space, as Little Toomai could see, the ground had been trampled down as hard as a brick floor. Some trees grew in the centre of the clearing, but their bark was rubbed away, and the white wood beneath showed all shiny and polished in the patches of moonlight. There were creepers hanging from the upper branches, and the bells of the flowers of the creepers, great waxy white things like convolvuluses, hung down fast asleep, but within the limits of the clearing there was not a single blade of green – nothing but the trampled earth. The moonlight showed it all iron-grey, except where some elephants stood upon it, and their shadows were inky black. Little Toomai looked, holding his breath, with his eyes starting out of his head, and as he looked, more and more and more elephants swung out into the open from between the tree-trunks. Little Toomai could only count up to ten, and he counted again and again on his fingers till he lost count of the tens, and his head began to swim. Outside the clearing he could hear them crashing in the undergrowth as they worked their way up the hillside, but as soon as they were within the circle of the tree-trunks they moved like ghosts.

There were white-tusked wild males, with fallen leaves and nuts and twigs lying in the wrinkles of their necks and the folds of their ears; fat slow-footed she-elephants, with restless, little pinky-black calves only three or four feet high running under their stomachs; young elephants with their tusks just beginning to show, and very proud of them; lanky, scraggy old-maid elephants, with their hollow anxious faces, and trunks like rough bark; savage old bull elephants, scarred from shoulder to flank with great weals and cuts of bygone fights, and the caked dirt of their solitary mud-baths dropping from their shoulders; and there was one with a broken tusk and the marks of the full-stroke, the terrible drawing scrape, of a tiger's claws on his side. They were standing head to head, or walking to and fro across the ground in couples, or rocking and swaying all by themselves – scores and scores of elephants. Toomai knew that so long as he lay still on Kala Nag's neck nothing would happen to him, for even in the rush and scramble of a keddah-drive a wild elephant does not reach up with his trunk and drag a man off the neck of a tame elephant. And these elephants were not thinking of men that night. Once they started and put their ears forward when they heard the chinking of a leg-iron in the forest, but it was Pudmini, Petersen Sahib's pet elephant, her chain snapped short off, grunting, snuffling up the hillside. She must have broken her pickets, and come straight from Petersen Sahib's camp. And Little Toomai saw another elephant, one that he did not know, with deep rope-galls on his back and breast He, too, must have run away from some camp in the hills about.

At last there was no sound of any more elephants moving in the forest, and Kala Nag rolled out from his station between the trees and went into the middle of the crowd, clucking and gurgling, and all the elephants began to talk in their own tongue, and to move about. Still lying down, Little Toomai looked down upon scores and scores of broad backs, and wagging ears, and tossing trunks, and little rolling eyes. He heard the click of tusks as they crossed other tusks by accident, and the dry rustle of trunks twined together, and the chafing of enormous sides and shoulders in the crowd, and the incessant flick and *hissh* of the great tails. Then a cloud came over the moon, and he sat in black darkness. But the quiet, steady hustling and pushing and gurgling went on just the same. He knew that there were elephants all round Kala Nag, and that there was no chance of backing him out of the assembly; so he set his teeth and shivered. In a keddah at least there was torch-light and shouting, but here he was all alone in the dark, and once a trunk came up and touched him on the knee. Then an elephant trumpeted, and they all took it up for five or ten terrible seconds. The dew from the trees above spattered down like rain on the unseen backs, and a dull booming noise began, not very loud at first, and Little Toomai could not tell what it was. But it grew and grew, and Kala Nag lifted up one fore foot and then the other, and brought them down on the ground – one-two, one-two, as steadily as trip-hammers. The elephants were stamping altogether now, and it sounded like a war-drum beaten at the mouth of a cave. The dew fell from the trees till there was no more left to fall, and the booming went on, and the ground rocked and shivered, and Little Toomai put his hands up to his ears to shut out the sound. But it was all one gigantic jar that ran through him – this stamp of hundreds of heavy feet on the raw earth. Once or twice he could feel Kala Nag and all the others surge forward a few strides, and the thumping would change to the crushing sound of juicy green things being bruised, but in a minute or two the boom of feet on hard earth began again. A tree was creaking and groaning somewhere near him. He put out his arm and felt the bark, but Kala Nag moved forward, still tramping, and he could not tell where he was in the clearing. There was no sound from the elephants, except once, when two or three little calves squeaked together. Then he heard a thump and a shuffle, and the booming went on. It must have lasted fully two hours, and Little Toomai ached in every nerve, but he knew by the smell of the night air that the dawn was coming.

The morning broke in one sheet of pale yellow behind the green hills, and the booming stopped with the first ray, as though the light had been an order. Before Little Toomai had got the ringing out of his head, before even he had shifted his position, there was not an elephant in sight except Kala Nag, Pudmini, and the elephant with the rope-galls, and there was neither sign nor rustle nor whisper down the hillsides to show where the others had gone. Little Toomai stared again and again. The clearing, as he remembered it, had grown in the night. More trees stood in the middle of it, but the undergrowth and the jungle-grass at the sides had been rolled back. Little Toomai stared once more. Now he understood the trampling.

The elephants had stamped out more room – had stamped the thick grass and juicy cane to trash, the trash into slivers, the slivers into tiny fibres, and the fibres into hard earth.

"*Wah!*" said Little Toomai, and his eyes were very heavy. "Kala Nag, my lord, let us keep by Pudmini and go to Petersen Sahib's camp, or I shall drop from thy neck."

The third elephant watched the two go away, snorted, wheeled round, and took his own path. He may have belonged to some little native king's establishment, fifty or sixty or a hundred miles away.

Two hours later, as Petersen Sahib was eating early breakfast, his elephants, who had been double-chained that night, began to trumpet, and Pudmini, mired to the shoulders, with Kala Nag, very footsore, shambled into the camp. Little Toomai's face was grey and pinched, and his hair was full of leaves and drenched with dew, but he tried to salute Petersen Sahib, and cried faintly: "The dance – the elephant-dance! I have seen it, and – I die!" As Kala Nag sat down, he slid off his neck in a dead faint.

But, since native children have no nerves worth speaking of, in two hours he was lying very contentedly in Petersen Sahib's hammock with Petersen Sahib's shooting-coat under his head, and a glass of warm milk, a little brandy, with a dash of quinine inside of him, and while the old hairy, scarred hunters of the jungles sat three deep before him, looking at him as though he were a spirit, he told his tale in short words, as a child will, and wound up with:

"Now, if I lie in one word, send men to see, and they will find that the Elephant-Folk have trampled down more room in their dance-room, and they will find ten and ten, and many times ten, tracks leading to that dance-room. They made more room with their feet. I have seen it. Kala Nag took me, and I saw. Also Kala Nag is very leg-weary!"

Little Toomai lay back and slept all through the long afternoon and into the twilight, and while he slept Petersen Sahib and Machua Appa followed the track of the two elephants for fifteen miles across the hills. Petersen Sahib had spent eighteen years in catching elephants, and he had only once before found such a dance-place. Machua Appa had no need to look twice at the clearing to see what had been done there, or to scratch with his toe in the packed, rammed earth.

"The child speaks truth," said he. "All this was done last night, and I have counted seventy tracks crossing the river. See, Sahib, where Pudmini's leg-iron cut the bark of that tree! Yes, she was there too." They looked at one another and up and down, and they wondered, for the ways of elephants are beyond the wit of any man, black or white, to fathom.

"Forty years and five," said Machua Appa, "have I followed my lord the elephant, but never have I heard that any child of man had seen what this child has seen. By all the Gods of the Hills, it is – what can we say?" And he shook his head.

When they got back to camp it was time for the evening meal. Petersen Sahib ate alone in his tent, but he gave orders that the camp should have two sheep and some fowls, as well as a double ration of flour and rice and salt, for he knew that there would be a feast. Big Toomai had come up hot-foot from the camp in the plains to search for his son and his elephant, and now that he had found them he looked at them as though he were afraid of them both. And there was a feast by the blazing camp-fires in front of the lines of picketed elephants, and Little Toomai was the hero of it all. And the big brown elephant-catchers, the trackers and drivers and ropers, and the men who know all the secrets of breaking the wildest elephants, passed him from one to the other, and they marked his forehead with blood from the breast of a newly killed jungle-cock, to show that he was a forester, initiated and free of all the jungles.

And at last, when the flames died down, and the red light of the logs made the elephants look as though they had been dipped in blood too, Machua Appa, the head of all the drivers of all the keddahs – Machua Appa, Petersen Sahib's other self, who had never seen a made road in forty years: Machua Appa, who was so great that he had no other name than Machua Appa – leaped to his feet, with Little Toomai held high in the air above his head, and shouted: "Listen, my brothers. Listen, too, you my lords in the lines there, for I, Machua Appa, am speaking! This little one shall no more be called Little Toomai, but Toomai of the Elephants, as his great grandfather was called before him. What never man has seen he has seen through the long night, and the favour of the Elephant-Folk and of the Gods of the Jungles is with him. He shall become a great tracker; he shall become greater than I, even I, Machua Appa! He shall follow the new trail, and the stale trail, and the mixed trail, with a clear eye! He shall take no harm in the keddah when he runs under their bellies to rope the wild tuskers. And if he slips before the feet of the charging bull-elephant, the bull-elephant shall know who he is and shall not crush him. *Aihai!* My lords in the chains" – he whirled up the line of pickets – "here is the little one that has seen your dances in your Widen places – the sight that never man saw! Give him honour, my lords! *Salaam karo*, my children. Make your salute to Toomai of the Elephants! Gunga Pershad, *ahaa!* Hira Guj, Birchi Guj, Kuttar Guj, *ahaa!* Pudmini – thou hast seen him at the dance, and thou too, Kala Nag, my pearl among elephants! *Ahaa!* Together! To Toomai of the Elephants. *Barrao!*"

And at that last wild yell the whole line flung up their trunks till the tips touched their foreheads, and broke out into the full salute – the crashing trumpet-peal that only the Viceroy of India hears, the salaamut of the keddah.

But it was all for the sake of Little Toomai, who had seen what never man had seen before – the dance of the elephants at night and alone in the heart of the Garo Hills!

Shiv and the Grasshopper

The Song that Toomai's Mother Sang to the Baby

Shiv, who poured the harvest and made the winds to blow,
Sitting at the doorways of a day of long ago,
Gave to each his portion, food and toil and fate,
From the king upon the *guddee* to the beggar at the gate.
    All things made he – Shiva the Preserver.
    Mahadeo! Mahadeo! He made all –
    Thorn for the camel, fodder for the kine,
    And mother's heart for sleepy head, O little son of mine!

Wheat he gave to rich folk, millet to the poor,
Broken scraps for holy men that beg from door to door.
Cattle to the tiger, carrion to the kite,
And rags and bones to wicked wolves without the wall at night
Naught he found too lofty, none he saw too low –
Parbati beside him watched them come and go,
Thought to cheat her husband, turning Shiv to jest,
Stole the little grasshopper and hid it in her breast!

    So she tricked him, Shiva the Preserver.
    Mahadeo! Mahadeo! Turn and see.
    Tall are the camels, heavy are the kine,
    But this was Least of Little Things, O little son of mine!

    When the dole was ended, laughingly she said:
    "Master of a million mouths, is riot one unfed?"
    Laughing, Shiv made answer: "All have had their part,
    Even he the little one, hidden 'neath thy heart."

From her breast she plucked it, Parbati the thief,
Saw the Least of Little Things gnawed a new-grown leaf.
Saw and feared and wondered, making prayer to Shiv,
Who hath surely given meat to all that live.
     All things made he – Shiva the Preserver.
     Mahadeo! Mahadeo! He made all –
     Thorn for the camel, fodder for the kine,
     And mother's heart for sleepy head, O little son of mine!

Servants of the Queen

You can work it out by fractions or by simple rule of three,
But the way of Tweedle-dum is not the way of Tweedle-dee.
You can twist it, you can turn it, you can plait it till you drop,
But the way of Pilly-Winky's *not* the way of Winkie-Pop!

It had been raining heavily for one whole month – raining on a camp of thirty thousand men and thousands of camels, elephants, horses, bullocks, and mules all gathered together at a place called Rawalpindi, to be reviewed by the Viceroy of India. He was receiving a visit from the Amir of Afghanistan – a wild king of a very wild country. And the Amir had brought with him for a bodyguard eight hundred men and horses who had never seen a camp or a locomotive before in their lives – savage men and savage horses from somewhere at the back of Central Asia. Every night a mob of these horses would be sure to break their heel-ropes and stampede up and down the camp through the mud in the dark, or the camels would break loose and run about and fall over the ropes of the tents, and you can imagine how pleasant that was for men trying to go to sleep. My tent lay far away from the camel lines, and I thought it was safe, but one night a man popped his head in and shouted: "Get out, quick! They're coming! My tent's gone!"

I knew who "they" were, so I put on my boots and waterproof and scuttled out into the slush. Little Vixen, my fox-terrier, went out through the other side, and then there was a roaring and a grunting and bubbling, and I saw the tent cave in, as the pole snapped, and begin to dance about like a mad ghost. A camel had blundered into it, and wet and angry as I

140

Every night a mob of these horses would be sure to break their heel-ropes and stampede up and down the camp.

was, I could not help laughing. Then I ran on, because I did not know how many camels might have got loose, and before long I was out of sight of the camp, ploughing my way through the mud. At last I fell over the tail-end of a gun, and by that knew I was somewhere near the artillery lines where the cannon were stacked at night. As I did not want to plowter about any more in the drizzle and the dark, I put my waterproof over the muzzle of one gun, and made a sort of wigwam with two or three rammers that I found, and lay along the tail of another gun, wondering where Vixen had got to, and where I might be. Just as I was getting ready to go to sleep I heard a jingle of harness and a grunt, and a mule passed me shaking his wet ears. He belonged to a screw-gun battery, for I could hear the rattle of the straps and rings and chains and things on his saddle-pad. The screw-guns are tiny little cannon made in two pieces, that are screwed together when the time comes to use them. They are taken up mountains, anywhere that a mule can find a road, and they are very useful for fighting in rocky country. Behind the mule there was a camel, with his big soft feet squelching and slipping in the mud, and his neck bobbing to and fro like a strayed hen's. Luckily, I knew enough of beast language – not wild-beast language, but camp-beast language, of course – from the natives to know what he was saying. He must have been the one that flopped into my tent, for he called to the mule: "What shall I do? Where shall I go? I have fought with a white Thing that waved, and it took a stick and hit me on the neck." (That was my broken tent-pole, and I was very glad to know it.) "Shall we run on?"

"Oh, it was you," said the mule, "you and your friends, that have been disturbing the camp? All right. You'll be beaten for this in the morning, but I may as well give you something on account now."

I heard the harness jingle as the mule backed and caught the camel two kicks in the ribs that rang like a drum. "Another time," he said, "you'll know better than to run through a mule-battery at night, shouting 'Thieves and fire!' Sit down, and keep your silly neck quiet."

The camel doubled up camel-fashion, like a two-foot rule, and sat down whimpering. There was a regular beat of hoofs in the darkness, and a big troop-horse cantered up as steadily as though he were on parade, jumped a gun-tail, and landed close to the mule.

"It's disgraceful," he said, blowing out his nostrils. "Those camels have racketed through our lines again – the third time this week. How's a horse to keep his condition if he isn't allowed to sleep? Who's here?"

"I'm the breech-piece mule of number two gun of the First Screw Battery," said the mule, "and the other's one of your friends. He's waked me up too. Who are you?"

"Number Fifteen, E troop, Ninth Lancers – Dick Cunliffe's horse. Stand over a little, there."

"Oh, beg your pardon," said the mule. "It's dark to see much. Aren't these camels too sickening for anything? I walked out of my lines to get a little peace and quiet here."

"My lords," said the camel humbly, "we dreamed bad dreams in the night, and we were very much afraid. I am only a baggage-camel of the 39th Native Infantry, and I am not as brave as you are, my lords."

"Then why didn't you stay and carry baggage for the 39th Native Infantry, instead of running all round the camp?" said the mule.

"They were such very bad dreams," said the camel. "I am sorry. Listen! What is that? Shall we run on again?"

"Sit down," said the mule, "or you'll snap your long stick-legs between the guns." He cocked one ear and listened. "Bullocks!" he said. "Gun-bullocks. On my word, you and your friends have waked the camp very thoroughly. It takes a good deal of prodding to put up a gun-bullock."

I heard a chain dragging along the ground, and a yoke of the great sulky white bullocks that drag the heavy siege-guns when the elephants won't go any nearer to the firing came shouldering along together. And almost stepping on the chain was another battery mule, calling wildly for "Billy."

"That's one of our recruits," said the old mule to the troop-horse. "He's calling for me. Here, youngster, stop squealing. The dark never hurt anybody yet."

The gun-bullocks lay down together and began chewing the cud, but the young mule huddled close to Billy.

"Things!" he said. "Fearful and horrible Things, Billy! They came into our lines while we were asleep. D'you think they'll kill us?"

"I've a very great mind to give you a number one kicking," said Billy. "The idea of a fourteen-hand mule with your training disgracing the battery before this gentleman!"

"Gently, gently!" said the troop-horse. "Remember they are always like this to begin with. The first time I ever saw a man (it was in Australia when I was a three-year-old) I ran for half a day, and if I'd seen a camel, I should have been running still."

Nearly all our horses for the English cavalry are brought to India from Australia, and are broken in by the troopers themselves.

"True enough," said Billy. "Stop shaking, youngster. The first time they put the full harness with all its chains on my back, I stood on my fore legs and kicked every bit of it off. I hadn't learned the *real* science of kicking then, but the battery said they had never seen anything like it."

"But this wasn't harness or anything that jingled," said the young mule. "You know I don't mind that now, Billy. It was things like trees, and they fell up and down the lines and bubbled, and my head-rope broke, and I couldn't find my driver, and I couldn't find you, Billy, so I ran off with – with these gentlemen."

"*Hm!*" said Billy. "As soon as I heard the camels were loose I came away on my own account. When a battery – a screw-gun – mule calls gun-bullocks gentlemen, he must be very badly shaken up. Who are you fellows on the ground there?"

The gun-bullocks rolled their cuds, and answered both together: "The seventh yoke of the first gun of the Big Gun Battery. We were asleep when the camels came, but when we were trampled on we got up and walked away. It is better to lie quiet in the mud than to be disturbed on good bedding. We told your friend here that there was nothing to be afraid of, but he knew so much that he thought otherwise. *Wah!*"

They went on chewing.

"That comes of being afraid," said Billy. "You get laughed at by gun-bullocks. I hope you like it, young 'un."

The young mule's teeth snapped, and I heard him say something about not being afraid of any beefy old bullock in the world, but the bullocks only clicked their horns together and went on chewing.

"Now, don't be angry after you've been afraid. That's the worst kind of cowardice," said the troop-horse. "Anybody can be forgiven for being scared in the night, *I* think, if they see things they don't understand. We've broken out of our pickets, again and again, four hundred and fifty of us, just because a new recruit got to telling tales of whip-snakes at home in Australia till we were scared to death of the loose ends of our head-ropes."

"That's all very well in camp," said Billy. "I'm not above stampeding myself, for the fun of the thing, when I haven't been out for a day or two, but what do you do on active service?"

"Oh, that's quite another set of new shoes," said the troop-horse. "Dick Cunliffe's on my back then, and drives his knees into me, and all I have to do is to watch where I am putting my feet, and to keep my hind legs well under me, and be bridle-wise."

"What's bridle-wise?" said the young mule.

"By the Blue Gums of the Back Blocks," snorted the troop-horse, "do you mean to say that you aren't taught to be bridle-wise in your business? How can you do anything, unless you can spin round at once when the rein is pressed on your neck? It means life or death to your man, and of course that's life and death to you. Get round with your hind legs under you the instant you feel the rein on your neck. If you haven't room to swing round, rear up a little and come round on your hind legs. That's being bridle-wise."

"We aren't taught that way," said Billy the mule, stiffly. "We're taught to obey the man at our head: step off when he says so, and step in when he says so. I suppose it comes to the same thing. Now, with all this fine fancy business and rearing, which must be very bad for your hocks, what do you *do?*"

"That depends," said the troop-horse. "Generally I have to go in among a lot of yelling, hairy men with knives – long shiny knives, worse than the farrier's knives – and I have to take care that Dick's boot is just touching the next man's boot without crushing it. I can see Dick's lance to the right of my right eye, and I know I'm safe. I shouldn't care to be the man or horse that stood up to Dick and me when we're in a hurry."

"Don't the knives hurt?" said the young mule.

"Well, I got one cut across the chest once, but that wasn't Dick's fault – "

"A lot I should have cared whose fault it was, if it hurt!" said the young mule.

"You must," said the troop-horse. "If you don't trust your man, you may as well run away at once. That's what some of our horses do, and I don't blame them. As I was saying, it wasn't Dick's fault. The man was lying on the ground, and I stretched myself not to tread on him, and he slashed up at me. Next time I have to go over a man lying down I shall step on him – hard."

"*Hm!*" said Billy. "It sounds very foolish. Knives are duty things at any time. The proper thing to do is to climb up a mountain with a well-balanced saddle, hang on by all four feet and your ears too, and creep and crawl and wriggle along, till you come out hundreds of feet above any one else, on a ledge where there's just room enough for your hoofs. Then you stand still and keep quiet – never ask a man to hold your head, young 'un – keep quiet while the guns are being put together, and then you watch the little poppy shells drop down into the tree-tops ever so far below."

"Don't you ever trip?" said the troop-horse.

"They say that when a mule trips you can split a hen's ear," said Billy. "Now and again *per-haps* a badly packed saddle will upset a mule, but it's very seldom. I wish I could show you our business. It's beautiful. Why, it took me three years to find out what the men were driving at. The science of the thing is never to show up against the sky-line, because, if you do, you may get fired at. Remember that, young 'un. Always keep hidden as much as possible, even if you have to go a mile out of your way. I lead the battery when it comes to that sort of climbing."

"Fired at without the chance of running into the people who are firing!" said the troop-horse, thinking hard. "I couldn't stand that. I should want to charge – with Dick."

"Oh, no, you wouldn't. You know that as soon as the guns are in position *they'll* do all the charging. That's scientific and neat, but knives – *pah!*"

The baggage-camel had been bobbing his head to and fro for some time past, anxious to get a word in edgeways. Then I heard him say, as he cleared his throat, nervously:

"I – I – I have fought a little, but not in that climbing way or that running way."

"No. Now you mention it," said Billy, "you don't look as though you were made for climbing or running – much. Well, how was it, old Hay-bales?"

"The proper way," said the camel. "We all sat down – "

"Oh, my crupper and breastplate!" said the troop-horse under his breath. "Sat down!"

"We sat down – a hundred of us," the camel went on, "in a big square, and the men piled our *kajawahs*, our packs and saddles, outside the square, and they fired over our backs, the men did, on all sides of the square."

"What sort of men? Any men that came along?" said the troop-horse. "They teach us in riding school to lie down and let our masters fire across us, but Dick Cunliffe is the only man I'd trust to do that. It tickles my girths, and, besides, I can't see with my head on the ground."

"What does it matter who fires across you?" said the camel. "There are plenty of men and plenty of other camels close by, and a great many clouds of smoke. I am not frightened then. I sit still and wait."

"And yet," said Billy, "you dream bad dreams and upset the camp at night. Well! Well! Before I'd lie down, not to speak of sitting down, and let a man fire across me, my heels and his head would have something to say to each other. Did you ever hear anything so awful as that?"

There was a long silence, and then one of the gun-bullocks lifted up his big head and said: "This is very foolish indeed. There is only one way of fighting."

"Oh, go on," said Billy. "*Please* don't mind me. I suppose you fellows fight standing on your tails?"

"Only one way," said the two together. (They must have been twins.) "This is that way. To put all twenty yoke of us to the big gun as soon as Two Tails trumpets." ("Two Tails" is camp-slang for the elephant.)

"What does Two Tails trumpet for?" said the young mule.

"To show that he is not going any nearer to the smoke on the other side. Two Tails is a great coward. Then we tug the big gun all together – *Heya – Hullah! Heeyah! Hullah! We* do not climb like cats nor run like calves. We go across the level plain, twenty yoke of us, till we are unyoked again, and we graze while the big guns talk across the plain to some town with mud walls, and pieces of the wall fall out, and the dust goes up as though many cattle were coming home."

"Oh! And you choose that time for grazing?" said the young mule.

"That time or any other. Eating is always good. We eat till we are yoked up again and tug the gun back to where Two Tails is waiting for it. Sometimes there are big guns in the city that speak back, and some of us are killed, and then there is all the more grazing for those that are left. This is Fate – nothing but Fate. None the less, Two Tails is a great coward. That is the proper way to fight. We are brothers from Hapur. Our father was a sacred bull of Shiva. We have spoken."

"Well, I've certainly learned something tonight," said the troop-horse. "Do you gentlemen of the screw-gun battery feel inclined to eat when you are being fired at with big guns, and Two Tails is behind you?"

"About as much as we feel inclined to sit down and let men sprawl all over us, or run into people with knives. I never heard such stuff. A mountain ledge, a well-balanced load, a driver you can trust to let you pick your own way, and I'm your mule. But – the other things – No!" said Billy, with a stamp of his foot.

"Of course," said the troop-horse, "everyone is not made in the same way; and I can quite see that your family, on your fathers side, would fail to understand a great many things."

"Never you mind my family on my father's side," said Billy angrily, for every mule hates to be reminded that his father was a donkey. "My father was a Southern gentleman, and he could pull down and bite and kick into rags every horse he came across. Remember that, you big brown Brumby!"

Brumby means wild horse without any breeding. Imagine the feelings of Ormonde if a 'bus-horse called him a cocktail, and you can imagine how the Australian horse felt. I saw the white of his eye glitter in the dark.

"See here, you son of an imported Málaga jackass," he said between his teeth, "I'd have you know that I'm related on my mother's side to Carbine, winner of the Melbourne Cup, and where I come from we aren't accustomed to being ridden over roughshod by any parrot-mouthed, pig-headed mule in a pop-gun pea-shooter battery. Are you ready?"

"On your hind legs!" squealed Billy. They both reared up facing each other, and I was expecting a furious fight, when a gurgly, nimbly voice called out of the darkness to the right: "Children, what are you fighting about there? Be quiet."

Both beasts dropped down with a snort of disgust, for neither horse nor mule can bear to listen to an elephant's voice.

"It's Two Tails!" said the troop-horse. "I can't stand him. A tail at each end isn't fair!"

"My feelings exactly," said Billy, crowding into the troop-horse for company. "We're very alike in some things."

"I suppose we've inherited them from our mothers," said the troop-horse. "It's not worth quarrelling about. Hi! Two Tails, are you tied up?"

"Yes," said Two Tails, with a laugh all up his trunk. "I'm picketed for the night. I've heard what you fellows have been saying. But don't be afraid. I'm not coming over."

The bullocks and the camel said, half aloud: "Afraid of Two Tails – what nonsense!" And the bullocks went on: "We are sorry that you heard, but it is true. Two Tails, why are you afraid of the guns when they fire?"

"Well," said Two Tails, rubbing one hind leg against the other, exactly like a little boy saying a poem, "I don't quite know whether you'd understand."

"We don't, but we have to pull the guns," said the bullocks.

"I know it, and I know you are a good deal braver than you think you are. But it's different with me. My battery captain called me a Pachydermatous Anachronism the other day."

"That's another way of fighting, I suppose?" said Billy, who was recovering his spirits.

"*You* don't know what that means, of course, but I do. It means betwixt and between, and that is just where I am. I can see inside my head what will happen when a shell bursts, and you bullocks can't."

"I can," said the troop-horse. "At least a little bit I try not to think about it."

"I can see more than you, and I *do* think about it. I know there's a great deal of me to take care of, and I know that nobody knows how to cure me when I'm sick. All they can do is to stop my driver's pay till I get well, and I can't trust my driver."

"Ah," said the troop-horse. "That explains it. I can trust Dick."

"You could put a whole regiment of Dicks on my back without making me feel any better. I know just enough to be uncomfortable, and not enough to go on in spite of it."

"We do not understand," said the bullocks.

"I know you don't. I'm not talking to you. You don't know what blood is."

"We do," said the bullocks. "It is red stuff that soaks into the ground and smells."

The troop-horse gave a kick and a bound and a snort.

"Don't talk of it," he said. "I can smell it now, just thinking of it. It makes me want to run – when I haven't Dick on my back."

"But it is not here," said the camel and the bullocks. "Why are you so stupid?"

"It's vile stuff," said Billy. "I don't want to run, but I don't want to talk about it."

"There you are!" said Two Tails, waving his tail to explain.

"Surely. Yes, we have been here all night," said the bullocks.

Two Tails stamped his foot till the iron ring on it jingled. "Oh, I'm not talking to *you*. You can't see inside your heads."

"No. We see out of our four eyes," said the bullocks. "We see straight in front of us."

"If I could do *that* and nothing else you wouldn't be needed to pull the big guns at all. If I was like my captain – he can see things inside his head before the firing begins, and he shakes all over, but he knows too much to run away – if I was like him I could pull the guns. But if I were as wise as all that I should never be here. I should be a king in the forest, as I used to be, sleeping half the day and bathing when I liked. I haven't had a good bath for a month."

"That's all very fine," said Billy, "but giving a thing a long name doesn't make it any better."

"*Hsh!*" said the troop-horse. "I think I understand what Two Tails means."

"You'll understand better in a minute," said Two Tails angrily. "Now you just explain to me why you don't like this!"

He began trumpeting furiously at the top of his trumpet.

"Stop that!" said Billy and the troop-horse together, and I could hear them stamp and shiver. An elephant's trumpeting is always nasty, especially on a dark night.

"I shan't stop," said Two Tails. "Won't you explain that, please? *Hhrrmph!*

Rrrt! Rrrmph! Rrrhha!" Then he stopped suddenly, and I heard a little whimper in the dark, and knew that Vixen had found me at last. She knew as well as I did that if there is one thing in the world the elephant is more afraid of than another it is a little barking dog, so she stopped to bully Two Tails in his pickets, and yapped round his big feet. Two Tails shuffled and squeaked. "Go away, little dog!" he said. "Don't snuff at my ankles, or I'll kick at you. Good little dog – nice little doggie, then! Go home, you yelping little beast! Oh, why doesn't some one take her away? She'll bite me in a minute."

"Seems to me," said Billy to the troop-horse, "that our friend Two Tails is afraid of most things. Now, if I had a full meal for every dog I've kicked across the parade-ground I should be as fat as Two Tails nearly."

I whistled, and Vixen ran up to me, muddy all over, and licked my nose, and told me a long tale about hunting for me all through the camp. I never let her know that I understood beast talk, or she would have taken all sorts of liberties. So I buttoned her into the breast of my overcoat, and Two Tails shuffled and stamped and growled to himself.

"Extraordinary! Most extraordinary!" he said. "It runs in our family. Now, where has that nasty little beast gone to?"

I heard him feeling about with his trunk.

"We all seem to be affected in various ways," he went on, blowing his nose. "Now, you gentlemen were alarmed, I believe, when I trumpeted."

"Not alarmed, exactly," said the troop-horse, "but it made me feel as though I had hornets where my saddle ought to be. Don't begin again."

"I'm frightened of a little dog, and the camel here is frightened by bad dreams in the night."

"It is very lucky for us that we haven't all got to fight in the same way," said the troop-horse.

"What I want to know," said the young mule, who had been quiet for a long time, "what *I* want to know is, why we have to fight at all."

"Because we're told to," said the troop-horse, with a snort of contempt.

"Orders," said Billy the mule, and his teeth snapped.

"*Hukm hai!* [It is an order]," said the camel with a gurgle, and Two Tails and the bullocks repeated: *"Hukm hai!"*

151

"Yes, but who gives the orders?" said the recruit-mule.

"The man who walks at your head – or sits on your back – or holds the nose-rope – or twists your tail," said Billy and the troop-horse and the camel and the bullocks one after the other.

"But who gives them the orders?"

"Now you want to know too much, young 'un," said Billy, "and that is one way of getting kicked. All you have to do is to obey the man at your head and ask no questions."

"He's quite right," said Two Tails. "I can't always obey, because I'm betwixt and between, but Billy's right. Obey the man next to you who gives the order, or you'll stop all the battery, besides getting a thrashing."

The gun-bullocks got up to go. "Morning is coming," they said. "We will go back to our lines. It is true that we only see out of our eyes, and we are not very clever, but still, we are the only people tonight who have not been afraid. Good night, you brave people."

Nobody answered, and the troop-horse said, to change the conversation: "Where's that little dog? A dog means a man somewhere about."

"Here I am," yapped Vixen, "under the gun-tail with my man. You big, blundering beast of a camel you, you upset our tent. My man's very angry."

"*Phew!*" said the bullocks. "He must be white!"

"Of course he is," said Vixen. "Do you suppose I'm looked after by a black bullock-driver?"

"*Huah! Ouach! Ugh!*" said the bullocks. "Let us get away quickly."

They plunged forward in the mud, and managed somehow to run their yoke on the pole of an ammunition-waggon, where it jammed.

"Now you *have* done it," said Billy calmly. "Don't struggle. You're hung up till daylight. What on earth's the matter?"

The bullocks went off into the long hissing snorts that Indian cattle give, and pushed and crowded and slued and stamped and slipped and nearly fell down in the mud, grunting savagely.

"You'll break your necks in a minute," said the troop-horse. "What's the matter with white men? I live with 'em."

"They – eat us! Pull!" said the near bullock. The yoke snapped with a twang, and they lumbered off together.

I never knew before what made Indian cattle so scared of Englishmen. We eat beef – a thing that no cattle-driver touches – and of course the cattle do not like it.

"May I be flogged with my own pad-chains! Who'd have thought of two big lumps like those losing their heads?" said Billy.

"Never mind. I'm going to look at this man. Most of the white men, I know, have things in their pockets," said the troop-horse.

"I'll leave you, then. I can't say I'm over-fond of 'em myself. Besides, white men who haven't a place to sleep in are more than likely to be thieves, and I've a good deal of Government property on my back. Come along, young 'un, and we'll go back to our lines. Good night, Australia! See you on parade tomorrow, I suppose. Good night, old Hay-bales! Try to control your feelings, won't you? Good night, Two Tails! If you pass us on the ground tomorrow, don't trumpet. It spoils our formation."

Billy the Mule stumped off with the swaggering limp of an old campaigner, as the troop-horse's head came nuzzling into my breast, and I gave him biscuits, while Vixen, who is a most conceited little dog, told him fibs about the scores of horses that she and I kept.

"I'm coming to the parade tomorrow in my dog-cart," she said. "Where will you be?"

"On the left hand of the second squadron. I set the time for all my troop, little lady," he said politely. "Now I must go back to Dick. My tail's all muddy, and he'll have two hours' hard work dressing me for parade."

The big parade of all the thirty thousand men was held that afternoon, and Vixen and I had a good place close to the Viceroy and the Amir of Afghanistan, with his high big black hat of astrachan wool and the great diamond star in the centre. The first part of the review was all sunshine, and the regiments went by in wave upon wave of legs all moving together, and guns all in a line, till our eyes grew dizzy. Then the cavalry came up, to the beautiful cavalry canter of "Bonnie Dundee," and Vixen cocked her ear where she sat on the dog-cart. The second squadron of the Lancers shot by, and there was the troop-horse, with his tail like spun silk, his head pulled into his breast, one ear forward and one back, setting the time for all his squadron, his legs going as smoothly as waltz-music. Then the big guns came by, and I saw Two Tails and two other elephants harnessed in line to a forty-pounder siege-gun while twenty yoke of oxen walked behind. The seventh pair had a new yoke, and they looked rather stiff and tired. Last came the screw-guns, and Billy the Mule carried himself as though he commanded all the troops, and his harness was oiled and polished till it winked. I gave a cheer all by myself for Billy the Mule, but he never looked right or left.

The rain began to fall again, and for a while it was too misty to see what the troops were doing. They had made a big half circle across the plain, and were spreading out into a line. That line grew and grew and grew till it was three-quarters of a mile long from wing to wing – one solid wall of men, horses, and guns. Then it came on straight towards the Viceroy and the Amir, and as it got nearer the ground began to shake, like the deck of a steamer when the engines are going fast.

Unless you have been there you cannot imagine what a frightening effect this steady come-down of troops has on the spectators, even when they know it is only a review. I looked at the Amir. Up till then he had not shown the shadow of a sign of astonishment or anything else, but now his eyes began to get bigger and bigger, and he picked up the reins on his horse's neck and looked behind him. For a minute it seemed as though he were going to draw his sword and slash his way out through the English men and women in the carriages at the back. Then the advance stopped dead, the ground stood still, the whole line saluted, and thirty bands began to play all together. That was the end of the review, and the regiments went off to their camps in the rain, and an infantry band struck up with:

> The animals went in two by two,
> Hurrah!
> The animals went in two by two,
> The elephant and the battery mul',
> and they all got into the Ark
> For to get out of the rain!

Then I heard an old, grizzled, long-haired Central Asian chief, who had come down with the Amir, asking questions of a native officer.

"Now," said he, "in what manner was this wonderful thing done?"

And the officer answered: "An order was given, and they obeyed."

"But are the beasts as wise as the men?" said the chief.

"They obey, as the men do. Mule, horse, elephant, or bullock, he obeys his driver, and the driver his sergeant, and the sergeant his lieutenant, and the lieutenant his captain, and the captain his major, and the major his colonel, and the colonel his brigadier commanding three regiments, and the brigadier the general, who obeys the Viceroy, who is the servant of the Empress. Thus it is done."

"Would it were so in Afghanistan!" said the chief, "for there we obey only our own wills."

"And for that reason," said the native officer, twirling his moustache, "your Amir whom you do not obey must come here and take orders from our Viceroy."

Parade-Song of the Camp-Animals

ELEPHANTS OF THE GUN-TEAM

We lent to Alexander the strength of Hercules,
The wisdom of our foreheads, the cunning of our knees;
We bowed our necks to service: they ne'er were loosed again –
Make way there – way for the ten-foot teams
    Of the forty-pounder train!

GUN-BULLOCKS

Those heroes in their harnesses avoid a cannon-ball,
And what they know of powder upsets them one and all;
Then *we* come into action and tug the guns again –
Make way there – way for the twenty yoke
    Of the forty-pounder train!

CAVALRY HORSES

By the brand on my shoulder, the finest of tunes
Is played by the Lancers, Hussars, and Dragoons,
And it's sweeter than "Stables" or "Water" to me –
The cavalry canter of "Bonnie Dundee"!

Then feed us and break us and handle and groom,
And give us good riders and plenty of room,
And launch us in column of squadron and see
The way of the war-horse to "Bonnie Dundee"!

SCREW-GUN MULES

As me and my companions were scrambling up a hill
The path was lost in rolling stones but we went forward still,
For we can wriggle and climb, my lads, and turn up everywhere,
Oh, it's our delight on a mountain height, with a leg or two to spare!

Good luck to every sergeant, then, that lets us pick our road;
Bad luck to all the driver-men that cannot pack a load:
For we can wriggle and climb, my lads, and turn up everywhere,
Oh it's our delight on a mountain height with a leg or two to spare!

COMMISSARIAT CAMELS

We haven't a camelty tune of our own
To help us trollop along,
But every neck is a hair-trombone
(*Rtt-ta-ta-ta!* is a hair-trombone!)
And this our marching-song:
Can't! Don't! Shan't! Won't!
Pass it along the line!
Somebody's pack has slid from his back,
Wish it were only mine!
Somebody's load has tipped off in the road –
Cheer for a halt and a row!
Urrr! Yarrh! Grr! Arrh!
Somebody's catching it now!

ALL THE BEASTS TOGETHER

Children of the camp are we,
Serving each in his degree;
Children of the yoke and goad,
Pack and harness, pad and load.

See our line across the plain,
Like a heel-rope bent again,
Reaching, writhing, rolling far,
Sweeping all away to war;
While the men that walk beside,
Dusty, silent, heavy-eyed,
Cannot tell why we or they
March and suffer day by day.
Children of the camp are we,
Serving each in his degree;
Children of the yoke and goad,
Pack and harness, pad and load!

Book II

How Fear Came

The stream is shrunk – the pool is dry,
And we be comrades, thou and I;
With fevered jowl and dusty flank
Each jostling each along the bank;
And by one drouthy fear made still,
Foregoing thought of quest or kill.
Now 'neath his dam the fawn may see,
The lean pack-wolf as cowed as he,
And the tall buck, unflinching, note
The fangs that tore his father's throat.
The pools are shrunk – the streams are dry,
And we be playmates, thou and I,
Till yonder cloud – good hunting! – loose
The rain that breaks our Water Truce.

The Law of the Jungle – which is by far the oldest law in the world – has arranged for almost every kind of accident that may befall the Jungle-People, till now its code is as perfect as time and custom can make it. If you have read the other stories about Mowgli, you will remember that he spent a great part of his life in the Seeonee Wolf Pack, learning the Law from Baloo the Brown Bear; and it was Baloo who told him, when the boy grew impatient at the constant orders, that the Law was like the giant creeper, because it dropped across every one's back and no one could escape. "When thou hast lived as long as I have, Little Brother, thou wilt see how all the jungle obeys at least one Law. And that will be no pleasant sight," said Baloo.

This talk went in at one ear and out at the other, for a boy who spends his life eating and sleeping does not worry about anything till it actually stares him in the face. But one year Baloo's words came true, and Mowgli saw all the jungle working under one Law.

It began when the winter rains failed almost entirely, and Sahi the Porcupine, meeting Mowgli in a bamboo thicket, told him that the wild yams were drying up. Now everybody knows that Sahi is ridiculously fastidious in his choice of food, and will eat nothing but the very best and ripest. So Mowgli laughed and said: "What is that to me?"

"Not much *now*," said Sahi, rattling his quills in a stiff, uncomfortable way, "but later we shall see. Is there any more diving into the deep rock-pool below the Bee Rocks, Little Brother?"

"No. The foolish water is going all away, and I do not wish to break my head," said Mowgli, who was quite sure he knew as much as any five of the Jungle-People put together.

"That is thy loss. A small crack might let in some wisdom." Sahi ducked quickly to prevent Mowgli from pulling his nose-bristles, and Mowgli told Baloo what Sahi had said. Baloo looked very grave, and mumbled half to himself: "If I were alone I would change my hunting-grounds now, before the others began to think. And yet – hunting among strangers ends in fighting – and they might hurt my man-cub. We must wait and see how the *mohwa* blooms."

That spring the *mohwa*-tree, that Baloo was so fond of, never flowered. The greeny, cream-coloured, wax blossoms were heat-killed before they were born, and only a few bad-smelling petals came down when he stood on his hind legs and shook the tree. Then, inch by inch, the untempered heat crept into the heart of the jungle, turning it yellow, brown, and at last black. The green growths in the sides of the ravines burned up to broken wires and curled films of dead stuff; the hidden pools sank down and caked over, keeping the last least footmark on their edges as if it had been cast in iron; the juicy-stemmed creepers fell away from the trees they clung to and died at their feet; the bamboos withered, clanking when the hot winds blew, and the moss peeled off the rocks deep in the jungle, till they were as bare and as hot as the quivering blue boulders in the bed of the stream.

The birds and the Monkey-People went north early in the year, for they

He hunted, too, for deep-boring grubs under the bark of the trees.

knew what was coming, and the deer and the wild pig broke far away into the perished fields of the villages, dying sometimes before the eyes of men too weak to kill them. Chil the Kite stayed and grew fat, for there was a great deal of carrion, and evening after evening he brought the news to the beasts, too weak to force their way to fresh hunting-grounds, that the sun was killing the jungle for three days' flight in every direction.

Mowgli, who had never known what real hunger meant, fell back on stale honey, three years old, scraped out of deserted rock-hives – honey black as a sloe, and dusty with dried sugar. He hunted, too, for deep-boring grubs under the bark of the trees, and robbed the wasps of their new broods. All the game in the jungle was no more than skin and bone, and Bagheera could kill thrice in a night and hardly get a full meal. But the want of water was the worst, for though the Jungle-People drink seldom they must drink deep.

And the heat went on and on, and sucked up all the moisture, till at last the main channel of the Wainganga was the only stream that carried a trickle of water between its dead banks. And when Hathi the Wild Elephant, who lives for a hundred years and more, saw a long, lean blue ridge of rock show dry in the very centre of the stream, he knew that he was looking at the Peace Rock, and then and there he lifted up his trunk and proclaimed the Water Truce, as his father before him had proclaimed it fifty years ago. The deer, wild pig, and buffalo took up the cry hoarsely, and Chil the Kite flew in great circles far and wide, whistling and shrieking the warning.

By the Law of the Jungle it is death to kill at the drinking-places when once the Water Truce has been declared. The reason for this is that drinking comes before eating. Every one in the jungle can scramble along somehow when only game is scarce, but water is water, and when there is but one source of supply, all hunting stops while the Jungle-People go there for their needs. In good seasons, when water was plentiful, those who came down to drink at the Wainganga – or anywhere else, for that matter – did so at the risk of their lives, and that risk made no small part of the fascination of the night's doings. To move down so cunningly that never a leaf stirred; to wade knee-deep in the roaring shallows that drown all noise from behind; to drink, looking backward over one shoulder, every muscle ready for the first desperate bound of keen terror; to roll on the sandy margin, and return, wet-muzzled and well plumped out, to the admiring herd, was a thing that all glossy-horned young bucks took a delight in, precisely because they knew that at any moment Bagheera or Shere Khan might leap upon them and bear them down. But now that life-and-death fun was ended, and the Jungle-People came up, starved and weary, to the shrunken river – tiger, bear, deer, buffalo, and pig together – drank the fouled waters, and hung above them, too exhausted to move off.

The deer and pig had tramped all day in search of something better than dried bark and withered leaves. The buffaloes had found no wallows to be cool in, and no green crops to steal. The snakes had left the jungle and come down to the river in the hope of catching a stray frog. They curled round wet stones, and never offered to strike when the snout of a rooting pig dislodged them. The river-turtles had long ago been killed by Bagheera, cleverest of hunters, and the fish had buried themselves deep in the cracked mud. Only the Peace Rock lay across the shallows like a long snake, and the little tired ripples hissed as they dried on its hot side.

It was here that Mowgli came nightly for the cool and the companion-ship. The most hungry of his enemies would hardly have cared for the boy then. His naked skin made him look more lean and wretched than any of his fellows. His hair was bleached to tow-colour by the sun; his ribs stood out like the ribs of a basket, and the lumps on his knees and elbows, where he was used to track on all fours, gave his shrunken limbs the look of knot-ted grass-stems. But his eye, under his matted forelock, was cool and quiet, for Bagheera, his adviser in this time of trouble, told him to move quietly, hunt slowly, and never, on any account, to lose his temper.

"It is an evil time," said the black panther, one furnace-hot evening, "but it will go if we can live till the end. Is thy stomach full, man-cub?"

"There is stuff in my stomach, but I get no good of it. Think you, Bagheera, the rains have forgotten us and will never come again?"

"Not I. We shall see the *mohwa* in blossom yet, and the little fawns all fat with new grass. Come down to the Peace Rock and hear the news. On my back, Little Brother."

"This is no time to carry weight. I can still stand alone, but – indeed we be no fatted bullocks, we two."

Bagheera looked along his ragged, dusty flank and whispered: "Last night I killed a bullock under the yoke. So low was I brought that I think I should not have dared to spring if he had been loose. *Wou!*"

Mowgli laughed. "Yes, we are great hunters now," said he. "I am very bold – to eat grubs." And the two came down together through the crackling undergrowth to the river bank and the lace-work of shoals that ran out from it in every direction.

"The water cannot live long," said Baloo, joining them. "Look across! Yonder are trails like the roads of Man."

On the level plain of the farther bank the stiff jungle-grass had died standing, and, dying, had mummied. The beaten tracks of the deer and the pig, all leading towards the river, had striped that colourless plain with dusty gullies driven through the ten-foot grass, and, early as it was, each long avenue was full of first-comers hastening to the water. You could hear the does and fawns coughing in the snuff-like dust.

Up-stream, at the bend of the sluggish pool around the Peace Rock, and warden of the Water Truce, stood Hathi the Wild Elephant, with his sons, gaunt and grey in the moonlight, rocking to and fro – always rocking. Below him a little were the vanguard of the deer; below these, again, the pig and the wild buffalo; and on the opposite bank, where the tall trees came down to the water's edge, was the place set apart for the Eaters of Flesh – the tiger, the wolves, the panther, the bear, and the others.

"We be under one Law, indeed," said Bagheera, wading into the water and looking across at the lines of clicking horns and staring eyes where the deer and the pig pushed each other to and fro. "Good hunting, all of you of my blood," he added, lying down at full length, one flank thrust out of the shallows. And then, between his teeth: "But for that which is the Law it would be *very* good hunting."

The quick-spread ears of the deer caught the last sentence, and a frightened whisper ran along the ranks. "The Truce! Remember the Truce!"

"Peace there, peace!" gurgled Hathi the Wild Elephant. "The Truce holds, Bagheera. This is no time to talk of hunting."

"Who should know better than I?" Bagheera answered, rolling his yellow eyes up-stream. "I am an eater of turtle – a fisher of frogs. *Ngaayah!* Would I could get good from chewing branches!"

"*We* wish so, very greatly," bleated a young fawn, who had only been born that spring, and did not at all like it. Wretched as the Jungle-People were, even Hathi could not help chuckling, while Mowgli, lying on his elbows in the warm water, laughed aloud, and beat up the foam with his feet.

"Well spoken, little bud-horn," Bagheera purred. "When the Truce ends that shall be remembered in thy favour." And he looked keenly through the darkness to make sure of recognizing the fawn again.

Gradually the talk spread up and down the drinking-places. You could hear the scuffling, snorting pig asking for more room, the buffaloes grunting among themselves as they lurched out across the sandbars, and the deer telling pitiful stories of their long footsore searches in quest of food. Now and again they asked some question of the Eaters of Flesh across the river, but all the news was bad, and the roaring hot wind of the jungle came and went, between the rocks and the rattling branches, and scattered twigs and dust on the water.

"The Men-Folk too, they die beside their ploughs," said a young sambur. "I passed three between sunset and night. They lay still, and their bullocks with them. We also shall lie still in a little."

"The river has fallen since last night," said Baloo. "O Hathi, hast thou ever seen the like of this drouth?"

"It will pass, it will pass," said Hathi, squirting water along his back and sides.

"We have one here that cannot endure long," said Baloo, and he looked towards the boy he loved.

"I?" said Mowgli indignantly, sitting up in the water. "I have no long fur to cover my bones, but – but if thy hide were pulled off, Baloo – "

Hathi shook all over at the idea, and Baloo said severely:

"Man-cub, that is not seemly to tell a Teacher of the Law. *Never* have I been seen without my hide."

"Nay, I meant no harm, Baloo, but only that thou art, as it were, like the cocoanut in the husk, and I am the same cocoanut all naked. Now that brown husk of thine – " Mowgli was sitting cross-legged, and explaining things with his forefinger in his usual way, when Bagheera put out a paddy paw and pulled him over backwards into the water.

"Worse and worse," said the black panther, as the boy rose spluttering. "First, Baloo is to be skinned and now he is a cocoanut. Be careful that he does not do what the ripe cocoanuts do."

"And what is that?" said Mowgli, off his guard for the minute, though that is one of the oldest catches in the jungle.

"Break thy head," said Bagheera quietly, pulling him under again.

"It is not good to make a jest of thy teacher," said the bear, when Mowgli had been ducked for the third time.

"Not good! What would ye have? That naked thing running to and fro makes a monkey-jest of those who have once been good hunters, and pulls the best of us by the whiskers for sport." This was Shere Khan, the Lame Tiger, limping down to the water. He waited a little to enjoy the sensation he made among the deer on the opposite bank; then he dropped his square, frilled head and began to lap, growling: "The jungle has become a whelping-ground for naked cubs now. Look at me, man-cub!"

Mowgli looked – stared, rather – as insolently as he knew how, and in a minute Shere Khan turned away uneasily. "Man-cub this, and man-cub that," he rumbled, going on with his drink. "The cub is neither man nor cub, or he would have been afraid. Next season I shall have to beg his leave for a drink. *Aurgh!*"

"That may come, too," said Bagheera, looking him steadily between the eyes. "That may come, too.... *Faugh*, Shere Khan! What new shame hast thou brought here?"

The Lame Tiger had dipped his chin and jowl in the water, and dark oily streaks were floating from it downstream.

"Man!" said Shere Khan coolly. "I killed an hour since." He went on purring and growling to himself.

The line of beasts shook and wavered to and fro, and a whisper went up that grew to a cry: "Man! Man! He has killed Man!" Then all looked towards Hathi the Wild Elephant, but he seemed not to hear. Hathi never does anything till the time comes, and that is one of the reasons why he lives so long.

"At such a season as this to kill Man! Was there no other game afoot?" said Bagheera scornfully, drawing himself out of the tainted water, and shaking each paw, cat-fashion, as he did so.

"I killed for choice – not for food." The horrified whisper began again, and Hathi's watchful little white eye cocked itself in Shere Khan's direction. "For choice," Shere Khan drawled. "Now come I to drink and make me clean again. Is there any to forbid?"

Bagheera's back began to curve like a bamboo in a high wind, but Hathi lifted up his trunk and spoke quietly.

"Thy kill was from choice?" he asked, and when Hathi asks a question it is best to answer.

"Even so. It was my right and my night. Thou knowest, O Hathi." Shere Khan spoke almost courteously.

"Yea, I know," Hathi answered. And, after a little silence: "Hast thou drunk thy fill?"

"For tonight, yes."

"Go, then. The river is to drink, and not to defile. None but the Lame Tiger would have boasted of his right at this season when – when we suffer together – Man and Jungle-People alike. Clean or unclean, get to thy lair, Shere Khan!"

The last words rang out like silver trumpets, and Hathi's three sons rolled forward half a pace, though there was no need. Shere Khan slunk away, not daring to growl, for he knew – what every one else knows – that when the last comes to the last Hathi is the master of the jungle.

"What is this right Shere Khan speaks of?" Mowgli whispered in Bagheera's ear. "To kill Man is *always* shameful. The Law says so. And yet Hathi says – "

"Ask him. I do not know, Little Brother. Right or no right, if Hathi had not spoken I would have taught that lame butcher his lesson. To come to the Peace Rock fresh from a kill of Man – and to boast of it – is a jackal's trick. Besides, he tainted the good water."

Mowgli waited for a minute to pick up his courage, because no one cared to address Hathi directly, and then he cried: "What is Shere Khan's right, O Hathi?" Both banks echoed his words, for all the people of the jungle are intensely curious, and they had just seen something that no one, except Baloo, who looked very thoughtful, seemed to understand.

"It is an old tale," said Hathi, "a tale older than the jungle. Keep silence along the banks, and I will tell that tale."

There was a minute or two of pushing and shouldering among the pigs and the buffalo, and then the leaders of the herds grunted, one after another: "We wait." And Hathi strode forward till he was almost knee-deep in the pool by the Peace Rock. Lean and wrinkled and yellow-tusked though he was, he looked what the jungle held him to be – their master.

"Ye know, children," he began, "that of all things ye most fear Man." There was a mutter of agreement.

"This tale touches thee, Little Brother," said Bagheera to Mowgli.

"I? I am of the pack – a hunter of the Free People," Mowgli answered. "What have I to do with Man?"

"And ye do not know why ye fear Man?" Hathi went on. "This is the reason. In the beginning of the jungle, and none know when that was, we of the jungle walked together, having no fear of one another. In those days there was no drouth, and leaves and flowers and fruit grew on the same tree, and we ate nothing at all except leaves and flowers and grass and fruit and bark."

"I am glad I was not born in those days," said Bagheera. "Bark is only good to sharpen claws."

"And the Lord of the Jungle was Tha, the First of the Elephants. He drew the jungle out of deep waters with his trunk, and where he made furrows in the ground with his tusks, there the rivers ran, and where he struck with his foot, there rose ponds of good water, and when he blew through his trunk – thus – the trees fell. That was the manner in which the jungle was made by Tha, and so the tale was told to me."

"It has not lost fat in the telling," Bagheera whispered, and Mowgli laughed behind his hand.

"In those days there was no corn or melons or pepper or sugar-cane, nor were there any little huts such as ye have all seen. And the Jungle-People knew nothing of Man, but lived in the jungle together, making one people. But presently they began to dispute over their food, though there was grazing enough for all. They were lazy. Each wished to eat where he lay, as sometimes we may do now when the spring rains are good. Tha, the First of the Elephants, was busy making new jungles and leading the rivers in their beds. He could not walk everywhere, so he made the First of the Tigers the master and the judge of the jungle, to whom the Jungle-

People should bring their disputes. In those days the First of the Tigers ate fruit and grass with the others. He was as large as I am, and he was very beautiful, in colour all over like the blossom of the yellow creeper. There was never stripe nor bar upon his hide in those good days when the jungle was new. All the Jungle-People came before him without fear, and his word was the Law of all the jungle. We were then, remember ye, one people. Yet, upon a night, there was a dispute between two bucks – a grazing-quarrel such as ye now try out with the head and the fore feet – and it is said that as the two spoke together before the First of the Tigers lying among the flowers, a buck pushed him with his horns, and the First of the Tigers forgot that he was the master and judge of the jungle, and, leaping upon that buck, broke his neck.

"Till that night never one of us had died, and the First of the Tigers, seeing what he had done, and being made foolish by the scent of the blood, ran away into the Marshes of the North, and we of the jungle, left without a judge, fell to fighting among ourselves. Tha heard the noise of it and came back. And some of us said this and some of us said that, but he saw the dead buck among the flowers, and asked who had killed, and we of the jungle would not tell because the smell of the blood made us foolish, even as that same smell makes us foolish today. We ran to and fro in circles, capering and crying out and shaking our heads. So therefore Tha gave an order to the trees that hang low, and to the trailing creepers of the jungle, that they should mark the killer of the buck that he should know him again. And Tha said: 'Who will now be master of the Jungle-People?' Then up leaped the grey ape who lives in the branches, and said: 'I will now be master of the jungle.' At this Tha laughed, and said: 'So be it,' and went away very angry.

"Children, ye know the grey ape. He was then as he is now. At the first he made a wise face for himself, but in a little while he began to scratch and to leap up and down, and when Tha returned he found the grey ape hanging, head down, from a bough, mocking those who stood below; and they mocked him again. And so there was no Law in the jungle – only foolish talk and senseless words.

"Then Tha called us all together and said: 'The first of your masters has brought Death into the jungle, and the second Shame. Now it is time there was a Law, and a Law that ye may not break. Now ye shall know Fear, and when ye have found him ye shall know that he is your master, and the rest shall follow.' Then we of the jungle said: 'What is Fear?' And Tha said: 'Seek till ye find.' So we went up and down the jungle seeking for Fear, and presently the buffaloes – "

"Ugh!" said Mysa, the leader of the buffaloes, from their sandbank.

"Yes, Mysa, it was the buffaloes. They came back with the news that in a cave in the jungle sat Fear, and that he had no hair, and went upon his hind legs. Then we of the jungle followed the herd till we came to that cave, and Fear stood at the mouth of it, and he was, as the buffaloes had said, hairless, and he walked upon his hinder legs. When he saw us he cried out, and his voice filled us with the fear that we have now, and we ran away, tramping upon and tearing each other because we were afraid. That night, it was told to me, we of the jungle did not lie down together as used to be our custom, but each tribe drew off by itself – the pig with the pig, the deer with the deer; horn to horn, hoof to hoof – like keeping to like, and so lay shaking in the jungle.

"Only the First of the Tigers was not with us, for he was still hidden in the marshes of the North, and when word was brought to him of the Thing we had seen in the cave, he said: 'I will go to this Thing and break his neck.' So he ran all the night till he came to the cave, but the trees and the creepers on his path, remembering the order Tha had given, let down their branches and marked him as he ran, drawing their fingers across his back, his flank, his forehead, and his jowl. Wherever they touched him there was a mark and a stripe upon his yellow hide. *And those stripes do his children wear to this day!* When he came to the cave, Fear, the Hairless One, put out his hand and called him the Striped One That Comes by Night,' and the First of the Tigers was afraid of the Hairless One, and ran back to the swamps howling."

Mowgli chuckled quietly here, his chin in the water.

"So loud did he howl that Tha heard him and said: 'What is the sorrow?' And the First of the Tigers, lifting up his muzzle to the new-made sky, which is now so old, said: 'Give me back my power, O Tha. I am made ashamed before all the jungle, and I have run away from a Hairless One, and he has called me a shameful name.' 'And why?' said Tha. 'Because I am smeared with the mud of the marshes,' said the First of the Tigers. 'Swim, then, and roll on the wet grass, and if it be mud it will surely wash away,' said Tha. And the First of the Tigers swam, and rolled, and rolled, till the jungle ran round and round before his eyes, but not one little bar upon his hide was changed, and Tha, watching him, laughed. Then the First of the Tigers said: 'What have I done that this comes to me?' Tha said: Thou hast killed the buck, and thou hast let Death loose in the jungle, and with Death has come Fear, so that the people of the jungle are afraid one of the other as thou art afraid of the Hairless One.' The First of the Tigers said: 'They will never fear me, for I knew them since the beginning.' Tha said: 'Go and see.' And the First of the Tigers ran to and fro, calling aloud to the deer and the pig and the sambur and the porcupine and all the Jungle-Peoples, but they all ran away from him who had been their judge, because they were afraid.

"Then the First of the Tigers came back, his pride was broken in him, and, beating his head upon the ground, he tore up the earth with all his feet and said: 'Remember that I was once the master of the jungle! Do not forget me, O Tha. Let my children remember that I was once without shame or fear!" And Tha said: 'This much will I do, because thou and I together saw the jungle made. For one night of each year it shall be as it was before the buck was killed – for thee and for thy children. In that one night, if ye meet the Hairless One – and his name is Man – ye shall not be afraid of him, but he shall be afraid of you as though ye were judges of the jungle and masters of all things. Show him mercy in that night of his fear, for thou hast known what Fear is.'

"Then the First of the Tigers answered: 'I am content.' But when next he drank he saw the black stripes upon his flank and his side, and he remembered the name that the Hairless One had given him, and he was angry. For a year he lived in the marshes, waiting till Tha should keep his promise. And upon a night when the Jackal of the Moon [the Evening Star] stood clear of the jungle, he felt that his night was upon him, and he went to that cave to meet the Hairless One. Then it happened as Tha promised, for the Hairless One fell down before him and lay along the ground, and the First of the Tigers struck him and broke his back, for he thought that there was but one such a Thing in the jungle, and that he had killed Fear.

173

Then, nosing above the kill, he heard Tha coming down from the woods of the North, and presently the voice of the First of the Elephants, which is the voice that we hear now – ”

The thunder was rolling up and down the dry, scarred hills, but it brought no rain – only heat-lightning that flickered behind the ridges – and Hathi went on:

"That was the voice he heard, and it said: 'Is this thy mercy?' The First of the Tigers licked his lips and said: 'What matter? I have killed Fear.' And Tha said: 'O blind and foolish! Thou hast untied the feet of Death, and he will follow thy trail till thou diest. Thou hast taught Man to kill!"

"The First of the Tigers, standing stiffly to his kill, said: 'He is as the buck was. There is no Fear. Now I will judge the Jungle-Peoples once more.'

"And Tha said: 'Never again shall the Jungle-Peoples come to thee. They shall never cross thy trail, nor sleep near thee, nor follow after thee, nor browse by thy lair. Only Fear shall follow thee, and with a blow that thou canst not see shall bid thee wait his pleasure. He shall make the ground to open under thy feet, and the creeper to twist about thy neck, and the tree-trunks to grow together about thee higher than thou canst leap, and at the last he shall take thy hide to wrap his cubs when they are cold. Thou hast shown him no mercy, and none will he show thee.'

"The First of the Tigers was very bold, for his night was still on him, and he said: 'The promise of Tha is the promise of Tha. He will not take away my night?' And Tha said: 'Thy one night is thine, as I have said, but there is a price to pay. Thou hast taught Man to kill, and he is no slow learner.'

"The First of the Tigers said: 'He is here under my foot, where his back is broken. Let the jungle know that I have killed Fear.'

"Then Tha laughed and said: 'Thou hast killed one of many, but thou thyself shalt tell the jungle – for thy night is ended!"

"So the day came, and from the mouth of the cave went out another Hairless One, and he saw the kill in the path, and the First of the Tigers above it, and he took a pointed stick – ”

"They throw a thing that cuts now," said Sahi, rustling down the bank, for Sahi was considered uncommonly good eating by the Gonds – they

"And throwing it, he struck the First of the Tigers deep in the flank."

called him Ho-Igoo – and he knew something of the wicked little Gondi axe that whirls across a clearing like a dragon-fly.

"It was a pointed stick, such as they set in the foot of a pit-trap," said Hathi. "And throwing it, he struck the First of the Tigers deep in the flank. Thus it happened as Tha said, for the First of the Tigers ran howling up and down the jungle till he tore out the stick, and all the jungle knew that the Hairless One could strike from far off, and they feared more than before. So it came about that the First of the Tigers taught the Hairless One to kill – and ye know what harm that has since done to all our peoples – through the noose, and the pitfall, and the hidden trap, and the flying stick, and the stinging fly that comes out of white smoke [Hathi meant the rifle], and the Red Flower that drives us into the open. Yet for one night in the year the Hairless One fears the tiger, as Tha promised, and never has the tiger given him cause to be less afraid. Where he finds him, there he kills him, remembering how the First of the Tigers was made ashamed. For the rest, Fear walks up and down the jungle by day and by night."

"*Ahi! Aoo!*" said the deer, thinking of what it all meant to them.

"And only when there is one great Fear over all, as there is now, can we of the jungle lay aside our little fears, and meet together in one place as we do now."

"For one night only does Man fear the tiger?" said Mowgli.

"For one night only," said Hathi.

"But I – but we – but all the jungle knows that Shere Khan kills Man twice and thrice in a moon."

"Even so. *Then* he springs from behind and turns his head aside as he strikes, for he is full of fear. If Man looked at him he would run. But on his night he goes openly down to the village. He walks between the houses and thrusts his head into the doorway, and the men fall on their faces, and there he does his kill. One kill in that night."

"Oh!" said Mowgli to himself, rolling over in the water. "*Now* I see why Shere Khan bade me look at him. He got no good of it, for he could not hold his eyes steady, and – and I certainly did not fall down at his feet. But then I am not a man, being of the Free People."

"*Umm!*" said Bagheera deep in his furry throat. "Does the tiger know his night?"

"Never till the Jackal of the Moon stands clear of the evening mist. Sometimes it falls in the dry summer and sometimes in the wet rains – this one night of the tiger. But for the First of the Tigers this would never have been, nor would any of us have known fear."

The deer grunted sorrowfully, and Bagheera's lips curled in a wicked smile. "Do men know this – tale?" said he.

"None know it except the tigers, and we, the elephants – the children of Tha. Now ye by the pools have heard it, and I have spoken."

Hathi dipped his trunk into the water as a sign that he did not wish to talk.

"But – but – but," said Mowgli, turning to Baloo, "why did not the First of the Tigers continue to eat grass and leaves and trees? He did but break the buck's neck. He did not *eat*. What led him to the hot meat?"

"The trees and the creepers marked him, Little Brother, and made him the striped thing that we see. Never again would he eat their fruit, but from that day he revenged himself upon the deer, and the others, the Eaters of Grass," said Baloo.

"Then *thou* knowest the tale. *Heh?* Why have I never heard?"

"Because the jungle is full of such tales. If I made a beginning there would never be an end to them. Let go my ear, Little Brother."

The Law of the Jungle

Just to give you an idea of the immense variety of the Jungle Law, I have translated into verse (Baloo always recited them in a sort of sing-song) a few of the laws that apply to the wolves. There are, of course, hundreds and hundreds more, but these will serve as specimens of the simpler rulings.

Now this is the Law of the Jungle – as old and as true as the sky;
And the wolf that shall keep it may prosper, but the wolf that shall break
it must die.
As the creeper that girdles the tree-trunk the Law runneth forward and
back –
For the strength of the pack is the wolf, and the strength of the wolf is the
pack.

Wash daily from nose-tip to tail-tip; drink deeply, but never too deep;
And remember the night is for hunting, and forget not the day is for
sleep.

The jackal may follow the tiger, but, cub, when thy whiskers are grown,
Remember the wolf is a hunter – go forth and get food of thine own.

Keep peace with the lords of the jungle – the tiger, the panther, and bear;
And trouble not Hathi the Silent, and mock not the boar in his lair.

When pack meets with pack in the jungle, and neither will go from the
trail,
Lie down till the leaders have spoken – it may be fair words shall prevail.

When ye fight with a wolf of the pack, ye must fight him alone and afar,
Lest others take part in the quarrel, and the pack be diminished by war.

The lair of the wolf is his refuge, and where he has made him his home,
Not even the head wolf may enter, not even the council may come.

The lair of the wolf is his refuge, but where he has digged it too plain,
The council shall send him a message, and so he shall change it again.

If ye kill before midnight, be silent, and wake not the woods with your
    bay,
Lest ye frighten the deer from the crop, and your brothers go empty
    away.

Ye may kill for yourselves, and your mates, and your cubs as they need,
    and ye can;
But kill not for pleasure of killing, and *seven times never kill Man!*

If ye plunder his kill from a weaker, devour not all in thy pride;
Pack-right is the right of the meanest; so leave him the head and the hide.

The kill of the pack is the meat of the pack. Ye must eat where it lies;
And no one may carry away of that meat to his lair, *or he dies.*

The kill of the wolf is the meat of the wolf. He may do what he will;
But, till he has given permission, the pack may not eat of that kill.

Cub-right is the right of the yearling. From all of his pack he may claim
Full-gorge when the killer has eaten; and none may refuse him the same.

Lair-right is the right of the mother. From all of her year she may claim
One haunch of each kill for her litter, and none may deny her the same.

Cave-right is the right of the father – to hunt by himself for his own:
He is freed of all calls to the pack; he is judged by the council alone.

Because of his age and his cunning, because of his gripe and his paw,
In all that the Law leaveth open, the word of your head wolf is Law.

Now these are the Laws of the Jungle, and many and mighty are they;
But the head and the hoof of the Law and the haunch and the hump is –
    Obey!

The Miracle of Purun Bhagat

The night we felt the Earth would move
 We stole and plucked him by the hand,
Because we loved him with the love
 That knows but cannot understand.

And when the roaring hillside broke,
 And all our world fell down in rain,
We saved him, we the Little-Folk;
 But lo! he will not come again!

Mourn now, we saved him for the sake
 Of such poor love as wild ones may.
Mourn ye! Our brother does not wake
 And his own kind drive us away!

Dirge of the Langurs.

There was once a man in India who was Prime Minister of one of the semi-independent native states in the north-western part of the country. He was a Brahmin, so high-caste that caste ceased to have any particular meaning for him, and his father had been an important official in the gay-coloured tag-rag and bob-tail of an old-fashioned Hindu Court. But as Purun Dass grew up he realised that the ancient order of things was changing, and that if any one wished to get on he must stand well with the English, and imitate all the English believed to be good. At the same time a native official must keep his own master's favour. This was a difficult game, but the quiet, close-mouthed young Brahmin, helped by a good English education at a Bombay university, played it coolly, and rose, step by step, to be Prime Minister of the kingdom. That is to say, he held more real power than his master, the Maharajah.

When the old king – who was suspicious of the English, their railways and telegraphs – died, Purun Dass stood high with his young successor, who had been tutored by an Englishman. And between them, though he always took care that his master should have the credit, they established schools for little girls, made roads, and started State dispensaries and shows of agricultural implements, and published a yearly blue-book on the "Moral and Material Progress of the State," and the Foreign Office and the Government of India were delighted. Very few native states take up English progress without reservations, for they will not believe, as Purun Dass showed he did, that what is good for the Englishman must be twice as good for the Asiatic. The Prime Minister became the honoured friend of viceroys and governors, and lieutenant-governors, and medical missionaries, and common missionaries, and hard-riding English officers who came to shoot in the State preserves, as well as of whole hosts of tourists who travelled up and down India in the cold weather, showing how things ought to be managed. In his spare time he would endow scholarships for the study of medicine and manufactures on strictly English lines, and write letters to the *Pioneer*, the greatest Indian daily paper, explaining his master's aims and objects.

At last he went to England on a visit, and had to pay enormous sums to the priests when he came back, for even so high-caste a Brahmin as Purun Dass lost caste by crossing the black sea. In London he met and talked with every one worth knowing – men whose names go all over the world – and saw a great deal more than he said. He was given honorary degrees by learned universities, and he made speeches and talked of Hindu social reform to English ladies in evening dress, till all London cried: "This is the most fascinating man we have ever met at dinner since cloths were first laid!"

When he returned to India there was a blaze of glory, for the Viceroy himself made a special visit to confer upon the Maharajah the Grand Cross of the Star of India – all diamonds and ribbons and enamel. And at the same ceremony, while the cannon boomed, Purun Dass was made a Knight

Commander of the Order of the Indian Empire, so that his name stood Sir Purun Dass, K.C.I.E.

That evening at dinner in the big Viceregal tent he stood up with the badge and the collar of the order on his breast, and replying to the toast of his master's health, made a speech that few Englishmen could have surpassed.

Next month, when the city had returned to its sunbaked quiet, he did a thing no Englishman would have dreamed of doing, for, so far as the world's affairs went, he died. The jewelled order of his knighthood returned to the Indian Government, and a new Prime Minister was appointed to the charge of affairs, and a great game of General Post began in all the subordinate appointments. The priests knew what had happened and the people guessed, but India is the one place in the world where a man can do as he pleases and nobody asks why. And the fact that Dewan Sir Purun Dass, K.C.I.E., had resigned position, palace, and power, and taken up the begging bowl and ochre-coloured dress of a Sannyasi or holy man, was considered nothing extraordinary. He had been, as the Old Law recommends, twenty years a youth, twenty years a fighter – though he had never carried a weapon in his life – and twenty years head of a household. He had used his wealth and his power for what he knew both to be worth; he had taken honour when it came his way; he had seen men and cities far and near, and men and cities had stood up and honoured him. Now he would let these things go, as a man drops the cloak he needs no longer.

Behind him, as he walked through the city gates, an antelope skin and brass-handled crutch under his arm, and a begging-bowl of polished brown *coco-de-mer* in his hand, barefoot, alone, with eyes cast on the ground – behind him they were firing salutes from the bastions in honour of his happy successor. Purun Dass nodded. All that life was ended, and he bore it no more ill-will or good-will than a man bears to a colourless dream of the night. He was a Sannyasi – a houseless, wandering mendicant, depending on his neighbours for his daily bread, and so long as there is a morsel to divide in India neither priest nor beggar starves. He had never in his life tasted meat, and very seldom eaten even fish. A five-pound-note would have covered his personal expenses for food through any one of the many years in which he had been absolute master of millions of money. Even when he was being lionised in London he had held before him his dream of peace and quiet – the long, white, dusty Indian road, printed all over with bare feet, the incessant, slow-moving traffic, and the sharp-smelling wood-smoke curling up under the fig-trees in the twilight, where the wayfarers sat at their evening meal.

When the time came to make that dream true the Prime Minister took the proper steps, and in three days you might more easily have found a bubble in the trough of the long Atlantic seas than Purun Dass among the roving, gathering, separating millions of India.

At night his antelope skin was spread where the darkness overtook him – sometimes in a Sannyasi monastery by the roadside; sometimes by a mud pillar shrine of Kala Pir, where the Yogis, who are another misty division of holy men, would receive him as they do those who know what castes and divisions are worth; sometimes on the outskirts of a little Hindu village, where the children would steal up with the food their parents had prepared; and sometimes on the pitch of the bare grazing-grounds where the flame of his stick fire waked the drowsy camels. It was all one to Purun Dass – or Purun Bhagat, as he called himself now. Earth, people, and food were all one. But, unconsciously, his feet drew him away northwards and eastwards; from the south to Rohtak; from Rohtak to Kurnool; from Kurnool to ruined Samanah, and then up-stream along the dried bed of the Gugger River that fills only when the rain falls in the hills, till, one day, he saw the far line of the great Himalayas.

Then Purun Bhagat smiled, for he remembered that his mother was of Rajput Brahmin birth, from Kulu way – a hill-woman, always homesick for the snows – and that the least touch of hill blood draws a man in the end back to where he belongs.

"Yonder," said Purun Bhagat, breasting the lower slopes of the Siwaliks, where the cacti stand up like seven-branched candlesticks, "yonder I shall sit down and get knowledge." And the cool wind of the Himalayas whistled about his ears as he trod the road that led to Simla.

The last time he had come that way it had been in state, with a clattering cavalry escort, to visit the gentlest and most affable of viceroys, and the two had talked for an hour together about mutual friends in London, and what the Indian common folk really thought of things. This time Purun

Bhagat paid no calls, but leaned on the rail of the mall, watching the glorious view of the plains spread out forty miles below, till a native Mohammedan policeman told him he was obstructing traffic. And Purun Bhagat salaamed reverently to the Law, because he knew the value of it, and was seeking for a Law of his own. Then he moved on, and slept that night in an empty hut at Chota Simla, which looks like the very last end of the earth, but it was only the beginning of his journey. He followed the Himalaya-Tibet road, the little ten-foot track that is blasted out of solid rock, or strutted out on timbers over gulfs a thousand feet deep; that dips into warm, wet, shut-in valleys, and climbs across bare, grassy hill-shoulders where the sun strikes like a burning-glass; or turns through dripping, dark forests where the tree-ferns dress the trunks from head to heel, and the pheasant calls to his mate. And he met Tibetan herdsmen with their dogs and flocks of sheep, each sheep with a little bag of borax on his back, and wandering woodcutters, and cloaked and blanketed lamas from Tibet, coming into India on pilgrimage, and envoys of little solitary hill-states, posting furiously on ring-streaked and piebald ponies, or the cavalcade of a rajah paying a visit. Or else for a long, clear day he would see nothing more than a black bear grunting and rooting down below in the valley. When he first started, the roar of the world he had left still rang in his ears, as the roar of a tunnel rings a little after the train has passed through. But when he had put the Mutteeanee Pass behind him that was all done, and Purun Bhagat was alone with himself, walking, wondering, and thinking, his eyes on the ground, and his thoughts with the clouds.

One evening he crossed the highest pass he had met till then – it had been a two days' climb – and came out on a line of snow-peaks that belted all the horizon – mountains from fifteen to twenty thousand feet high, looking almost near enough to hit with a stone, though they were fifty or sixty miles away. The pass was crowned with dense, dark forest – deodar, walnut, wild cherry, wild olive, and wild pear, but mostly deodar, which is the Himalayan cedar; and under the shadow of the deodars stood a deserted shrine to Kali – who is Durga, who is Sitala, who is sometimes worshipped against the smallpox.

Purun Dass swept the stone floor clean, smiled at the grinning statue, made himself a little mud fireplace at the back of the shrine, spread his antelope skin on a bed of fresh pine needles, tucked his *bairagi* – his brass-handled crutch – under his armpit, and sat down to rest.

Immediately below him the hillside fell away, clean and cleared for fifteen hundred feet, to where a little village of stone-walled houses, with roofs of beaten earth, clung to the steep tilt. All round it tiny terraced fields lay out like aprons of patchwork on the knees of the mountain, and cows no bigger than beetles grazed between the smooth stone circles of the threshing-floors. Looking across the valley the eye was deceived by the size of things, and could not at first realise that what seemed to be low scrub, on the opposite mountain-flank, was in truth a forest of hundred-foot pines. Purun Bhagat saw an eagle swoop across the enormous hollow, but the great bird dwindled to a dot ere it was half-way over. A few bands of scattered clouds strung up and down the valley, catching on a shoulder of the hills, or rising up and dying out when they were level with the head of the pass. And "Here shall I find peace," said Purun Bhagat.

Now, a hill-man makes nothing of a few hundred feet up or down, and as soon as the villagers saw the smoke in the deserted shrine, the village priest climbed up the terraced hillside to welcome the stranger.

When he met Purun Bhagat's eyes – the eyes of a man used to control thousands – he bowed to the earth, took the begging-bowl without a word, and returned to the village, saying: "We have at last a holy man. Never have I seen such a man. He is of the plains – but pale coloured – a Brahmin of the Brahmins." Then all the housewives of the village said: "Think you he will stay with us?" And each did her best to cook the most savoury meal for the Bhagat. Hill-food is very simple, but with buckwheat and Indian corn, and rice and red pepper, and little fish out of the stream in the little valley, and honey from the flue-like hives built in the stone walls, and dried apricots, and turmeric, and wild ginger, and bannocks of flour, a devout woman can make good things. And it was a full bowl that the priest carried to the Bhagat. Was he going to stay? asked the priest. Would he need a *chela* – a disciple – to beg for him? Had he a blanket against the cold weather? Was the food good?

Purun Bhagat ate, and thanked the giver. It was in his mind to stay. That was sufficient, said the priest. Let the begging-bowl be placed outside the shrine, in the hollow made by those two twisted roots, and daily should the Bhagat be fed, for the village felt honoured that such a man – he looked timidly into the Bhagat's face – should tarry among them.

That day saw the end of Purun Bhagat's wanderings. He had come to the place appointed for him – the silence and the space. After this, time stopped, and he, sitting at the mouth of the shrine, could not tell whether he were alive or dead: a man with control of his limbs, or a part of the hills, and the clouds, and the shifting rain, and sunlight. He would repeat a Name softly to himself a hundred hundred times, till, at each repetition, he seemed to move more and more out of his body, sweeping up to the doors of some tremendous discovery. But, just as the door was opening, his body would drag him back, and, with grief, he felt he was locked up again in the flesh and bones of Purun Bhagat.

Every morning the filled begging-bowl was laid silently in the crotch of the roots outside the shrine. Sometimes the priest brought it; sometimes a Ladakhi trader, lodging in the village, and anxious to get merit, trudged up the path. But, more often, it was the woman who had cooked the meal overnight, and she would murmur, hardly above her breath: "Speak for me before the gods, Bhagat. Speak for such a one, the wife of so-and-so!" Now and then some bold child would be allowed the honour, and Purun Bhagat would hear him drop the bowl and run as fast as his little legs could carry him, but the Bhagat never came down to the village. It was laid out like a map at his feet. He could see the evening gatherings held on the circle of the threshing-floors, because that was the only level ground; could see the wonderful unnamed green of the young rice, the indigo blues of the Indian corn; the dock-like patches of buckwheat, and, in its season, the red bloom of the amaranth, whose tiny seeds, being neither grain nor pulse, made a food that can be lawfully eaten by Hindus in time of fasts.

When the year turned, the roofs of the huts were all little squares of purest gold, for it was on the roofs that they laid out their cobs of the corn to dry. Hiving and harvest, rice-sowing and husking, passed before his eyes, all embroidered down there on the many-sided fields, and he thought of them all, and wondered what they all led to at the long last.

Even in populated India a man cannot a day sit still before the wild things run over him as though he were a rock. And in that wilderness very soon the wild things, who knew Kali's shrine well, came back to look at

the intruder. The langurs, the big, grey-whiskered monkeys of the Himalayas, were, naturally, the first, for they are alive with curiosity. And when
they had upset the begging-bowl, and rolled it round the floor, and tried
their teeth on the brass-handled crutch, and made faces at the antelope skin,
they decided that the human being who sat so still was harmless. At evening,
they would leap down from the pines, and beg with their hands for things
to eat, and then swing off in graceful curves. They liked the warmth of the
fire, too, and huddled round it till Purun Bhagat had to push them aside to
throw on more fuel, and in the morning, as often as not, he would find a
furry ape sharing his blanket. All day long, one or other of the tribe would
sit by his side, staring out at the snows, crooning and looking unspeakably
wise and sorrowful.

After the monkeys came the barasingha, that big deer which is like our
red deer, but stronger. He wished to rub off the velvet of his horns against
the cold stones of Kali's statue, and stamped his feet when he saw the man
at the shrine. But Purun Bhagat never moved, and, little by little, the royal
stag edged up and nuzzled his shoulder. Purun Bhagat slid one cool hand
along the hot antlers, and the touch soothed the fretted beast, who bowed
his head, and Purun Bhagat very softly rubbed and ravelled off the velvet.
Afterwards, the barasingha brought his doe and fawn – gentle things that
mumbled on the holy man's blanket – or would come alone at night, his
eyes green in the fire-flicker, to take his share of fresh walnuts. At last, the
musk-deer, the shyest and almost the smallest of the deerlets, came, too, her
big, rabbity ears erect; even brindled, silent *mushick-nabha* must needs find
out what the light in the shrine meant, and drop her moose-like nose into
Purun Bhagat's lap, coming and going with the shadows of the fire. Purun
Bhagat called them all "my brothers," and his low call of *"Bhai! Bhai!"*
would draw them from the forest at noon if they were within earshot. The
Himalayan black bear, moody and suspicious – Sona, who has the V-shaped
white mark under his chin – passed that way more than once. And since
the Bhagat showed no fear, Sona showed no anger, but watched him, and
came closer, and begged a share of the caresses, and a dole of bread or wild
berries. Often, in the still dawns, when the Bhagat would climb to the very
crest of the notched pass to watch the red day walking along the peaks of
the snows, he would find Sona shuffling and grunting at his heels, thrusting

a curious fore paw under fallen trunks, and bringing it away with a *whoof* of impatience. Or his early steps would wake Sona where he lay curled up, and the great brute, rising erect, would think to fight, till he heard the Bhagat's voice and knew his best friend.

Nearly all hermits and holy men who live apart from the big cities have the reputation of being able to work miracles with the wild things, but all the miracle lies in keeping still, in never making a hasty movement, and, for a long time, at least, in never looking directly at a visitor. The villagers saw the outlines of the barasingha stalking like a shadow through the dark forest behind the shrine; saw the minaul, the Himalayan pheasant, blazing in her best colours before Kali's statue, and the langurs on their haunches, inside, playing with the walnut shells. Some of the children, too, had heard Sona singing to himself, bear-fashion, behind the fallen rocks, and the Bhagat's reputation as miracle-worker stood firm.

Yet nothing was farther from his mind than miracles. He believed that all things were one big Miracle, and when a man knows that much he knows something to go upon. He knew for a certainty that there was nothing great and nothing little in this world, and day and night he strove to think out his way into the heart of things, back to the place whence his soul had come.

So thinking, his untrimmed hair fell down about his shoulders, the stone slab at the side of the antelope skin was dented into a little hole by the foot of his brass-handled crutch, and the place between the tree-trunks, where the begging-bowl rested day after day, sank and wore into a hollow almost as smooth as the brown shell itself, and each beast knew his exact place at the fire. The fields changed their colours with the seasons; the threshing-floors filled and emptied, and filled again and again; and again and again, when winter came, the langurs frisked among the branches feathered with light snow, till the mother monkeys brought their sad-eyed little babies up from the warmer valleys with the spring. There were few changes in the village. The priest was older, and many of the little children who used to come with the begging-dish sent their own children now. And when you asked of the villagers how long their holy man had lived in Kali's shrine at the head of the pass, they answered: "Always."

Then came such summer rains as had not been known in the hills for many seasons. Through three good months the valley was wrapped in cloud and soaking mist – steady, unrelenting downfall, breaking off into thunder-shower after thunder-shower. Kali's shrine stood above the clouds, for the most part, and there was a whole month in which the Bhagat never caught a glimpse of his village. It was packed away under a white floor of cloud that swayed and shifted and rolled on itself and bulged upwards, but never broke from its piers – the streaming flanks of the valley.

All that time he heard nothing but the sound of a million little waters, overhead from the trees, and underfoot along the ground, soaking through the pine-needles, dripping from the tongues of draggled fern, and spouting in newly torn muddy channels down the slopes. Then the sun came out, and drew forth the good incense of the deodars and the rhododendrons, and that far-off, clean smell the Hill-People call "the smell of the snows." The hot sunshine lasted for a week, and then the rains gathered together for their last downpour, and the water fell in sheets that flayed off the skin of the ground and leaped back in mud. Purun Bhagat heaped his fire high that night, for he was sure his brothers would need warmth, but never a beast came to the shrine, though he called and called till he dropped asleep, wondering what had happened in the woods.

It was in the black heart of the night, the rain drumming like a thousand drums, that he was roused by a plucking at his blanket, and, stretching out, felt the little hand of a langur. "It is better here than in the trees," he said sleepily, loosening a fold of blanket. "Take it and be warm." The monkey caught his hand and pulled hard. "It is food, then?" said Purun Bhagat "Wait a while, and I will prepare some." As he kneeled to throw fuel on the fire the langur ran to the door of the shrine, crooned, and ran, back again, plucking at the man's knee.

"What is it? What is thy trouble, Brother?" said Purun Bhagat, for the langur's eyes were full of things that he could not tell. "Unless one of thy caste be in a trap – and none set traps here – I will not go into that weather. Look, Brother, even the barasingha comes for shelter."

The deer's antlers clashed as he strode into the shrine, clashed against the grinning statue of Kali. He lowered them in Purun Bhagat's direction and stamped uneasily, hissing through his half-shut nostrils.

"*Hai! Hai! Hai!*" said the Bhagat, snapping his fingers. "Is *this* payment for a night's lodging?" But the deer pushed him towards the door, and as he did so Purun Bhagat heard the sound of something opening with a sigh, and saw two slabs of the floor draw away from each other, while the sticky earth below smacked its lips.

"Now I see," said Purun Bhagat. "No blame to my brothers that they did not sit by the fire tonight. The mountain is falling. And yet – why should I go?" His eye fell on the empty begging-bowl, and his face changed. "They have given me good food daily since – since I came, and, if I am not swift, tomorrow there will not be one mouth in the valley. Indeed, I must go and warn them below. Back there, Brother! Let me get to the fire."

The barasingha backed unwillingly as Purun Bhagat drove a torch deep into the flame, twirling it till it was well lit. "Ah! Ye came to warn me," he said, rising. "Better than that we shall do, better than that. Out, now, and lend me thy neck, Brother, for I have but two feet."

He clutched the bristling withers of the barasingha with his right hand, held the torch away with his left, and stepped out of the shrine into the desperate night. There was no breath of wind, but the rain nearly drowned the torch as the great deer hurried down the slope, sliding on his haunches. As soon as they were clear of the forest more of the Bhagat's brothers joined them. He heard, though he could not see, the langurs pressing about him, and behind them the *uhh! uhh!* of Sona. The rain matted his long white hair into ropes; the water splashed beneath his bare feet, and his yellow robe clung to his frail old body, but he stepped down steadily, leaning against the barasingha. He was no longer a holy man, but Sir Purun Dass, K.C.I.E., Prime Minister of no small State, a man accustomed to command, going out to save life. Down the steep plashy path they poured all together, the Bhagat and his brothers, down and down till the deer clicked and stumbled on the wall of a threshing-floor, and snorted because he smelled Man. Now they were at the head of the one crooked village street, and the Bhagat beat with his crutch at the barred windows of the blacksmith's house as his torch blazed up in the shelter of the eaves. "Up and out!" cried Purun Bhagat, and he did not know his own voice, for it was years since he had spoken aloud to a man. "The hill falls! The hill is falling! Up and out, oh, you within!"

"It is our Bhagat," said the blacksmith's wife. "He stands among his beasts. Gather the little ones and give the call."

It ran from house to house, while the beasts, cramped in the narrow way, surged and huddled round the Bhagat, and Sona puffed impatiently.

The people hurried into the street – they were no more than seventy souls all told – and in the glare of their torches they saw their Bhagat holding back the terrified barasingha, while the monkeys plucked piteously at his skirts, and Sona sat on his haunches and roared.

"Across the valley and up the next hill!" shouted Purun Bhagat. "Leave none behind! We follow!"

Then the people ran as only Hill-Folk can run, for they knew that in a landslip you must climb for the highest ground across the valley. They fled, splashing through the little river at the bottom, and panted up the terraced fields on the far side, while the Bhagat and his brethren followed. Up and up the opposite mountain they climbed, calling to each other by name – the roll-call of the village – and at their heels toiled the big barasingha, weighted by the failing strength of Purun Bhagat. At last the deer stopped in the shadow of a deep pine-wood, five hundred feet up the hillside. His instinct, that had warned him of the coming slide, told him he would be safe here.

Purun Bhagat dropped fainting by his side, for the chill of the rain and that fierce climb were killing him. But first he called to the scattered torches ahead: "Stay and count your numbers." Then, whispering to the deer as he saw the lights gather in a cluster: "Stay with me, Brother. Stay – till – I – go!"

There was a sigh in the air that grew to a mutter, and a mutter that grew to a roar, and a roar that passed all sense of hearing, and the hillside on which the villagers stood was hit in the darkness, and rocked to the blow. Then a note as steady, deep, and true as the deep C of the organ drowned everything for perhaps five minutes, while the very roots of the pines quivered to it. It died away, and the sound of the rain falling on miles of hard ground and grass changed to the muffled drums of water on soft earth. That told its own tale.

Never a villager – not even the priest – was bold enough to speak to the Bhagat who had saved their lives. They crouched under the pines and waited till the day. When it came they looked across the valley, and saw that what had been forest, and terraced field, and track-threaded grazing-ground was one raw, red, fan-shaped smear, with a few trees flung head-down on the scarp. That red ran high up the hill of their refuge, damming back the little river, which had begun to spread into a brick-coloured lake. Of the village, of the road to the shrine, of the shrine itself, and the forest behind, there was no trace. For one mile in width and two thousand feet in sheer depth the mountain-side had come away bodily, planed clean from head to heel.

And the villagers, one by one, crept through the wood to pray before their Bhagat. They saw the barasingha standing over him, who fled when they came near, and they heard the langurs wailing in the branches, and Sona moaning up the hill. But their Bhagat was dead, sitting cross-legged, his back against a tree, his crutch under his armpit, and his face turned to the north-east.

The priest said: "Behold a miracle after a miracle, for in this very attitude must all Sannyasis be buried! Therefore, where he now is we will build the temple to our holy man."

They built the temple before a year was ended, a little stone and earth shrine, and they called the hill the Bhagat's Hill, and they worship there with lights and flowers and offerings to this day. But they do not know that the saint of their worship is the late Sir Purun Dass, K.C.I.E., D.C.L., Ph.D., etc., once Prime Minister of the progressive and enlightened State of Mohiniwala, and honorary or corresponding member of more learned and scientific societies than will ever do any good in this world or the next.

A Song of Kabir

Oh, light was the world that he weighed in his hands!
Oh, heavy the tale of his fiefs and his lands!
He has gone from the *guddee* and put on the shroud,
And departed in guise of *bairagi* avowed!

Now the white road to Delhi is mat for his feet,
The *sal* and the *kikar* must guard him from heat;
His home is the camp, and the waste, and the crowd –
He is seeking the Way, a *bairagi* avowed!

He has looked upon Man and his eyeballs are clear
(There was One; there is One, and but One, saith Kabir);
The Red Mist of Doing is thinned to a cloud –
He has taken the Path, a *bairagi* avowed!

To learn and discern of his brother the clod,
Of his brother the brute, and his brother the God.
He has gone from the council and put on the shroud
("Can ye hear?" saith Kabir), a *bairagi* avowed!

Letting in the Jungle

Veil them, cover them, wall them round,
    Blossom and creeper and weed,
Let us forget the sight and the sound,
    And the smell and the touch of the breed!

Fat black ash by the altar-stone
    Here is the white-foot rain!
And the does bring forth in the fields unsown,
    And none may affright them again;
And the blind walls crumble, unknown, o'erthrown,
    And none may inhabit again!

You will remember, if you have read the tales in the first *Jungle Book*, that after Mowgli had pinned Shere Kahn's hide to the Council Rock, he told as many as were left of the Seeonee Pack that henceforward he would hunt in the jungle alone; and the four children of Mother and Father Wolf said that they would hunt with him. But it is not easy to change all one's life at once – particularly in the jungle. The first thing Mowgli did, when the disorderly pack had slunk off, was to go to the home-cave, and sleep for a day and a night. Then he told Mother Wolf and Father Wolf as much as they could understand of his adventures among men. And when he made the morning sun flicker up and down the blade of his skinning-knife – the same he had skinned Shere Khan with – they said he had learnt something. Then Akela and Grey Brother had to explain their share of the great buffalo-drive in the ravine, and Baloo toiled up the hill to hear all about it, and Bagheera scratched himself all over with pure delight at the way in which Mowgli had managed his war.

It was long after sunrise, but no one dreamed of going to sleep, and from time to time, Mother Wolf would throw up her head, and sniff a deep snuff of satisfaction as the wind brought her the smell of the tiger-skin on the Council Rock.

"But for Akela and Grey Brother here," Mowgli said, at the end, "I could have done nothing. Oh, Mother, Mother! If thou hadst seen the blue herd-bulls pour down the ravine, or hurry through the gates when the man pack flung stones at me!"

"I am glad I did not see that last," said Mother Wolf, stiffly. "It is not *my* custom to suffer my cubs to be driven to and fro like jackals! *I* would have taken a price from the man pack, but I would have spared the woman who gave thee the milk. Yes, I would have spared her alone."

"Peace, peace, Raksha!" said Father Wolf, lazily. "Our frog has come back again – so wise that his own father must lick his feet. And what is a cut, more or less, on the head? Leave Man alone." Baloo and Bagheera both echoed: "Leave Man alone."

Mowgli, his head on Mother Wolf's side, smiled contentedly, and said that, for his own part, he never wished to see, or hear, or smell Man again.

"But what," said Akela, cocking one ear, "but what if men do not leave thee alone, Little Brother?"

"We be *five*," said Grey Brother, looking round at the company, and snapping his jaws on the last word.

"We also might attend to that hunting," said Bagheera, with a little *switch-switch* of his tail, looking at Baloo. "But why think of Man now, Akela?"

"For this reason," the Lone Wolf answered. "When that yellow thief's hide was hung up on the rock, I went back along our trail to the village, stepping in my tracks, turning aside, and lying down, to make a mixed trail in case any should follow us. But when I had fouled the trail so that I myself hardly knew it again, Mang the Bat came hawking between the trees, and hung up above me. Said Mang: 'The village of the man pack, where they cast out the man-cub, hums like a hornet's nest.'"

"It was a big stone that I threw," chuckled Mowgli, who had often amused himself by throwing ripe pawpaws into a hornet's nest, and racing to the nearest pool before the hornets caught him.

"I asked of Mang what he had seen. He said that the Red Flower blossomed at the gate of the village, and men sat about it carrying guns. Now *I* know, for I have good cause" – Akela looked here at the old dry scars on his flank and side – "that men do not carry guns for pleasure. Presently, Little Brother, a man with a gun follows our trail – if, indeed, he be not already on it."

"But why should he? Men have cast me out. What more do they need?" said Mowgli angrily.

"Thou art a man, Little Brother," Akela returned. "It is not for us, the Free Hunters, to tell thee what thy brethren do, or why."

He had just time to snatch up his paw as the skinning-knife cut deep into the ground below. Mowgli struck quicker than an average human eye could follow, but Akela was a wolf, and even a dog, who is very far removed from the wild wolf, his ancestor, can be waked out of deep sleep by a cartwheel touching his flank, and can spring away unharmed before that wheel comes on.

"Another time," Mowgli said, quietly, returning the knife to its sheath, "speak of the man pack and of Mowgli in *two* breaths – not one."

"*Phff!* That is a sharp tooth," said Akela, snuffing at the blade's cut in the earth, "but living with the man pack has spoiled thine eye, Little Brother. I could have killed buck while thou wast striking."

Bagheera sprang to his feet, thrust up his head as far as he could, sniffed, and stiffened through every curve in his body. Grey Brother followed his example quickly, keeping a little to his left to get the wind that was blowing from the right, while Akela bounded fifty yards upwind, and, half-crouching, stiffened too. Mowgli looked on enviously. He could smell things as very few human beings could, but he had never reached the hair-trigger-like sensitiveness of a jungle nose, and his three months in the smoky village had put him back sadly. However, he dampened his finger, rubbed it on his nose, and stood erect to catch the upper scent, which, though the faintest, is the truest.

"Man!" Akela growled, dropping on his haunches.

"Buldeo!" said Mowgli, sitting down. "He follows our trail, and yonder is the sunlight on his gun. Look!"

It was no more than a splash of sunlight, for a fraction of a second, on the brass clamps of the old Tower musket, but nothing in the jungle winks with just that flash, except when the clouds race over the sky. Then a piece of mica, or a little pool, or even a highly polished leaf will flash like a heliograph. But that day was cloudless and still.

"I knew men would follow," said Akela, triumphantly. "Not for nothing have I led the pack!"

Mowgli's four wolves said nothing, but ran down hill on their bellies, melting into the thorn and under-brush.

"Whither go ye, and without word?" Mowgli called.

"*Hsh!* We roll his skull here before midday!" Grey Brother answered.

"Back! Back and wait! Man does not eat Man!" Mowgli shrieked.

"Who was a wolf but now? Who drove the knife at me for thinking he might be a man?" said Akela, as the Four turned back sullenly and dropped to heel.

"Am I to give reason for all I choose to do?" said Mowgli, furiously.

"That is Man! There speaks Man!" Bagheera muttered under his whiskers. "Even so did men talk round the king's cages at Oodeypore. We of the jungle know that Man is wisest of all. If we trusted our ears we should know that of all things he is most foolish." Raising his voice, he added: "The man-cub is right in this. Men hunt in packs. To kill one, unless we know what the others will do, is bad hunting. Come, let us see what this man means towards us."

"We will not come," Grey Brother growled. "Hunt alone, Little Brother. *We* know our own minds! The skull would have been ready to bring by now."

Mowgli had been looking from one to the other of his friends, his chest heaving and his eyes full of tears. He strode forward, and, dropping on one knee, said: "Do I not know my mind? Look at me!"

They looked uneasily, and when their eyes wandered, he called them back again and again, till their hair stood up all over their bodies, and they trembled in every limb, while Mowgli stared and stared.

"Now," said he, "of us five, which is leader?"

"Thou art leader, Little Brother," said Grey Brother, and he licked Mowgli's foot.

"Follow, then," said Mowgli, and the Four followed at his heels with their tails between their legs.

"This comes of living with the man pack," said Bagheera, slipping down after them. "There is more in the jungle now than Jungle Law, Baloo."

The old bear said nothing, but he thought many things.

Mowgli cut across noiselessly through the jungle, at right angles to Buldeo's path, till, parting the undergrowth, he saw the old man, his musket on his shoulder, running up the two-day-old trail at a dog-trot.

You will remember that Mowgli had left the village with the heavy weight of Shere Khan's raw hide on his shoulders, while Akela and Grey Brother trotted behind, so that the trail was very clearly marked. Presently Buldeo came to where Akela, as you know, had gone back and mixed it all up. Then he sat down, and coughed and grunted, and made little casts round and about into the jungle to pick it up again, and all the time he could have thrown a stone over those who were watching him. No one can be so silent as a wolf when he does not care to be heard, and Mowgli, though the wolves thought he moved very clumsily, could come and go like a shadow. They ringed the old man as a school of porpoises ring a steamer at full speed, and as they ringed him they talked unconcernedly, for their speech began below the lowest end of the scale that untaught human beings can hear. (The other end is bounded by the high squeak of Mang the Bat, which very many people cannot catch at all. From that note all the bird and bat and insect talk takes on.)

"This is better than any kill," said Grey Brother, as Buldeo stooped and peered and puffed. "He looks like a lost pig in the jungles by the river. What does he say?" Buldeo was muttering savagely.

Mowgli translated. "He says that packs of wolves must have danced round me. He says that he never saw such a trail in his life. He says he is tired."

"He will be rested before he picks it up again," said Bagheera coolly, as he slipped round a tree-trunk, in the game of blind-man's-buff that they were playing. *Now*, what does the lean thing do?"

"Eat or blow smoke out of his mouth. Men always play with their mouths," said Mowgli. And the silent trailers saw the old man fill and light,

*Mowgli cut noiselessly through the jungle at right-angles
to Buldeo's path.*

and puff at a water-pipe, and they took good note of the smell of the tobacco, so as to be sure of Buldeo in the darkest night, if necessary.

Then a little knot of charcoal-burners came down the path, and naturally halted to speak to Buldeo, whose fame as a hunter reached for at least twenty miles round. They all sat down and smoked, and Bagheera and the others came up and watched while Buldeo began to tell the story of Mowgli the Devil-Child from one end to another, with additions and inventions. How he himself had really killed Shere Khan; and how Mowgli had turned himself into a wolf, and fought with him all the afternoon, and changed into a boy again and bewitched Buldeo's rifle, so that the bullet turned the corner, when he pointed it at Mowgli, and killed one of Buldeo's own buffaloes; and how the village, knowing him to be the bravest hunter in Seeonee, had sent him out to kill this devil-child. But meantime the village had got hold of Messua and her husband, who were undoubtedly the father and mother of this devil-child, and had barricaded them in their own hut, and presently would torture them to make them confess they were witch and wizard, and then they would be burned to death.

"When?" said the charcoal-burners, because they would very much like to be present at the ceremony.

Buldeo said that nothing would be done till he returned, because the village wished him to kill the jungle boy first. After that they would dispose of Messua and her husband, and divide their land and buffaloes among the village. Messua's husband had some remarkably fine buffaloes, too. It was an excellent thing to destroy wizards, Buldeo thought, and people who entertained wolf-children out of the jungle were clearly the worst kind of witches.

But, said the charcoal-burners, what would happen if the English heard of it? The English, they had been told, were a perfectly mad people, who would not let honest farmers kill witches in peace.

Why, said Buldeo, the head-man of the village would report that Messua and her husband had died of snakebite. That was all arranged, and the only thing now was to kill the wolf-child. They did not happen to have seen anything of such a creature?

The charcoal-burners looked round cautiously, and thanked their stars they had not, but they had no doubt that so brave a man as Buldeo would find him if any one could. The sun was getting rather low, and they had an idea that they would push on to Buldeo's village and see the wicked witch. Buldeo said that, though it was his duty to kill the devil-child he could not think of letting a party of unarmed men go through the jungle, which might reveal the wolf-demon at any minute, without his escort. He, therefore, would accompany them, and if the sorcerer's child appeared – well, he would show them how the best hunter in Seeonee dealt with such things. The Brahmin, he said, had given him a charm against the creature that made everything perfectly safe.

"What says he? What says he? What says he?" the wolves repeated every few minutes. And Mowgli translated until he came to the witch part of the story, which was a little beyond him, and then he said that the man and woman who had been so kind to him were trapped.

"Do men trap men?" said Grey Brother.

"So he says. I cannot understand the talk. They are all mad together. What have Messua and her man to do with me that they should be put in a trap, and what is all this talk about the Red Flower? I must look to this. Whatever they would do to Messua they will not do till Buldeo returns. And so – " Mowgli thought hard with his fingers playing round the haft of his skinning-knife, while Buldeo and the charcoal-burners went off very valiantly in single file.

"I go hot-foot back to the man pack," Mowgli said at last.

"And those?" said Grey Brother, looking hungrily after the brown backs of the charcoal-burners.

"Sing them home," said Mowgli with a grin. "I do not wish them to be at the village gate till it is dark. Can ye hold them?"

Grey Brother bared his white teeth in contempt. "We can head them round and round in circles like tethered goats – if I know Man."

"That I do not need. Sing to them a little lest they be lonely on the road, and, Grey Brother, the song need not be of the sweetest. Go with them, Bagheera, and help make that song. When night is laid down, meet me by the village – Grey Brother knows the place."

"It is no light hunting to track for a man-cub. When shall I sleep?" said Bagheera, yawning, though his eyes showed he was delighted with the amusement. "Me to sing to naked men! But let us try."

He lowered his head so that the sound would travel, and cried a long, long "Good hunting" – a midnight call in the afternoon, which was quite awful enough to begin with. Mowgli heard it rumble, and rise, and fall, and die off in a creepy sort of whine behind him, and laughed to himself as he ran through the jungle. He could see the charcoal-burners huddled in a knot, old Buldeo's gun-barrel waving, like a banana-leaf, to every point of the compass at once. Then Grey Brother gave the *Ya-la-hi! Yalaha!* call for the buck-driving, when the pack drives the nilghai, the big blue cow, before them, and it seemed to come from the very ends of the earth, nearer, and nearer, and nearer, till it ended in a shriek snapped off short. The other three answered, till even Mowgli could have vowed that the full pack was in full cry, and then they all broke into the magnificent morning-song in the jungle, with every turn, and flourish, and grace-note, that a deep-mouthed wolf of the pack knows. This is a rough rendering of the song, but you must imagine what it sounds like when it breaks the afternoon hush of the jungle:

> One moment past our bodies cast
>   No shadow on the plain;
> Now clear and black they stride our track,
>   And we run home again.
> In morning-hush, each rock and bush
>   Stands hard, and high, and raw:
> Then give the call: *"Good rest to all*
>   *That keep the Jungle Law!"*
>
> Now horn and pelt our peoples melt
>   In covert to abide;
> Now crouched and still, to cave and hill
>   Our jungle barons glide.
> Now, stark and plain, Man's oxen strain,
>   That draw the new-yoked plough;
> Now stripped and dread the dawn is red
>   Above the lit *talao.*

Ho! Get to lair! The sun's aflare
    Behind the breathing grass:
And creaking through the young bamboo
    The warning whispers pass.
By day made strange, the woods we range
    With blinking eyes we scan;
While down the skies the wild duck cries:
    "The day – the day to Man!"

The dew is dried that drenched our hide,
    Or washed about our way;
And where we drank, the puddled bank
    Is crisping into clay.
The traitor dark gives up each mark
    Of stretched or hooded claw;
Then hear the call: *"Good rest to all*
    That keep the Jungle Law!"

But no translation can give the effect of it, or the yelping scorn the four threw into every word of it, as they heard the trees crash when the men hastily climbed up into the branches, and Buldeo began repeating incantations and charms. Then they lay down and slept, for like all who live by their own exertions, they were of a methodical cast of mind, and no one can work well without sleep.

Meantime, Mowgli was putting the miles behind him, nine to the hour, swinging on, delighted to find himself so fit after all his cramped months among men. The one idea in his head was to get Messua and her husband out of the trap, whatever it was, for he had a natural mistrust of traps. Later on, he promised himself, he would begin to pay his debts to the village at large.

It was at twilight when he saw the well-remembered grazing-grounds, and the *dhâk-tree* where Grey Brother had waited for him on the morning that he killed Shere Khan. Angry as he was at the whole breed and community of Man, something jumped up in his throat and made him catch his breath when he looked at the village roofs. He noticed that every one had come in from the fields unusually early, and that, instead of getting to their

Stooping over the man and the woman, he cut their thongs.

evening cooking, they gathered in a crowd under the village tree, and chattered, and shouted.

"Men must always be making traps for men, or they are not content," said Mowgli. "Two nights ago it was Mowgli – but that night seems many rains old. Tonight it is Messua and her man. Tomorrow, and for very many nights after, it will be Mowgli's turn again."

He crept along outside the wall till he came to Messua's hut, and looked through the window into the room. There lay Messua, gagged, and bound hand and foot, breathing hard, and groaning. Her husband was tied to the gaily painted bedstead. The door of the hut that opened into the street was shut fast, and three or four people were sitting with their backs to it.

Mowgli knew the manners and customs of the villagers very fairly. He argued that so long as they could eat, and talk, and smoke, they would not do anything else, but as soon as they had fed they would begin to be dangerous. Buldeo would be coming in before long, and if his escort had done its duty Buldeo would have a very interesting tale to tell. So he went in through the window, and, stooping over the man and the woman, cut their thongs, pulling out the gags, and looked round the hut for some milk.

Messua was half wild with pain and fear (she had been beaten and stoned all the morning), and Mowgli put his hand over her mouth just in time to stop a scream. Her husband was only bewildered and angry, and sat picking dust and things out of his torn beard.

"I knew – I knew he would come," Messua sobbed at last. "Now do I *know* that he is my son." And she caught Mowgli to her heart. Up to that time Mowgli had been perfectly steady, but here he began to tremble all over, and that surprised him immensely.

"Why are these thongs? Why have they tied thee?" he asked, after a pause.

"To be put to the death for making a son of thee – what else?" said the man, sullenly. "Look! I bleed."

Messua said nothing, but it was at *her* wounds that Mowgli looked, and they heard him grit his teeth when he saw the blood.

"Whose work is this?" said he. "There is a price to pay."

"The work of all the village. I was too rich. I had too many cattle. *Therefore* she and I are witches, because we gave thee shelter."

"I do not understand. Let Messua tell the tale."

"I gave thee milk, Nathoo. Dost thou remember?" Messua said, timidly. "Because thou wast my son, whom the tiger took, and because I loved thee very dearly. They said that I was thy mother, the mother of a devil, and therefore worthy of death."

"And what is a devil?" said Mowgli. "Death I have seen."

The man looked up gloomily under his eyebrows, but Messua laughed. "See!" she said to her husband. "I knew – I said that he was no sorcerer! He is my son – my son!"

"Son or sorcerer, what good will that do us?" the man answered. "We be as dead already."

"Yonder is the road through the jungle." Mowgli pointed through the window. "Your hands and feet are free. Go now."

"We do not know the jungle, my son, as – as thou knowest," Messua began. "I do not think that I could walk far."

"And the men and women would be upon our backs and drag us here again," said the husband.

"*Hm!*" said Mowgli, and he tickled the palm of his hand with the tip of his skinning-knife. "I have no wish to do harm to any one of this village – *yet*. But I do not think they will stay thee. In a little while they will have much to think upon. Ah!" He lifted his head and listened to shouting and trampling outside. "So they have let Buldeo come home at last?"

"He was sent out this morning to kill thee," Messua cried. "Didst thou meet him?"

"Yes – we – I met him. He has a tale to tell, and while he is talking it there is time to do much. But first I will learn what they mean. Think where ye would go, and tell me when I come back."

He bounded through the window and ran along again outside the wall of the village till he came within earshot of the crowd round the peepul-tree. Buldeo was lying on the ground, coughing and groaning, and every one was asking him questions. His hair had fallen about his shoulders; his hands and legs were skinned from climbing up trees, and he could hardly speak, but he felt the importance of his position keenly. From time to time he said something about devils and singing devils, and magic enchantment, just to give the crowd a taste of what was coming. Then he called for water.

"*Bah!*" said Mowgli. "Chatter – chatter! Talk, talk! Men are blood-brothers of the *Bandar-log*. Now he must wash his mouth with water; now he must blow smoke; and when all that is done he has still his story to tell. They are very wise people – men. They will leave no one to guard Messua till their ears are stuffed with Buldeo's tales. And – I grow as lazy as they!"

He shook himself and glided back to the hut. Just as he was at the window he felt a touch on his foot.

"Mother," said he, for he knew that tongue well, "what dost *thou* here?"

"I heard my children singing through the woods, and I followed the one I loved best. Little Frog, I have a desire to see that woman who gave thee milk," said Mother Wolf, all wet with the dew.

"They have bound and mean to kill her. I have cut those ties, and she goes with her man through the jungle."

"I also will follow. I am old, but not yet toothless." Mother Wolf reared herself up on end, and looked through the window into the dark of the hut.

In a minute she dropped noiselessly, and all she said was: "I gave thee thy first milk, but Bagheera speaks truth: Man goes to Man at the last."

"Maybe," said Mowgli, with a very unpleasant look on his face, "but tonight I am very far from that trail. Wait here, but do not let her see."

"*Thou* wast never afraid of *me*, little frog," said Mother Wolf, backing into the high grass, and blotting herself out, as she knew how.

"And now," said Mowgli, cheerfully, as he swung into the hut again, "they are all sitting round Buldeo, who is saying that which did not happen. When his talk is finished, they say they will assuredly come here with the Red – with fire and burn you both. And then?"

"I have spoken to my man," said Messua. "Khanhiwara is thirty miles from here, but at Khanhiwara we may find the English – "

"And what pack are they?" said Mowgli.

"I do not know. They be white, and it is said that they govern all the land, and do not suffer people to burn or beat each other without witnesses. If we can get thither tonight we live. Otherwise we die."

"Live then. No man passes the gates tonight. But what does *he* do?" Messua's husband was on his hands and knees digging up the earth in one corner of the hut.

"It is his little money," said Messua. "We can take nothing else."

"Ah, yes. The stuff that passes from hand to hand and never grows warmer. Do they need it outside this place also?" said Mowgli.

The man stared angrily. "He is a fool, and no devil," he muttered. "With the money I can buy a horse. We are too bruised to walk far, and the village will follow us in an hour."

"I say they will *not* follow till I choose, but a horse is well thought of, for Messua is tired." Her husband stood up and knotted the last of the rupees into his waist-cloth. Mowgli helped Messua through the window, and the cool night air revived her, but the jungle in the starlight looked very dark and terrible.

"Ye know the trail to Khanhiwara?" Mowgli whispered.

They nodded.

"Good. Remember, now, not to be afraid. And there is no need to go quickly. Only – only there may be some small singing in the jungle behind you and before."

"Think you we would have risked a night in the jungle through anything less than the fear of burning? It is better to be killed by beasts than by men," said Messua's husband. But Messua looked at Mowgli and smiled.

"I say," Mowgli went on, just as though he were Baloo repeating an old Jungle Law for the hundredth time to an inattentive cub, "I say that not a tooth in the jungle is bared against you, not a foot in the jungle is lifted against you. Neither man nor beast shall stay you till you come within eye-shot of Khanhiwara. There will be a watch about you." He turned quickly to Messua, saying: "*He* does not believe, but thou wilt believe?"

"Aye, surely, my son. Man, ghost, or wolf of the jungle, I believe."

"*He* will be afraid when he hears my people singing. Thou wilt know and understand. Go now, and slowly, for there is no need of any haste. The gates are shut."

Messua flung herself sobbing at Mowgli's feet, but he lifted her very quickly with a shiver. Then she hung about his neck and called him every name of blessing she could think of, but her husband looked enviously across his fields, and said: "*If* we reach Khanhiwara, and I get the ear of the English, I will bring such a law-suit against the Brahmin and old Buldeo and the others as shall eat this village to the bone. They shall pay me twice over for my crops untilled and my buffaloes unfed. I will have a great justice."

Mowgli laughed. "I do not know what justice is, but – come thou back next rains and see what is left."

They went off towards the jungle, and Mother Wolf leaped from her place of hiding.

"Follow!" said Mowgli. "And look to it that all the jungle knows these two are safe. Give tongue a little. I would call Bagheera."

The long, low howl rose and fell, and Mowgli saw Messua's husband flinch and turn, half minded to run back to the hut.

"Go on," Mowgli shouted, cheerfully. "I said there might be singing. That call will follow up to Khanhiwara. It is the favour of the jungle."

Messua urged her husband forward, and the darkness shut down on them and Mother Wolf as Bagheera rose up almost under Mowgli's feet, trembling with delight of the night that drives the Jungle-People wild.

"I am ashamed of thy brethren," he said, purring.

"What? Did they not sing sweetly to Buldeo?" said Mowgli.

"Too well! Too well! They made even *me* forget my pride, and, by the broken lock that freed me, I went singing through the jungle as though I were out wooing in the spring! Didst thou not hear us?"

"I had other game afoot. Ask Buldeo if he liked the song. But where are the Four? I do not wish one of the man pack to leave the gates tonight."

"What need of the Four, then?" said Bagheera, shifting from foot to foot, his eyes ablaze, and purring louder than ever. "I can hold them, Little Brother. Is it killing at last? The singing and the sight of the men climbing up the trees have made me very ready. Who is Man that we should care for him – the naked brown digger, the hairless and toothless, the eater of earth? I have followed him all day – at noon – in the white sunlight. I herded him as the wolves herd buck. I am Bagheera! Bagheera! Bagheera! As I dance with my shadow so I danced with those men. Look!" The great panther leaped as a kitten leaps at a dead leaf whirling overhead, struck left and right into the empty air, that sung under the strokes, landed noiselessly, and leaped again and again, while the half purr, half growl gathered head as steam rumbles in a boiler. "I am Bagheera – -in the jungle – in the night, and my strength is in me. Who shall stay my stroke? Man-cub, with one blow of my paw I could beat thy head flat as a dead frog in the summer!"

"Strike, then!" said Mowgli, in the dialect of the village, *not* the talk of the jungle. And the human words brought Bagheera to a full stop, flung back on his haunches that quivered under him, his head just at the level of Mowgli's. Once more Mowgli stared, as he had stared at the rebellious cubs, full into the beryl-green eyes, till the red glare behind their green went out like the light of a lighthouse shut off twenty miles across the sea, till the eyes dropped, and the big head with them – dropped lower and lower, and the red rasp of a tongue grated on Mowgli's instep.

"Brother – Brother – Brother!" the boy whispered, stroking steadily and lightly from the neck along the heaving back. "Be still, be still! It is the fault of the night, and no fault of thine."

"It was the smells of the night," said Bagheera, penitently. "This air cries aloud to me. But how dost *thou* know?"

Of course the air round an Indian village is full of all kinds of smells, and to any creature who does nearly all his thinking through his nose, smells are as maddening as music and drugs are to human beings. Mowgli gentled the panther for a few minutes longer, and he lay down like a cat before a fire, his paws tucked under his breast, and his eyes half shut.

"Thou art of the jungle and *not* of the jungle," he said at last. "And I am only a black panther. But I love thee, Little Brother."

"They are very long at their talk under the tree," Mowgli said, without noticing the last sentence. "Buldeo must have told many tales. They should come soon to drag the woman and her man out of the trap and put them into the Red Flower. They will find that trap sprung. Ho! Ho!"

"Nay, listen," said Bagheera. "The fever is out of my blood now. Let them find *me* there! Few would leave their houses after meeting me. It is not the first time I have been in a cage, and I do not think they will tie *me* with cords."

"Be wise, then," said Mowgli, laughing, for he was beginning to feel as reckless as the panther, who had glided into the hut.

"*Pah!*" Bagheera puffed. "This place is rank with Man, but here is just such a bed as they gave me to lie upon in the king's cages at Oodeypore.

Now I lie down." Mowgli heard the strings of the cot crack under the great brute's weight. "By the broken lock that freed me, they will think they have caught big game! Come and sit beside me, Little Brother. We will give them 'good hunting' together!"

"No, I have another thought in my stomach. The man pack shall not know what share I have in the sport. Make thine own hunt. I do not wish to see them."

"Be it so," said Bagheera. "Now they come!"

The conference under the peepul-tree had been growing noisier and noisier, at the far end of the village. It broke in wild yells, and a rush up the street of men and women, waving clubs and bamboos and sickles and knives. Buldeo and the Brahmin were at the head of it, but the mob was close at their heels, and they cried: "The witch and the wizard! Let us see if hot coins will make them confess! Burn the hut over their heads! We will teach them to shelter wolf-devils! Nay, beat them first! Torches! More torches! Buldeo, heat the gun-barrel!"

Here was some little difficulty with the catch of the door. It had been very firmly fastened, but the crowd tore it away bodily, and the light of the torches streamed into the room where, stretched at full length on the bed, his paws crossed and lightly hung down over one end, black as the pit and terrible as a demon, was Bagheera. There was one half-minute of desperate silence, as the front ranks of the crowd clawed and tore their way back from the threshold, and in that minute Bagheera raised his head and yawned – elaborately, carefully, and ostentatiously – as he would yawn when he wished to insult an equal. The fringed lips drew back and up; the red tongue curled; the lower jaw dropped and dropped till you could see half-way down the hot gullet; and the gigantic dogteeth stood clear to the pit of the gums till they rang together, upper and under, with the snick of steel-faced wards shooting home round the edges of a safe. Next minute the street was empty. Bagheera had leaped back through the window, and stood at Mowgli's side, while a yelling, screaming torrent scrambled and tumbled one over another in their panic haste to get to their huts.

"They will not stir till the day comes," said Bagheera, quietly. "And now?"

The silence of the afternoon sleep seemed to have overtaken the village, but, as they listened, they could hear the sound of heavy grain-boxes being dragged over earthen floors and pushed against doors. Bagheera was quite right. The village would not stir till daylight. Mowgli sat still and thought, and his face grew darker and darker.

"What have I done?" said Bagheera, at last, fawning.

"Nothing but great good. Watch them now till the day. I sleep." Mowgli ran off into the jungle, and dropped across a rock, and slept and slept the day round, and the night back again.

When he waked, Bagheera was at his side, and there lay a newly killed buck at his feet. Bagheera watched curiously while Mowgli went to work with his skinning-knife, ate and drank, and turned over with his chin in his hands.

"The man and the woman came safe within eye-shot of Khanhiwara," Bagheera said. "Thy mother sent the word back by Chil. They found a horse before midnight of the night they were freed, and went very quickly. Is not that well?"

"That is well," said Mowgli.

"And thy man pack in the village did not stir till the sun was high this morning. Then they ate their food and ran back quickly to their houses."

"Did they, by chance, see thee?"

"It may have been. I was rolling in the dust before the gate at dawn, and I may have made also some small song to myself. Now, Little Brother, there is nothing more to do. Come hunting with me and Baloo. He has new hives that he wishes to show, and we all desire thee back again as of old. Take off that look which makes even *me* afraid. The man and woman will not be put into the Red Flower, and all goes well in the jungle. Is it not true? Let us forget the man pack."

"They shall be forgotten – in a little while. Where does Hathi feed tonight?"

"Where he chooses. Who can answer for the Silent One? But why? What is there Hathi can do which we cannot?"

"Bid him and his three sons come here to me."

"But, indeed, and truly, Little Brother, it is not – it is not seemly to say 'Come' and 'Go' to Hathi. Remember, he is the master of the jungle, and before the man pack changed the look on thy face, he taught thee a Master Word of the jungle."

"That is all one. I have a Master Word for him now. Bid him come to Mowgli the Frog, and if he does not hear at first, bid him come because of the sack of the fields of Bhurtpore."

"The sack of the fields of Bhurtpore," Bagheera repeated two or three times to make sure. "I go. Hathi can but be angry at the worst, and I would give a moon's hunting to hear a Master Word that compels the Silent One."

He went away, leaving Mowgli stabbing furiously with his skinning-knife into the earth. Mowgli had never seen human blood in his life before till he had seen, and – what meant much more to him – smelled Messua's blood on the thongs that bound her. And Messua had been kind to him, and, so far as he knew anything about love, he loved Messua as completely as he hated the rest of mankind. But deeply as he loathed them, their talk, their cruelty, and their cowardice, not for anything the jungle had to offer could he bring himself to take a human life, and have that terrible scent of blood back again in his nostrils. His plan was simpler but much more thorough, and he laughed to himself when he thought that it was one of old Buldeo's tales told under the peepul-tree in the evening that had put the idea into his head.

"It *was* a Master Word," Bagheera whispered in his ear. "They were feeding by the river, and they obeyed as though they were bullocks. Look, where they come now!"

Hathi and his three sons had appeared in their usual way, without a sound. The mud of the river was still fresh on their flanks, and Hathi was thoughtfully chewing the green stem of a young plantain-tree that he had gouged up with his tusks. But every line in his vast body showed to Bagheera, who could see things when he came across them, that it was not the master of the jungle speaking to a man-cub, but one who was afraid coming before one who was not. His three sons rolled side by side, behind their father.

Mowgli hardly lifted his head as Hathi gave him "Good hunting." He kept him swinging and rocking, and shifting from one foot to another, for a long time before he spoke, and when he opened his mouth it was to Bagheera, not to the elephants.

"I will tell a tale that was told to me by the hunter ye hunted today," said Mowgli. "It concerns an elephant, old and wise, who fell into a trap, and the sharpened stake in the pit scarred him from a little above his heel to the crest of his shoulder, leaving a white mark." Mowgli threw out his hand, and as Hathi wheeled the moonlight showed a long white scar on his slaty side, as though he had been struck with a red-hot whip. "Men came to take him from the trap," Mowgli continued, "but he broke his ropes, for he was strong, and he went away till his wound was healed. Then came he, angry, by night to the fields of those hunters. And I remember now that he had three sons. These things happened many, many rains ago, and very far away – among the fields of Bhurtpore. What came to those fields at the next reaping, Hathi?"

"They were reaped by me and by my four sons," said Hathi.

"And to the ploughing that follows the reaping?" said Mowgli.

"There was no ploughing," said Hathi.

"And to the men that live by the green crops on the ground?" said Mowgli.

"They went away."

"And to the huts in which the men slept?" said Mowgli. "We tore the roofs to pieces, and the jungle swallowed up the walls," said Hathi.

"And what more, besides?" said Mowgli.

"As much good ground as I can walk over in two nights from the east to the west, and from the north to the south as much as I can walk over in three nights, the jungle took. We let in the jungle upon five villages, and in those villages, and in their lands, the grazing-ground and the soft crop-grounds, there is not one man today who gets his food from the ground. That was the sack of the fields of Bhurtpore, which I and my three sons did. And now I ask, man-cub, how the news of it came to thee?" said Hathi.

"A man told me. And now I see even Buldeo can speak truth. It was well done, Hathi with the white mark, but the second time it shall be done better, for the reason that there is a man to direct. Thou knowest the village of the man pack that cast me out? They are idle, senseless, and cruel; they play with their mouths, and they do not kill their weaker for food, but for sport. When they are full-fed they would throw their own breed into the Red

Flower. This I have seen. It is not well that they should live here any more. I hate them!"

"Kill, then," said the youngest of Hathi's three sons, picking up a tuft of grass, dusting it against his fore legs, and throwing it away, while his little red eyes glanced furtively from side to side.

"What good are white bones to me?" Mowgli answered furiously. "Am I the cub of a wolf to play in the sun with a raw head? I have killed Shere Khan, and his hide rots on the Council Rock, but – but I do not know whither Shere Khan is gone, and my stomach is still empty. Now I will take that which I can see and touch. Let in the jungle upon that village, Hathi!"

Bagheera shivered, and cowered down. He could understand, if the worst came to the worst, a quick rush down the village street, and a right and left blow into a crowd, or a crafty killing of men as they ploughed in the twilight, but this scheme for deliberately blotting out an entire village from the eyes of man and beast frightened him. Now he saw why Mowgli had sent for Hathi. No one but the long-lived elephant could plan and carry through such a war.

"Let them run as the men ran from the fields of Bhurtpore, till we have the rain-water for the only plough, and the noise of the rain on the thick leaves for the pattering of their spindles – till Bagheera and I lair in the house of the Brahmin, and the buck drink at the tank behind the temple! Let in the jungle, Hathi!"

"But I – but we have no quarrel with them, and it needs the red rage of great pain ere we tear down the places where men sleep," said Hathi, rocking doubtfully.

"Are ye the only Eaters of Grass in the jungle? Drive in your peoples. Let the deer and the pig and the nilghai look to it. Ye need never show a hand's-breadth of hide till the fields are naked. Let in the jungle, Hathi!"

"There will be no killing? My tusks were red at the sack of the fields of Bhurtpore, and I would not wake that smell again."

"Nor I. I do not wish even their bones to lie on our clean earth. Let them go find a fresh lair. They cannot stay here! I have seen and smelled the blood of the woman that gave me food – the woman whom they would have killed but for me. Only the smell of the new grass on their

215

door-steps can take away that smell. It burns in my mouth. Let in the jungle, Hathi!"

"Ah!" said Hathi. "So did the scar of the stake burn on my hide till we watched their villages die under in the spring growth. Now I see. Thy war shall be our war. We will let in the jungle."

Mowgli had hardly time to catch his breath – he was shaking all over with rage and hate – before the place where the elephants had stood was empty, and Bagheera was looking at him with terror.

"By the broken lock that freed me!" said the black panther at last. "Art *thou* the naked thing I spoke for in the pack when all was young? Master of the jungle, when my strength goes, speak for me – speak for Baloo – speak for us all! We are cubs before thee! Snapped twigs under foot! Fawns that have lost their doe!"

The idea of Bagheera being a stray fawn upset Mowgli altogether, and he laughed and caught his breath, and sobbed and laughed again, till he had to jump into a pool to make himself stop. Then he swam round and round, ducking in and out of the bars of the moonlight like the frog, his namesake.

By this time Hathi and his three sons had turned, each to one point of the compass, and were striding silently down the valleys a mile away. They went on and on for two days' march – that is to say, a long sixty miles – through the jungle, while every step they took, and every wave of their trunks, was known and noted and talked over by Mang and Chil and the Monkey-People and all the birds. Then they began to feed, and fed quietly for a week or so. Hathi and his sons are like Kaa the Rock Python. They never hurry till they have to.

At the end of that time – and none knew who had started it – a rumour went through the jungle that there was better food and water to be found in such and such a valley. The pigs – who, of course, will go to the ends of the earth for a full meal – moved first by companies, scuffling over the rocks, and the deer followed, with the little wild foxes that live on the dead and dying of the herds; and the heavy-shouldered nilghai moved parallel with the deer, and the wild buffaloes of the swamps came after the nilghai. The least little thing would have turned the scattered, straggling droves that grazed and sauntered and drank and grazed again, but whenever there was an alarm some one would rise up and soothe them. At one time it would be Sahi the Porcupine, full of news of good feed just a little farther on; at another Mang would cry cheerily and flap down a glade to show it was all empty; or Baloo, his mouth full of roots, would shamble alongside a wavering line and half frighten, half romp it clumsily back to the proper road. Very many creatures broke back or ran away or lost interest, but very many were left to go forward. At the end of another ten days or so the situation was this; The deer and the pig and the nilghai were milling round and round in a circle of eight or ten miles' radius, while the Eaters of Flesh skirmished round its edge. And the centre of that circle was the village, and round the village the crops were ripening, and in the crops sat men on what they call *machans* – platforms like pigeon-perches, made of sticks at the top of four poles – to scare away birds and other stealers. Then the deer were coaxed no more. The Eaters of Flesh were close behind them, and forced them forward and inward.

It was a dark night when Hathi and his three sons slipped down from the jungle, and broke off the poles of the *machans* with their trunks, and they fell as a snapped stalk of hemlock in bloom falls, and the men that tumbled from them heard the deep gurgling of the elephants in their ears. Then the vanguard of the bewildered armies of the deer broke down and flooded into the village grazing-grounds and the ploughed fields; and the sharp-hoofed, rooting wild pig came with them, and what the deer left the pig spoiled, and from time to time an alarm of wolves would shake the herds, and they would rush to and fro desperately, treading down the young barley, and cutting flat the banks of the irrigating channels. Before the dawn broke the pressure on the outside of the circle gave way at one point. The Eaters of Flesh had fallen back and left an open path to the south, and drove upon drove of buck fled along it. Others, who were bolder, lay up in the thickets to finish their meal next night.

But the work was practically done. When the villagers looked in the morning they saw their crops were lost. That meant death if they did not get away, for they lived year in and year out as near to starvation as the jungle was near to them. When the buffaloes were sent to graze the hungry brutes found that the deer had cleared the grazing-grounds, and so wandered into the jungle and drifted off with their wild mates; and when twilight fell the three or four ponies that belonged to the village lay in their stables with

217

their heads beaten in. Only Bagheera could have given those strokes, and only Bagheera would have thought of insolently dragging the last carcass to the open street.

The villagers had no heart to make fires in the fields that night, so Hathi and his three sons went gleaning among what was left, and where Hathi gleans there is no need to follow. The men decided to live on their stored seed-corn until the rains had fallen, and then to take work as servants till they could catch up with the lost year. But as the grain-dealer was thinking of his well-filled crates of corn, and the prices he would levy at the sale of it, Hathi's sharp tusks were picking out the corner of his mud-house, and smashing up the big wicker-chest, leeped with cow-dung, where the precious stuff lay.

When that last loss was discovered, it was the Brahmin's turn to speak. He had prayed to his own gods without answer. It might be, he said, that, unconsciously, the village had offended some one of the gods of the jungle, for, beyond doubt, the jungle was against them. So they sent for the head-man of the nearest tribes of wandering Gonds – little, wise, and very black hunters, living in the deep jungle, whose fathers came of the oldest race in India – the aboriginal owners of the land. They made the Gond welcome with what they had, and he stood on one leg, his bow in his hand, and two or three poisoned arrows stuck through his top-knot, looking half afraid and half contemptuously at the anxious villagers and their ruined fields. They wished to know whether his gods – the Old Gods – were angry with them, and what sacrifices should be offered. The Gond said nothing, but picked up a trail of the *karela*, the vine that bears the bitter wild gourd, and laced it to and fro across the temple door in the face of the staring red Hindu image. Then he pushed with his hand in the open air along the road to Khanhiwara, and went back to his jungle, and watched the Jungle-People drifting through it. He knew that when the jungle moves only white men can hope to turn it aside.

There was no need to ask his meaning. The wild gourd would grow where they had worshipped their god, and the sooner they saved themselves the better.

But it is hard to tear a village from its moorings. They stayed on as long as any summer food was left to them, and they tried to gather nuts in the jungle, but shadows with glaring eyes watched them, and rolled before them even at mid-day, and when they ran back afraid to their walls, on the tree-trunks they had passed not five minutes before the bark would be striped and chiselled with the stroke of some great taloned paw. The more they kept to their village, the bolder grew the wild things that gambolled and bellowed on the grazing-grounds by the Wainganga. They had no heart to patch and plaster the rear walls of the empty byres that backed on to the jungle; the wild pig trampled them down, and the knotty-rooted vines hurried after and threw their elbows over the new-won ground, and the coarse grass bristled behind the vines. The unmarried men ran away first, and carried the news far and near that the village was doomed. Who could fight, they said, against the jungle, or the gods of the jungle, when the very village cobra had left his hole in the platform under the peepul? So their little commerce with the outside world shrank as the trodden paths across the open grew fewer and fainter. And the nightly trumpetings of Hathi and his three sons ceased to trouble them; they had no more to go. The crop on the ground and the seed in the ground had been taken. The outlying fields were already losing their shape, and it was time to throw themselves on the charity of the English at Khanhiwara.

Native fashion, they delayed their departure from one day to another till the first rains caught them and the unmended roofs let in a flood, and the grazing-ground stood ankle deep, and all green things came on with a rush after the heat of the summer. Then they waded out – men, women, and children – through the blinding hot rain of the morning, but turned naturally for one farewell look at their homes.

They heard, as the last burdened family filed through the gate, a crash of falling beams and thatch behind the walls. They saw a shiny, snaky black trunk lifted for an instant, scattering sodden thatch. It disappeared, and there was another crash, followed by a squeal. Hathi had been plucking off the roofs of the huts as you pluck water-lilies, and a rebounding beam had pricked him. He needed only this to unchain his full strength, for of all things in the jungle the wild elephant enraged is the most wantonly destructive. He kicked backwards at a mud wall that crumbled at the stroke, and, crumbling, melted to yellow mud under the torrents of rain. Then he wheeled and squealed, and tore through the narrow streets, leaning against the huts right and left, shivering the crazy doors, and crumpling up the eaves, while his three sons raged behind as they had raged at the sack of the fields of Bhurtpore.

"The jungle will swallow these shells," said a quiet voice in the wreckage. "It is the outer walls that must lie down." And Mowgli, with the rain sluicing over his bare shoulders and arms, leaped back from a wall that was settling like a tired buffalo.

"All in good time," panted Hathi. "Oh, but my tusks were red at Bhurtpore! To the outer wall, children! With the head! Together! Now!"

The four pushed side by side. The outer wall bulged, split, and fell, and the villagers, dumb with horror, saw the savage, clay-streaked heads of the wreckers in the ragged gap. Then they fled, houseless and foodless, down the valley, as their village, shredded and tossed and trampled, melted behind them.

A month later the place was a dimpled mound, covered with soft, green young stuff, and by the end of the rains there was the roaring jungle in full blast on the spot that had been under plough not six months before.

Mowgli's Song against People

I will let loose against you the fleet-footed vines –
I will call in the jungle to stamp out your lines!
    The roofs shall fade before it,
      The house-beams shall fall,
    And the *karela*, the bitter *karela*,
      Shall cover it all!

In the gates of these your councils my
          people shall sing,
In the doors of these your garners the
          Bat-Folk shall cling;
    And the snake shall be your watchman,
      By a hearthstone unswept;
    For the *karela*, the bitter *karela*,
      Shall fruit where ye slept!

Ye shall not see my strikers; ye shall hear them and guess;
By night, before the moon-rise, I will send for my cess,
    And the wolf shall be your herdsman
      By a landmark removed,
    For the *karela*, the bitter *karela*,
      Shall seed where ye loved!

I will reap your fields before you at the hands of a host;
Ye shall glean behind my reapers for the bread that is lost;
   And the deer shall be your oxen
    By a headland untilled,
  For the *karela*, the bitter *karela*,
    Shall leaf where ye build!

I have untied against you the club-footed vines,
I have sent in the jungle to swamp out your lines.
The trees – the trees are on you!
  The house-beams shall fall,
And the *karela*, the bitter *karela*,
  Shall cover you all!

The Undertakers

When ye say to Tabaqui: "My Brother!" When ye call the hyena to meat,
Ye may cry the full truce with Jacala – the belly that runs on four feet.

Jungle Law

"Respect the Aged!"

It was a thick voice – a muddy voice that would have made you shudder – a voice like something soft breaking in two. There was a quaver in it, a croak and a whine.

"Respect the aged! O companions of the river – respect the aged!"

Nothing could be seen on the broad reach of the river except a little fleet of square-sailed, wooden-pinned barges, loaded with building-stone, that had just come under the railway bridge, and were driving down-stream. They put their clumsy helms over to avoid the sandbar made by the scour of the bridge-piers, and as they passed, three abreast, the horrible voice began again:

"O Brahmins of the river – respect the aged and infirm!"

A boatman turned where he sat on the gunwale, lifted up his hand, said something that was not a blessing, and the boats creaked on through the twilight. The broad Indian river, that looked more like a chain of little lakes than a stream, was as smooth as glass, reflecting the sandy-red sky in mid-channel, but splashed with patches of yellow and dusky purple near and under the low banks. Little creeks ran into it in the wet season, but now their dry mouths hung clear above water-line. On the left shore, almost under the railway bridge, stood a mud and brick and thatch and stick village, whose main street, full of cattle going back to their byres, ran straight to the river, and ended in a sort of rude brick pier-head, where people who wanted to wash could wade in step by step. That was the ghat of the village of Mugger-Ghat.

Night was falling fast over the fields of lentils and rice and cotton in the low-lying grounds yearly flooded by the river, over the reeds that fringed the elbow of the bend, and the tangled jungle of the grazing-grounds behind the still reeds. The parrots and crows, who had been chattering and shouting over their evening drink, had flown inland to roost, crossing the out-going battalions of the flying-foxes, and cloud upon cloud of water-birds came whistling and "honking" to the cover of the reed-beds. There were geese, barrel-headed and black-backed, teal, widgeon, mallard and sheldrake, with curlews, and here and there a flamingo.

A lumbering adjutant-crane brought up the rear, flying as though each slow stroke would be his last.

"*Respect the aged! Brahmins of the river – respect the aged!*"

The adjutant half turned his head, sheered a little in the direction of the voice, and landed stiffly on the sandbar below the bridge. Then you saw what a ruffianly brute he really was. His back-view was immensely respectable, for he stood nearly six feet high, and looked rather like a very proper bald-headed parson. In front it was different, for his Ally Sloper-like head and neck had not a feather to them, and there was a horrible raw-skin pouch on his neck under his chin – a hold-all for the things his pick-axe beak might steal. His legs were long and thin and skinny, but he moved them delicately, and looked at them with pride as he preened down his ashy-grey tail-feathers, glanced over the smooth of his shoulder, and stiffened into "Stand at attention."

A mangy little jackal, who had been yapping hungrily on a low bluff, cocked up his ears and tail, and scuttered across the shallows to join the adjutant.

He was the lowest of his caste – not that the best of jackals are good for much, but this one was peculiarly low, being half a beggar, half a criminal – a cleaner-up of village rubbish-heaps, desperately timid or wildly bold, everlastingly hungry, and full of cunning that never did him any good.

"*Ugh!*" he said, shaking himself dolefully as he landed. "May the red mange destroy the dogs of this village! I have three bites for each flea upon me, and all because I looked – only looked, mark you – at an old shoe in a cow-byre. Can I eat mud?" He scratched himself under his left ear.

"I heard," said the adjutant, in a voice like a blunt saw going through a thick board, "I *heard* there was a new-born puppy in that same shoe."

"To hear is one thing, to know is another," said the jackal, who had a very fair knowledge of proverbs, picked up by listening to men round the village fires of an evening.

"Quite true. So, to make sure, I took care of that puppy while the dogs were busy elsewhere."

"They were *very* busy," said the jackal. "Well, I must not go to the village hunting for scraps yet a while. And so there truly was a blind puppy in that shoe?"

"It is here," said the adjutant, squinting over his beak at his full pouch. "A small thing, but acceptable now that charity is dead in the world."

"*Ahai!* The world is iron in these days," wailed the jackal. Then his restless eye caught the least possible ripple on the water, and he went on quickly: "Life is hard for us all, and I doubt not that even our excellent master, the Pride of the Ghat and the Envy of the River – "

"A liar, a flatterer, and a jackal were all hatched out one egg," said the adjutant to nobody in particular, for he was rather a fine sort of a liar on his own account when he took the trouble.

"Yes, the Envy of the River," the jackal repeated, raising his voice. "Even he, I doubt not, finds that since the bridge has been built good food is more scarce. But on the other hand, though I would by no means say this to his noble face, he is so wise and so virtuous – as I, alas! am not – "

"When the jackal says that he is grey, how black must the jackal be!" muttered the adjutant. He could not see what was coming.

"That *his* food never fails, and in consequence – "

There was a soft grating sound as though a boat had just touched in shoal water. The jackal spun round quickly and faced (it is always best to face) the creature he had been talking about. It was a twenty-four-foot crocodile, cased in what looked like treble-riveted boiler-plate, studded and keeled and crested, the yellow points of his upper teeth just overhanging his beautifully fluted lower jaw. It was the blunt-nosed mugger of Mugger-Ghat, older than any man in the village, who had given his name to the village, the demon of the ford before the railway bridge came – murderer, man-eater, and local fetish in one. He lay with his chin in the shallows, keeping his place by an almost invisible rippling of his tail, and well the jackal knew that one stroke of that same tail in the water could carry the mugger up the bank with the rush of a steam-engine.

"Auspiciously met, Protector of the Poor!" he fawned, backing at every word. "A delectable voice was heard, and we came in the hopes of sweet conversation. My tailless presumption, while waiting here, led me, indeed, to speak of thee. It is my hope that nothing was overheard."

Now the jackal had spoken just to be listened to, for he knew flattery was the best way of getting things to eat, and the mugger knew that the jackal had spoken for this end, and the jackal knew that the mugger knew, and the mugger knew that the jackal knew that the mugger knew, and so they were all very contented together.

The old brute pushed and panted and grunted up the bank, mumbling: "Respect the aged and infirm!" And all the time his little eyes burned like coals under the heavy horny eyelids on the top of his triangular head, as he shoved his bloated barrel-body along between his crutched legs. Then he settled down, and accustomed as the jackal was to his ways, he could not help starting, for the hundredth time, when he saw how exactly the mugger imitated a log adrift on the bar. He had even taken pains to lie at the exact angle a naturally stranded log would make with the water, having regard to the current of the season at the time and place. All this was only a matter of habit, of course, because the mugger had come ashore for plea-sure. But a crocodile is never quite full, and if the jackal had been deceived by the likeness he would not have lived to philosophise over it.

"My child, I heard nothing," said the mugger, shutting one eye. "The water was in my ears, and also I was faint with hunger. Since the railway bridge was built my people at my village have ceased to love me, and that is breaking my heart."

"Ah, shame!" said the jackal. "So noble a heart, too! But men are all alike to my mind."

"Nay, there are very great differences indeed," the mugger answered, gently. "Some are as lean as boat-poles. Others again are fat as young ja —— dogs. Never would I causelessly revile men. They are of all fashions,

*It was a twenty-four foot crocodile, cased in what looked like
treble-riveted boiler plate.*

but the long years have shown me that, one with another, they are very good. Men, women, and children – I have no fault to find with them. And remember, child, he who rebukes the world is rebuked by the world."

"Flattery is worse than an empty tin can in the belly. But that which we have just heard is wisdom," said the adjutant, bringing down one foot.

"Consider, though, their ingratitude to this excellent one," began the jackal, tenderly.

"Nay, nay, not ingratitude!" the mugger said. "They do not think for others, that is all. But I have noticed, lying at my station below the ford, that the stairs of the new bridge are cruelly hard to climb, both for old people and young children. The old, indeed, are not so worthy of consideration, but I am grieved – I am truly grieved – on account of the small fat children. Still, I think, in a little while, when the newness of the bridge has worn away, we shall see my people's bare brown legs bravely splashing through the ford as before. Then the old mugger will be honoured again."

"But surely I saw marigold wreaths floating off the edge of the ghat only this noon," said the adjutant. Marigold wreaths are a sign of reverence all India over.

"An error – an error. It was the wife of the sweetmeat-seller. She loses her eyesight year by year, and cannot tell a log from me – the mugger of the ghat! I saw the mistake when she threw the garland, for I was lying at the very foot of the ghat, and had she taken another step I might have shown her some little difference. Yet she meant well, and we must consider the spirit of the offering."

"What profit are marigold wreaths when one is on the rubbish-heap?" said the jackal, hunting for fleas, but keeping one wary eye on his Protector of the Poor.

"True, but they have not yet begun to make the rubbish-heap that shall carry me. Five times have I seen the river draw back from the village and make new land at the foot of the street. Five times have I seen the village rebuilt on the banks, and I shall see it built yet five times more. I am no faithless, fish-hunting gavial, I, at Kasi today and Prayag tomorrow, as the saying is, but the true and constant watcher of the ford. It is not for nothing, child, that the village bears my name, and 'he who watches long,' as the saying is, 'shall at last have his reward.'"

"*I* have watched long – very long – nearly all my life, and my reward has been bites and blows," said the jackal.

"Ho! Ho! Ho!" roared the adjutant.

> "In August was the jackal born;
> The rains fell in September;
> 'Now such a fearful flood as this,'
> Said he, 'I can't remember!'"

There is one very unpleasant peculiarity about the adjutant. At uncertain times he suffers from acute attacks of the fidgets or cramp in his legs, and though he is more virtuous to behold than any of the cranes, who are all immensely respectable, he flies off into wild, cripple-stilt war-dances, half opening his wings and bobbing his bald head up and down, while for reasons best known to himself he is very careful to time his worst attacks with his nastiest remarks. At the last word of his song he came to attention again, ten times adjutaunter than before.

The jackal winced, though he was full three seasons old, but one cannot resent an insult from a person with a beak a yard long, and the power of driving it like a javelin. The adjutant was a most notorious coward, but the jackal was worse.

"We must live before we can learn," said the mugger, "and there is this to say: Little jackals are very common, child, but such a mugger as I am is not common. For all that I am not proud, since pride is destruction; but take notice, it is Fate, and against his Fate no one who swims or walks or runs should say anything at all. I am well contented with Fate. With good luck, a keen eye, and the custom of considering whether a creek or a back-water has an outlet to it ere you ascend, much may be done."

"Once I heard that even the Protector of the Poor made a mistake," said the jackal viciously.

"True, but there my Fate helped me. It was before I had come to my full growth – before the last famine but three (by the Right and Left of Ganga – how full the streams used to be in those days!). Yes, I was young and unthinking, and when the flood came, who was so pleased as I? A little made me very happy then. The village was deep in flood, and I swam above the ghat and went far inland, up to the rice-fields, and they were deep in good mud. I remember also a pair of bracelets (glass they were, and troubled me not a little) that I found that evening. Yes, glass bracelets, and, if my memory serves me well, a shoe. I should have shaken off both shoes, but I was hungry. I learned better later. Yes. And so I fed and rested me, but when I was ready to go to the river again the flood had fallen, and I walked through the mud of the main street. Who but I? Came out all my people, priests and women and children, and I looked upon them with benevolence. The mud is not a good place to fight in. Said a boatman: 'Get axes and kill him, for he is the mugger of the ford.' 'Not so,' said the Brahmin. 'Look, he is driving the flood before him! He is the godling of the village.' Then they threw many flowers at me, and by happy thought one led a goat across the road."

"How good – how very good is goat!" said the jackal.

"Hairy – too hairy, and when found in the water more than likely to hide a cross-shaped hook. But that goat I accepted, and went down to the ghat in great honour. Later, my Fate sent me the boatman who had desired to cut off my tail with an axe. His boat grounded upon an old shoal which you would not remember."

"We are not *all* jackals here," said the adjutant. "Was it the shoal made where the stone-boats sank in the year of the great drouth – a long shoal that lasted three floods?"

"There were two," said the mugger. "An upper and a lower shoal."

"Aye, I forgot. A channel divided them, and later dried up again," said the adjutant, who prided himself on his memory.

"On the lower shoal, children, my well-wisher's craft grounded. He was sleeping in the bows, and, half awake, leaped over to his waist – no, it was no more than to his knees – to push off. His empty boat went on and touched again below the next reach, as the river ran then. I followed, because I knew men would come out to drag it ashore."

"And did they do so?" said the jackal, a little awe-stricken. This was hunting on a scale that impressed him.

"There and lower down they did. I went no farther, but that gave me three in one day – well-fed *manjis* [boatmen] all, and, except in the case of the last (then I was careless), never a cry to warn those on the bank."

"Ah, noble sport! But what cleverness and great judgment it requires!" said the jackal.

"Not cleverness, child, but thought. A little thought in life is like salt upon rice, as the boatmen say, and I have thought deeply always. The gavial, my cousin, the fish-eater, has told me how hard it is for him to follow his fish, and how one fish differs from the other, and how he must know them all, both together and apart. I say that is wisdom, but, on the other hand, my cousin, the gavial, lives among his people. *My* people do not swim in companies, with their mouths out of the water, as Rewa does; nor do they constantly rise to the surface of the water, and turn over on their sides, like Mohoo and little Chapta; nor do they gather in shoals after flood, like Batchua and Chilwa."

"All are very good eating," said the adjutant, clattering his beak.

"So my cousin says, and makes a great to-do over hunting them, but they do not climb the banks to escape his sharp nose. *My* people are otherwise. Their life is on the land, in the houses, among the cattle. I must know what they do, and what they are about to do, and, adding the tail to the trunk, as the saying is, I make up the whole elephant. Is there a green branch and an iron ring hanging over a doorway? The old mugger knows that a boy has been born in that house, and must some day come down to the ghat to play. Is a maiden to be married? The old mugger knows, for he sees the men carry gifts back and forth; and she, too, comes down to the ghat to bathe before her wedding, and – he is there. Has the river changed its channel, and made new land where there was only sand before? The mugger knows."

"Now, of what use is that knowledge?" said the jackal. "The river has shifted even in my little life." Indian rivers are nearly always moving about in their beds, and will shift, sometimes, as much as two or three miles in a season, drowning the fields on one bank, and spreading good silt on the other.

"There is no knowledge so useful," said the mugger, "for new land means new quarrels. The mugger knows. Oho! The mugger knows. As soon as the water has drained off, he creeps up the little creeks that men think would not hide a dog, and there he waits. Presently comes a farmer saying he will plant cucumbers here, and melons there, in the new land that the river has given him. He feels the good mud with his bare toes. Anon comes another, saying he will put onions, and carrots, and sugar-cane in such and such places. They meet as boats adrift meet, and each rolls his eye at the other under the big blue turban. The old mugger sees and hears. Each calls the other 'Brother,' and they go to mark out the boundaries of the new land. The mugger hurries with them from point to point, shuffling very low through the mud. Now they begin to quarrel! Now they say hot words! Now they pull turbans! Now they lift up their *lathis* [clubs], and at last one falls backwards into the mud, and the other runs away. When he comes back the dispute is settled as the iron-bound bamboo of the loser witnesses. Yet they are not grateful to the mugger. No, they cry 'Murder!" And their families fight with sticks, twenty a-side. My people are good people – upland Jats – Malwais of the Bet. They do not give blows for sport, and, when the fight is done, the old mugger waits far down the river, out of sight of the village, behind the *kikar-scrub* yonder. Then come they down, my broad-shouldered Jats – eight or nine together under the stars, bearing the dead man upon a bed. They are old men with grey beards, and voices as deep as mine. They light a little fire – ah! how well I know that fire! – and they drink tobacco, and they nod their heads together forward in a ring, or sideways towards the dead man upon the bank. They say the English Law will come with a rope for this matter, and that such a man's family will be ashamed, because such a man must be hanged in the great square of the jail. Then say the friends of the dead: 'Let him hang!" And the talk is all to do over again – once, twice, twenty times in the long night. Then says one, at last: 'The fight was a fair fight. Let us take blood-money, a little more than is offered by the slayer, and we will say no more about it.' Then do they haggle over the blood-money, for the dead was a strong man, leaving many sons. Yet before *amratvela* [sunrise] they put the fire to him a little, as the custom is, and the dead man comes to me, and *he* says no more about it. Aha! My children, the mugger knows – the mugger knows – and my Malwai Jats are a good people!"

"They are too close – too narrow in the hand for my crop," croaked the adjutant. "They waste not the polish on the cow's horn, as the saying is, and, again, who can glean after a Malwai?"

"Ah, I – glean – *them*," said the mugger.

"Now, in Calcutta of the South, in the old days," the adjutant went on, "everything was thrown into the streets, and we picked and chose. Those were dainty seasons. But today they keep their streets as clean as the outside of an egg, and my people fly away. To be clean is one thing; to dust, sweep, and sprinkle seven times a day wearies the very gods themselves."

"There was a down-country jackal had it from a brother, who told me, that in Calcutta of the South all the jackals were as fat as otters in the rains," said the jackal, his mouth watering at the bare thought of it.

"Ah, but the white-faces are there – the English – and they bring dogs from somewhere down the river, in boats – big fat dogs – to keep these same jackals lean," said the adjutant.

"They are, then, as hard-hearted as these people? I might have known. Neither earth, sky, nor water shows charity to a jackal. I saw the tents of a white-face last season, after the rains, and also I took a new yellow bridle to eat. The white-faces do not dress their leather in the proper way. It made me very sick."

"That was better than my case," said the adjutant. "When I was in my third season, a young and a bold bird, I went down to the river where the big boats come in. The boats of the English are thrice as big as this village."

"He has been as far as Delhi, and says all the people there walk on their heads," muttered the jackal. The mugger opened his left eye, and looked keenly at the adjutant.

"It is true," the big bird insisted. "A liar only lies when he hopes to be believed. No one who had not seen those boats *could* believe this truth."

"*That* is more reasonable," said the mugger. "And then?"

"From the insides of this boat they were taking out great pieces of white stuff, which, in a little while, turned to water. Much split off, and fell about on the shore, and the rest they swiftly put into a house with thick walls. But a boatman, who laughed, took a piece no larger than a small dog, and threw it to me. I – all my people – swallow without reflection, and that piece I swallowed as is our custom. Immediately I was afflicted with an excessive cold, which, beginning in my crop, ran down to the extreme end of my toes, and deprived me even of speech, while the boatmen laughed at me. Never have I felt such cold. I danced in my grief and amazement till I could recover my breath, and then I danced and cried out against the falseness of this world, and the boatmen derided me till they fell down. The chief wonder of the matter, setting aside that marvellous coldness, was that there was nothing at all in my crop when I had finished my lamentings!"

The adjutant had done his very best to describe his feelings after swallowing a seven-pound lump of Wenham Lake ice, off an American ice-ship, in the days before Calcutta made her ice by machinery. But as he did not know what ice was, and as the mugger and the jackal knew rather less, the tale missed fire.

"Anything," said the mugger, shutting his left eye again, "*anything* is possible that comes out of a boat thrice the size of Mugger-Ghat. My village is not a small one."

There was a whistle overhead on the bridge, and the *Delhi Mail* slid across, all the carriages gleaming with light, and the shadows faithfully following along the river. It clanked away into the dark again, but the mugger and the jackal were so well used to it that they never turned their heads.

"Is that anything less wonderful than a boat thrice the size of Mugger-Ghat?" said the bird, looking up.

"I saw that built, child. Stone by stone I saw the bridge-piers rise, and when the men fell off (they were wondrous sure-footed for the most part – but *when* they fell) I was ready. After the first pier was made they never thought to look down the stream for the body to burn. There, again, I saved much trouble. There was nothing strange in the building of the bridge," said the mugger.

"But that which goes across, pulling the roofed carts, *that* is strange," the adjutant repeated.

"It is, past any doubt, a new breed of bullock. Some day it will not be able to keep its foothold up yonder, and will fall as the men did. The old mugger will then be ready."

The jackal looked at the adjutant, and the adjutant looked at the jackal. If there was one thing they were more certain of than another, it was that the engine was everything in the wide world except a bullock. The jackal had watched it time and again from the aloe hedges at the side of the line, and the adjutant had seen engines since the first engine ran in India. But the mugger had only looked up at the thing from below, where the brass dome seemed rather like a bullock's hump.

"*M* – yes, a new kind of bullock," the mugger repeated ponderously, to make himself quite sure in his own mind; and "Certainly it is a bullock," said the jackal.

"And again it might be – " began the mugger pettishly.

"Certainly – most certainly," said the jackal, without waiting for the other to finish.

"What?" said the mugger angrily, for he could feel that the others knew more than he did. "What might it be? *I* never finished my words. You said it was a bullock."

"It is anything the Protector of the Poor pleases. I am *his* servant – not the servant of the thing that crosses the river."

"Whatever it is, it is white-face work," said the adjutant, "and for my own part, I would not lie out upon a place so near to it as this bar."

"You do not know the English as I do," said the mugger. "There was a white-face here when the bridge was built, and he would take a boat in the evenings and shuffle with his feet on the bottom-boards, and whisper: 'Is he here? Is he there? Bring me my gun.' I could hear him before I could see him – each sound that he made – creaking and puffing and rattling his gun, up and down the river. As surely as I had picked up one of his workmen, and thus saved great charges in wood for the burning, so surely would he come down to the ghat, and shout in a loud voice that he would hunt me, and rid the river of me – the mugger of Mugger-Ghat! *Me!* Children, I have swum under the bottom of his boat for hour after hour, and heard him fire his gun at logs, and when I was well sure he was wearied, I have risen by his side and snapped my jaws in his face. When the bridge was finished he went away. All the English hunt in that fashion, except when they are hunted."

"Who hunts the white-faces?" yapped the jackal, excitedly.

"No one now, but I have hunted them in my time."

"I remember a little of that hunting. I was young then," said the adjutant, clattering his beak significantly.

"I was well established here. My village was being built for the third time, as I remember, when my cousin, the gavial, brought me word of rich waters above Benares. At first I would not go, for my cousin, who is a fish-eater, does not always know the good from the bad. But I heard my people talking in the evenings, and what they said made me certain."

"And what did they say?" the jackal asked.

"They said enough to make me, the mugger of Mugger-Ghat, leave water and take to my feet. I went by night, using the littlest streams as they served me, but it was the beginning of the hot weather and all streams were low. I crossed dusty roads; I went through tall grass; I climbed hills in the moonlight. Even rocks did I climb, children – consider this well! I crossed the tail of Sirhind, the waterless, before I could find the set of the little rivers that flow Gangaward. I was a month's journey from my own people and the banks that I knew. That was very marvellous!"

"What food on the way?" said the jackal, who kept his soul in his little stomach, and was not a bit impressed by the mugger's land travels.

"That which I could find – *cousin*," said the mugger slowly, dragging each word.

Now you do not call a man a cousin in India unless you think you can establish some kind of blood-relationship, and as it is only in old fairy-tales that the mugger ever marries a jackal, the jackal knew for what reason he had been suddenly lifted into the mugger's family circle. If they had been alone he would not have cared, but the adjutant's eyes twinkled with mirth at the ugly jest.

"Assuredly, Father, I might have known," said the jackal. A mugger does not care to be called a father of jackals, and the mugger of Mugger-Ghat said as much – and a great deal more which there is no use in repeating here.

"The Protector of the Poor has claimed kinship. How can I remember the precise degree? Moreover, we eat the same food. He has said it," was the jackal's reply.

That made matters rather worse, for what the jackal hinted at was that the mugger must have eaten his food on that land-march fresh, and fresh every day, instead of keeping it by him till it was in a fit and proper condition, as every self-respecting mugger and most wild beasts do when they can. Indeed, one of the worst terms of contempt along the river-bed is "eater of fresh meat." It is nearly as bad as calling a man a cannibal.

"That food was eaten thirty seasons ago," said the adjutant, quietly. "If we talk for thirty seasons more it will never come back. Tell us, now, what happened when the good waters were reached after thy most wonderful land-journey. If we listened to the howling of every jackal the business of the town would stop, as the saying is."

The mugger must have been grateful for the interruption, because he went on, with a rush:

"By the Right and Left of Ganga! When I came there never did I see such waters!"

"Were they better, then, than the big flood of last season?" said the jackal.

"Better! That flood was no more than comes every five years – a handful of drowned strangers, some chickens, and a dead bullock in muddy water with cross-currents. But the season I think of, the river was low, smooth, and even, and, as the gavial had warned me, the dead English came down, touching each other. I got my girth in that season – my girth and my depth. From Agra, by Etawah and the broad waters by Allahabad – "

"Oh, the eddy that set under the walls of the fort at Allahabad!" said the adjutant. "They came in there like widgeon to the reeds, and round and round they swung – thus!"

He went off into his horrible dance again, while the jackal looked on enviously. He naturally could not remember the terrible year of the Mutiny they were talking about. The mugger continued:

"Yes, by Allahabad one lay still in the slack-water and let twenty go by to pick one; and, above all, the English were not cumbered with jewelry and nose-rings and anklets as my women are nowadays. To delight in ornaments is to end with a rope for necklace, as the saying is. All the muggers of all the rivers grew fat then, but it was my Fate to be fatter than them all. The news was that the English were being hunted into the rivers, and by the Right and Left of Ganga, we believed it was true! So far as I went south I believed it to be true, and I went down-stream beyond Monghyr and the tombs that look over the river."

"I know that place," said the adjutant. "Since those days Monghyr is a lost city. Very few live there now."

"Thereafter I worked up-stream very slowly and lazily, and a little above Monghyr there came down a boatful of white-faces – alive! They were, as I remember, women, lying under a cloth spread over sticks, and crying aloud. There was never a gun fired at us watchers of the fords in those days.

All the guns were busy elsewhere. We could hear them day and night inland, coming and going as the wind shifted. I rose up full before the boat, because I had never seen white-faces alive, though I knew them well – otherwise. A naked white child kneeled by the side of that boat, and stooping over, must needs try to trail his hands in the river. It is a pretty thing to see how a child loves running water. I had fed that day, but there was a little unfilled space within me. Still, it was for sport and not for food that I rose at the child's hands. They were so clear a mark that I did not even look when I closed, but they were so small that though my jaws rang true – I am sure of that – the child drew them up swiftly, unhurt. They must have passed between tooth and tooth – those small white hands. I should have caught him crosswise at the elbows, but, as I said, it was only for sport and desire to see new things that I rose at all. They cried out one after another in the boat, and presently I rose again to watch them. The boat was too heavy to push over. They were only women, but he who trusts a woman will walk on duckweed in a pool, as the saying is. And by the Right and Left of Ganga – that is truth!"

"Once a woman gave me some dried skin from a fish," said the jackal. "I had hoped to get her baby, but horse-food is better than the kick of a horse, as the saying is. What did thy woman do?"

"She fired at me with a short gun of a kind I have never seen before or since. Five times, one after another" [the mugger must have met with an old-fashioned revolver] – "and I stayed open-mouthed and gaping, my head in the smoke. Never did I see such a thing. Five times, as swiftly as I wave my tail – thus!"

The jackal, who had been growing more and more interested in the story, had just time to leap back as the huge tail swung by like a scythe.

"Not before the fifth shot," said the mugger, as though he had never dreamed of stunning one of his listeners, "not before the fifth shot did I sink, and I rose in time to hear a boatman telling all those white women that I was most certainly dead. One bullet had gone under a neck-plate of mine. I know not if it is there still, for the reason I cannot turn my head. Look and see, child. It will show that my tale is true."

"I?" said the jackal. "Shall an eater of old shoes, a bone-cracker, presume to doubt the word of the Envy of the River? May my tail be bitten off by blind puppies if the shadow of such a thought has crossed my humble mind. The Protector of the Poor has condescended to inform me, his slave, that once in his life he has been wounded by a woman. That is sufficient, and I will tell the tale to all my children, asking for no proof."

"Over-much civility is sometimes no better than over-much discourtesy, for, as the saying is, one can choke a guest with curds. I do *not* desire that any children of thine should know that the mugger of Mugger-Ghat took his only wound from a woman. They will have much else to think of if they get their meat as miserably as does their father."

"It is forgotten long ago! It was never said! There never was a white woman! There was no boat! Nothing whatever happened at all."

The jackal waved his brush to show how completely everything was wiped out of his memory, and sat down with an air.

"Indeed, very many things happened," said the mugger, beaten in his second attempt that night to get the better of his friend. (Neither bore malice, however. Eat and be eaten was fair law along the river, and the jackal came in for his share of plunder when the mugger had finished a meal.) "I left that boat and went up-stream, and, when I had reached Arrah and the back-waters behind it, there were no more dead English. The river was empty for a while. Then came one or two dead, in red coats, not English, but of one kind all – Hindus and Purbeeahs – then five and six abreast, and at last, from Arrah to the north beyond Agra, it was as though whole villages had walked into the water. They came out of little creeks one after another, as the logs come down in the rains. When the river rose they rose also in companies from the shoals they had rested upon, and the falling flood dragged them with it across the fields and through the jungle by the long hair. All night, too, going north, I heard the guns, and by day the shod feet of men crossing fords, and that noise which a heavy cartwheel makes on sand under water, and every ripple brought more dead. At last even I was afraid, for I said: 'If this thing happens to men, how shall the mugger of Mugger-Ghat escape?' There were boats, too, that came up behind me without sails, burning continually, as the cotton-boats sometimes burn, but never sinking."

"Ah!" said the adjutant "Boats like those come to Calcutta of the South. They are tall and black, they beat up the water behind them with a tail, and they – "

"Are thrice as big as my village. *My* boats were low and white; they beat up the water on either side of them, and were no larger than the boats of one who speaks truth should be. They made me very afraid, and I left water and went back to this my river, hiding by day and walking by night, when I could not find little streams to help me. I came to my village again, but I did not hope to see any of my people there. Yet they were ploughing and sowing and reaping, and going to and fro in their fields as quietly as their own cattle."

"Was there still good food in the river?" said the jackal.

"More than I had any desire for. Even I – and I do not eat mud – even *I* was tired, and, as I remember, a little frightened of this constant coming down of the silent ones. I heard my people say in my village that all the English were dead, but those that came, face down, with the current were *not* English, as my people saw. Then my people said that it was best to say nothing at all, but to pay the tax and plough the land. After a long time the river cleared, and those that came down it had been clearly drowned by the floods, as I could well see, and, though it was not so easy then to get food, I was heartily glad. A little killing here and there is no bad thing – but even the mugger is sometimes satisfied, as the saying is."

"Marvellous! Most truly marvellous!" said the jackal. "I am become fat through merely hearing about so much good eating. And afterwards what, if it be permitted to ask, did the Protector of the Poor do?"

"I said to myself – and by the Right and Left of Ganga! I locked my jaws on that vow – I said I would never go roving any more. So I lived by the ghat, very close to my own people, and I watched over them year after year, and they loved me so much that they threw marigold wreaths at my head whenever they saw it lift. Yes, and my Fate has been very kind to me, and all the river is good enough to respect my poor and infirm presence. Only – "

"No one is all happy from his beak to his tail," said the adjutant, sympathetically. "What does the mugger of Mugger-Ghat need more?"

"That little white child which I did not get," said the mugger, with a deep sigh. "He was very small, but I have not forgotten. I am aged now, but before I die it is my desire to try one new thing. It is true they are a heavy-footed, noisy, and foolish people, and the sport would be small, but I remember the old days above Benares, and, if the child lives, he will

remember still. It may be he goes up and down the bank of some river telling how he once passed his hands between the teeth of the mugger of
Mugger-Ghat, and lived to make a tale of it. My Fate has been very kind,
but that plagues me sometimes in my dreams – the thought of the little
white child in the bows of that boat." He yawned, and closed his jaws. "And
now I will rest and think. Keep silent, my children, and respect the aged."

He turned stiffly, and shuffled to the top of the sandbar, while the jackal
drew back with the adjutant to the shelter of a tree stranded on the end
nearest the railway bridge.

"That was a pleasant and profitable life," he grinned, looking up inquir-
ingly at the bird who towered above him. "And not once, mark you, did
he think fit to tell me where a morsel might have been left along the banks.
Yet I have told *him* a hundred times of good things wallowing down-stream.
How true is the saying: 'All the world forgets the jackal and the barber
when the news has been told!' Now he is going to sleep! *Arrah!*"

"How can a jackal hunt with a mugger?" said the adjutant, coolly. "Big
thief and little thief – it is easy to say who gets the pickings."

The jackal turned, whining impatiently, and was going to curl himself
up under the tree-trunk, when suddenly he cowered, and looked up through
the draggled branches at the bridge almost above his head.

"What now?" said the adjutant, opening one wing uneasily.

"Wait till we see. The wind blows from us to them, but they are not
looking for us – those two men."

"Men, is it? My office protects me. All India knows I am holy." The
adjutant, being a first-class scavenger, is allowed to go where he pleases,
and so this one never flinched.

"I am not worth a blow from anything better than an old shoe," said
the jackal, and listened again. "Hark to that footfall!" he went on. "That
was no country leather, but the shod foot of a white-face. Listen again! Iron
hits iron up there! It is a gun! Friend, those heavy-footed, foolish English
are coming to speak with the mugger."

"Warn him, then. He was called Protector of the Poor by some one not
unlike a starving jackal but a little time ago."

"Let my cousin protect his own hide. He has told me again and again
there is nothing to fear from the white-faces. They must be white-faces. Not

a villager of Mugger-Ghat would dare to come after him. See, I said it was a gun! Now, with good luck, we shall feed before daylight. He cannot hear well out of water, and – this time it is not a woman!"

A shiny barrel glittered for a minute in the moonlight on the girders. The mugger was lying on the sandbar as still as his own shadow, his fore feet spread out a little, his head dropped between them, snoring like a – mugger.

A voice on the bridge whispered: "It's an odd shot – straight down almost – but as safe as houses. Better try behind the neck. Golly! What a brute! The villagers will be wild if he's shot, though. He's the *deota* [godling] of these parts."

"I don't care a rap," another voice answered. "He took about fifteen of my best coolies while the bridge was building, and it's time he was put an end to. I've been after him in a boat for weeks. Stand by with the Martini as soon as I've given him both barrels of this."

"Mind the kick, then. A double four-bore's no joke."

"That's for him to decide. Here goes!"

There was a roar like the sound of a small cannon (the biggest sort of elephant-rifle is not very different from some artillery), and a double streak of flame, followed by the stinging crack of a Martini, whose long bullet makes nothing of a crocodile's plates. But the explosive bullets did the work. One of them struck just behind the mugger's neck, a hand's breadth to the left of the backbone, while the other burst a little lower down, at the beginning of the tail. In ninety-nine cases out of a hundred a mortally wounded crocodile can scramble off for deep water and get away, but the mugger of Mugger-Ghat was literally broken into three pieces. He hardly moved his head before the life went out of him, and he lay as flat as the jackal.

"Thunder and lightning! Lightning and thunder!" said that miserable little beast. "Has the thing that pulls the covered carts over the bridge tumbled at last?"

"It is no more than a gun," said the adjutant, though his very tail-feathers quivered. "Nothing more than a gun. He is certainly dead. Here come the white-faces."

The two Englishmen had hurried down from the bridge and across to the sandbar, where they stood admiring the length of the mugger. Then a native with an axe cut off the big head, and four men dragged it across the spit.

"The last time that I had my hand in a mugger's mouth," said one of the Englishmen, stooping down (he was the man who had built the bridge), "it was when I was about five years old – coming down the river by boat to Monghyr. I was a Mutiny baby, as they call it. Poor Mother was in the boat, too, and she often told me how she fired Dad's old pistol at the beast's head."

"Well, you've certainly had your revenge on the chief of the clan – even if the gun has made your nose bleed. Hi, you boatmen! Haul that head up the bank, and we'll boil it for the skull. The skin's too knocked about to keep. Come along to bed now. This was worth sitting up all night for, wasn't it?"

Curiously enough, the jackal and the adjutant made the very same remark not three minutes after the men had left.

A Ripple Song

Once a ripple came to land
  In the golden sunset burning –
Lapped against a maiden's hand,
  By the ford returning.

Dainty foot and gentle breast –
Safe across be glad and rest.
"Maiden, wait," the ripple saith.
"Wait a while, for I am Death!"

"Where my lover calls I go –
  Shame it were to treat him coldly –
'Twas a fish that circled so,
  Turning over boldly."

Dainty foot and tender heart,
Wait the loaded ferry-cart.
"Wait, ah, wait!" the ripple saith.
"Maiden, wait, for I am Death!"

"When my lover calls I haste –
  Dame Disdain was never wedded!"
Ripple – ripple round her waist,
  Clear the current eddied.

Foolish heart and faithful hand,
Little feet that touched no land.
Far away the ripple fled,
Ripple – ripple – running red!

The King's Ankus

These are the four that are never content: that have never been filled since
    the dews began –
Jacala's mouth, and the glut of the kite, and the hands of the ape, and the
    eyes of Man.

Jungle Saying

Kaa, the big rock python, had changed his skin for perhaps the two hundredth time since his birth, and Mowgli, who never forgot that he owed his life to Kaa for a night's work at the Cold Lairs, which you may perhaps remember, went to congratulate him. Skin-changing always makes a snake moody and depressed till the new skin begins to shine and look beautiful. Kaa never made sport of Mowgli any more, but accepted him, as the other Jungle-People did, for the master of the jungle, and brought him all the news that a python of his size would naturally hear. What Kaa did not know about the Middle Jungle, as they call it – the life that runs close to the earth or under it, the boulder, burrow, and the tree-bole life – might have been written upon the smallest of his scales.

That afternoon Mowgli was sitting in the circle of Kaa's great coils, fingering the flaked and broken old skin that lay all looped and twisted among the rocks just as Kaa had left it. Kaa had very courteously packed himself under Mowgli's broad, bare shoulders, so that the boy was really resting in a living arm-chair.

"Even to the scales of the eyes it is perfect," said Mowgli, under his breath, playing with the old skin. "Strange to see the covering of one's own head at one's own feet."

"Aye, but I lack feet," said Kaa. "And since this is the custom of all my people, I do not find it strange. Does thy skin never feel old and harsh?"

"Then go I and wash, Flathead. But, it is true, in the great heats I have wished I could slough my skin without pain, and run skinless."

"I wash, and *also* I take off my skin. How looks the new coat?"

Mowgli ran his hand down the diagonal checkerings of the immense back. "The turtle is harder-backed, but not so gay," he said judgmatically. "The frog, my name-bearer, is more gay, but not so hard. It is very beautiful to see – like the mottling in the mouth of a lily."

"It needs water. A new skin never comes to full colour before the first bath. Let us go bathe."

"I will carry thee," said Mowgli, and he stooped down, laughing, to lift the middle section of Kaa's great body, just where the barrel was thickest. A man might just as well have tried to heave up a two-foot water-main, and Kaa lay still, puffing with quiet amusement. Then their regular evening game began – the boy in the flush of his great strength, and the python in his sumptuous new skin, standing up one against the other for a wrestling match – a trial of eye and strength. Of course, Kaa could have crushed a dozen Mowglis had he let himself go, but he played carefully, and never loosed one-tenth of his power. Ever since Mowgli was strong enough to endure a little rough handling, Kaa had taught him this game, and it suppled his limbs as nothing else could. Sometimes Mowgli would stand lapped almost to his throat in Kaa's shifting coils, striving to get one arm free and catch him by the throat. Then Kaa would give way limply, and Mowgli, with both quick-moving feet, would try to cramp the purchase of that huge tail as it flung backwards feeling for a rock or a stump. They would rock to and fro, head to head, each waiting for his chance, till the beautiful, statue-like group melted in a whirl of black-and-yellow coils and struggling legs and arms, to rise up again and again. "Now! Now! Now!" said Kaa, making feints with his head that even Mowgli's quick hand could not turn aside. "Look! I touch thee here, Little Brother! Here, and here! Are thy hands numb? Here again!"

The game always ended in one way – with a straight, driving blow of the head that knocked the boy over and over. Mowgli could never learn the guard for that lightning lunge, and, as Kaa said, there was not the least use in trying.

"Good hunting!" Kaa grunted at last, and Mowgli, as usual, was shot away half a dozen yards, gasping and laughing. He rose with his fingers full of grass, and followed Kaa to the wise snake's pet bathing-place – a deep, pitch-black pool surrounded with rocks, and made interesting by sunken tree-stumps. The boy slipped in, jungle fashion, without a sound, and dived across; rose, too, without a sound, and turned on his back, his arms behind his head, watching the moon rising above the rocks, and breaking up her reflection in the water with his toes. Kaa's diamond-shaped head cut the pool like a razor, and came out to rest on Mowgli's shoulder. They lay still, soaking luxuriously in the cool water.

"It is *very* good," said Mowgli at last, sleepily. "Now, in the man pack, at this hour, as I remember, they laid them down upon hard pieces of wood in the inside of a mud-trap, and, having carefully shut out all the clean winds, drew foul cloth over their heavy heads, and made evil songs through their noses. It is better in the jungle."

A hurrying cobra slipped down over a rock and drank, gave them "Good hunting!" and went away.

"*Sssh!*" said Kaa, as though he had suddenly remembered something. "So the jungle gives thee all that thou hast ever desired, Little Brother?"

"Not all," said Mowgli, laughing, "else there would be a new and strong Shere Khan to kill once a moon. *Now*, I could kill with my own hands, asking no help of buffaloes. And also I have wished the sun to shine in the middle of the rains, and the rains to cover the sun in the deep of summer; and also I have never gone empty but I wished that I had killed a goat; and also I have never killed a goat but I wished it had been buck; nor buck but I wished it had been nilghai. But thus do we feel, all of us."

"Thou hast no other desire?" the big snake demanded. "What more can I wish? I have the jungle, and the favour of the jungle! Is there more between sunrise and sunset?"

"Now, the cobra said – " Kaa began.

"What cobra? He that went away just now said nothing. He was hunting."

"It was another."

"Hast thou many dealings with the Poison-People? I give them their own path. They carry death in the fore tooth, and that is not good – for they are so small. But what hood is this thou hast spoken with?"

Kaa rolled slowly in the water like a steamer in a beam sea. "Three or four moons since," said he, "I hunted in the Cold Lairs, which place, may be, thou hast not forgotten. And the thing I hunted fled shrieking past the tanks and to that house whose side I once broke for thy sake, and ran into the ground."

"But the people of the Cold Lairs do not live in burrows." Mowgli knew that Kaa was talking of the Monkey-People.

"This thing was not living, but seeking to live," Kaa replied, with a quiver of his tongue. "He ran into a burrow that led very far. I followed, and having killed, I slept. When I waked I went forward."

"Under earth?"

"Even so. Coming at last upon a white hood [a white cobra], who spoke of things beyond my knowledge, and showed me many things I had never before seen."

"New game? Was it good hunting?" Mowgli turned quickly on his side.

"It was no game, and would have broken all my teeth, but the white hood said that a man – he spoke as one that knew the breed – that a man would give the hot breath under his ribs for only the sight of those things."

"We will look," said Mowgli. "I now remember that I was once a man."

"Slowly – slowly. It was haste killed the yellow snake that ate the sun. We two spoke together under the earth, and I spoke of thee, naming thee as a man. Said the white hood (and he is indeed as old as the jungle): 'It is long since I have seen a man. Let him come, and he shall see all these things, for the least of which very many men would die.'"

"That *must* be new game. And yet the Poison-People do not tell us when game is afoot. They are unfriendly folk."

"It is *not* game. It is – it is – I cannot say what it is."

"We will go there. I have never seen a white hood, and I wish to see the other things. Did he kill them?"

"They are all dead things. He says he is the keeper of them all."

"Ah! As a wolf stands above meat he has taken to his own lair. Let us go."

Mowgli swam to the bank, rolled in the grass to dry himself, and the two set off for the Cold Lairs, the deserted city of which you may have heard. Mowgli was not in the least afraid of the Monkey-People in those days, but the Monkey-People had the liveliest horror of Mowgli. Their tribes, however, were raiding in the jungle, and so the Cold Lairs stood empty and silent in the moonlight. Kaa led up to the ruins of the queen's pavilion that stood on the terrace, slipped over the rubbish, and dived down the half-choked staircase that went underground from the centre of the pavilion. Mowgli gave the Snake Call – "We be of one blood, ye and I" – and followed on his hands and knees. They crawled a long distance down a sloping passage that turned and twisted several times, and at last came to where the root of some great tree, growing thirty feet overhead, had forced out a solid stone in the wall. They crept through the gap, and found themselves in a large vault, whose domed roof had been also broken away by tree-roots so that a few streaks of light dropped down into the darkness.

"A safe lair," said Mowgli, rising to his firm feet, "but over-far to visit daily. And now what do we see?"

"Am I nothing?" said a voice in the middle of the vault, and Mowgli saw something white move, till, little by little, there stood up the hugest cobra he had ever set eyes on – a creature nearly eight feet long, and bleached by being in darkness to an old ivory-white. Even the spectacle marks of his spread hood had faded to a faint yellow. His eyes were as red as rubies, and altogether he was most wonderful to see.

"Good hunting!" said Mowgli, who carried his manners with his knife, and that never left him.

"What of the city?" said the white cobra, without answering the greeting. "What of the great, the walled city – the city of a hundred elephants and twenty thousand horses, and cattle past counting – the city of the King of Twenty Kings? I grow deaf here, and it is long since I heard the war-gongs."

"The jungle is above our heads," said Mowgli. "I know only Hathi and his sons among elephants. Bagheera has slain all the horses in one village, and – what is a king?"

"I told thee," said Kaa softly to the cobra. "I told thee, four moons ago, that thy city was not."

"The city – the great city of the forest whose gates are guarded by the king's towers – can never pass. They built it before my father's father came from the egg, and it shall endure when my sons' sons are as white as I. Salomdhi, son of Chandrabija, son of Viyeja, son of Yegasuri, built it in the days of Bappa Rawal. Whose cattle are *ye?*"

"It is a lost trail," said Mowgli, turning to Kaa. "I know not his talk."

"Nor I. He is very old. Father of Cobras, there is only the jungle here, as it has been since the beginning."

"Then who is *he,*" said the white cobra, "sitting down before me, unafraid, knowing not the name of the king, talking our talk through a man's lips? Who is he with the knife and the snake's tongue?"

"Mowgli they call me," was the answer. "I am of the jungle. The wolves are my people, and Kaa here is my brother. Father of Cobras, who art thou?"

"I am the warden of the king's treasure. Kurrun Raja built the stone above me, in the days when my skin was dark, that I might teach death to those who came to steal. Then they let down the treasure through the stone, and I heard the song of the Brahmins my masters."

"*Umm!*" said Mowgli to himself. "I have dealt with one Brahmin already, in the man pack, and – I know what I know. Evil comes here in a little."

"Five times since my wardship has the stone been lifted, but always to let down more, and never to take away. There are no riches like these riches – the treasures of a hundred kings. But it is long and long since the stone was last moved, and I think that my city has forgotten."

"There is no city. Look up. Yonder are the roots of the great trees tearing the stones apart. Trees and men do not grow together," Kaa insisted.

"Twice and thrice have men found their way here," the white cobra answered savagely, "but they never spoke till I came upon them groping in the dark, and then they cried only a little time. But *ye* come with lies, man and snake both, and would have me believe that my city is not, and that my wardship ends. Little do men change in the years. But *I* change never! Till the stone is lifted, and the Brahmins come down singing the songs that I know, and feed me with warm milk, and take me to the light again, I – I

– *I*, and no other, am the warden of the king's treasure! The city is dead, ye say, and here are the roots of the trees? Stoop down, then, and take what ye will. Earth has no treasure like these. Man with the snake's tongue, if thou canst go alive by the way that thou hast entered at, the lesser kings will be thy servants!"

"Again the trail is lost," said Mowgli, coolly. "Can any jackal have burrowed so deep and bitten this great whitehood? He is surely mad. Father of Cobras, I see nothing here to take away."

"By the gods of the sun and moon, it is the madness of death upon the boy!" hissed the cobra. "Before thine eyes close I will allow thee this favour. Look thou, and see what man has never seen before!"

"They do not well in the jungle who speak to Mowgli of favours," said the boy, between his teeth, "but the dark changes all, as I know. I will look, if that please thee."

He stared with puckered-up eyes round the vault, and then lifted up from the floor a handful of something that glittered.

"Oho!" said he. "This is like the stuff they play with in the man pack. Only this is yellow and the other was brown."

He let the gold pieces fall, and moved forward. The floor of the vault was buried some five or six feet deep in coined gold and silver that had burst from the sacks it had been originally stored in, and, in the long years, the metal had packed and settled as sand packs at low tide. On it and in it, and rising through it, as wrecks lift through the sand, were jewelled elephant-howdahs of embossed silver, studded with plates of hammered gold, and adorned with carbuncles and turquoises. There were palanquins and litters for carrying queens, framed and braced with silver and enamel, with jade-handled poles and amber curtain-rings; there were golden candlesticks hung with pierced emeralds that quivered on the branches; there were studded images, five feet high, of forgotten gods, silver with jewelled eyes; there were coats of mail, gold inlaid on steel, and fringed with rotted and blackened seed-pearls; there were helmets, crested and beaded with pigeon's-blood rubies; there were shields of lacquer, of tortoise-shell, and rhinoceros-hide, strapped and bossed with red gold and set with emeralds at the edge; there were sheaves of diamond-hilted swords, daggers, and hunting-knives; there were golden sacrificial bowls and ladles, and portable altars of a shape that never sees the light of day; there were jade cups and bracelets; there were incense-burners, combs, and pots for perfume, henna, and eye-powder, all in embossed gold; there were nose-rings, armlets, head-bands, finger-rings, and girdles past any counting; there were belts seven fingers broad, of square-cut diamonds and rubies, and wooden boxes, trebly clamped with iron, from which the wood had fallen away in powder, showing the pile of uncut star-sapphires, opals, cat's-eyes, sapphires, rubies, diamonds, emeralds, and garnets within.

The white cobra was right. No mere money would begin to pay the value of this treasure, the sifted pickings of centuries of war, plunder, trade, and taxation. The coins alone were priceless, leaving out of count all the precious stones, and the dead weight of the gold and silver alone might be two or three hundred tons. Every native ruler in India today, however poor, has a hoard to which he is always adding. And, though once in a long while, some enlightened prince may send off forty or fifty bullock-cart loads of silver to be exchanged for Government securities, the bulk of them keep their treasure and the knowledge of it very closely to themselves.

But Mowgli naturally did not understand what these things meant. The knives interested him a little, but they did not balance as well as his own, and so he dropped them. At last he found something really fascinating laid on the front of a howdah half buried in the coins. It was a two-foot *ankus*, or elephant-goad – something like a small boat-hook. The top was one round shining ruby, and eight inches of the handle below it were studded with rough turquoises close together, giving a most satisfactory grip. Below them was a rim of jade with a flower-pattern running round it – only the leaves were emeralds, and the blossoms were rubies sunk in the cool, green stone. The rest of the handle was a shaft of pure ivory, while the point – the spike and hook – was gold-inlaid steel with pictures of elephant-catching: and the pictures attracted Mowgli, who saw that they had something to do with his friend Hathi.

The white cobra had been following him closely.

"Is it not worth dying to behold?" he said. "Have I not done thee a great favour?"

"I do not understand," said Mowgli. "The things are hard and cold, and by no means good to eat. But this" – he lifted the *ankus* – "I desire to take away, that I may see it in the sun. Thou sayest they are all thine. Wilt thou give it to me, and I will bring thee frogs to eat?"

The white cobra fairly shook with evil delight. "Assuredly I will give it," he said. "All that is here I will give thee – till thou goest away."

"But I go now. This place is dark and cold, and I wish to take the thorn-pointed thing to the jungle."

"Look by thy foot! What is that there?"

Mowgli picked up something white and smooth. "It is the bone of a man's head," he said quietly. "And here are two more."

"They came to take the treasure away many years ago. I spoke to them in the dark, and they lay still."

"But what do I need of this that is called treasure? If thou wilt give me the *ankus* to take away, it is good hunting. If not, it is good hunting none the less. I do not fight with the Poison-People, and I was also taught the Master Word of thy tribe."

"There is but one Master Word here. It is mine!"

Kaa flung himself forward with blazing eyes. "Who bade me bring the man?" he hissed.

"I surely," the old cobra lisped. "It is long since I have seen Man, and this man speaks our tongue."

"But there was no talk of killing. How can I go to the jungle and say that I have led him to his death?" said Kaa.

"I talk not of killing till the time. And as to thy going or not going, there is the hole in the wall. Peace, now, thou fat monkey-killer! I have but to touch thy neck, and the jungle will know thee no longer. Never man came here that went away with the breath under his ribs. I am the warden of the treasure of the king's city!"

"But, thou white worm of the dark, I tell thee there is neither king nor city! The jungle is all about us!" cried Kaa.

"There is still the treasure. But this can be done. Wait a while, Kaa of the Rocks, and see the boy run. There is room for great sport here. Life is good. Run to and fro a while, and make sport, boy!"

Mowgli put his hand on Kaa's head quietly.

"The white thing has dealt with men of the man pack until now. He does not know me," he whispered. "He has asked for this hunting. Let him have it." Mowgli had been standing with the *ankus* held point down. He flung it from him quickly, and it dropped crossways just behind the great snake's hood, pinning him to the floor. In a flash, Kaa's weight was upon the writhing body, paralysing it from hood to tail. The red eyes burned, and the six spare inches of the head struck furiously right and left.

"Kill!" said Kaa, as Mowgli's hand went to his knife.

"No," he said, as he drew the blade, "I will never kill again save for food. But look you, Kaa!" He caught the snake behind the hood, forced the mouth open with the blade of the knife, and showed the terrible poison-fangs of the upper jaw lying black and withered in the gum. The white cobra had outlived his poison, as a snake will. "*Thuu*" [It is dried up],[1] said Mowgli, and motioning Kaa away, he picked up the *ankus*, setting the white cobra free.

"The king's treasure needs a new warden," he said gravely. "Thuu, thou hast not done well. Run to and fro and make sport, Thuu!"

"I am shamed. Kill me!" hissed the white cobra.

"There has been too much talk of killing. We will go now. I take the thorn-pointed thing, Thuu, because I have fought and worsted thee."

"See, then, that the thing does not kill thee at last. It is Death! Remember, it is Death! There is enough in that thing to kill the men of all my city. Not long wilt thou hold it, Jungle Man, nor he who takes it from thee. They will kill, and kill, and kill for its sake! My strength is dried up, but the *ankus* will do my work. It is Death! It is Death! It is Death!"

Mowgli crawled out through the hole into the passage again, and the last that he saw was the white cobra striking furiously with his harmless fangs at the stolid golden faces of the gods that lay on the floor, and hissing, "It is Death!"

They were glad to get to the light of day once more. And when they were back in their own jungle and Mowgli made the *ankus* glitter in the morning light, he was almost as pleased as though he had found a bunch of new flowers to stick in his hair.

---

[1] Literally, a rotted tree stump.

"This is brighter than Bagheera's eyes," he said delightedly, as he twirled the ruby. "I will show it to him. But what did the Thuu mean when he talked of death?"

"I cannot say. I am sorrowful to my tail's tail that he felt not thy knife. There is always evil at the Cold Lairs – above ground and below. But now I am hungry. Dost thou hunt with me this dawn?" said Kaa.

"No, Bagheera must see this thing. Good hunting!" Mowgli danced off, flourishing the great *ankus*, and stopping from time to time to admire it, till he came to that part of the jungle Bagheera chiefly used, and found him drinking after a heavy kill. Mowgli told him all his adventures from beginning to end, and Bagheera sniffed at the *ankus* between whiles. When Mowgli came to the white cobra's last words, Bagheera purred approvingly.

"Then the white hood spoke the thing which is?" Mowgli asked quickly.

"I was born in the king's cages at Oodeypore, and it is in my stomach that I know some little of Man. Very many men would kill thrice in a night for the sake of that one red stone alone."

"But the stone makes it heavy to the hand. My little bright knife is better, and – See! The red stone is not good to eat. Then *why* would they kill?"

"Mowgli, go thou and sleep. Thou hast lived among men, and – "

"I remember. Men kill because they are not hunting – for idleness and pleasure. Wake again, Bagheera. For what use was this thorn-pointed thing made?"

Bagheera half opened his eyes – he was very sleepy – with a malicious twinkle.

"It was made by men to thrust into the head of the sons of Hathi, so that the blood should pour out. I have seen the like in the streets of Oodeypore, before our cages. That thing has tasted the blood of many such as Hathi."

"But why do they thrust into the heads of elephants?"

"To teach them Man's Law. Having neither claws nor teeth, men make these things – and worse."

"Always more blood when I come near, even to the things the man pack have made!" said Mowgli disgustedly. He was a little tired of the weight of the *ankus*. "If I had known this, I would not have taken it. First it was Messua's blood on the thongs, and now it is Hathi's. I will use it no more. Look!"

The *ankus* flew sparkling, and buried itself point down fifty yards away, between the trees. "So my hands are clean of Death," said Mowgli, rubbing his hands on the fresh, moist earth. "The Thuu said Death would follow me. He is old and white and mad."

"White or black, or death or life, *I* am going to sleep, Little Brother. I cannot hunt all night and howl all day, as do some folk."

Bagheera went off to a hunting-lair that he knew, about two miles off. Mowgli made an easy way for himself up a convenient tree, knotted three or four creepers together, and in less time than it takes to tell was swinging in a hammock fifty feet above ground. Though he had no positive objection to strong daylight, Mowgli followed the custom of his friends, and used it as little as he could. When he waked among the very loud-voiced peoples that live in the trees, it was twilight once more, and he had been dreaming of the beautiful pebbles he had thrown away.

"At least I will look at the thing again," he said, and slid down a creeper to the earth. But Bagheera was before him. Mowgli could hear him snuffing in the half light.

"Where is the thorn-pointed thing?" cried Mowgli.

"A man has taken it. Here is his trail."

"Now we shall see whether the Thuu spoke truth. If the pointed thing is Death, that man will die. Let us follow."

"Kill first," said Bagheera. "An empty stomach makes a careless eye. Men go very slowly, and the jungle is wet enough to hold the lightest mark."

They killed as soon as they could, but it was nearly three hours before they finished their meat and drink and buckled down to the trail. The Jungle-People know that nothing makes up for being hurried over your meals.

"Think you the pointed thing will turn in the man's hand and kill him?" Mowgli asked. "The Thuu said it was Death."

"We shall see when we find," said Bagheera, trotting with his head low. "It is single-foot" [he meant that there was only one man], "and the weight of the thing has pressed his heel far into the ground."

"*Hai!* This is as clear as summer lightning," Mowgli answered, and they fell into the quick, choppy trail-trot in and out through the checkers of the moonlight, following the marks of those two bare feet.

"Now he runs swiftly," said Mowgli. "The toes are spread apart." They went on over some wet ground. "Now why does he turn aside here?"

"Wait!" said Bagheera, and flung himself forward with one superb bound as far as ever he could. The first thing to do when a trail ceases to explain itself is to cast forward without leaving your own confusing foot-marks on the ground. Bagheera turned as he landed, and faced Mowgli, crying: "Here comes another trail to meet him. It is a smaller foot, this second trail, and the toes turn inward."

Then Mowgli ran up and looked. "It is the foot of a Gond hunter," he said. "Look! Here he dragged his bow on the grass. That is why the first trail turned aside so quickly. Big Foot hid from Little Foot."

"That is true," said Bagheera. "Now, lest by crossing each other's tracks we foul the signs, let each take one trail. I am Big Foot, Little Brother, and thou art Little Foot, the Gond."

Bagheera leaped back to the original trail, leaving Mowgli stooping above the curious in-toed track of the wild little man of the woods.

"Now," said Bagheera, moving step by step along the chain of footprints, "I, Big Foot, turn aside here. Now I hide me behind a rock and stand still, not daring to shift my feet. Cry thy trail, Little Brother."

"Now I, Little Foot, come to the rock," said Mowgli, running up his trail. "Now sit I down under the rock, leaning upon my right hand, and resting my bow between my toes. I wait long, for the mark of my feet is deep here."

"I also," said Bagheera, hidden behind the rock. "I wait, resting the end of the thorn-pointed thing upon a stone. It slips, for here is a scratch upon the stone. Cry thy trail, Little Brother."

"One, two twigs and a big branch are broken here," said Mowgli, in an undertone. "Now, how shall I cry *that?* Ah! It is plain now. I, Little Foot, go away making noises and tramplings so that Big Foot may hear me." He moved away from the rock pace by pace among the trees, his voice rising in the distance as he approached a little cascade. "I – go – far – away – to – where – the – noise – of – falling – water – covers – my – noise. And – here – I – wait. Cry thy trail, Bagheera, Big Foot!"

The panther had been casting in every direction to see how Big Foot's trail led away from behind the rock. Then he gave tongue.

"I come from behind the rock upon my knees, dragging the thorn-pointed thing. Seeing no one, I run. I, Big Foot, run swiftly. The trail is clear. Let each follow his own. I run!"

Bagheera swept on along the clearly marked trail, and Mowgli followed the steps of the Gond. For a time there was silence in the jungle.

"Where art thou, Little Foot?" cried Bagheera. Mowgli's voice answered him not fifty yards to the right.

"*Um!*" said the panther, with a deep cough. "The two run side by side, drawing nearer!"

They raced on another half mile, always keeping about the same distance, till Mowgli, whose head was not so close to the ground as Bagheera's, cried: "They have met. Good hunting – look! Here stood Little Foot, with his knee on a rock – and yonder is Big Foot."

Not ten yards in front of them, stretched across a pile of broken rocks, lay the body of a villager of the district, a lean, small-feathered Gond arrow through his back and breast.

"Was the Thuu so old and so mad, Little Brother?" said Bagheera, gently. "Here is one death, at least."

"Follow on. But where is the drinker of elephant's blood – the red-eyed thorn?"

"Little Foot has it – perhaps. It is single-foot again now."

The single trail of a light man who had been running quickly and bearing a burden on his left shoulder held on round a long, low spur of dried grass, where each footfall seemed to the sharp eyes of the trackers marked in hot iron.

Neither spoke till the trail ran up to the ashes of a camp-fire hidden in a ravine.

"Again!" said Bagheera, checking as though he had been turned into stone.

The body of a little wizened Gond lay with its feet in the ashes, and Bagheera looked enquiringly at Mowgli.

"That was done with a bamboo," said the boy, after one glance. "I have used such a thing among the buffaloes when I served the man pack. The Father of Cobras – I am sorrowful that I made a jest of him – knew the breed well, as I might have known. Said I not that men kill for idleness?"

"Indeed, they killed for the sake of red and blue stones," Bagheera answered. "Remember, *I* was in the king's cages at Oodeypore."

"One, two, three, four tracks," said Mowgli, stooping over the ashes. "Four tracks of men with shod feet. They do not go so quickly as Gonds. Now, what evil had the little woodman done to them? See, they talked together, all five, standing up, before they killed him. Bagheera, let us go back. My stomach is heavy in me, and yet it dances up and down like an oriole's nest at the end of a branch."

"It is no good hunting to leave game afoot. Follow!" said the panther. "Those eight shod feet have not gone far."

No more was said for fully an hour, as they took up the broad trail of the four men with shod feet.

It was clear, hot daylight now, and Bagheera said: "I smell smoke."

"Men are always more ready to eat than to run," Mowgli answered, trotting in and out between the low scrub bushes of the new jungle they were exploring. Bagheera, a little to his left, made an indescribable noise in his throat.

"Here is one that is done with feeding," said he. A tumbled bundle of gay-coloured clothes lay under a bush, and round it was some spilt flour.

"That was done by the bamboo again," said Mowgli. "See! That white dust is what men eat. They have taken the kill from this one – he carried their food – and given him for a kill to Chil the Kite."

"It is the third," said Bagheera.

"I will go with new, big frogs to the Father of Cobras, and feed him fat," said Mowgli to himself. "This drinker of elephant's blood is Death himself – but still I do not understand!"

"Follow!" said Bagheera.

They had not gone half a mile farther when they heard Ko the Crow singing a death-song in the top of a tamarisk under whose shade three men were lying. A half-dead fire smoked in the centre of the circle, beneath an iron plate which held a blackened and burned cake of unleavened bread. Close to the fire, and blazing in the sunshine, lay the ruby-and-turquoise *ankus*.

"The thing works quickly; all ends here," said Bagheera. "How did *these* die, Mowgli? There is no mark on any."

A Jungle-dweller gets to learn by experience as much as many doctors know of poisonous plants and berries. Mowgli sniffed the smoke that came up from the fire, broke off a morsel of the blackened bread, tasted it, and spat it out again.

"Apple of Death," he coughed. "The first must have made it ready in the food for *these*, who killed him, having first killed the Gond."

"Good hunting, indeed! The kills follow close," said Bagheera.

"Apple of Death" is what the Jungle call thorn-apple or dhatura, the readiest poison in all India.

"What now?" said the panther. "Must thou and I kill each other for yonder red-eyed slayer?"

"Can it speak?" said Mowgli in a whisper. "Did I do it a wrong when I threw it away? Between us two it can do no wrong, for we do not desire what men desire. If it be left here, it will assuredly continue to kill men one after another as fast as nuts fall in a high wind. I have no love to men, but even I would not have them die six in a night."

"What matter? They are only men. They killed one another, and were well pleased," said Bagheera. "That first little woodman hunted well."

"They are cubs none the less; and a cub will drown himself to bite the moon's light on the water. The fault was mine," said Mowgli, who spoke as though he knew all about everything. "I will never again bring into the Jungle strange things – not though they be as beautiful as flowers. This," – he handled the ankus gingerly – "goes back to the Father of Cobras. But first we must sleep, and we cannot sleep near these sleepers. Also we must bury *him*, lest he run away and kill another six. Dig me a hole under that tree."

"But, Little Brother," said Bagheera, moving off to the spot, "I tell thee it is no fault of the blood-drinker. The trouble is with the men."

"All one," said Mowgli. "Dig the hole deep. When we wake I will take him up and carry him back."

Two nights later, as the White Cobra sat mourning in the darkness of the vault, ashamed, and robbed, and alone, the turquoise ankus whirled through the hole in the wall, and clashed on the floor of golden coins.

"Father of Cobras," said Mowgli (he was careful to keep the other side of the wall), "get thee a young and ripe one of thine own people to help thee guard the King's Treasure, so that no man may come away alive any more."

"Ah-ha! It returns, then. I said the thing was Death. How comes it that thou are still alive?" the old Cobra mumbled, twining lovingly round the ankus-haft.

"By the Bull that bought me, I do not know! That thing has killed six times in a night. Let him go out no more."

The Song of the Little Hunter

Ere Mor the Peacock flutters, ere the Monkey-People cry,
    Ere Chil the Kite swoops down a furlong sheer,
Through the jungle very softly flits a shadow and a sigh –
    He is Fear, O Little Hunter, he is Fear!
Very softly down the glade runs a waiting, watching shade,
    And the whisper spreads and widens far and near;
And the sweat is on thy brow, for he passes even now –
    He is Fear, O Little Hunter, he is Fear!

Ere the moon has climbed the mountain, ere the rocks are ribbed with
        light,
    When the downward-dipping tails are dank and drear,
Comes a breathing hard behind thee, *snuffle-snuffle* through the night –
    It is Fear, O Little Hunter, it is Fear!
On thy knees and draw the bow; bid the shrilling arrow go;
    In the empty mocking thicket plunge the spear;
But thy hands are loosed and weak, and the blood has left thy cheek –
    It is Fear, O Little Hunter, it is Fear!

When the heat-cloud sucks the tempest, when the slivered pine trees fall,
    When the blinding, blaring rain-squalls lash and veer;
Through the trumpets of the thunder rings a voice more loud than all –
    It is Fear, O Little Hunter, it is Fear!

Now the spates are banked and deep; now the footless boulders leap;
    Now the lightning shows each littlest leaf-rib clear,
But thy throat is shut and dried, and thy heart against thy side
    Hammers: Fear, O Little Hunter – this is Fear!

Quiquern

The People of the Eastern Ice, they are melting like the snow –
They beg for coffee and sugar; they go where the white men go.
The People of the Western Ice, they learn to steal and fight –
They sell their furs to the trading-post; they sell their soul to the white.

The People of the Southern Ice, they trade with the whaler's crew;
Their women have many ribbons, but their tents are torn and few.
But the People of the Elder Ice, beyond the white man's ken –
Their spears are made of the narwhal horn, and they are the last of
    the Men.

Translation

"He has opened his eyes. Look!"
    "Put him in the skin again. He will be a strong dog. On the fourth month we will name him."

"For whom?" said Amoraq.

Kadlu's eye rolled round the skin-lined snow-house till it came to fourteen-year-old Kotuko sitting on the sleeping-bench, making a button out of walrus ivory. "Name him for me," said Kotuko, with a grin. "I shall need him some one day."

Kadlu grinned back till his eyes were almost buried in the fat of his flat cheeks, and nodded to Amoraq, while the puppy's fierce mother whined to see her baby wriggling far from reach in the little sealskin pouch hung above the warmth of the blubber-lamp. Kotuko went on with his carving, and

Kadlu threw a rolled bundle of leather dog-harnesses into a tiny little room that opened from one side of the house, slipped off his heavy deerskin hunting-suit, put it into a whalebone net that hung above another lamp, and dropped down on the sleeping-bench to whittle at a piece of frozen seal-meat till Amoraq, his wife, should bring the regular dinner of boiled meat and blood-soup. He had been out since early dawn at the seal-holes eight miles away, and had come home with three big seal. Half-way down the long low snow passage or tunnel that led to the inner door of the house you could hear snappings and yelpings, as the dogs of his sleigh-team, released from the day's work, scuffled for warm places.

When the yelpings grew too loud Kotuko lazily rolled off the sleeping-bench and picked up a whip with an eighteen-inch handle of springy whalebone, and twenty-five feet of heavy plaited thong. He dived into the passage, where it sounded as though all the dogs were eating him alive, but that was no more than their regular grace before meals. When he crawled out at the far end, half a dozen furry heads followed him with their eyes as he went to a sort of gallows of whale jawbones, from which the dog's meat was hung, split off the frozen stuff in big lumps with a broad-headed spear, and waited, his whip in one hand and the meat in the other. Each beast was called by name – the weakest first, and woe betide any dog that moved out of his turn, for the tapering lash would shoot out like thonged lightning and flick away an inch or so of hair and hide. Each beast simply growled, snapped once, choked over his portion, and hurried back to the passage, while the boy stood up on the snow under the blazing Northern Lights and dealt out justice. The last to be served was the big black leader of the team, who kept order when the dogs were harnessed, and to him Kotuko gave a double allowance of meat as well as an extra crack of the whip.

"Ah!" said Kotuko, coiling up the lash, "I have a little one over the lamp that will make a great many howlings. *Sarpok!* Get in!"

He crawled back over the huddled dogs, dusted the dry snow from his furs with the whalebone beater that Amoraq kept by the door, tapped the skin-lined roof of the house to shake off any icicles that might have fallen from the dome of snow above, and curled up on the bench. The dogs in the passage snored and whined in their sleep, the boy-baby in Amoraq's deep fur hood kicked and choked and gurgled, and the mother of the newly named puppy lay at Kotuko's side, her eyes fixed on the bundle of sealskin, warm and safe above the broad yellow flame of the lamp.

And all this happened far away to the north, beyond Labrador, beyond Hudson Strait where the great tides throw the ice about – north of Melville Peninsula – north even of the narrow Fury and Hecla Strait – on the north shore of Baffin Land where Bylot Island stands above the ice of Lancaster Sound like a pudding-bowl wrong side up. North of Lancaster Sound there is little we know anything about, except North Devon and Ellesmere Land, but even there live a few scattered people, next door, as it were, to the very Pole.

Kadlu was an Innuit – what you call an Esquimau – and his tribe, some thirty persons, all told, belonged to the Tununirmiut – "the country lying at the back of something." On the maps that desolate coast is written Navy Board Inlet, but the Innuit name is best because that country lies at the very back of everything in the world. For nine months of the year there is only ice and snow and gale after gale, with a cold no one can realise who has never seen the thermometer go down even to zero. For six months of those nine it is dark, and that is what makes it so horrible. In the three months of summer it only freezes every other day and every night, and then the snow begins to weep away from the southerly slopes, and a few ground-willows put out their woolly buds, a tiny stonecrop or so makes believe to blossom, beaches of fine gravel and rounded stones run down to the open sea, and polished boulders and streaked rocks lift up above the granulated snow. But all that goes in a few weeks, and the wild winter locks down again on the land, while at sea the ice tears up and down the offing, jamming and ramming, and splitting and hitting, and pounding and grounding till it all freezes together, ten feet thick, from the shore outward to deep water.

In the winter Kadlu would follow the seal to the edge of this land-ice and spear them as they came up to breathe at their blow-holes. The seal must have open sea-water to live and catch fish in, and the ice would sometimes run eighty miles without a break from the nearest land. In the spring he and his people retreated from the thawing ice to the rocky main-land, where they put up tents of skins and snared the sea-birds, or speared the young seal basking on the beaches. Later, they would go south into Baffin Land after the reindeer and to get their year's store of salmon from the hundreds of streams and lakes of the interior, coming back north in September or October for the musk-ox hunting and the regular winter sealery. This travelling was done with dog-sleighs, twenty and thirty miles a day, or sometimes down the coast in big skin "woman-boats", when the dogs and the babies lay among the feet of the rowers, and the women sang songs as they glided from cape to cape over the glassy, cold waters. All the luxuries that the Tununirmiut knew came from the south – drift-wood for sleigh-runners, rod-iron for harpoon-tips, steel knives, tin kettles that cooked food much better than the old soapstone affairs, flint and steel, and even matches, coloured ribbons for the women's hair, little cheap mirrors, and red cloth for the edging of deerskin dress-jackets. Kadlu traded the rich creamy-twisted narwhal horn and musk-ox teeth (these are just as valuable as pearls) to the Southern Innuit, and they in turn traded with the whalers and the missionary posts of Exeter and Cumberland sounds. And so the chain went on till a kettle picked up by a ship's cook in the Bhendy Bazaar might end its days over a blubber lamp somewhere on the cool side of the Arctic Circle.

Kadlu being a good hunter was rich in iron harpoons, snow-knives, bird-darts, and all the other things that make life easy up there in the great cold, and he was the head of his tribe, or, as they say, "the man who knows all about it by practice". This did not give him any authority, except now and then he could advise his friends to change their hunting-grounds, but Kotuko used it to domineer a little, in the lazy fat Innuit fashion, over the other boys when they came out at night to play ball in the moonlight, or to sing the Child's Song to the Aurora Borealis.

But at fourteen an Innuit feels himself a man, and Kotuko was tired of making snares for wild-fowl and kit-foxes, and very tired of helping the women to chew seal and deerskins (that supple them as nothing else can) the long day through while the men were out hunting. He wanted to go into the *quaggi*, the Singing-House, when the hunters gathered there for their mysteries, and the *angekok*, the sorcerer, frightened them into the most delightful fits after the lamps were put out, and you could hear the Spirit of the Reindeer stamping on the roof, and when a spear was thrust out into the open black night it came back covered with hot blood. He wanted to throw his big boots into the net with the tired air of the head of a family, and to gamble with the hunters when they dropped in of an evening and played a sort of home-made roulette with a tin pot and a nail. There were hundreds of things that he wanted to do, but the grown men laughed at him and said: "Wait till you have been in the buckle, Kotuko. Hunting is not *all* catching."

Now that his father had named a puppy for him things looked brighter. An Innuit does not waste a good dog on his son till the boy knows something of dog-driving, and Kotuko was more than sure that he knew more than everything.

If the puppy had not had an iron constitution he would have died from over-stuffing and over-handling. Kotuko made him a tiny harness with a trace to it, and hauled him all over the house-floor shouting: "*Aua! Ja aua!*" [Go to the right.] "*Choiachoi, ja choiachoi!*" [Go to the left.] "*Ohaha!*" [Stop.] The puppy did not like it at all, but being fished for in this way was pure happiness beside being put to the sleigh for the first time. He just sat down on the snow and played with the seal-hide trace that ran from his harness to the *pitu*, the big thong in the bows of the sleigh. Then the team started and the puppy found the heavy ten-foot sleigh running up his back and dragging him along the snow, while Kotuko laughed till the tears ran down his face. There followed days and days of the cruel whip that hisses like the wind over ice, and his companions all bit him because he did not know his work, and the harness chafed him, and he was not allowed to sleep with Kotuko any more, but had to take the coldest place in the passage. It was a sad time for the puppy.

The boy learned, too, as fast as the dog, though a dog-sleigh is a heart-breaking thing to manage. Each beast is harnessed – the weakest nearest to the driver – by his own separate trace, which runs under his left fore leg to the main thong, where it is fastened by a sort of button and loop which can be slipped by a turn of the wrist, thus freeing one dog at a time. This is very necessary, because young dogs often get the trace between their hind legs, where it cuts to the bone. And they one and all *will* go visiting their friends as they run, jumping in and out among the traces. Then they fight, and the result is more mixed than a wet fishing-line next morning. A great deal of trouble can be avoided by scientific use of the whip. Every Innuit boy prides himself as being a master of the long lash, but it is easy to flick at a mark on the ground and difficult to lean forward and catch a shirking dog just behind the shoulders when the sleigh is going at full speed. If you call one dog's name for "visiting" and accidentally lash another the two will fight it out at once, and stop all the others. Again, if you travel with a companion and begin to talk, or by yourself and sing, the dogs will halt, turn round, and sit down and hear what you have to say. Kotuko was run away from once or twice through forgetting to block the sleigh when he stopped, and he broke many lashings and ruined a few thongs ere he could be trusted with a full team of eight and the light sleigh. Then he felt himself a person of consequence, and on smooth black ice, with a bold heart and a quick elbow, he smoked along over the levels as fast as a pack in full cry. He would go ten miles to the seal-holes, and when he was on the hunting-grounds he would twitch a trace loose from the *pitu* and free the big black leader, who was then the cleverest dog in the team. As soon as the dog had scented a breathing-hole Kotuko would reverse the sleigh, driving a couple of sawed-off antlers that stuck up like perambulator handles deep into the snow, so that the team could not get away. Then he would crawl forward inch by inch and wait till the seal came up to breathe. Then he would stab down swiftly with his spear and running line, and presently would haul his seal on to the lip of the ice while the black leader came up and helped to pull the carcass across the ice to the sleigh. That was the time when the harnessed dogs yelled and foamed with excitement, and Kotuko laid the long lash like a red-hot bar across all their faces till the carcass froze stiff. Going home was the heavy work. The loaded sleigh had to be humoured among the rough ice, and the dogs sat down and looked hungrily at the seal instead of pulling. At last they would strike the well-worn sleigh-road to the village, and *toodle-ki-yi* along the ringing ice, heads down and tails up, while Kotuko struck up the "*Angutivun tai-na tau-na-ne taina*" (the Song of the Returning Hunter), and voices hailed him from house to house under all that dim, star-litten sky.

When Kotuko, the dog, came to his full growth, he enjoyed himself, too. He fought his way up the team steadily, fight after fight, till one fine evening over their food he tackled the big black leader (Kotuko, the boy, saw fair play) and made second dog of him, as they say. So he was promoted to the long thong of the leading dog, running five feet in advance of all the others: it was his bounden duty to stop all fighting, in harness or out of it, and he wore a collar of copper wire, very thick and heavy. On special occasions he was fed with cooked food inside the house, and sometimes was allowed to sleep on the bench with Kotuko. He was a good seal-dog, and would keep a musk-ox at bay by running round him and snapping at his heels. He would even – and this for a sleigh-dog is the last proof of bravery – he would even stand up to the gaunt Arctic wolf, whom all dogs of the north, as a rule, fear beyond anything that walks the snow. He and his master – they did not count the team of ordinary dogs as company – hunted together, day after day and night after night – fur-wrapped boy and savage, long-haired, narrow-eyed, white-fanged, yellow brute. All an Innuit has to do is to get food and skins for himself and his family. The women-folk make the skins into clothing, and occasionally help in trapping small game, but the bulk of the food – and they eat enormously – must be found by the men. If the supply fails there is no one up there to buy or beg or borrow from. The people must die.

An Innuit does not think of these chances till he is forced to. Kadlu, Kotuko, Amoraq, and the boy-baby who kicked about the fur hood and chewed pieces of blubber all day, were as happy together as any family in the world. They came of a very gentle race – an Innuit seldom loses his temper, and almost never strikes a child – who did not know exactly what telling a real lie meant, still less how to steal. They were content to spear their living out of the heart of the bitter, hopeless cold; to smile oily smiles, and tell queer ghost- and fairy-tales of evenings; and eat till they could eat no more, and sing the endless woman's song, "*Amna aya, aya amna, ah! ah!*" through the long lamp-lighted days as they mended their clothes and hunting gear.

But one terrible winter everything betrayed them. The Tununirmiut returned from the yearly salmon fishing and made their houses on the fresh ice to the north of Bylot Island, ready to go after the seal as soon as the sea froze. But it was an early and savage autumn. All through September there were continuous gales that broke up the smooth seal-ice where it was only four or five feet thick and forced it inland, and piled a great barrier some twenty miles broad of lumped and ragged and needly ice, over which it was impossible to draw the sleighs. The edge of the floe off which the seal were used to fishing in winter lay perhaps twenty miles beyond this barrier and out of reach of the Tununirmiut. Even so, they might have managed to scrape through the winter on their stock of frozen salmon and stored blubber and what the traps gave them, but in December one of their hunters came across a *tupik*, a skin-tent, of three women and a girl nearly dead, whose men had come down from the far north and been crushed in their little skin hunting-boats while they were out after the long-horned narwhal. Kadlu, of course, could only distribute the women among the huts of the winter village, for no Innuit dare refuse a meal to a stranger. He never knows when his own turn may come to beg. Amoraq took the girl, who was about fourteen, into her own house as a sort of servant. From the cut of her sharp-pointed hoop, and the long diamond pattern of her white deer-skin leggings, they supposed she came from Ellesmere Land. She had never seen tin cooking-pots or wooden-shod sleighs before, but Kotuko, the boy, and Kotuko, the dog, were rather fond of her.

Then all the foxes went south, and even the wolverine, that growling, blunt-headed little thief of the snow, did not take the trouble to follow the line of empty traps that Kotuko set. The tribe lost a couple of their best hunters, who were badly crippled in a fight with a musk-ox, and this threw more work on the others. Kotuko went out, day after day, with a light hunting-sleigh and six or seven of the strongest dogs, looking till his eyes ached for some patch of clear ice where a seal might, perhaps, have scratched a breathing-hole. Kotuko, the dog, ranged far and wide, and in the dead stillness of the ice-fields Kotuko, the boy, could hear his half-choked whine of excitement, above a seal-hole three miles away, as plainly as though he were at his elbow. When the dog found a hole the boy would build himself a little low snow wall to keep off the worst of the bitter wind, and there he would wait ten, twelve, twenty hours for the seal to come up to breathe, his eyes glued to the tiny mark he had made above the hole to guide the downward thrust of his harpoon, a little sealskin mat under his feet, and his legs tied together in the *tutareang* – the buckle that the old hunters had talked about. This helps to keep a man's legs from twitching as he waits and waits and waits for the quick-eared seal to rise. Though there is no excitement in it, you can easily believe that the sitting still in the buckle, with the thermometer perhaps forty degrees below zero, is the hardest work an Innuit knows. When a seal was caught, Kotuko, the dog, would bound forward, his trace trailing behind him, and help to pull the body to the sleigh where the tired and hungry dogs lay sullenly under the lee of the broken ice.

A seal did not go very far, for each mouth in the little village had a right to be filled, and neither bone, hide, nor sinew was wasted. The dogs' meat was taken for human use, and Amoraq fed the team with pieces of old summer skin-tents raked out from under the sleeping-bench, and they howled and howled again, and waked to howl hungrily. One could tell by the lamps in the huts that famine was near. In good seasons, when blubber was plentiful, the light in the boat-shaped bowls would be two feet high – cheerful, oily, and yellow. Now it was a bare six inches: Amoraq carefully pricked down the moss wick when an unwatched flame brightened for a moment, and the eyes of all the family followed her hand. The horror of famine up there in the great cold is not so much dying as dying in the dark. All the Innuit dread the dark that presses on them without a break for six months in each year, and when the lamps are low in the houses the minds of people begin to be shaken and confused.

But worse was to come.

The underfed dogs snapped and growled in the passages, glaring at the cold stars and snuffing into the bitter wind night after night. When they stopped howling the silence fell down again as solid and as heavy as a snowdrift against a door, and men could hear the beating of their blood in the thin passages of the ear and the thumping of their own hearts that sounded as loud as the noise of sorcerers' drums beaten across the snow. One night Kotuko, the dog, who had been unusually sullen in harness, leaped up and pushed his head against Kotuko's knee. Kotuko patted him, but the dog still pushed blindly forward, fawning. Then Kadlu waked and gripped the heavy wolf-like head and stared into the glassy eyes. The dog whimpered as though he were afraid, and shivered between Kadlu's knees. The hair rose about his neck and he growled as though a stranger were at the door, then he barked joyously and rolled on the ground and bit at Kotuko's boot like a puppy.

"What is it?" said Kotuko, for he was beginning to be afraid.

"The sickness," Kadlu answered. "It is the dog-sickness." Kotuko the dog lifted his nose and howled and howled again.

"I have not seen this before. What will he do?" said Kotuko.

Kadlu shrugged one shoulder a little and crossed the hut for his short stabbing-harpoon. The big dog looked at him, howled again, and slunk away down the passage, while the other dogs drew aside right and left to give him ample room. When he was out on the snow he barked furiously, as though on the trail of a musk-ox, and, barking and leaping and frisking, passed out of sight. His trouble was not hydrophobia but simple plain madness. The cold and the hunger, and above all the dark, had turned his head, and when the terrible dog-sickness once shows itself in a team it spreads like wild-fire. Next hunting day another dog sickened, and was killed then and there by Kotuko as he bit and struggled among the traces. Then the black second-dog who had been the leader in the old days suddenly gave tongue on an imaginary reindeer track, and when they slipped him from the *pitu* he flew at the throat of an ice-cliff, and ran away as his leader had done, his harness on his back. After that no one would take the dogs out again. They needed them for something else, and the dogs knew it, and though they were tied down and fed by hand their eyes were full of despair and fear. To make things worse the old women began to tell ghost-tales, and to say that they had met the spirits of the dead hunters lost that autumn who prophesied all sorts of horrible things.

Kotuko grieved more for the loss of his dog than anything else, for though an Innuit eats enormously he also knows how to starve. But the hunger, the darkness, the cold, and the exposure told on his strength, and he began to hear voices inside his head, and to see people, who were not there, out of the tail of his eye. One night – he had unbuckled himself after ten hours waiting above a "blind" seal-hole, and was staggering back to the village faint and dizzy – he halted to lean his back against a boulder, which happened to be supported like a rocking-stone on a single jutting point of ice. His weight disturbed the balance of the thing, it rolled over ponderously, and as Kotuko sprang aside to avoid it, slid after him, squeaking and hissing on the ice-slope.

That was enough for Kotuko. He had been brought up to believe that every rock and boulder had its owner (its *inua*), who was generally a one-eyed kind of a Woman-Thing called a *tornaq*, and that when a *tornaq* meant to help a man she rolled after him inside her stone house, and asked him whether he would take her for a guardian spirit. (In summer thaws the ice-propped rocks and boulders roll and slip all over the face of the land, so you can easily see how the idea of live stones arose.) Kotuko heard the blood beating in his ears as he had heard it all day, and he thought that was the *tornaq* of the stone speaking to him. Before he reached home he was quite certain that he had held a long conversation with her, and as all his people believed that this was quite possible no one contradicted him.

"She said to me: 'I jump down, I jump down from my place on the snow,'" cried Kotuko with hollow eyes, leaning forward in the half-lighted hut. "She said: 'I will be a guide.' She says: 'I will guide you to the good seal-holes.' Tomorrow I go out and the *tornaq* will guide me."

Then the *angekok*, the village sorcerer, came in and Kotuko told him the tale a second time. It lost nothing in the telling.

"Follow the *tornait* [the spirits of the stones] and they will bring us food again," said the *angekok*.

Now the girl from the north had been lying near the lamp, eating very little and saying less for days past, but when Amoraq and Kadlu next morning packed and lashed a little hand-sleigh for Kotuko, and loaded it with his hunting-gear and as much blubber and frozen seal-meat as they could spare, she took the pulling-rope, and stepped out boldly at the boy's side.

"Your house is my house," she said, as the little bone-shod sleigh squeaked and bumped behind them in the awful Arctic night.

"My house is your house," said Kotuko, "but *I* think that we shall both go to Sedna together."

Now Sedna is the Mistress of the Underworld, and the Innuit believe that every one who dies must spend a year in her horrible country before going to Quadliparmiut, the Happy Place, where it never freezes and fat reindeer trot up when you call.

Through the village people were shouting: "The *tornait* have spoken to Kotuko. They will show him open ice. He will bring us the seal again." Their voices were soon swallowed up by the cold empty dark, and Kotuko and the girl shouldered close together as they strained on the pulling-rope or humoured the sleigh through the ice, in the direction of the Polar Sea. Kotuko insisted that the *tornaq* of the stone had told him to go north, and so north they went under Tuktuqdjung the Reindeer – those stars that we call the Great Bear.

No European could have made five miles a day over the ice-rubbish and the sharp-edged drifts. But those two knew exactly the turn of the wrist that coaxes a sleigh round a hummock, the jerk that neatly lifts it out of an ice-crack, and the exact strength that goes to the few quiet strokes of the spear-head that make a path possible when everything looks hopeless.

The girl said nothing, but bowed her head, and the long wolverine-fur fringe of her ermine hood blew across her broad, dark face. The sky above them was an intense velvety black, changing to bands of Indian red on the horizon, where the great stars burned like street-lamps. From time to time a greenish wave of the Northern Lights would roll across the hollow of the high heavens, flick like a flag and disappear, or a meteor would crackle from darkness to darkness trailing a shower of sparks behind. Then they could see the ridged and furrowed surface of the floe all tipped and laced with strange colours – red, copper, and bluish – but in the ordinary starlight everything turned to one frost-bitten grey. The floe, as you will remember, had been battered and tormented by the autumn gales till it was one frozen earthquake. There were gullies and ravines; and holes like gravel-pits cut in ice, lumps and scattered pieces frozen down to the original floor of the floe; blotches of old black ice that had been thrust under the floe in some gale, and heaved up again; roundish boulders of ice; saw-like edges of ice carved by the snow that flies before the wind and sunk pits where thirty or forty acres lay five or six feet below the level of the rest of the field. From a little distance you might have taken the lumps for seal, or walrus, over-turned sleighs, or men on a hunting expedition, or even the great Ten-legged White Spirit-Bear himself, but in spite of these fantastic shapes, all on the very edge of starting into life, there was neither sound nor the least faint echo of sound. And through this silence and through this waste where the sudden lights flapped and went out again, the sleigh and the two that pulled it crawled like things in a nightmare – a nightmare of the end of the world at the end of the world.

When they were tired Kotuko would make what the hunters call a "half-house," a very small snow hut, into which they would huddle with the travelling lamp, and try to thaw out the frozen seal-meat. When they had slept, the march began again – thirty miles a day to get five miles northward. The girl was always very silent, but Kotuko muttered to himself and broke out into songs he had learned in the Singing-House – summer songs, and reindeer and salmon songs – all horribly out of place at that season. He would declare that he heard the *tornaq* growling to him, and would run wildly up a hummock tossing his arms and speaking in loud threatening tones. To tell the truth, Kotuko was very nearly crazy for the time being, but the girl was sure that he was being guided by his guardian spirit, and that everything would come right. She was not surprised, therefore, when at the end of the fourth march, Kotuko, whose eyes were burning like fireballs in his head, told her that his *tornaq* was following them across the snow in the shape of a two-headed dog. The girl looked where Kotuko pointed, and some Thing seemed to slip into a ravine. It was certainly not human, but everybody knew that the *tornait* preferred to appear in the shape of bear and seal and such like.

It might have been the Ten-legged White Spirit-Bear himself, or it might have been anything, for Kotuko and the girl were so starved that their eyes were untrustworthy. They had trapped nothing and seen no trace of game since they had left the village; their food would not hold out for another week, and there was a gale coming. A polar storm will blow for ten days without a break, and all that while it is certain death to be abroad. Kotuko laid up a snow-house large enough to take in the hand-sleigh (it is never wise to be separated from your meat), and while he was shaping the last irregular block of ice that makes the keystone of the roof he saw a Thing looking at him from a little cliff of ice half a mile away. The air was hazy, and the Thing seemed to be forty feet long and ten feet high, with twenty feet of tail and a shape that quivered all along the outlines. The girl saw it too, but instead of crying aloud with terror, said quietly: "That is Quiquern. What comes after?"

"He will speak to me," said Kotuko, but the snow-knife trembled in his hand as he spoke, because however much a man may believe that he is a friend of strange and ugly spirits he seldom likes to be taken quite at his

275

word. Quiquern, too, is the phantom of a gigantic toothless dog without any hair, who is supposed to live in the far north, and to wander about the country just before things are going to happen. They may be pleasant or unpleasant things, but not even the sorcerers care to speak about Quiquem. He makes the dogs go mad. Like the Spirit-Bear he has several extra pairs of legs – six or eight – and this Thing jumping up and down in the haze had more legs than any real dog needed.

Kotuko and the girl huddled into their hut quickly. Of course if Quiquem had wanted them he could have torn it to pieces above their heads, but the sense of a foot-thick snow-wall between themselves and the wicked dark was great comfort. The gale broke with a shriek of wind like the shriek of a train, and for three days and three nights it held, never varying one point and never lulling even for a minute. They fed the stone-lamp between their knees and nibbled at the half-warm seal-meat, and watched the black soot gather on the roof for seventy-two long hours. The girl counted up the food in the sleigh; there was not more than two days' supply, and Kotuko looked over the iron heads and the deer-sinew fastenings of his harpoon and his seal-lance and his bird-dart. There was nothing else to do.

"We shall go to Sedna soon – very soon," the girl whispered. "In three days we shall lie down and go. Will your *tornaq* do nothing? Sing her an *angekok's* song to make her come here."

He began to sing in the high-pitched howl of the magic songs, and the gale went down slowly. In the middle of his song the girl started, laid her mittened hand and then her head to the ice floor of the hut. Kotuko followed her example, and the two kneeled staring into each other's eyes, and listening with every nerve. He ripped a thin sliver of whale-bone from the rim of a bird-snare that lay on the sleigh, and after straightening set it up upright in a little hole in the ice, firming it down with his mitten. It was almost as delicately adjusted as a compass-needle, and now, instead of listening, they watched. The thin rod quivered a little – the least little jar in the world – then vibrated steadily for a few seconds, came to rest, and vibrated again, this time nodding to another point of the compass.

"Too soon!" said Kotuko. "Some big floe has broken far away outside."

The girl pointed at the rod and shook her head. "It is the big breaking," she said. "Listen to the ground-ice. It knocks."

When they kneeled this time they heard the most curious muffled grunts and knockings apparently under their feet. Sometimes it sounded as though a blind puppy were squeaking above the lamp; then as if a stone were being ground on hard ice; and again, like muffled blows on a drum; but all dragged out and made small, as though they had travelled through a little horn a weary distance away.

"We shall not go to Sedna lying down," said Kotuko. "It is the breaking. The *tornaq* has cheated us. We shall die."

All this may sound absurd enough, but the two were face to face with a very real danger. The three days' gale had driven the deep water of Baffin Bay southerly, and piled it on to the edge of the far-reaching land-ice that stretches from Bylot Island to the west. Also, the strong current which sets east out of Lancaster Sound carried with it mile upon mile of what they call pack-ice – rough ice that has not frozen into fields. And this pack was bombarding the floe at the same time that the swell and heave of the storm-worked sea was weakening and undermining it. What Kotuko and the girl had been listening to were the faint echoes of that fight thirty or forty miles away, and the tell-tale little rod quivered to the shock of it.

Now, as the Innuit say, when the ice once wakes after its long winter sleep there is no knowing what may happen, for solid floe-ice changes shape almost as quickly as a cloud. The gale was evidently a spring gale sent out of time and anything was possible.

Yet the two were happier in their minds than before. If the floe broke up there would be no more waiting and suffering. Spirits, goblins, and witch-people were moving about on the racking ice, and they might find themselves stepping into Sedna's country side by side with all sorts of wild Things, the flush of excitement still on them. When they left the hut after the gale, the noise on the horizon was steadily growing, and the tough ice moaned and buzzed all round them.

"It is still waiting," said Kotuko.

On the top of a hummock sat or crouched the eight-legged Thing that they had seen three days before – and it howled horribly.

"Let us follow," said the girl. "It may know some way that does not lead to Sedna." But she reeled from weakness as she took the pulling-rope. The Thing moved off slowly and clumsily across the ridges, heading always towards the westward and the land, and they followed while the growling thunder at the edge of the floe rolled nearer and nearer. The floe's lip was split and cracked in every direction for three or four miles inland, and great pans of ten-foot-thick ice, from a few yards to twenty acres square, were jolting and ducking and surging into one another and into the yet unbroken floe as the heavy swell took and shook and spouted between them. This battering-rain ice was, so to speak, the first army that the sea was flinging against the floe. The incessant crash and jar of these cakes almost drowned the ripping sound of sheets of pack-ice driven bodily under the floe as cards are hastily pushed under a tablecloth. Where the water was shallow these sheets would be piled one atop of the other till the bottommost touched mud fifty feet down and the discoloured sea banked behind the muddy ice till the increasing pressure drove all forward again. In addition to the floe and the pack-ice, the gale and the currents were bringing down true bergs, sailing mountains of ice, snapped off from the Greenland side of things or the north shore of Melville Bay. They pounded in solemnly, the waves breaking white round them, and advanced on the floe like an old-time fleet under full sail. But a berg that seemed ready to carry the world before it would ground helplessly, reel over, and wallow in a lather of foam and mud, and flying frozen spray, while a much smaller and lower one would rip and ride into the flat floe, flinging tons of rubbish on either side, and cutting a track a mile long before it was stopped. Some fell like swords, shearing a raw-edged canal, and others splintered into a shower of blocks, weighing scores of tons apiece, that whirled and skirled among the hummocks. Others, again, rose up bodily out of the water when they shoaled, twisted as though in pain, and fell solidly on their sides, while the sea threshed over their shoulders. This trampling and crowding and bending and buckling and arching of the ice into every possible shape was going on as far as the eye could reach all along the north line of the floe. From where Kotuko and the girl were, the confusion looked no more than an uneasy rippling crawling movement under the horizon, but it came towards them each moment, and they could hear far away to landward a heavy booming, as it might have been the boom of artillery through a fog. That showed that the floe was being jammed home against the iron cliffs of Bylot Island, the land to the southward, behind them.

"This has never been before," said Kotuko, staring stupidly. "This is not the time. How can the floe break *now*?"

"Follow *that!*" the girl cried, pointing to the Thing half limping, half running distractedly before them. They followed, tugging the hand-sleigh, while nearer and nearer came the roaring march of the ice. At last the fields round them cracked and starred in every direction, and the cracks opened and snapped like the teeth of wolves. But where the Thing rested, on a mound of old and scattered ice-blocks some fifty feet high, there was no motion. Kotuko leaped forward wildly, dragged the girl after him, and crawled to the bottom of the mound. The talking of the ice grew louder and louder round them, but the mound stayed fast, and as the girl looked at him he threw his right elbow upwards and outwards, making the Innuit sign for land in the shape of an island. And land it was that the eight-legged limping Thing had led them to – some granite-tipped, sand-beached islet off the coast, shod and sheathed and masked with ice so that no man could have told it from the floe, but at the bottom solid earth, and no shifting ice. The smashing and rebound of the floes as they grounded and splintered marked the borders of it, and a friendly shoal ran out to the northward, turning aside the rush of the heaviest ice exactly as a ploughshare turns over loam. There was a danger, of course, that some heavily squeezed ice-field might shoot up the beach and plane off the top of the islet bodily, but that did not trouble Kotuko and the girl, when they made their snow-house and began to eat, and heard the ice hammer and skid along the beach. The Thing had disappeared, and Kotuko was talking excitedly about his power over spirits as he crouched round the lamp. In the middle of his wild sayings the girl began to laugh and rock herself backwards and forwards.

Behind her shoulder, crawling into the hut crawl by crawl, there were two heads, one yellow and one black, that belonged to two of the most sorrowful and ashamed dogs that ever you saw. Kotuko, the dog, was one and the black leader was the other. Both were now fat, well-looking, and quite restored to their proper minds, but coupled to each other in an extraordinary fashion. When the black leader ran off, you remember, his harness was still on him. He must have met Kotuko, the dog, and played or fought with him, for his shoulder-loop had caught in the plaited copper wire of Kotuko's collar, and had drawn tight, so that neither dog could get at the trace to gnaw it apart, but each was fastened sidelong to his neighbour's neck. That, with the freedom of hunting on their own account, must have helped to cure their madness. They were very sober.

The girl pushed the two shame-faced creatures towards Kotuko, and, sobbing with laughter, cried: "That is Quiquern, who led us to safe ground. Look at his eight legs and double head!"

Kotuko cut them free, and they fell into his arms, yellow and black together, trying to explain how they had got their senses back again. Kotuko ran a hand down their ribs, which were round and well clothed. "They have found food," he said, with a grin. "I do not think we shall go to Sedna so soon. My *tornaq* sent these. The sickness has left them."

As soon as they had greeted Kotuko these two, who had been forced to sleep and eat and hunt together for the past few weeks, flew at each other's throats, and there was a beautiful battle in the snow-house. "Empty dogs do not fight," Kotuko said. "They have found the seal. Let us sleep. We shall find food."

When they waked there was open water on the north beach of the island, and all the loosened ice had been driven landward. The first sound of the surf is one of the most delightful that the Innuit can hear, for it means that spring is on the road. Kotuko and the girl took hold of hands and smiled. The clear full roar of the surge among the ice reminded them of salmon and reindeer time and the smell of blossoming ground-willows. Even as they looked the sea began to skim over between the floating cakes of ice, so intense was the cold, but on the horizon there was a vast red glare, and that was the light of the sunken sun. It was more like hearing him yawn in his sleep than seeing him rise, and the glare lasted for only a few minutes, but it marked the turn of the year. Nothing, they felt, could alter that.

Kotuko found the dogs fighting outside over a fresh-killed seal who was following the fish that a gale always disturbs. He was the first of some twenty or thirty seal that landed on the island in the course of the day, and, till the sea froze hard, there were hundreds of keen black heads rejoicing in the shallow free water and floating about with the floating ice.

It was good to eat seal-liver again; to fill the lamps recklessly with blubber and watch the flame blaze three feet in the air; but as soon as the new sea-ice bore, Kotuko and the girl loaded the hand-sleigh and made the two dogs pull as they had never pulled in their lives, for they feared what might have happened in their village. The weather was as pitiless as ever, but it is easier to draw a sleigh loaded with good food than to hunt starving. They left five-and-twenty seal carcasses buried in the ice of the beach all ready for use and hurried back to their people. The dogs showed them the way as soon as Kotuko told them what was expected, and though there was no sign of a landmark, in two days they were giving tongue outside Kadlu's village. Only three dogs answered them; the others had been eaten, and the houses were nearly dark. But when Kotuko shouted, "*Ojo!*" [boiled meat] weak voices answered, and when he called the roll-call of the village name by name, very distinctly, there were no gaps in it.

An hour later the lamps blazed in Kadlu's house, snow-water was heating, the pots were beginning to simmer, and the snow was dripping from the roof as Amoraq made ready a meal for all the village, and the boy-baby chewed at a strip of rich nutty blubber, and the hunters slowly and methodically filled themselves to the very brim with seal-meat. Kotuko and the girl told their tale. The two dogs sat between them, and whenever their names came in they cocked an ear apiece and looked most thoroughly ashamed of themselves. A dog who has once gone mad and recovered, the Innuit say, is safe against all further attacks.

"So the *tornaq* did not forget us," said Kotuko. "The storm blew; the ice broke, and the seal swam in behind the fish that were frightened by the storm. Now the new seal-holes are not two days' distant. Let the good hunters go tomorrow and bring back the seal I have speared – twenty-five seal buried in the ice. When we have eaten those we will all follow the seal on the floe."

"What do *you* do?" said the village sorcerer, in the same sort of voice as he used to Kadlu, richest of the Tununirmiut.

Kotuko looked at the girl from the north and said quietly: "*We* build a house." He pointed to the northwest side of Kadlu's house, for that is the side on which the married son or daughter always lives.

The girl turned her hands, palm upward, with a little despairing shake of her head. She was a foreigner, picked up starving, and she could bring nothing to house-keeping.

Amoraq jumped from the bench where she sat and began to sweep things into the girl's lap – stone-lamps, iron skin-scrapers, tin kettles, deerskins embroidered with musk-ox teeth, and real canvas-needles such as sailors use – the finest dowry ever given on the far edge of the Arctic Circle, and the girl from the north bowed her head down to the very floor.

"Also these!" said Kotuko, laughing and signing to the dogs, who thrust their cold muzzles into the girl's face.

"Ah," said the *angekok*, with an important cough, as though he had been thinking it all over. "As soon as Kotuko left the village I went to the Sing-ing-House and sang magic. I sang all the long nights and called upon the Spirit of the Reindeer. *My* singing made the gale blow that broke the ice and drew the two dogs towards Kotuko when the ice would have crushed his bones. *My* song drew the seal in behind the broken ice. My body lay still in the *quaggi*, but my spirit ran about on the ice and guided Kotuko and the dogs in all the things they did. *I* did it."

Everybody was full and sleepy, so no one contradicted, and the *angekok* helped himself to yet another lump of boiled meat and lay down to sleep with the others, in the warm, well-lighted, oil-smelling home.

Now Kotuko, who drew very well in the Innuit style, scratched pictures of all these adventures on a long flat piece of ivory with a hole at one end. When he and the girl went north to Ellesmere Land in the year of the Wonderful Open Winter, he left the picture-story with Kadlu, who lost it in the shingle when his dog-sleigh broke down one summer on the beach of Lake Nettilling at Nikosiring, and there a Lake Innuit found it next spring and sold it to a man at Imigen who was interpreter on a Cumberland Sound whaler, and he sold it to Hans Olsen, who was afterwards a quar-termaster on board a big steamer that took tourists to the North Cape in Norway. When the tourist season was over the steamer ran between London and Australia, stopping at Ceylon, and there Olsen sold the ivory to a Cingalese jeweller for two imitation sapphires. I found it under some rubbish in a house at Colombo, and have translated it from one end to the other.

Angutivun Tania

This is a very free translation of the Song of the Returning Hunter, as the men used to sing it after seal-spearing. The Innuit always repeat things over and over again.

> Our gloves are stiff with the frozen blood,
> Our furs with the drifted snow,
> As we come in with the seal – the seal!
> In from the edge of the floe.
>
> *Au jana! Aua! Oho! Haq!*
> And the yelping dog-teams go,
> And the long whips crack, and the men come back,
> Back from the edge of the floe!
>
> We tracked the seal to his secret place,
> We heard him scratch below,
> We made our mark, and we watched beside,
> Out on the edge of the floe.
>
> We raised our lance when he rose to breathe,
> We drove it downward – so!
> And we played him thus, and we killed him thus,
> Out on the edge of the floe.
>
> Our gloves are glued with the frozen blood,
> Our eyes with the drifting snow;
> But we come back to our wives again,
> Back from the edge of the floe!

Au jana! Aua! Oha! Haq!
  And the yelping dog-team go,
And the wives can hear their men come back,
  Back from the edge of the floe.

Red Dog

For our white and our excellent nights – for the nights of swift running,
    Fair ranging, far-seeing, good hunting, sure cunning!
For the smells of the dawning, untainted ere dew has departed!
For the rush through the mist, and the quarry blend-started!
For the cry of our mates when the sambur has wheeled and is standing at
      bay,
        For the risk and the riot of night!
        For the sleep at the lair-mouth by day –
        It is met, and we go to the fight.
            Bay! O bay!

It was after the letting in of the jungle that the pleasantest part of Mowgli's life began. He had the good conscience that comes from paying a just debt, and all the jungle was his friend, for all the jungle was afraid of him. The things that he did and saw and heard when he was wandering from one people to another, with or without his four companions, would make many, many stories, each as long as this one. So you will never be told how he met and escaped from the Mad Elephant of Mandla, who killed two-and-twenty bullocks drawing eleven carts of coined silver to the Government Treasury, and scattered the shiny rupees in the dust; how he fought Jacala the Crocodile all one long night in the Marshes of the North, and broke his skinning-knife on the brute's back-plates; how he found a new and longer knife round the neck of a man who had been killed by a wild boar, and how he tracked that boar and killed him as a fair price for the knife; how he was caught up in the Great Famine by the moving of the deer, and nearly crushed to death in the swaying hot herds; how he saved Hathi the Silent from being caught in a pit with a stake at the bottom, and how next day he himself fell into a very cunning leopard-trap, and how Hathi broke the thick wooden bars to pieces about him; how he milked the wild buffaloes in the swamp, and how –

But we must tell one tale at a time. Father and Mother Wolf died, and Mowgli rolled a big boulder against the mouth of the cave and cried the Death Song over them, and Baloo grew very old and stiff, and even Bagheera, whose nerves were steel and whose muscles were iron, seemed slower at the kill. Akela turned from grey to milky white with pure age; his ribs stuck out, and he walked as though he had been made of wood, and Mowgli killed for him. But the young wolves, the children of the disbanded Seeonee Pack, throve and increased, and when there were some forty of them, masterless, clean-footed five-year-olds, Akela told them that they ought to gather themselves together and follow the Law, and run under one head, as befitted the Free People.

This was not a matter in which Mowgli gave advice, for, as he said, he had eaten sour fruit, and he knew the tree it hung from; but when Phao, son of Phaona (his father was the Grey Tracker in the days of Akela's headship), fought his way to the leadership of the pack according to the Jungle Law, and when the old calls and the old songs began to ring under the stars once more, Mowgli came to the Council Rock for memory's sake. If he chose to speak the pack waited till he had finished, and he sat at Akela's side on the rock above Phao. Those were the days of good hunting and good sleeping. No stranger cared to break into the jungles that belonged to Mowgli's people, as they called the pack, and the young wolves grew fat and strong, and there were many cubs to bring to the looking-over. Mowgli always attended a looking-over, for he remembered the night when a black panther brought a naked brown baby into the pack, and the long call, "Look, look well, O wolves," made his heart flutter with strange feelings. Otherwise, he would be far away in the jungle, tasting, touching, seeing, and feeling new things.

One twilight when he was trotting leisurely across the ranges to give Akela the half of a buck that he had killed, while his four wolves were jogging behind him, sparring a little and tumbling one over another for joy of being alive, he heard a cry that he had not heard since the bad days of Shere Khan. It was what they call in the jungle the *Pheeal*, a kind of shriek that the jackal gives when he is hunting behind a tiger, or when there is some big killing afoot. If you can imagine a mixture of hate, triumph, fear, and despair, with a kind of leer running through it, you will get some notion of the *Pheeal* that rose and sank and wavered and quivered far away across the Wainganga. The Four began to bristle and growl. Mowgli's hand went to his knife and he too checked as though he had been turned into stone.

"There is no Striped One would dare kill here," he said, at last.

"That is not the cry of the Forerunner," said Grey Brother. "It is some great killing. Listen!"

It broke out again, half sobbing and half chuckling, just as though the jackal had soft human lips. Then Mowgli drew a deep breath, and ran to the Council Rock, overtaking on his way hurrying wolves of the pack. Phao and Akela were on the rock together, and below them, every nerve strained, sat the others. The mothers and the cubs were cantering to their lairs, for when the *Pheeal* cries is no time for weak things to be abroad.

They could hear nothing except the Wainganga gurgling in the dark and the evening winds among the tree-tops, till suddenly across the river a wolf called. It was no wolf of the pack, for those were all at the rock. The note changed to a long despairing bay; and "Dhole!" it said, "Dhole! Dhole! Dhole!" In a few minutes they heard tired feet on the rocks, and a gaunt, dripping wolf, streaked with red on his flanks, his right fore paw useless, and his jaws white with foam, flung himself into the circle and lay gasping at Mowgli's feet.

"Good hunting? Under whose headship?" said Phao gravely.

"Good hunting! Won-tolla am I," was the answer. He meant that he was a solitary wolf, fending for himself, his mate, and his cubs in some lonely lair. Won-tolla means an outlier – one who lies out from any pack. When he panted they could see his heart shake him backwards and forwards.

"What moves?" said Phao, for that is the question all the jungle asks after the *Pheeal*.

"The dholes, the dholes of the Dekkan – Red Dog the Killer! They came north from the south saying the Dekkan was empty and killing out by the way. When this moon was new there were four to me – my mate and three cubs. She would teach them to kill on the grass plains, hiding to drive the buck, as we do who are of the open. At midnight I heard them together, full tongue on the trail. At the dawn-wind I found them stiff in the grass – four, Free People, four when this moon was new! Then sought I my blood-right and found the dhole."

"How many?" said Mowgli. The pack growled deep in their throats.

"I do not know. Three of them will kill no more, but at the last they drove me like the buck, on three legs they drove me. Look, Free People!"

He thrust out his mangled fore foot, all dark with dried blood. There were cruel bites low down on his side, and his throat was torn and worried.

"Eat," said Akela, rising up from the meat Mowgli had brought him. The outlier flung himself on it famishing.

"This shall be no loss," he said humbly when he had taken off the edge of his hunger. "Give me a little strength, Free People, and I also will kill! My lair is empty that was full when this moon was new, and the blood-debt is not all paid."

Phao heard his teeth crack on a haunch-bone and grunted approvingly.

"We shall need those jaws," said he. "Were their cubs with the dholes?"

"Nay, nay. Red hunters all – grown dogs of their pack, heavy and strong."

That meant that the dhole, the red hunting-dog of the Dekkan, was moving to fight, and the wolves knew well that even the tiger will surrender a new kill to the dholes. They drive straight through the jungle, and what they meet they pull down and tear to pieces. Though they are not as big nor half as cunning as the wolf, they are very strong and very numerous. The dholes, for instance, do not begin to call themselves a pack till they are a hundred strong, whereas forty wolves make a very fair pack. Mowgli's wanderings had taken him to the edge of the high grassy downs of the Dekkan, and he had often seen the fearless dholes sleeping and playing and scratching themselves among the little hollows and tussocks that they use for lairs. He despised and hated them because they did not smell like the Free People, because they did not live in caves, and, above all, because they had hair between their toes while he and his friends were clean-footed. But he knew, for Hathi had told him, what a terrible thing a dhole hunting-pack was. Hathi himself moves aside from their line, and until they are all killed, or till game is scarce, they go forward killing as they go.

Akela knew something of the dholes, too. He said to Mowgli quietly: "It is better to die in the full pack than leaderless and alone. It is good hunting, and – my last. But, as men live, thou hast very many more nights and days, Little Brother. Go north and lie down, and if any wolf live after the dhole has gone by he shall bring thee word of the fight."

"Ah," said Mowgli, quite gravely, "must I go to the marshes and catch little fish and sleep in a tree, or must I ask help of the *Bandar-log* and eat nuts while the pack fights below?"

"It is to the death," said Akela. "Thou hast never met the dholes – the Red Killers. Even the Striped One – "

"*Aowa! Aowa!*" said Mowgli pettingly. "I have killed one striped ape. Listen now: There was a wolf, my father, and there was a wolf, my mother, and there was an old grey wolf (not too wise: he is white now) was my father and my mother. Therefore I – " He raised his voice. "I say that when the dholes come, and if the dholes come, Mowgli and the Free People are of one skin for that hunting. And I say, by the bull that bought me, by the bull Bagheera paid for me in the old days which ye of the pack do not remember, *I* say, that the trees and the river may hear and hold fast if I forget. *I* say that this my knife shall be as a tooth to the pack – and I do not think it is so blunt. This is my word which has gone from me."

"Thou dost not know the dhole, man with a wolfs tongue," Won-tolla cried. "I look only to clear my blood debt against them ere they have me in many pieces. They move slowly, killing out as they go, but in two days a little strength will come back to me and I turn again for my blood-debt. But for *ye*, Free People, my counsel is that ye go north and eat but little for a while till the dhole are gone. There is no sleep in this hunting."

"Hear the Outlier!" said Mowgli with a laugh. "Free People, we must go north and eat lizards and rats from the bank, lest by any chance we meet the dhole. He must kill out our hunting-grounds while we lie hid in the north till it please him to give us our own again. He is a dog – and the pup of a dog – red, yellow-bellied, lairless, and haired between every toe! He counts his cubs six and eight at the litter, as though he were

Chikai, the little leaping rat. Surely we must run away, Free People, and beg leave of the peoples of the north for the offal of dead cattle! Ye know the saying: 'North are the vermin; South are the lice. *We* are the jungle.' Choose ye, O choose. It is good hunting! For the pack – for the full pack – for the lair and the litter; for the in-kill and the out-kill; for the mate that drives the doe and the little, little cub within the cave, it is met – it is met – it is met!"

The pack answered with one deep crashing bark that sounded in the night like a tree falling. "It is met," they cried.

"Stay with these," said Mowgli to his Four. "We shall need every tooth. Phao and Akela must make ready the battle. I go to count the dogs."

"It is death!" Won-tolla cried, half rising. "What can such a hairless one do against the Red Dog. Even the Striped One, remember – "

"Thou art indeed an outlier," Mowgli called back, "but we will speak when the dholes are dead. Good hunting all!"

He hurried off into the darkness, wild with excitement, hardly looking where he set foot, and the natural consequence was that he tripped full length over Kaa's great coils where the python lay watching a deer-path near the river.

"*Kssha!*" said Kaa angrily. "Is this jungle work to stamp and ramp and undo a night's hunting – when the game are moving so well, too?"

"The fault was mine," said Mowgli, picking himself up. "Indeed I was seeking thee, Flathead, but each time we meet thou art longer and broader by the length of my arm. There is none like thee in the jungle, wise, old, strong, and most beautiful Kaa."

"Now whither does *this* trail lead?" Kaa's voice was gentler. "Not a moon since there was a manling with a knife threw stones at my head and called me bad little tree-cat names because I lay asleep in the open."

"Aye, and turned every driven deer to all the winds, and Mowgli was hunting, and this same Flathead was too deaf to hear his whistle and leave the deer-roads free," Mowgli answered composedly, sitting down among the painted coils.

"Now this same manling comes with soft, tickling words to this same Flathead, telling him that he is wise, and strong, and beautiful, and this same old Flathead believes and coils a place, thus, for this same stone-throwing manling and.... Art thou at ease now? Could Bagheera give thee so good a resting-place?"

Kaa had, as usual, made a sort of soft half-hammock of himself under Mowgli's weight. The boy reached out in the darkness and gathered in the supple cable-like neck till Kaa's head rested on his shoulder, and then he told him all that had happened in the jungle that night.

"Wise I may be," said Kaa at the end, "but deaf I surely am. Else I should have heard the *Pheeal*. Small wonder the eaters-of-grass are uneasy. How many be the dholes?"

"I have not seen yet. I came hot-foot to thee. Thou art older than Hathi. But, oh, Kaa" – here Mowgli wriggled with joy, "it will be good hunting! Few of us will see another moon."

"Dost *thou* strike in this? Remember thou art a man, and remember what pack cast thee out. Let the wolf look to the dog. *Thou* art a man."

"Last year's nuts are this year's black earth," said Mowgli. "It is true that I am a man, but it is in my stomach that this night I have said that I am a wolf. I called the river and the trees to remember. I am of the Free People, Kaa, till the dholes have gone by."

"Free People," Kaa grunted. "Free thieves! And thou hast tied thyself into the death-knot for the sake of the memory of dead wolves! This is no good hunting."

"It is my word which I have spoken. The trees know, the river knows. Till the dholes have gone by my word comes not back to me."

"*Ngssh!* That changes all trails. I had thought to take thee away with me to the northern marshes, but the word even the word of a little, naked, hairless manling – is the word. Now I, Kaa, say – "

"Think well, Flathead, lest thou tie thyself into the death-knot also. I need no word from thee, for well I know – "

"Be it so, then," said Kaa. "I will give no word. But what is in thy stomach to do when the dhole come?"

"They must swim the Wainganga. I thought to meet them with my knife in the shallows, the pack behind me, and so stabbing and thrusting we might turn them down-stream, or cool their throats a little."

"The dhole do not turn and their throats are hot," said Kaa. "There will be neither manling nor wolf-cub when that hunting is done, but only dry bones."

"*Alala!* If we die we die. It will be most good hunting. But my stomach is young, and I have not seen many rains. I am not wise nor strong. Hast thou a better plan, Kaa?"

"I have seen a hundred and a hundred rains. Ere Hathi cast his milk-tushes my trail was big in the dust. By the First Egg, I am older than many trees, and I have seen all that the jungle has done."

"But *this* is new hunting," said Mowgli. "Never before have the dhole crossed our trail."

"What is has been. What will be is no more than a forgotten year striking backwards. Be still while I count those my years."

For a long hour Mowgli lay back among the coils, playing with his knife, while Kaa, his head motionless on the ground, thought of all that he had seen and known since the day he came from the egg. The light seemed to go out of his eyes and leave them like stale opals, and now and again he made little stiff passes with his head to right and left, as though he were hunting in his sleep. Mowgli dozed quietly, for he knew that there is nothing like sleep before hunting, and he was trained to take it at any hour of the day or night.

Then he felt Kaa grow bigger and broader below him as the huge python puffed himself out, hissing with the noise of a sword drawn from a steel scabbard.

"I have seen all the dead seasons," Kaa said at last, "and the great trees and the old elephants and the rocks that were bare and sharp-pointed ere the moss grew. Art *thou* still alive, manling?"

"It is only a little after moonrise," said Mowgli. "I do not understand – "

"*Hssh!* I am again Kaa. I knew it was but a little time. Now we will go to the river, and I will show thee what is to be done against the dhole."

He turned, straight as an arrow, for the main stream of the Wainganga, plunging in a little above the pool that hid the Peace Rock, Mowgli at his side.

"Nay, do not swim. I go swiftly. My back, Little Brother."

Mowgli tucked his left arm round Kaa's neck, dropped his right close to his body, and straightened his feet. Then Kaa breasted the current as he alone could, and the ripple of the checked water stood up in a frill round Mowgli's neck and his feet were waved to and fro in the eddy under the python's lashing sides. A mile or so above the Peace Rock the Wainganga narrows between a gorge of marble rocks from eighty to a hundred feet high, and the current runs like a mill-race between and over all manner of ugly stones. But Mowgli did not trouble his head about the water: no water in the world could have given him a moment's fear. He was looking at the gorge on either side and sniffing uneasily, for there was a sweetish-sourish smell in the air, very like the smell of a big ant-hill on a hot day. Instinctively he lowered himself in the water, only raising his head to breathe, and Kaa came to anchor with a double twist of his tail round a sunken rock, holding Mowgli in the hollow of a coil, while the water raced by.

"This is the Place of Death," said the boy. "Why do we come here?"

"They sleep," said Kaa. "Hathi will not turn aside for the Striped One. Yet Hathi and the Striped One together turn aside for the dhole, and the dhole, they say, turn aside for nothing. And yet for whom do the Little People of the Rocks turn aside? Tell me, master of the jungle, who is the master of the jungle?"

"These," Mowgli whispered. "It is the Place of Death. Let us go."

"Nay, look well, for they are asleep. It is as it was when I was not the length of thy arm."

The split and weather-worn rocks of the gorge of the Wainganga had been used since the beginning of the jungle by the Little People of the Rocks – the busy, furious, black, wild bees of India. And, as Mowgli knew well, all trails turned off half a mile away from their country. For centuries the Little People had hived and swarmed from cleft to cleft and swarmed again, staining the white marble with stale honey, and made their combs tall and deep and black in the dark of the inner caves, and neither man nor beast nor fire nor water had ever touched them. The length of the gorge on both sides was hung as it were with black shimmery velvet curtains, and Mowgli sank as he looked, for those were the clotted millions of the sleeping bees. There were other lumps and festoons and things like decayed tree-trunks studded on the face of the rock – the old comb of past years, or new cities built in the shadow of the windless gorge – and huge masses of spongy, rotten trash had rolled down and stuck among the trees and creepers that clung to the rock-face. As he listened he heard more than once the rustle and slide of a honey-loaded comb turning over or falling away somewhere in the dark galleries. Then a booming of angry wings and the sullen drip, drip, drip, of the wasted honey, guttering along till it lipped over some ledge in the open and sluggishly trickled down on the twigs. There was a tiny little beach, not five feet broad, on one side of the river, and that was piled high with the rubbish of uncounted years. There lay dead bees, drones, sweepings, stale combs, and wings of marauding moths and beetles that had strayed in after honey, all tumbled in smooth piles of the finest black dust. The mere sharp smell of it was enough to frighten anything that had no wings, and knew what the Little People were.

Kaa moved up-stream again till he came to a sandbar at the head of the gorge.

"Here is this season's kill," said he. "Look!"

On the bank lay the skeletons of a couple of young deer and a buffalo. Mowgli could see that no wolf nor jackal had touched the bones, which were laid out naturally.

"They came beyond the line, they did not know," murmured Mowgli, "and the Little People killed them. Let us go ere they awake."

"They do not wake till the dawn," said Kaa. "Now I will tell thee. A hunted buck from the south, many, many rains ago, came hither from the south, not knowing the jungle, a pack on his trail. Being made blind by fear he leaped from above, the pack running by sight, for they were hot and blind on the trail. The sun was high, and the Little People were many and very angry. Many, too, were those of the pack who leaped into the Wainganga, but they were dead ere they took water. Those who did not leap died also in the rocks above. But the buck lived."

"How?"

"Because he came first, running for his life, leaping ere the Little People were aware, and was in the river when they gathered to kill. The pack, following, was altogether lost under the weight of the Little People, who had been roused by the feet of that buck."

"The buck lived?" Mowgli repeated slowly.

"At least he did not die *then*, though none waited his coming down with a strong body to hold him safe against the water, as a certain old fat, deaf, yellow Flat-head would wait for a manling – yea, though there were all the dhole of the Dekkan on his trail. What is in thy stomach?"

Kaa's head lay on Mowgli's wet shoulder, and his tongue quivered by the boy's ear. There was a long silence before Mowgli whispered:

"It is to pull the very whiskers of Death, but – Kaa, thou art, indeed, the wisest of all the jungle."

"So many have said. Look now, if the dhole follow thee – "

"As surely they will follow. Ho! Ho! I have many little thorns under my tongue to prick into their hides."

"If they follow thee hot and blind, looking only at thy shoulders, those who do not die up above will take water either here or lower down, for the Little People will rise up and cover them. Now the Wainganga is hungry water, and they will have no Kaa to hold them, but will go down, such as live, to the shallows by the Seeonee lairs, and there thy pack may meet them by the throat."

"*Ahai! Eowawa!* Better could not be till the rains fall in the dry season. There is now only the little matter of the run and the leap. I will make me known to the dholes, so that they shall follow me very closely."

"Hast thou seen the rocks above thee? From the landward side?"

"Indeed no. That I had forgotten."

"Go look. It is all rotten ground, cut and full of holes. One of thy clumsy feet set down without seeing would end the hunt. See, I leave thee here, and for thy sake only I will carry word to the pack that they may know where to look for the dholes. For myself, I am not of one skin with *any* wolf."

When Kaa disliked an acquaintance he could be more unpleasant than any of the Jungle-People, except perhaps Bagheera. He swam down-stream, and opposite the rock he came on Phao and Akela listening to the night noises.

"*Hssh!* dogs," he said cheerfully. "The dholes will come down-stream. If ye be not afraid ye can kill them in the shallows."

"When come they?" said Phao. "And where is my man-cub?" said Akela.

"They come when they come," said Kaa. "Wait and see. As for *thy* man-cub, from whom thou hast taken his word and so laid him open to Death, *thy* man-cub is with *me*, and if he be not already dead the fault is none of thine, bleached dog! Wait here for the dhole, and be glad that the man-cub and I strike on thy side."

Kaa flashed up-stream again and moored himself in the middle of the gorge, looking upwards at the line of the cliff. Presently he saw Mowgli's head move against the stars. Then there was a whizz in the air, the keen clean *schloop* of a body falling feet first. Next minute the body was at rest again in the loop of Kaa's body.

"It is no leap by night," said Mowgli quietly. "I have jumped twice as far for sport, but that is an evil place above – low bushes and gullies that go down deep – all full of the Little People. I have put big stones one above the other by the side of three gullies. These I shall throw down with my feet in running, and the Little People will rise up behind me angry."

"That is man's cunning," said Kaa. "Thou art wise, but the Little People are always angry."

"Nay, at twilight all wings near and far rest for a while. I will play with the dholes at twilight, for the dholes hunt best by day. They follow now Won-tolla's blood-trail."

"Chil does not leave a dead ox, nor the dholes a blood-trail," said Kaa.

"Then I will make him a new blood-trail – of his own blood if I can, and give him dirt to eat. Thou wilt stay here, Kaa, till I come with my dholes?"

"Aye, but what if they kill thee in the jungle, or the Little People kill thee before thou canst leap down to the river?"

"When tomorrow comes we will kill tomorrow," said Mowgli, quoting a jungle saying; and again, "When I am dead it is time to sing the Death-Song. Good hunting, Kaa."

He loosed his arm from the python's neck and went down the gorge like a log in a freshet, paddling towards the far bank, where he found slack water, and laughing aloud from sheer happiness. There was nothing Mowgli liked better than, as he himself said, "to pull the whiskers of Death" and make the jungle feel that he was their overlord. He had often, with Baloo's help, robbed bees' nests in single trees, and he knew that the Little People disliked the smell of wild garlic. So he gathered a small bundle of it, tied it up with a bark string, and then followed Won-tolla's blood-trail as it ran southerly from the lairs, for some five miles, looking at the trees with his head on one side and chuckling as he looked.

"Mowgli the Frog have I been," said he to himself, "Mowgli the Wolf have I said that I am. Now Mowgli the Ape must I be before I am Mowgli the Buck. At the end I shall be Mowgli the Man. Ho!" And he slid his thumb along the eighteen-inch blade of his knife.

Won-tolla's trail, all rank with dark blood-spots, ran under a forest of thick trees that grew close together and stretched away north-eastward, gradually growing thinner and thinner to within two miles of the Bee Rocks. From the last tree to the low scrub of the Bee Rocks was open country, where there was hardly cover enough to hide a wolf. Mowgli trotted along under the trees, judging distances between branch and branch, occasionally climbing up a trunk and taking a trial leap from one tree to another, till he came to the open ground, which he studied very carefully for an hour. Then he turned, picked up Won-tolla's trail where he had left it, settled himself in a tree with an outrunning branch some eight feet from the ground, hung his bunch of garlic in a safe crotch, and sat still sharpening his knife on the sole of his foot.

A little before mid-day, when the sun was very warm, he heard the patter of feet and smelled the abominable smell of the dhole pack as they trotted steadily and pitilessly along Won-tolla's trail. Seen from above the red dhole does not look half the size of a wolf, but Mowgli knew how strong his feet and jaws were. He watched the sharp bay head of the leader snuffing along the trail and gave him "Good hunting!"

The brute looked up and his companions halted behind him, scores and scores of red dogs with low-hung tails, heavy shoulders, weak quarters, and bloody mouths. The dholes are a very silent people as a rule, and they have no manners even in their own Dekkan. Fully two hundred must have gathered below him, but he could see that the leaders sniffed hungrily on Won-tolla's trail, and tried to drag the pack forward. That would never do, or they would be at the lairs in broad daylight, and Mowgli meant to hold them under his tree till twilight.

"By whose leave do ye come here?" said Mowgli.

"All jungles are our jungle," was the reply, and the dhole that gave it bared his white teeth. Mowgli looked down with a smile and imitated perfectly the sharp chitter-chatter of Chikai, the leaping rat of the Dekkan, meaning the dholes to understand that he considered them no better than Chikai. The pack closed up round the tree-trunk and the leader bayed savagely, calling Mowgli a tree-ape. For an answer Mowgli stretched down one naked leg and wriggled his bare toes just above the leader's head. That was enough, and more than enough to wake the pack to stupid rage. Those who have hair between their toes do not care to be reminded of it. Mowgli caught his foot away as the leader leaped and said sweetly: "Dog, red dog! Go back to the Dekkan and eat lizards. Go to Chikai thy brother, dog, dog, red, red dog! There is hair between every toe!" He twiddled his toes a second time.

"Come down ere we starve thee out, hairless ape," yelled the pack, and this was exactly what Mowgli wanted. He laid himself down along the branch, his cheek to the bark, his right arm free, and for some five minutes he told the pack what he thought and knew about them, their manners, their customs, their mates, and their puppies. There is no speech in the world so rancorous and so stinging as the language the Jungle-People use to show scorn and contempt. When you come to think of it you will see how this must be so. As Mowgli told Kaa, he had many little thorns under his tongue, and slowly and deliberately he drove the dholes from silence to growls, from growls to yells, and from yells to hoarse slavery ravings. They tried to answer his taunts, but a cub might as well have tried to answer Kaa in a rage, and all the while Mowgli's right hand lay crooked at his side, ready for action, his feet locked round the branch. The big bay leader had leaped many times into the air, but Mowgli dared not risk a false blow. At last, made furious beyond his natural strength, he bounded up seven or eight feet clear of the ground. Then Mowgli's hand shot out like the head of a tree-snake, and gripped him by the scruff of his neck, and the branch shook with the jar as his weight fell back, and Mowgli was almost wrenched on to the ground. But he never loosed his grip, and inch by inch he hauled the beast, hanging like a drowned jackal, up on the branch. With his left hand he reached for his knife and cut off the red, bushy tail, flinging the dhole back to earth again. That was all he needed. The dholes would not go forward on Won-tolla's trail now till they had killed Mowgli, or Mowgli had killed them. He saw them settle down in circles with a quiver of the haunches that meant revenge to the death, and so he climbed to a higher crotch, settled his back comfortably and went to sleep.

After three or four hours he waked and counted the pack. They were all there, silent, husky, and dry, with eyes of steel. The sun was beginning to sink. In half an hour the Little People of the Rocks would be ending their labours, and, as you know, the dhole does not fight well in the twilight.

"I did not need such faithful watchers," he said, standing up on a branch, "but I will remember this. Ye be true dholes, but to my thinking too much of one kind. For that reason I do not give the big lizard-eater his tail again. Art thou not pleased, Red Dog?"

"I myself will tear out thy stomach," yelled the leader, biting the foot of the tree.

"Nay, but consider, wise rat of Dekkan. There will now be many litters of little tailless red dogs, yea, with raw red stumps that sting when the sand is hot. Go home, Red Dog, and cry that an ape has done this. Ye will not go? Come then with me, and I will make ye very wise."

He moved monkey-fashion into the next tree, and so on and the next and the next, the pack following with lifted hungry heads. Now and then he would pretend to fall, and the pack would tumble one over the other in their haste to be in at the death. It was a curious sight – the boy with the knife that shone in the low sunlight as it sifted through the upper branches, and the silent pack with their red coats all aflame huddling and following below. When he came to the last tree he took the garlic and rubbed himself all over carefully, and the dholes yelled with scorn. "Ape with a wolf's tongue, dost thou think to cover thy scent?" they said. "We will follow to the death."

"Take thy tail," said Mowgli, flinging it back along the course he had taken. The pack naturally rushed back a little when they smelt the blood. "And follow now – to the death!"

He had slipped down the tree-trunk, and headed like the wind in bare feet for the Bee Rocks, before the dholes saw what he would do.

They gave one deep howl and settled down to the long lobbing canter that can, at the last, run down anything that lives. Mowgli knew their pack pace to be much slower than that of the wolves, or he would never have risked a two-mile run in full sight. They were sure that the boy was theirs at last, and he was sure that he had them to play with as he pleased. All his trouble was to keep them sufficiently hot behind him to prevent them turning off too soon. He ran cleanly, evenly, and springily, the tail-less leader not five yards behind him, and the pack stringing out over perhaps a quarter of a mile of ground, crazy and blind with the rage of slaughter. So he kept his distance by ear, reserving his last effort for the rush across the Bee Rocks.

The Little People had gone to sleep in the early twilight, for it was not the season of late blossoming flowers. But as Mowgli's first footfalls rang hollow on the hollow ground he heard a sound as though all the earth were humming. Then he ran as he had never run in his life below, spurned aside one – two – three of the piles of stones into the dark sweet-smelling gullies; heard a roar like the roar of the sea in a cave, saw with the tail of his eye the air grow dark behind him, saw the current of the Wainganga far below, and a flat, diamond-shaped head in the water; leaped outward with all his strength, the tailless dhole snapping at his shoulder in mid-air, and dropped feet first to the safety of the river, breathless and triumphant. There was not a sting on his body, for the smell of the garlic had checked the Little People for just the few seconds that carried him across the rocks. When he rose Kaa's coils were steadying him and things were bounding over the edge of the cliff – great lumps, it seemed, of clustered bees falling like plummets, and as each lump touched water the bees flew upward and the body of a dhole whirled down-stream. Overhead they could hear furious short yells that were drowned in a roar like thunder – the roar of the wings of the Little People of the Rocks. Some of the dholes, too, had fallen into the gullies that communicated with the underground caves, and there choked, and fought, and snapped among the tumbled honeycombs, and at last, borne up dead on the heaving waves of bees beneath them, shot out of some hole in the river-face, to roll over on the black rubbish heaps. There were dholes who had leaped short into the trees on the cliffs, and the bees blotted out their shapes, but the greater number of them, maddened by the stings, had flung themselves into the river, and, as Kaa said, the Wainganga was hungry water.

Overhead they could hear furious short yells that were drowned in a roar like thunder.

Kaa held Mowgli fast till the boy had recovered his breath.

"We may not stay here," he said. "The Little People are roused indeed. Come!"

Swimming low and diving as often as he could, Mowgli went down the river with the knife in his hand.

"Slowly, slowly!" said Kaa. "One tooth does not kill a hundred unless it be a cobra's, and many of the dholes took water swiftly when they saw the Little People rise. *They* are unhurt."

"The more work for my knife, then. *Phai!* How the Little People follow." Mowgli sank again. The face of the water was blanketed with wild bees buzzing sullenly and stinging all they found.

"Nothing was ever yet lost by silence," said Kaa – no sting could penetrate his scales – "and thou hast all the long night for the hunting. Hear them howl!"

Nearly half the pack had seen the trap their fellows rushed into, and, turning sharp aside, had flung themselves into the water where the gorge broke down in steep banks. Their cries of rage and their threats against the "tree-ape" who had brought them to their shame mixed with the yells and growls of those who had been punished by the Little People. To remain ashore was death, and every dhole knew it. The pack was swept along the current, down and down to the rocks of the Peace Pool, but even there the angry Little People followed and forced them to the water again. Mowgli could hear the voice of the tailless leader bidding his people hold on and kill out every wolf in Seeonee. But he did not waste his time in listening.

"One kills in the dark behind us!" snapped a dhole. "Here is tainted water!"

Mowgli had dived forward like an otter, twitched a struggling dhole under water before he could open his mouth, and dark, oily rings rose in the Peace Pool as the body plopped up, turning on its side. The dholes tried to turn, but the current forced them by, and the Little People darted at their heads and ears, and they could hear the challenge of the Seeonee Pack growing louder and deeper in the gathering darkness ahead. Again Mowgli dived, and again a dhole went under and rose dead, and again the clamour broke out at the rear of the pack, some howling that it was best to go ashore, others calling on their leader to lead them back to the Dekkan, and others bidding Mowgli show himself and be killed.

"They come to the fight with two stomachs and many voices," said Kaa. "The rest is with thy brethren below yonder. The Little People go back to sleep, and I will turn also. I do not help wolves."

A wolf came running along the bank on three legs, leaping up and down, laying his head sideways close to the ground, hunching his back, and breaking a couple of feet into the air, as though he were playing with his cubs. It was Won-tolla the Outlier and he said never a word, but continued his horrible sport beside the dholes. They had been long in the water now, and were swimming laboriously, their coats drenched and heavy, and their bushy tails dragging like sponges, so tired and shaken that they, too, were silent, watching the pair of blazing eyes that moved abreast of them.

"This is no good hunting," said one at last.

"Good hunting!" said Mowgli as he rose boldly at the brute's side and sent the long knife home behind the shoulder, pushing hard to avoid the dying snap.

"Art thou there, man-cub?" said Won-tolla, from the bank.

"Ask of the dead, Outlier," Mowgli replied. "Have none come downstream? I have filled these dogs' mouths with dirt. I have tricked them in the broad daylight, and their leader lacks his tail, but here be some few for thee still. Whither shall I drive them?"

"I will wait," said Won-tolla. "The long night is before me, and I shall see well."

Nearer and nearer came the bay of the Seeonee wolves. "For the pack, for the full pack it is met!" And a bend in the river drove the dholes forward among the sands and shoals opposite the Seeonee lairs.

Then they saw their mistake. They should have landed half a mile higher up and rushed the wolves on dry ground. Now it was too late. The bank was lined with burning eyes, and except for the horrible *Pheeal* cry that had never stopped since sundown there was no sound in the jungle. It seemed as though Won-tolla was fawning on them to come ashore; and "Turn and take hold!" said the leader of the dholes. The entire pack flung themselves at the shore, threshing and squattering through the shoal water till the face of the Wainganga was all white and torn, and the great ripples went from side to side like bow-waves from a boat. Mowgli followed the rush, stabbing and slicing as the dholes, huddled together, rushed up the river-beach in a wave.

Then the long fight began, heaving and straining and splitting and scattering and narrowing and broadening along the red wet sands, and over and between the tangled tree-roots, and through and among the bushes, and in and out of the grass clumps, for even now the dholes were two to one. But they met wolves fighting for all that made the pack, and not only the short, deep-chested white-tusked hunters of the pack, but the wild-eyed *lahinis* – the she-wolves of the lair, as the saying is – fighting for their litters, with here and there a yearling wolf, his first coat still half woolly, tugging and grappling by their sides. A wolf, you must know, flies at the throat or snaps at the flank, while a dhole by preference bites low, so when the dholes were struggling out of the water and had to raise their heads the odds were with the wolves; on dry land the wolves suffered, but in the water or on land Mowgli's knife came and went the same. The Four had worked their way to his aid. Grey Brother, crouched between the boy's knees, protected his stomach, while the others guarded his back and either side, or stood over him when the shock of a leaping, yelling dhole who had thrown himself on the steady blade bore him down. For the rest, it was one tangled confusion – a locked and swaying mob that moved from right to left and from, left to right along the bank, and also ground round and round slowly on its own centre. Here would be a heaving mound, like a water-blister in a whirlpool, which would break like a water-blister, and throw up four or five mangled dogs, each striving to get back to the centre; here would be a single wolf borne down by two or three dholes dragging them forward, and sinking the while; here a yearling cub would be held up by the pressure round him, though he had been killed early in the fight, while his mother, crazed with dumb rage, rolled over snapping and passing on; and in the middle of the thickest fight, perhaps, one wolf and one dhole, forgetting everything else, would be manoeuvring for first hold till they were swept away by a rush of yelling fighters. Once Mowgli passed Akela, a dhole on either flank, and his all but toothless jaws closed over the loins of a third; and once he saw Phaon, his teeth set in the throat of a dhole, tugging the unwilling beast forward till the yearlings could finish him. But the bulk of the fight was blind flurry and smother in the dark; hit, trip, and tumble, yelp, groan, and worry-worry-worry round him and behind him and above him.

As the night wore on the quick giddy-go-round motion increased. The dholes were wearied and afraid to attack the stronger wolves, though they did not yet dare to run away, but Mowgli felt that the end was coming soon, and contented himself with striking to cripple. The yearlings were growing bolder; there was time to breathe; and now the mere flicker of the knife would sometimes turn a dhole aside.

"The meat is very near the bone," Grey Brother gasped. He was bleeding from a score of flesh-wounds.

"But the bone is yet to be cracked," said Mowgli. "*Aowawa! Thus* do we do in the jungle!" The red blade ran like a flame along the side of a dhole whose hind quarters were hidden by the weight of a clinging wolf.

"My kill!" snorted the wolf through his wrinkled nostrils. "Leave him to me!"

"Is thy stomach *still* empty, Outlier?" said Mowgli. Won-tolla was fearfully punished, but his grip had paralysed the dhole, who could not turn round and reach him.

"By the bull that bought me," Mowgli cried, with a bitter laugh, "it is the tailless one!" And indeed it was the big bay-coloured leader.

"It is not wise to kill cubs and *lahinis*," Mowgli went on philosophically, wiping the blood out of his eyes, "unless one also kills the lair-father, and it is in my stomach that this lair-father kills thee."

A dhole leaped to his leader's aid, but before his teeth had found Won-tolla's flank, Mowgli's knife was in his chest, and Grey Brother took what was left.

"And thus do we do in the jungle," said Mowgli.

Won-tolla said not a word, only his jaws were closing and closing on the backbone as life ebbed. The dhole shuddered, his head dropped and he lay still, and Won-tolla dropped above him.

"*Huh!* The blood-debt is paid," said Mowgli. "Sing the song, Won-tolla."

"He hunts no more," said Grey Brother, "and Akela too is silent, this long time."

"The bone is cracked!" thundered Phao, son of Phaon. "They go! Kill, kill out, O hunters of the Free People!"

Dhole after dhole was slinking away from those dark and bloody sands to the river, to the thick jungle, upstream or down-stream as he saw the road clear.

"The debt! The debt!" shouted Mowgli. "Pay the debt! They have slain the Lone Wolf! Let not a dog go!"

He was flying to the river, knife in hand, to check any dhole who dared to take water, when, from under a mound of nine dead, rose Akela's head and fore quarters, and Mowgli dropped on his knees beside the Lone Wolf.

"Said I not it would be my last fight?" Akela gasped. "It is good hunting. And thou, Little Brother?"

"I live, having killed many."

"Even so. I die, and I would – I would die by thee, Little Brother."

Mowgli took the terrible scarred head on his knees, and put his arms round the torn neck.

"It is long since the old days of Shere Khan and a man-cub that rolled naked in the dust," coughed Akela.

"Nay, nay, I am a wolf. I am of one skin with the Free People," Mowgli cried. "It is no will of mine that I am a man."

"Thou art a man, Little Brother, wolfling of my watching. Thou art all a man, or else the pack had fled before the dhole. My life I owe to thee, and today thou hast saved the pack even as once I saved thee. Hast thou forgotten? All debts are paid now. Go to thine own people. I tell thee again, eye of my eye, this hunting is ended. Go to thine own people."

"I will never go. I will hunt alone in the jungle. I have said it."

"After the summer come the rains, and after the rains come the spring. Go back before thou art driven."

"Who will drive me?"

"Mowgli will drive Mowgli. Go back to thy people. Go to Man."

"When Mowgli drives Mowgli I will go," Mowgli answered.

"There is no more for thee," said Akela. "Now I would speak to my kind. Little Brother, canst thou raise me to my feet? I also am a leader of the Free People."

Very carefully and gently Mowgli raised Akela to his feet, both arms round him, and the Lone Wolf drew a deep breath and began the Death-Song that a leader of the pack should sing when he dies. It gathered strength as he went on, lifting and lifting and ringing far across the river, till it came to the last "Good hunting!" and Akela shook himself clear of Mowgli for an instant, and leaping into the air, fell backwards dead upon his last and most terrible kill.

Mowgli sat with his head on his knees, careless of anything else, while the last of the dying dholes were being overtaken and run down by the merciless *lahinis*. Little by little the cries died away, and the wolves came back limping as their wounds stiffened to take stock of the dead. Fifteen of the pack, as well as half a dozen *lahinis*, were dead by the river, and of the others not one was unmarked. Mowgli sat through it all till the cold daybreak, when Phao's wet red muzzle was dropped in his hand, and Mowgli drew back to show the gaunt body of Akela.

"Good hunting!" said Phao, as though Akela were still alive, and then over his bitten shoulder to the others: "Howl, dogs! A wolf has died tonight!"

But of all the pack of two hundred fighting dholes, red dogs of the Dekkan, whose boast is that no living thing in the jungle dare stand before them, not one returned to the Dekkan to carry that news.

Chil's Song

This is the song that Chil sang as the kites dropped down one after another to the river-bed, when the great fight was finished. Chil is good friends with everybody, but he is a cold-blooded kind of creature at heart, because he knows that almost everybody in the jungle comes to him in the long run.

These were my companions going forth by night,
  (Chil! Look you, for Chil!)
Now come I to whistle them the ending of the fight.
  (Chil! Vanguards of Chil!)
Word they gave me overhead of quarry newly slain,
Word I gave them underfoot of buck upon the plain.
Here's an end of every trail – they shall not speak again!

They that gave the hunting-cry – they that followed fast –
  (Chil! Look you, for Chil!)
They that bade the sambur wheel, and pinned him as he passed –
  (Chil! Vanguards of Chil!)
They that lagged behind the scent – they that ran before,
They that shunned the level horn – they that overbore,
Here's an end of every trail – they shall not follow more.

These were my companions. Pity 'twas they died!
  (Chil! Look you, for Chil!)
Now come I to comfort them that knew them in their pride.
  (Chil! Vanguards of Chil!)
Tattered flank and sunken eye, open mouth and red,
Locked and lank and lone they lie, the dead upon their dead.
Here's an end of every trail – and here my hosts are fed!

The Spring Running

Man goes to Man! Cry the challenge through the jungle!
   He that was our brother goes away.
Hear, now, and judge, O ye people of the jungle,
   Answer, who shall turn him – who shall stay?

Man goes to Man! He is weeping in the jungle.
   He that was our brother sorrows sore!
Man goes to Man! (Oh, we loved him in the jungle!)
   To the man-trail where we may not follow more.

The second year after the great fight with Red Dog and the death of Akela, Mowgli must have been nearly seventeen years old. He looked older, for hard exercise, the best of good eating, and baths whenever he felt in the least hot or dusty had given him strength and growth far beyond his age. He could swing by one hand from a top branch for half an hour at a time, when he had occasion to look along the tree-roads. He could stop a young buck in mid-gallop and throw him sideways by the head. He could even jerk over the big blue wild boars that lived in the Marshes of the North. The Jungle-People, who used to fear him for his wits, feared him now for his mere strength, and when he moved quietly on his own affairs the whisper of his coming cleared the wood-path. And yet the look in his eyes was always gentle. Even when he fought his eyes never glazed as Bagheera's did. They only grew more and more interested and excited, and that was one of the things that Bagheera himself did not understand.

He asked Mowgli about it, and the boy laughed and said: "When I miss the kill I am angry. When I must go empty for two days I am very angry. Do not my eyes talk then?"

"The mouth is hungry," said Bagheera, "but the eyes say nothing. Hunting, eating, or swimming, it is all one – like a stone in wet or dry weather." Mowgli looked at him lazily from under his long eyelashes, and, as usual, the panther's head dropped. Bagheera knew his master.

They were lying out far up the side of a hill overlooking the Wainganga, and the morning mists lay below them in bands of white and green. As the sun rose they changed into bubbling seas of red and gold, churned off and let the low rays stripe the dried grass on which Mowgli and Bagheera were resting. It was the end of the cold weather, the leaves and the trees looked worn and faded, and there was a dry ticking rustle when the wind blew. A little leaf tap-tap-tapped furiously against a twig as a single leaf caught in a current will. It roused Bagheera, for he snuffed the morning air with a deep hollow cough, threw himself on his back, and struck with his fore paws at the nodding leaf above.

"The year turns," he said. "The jungle goes forward. The Time of New Talk is near. That leaf knows. It is very good."

"The grass is dry," Mowgli answered, pulling up a tuft. "Even Eye-of-the-Spring [that is a little, trumpet-shaped, waxy red flower that runs in and out among the grasses] – even Eye-of-the-Spring is shut and…. Bagheera, *is* it well for the Black Panther so to lie on his back and beat with his paws in the air as though he were the tree-cat?"

"*Aowh!*" said Bagheera. He seemed to be thinking of other things.

"I say, *is* it well for the Black Panther so to mouth and cough and howl and roll? Remember, we be the masters of the jungle, thou and I."

"Indeed, yes. I hear, man-cub." Bagheera rolled over hurriedly, and sat up, the dust on his ragged black flanks. (He was just casting his winter coat.) "We be surely the masters of the jungle! Who is so strong as Mowgli? Who so wise?" There was a curious drawl in the voice that made Mowgli turn to see whether by any chance the black panther were making fun of him, for the jungle is full of words that sound like one thing but mean another. "I said we be beyond question the masters of the jungle," Bagheera repeated. "Have I done wrong? I did not know that the man-cub no longer lay upon the ground. Does he fly, then?"

Mowgli sat with his elbows on his knees looking out across the valley at the daylight. Somewhere down in the woods below a bird was trying over in a husky, reedy voice the first few notes of his spring song. It was no more than a shadow of the full-throated tumbling call he would be crying later, but Bagheera heard it.

"I said the Time of New Talk was near," growled the panther, switching his tail.

"I hear," Mowgli answered. "Bagheera, why dost thou shake all over? The sun is warm."

"That is Ferao, the scarlet woodpecker," said Bagheera. "*He* has not forgotten. Now I too must remember my song." And he began purring and crooning to himself, harking back dissatisfied again and again.

"There is no game afoot," said Mowgli, lazily.

"Little Brother, are *both* thine ears stopped? That is no killing-word but my song that I make ready against the need."

"I had forgotten. I shall know when the Time of New Talk is here, because then thou and the others run away and leave me single-foot." Mowgli spoke rather savagely.

"But, indeed, Little Brother," Bagheera began, "we do not always – "

"I say ye do," said Mowgli, shooting out his forefinger angrily. "Ye *do* run away, and I, who am the master of the jungle, must needs walk single-foot. How was it last season, when I would gather sugar-cane from the fields of a man pack? I sent a runner – I sent thee! – to Hathi bidding him to come upon such a night and pluck the sweet grass for me with his trunk."

"He came only two nights later," said Bagheera, cowering a little, "and of that long sweet grass that pleased thee so, he gathered more than any man-cub could eat in all the nights of the rains. His was no fault of mine."

"He did not come upon the night when I sent him the word. No, he was trumpeting and running and roaring through valleys in the moonlight. His trail was like the trail of three elephants, for he would not hide among the trees. He danced in the moonlight before the houses of the man pack. I saw him, and yet he would not come to me; and *I* am the master of the jungle!"

"It was the Time of New Talk," said the panther, always very humble. "Perhaps, Little Brother, thou didst not that time call him by a Master Word? Listen to Ferao!"

Mowgli's bad temper seemed to have boiled itself away. He lay back with his head on his arms, his eyes shut. "I do not know – nor do I care," he said sleepily. "Let us sleep, Bagheera. My stomach is heavy in me. Make me a rest for my head."

The panther lay down again with a sigh, because he could hear Ferao practising and repractising his song against the Spring-time of New Talk, as they say.

In an Indian jungle the seasons slide one into the other almost without division. There seem to be only two – the wet and the dry – but if you look closely below the torrents of rain and the clouds of char and dust you will find all four going round in their regular order. Spring is the most wonderful, because she has not to cover a clean bare field with new leaves and flowers, but to drive before her and to put away the hanging-on, over-surviving raffle of half-green things which the gentle winter has suffered to live, and to make the partly dressed, stale earth feel new and young once more. And this she does so well that there is no spring in the world like the jungle spring.

There is one day when all things are tired, and the very smells as they drift on the heavy air are old and used. One cannot explain, but it feels so. Then there is another day – to the eye nothing whatever has changed – when all the smells are new and delightful and the whiskers of the Jungle-People quiver to their roots, and the winter hair comes away from their sides in long draggled locks. Then, perhaps, a little rain falls, and all the trees and the bushes and the bamboos and the mosses and the juicy-leaved plants wake with a noise of growing that you can almost hear, and under this noise runs, day and night, a deep hum. *That* is the noise of the spring – a vibrating boom which is neither bees nor falling water nor the wind in the tree-tops, but the purring of the warm, happy world.

Up to this year Mowgli had always delighted in the turn of the seasons. It was he who generally saw the first Eye-of-the-Spring deep down among the grasses, and the first bank of spring clouds which are like nothing else in the jungle. His voice could be heard in all sorts of wet star-lighted blossoming places, helping the big frogs through their choruses, or mocking the little upside-down owls that hoot through the white nights. Like all his people, spring was the season he chose for his fittings – moving for mere joy of rushing through the warm air, thirty, forty, or fifty miles between twilight and the morning star, and coming back panting and laughing and wreathed with strange flowers. The Four did not follow him on these wild ringings of the jungle, but went off to sing songs with other wolves. The Jungle-People are very busy in the spring, and Mowgli could hear them grunting and screaming and whistling according to their kind. Their voices then are different from their voices at other times of the year, and that is one of the reasons why spring is called the Time of New Talk.

But that spring, as he told Bagheera, his stomach was new in him. Ever since the bamboo shoots turned spotty-brown he had been looking forward to the morning when the smells should change. But when that morning came, and Mor the Peacock, blazing in bronze and blue and gold, cried it aloud all along the misty woods, and Mowgli opened his mouth to send on the cry, the words choked between his teeth, and a feeling came over him that began at his toes and ended in his hair – a feeling of pure unhappiness – and he looked himself over to be sure that he had not trodden on a thorn. Mor cried the new smells, the other birds took it over, and from the rocks by the Wainganga he heard Bagheera's hoarse scream – something between the scream of an eagle and the neighing of a horse. There was a yelling and scattering of *Bandar-log* in the new-budding branches above, and there stood Mowgli, his chest filled to answer Mor, sinking in little gasps as the breath was driven out of it by this unhappiness.

He stared, but he could see no more than the mocking *Bandar-log* scudding through the trees, and Mor, his tail spread in full splendour, dancing on the slopes below.

"The smells have changed," screamed Mor. "Good hunting, Little Brother! Where is thy answer?"

"Little Brother, good hunting!" whistled Chil the Kite and his mate swooping down together. The two baffed under Mowgli's nose so close that a pinch of downy white feathers brushed out.

A light spring rain – elephant-rain they call it – drove across the jungle in a belt half a mile wide, left the new leaves wet and nodding behind, and died out in a double rainbow and a light roll of thunder. The spring-hum broke out for a minute and was silent, but all the Jungle-Folk seemed to be giving tongue at once. All except Mowgli.

"I have eaten good food," he said to himself. "I have drunk good water. Nor does my throat burn and grow small, as it did when I bit the blue-spotted root that Oo the Turtle said was clean food. But my stomach is heavy, and I have, for no cause, given very bad talk to Bagheera and others, people of the jungle and my people. Now, too, I am hot and now I am cold, and now I am neither hot nor cold, but angry with that which I cannot see. *Huhu!* It is time to make a running! Tonight I will cross the ranges; yes, I will make a spring running to the Marshes of the North and back again. I have hunted too easily too long. The Four shall come with me, for they grow as fat as white grubs."

He called, but never one of the Four answered. They were far beyond earshot, singing over the spring songs – the moon and sambur songs – with the wolves of the pack, for in the spring-time the Jungle-People make little difference between the day and the night. He gave the sharp barking note, but his only answer was the mocking *maiou* of the little spotted tree-cat winding in and out among the branches for early birds' nests. At this he shook all over with rage and half drew his knife. Then he became very haughty, though there was no one to see him, and stalked severely down the hillside, chin up and eyebrows down. But never a single one of his people asked him a question, for they were all too busy with their own affairs.

"Yes," said Mowgli to himself, though in his heart he knew that he had no reason. "Let the red dhole come from the Dekkan or the Red Flower dance among the bamboos, and all the jungle runs whining to Mowgli calling him great elephant names. But now, because Eye-of-the-Spring is red, and Mor, forsooth, must show his naked legs in some spring-dance, the jungle goes mad as Tabaqui.... By the bull that bought me, am I the master of the jungle or am I not? Be silent! What do ye here?"

A couple of young wolves of the pack were cantering down a path look-ing for open ground in which to fight. (You will remember that the Law of the Jungle forbids fighting where the pack can see.) Their neck-bristles were as stiff as wire, and they bayed, furiously crouching for the first grapple. Mowgli leaped forward, caught one outstretched throat in either hand, expecting to fling the creatures backwards, as he had often done in games or pack hunts. But he had never before interfered with a spring fight. The two leaped forward and dashed him aside to the earth, and without a word to waste rolled over and over close locked.

Mowgli was on his feet almost before he fell, his knife and his white teeth were bared, and at that minute he would have killed both for no reason but that they were fighting when he wished them to be quiet, although every wolf has full right under the Law to fight. He danced round them with lowered shoulders and quivering hand ready to send in a double blow when the first flurry of the scuffle should be over, but while he waited the strength seemed to go out of his body, the knife point lowered, and he sheathed the knife and watched.

"I have eaten poison," he said at last. "Since I broke up the council with the Red Flower – since I killed Shere Khan none of the pack could fling me aside. And these be only tail-wolves in the pack, little hunters. My strength is gone from me, and presently I shall die. O, Mowgli, why dost thou not kill them both?"

The fight went on till one wolf ran away, and Mowgli was left alone on the torn and bloody ground, looking now at his knife, and now at his legs and arms, while the feeling of unhappiness he had never known before covered him as water covers a log.

He killed early that evening and ate but little, so as to be in good fettle for his spring running, and he ate alone because all the Jungle-People were away singing or fighting. It was a perfect white night, as they call it. All green things seemed to have made a month's growth since the morning. The branch that was yellow-leaved the day before dripped sap when Mowgli broke it. The mosses curled deep and warm over his feet, the young grass had no cutting edges, and all the voices of the jungle boomed like one deep harp-string touched by the moon – the full Moon of New Talk, who splashed her light full on rock and pool, slipped it between trunk and creeper, and sifted it through the million leaves. Unhappy as he was, Mowgli sang aloud with pure delight as he settled into his stride. It was more like flying than anything else, for he had chosen the long downward slope that leads to the northern marshes through the heart of the main jungle, where the springy ground deadened the fall of his feet. A man-taught man would have picked his way with many stumbles through the cheating moonlight, but Mowgli's muscles, trained by years of experience, bore him up as though he were a feather. When a rotten log or a hidden stone turned under his foot he saved himself, never checking his pace, without effort and without thought. When he tired of ground-going he threw up his hands monkey-fashion to the nearest creeper, and seemed to float rather than to climb up into the thin branches, whence he would follow a tree-road till his mood changed, and he shot downwards in a long leafy curve to the levels again. There were still hot hollows surrounded by wet rocks where he could hardly breathe for the heavy scents of the night-flowers, and the bloom along the creeper-buds; dark avenues where the moonlight lay in belts as regular as chequered marbles in a church aisle; thickets where the wet young growth stood breast-high about him and threw its arms round his waist; and hilltops crowned with broken rock, where he leaped from stone to stone above the lairs of the frightened little foxes. He would hear, very faint and far off, the *chug-drug* of a boar sharpening his tusks on a bole; and later would come across the great brute all alone, scribing and rending the red bark of a tree, his mouth dripping with foam and his eyes blazing like fire. Or he would turn aside to the sound of clashing horns and hissing grunts and dash past a couple of furious sambur, staggering to and fro with lowered heads, striped with blood that shows black in the moonlight. Or at some rushing ford he would hear Jacala the Crocodile bellowing like a bull, or disturb a knot of the Poison-People, but before they could strike he would be away and across the glistening shingle, and deep into the jungle again.

So he ran, sometimes shouting, sometimes singing to himself, the happiest thing in all the jungle that night, till the smell of the flowers warned him that he was near the marshes, and those lay far beyond his farthest hunting-grounds.

Here, again, a man-trained man would have sunk over his head in three strides, but Mowgli's feet had eyes in them and they passed him from tussock to tussock and clump to quaking clump without asking help from the eyes in his head. He headed out to the middle of the swamp, disturbing the duck as he ran, and sat down on a moss-coated tree-trunk lapped in the black water. The marsh was awake all round him, for in the spring the Bird-People sleep very lightly, and companies of them were coming or going the night through. But no one took any notice of Mowgli sitting among the tall reeds humming songs without words and looking at the soles of his hard brown feet in case of neglected thorns. All his unhappiness seemed to have been left behind in his own jungle, and he was just beginning a song when it came back again – ten times worse than before. To make all worse the moon was setting.

This time Mowgli was frightened. "It is here also!" he said half aloud. "It has followed me," and he looked over his shoulder to see whether the It were not standing behind him. "There is no one here." The night noises in the marsh went on, but never bird or beast spoke to him, and the new feeling of misery grew.

"I have eaten poison," he said, in an awe-stricken voice. "It must be that carelessly I have eaten poison, and my strength is going from me. I was afraid – and yet it was not *I* that was afraid – Mowgli was afraid when the two wolves fought. Akela, or even Phao, would have silenced them, yet Mowgli was afraid. That is sure sign I have eaten poison.... But what do they care in the jungle? They sing and howl and fight, and run in companies under the moon, and I – *Hai mai!* – I am dying in the marshes, of that poison which I have eaten." He was so sorry for himself that he nearly wept. "And after," he went on, "they will find me lying in the black water. Nay, I will go back to my own jungle and I will die upon the Council Rock, and Bagheera whom I love, if he is not screaming in the valley, Bagheera, perhaps, may watch by what is left for a little, lest Chil use me as he used Akela."

A large warm tear splashed down on his knee, and, miserable as he was, Mowgli felt happy that he was so miserable, if you can understand that upside-down sort of happiness. "As Chil the Kite used Akela," he repeated, "on the night I saved the pack from Red Dog." He was quiet for a little, thinking of the last words of the Lone Wolf, which you, of course, remember. "Now Akela said to me many foolish things before he died, for when we die our stomachs change. He said.... None the less, I *am* of the jungle!"

In his excitement, as he remembered the fight on Wainganga bank, he shouted the last words aloud, and a wild buffalo-cow among the reeds sprang to her knees, snorting: "Man!"

"*Uhh!*" said Mysa the Wild Buffalo (Mowgli could hear him turn in his wallow), "*that* is no man. It is only the hairless wolf of the Seeonee Pack. On such nights runs he to and fro."

"*Uhh!*" said the cow, dropping her head again to graze, "I thought it was Man."

"I say no. Oh, Mowgli, is it danger?" lowed Mysa.

"Oh, Mowgli, is it danger?" the boy called back mockingly. "That is all Mysa thinks for: Is it danger? But for Mowgli, who goes to and fro in the jungle by night watching, what care ye?"

"How loud he cries?" said the cow.

"Thus do they cry," Mysa answered contemptuously, "who having torn the grass up know not how to eat it."

"For less than this," Mowgli groaned to himself, "for less than this even last rains I had pricked Mysa out of his wallow and ridden him through the swamp on a rush halter." He stretched his hand to break one of the feathery reeds, but drew it back with a sigh. Mysa went on steadily chewing the cud and the long grass ripped where the cow grazed. "I will not die *here,*" he said angrily. "Mysa, who is of one blood with Jacala and the pig, would mock me. Let us go beyond the swamp, and see what comes. Never have I run such a spring running – hot and cold together. Up, Mowgli!"

He could not resist the temptation of stealing across the reeds to Mysa and pricking him with the point of his knife. The great dripping bull broke out of his wallow like a shell exploding, while Mowgli laughed till he sat down.

"Say now that the hairless wolf of the Seeonee Pack once herded thee, Mysa," he called.

"Wolf! *Thou?*" the bull snorted, stamping in the mud. "All the jungle knows thou wast a herder of tame cattle – such a man's brat as shouts in the dust by the crops yonder. *Thou* of the jungle! What hunter would have crawled like a snake among the leeches, and for a muddy jest – a jackal's jest – have shamed me before my cow? Come to firm ground, and I will – I will...." Mysa frothed at the mouth, for he has nearly the worst temper of any one in the jungle.

Mowgli watched him puff and blow with eyes that never changed. When he could make himself heard through the spattering mud-shower, he said: "What man pack lair here by the marshes, Mysa? This is new jungle to me."

"Go north, then," roared the angry bull, for Mowgli had pricked him rather sharply. "It was a naked cowherd's jest. Go and tell them at the village at the foot of the marsh."

"The man pack do not love jungle-tales, nor do I think, Mysa, that a scratch more or less on thy hide is any matter for a council. But I will go and look at this village. Yes, I will go. Softly now! It is not every night that the master of the jungle comes to herd thee."

He stepped out to the shivering ground on the edge of the marsh, well knowing that Mysa would never charge over it, and laughed, as he ran, to think of the bull's anger.

"My strength is not altogether gone," he said. "It may be the poison is not to the bone. There is a star sitting low yonder." He looked at it steadily between half-shut hands. "By the bull that bought me, it is the Red Flower – the Red Flower that I lay beside before – before I came even to the first Seeonee Pack! Now that I have seen I will finish the running."

The marsh ended in a broad plain where a light twinkled. It was a long time since Mowgli had concerned himself with the doings of men, but this night the glimmer of the Red Flower drew him forward as if it had been new game.

"I will look," said he, "and I will see how far the man pack has changed."

Forgetting that he was no longer in his own jungle where he could do what he pleased, he trod carelessly through the dew-loaded grasses till he came to the hut where the light stood. Three or four yelping dogs gave tongue, for he was on the outskirts of a village.

"Ho!" said Mowgli, sitting down noiselessly, after sending back a deep wolf-growl that silenced the curs. "What comes will come. Mowgli, what hast thou to do any more with the lairs of the man pack?" He rubbed his mouth, remembering where a stone had struck it years ago when the other man pack had cast him out.

The door of the hut opened and a woman stood peering out into the darkness. A child cried, and the woman said over her shoulder: "Sleep. It was but a jackal that waked the dogs. In a little time morning comes."

Mowgli in the grass began to shake as though he had the fever. He knew that voice well, but to make sure he cried softly, surprised to find how man's talk came back: "Messua! O Messua!"

"Who calls?" said the woman, a quiver in her voice.

"Hast thou forgotten?" said Mowgli. His throat was dry as he spoke.

"If it be *thou*, what name did I give thee? Say!" She had half shut the door, and her hand was clutching at her breast.

"Nathoo! Ohé Nathoo!" said Mowgli, for, as you know, that was the name Messua gave him when he first came to the man pack.

"Come, my son," she called, and Mowgli stepped into the light, and looked full at Messua, the woman who had been good to him, and whose life he had saved from the man pack so long before. She was older, and her hair was grey, but her eyes and her voice had not changed. Woman-like, she expected to find Mowgli where she had left him, and her eyes travelled upwards in a puzzled fashion from his chest to his head, that touched the top of the door.

"My son," she stammered, and then sinking to his feet: "But it is no longer my son. It is a godling of the woods! *Ahai!*"

As he stood in the red light of the oil-lamp, strong, tall, and beautiful, his long black hair sweeping over his shoulders, the knife swinging at his neck, and his head crowned with a wreath of white jasmine, he might easily have been mistaken for some wild god of a jungle legend. The child half asleep on a cot sprang up and shrieked aloud with terror. Messua turned to soothe him while Mowgli stood still, looking in at the water-jars and cooking-pots, the grain-bin and all the other human belongings that he found himself remembering so well.

"What wilt thou eat or drink?" Messua murmured. "This is all thine. We owe our lives to thee. But art thou him I called Nathoo, or a godling, indeed?"

"I am Nathoo," said Mowgli, "I am very far from my own place. I saw this light and came hither. I did not know thou wast here."

"After we came to Khanhiwara," Messua said timidly, "the English would have helped us against those villagers that sought to burn us. Rememberest thou?"

"Indeed, I have not forgotten."

"But when the English Law was made ready we went to the village of those evil people and it was no more to be found."

"That also I remember," said Mowgli, with a quiver of the nostril.

"My man, therefore, took service in the fields, and at last, for indeed he was a strong man, we held a little land here. It is not so rich as the old village, but we do not need much – we two."

"Where is he – the man that dug in the dirt when he was afraid on that night?"

"He is dead – a year."

"And he?" Mowgli pointed to the child.

"My son that was born two rains ago. If thou art a godling give him the favour of the jungle that he may be safe among thy – thy people as we were safe on that night."

She lifted up the child, who, forgetting his fright, reached out to play with the knife that hung on Mowgli's chest, and Mowgli put the little fingers aside very carefully.

"And if thou art Nathoo whom the tigers carried away," Messua went on choking, "he is then thy younger brother. Give him an elder brother's blessing."

"*Hai mai!* What do I know of the thing called a blessing? I am neither a godling nor his brother, and – O Mother, Mother, my heart is heavy in me." He shivered as he set down the child.

"Like enough," said Messua, bustling among the cooking-pots. "This comes of running about the marshes by night. Beyond question, a fever has soaked thee to the marrow." Mowgli smiled a little at the idea of anything in the jungle hurting him. "I will make a fire and thou shalt drink warm milk. Put away the jasmine wreath, the smell is heavy in so small a place."

Mowgli sat down, muttering, his face in his hands. All manner of strange feelings were running over him, exactly as though he had been poisoned, and he felt dizzy and a little sick. He drank the warm milk in long gulps, Messua patting him on the shoulder from time to time, not quite sure whether he were her son Nathoo of the long-ago days or some wonderful jungle being, but glad to feel that he was at least flesh and blood.

"Son," she said at last. Her eyes were full of pride. "Have any told thee that thou art beautiful beyond all men?"

"Hah?" said Mowgli, for of course he had never heard anything of the kind. Messua laughed softly and happily. The look in his face was enough for her.

"I am the first, then? It is right, though it comes seldom, that a mother should tell her son these good things. Thou art very beautiful. Never have I looked upon such a man."

Mowgli twisted his head and tried to see over his own hard shoulder, and Messua laughed again so long that Mowgli, not knowing why, was forced to laugh with her, and the child ran from one to the other laughing too.

"Nay, thou must not mock thy brother," said Messua catching him to her breast. "When thou art one-half as fair we will marry thee to the young-est daughter of a king and thou shalt ride great elephants."

Mowgli could not understand one word in three of the talk here; the warm milk was taking effect on him after his forty-mile run; so he curled up and in a minute was deep asleep, and Messua put the hair back from his eyes, threw a cloth over him and was happy. Jungle-fashion, he slept out the rest of that night and all the next day, for his instincts, which never wholly slept, warned him there was nothing to fear. He waked at last with a bound that shook the hut, for the cloth over his face made him dream of traps, and there he stood, his hand on his knife, the sleep all heavy in his rolling eyes, ready for any fight.

Messua laughed and set the evening meal before him. There were only a few coarse cakes baked over the smoky fire, some rice, and a lump of sour preserved tamarinds – just enough to go on with till he could get to his evening kill. The smell of the dew in the marshes made him hungry and restless. He wanted to finish his spring running, but the child insisted on sitting in his arms, and Messua would have it that his long blue-black hair must be combed out. So she sang as she combed, foolish little baby songs, now calling Mowgli her son, and now begging him to give some of his jungle-power to the child. The hut door was closed, but Mowgli heard a sound he knew well, and saw Messua's jaw drop with horror as a great grey paw came under the bottom of the door, and Grey Brother outside whined a muffled and penitent whine of anxiety and fear.

"Out and wait. Ye would not come when I called," said Mowgli in jungle-talk, never turning his head, and the great grey paw disappeared.

"Do not – do not bring thy – thy servants with thee," said Messua. "I – we have always lived at peace with the jungle."

"It is peace," said Mowgli, rising. "Think of that night on the road to Khanhiwara. There were scores of such folk before thee and behind thee. But I see that even in spring-time the Jungle-People do not always forget. Mother, I go."

Messua drew aside humbly – he was indeed a wood-god she thought – but as his hand was on the door the mother in her made her throw her arms round Mowgli's neck again and again.

"Come back!" she whispered. "Son or no son, come back, for I love thee – and look, he too grieves."

The child was crying because the man with the shiny knife was going away.

"Come back again," Messua repeated. "By night or by day this door is never shut to thee."

Mowgli's throat worked as though the cords in it were being pulled, and his voice seemed to be dragged from it as he answered: "I will surely come back."

"And now," he said, as he put aside the head of the fawning wolf on the threshold, "I have a little cry against thee, Grey Brother. Why came ye not, all Four, when I called so long ago?"

"So long ago? It was but last night. I – we – were singing in the jungle, the new songs, for this is the Time of New Talk. Rememberest thou?"

"Truly, truly."

"And as soon as the songs were sung," Grey Brother went on earnestly, "I followed thy trail. I ran from all the others and followed hot-foot. But, O Little Brother, what hast *thou* done – eating and sleeping with the man pack?"

"If ye had come when I called this had never been," said Mowgli, running much faster.

"And now what is to be?" said Grey Brother.

The girl screamed, for she thought she had seen a spirit.

Mowgli was going to answer when a girl in a white cloth came down some path that led from the outskirts of the village. Grey Brother dropped out of sight at once and Mowgli backed noiselessly into a field of high-springing crops. He could almost have touched her with his hand when the warm green stalks closed before his face and he disappeared like a ghost. The girl screamed, for she thought she had seen a spirit, and then she gave a deep sigh. Mowgli parted the stalks with his hands and watched her till she was out of sight.

"And now I do not know," he said, sighing in his turn. "*Why* did ye not come when I called?"

"We follow thee – we follow thee," Grey Brother mumbled, licking at Mowgli's heel. "We follow thee always except in the Time of the New Talk."

"And would ye follow me to the man pack?" Mowgli whispered.

"Did I not follow thee on the night that our old pack cast thee out? Who waked thee lying among the crops?"

"Aye, but again?"

"Have I not followed thee tonight?"

"Aye, but again and again, and it may be again, Grey Brother?"

Grey Brother was silent. When he spoke he growled to himself: "The Black One spoke truth."

"And he said?"

"Man goes to Man at the last. Raksha our mother said – "

"So also said Akela on the night of Red Dog," Mowgli muttered.

"So also said Kaa, who is wiser than us all."

"What dost thou say, Grey Brother?"

"They cast thee out once, with bad talk. They cut thy mouth with stones. They sent Buldeo to slay thee. They would have thrown thee into the Red Flower. Thou, and not I, hast said that they are evil and senseless. Thou and not I – I follow my own people – didst let in the jungle upon them. Thou and not I didst make song against them more bitter even than our song against Red Dog."

"I ask thee what *thou* sayest?"

They were talking as they ran. Grey Brother cantered on a while without replying, and then he said between bound and bound as it were: "Man-cub – master of the jungle – son of Raksha – lair-brother to me – though I forget for a little while in the spring, thy trail is my trail, thy lair is my lair, thy kill is my kill, and thy death-fight is my death-fight. I speak for the Three. But what wilt thou say to the jungle?"

"That is well thought. Between the sight and the kill it is not good to wait. Go before and cry them all to the Council Rock, and I will tell them what is in my stomach. But they may not come – in the Time of the New Talk they may forget me."

"Hast thou then forgotten, nothing?" snapped Grey Brother over his shoulder, as he laid himself down to gallop, and Mowgli followed, thinking.

At any other season his news would have called all the jungle together with bristling necks, but now they were busy hunting and fighting and killing and singing. From one to another Grey Brother ran, crying: "The master of the jungle goes back to Man. Come to the Council Rock!" And the happy, eager people only answered: "He will return in the summer heats. The rains will drive him to lair. Run and sing with us, Grey Brother."

"But the master of the jungle goes back to Man," Grey Brother would repeat.

"*Eee – Yowa?* Is the Time of New Talk any less good for that?" they would reply. So when Mowgli, heavy-hearted, came up through the well-remembered rocks to the place where he had been brought into the pack, he found only the Four, Baloo, who was nearly blind with age, and the heavy, cold-blooded Kaa, coiled round Akela's empty seat.

"Thy trail ends here, then, manling?" said Kaa, as Mowgli threw himself down, his face in his hands. "Cry thy cry. We be of one blood, thou and I – man and snake together."

"Why was I not torn in two by Red Dog?" the boy moaned. "My strength is gone from me, and it is not the poison. By night and by day I hear a double step upon my trail. When I turn my head it is as though one had hidden himself from me that instant. I go to look behind the trees and he is not there. I call and none cry again, but it is as though one listened and kept back the answer. I lie down, but I do not rest. I run the spring running, but I am not made still. I bathe, but I am not made cool. The kill sickens me, but I have no heart to fight except I kill. The Red Flower is in my body, my bones are water – and – I know not what I know."

"What need of talk?" said Baloo, slowly, turning his head to where Mowgli lay. "Akela by the river said it, that Mowgli should drive Mowgli back to the man pack. I said it. But who listens now to Baloo? Bagheera – where is Bagheera this night? He knows also. It is the Law."

"When we met at the Cold Lairs, manling, I knew it," said Kaa, turning a little in his mighty coils. "Man goes to Man at the last, though the jungle does not cast him out."

The Four looked at one another and at Mowgli, puzzled but obedient.

"The jungle does not cast me out, then?" Mowgli stammered.

Grey Brother and the Three growled furiously, beginning: "So long as we live none shall dare – " But Baloo checked them.

"I taught thee the Law. It is for me to speak," he said, "and though I cannot now see the rocks before me, I see far. Little frog, take thine own trail; make thy lair with thine own blood and pack and people; but when there is need of foot or tooth or eye or a word carried swiftly by night, remember, master of the jungle, the jungle is thine at call."

"The Middle Jungle is thine also," said Kaa. "I speak for no small people."

"*Hai mai*, my brothers," cried Mowgli, throwing up his arms with a sob. "I know not what I know, I would not go, but I am drawn by both feet. How shall I leave these nights?"

"Nay, look up, Little Brother," Baloo repeated. "There is no shame in this hunting. When the honey is eaten we leave the empty hive."

"Having cast the skin," said Kaa, "we may not creep into it afresh. It is the Law."

"Listen, dearest of all to me," said Baloo. "There is neither word nor will here to hold thee back. Look up! Who may question the master of the jungle? I saw thee playing among the white pebbles yonder when thou wast a little frog; and Bagheera, that bought thee for the price of a young bull newly killed, saw thee also. Of that looking-over we two only remain, for Raksha, thy lair-mother, is dead with thy lair-father; the old wolf pack is long since dead; thou knowest whither Shere Khan went, and Akela died among the dholes; where but for thy wisdom and strength the second Seeonee Pack would also have died. There remain nothing but old bones. It is no longer the man-cub that asks leave of his pack, but the master of the jungle that changes his trail. Who shall question man in his ways?"

"But Bagheera and the bull that bought me," said Mowgli. "I would not – "

His words were cut short by a roar and a crash in the thicket below, and Bagheera, light, strong, and terrible as always.

"*Therefore,*" he said, stretching out a dripping right paw, "I did not come. It was a long hunt, but he lies dead in the bushes now – a bull in his second year – the bull that frees thee, Little Brother. All debts are paid now. For the rest, my word is Baloo's word." He licked Mowgli's foot. "Remember Bagheera loved thee," he cried and bounded away. At the foot of the hill he cried again long and loud: "Good hunting on a new trail, master of the jungle! Remember Bagheera loved thee."

"Thou hast heard," said Baloo. "There is no more. Go now, but first come to me. O wise little frog, come to me!"

"It is hard to cast the skin," said Kaa, as Mowgli sobbed and sobbed with his head on the blind bear's side and his arms round his neck, while Baloo tried feebly to lick his feet.

"The stars are thin," said Grey Brother, snuffing at the dawn-wind. "Where shall we lair today? For, from now, we follow new trails."

And this is the last of the Mowgli stories.

The Outsong

This is the song that Mowgli heard behind him in the jungle till he came to Messua's door again.

BALOO

For the sake of him who showed
One wise frog the jungle-road,
Keep the Law the man pack make –
For thy blind old Baloo's sake!
Clean or tainted, hot or stale,
Hold it as it were the trail,
Through the day and through the night,
Questing neither left nor right.
For the sake of him who loves
Thee beyond all else that moves,
When thy pack would make thee pain,
Say: "Tabaqui sings again."
When thy pack would work thee ill,
Say: "Shere Khan is yet to kill."
When the knife is drawn to slay,
Keep the Law and go thy way.
(Root and honey, palm and spathe,
Guard a cub from harm and scathe.)
Wood and water, wind and tree,
Jungle-favour go with thee!

KAA

Anger is the egg of fear –
Only lidless eyes are clear.
Cobra-poison none may leech;
Even so with cobra-speech.
Open talk shall call to thee
Strength whose mate is courtesy.
Send no lunge beyond thy length;
Lend no rotten bough thy strength.
Gauge thy gape with buck or goat,
Lest thine eye should choke thy throat.
After gorging, wouldst thou sleep?
Look thy den is hid and deep,
Lest a wrong, by thee forgot,
Draw thy killer to the spot.
East and West and North and South,
Wash thy skin and close thy mouth.
(Pit and rift and blue pool-brim
Middle Jungle follow him!)
Wood and water, wind and tree,
Jungle-favour go with thee!

BAGHEERA

In the cage my life began;
Well I know the ways of Man.
By the broken lock that freed –
Man-cub 'ware the man-cub's breed!
Scenting-dew or starlight pale,
Choose no idle tree-cat trail.
Pack or council, hunt or den,
Cry no truce with Jackal-Men.
Feed them silence when they say:
"Come with us an easy way."

330

Feed them silence when they seek
Help of thine to hurt the weak.
Make no *bandar's* boast of skill;
Hold thy peace above the kill.
Let nor call nor song nor sign
Turn thee from thy hunting-line.
(Morning mist or twilight clear
Serve him, wardens of the deer!)
Wood and water, wind and tree,
Jungle-favour go with thee!

THE THREE

On the trail that thou must tread
To the threshold of our dread,
Where the flower blossoms red;
Through the nights when thou shalt lie
Prisoned from our mother-sky,
Hearing us, thy loves, go by;
In the dawns, when thou shalt wake
To the toil thou canst not break,
Heartsick for the jungle's sake;
Wood and water, wind and tree,
Jungle-favour go with thee!

Kim

Chapter 1

O ye who tread the Narrow Way
By Tophet-flare to Judgement Day,
Be gentle when "the heathen" pray
To Buddha at Kamakura!
                                    Buddha at Kamakura

He sat, in defiance of municipal orders, astride the gun Zam-Zammah on her brick platform opposite the old Ajaib-Gher – the Wonder House, as the natives call the Lahore Museum. Who hold Zam-Zammah, that "fire-breathing dragon", hold the Punjab; for the great green-bronze piece is always first of the conqueror's loot.

There was some justification for Kim – he had kicked Lala Dinanath's boy off the trunnions – since the English held the Punjab and Kim was English. Though he was burned black as any native; though he spoke the vernacular by preference, and his mother-tongue in a clipped uncertain singsong; though he consorted on terms of perfect equality with the small boys of the bazaar; Kim was white – a poor white of the very poorest. The half-caste woman who looked after him (she smoked opium, and pretended to keep a secondhand furniture shop by the square where the cheap cabs wait) told the missionaries that she was Kim's mother's sister; but his mother had been nursemaid in a colonel's family and had married Kimball O'Hara, a young colour-sergeant of the Mavericks, an Irish regiment. He afterwards took a post on the Sind, Punjab, and Delhi Railway, and his regiment went home without him. The wife died of cholera in Ferozepore, and O'Hara fell to drink and loafing up and down the line with the keen-eyed three-year-old baby. Societies and chaplains, anxious for the child, tried to catch him, but O'Hara drifted away, till he came across the woman who took opium and learned the taste from her, and died as poor whites do in India. His estate at death consisted of three papers – one he called his "*ne varietur*" because those words were written below his signature thereon, and another his "clearance certificate". The third was Kim's birth certificate. Those things, he was used to say, in his glorious opium hours, would yet make little Kimball a man. On no account was Kim to part with them, for they belonged to a great piece of magic – such magic as men practised over yonder behind the museum, in the big blue and white Jadoo-Gher – the Magic House, as we name the Masonic Lodge. It would, he said, all come right some day, and Kim's horn would be exalted between pillars – monstrous pillars – of beauty and strength. The Colonel himself, riding on a horse, at the head of the finest regiment in the world, would attend to Kim – little Kim that should have been better off than his father. Nine hundred first-class devils, whose God was a Red Bull on a green field, would attend to Kim, if they had not forgotten O'Hara – poor O'Hara that was gang foreman on the Ferozepore line. Then he would weep bitterly in the broken rush chair on the veranda. So it came about after his death that the woman sewed parchment, paper, and birth certificate into a leather amulet-case which she strung round Kim's neck.

"And some day," she said, confusedly remembering O'Hara's prophecies, "there will come for you a great Red Bull on a green field, and the Colonel riding on his tall horse, yes, and" – dropping into English – "nine hundred devils."

"Ah," said Kim, "I shall remember. A Red Bull and a Colonel on a horse will come, but first, my father said, will come the two men making ready the ground for these matters. That is how my father said they always did; and it is always so when men work magic."

If the woman had sent Kim up to the local Jadoo-Gher with those papers, he would, of course, have been taken over by the Provincial Lodge and sent to the Masonic Orphanage in the Hills; but what she had heard of magic she distrusted. Kim, too, held views of his own. As he reached the years of indiscretion, he learned to avoid missionaries and white men of serious aspect who asked who he was, and what he did. For Kim did nothing with an immense success. True, he knew the wonderful walled city of Lahore from the Delhi Gate to the outer Fort Ditch; was hand in glove with men who led lives stranger than anything Haroun al Raschid dreamed of; and he lived in a life wild as that of the Arabian Nights, but missionaries and secretaries of charitable societies could not see the beauty of it. His nickname through the wards was "Little Friend of all the World'; and very often, being lithe and inconspicuous, he executed commissions by night on the crowded house-tops for sleek and shiny young men of fashion. It was intrigue, of course – he knew that much, as he had known all evil since he could speak – but what he loved was the game for its own sake – the stealthy prowl through the dark gullies and lanes, the crawl up a water-pipe, the sights and sounds of the women's world on the flat roofs, and the headlong flight from house-top to house-top under cover of the hot dark. Then there were holy men, ash-smeared *fakirs* by their brick shrines under the trees at the riverside, with whom he was quite familiar – greeting them as they returned from begging tours, and, when no one was by, eating from the same dish. The woman who looked after him insisted with tears that he should wear Euro-pean clothes – trousers, a shirt, and a battered hat. Kim found it easier to slip into Hindu or Muhammadan garb when engaged on certain businesses. One of the young men of fashion – he who was found dead at the bottom of a well on the night of the earthquake – had once given him a complete suit of Hindu kit, the costume of a low-caste street boy, and Kim stored it in a secret place under some baulks in Nila Ram's timber-yard, beyond the Punjab High Court, where the fragrant deodar logs lie seasoning after they have driven down the Ravi. When there was business or frolic afoot, Kim would use his properties, returning at dawn to the veranda, all tired out from shouting at the heels of a marriage procession, or yelling at a Hindu festival. Sometimes there was food in the house, more often there was not, and then Kim went out again to eat with his native friends.

As he drummed his heels against Zam-Zammah he turned now and again from his king-of-the-castle game with little Chota Lal and Abdullah the sweetmeat-seller's son, to make a rude remark to the native policeman on guard over the rows of shoes at the museum door. The big Punjabi grinned tolerantly: he knew Kim of old. So did the water-carrier, sluicing water on the dry road from his goatskin bag. So did Jawahir Singh, the museum carpenter, bent over new packing-cases. So did everybody in sight except the peasants from the country, hurrying up to the Wonder House to view the things that men made in their own province and elsewhere. The museum was given up to Indian arts and manufactures, and anybody who sought wisdom could ask the Curator to explain.

"Off! Off! Let me up!" cried Abdullah, climbing up Zam-Zammah's wheel.

"Thy father was a pastry-cook, Thy mother stole the ghee," sang Kim. "All Mussulmans fell off Zam-Zammah long ago!"

"Let *me* up!" shrilled little Chota Lal in his gilt-embroidered cap. His father was worth perhaps half a million sterling, but India is the only democratic land in the world.

"The Hindus fell off Zam-Zammah too. The Mussulmans pushed them off. Thy father was a pastry-cook –"

He stopped; for there shuffled round the corner, from the roaring Motee Bazaar, such a man as Kim, who thought he knew all castes, had never seen. He was nearly six feet high, dressed in fold upon fold of dingy stuff like horse-blanketing, and not one fold of it could Kim refer to any known trade or profession. At his belt hung a long open-work iron pen-case and a wooden rosary such as holy men wear. On his head was a gigantic sort of tam-o'-shanter. His face was yellow and wrinkled, like that of Fook Shing, the Chinese bootmaker in the bazaar. His eyes turned up at the corners and looked like little slits of onyx.

"Who is that?" said Kim to his companions.

"Perhaps it is a man," said Abdullah, finger in mouth, staring.

"Without doubt," returned Kim; "but he is no man of India that *I* have ever seen."

"A priest, perhaps," said Chota Lal, spying the rosary. "See! He goes into the Wonder House!"

"Nay, nay," said the policeman, shaking his head. "I do not understand your talk." The constable spoke Punjabi. "O friend of all the World, what does he say?"

"Send him hither," said Kim, dropping from Zam-Zammah, flourishing his bare heels. "He is a foreigner, and thou art a buffalo."

The man turned helplessly and drifted towards the boys. He was old,

'Who is that?', said Kim to his companions.

and his woollen gaberdine still reeked of the stinking artemisia of the mountain passes.

"O Children, what is that big house?" he said in very fair Urdu.

"The Ajaib-Gher, the Wonder House!" Kim gave him no title – such as Lala or Mian. He could not divine the man's creed.

"Ah! The Wonder House! Can any enter?"

"It is written above the door – all can enter."

"Without payment?"

"I go in and out. *I* am no banker," laughed Kim.

"Alas! I am an old man. I did not know." Then, fingering his rosary, he half turned to the museum.

"What is your caste? Where is your house? Have you come far?" Kim asked.

"I came by Kulu – from beyond the Kailas – but what know you? From the Hills where" – he sighed – "the air and water are fresh and cool."

"Aha! Khitai [a Chinaman]," said Abdullah proudly. Fook Shing had once chased him out of his shop for spitting at the joss above the boots.

"Pahari [a hillman]," said little Chota Lal.

"Aye, child – a hillman from hills thou'lt never see. Didst hear of Bhoti-yal [Tibet]? I am no Khitai, but a Bhotiya [Tibetan], since you must know – a lama – or, say, a guru in your tongue."

"A guru from Tibet," said Kim. "I have not seen such a man. They be Hindus in Tibet, then?"

"We be followers of the Middle Way, living in peace in our lamasseries, and I go to see the Four Holy places before I die. Now do you, who are children, know as much as I do who am old." He smiled benignantly on the boys.

"Hast thou eaten?"

He fumbled in his bosom and drew forth a worn wooden begging-bowl. The boys nodded. All priests of their acquaintance begged.

"I do not wish to eat yet." He turned his head like an old tortoise in the sunlight. "Is it true that there are many images in the Wonder House of Lahore?" He repeated the last words as one making sure of an address.

"That is true," said Abdullah. "It is full of heathen *būts*. Thou also art an idolater."

"Never mind *him*," said Kim. "That is the government's house and there is no idolatry in it, but only a sahib with a white beard. Come with me and I will show."

"Strange priests eat boys," whispered Chota Lal.

"And he is a stranger and a *būts-parast* [idolater]," said Abdullah, the Muhammadan.

Kim laughed. "He is new. Run to your mothers' laps, and be safe. Come!"

Kim clicked round the self-registering turnstile; the old man followed and halted amazed. In the entrance-hall stood the larger figures of the Greco-Buddhist sculptures done, savants know how long since, by forgotten workmen whose hands were feeling, and not unskilfully, for the mysteriously transmitted Grecian touch. There were hundreds of pieces, friezes of figures in relief, fragments of statues and slabs crowded with figures that had encrusted the brick walls of the Buddhist *stupas* and *viharas* of the North Country and now, dug up and labelled, made the pride of the museum. In open-mouthed wonder the lama turned to this and that, and finally checked in rapt attention before a large alto-relief representing a coronation or apotheosis of the Lord Buddha. The Master was represented seated on a lotus the petals of which were so deeply undercut as to show almost detached. Round him was an adoring hierarchy of kings, elders, and old-time Buddhas. Below were lotus-covered waters with fishes and water-birds. Two butterfly-winged *dewas* held a wreath over his head; above them another pair supported an umbrella surmounted by the jewelled headdress of the Bodhisat.

"The Lord! The Lord! It is Sakya Muni himself," the lama half sobbed; and under his breath began the wonderful Buddhist invocation:

> "To Him the Way, the Law, apart
> Whom Maya held beneath her heart,
> Ananda's Lord, the Bodhisat."

"And he is here! The Most Excellent Law is here also. My pilgrimage is well begun. And what work! What work!"

"Yonder is the sahib," said Kim, and dodged sideways among the cases of the arts and manufactures wing. A white-bearded Englishman was looking at the lama, who gravely turned and saluted him and after some fumbling drew forth a notebook and a scrap of paper.

"Yes, that is my name," smiling at the clumsy, childish print.

"One of us who had made pilgrimage to the Holy Places – he is now Abbot of the Lung-Cho Monastery – gave it me," stammered the lama. "He spoke of these." His lean hand moved tremulously round.

"Welcome, then, O lama from Tibet. Here be the images, and I am here" – he glanced at the lama's face – "to gather knowledge. Come to my office awhile." The old man was trembling with excitement.

The office was but a little wooden cubicle partitioned off from the sculpture-lined gallery. Kim laid himself down, his ear against a crack in the heat-split cedar door, and, following his instinct, stretched out to listen and watch.

Most of the talk was altogether above his head. The lama, haltingly at first, spoke to the Curator of his own lamassery, the Such-zen, opposite the Painted Rocks, four months" march away. The Curator brought out a huge book of photos and showed him that very place, perched on its crag, over-looking the gigantic valley of many-hued strata.

"Ay, ay!" The lama mounted a pair of horn-rimmed spectacles of Chinese work. "Here is the little door through which we bring wood before winter. And thou the English know of these things? He who is now Abbot of Lung-Cho told me, but I did not believe. The Lord – the Excellent One – he has honour here too? And his life is known?"

"It is all carven upon the stones. Come and see, if thou art rested."

Out shuffled the lama to the main hall, and, the Curator beside him, went through the collection with the reverence of a devotee and the appreciative instinct of a craftsman.

Incident by incident in the beautiful story he identified on the blurred stone, puzzled here and there by the unfamiliar Greek convention, but delighted as a child at each new trove. Where the sequence failed, as in the Annunciation, the Curator supplied it from his mound of books French and German, with photographs and reproductions.

Here was the devout Asita, the pendant of Simeon in the Christian story, holding the Holy Child on his knee while mother and father listened; and here were incidents in the legend of the cousin Devadatta. Here was the wicked woman who accused the Master of impurity, all confounded; here was the teaching in the Deer-park; the miracle that stunned the fire-worshippers; here was the Bodhisat in royal state as a prince; the miraculous birth; the death at Kusinagara, where the weak disciple fainted; while there were almost countless repetitions of the meditation under the Bodhi tree; and the adoration of the alms-bowl was everywhere. In a few minutes the Curator saw that his guest was no mere bead-telling mendicant, but a scholar of parts. And they went at it all over again, the lama taking snuff, wiping his spectacles, and talking at railway speed in a bewildering mixture of Urdu and Tibetan. He had heard of the travels of the Chinese pilgrims, Fu-Hiouen and Hwen-Tsiang, and was anxious to know if there was any translation of their record. He drew in his breath as he turned helplessly over the pages of Beal and Stanislas Julien. "Tis all here. A treasure locked." Then he composed himself reverently to listen to fragments hastily rendered into Urdu. For the first time he heard of the labours of European scholars, who by the help of these and a hundred other documents have identified the Holy Places of Buddhism. Then he was shown a mighty map, spotted and traced with yellow. The brown finger followed the Curator's pencil from point to point. Here was Kapilavastu, here the Middle Kingdom, and here Mahabodhi, the Mecca of Buddhism; and here was Kusinagara, sad place of the Holy One's death. The old man bowed his head over the sheets in silence for a while, and the Curator lit another pipe. Kim had fallen asleep. When he waked, the talk, still in spate, was more within his comprehension.

"And thus it was, O Fountain of Wisdom, that I decided to go to the Holy Places which his foot had trod – to the Birthplace, even to Kapila; then to Mahabodhi, which is Buddh Gaya – to the Monastery – to the Deer-park – to the place of his death."

The lama lowered his voice. "And I come here alone. For five – seven – eighteen – forty years it was in my mind that the Old Law was not well followed; being overlaid, as thou knowest, with devildom, charms, and idolatry. Even as the child outside said but now. Ay, even as the child said, with *būts parasti*."

"So it comes with all faiths."

"Thinkest thou? The books of my lamassery I read, and they were dried pith; and the later ritual with which we of the Reformed Law have cumbered ourselves – that, too, had no worth to these old eyes. Even the followers of the Excellent One are at feud on feud with one another. It is all illusion. Ay, *maya*, illusion. But I have another desire" – the seamed yellow face drew within three inches of the Curator, and the long forefinger nail tapped on the table. "Your scholars, by these books, have followed the Blessed Feet in all their wanderings; but there are things which they have not sought out. I know nothing – nothing do I know – but I go to free myself from the Wheel of Things by a broad and open road." He smiled with most simple triumph. "As a pilgrim to the Holy Places I acquire merit. But there is more. Listen to a true thing. When our gracious Lord, being as yet a youth, sought a mate, men said, in his father's court, that he was too tender for marriage. Thou knowest?"

The Curator nodded, wondering what would come next.

"So they made the triple trial of strength against all comers. And at the test of the Bow, our Lord first breaking that which they gave him, called for such a bow as none might bend. Thou knowest?"

"It is written. I have read."

"And, overshooting all other marks, the arrow passed far and far beyond sight. At the last it fell; and, where it touched earth, there broke out a stream which presently became a River, whose nature, by our Lord's beneficence, and that merit he acquired ere he freed himself, is that whoso bathes in it washes away all taint and speckle of sin."

"So it is written," said the Curator sadly.

The lama drew a long breath. "Where is that River? Fountain of Wisdom, where fell the arrow?"

"Alas, my brother, I do not know," said the Curator.

"Nay, if it please thee to forget – the one thing only that thou hast not told me. Surely thou must know? See, I am an old man! I ask with my head between thy feet, O Fountain of Wisdom. We *know* he drew the bow! We *know* the arrow fell! We *know* the stream gushed! Where, then, is the River? My dream told me to find it. So I came. I am here. But where is the River?"

"If I knew, think you I would not cry it aloud?"

"By it one attains freedom from the Wheel of Things," the lama went on, unheeding. "The River of the Arrow! Think again! Some little stream,

KIM

maybe – dried in the heats? But the Holy One would never so cheat an old man."

"I do not know. I do not know."

The lama brought his thousand-wrinkled face once more a handsbreadth from the Englishman's. "I see thou dost not know. Not being of the Law, the matter is hid from thee."

"Ay – hidden – hidden."

"We are both bound, thou and I, my brother. But I" – he rose with a sweep of the soft thick drapery – "I go to cut myself free. Come also!"

"I am bound," said the Curator. "But whither goest thou?"

"First to Kashi [Benares]: where else? There I shall meet one of the pure faith in a Jain temple of that city. He also is a Seeker in secret, and from him haply I may learn. Maybe he will go with me to Buddh Gaya. Thence north and west to Kapilavastu, and there will I seek for the River. Nay, I will seek everywhere as I go – for the place is not known where the arrow fell."

"And how wilt thou go? It is a far cry to Delhi, and farther to Benares."

"By road and the trains. From Pathânkot, having left the hills, I came hither in a *te-rain*. It goes swiftly. At first I was amazed to see those tall poles by the side of the road snatching up and snatching up their threads" – he illustrated the stoop and whirl of a telegraph-pole flashing past the train. "But later, I was cramped and desired to walk, as I am used."

"And thou art sure of thy road?" said the Curator.

"Oh, for that one but asks a question and pays money, and the appointed persons despatch all to the appointed place. That much I knew in my lamassery from sure report," said the lama proudly.

"And when dost thou go?" The Curator smiled at the mixture of old-world piety and modern progress that is the note of India today.

"As soon as may be. I follow the places of his life till I come to the River of the Arrow. There is, moreover, a written paper of the hours of the trains that go south."

"And for food?" Lamas, as a rule, have a good store of money somewhere about them, but the Curator wished to make sure.

"For the journey, I take up the Master's begging-bowl. Yes. Even as he went so go I, forsaking the ease of my monastery. There was with

345

me when I left the hills a *chela* [disciple] who begged for me as the Rule demands, but halting in Kulu awhile a fever took him and he died. I have now no *chela*, but I will take the alms-bowl and thus enable the charitable to acquire merit." He nodded his head valiantly. Learned doctors of a lamassery do not beg, but the lama was an enthusiast in this quest.

"Be it so," said the Curator, smiling. "Suffer me now to acquire merit. We be craftsmen together, thou and I. Here is a new book of white English paper: here be sharpened pencils two and three – thick and thin, all good for a scribe. Now lend me thy spectacles."

The Curator looked through them. They were heavily scratched, but the power was almost exactly that of his own pair, which he slid into the lama's hand, saying: "Try these."

"A feather! A very feather upon the face!" The old man turned his head delightedly and wrinkled up his nose. "How scarcely do I feel them! How clearly do I see!"

"They be *bilaur* – crystal – and will never scratch. May they help thee to thy River, for they are thine."

"I will take them and the pencils and the white notebook," said the lama, "as a sign of friendship between priest and priest – and now –" He fumbled at his belt, detached the open work iron pen-case, and laid it on the Curator's table. "That is for a memory between thee and me – my pen-case. It is something old – even as I am."

It was a piece of ancient design, Chinese, of an iron that is not smelted these days; and the collector's heart in the Curator's bosom had gone out to it from the first. For no persuasion would the lama resume his gift.

"When I return, having found the River, I will bring thee a written picture of the Padma Samthora – such as I used to make on silk at the lamassery. Yes – and of the Wheel of Life," he chuckled, "for we be craftsmen together, thou and I."

The Curator would have detained him: they are few in the world who still have the secret of the conventional brush-pen Buddhist pictures which are, as it were, half written and half drawn. But the lama strode out, head high in air, and pausing an instant before the great statue of a Bodhisat in meditation, brushed through the turnstiles.

Kim followed like a shadow. What he had overheard excited him wildly. This man was entirely new to all his experience, and he meant to investigate further, precisely as he would have investigated a new building or a strange festival in Lahore city. The lama was his trove, and he purposed to take possession. Kim's mother had been Irish too.

The old man halted by Zam-Zammah and looked round till his eye fell on Kim. The inspiration of his pilgrimage had left him for a while, and he felt old, forlorn, and very empty.

"Do not sit under that gun," said the policeman loftily.

"Huh! Owl!" was Kim's retort on the lama's behalf. "Sit under that gun if it please thee. When didst thou steal the milk-woman's slippers, Dunnoo?"

That was an utterly unfounded charge sprung on the spur of the moment, but it silenced Dunnoo, who knew that Kim's clear yell could call up legions of bad bazaar boys if need arose.

"And whom didst thou worship within?" said Kim affably, squatting in the shade beside the lama.

"I worshipped none, child. I bowed before the Excellent Law."

Kim accepted this new god without emotion. He knew already a few score.

"And what dost thou do?"

"I beg. I remember now it is long since I have eaten or drunk. What is the custom of charity in this town? In silence, as we do of Tibet, or speaking aloud?"

"Those who beg in silence starve in silence," said Kim, quoting a native proverb. The lama tried to rise, but sank back again, sighing for his disciple, dead in faraway Kulu. Kim watched – head to one side, considering and interested.

"Give me the bowl. I know the people of this city – all who are charitable. Give, and I will bring it back filled."

Simply as a child the old man handed him the bowl.

"Rest, thou. I know the people."

He trotted off to the open shop of a *kunjri*, a low-caste vegetable-seller, which lay opposite the belt-tramway line down the Motee Bazaar. She knew Kim of old.

"Oho, hast thou turned yogi with thy begging-bowl?" she cried.

"Nay," said Kim proudly. "There is a new priest in the city – a man such as I have never seen."

"Old priest – young tiger," said the woman angrily. "I am tired of new priests! They settle on our wares like flies. Is the father of my son a well of charity to give to all who ask?"

"No," said Kim. "Thy man is rather *yagi* [bad-tempered] than yogi [a holy man]. But this priest is new. The sahib in the Wonder House has talked to him like a brother. O my mother, fill me this bowl. He waits."

"That bowl indeed! That cow-bellied basket! Thou hast as much grace as the holy bull of Shiv. He has taken the best of a basket of onions already, this morn; and forsooth, I must fill thy bowl. He comes here again."

The huge, mouse-coloured Brahmini bull of the ward was shouldering his way through the many-coloured crowd, a stolen plantain hanging out of his mouth. He headed straight for the shop, well knowing his privileges as a sacred beast, lowered his head, and puffed heavily along the line of baskets ere making his choice. Up flew Kim's hard little heel and caught him on his moist blue nose. He snorted indignantly, and walked away across the tram-rails, his hump quivering with rage.

"See! I have saved more than the bowl will cost thrice over. Now, mother, a little rice and some dried fish atop – yes, and some vegetable curry."

A growl came out of the back of the shop, where a man lay.

"He drove away the bull," said the woman in an undertone. "It is good to give to the poor." She took the bowl and returned it full of hot rice.

"But my yogi is not a cow," said Kim gravely, making a hole with his fingers in the top of the mound. "A little curry is good, and a fried cake, and a morsel of conserve would please him, I think."

"It is a hole as big as thy head," said the woman fretfully. But she filled it, none the less, with good, steaming vegetable curry, clapped a fried cake atop, and a morsel of clarified butter on the cake, dabbed a lump of sour tamarind conserve at the side; and Kim looked at the load lovingly.

"That is good. When I am in the bazaar the bull shall not come to this house. He is a bold beggar-man."

"And thou?" laughed the woman. "But speak well of bulls. Hast thou not told me that some day a Red Bull will come out of a field to help thee?

Now hold all straight and ask for the holy man's blessing upon me. Perhaps, too, he knows a cure for my daughter's sore eyes. Ask him that also, O thou Little Friend of all the World."

But Kim had danced off ere the end of the sentence, dodging pariah dogs and hungry acquaintances.

"Thus do we beg who know the way of it," said he proudly to the lama, who opened his eyes at the contents of the bowl. "Eat now and – I will eat with thee. Ohé, *bhisti*!" he called to the water-carrier, sluicing the crotons by the museum. "Give water here. We men are thirsty."

"We men!" said the *bhisti*, laughing. "Is one skinful enough for such a pair? Drink, then, in the name of the Compassionate."

He loosed a thin stream into Kim's hands, who drank native-fashion; but the lama must needs pull out a cup from his inexhaustible upper draperies and drink ceremonially.

"*Pardesi* [a foreigner]," Kim explained, as the old man delivered in an unknown tongue what was evidently a blessing.

They ate together in great content, clearing the begging-bowl. Then the lama took snuff from a portentous wooden snuff-gourd, fingered his rosary awhile, and so dropped into the easy sleep of age, as the shadow of Zam-Zammah grew long.

Kim loafed over to the nearest tobacco-seller, a rather lively young Muhammadan woman, and begged a rank cigar of the brand that they sell to students of the Punjab University who copy English customs. Then he smoked and thought, knees to chin, under the belly of the gun, and the outcome of his thoughts was a sudden and stealthy departure in the direction of Nila Ram's timber-yard.

The lama did not wake till the evening life of the city had begun with lamp-lighting and the return of white-robed clerks and subordinates from the government offices. He stared dizzily in all directions, but none looked at him save a Hindu urchin in a dirty turban and Isabella-coloured clothes. Suddenly he bowed his head on his knees and wailed.

"What is this?" said the boy, standing before him. "Hast thou been robbed?"

"It is my new *chela* [disciple] that is gone away from me, and I know not where he is."

"And what like of man was thy disciple?"

"It was a boy who came to me in place of him who died, on account of the merit which I had gained when I bowed before the Law within there." He pointed towards the museum. "He came upon me to show me a road which I had lost. He led me into the Wonder House, and by his talk emboldened me to speak to the Keeper of the Images, so that I was cheered and made strong. And when I was faint with hunger he begged for me, as would a *chela* for his teacher. Suddenly was he sent. Suddenly has he gone away. It was in my mind to have taught him the Law upon the road to Benares."

Kim stood amazed at this, because he had overheard the talk in the museum, and knew that the old man was speaking the truth, which is a thing a native on the road seldom presents to a stranger.

"But I see now that he was but sent for a purpose. By this I know that I shall find a certain River for which I seek."

"The River of the Arrow?" said Kim, with a superior smile.

"Is this yet another Sending?" cried the lama. "To none have I spoken of my search, save to the Priest of the Images. Who art thou?"

"Thy *chela*," said Kim simply, sitting on his heels. "I have never seen any one like to thee in all this my life. I go with thee to Benares. And, too, I think that so old a man as thou, speaking the truth to chance-met people at dusk, is in great need of a disciple."

"But the River – the River of the Arrow?"

"Oh, that I heard when thou wast speaking to the Englishman. I lay against the door."

The lama sighed. "I thought thou hadst been a guide permitted. Such things fall sometimes – but I am not worthy. Thou dost not, then, know the River?"

"Not I." Kim laughed uneasily. "I go to look for – for a bull – a Red Bull on a green field who shall help me." Boy-like, if an acquaintance had a scheme, Kim was quite ready with one of his own; and, boy-like, he had really thought for as much as twenty minutes at a time of his father's prophecy.

"To what, child?" said the lama.

"God knows, but so my father told me. I heard thy talk in the Wonder House of all those new strange places in the Hills, and if one so old and so little – so used to truth-telling – may go out for the small matter of a river, it seemed to me that I too must go a-travelling. If it is our fate to find those things we shall find them – thou, thy River; and I, my Bull, and the Strong Pillars and some other matters that I forget."

"It is not pillars but a Wheel from which I would be free," said the lama.

"That is all one. Perhaps they will make me a king," said Kim, serenely prepared for anything.

"I will teach thee other and better desires upon the road," the lama replied in the voice of authority. "Let us go to Benares."

"Not by night. Thieves are abroad. Wait till the day."

"But there is no place to sleep." The old man was used to the order of his monastery, and though he slept on the ground, as the Rule decrees, preferred a decency in these things.

"We shall get good lodging at the Kashmir Serai," said Kim, laughing at his perplexity. "I have a friend there. Come!"

The hot and crowded bazaars blazed with light as they made their way through the press of all the races in upper India, and the lama mooned through it like a man in a dream. It was his first experience of a large manufacturing city, and the crowded tramcar with its continually squealing brakes frightened him. Half pushed, half towed, he arrived at the high gate of the Kashmir Serai: that huge open square over against the railway station, surrounded with arched cloisters, where the camel and horse caravans put up on their return from central Asia. Here were all manner of northern folk, tending tethered ponies and kneeling camels; loading and unloading bales and bundles; drawing water for the evening meal at the creaking well windlasses; piling grass before the shrieking, wild-eyed stallions; cuffing the surly caravan dogs; paying off camel-drivers; taking on new grooms; swearing, shouting, arguing, and chaffering in the packed square. The cloisters, reached by three or four masonry steps, made a haven of refuge around this turbulent sea. Most of them were rented to traders, as we rent the arches of a viaduct; the space between pillar and pillar being bricked or boarded off into rooms, which were guarded by heavy wooden doors and cumbrous native padlocks. Locked doors showed that the owner was away, and a few rude – sometimes very rude – chalk or paint scratches told where he had gone. Thus: "Lutuf Ullah is gone to Kurdistan." Below, in coarse verse: "O Allah, who sufferest lice to live on the coat of a Kabuli, why hast thou allowed this louse Lutuf to live so long?"

Kim, fending the lama between excited men and excited beasts, sidled along the cloisters to the far end, nearest the railway station, where Mahbub Ali, the horse-trader, lived when he came in from that mysterious land beyond the Passes of the North.

Kim had had many dealings with Mahbub in his little life – especially between his tenth and his thirteenth year – and the big burly Afghan, his beard dyed scarlet with lime (for he was elderly and did not wish his grey hairs to show), knew the boy's value as a gossip. Sometimes he would tell Kim to watch a man who had nothing whatever to do with horses: to follow him for one whole day and report every soul with whom he talked. Kim would deliver himself of this tale at evening, and Mahbub would listen without a word or gesture. It was intrigue of some kind, Kim knew; but its worth lay in saying nothing whatever to any one except Mahbub, who gave him beautiful meals all hot from the cookshop at the head of the serai, and once as much as eight annas in money.

"He is here," said Kim, hitting a bad-tempered camel on the nose. "Ohé, Mahbub Ali!" He halted at a dark arch and slipped behind the bewildered lama.

The horse-trader, his deep, embroidered Bokhariot belt unloosed, was lying on a pair of silk carpet saddlebags, pulling lazily at an immense silver hookah. He turned his head very slightly at the cry; and seeing only the tall silent figure, chuckled in his deep chest.

"Allah! A lama! A Red Lama! It is far from Lahore to the Passes. What dost thou do here?"

The lama held out the begging-bowl mechanically.

"God's curse on all unbelievers!" said Mahbub. "I do not give to a lousy Tibetan; but ask my Baltis over yonder behind the camels. They may value your blessings. Oh, horse-boys, here is a countryman of yours. See if he be hungry."

A shaven, crouching Balti, who had come down with the horses, and who was nominally some sort of degraded Buddhist, fawned upon the priest, and in thick gutturals besought the Holy One to sit at the horse-boys' fire.

"Go!" said Kim, pushing him lightly, and the lama strode away, leaving Kim at the edge of the cloister.

"Go!" said Mahbub Ali, returning to his hookah. "Little Hindu, run away. God's curse on all unbelievers! Beg from those of my tail who are of thy faith."

"Maharaj," whined Kim, using the Hindu form of address, and thoroughly enjoying the situation; "my father is dead – my mother is dead – my stomach is empty."

"Beg from my men among the horses, I say. There must be some Hindus in my tail."

"Oh, Mahbub Ali, but am *I* a Hindu?" said Kim in English.

The trader gave no sign of astonishment, but looked under shaggy eyebrows.

"Little Friend of all the World," said he, "what is this?"

"Nothing. I am now that holy man's disciple; and we go a pilgrimage together – to Benares, he says. He is quite mad, and I am tired of Lahore city. I wish new air and water."

"But for whom dost thou work? Why come to me?" The voice was harsh with suspicion.

"To whom else should I come? I have no money. It is not good to go about without money. Thou wilt sell many horses to the officers. They are very fine horses, these new ones: I have seen them. Give me a rupee, Mahbub Ali, and when I come to my wealth I will give thee a bond and pay."

"Um!" said Mahbub Ali, thinking swiftly. "Thou hast never before lied to me. Call that lama – stand back in the dark."

"Oh, our tales will agree," said Kim, laughing.

"We go to Benares," said the lama, as soon as he understood the drift of Mahbub Ali's questions. "The boy and I. I go to seek for a certain River."

"Maybe – but the boy?"

"He is my disciple. He was sent, I think, to guide me to that River. Sitting under a gun was I when he came suddenly. Such things have befallen the fortunate to whom guidance was allowed. But I remember now, he said he was of this world – a Hindu."

"And his name?"

"That I did not ask. Is he not my disciple?"

"His country – his race – his village? Mussulman – Sikh – Hindu – Jain – low caste or high?"

"Why should I ask? There is neither high nor low in the Middle Way. If he is my *chela* – does – will – can any one take him from me? For, look you, without him I shall not find my River." He wagged his head solemnly.

"None shall take him from thee. Go, sit among my Baltis," said Mahbub Ali, and the lama drifted off, soothed by the promise.

"Is he not quite mad?" said Kim, coming forward to the light again. "Why should I lie to thee, Hajji?"

Mahbub puffed his hookah in silence. Then he began, almost whispering: "Umballa is on the road to Benares – if indeed ye two go there."

"Tck! Tck! I tell thee he does not know how to lie – as we two know."

"And if thou wilt carry a message for me as far as Umballa, I will give thee money. It concerns a horse – a white stallion which I have sold to an officer upon the last time I returned from the passes. But then – stand nearer and hold up hands as begging – the pedigree of the white stallion was not fully established, and that officer, who is now at Umballa, bade me make it clear." (Mahbub here described the house and the appearance of the officer.) "So the message to that officer will be: 'The pedigree of the white stallion is fully established.' By this will he know that thou comest from me. He will then say 'What proof hast thou?' and thou wilt answer: 'Mahbub Ali has given me the proof.' "

"And all for the sake of a white stallion," said Kim, with a giggle, his eyes aflame.

"That pedigree I will give thee now – in my own fashion and some hard words as well." A shadow passed behind Kim, and a feeding camel. Mahbub Ali raised his voice.

"Allah! Art thou the only beggar in the city? Thy mother is dead. Thy father is dead. So is it with all of them. Well, well –" He turned as feeling on the floor beside him and tossed a flap of soft, greasy Mussulman bread to the boy. "Go and lie down among my horse-boys for tonight – thou and the lama. Tomorrow I may give thee service."

Kim slunk away, his teeth in the bread, and, as he expected, he found a small wad of folded tissue-paper wrapped in oilskin, with three silver rupees – enormous largesse. He smiled and thrust money and paper into his leather amulet-case. The lama, sumptuously fed by Mahbub's Baltis, was already asleep in a corner of one of the stalls. Kim lay down beside him and laughed. He knew he had rendered a service to Mahbub Ali, and not for one little minute did he believe the tale of the stallion's pedigree.

But Kim did not suspect that Mahbub Ali, known as one of the best horse-dealers in the Punjab, a wealthy and enterprising trader, whose caravans penetrated far and far into the Back of Beyond, was registered in one of the locked books of the Indian Survey Department as C25 1B. Twice or thrice yearly C25 would send in a little story, baldly told but most interesting, and generally – it was checked by the statements of R17 and M4 – quite true. It concerned all manner of out-of-the-way mountain principalities, explorers of nationalities other than English, and the gun trade – was, in brief, a small portion of that vast mass of "information received" on which the Indian government acts. But, recently, five confederated kings, who had no business to confederate, had been informed by a kindly Northern Power that there was a leakage of news from their territories into British India. So those kings" prime ministers were seriously annoyed and took steps, after the oriental fashion. They suspected, among many others, the bullying, red-bearded horse-dealer whose caravans ploughed through their fastnesses belly-deep in snow. At least, his caravan that season had been ambushed and shot at twice on the way down, when Mahbub's men accounted for three strange ruffians who might, or might not, have been hired for the job. Therefore Mahbub had avoided halting at the insalubrious city of Peshawar, and had come through without stop to Lahore, where, knowing his country-people, he anticipated curious developments.

And there was that on Mahbub Ali which he did not wish to keep an hour longer than was necessary – a wad of closely folded tissue-paper, wrapped in oilskin – an impersonal, unaddressed statement, with five microscopic pin-holes in one corner, that most scandalously betrayed the five confederated kings, the sympathetic Northern Power, a Hindu banker in Peshawar, a firm of gun-makers in Belgium, and an important, semi-independent Muhammadan ruler to the south. This last was R17's work, which Mahbub had picked up beyond the Dora Pass and was carrying in for R17, who, owing to circumstances over which he had no control, could not leave his post of observation. Dynamite was milky and innocuous beside that report of C25; and even an Oriental, with an Oriental's views of the value of time, could see that the sooner it was in the proper hands the better. Mahbub had no particular desire to die by violence, because two or three family blood-feuds across the border hung unfinished on his hands, and when these scores were cleared he intended to settle down as a more or less virtuous citizen. He had never passed the serai gate since his arrival two days ago, but had been ostentatious in sending telegrams to Bombay, where he banked some of his money; to Delhi, where a sub-partner of his own clan was selling horses to the agent of a Rajputana state; and to Umballa, where an Englishman was excitedly demanding the pedigree of a white stallion. The public letter-writer, who knew English, composed excellent telegrams, such as: – "Creighton, Laurel Bank, Umballa. – Horse is Arabian as already advised. Sorrowful delayed pedigree which am translating." And later to the same address: "Much sorrowful delay. Will forward pedigree." To his sub-partner at Delhi he wired: "Lutuf Ullah. – Have wired two thousand rupees your credit Luchman Narain's bank." This was entirely in the way of trade, but every one of those telegrams was discussed and re-discussed, by parties who conceived themselves to be interested, before they went over to the railway station in charge of a foolish Balti, who allowed all sorts of people to read them on the road.

When, in Mahbub's own picturesque language, he had muddied the wells of inquiry with the stick of precaution, Kim had dropped on him, sent from Heaven; and, being as prompt as he was unscrupulous, Mahbub Ali, used to taking all sorts of gusty chances, pressed him into service on the spot.

A wandering lama with a low-caste boy-servant might attract a moment's interest as they wandered about India, the land of pilgrims; but no one would suspect them or, what was more to the point, rob.

He called for a new light-ball to his hookah, and considered the case. If the worst came to the worst, and the boy came to harm, the paper would incriminate nobody. And he would go up to Umballa leisurely and – at a certain risk of exciting fresh suspicion – repeat his tale by word of mouth to the people concerned.

... he pursued the Flower of Delight with the feet of intoxication till he fell flat among the cushions.

But R17's report was the kernel of the whole affair, and it would be distinctly inconvenient if that failed to come to hand. However, God was great, and Mahbub Ali felt he had done all he could for the time being. Kim was the one soul in the world who had never told him a lie. That would have been a fatal blot on Kim's character if Mahbub had not known that to others, for his own ends or Mahbub's business, Kim could lie like an Oriental.

Then Mahbub Ali rolled across the serai to the Gate of the Harpies who paint their eyes and trap the stranger, and was at some pains to call on the one girl who, he had reason to believe, was a particular friend of a smoothfaced Kashmiri pundit who had waylaid his simple Balti in the matter of the telegrams. It was an utterly foolish thing to do; because they fell to drinking perfumed brandy against the Law of the Prophet, and Mahbub grew wonderfully drunk, and the gates of his mouth were loosened, and he pursued the Flower of Delight with the feet of intoxication till he fell flat among the cushions, where the Flower of Delight, aided by a smooth-faced Kashmiri pundit, searched him from head to foot most thoroughly.

About the same hour Kim heard soft feet in Mahbub's deserted stall. The horse-trader, curiously enough, had left his door unlocked, and his men were busy celebrating their return to India with a whole sheep of Mahbub's bounty. A sleek young gentleman from Delhi, armed with a bunch of keys which the Flower had unshackled from the senseless one's belt, went through every single box, bundle, mat, and saddlebag in Mahbub's possession even more systematically than the Flower and the pundit were searching the owner.

"And I think," said the Flower scornfully an hour later, one rounded elbow on the snoring carcass, "that he is no more than a pig of an Afghan horse-dealer, with no thought except women and horses. Moreover, he may have sent it away by now – if ever there were such a thing."

"Nay – in a matter touching Five Kings it would be next his black heart," said the pundit. "Was there nothing?"

The Delhi man laughed and resettled his turban as he entered. "I searched between the soles of his slippers as the Flower searched his clothes. This is not the man but another. I leave little unseen."

"They did not say he was the very man," said the pundit thoughtfully. "They said, 'Look if he be the man, since our counsels are troubled.' "

"That north country is full of horse-dealers as an old coat of lice. There is Sikander Khan, Nur Ali Beg, and Farrukh Shah – all heads of *kafilas* [caravans] – who deal there," said the Flower.

"They have not yet come in," said the pundit. "Thou must ensnare them later."

"Phew!" said the Flower with deep disgust, rolling Mahbub's head from her lap. "I earn my money. Farrukh Shah is a bear, Ali Beg a swashbuckler, and old Sikander Khan – yaie! Go! I sleep now. This swine will not stir till dawn."

When Mahbub woke, the Flower talked to him severely on the sin of drunkenness. Asiatics do not wink when they have outmanoeuvred an enemy, but as Mahbub Ali cleared his throat, tightened his belt, and staggered forth under the early morning stars, he came very near to it.

"What a colt's trick!" said he to himself. "As if every girl in Peshawar did not use it! But 'twas prettily done. Now God he knows how many more there be upon the Road who have orders to test me – perhaps with the knife. So it stands that the boy must go to Umballa – and by rail – for the writing is something urgent. I abide here, following the Flower and drinking wine as an Afghan coper should."

He halted at the stall next but one to his own. His men lay there heavy with sleep. There was no sign of Kim or the lama.

"Up!" He stirred a sleeper. "Whither went those who lay here last even – the lama and the boy? Is aught missing?"

"Nay," grunted the man, "the old madman rose at second cockcrow saying he would go to Benares, and the young one led him away."

"The curse of Allah on all unbelievers!" said Mahbub heartily, and climbed into his own stall, growling in his beard.

But it was Kim who wakened the lama – Kim with one eye laid against a knot-hole in the planking, who had seen the Delhi man's search through the boxes. This was no common thief that turned over letters, bills, and saddles – no mere burglar who ran a little knife sideways into the soles of Mahbub's slippers, or picked the seams of the saddlebags so deftly. At first Kim had been minded to give the alarm – the long-drawn *cho-or – choor!*

[thief! thief!] that sets the serai ablaze of nights; but he looked more carefully, and, hand on amulet, drew his own conclusions.

"It must be the pedigree of that made-up horse lie," said he, "the thing that I carry to Umballa. Better that we go now. Those who search bags with knives may presently search bellies with knives. Surely there is a woman behind this. Hai! Hai!" in a whisper to the light-sleeping old man. "Come. It is time – time to go to Benares."

The lama rose obediently, and they passed out of the serai like shadows.

Chapter 2

And whoso will, from Pride released,
Contemning neither creed nor priest,
May feel the Soul of all the East
   About him at Kamakura.
                   Buddha at Kamakura

They entered the fort-like railway station, black in the end of night; the electrics sizzling over the goods-yard where they handle the heavy northern grain traffic.

"This is the work of devils!" said the lama, recoiling from the hollow echoing darkness, the glimmer of rails between the masonry platforms, and the maze of girders above. He stood in a gigantic stone hall paved, it seemed, with the sheeted dead – third-class passengers who had taken their tickets overnight and were sleeping in the waiting-rooms. All hours of the twenty-four are alike to Orientals, and their passenger traffic is regulated accordingly.

"This is where the fire-carriages come. One stands behind that hole" – Kim pointed to the ticket-office – "who will give thee a paper to take thee to Umballa."

"But we go to Benares," he replied petulantly.

"All one. Benares then. Quick: she comes!"

"Take thou the purse."

The lama, not so well used to trains as he had pretended, started as the 3.25 a.m. southbound roared in. The sleepers sprang to life, and the station filled with clamour and shoutings, cries of water and sweetmeat vendors,

361

shouts of native policemen, and shrill yells of women gathering up their baskets, their families, and their husbands.

"It is the train – only the *te-rain*. It will not come here. Wait!" Amazed at the lama's immense simplicity (he had handed him a small bag full of rupees), Kim asked and paid for a ticket to Umballa. A sleepy clerk grunted and flung out a ticket to the next station, just six miles distant.

"Nay," said Kim, scanning it with a grin. "This may serve for farmers, but I live in the city of Lahore. It was cleverly done, babu. Now give the ticket to Umballa."

The babu scowled and dealt the proper ticket.

"Now another to Amritzar," said Kim, who had no notion of spending Mahbub Ali's money on anything so crude as a paid ride to Umballa. "The price is so much. The small money in return is just so much. I know the ways of the *te-rain*… Never did yogi need *chela* as thou dost," he went on merrily to the bewildered lama. "They would have flung thee out at Mian Mir but for me. This way! Come!" He returned the money, keeping only one anna in each rupee of the price of the Umballa ticket as his commission – the immemorial commission of Asia.

The lama jibbed at the open door of a crowded third-class carriage. "Were it not better to walk?" said he weakly.

A burly Sikh artisan thrust forth his bearded head. "Is he afraid? Do not be afraid. I remember the time when *I* was afraid of the *te-rain*. Enter! This thing is the work of the government."

"I do not fear," said the lama. "Have ye room within for two?"

"There is no room even for a mouse," shrilled the wife of a well-to-do cultivator – a Hindu Jat from the rich Jullundur district. Our night trains are not as well looked after as the day ones, where the sexes are very strictly kept to separate carriages.

"Oh, mother of my son, we can make space," said the blue-turbaned husband. "Pick up the child. It is a holy man, seest thou?"

"And my lap full of seventy times seven bundles! Why not bid him sit on my knee, Shameless? But men are ever thus!" She looked round for approval. An Amritzar courtesan near the window sniffed behind her head drapery.

"Enter! Enter!" cried a fat Hindu moneylender, his folded account-book in a cloth under his arm. With an oily smirk: "It is well to be kind to the poor."

"Ay, at seven per cent a month with a mortgage on the unborn calf," said a young Dogra soldier going south on leave; and they all laughed.

"Will it travel to Benares?" said the lama.

"Assuredly. Else why should we come? Enter, or we are left," cried Kim.

"See!" shrilled the Amritzar girl. "He has never entered a train. Oh, see!"

"Nay, help," said the cultivator, putting out a large brown hand and hauling him in. "Thus is it done, father."

"But – but – I sit on the floor. It is against the Rule to sit on a bench," said the lama. "Moreover, it cramps me."

"I say," began the moneylender, pursing his lips, "that there is not one rule of right living which these *te-rains* do not cause us to break. We sit, for example, side by side with all castes and peoples."

"Yea, and with most outrageously shameless ones," said the wife, scowling at the Amritzar girl making eyes at the young sepoy.

"I said we might have gone by cart along the road," said the husband, "and thus saved some money."

"Yes – and spent twice over what we saved on food by the way. That was talked out ten thousand times."

"Ay, by ten thousand tongues," grunted he.

"The Gods help us poor women if we may not speak. Oho! He is of that sort which may not look at or reply to a woman." For the lama, constrained by his Rule, took not the faintest notice of her. "And his disciple is like him?"

"Nay, mother," said Kim most promptly. "Not when the woman is well-looking and above all charitable to the hungry."

"A beggar's answer," said the Sikh laughing. "Thou hast brought it on thyself, sister!" Kim's hands were crooked in supplication.

"And whither goest thou?" said the woman, handing him the half of a cake from a greasy package.

"Even to Benares."

"Jugglers belike?" the young soldier suggested. "Have ye any tricks to pass the time? Why does not that yellow man answer?"

363

"Because," said Kim stoutly, "he is holy, and thinks upon matters hidden from thee."

"That may be well. We of the Ludhiana Sikhs" – he rolled it out sonorously – "do not trouble our heads with doctrine. We fight."

"My sister's brother's son is *naik* [corporal] in that regiment," said the Sikh craftsman quietly. "There are also some Dogra companies there." The soldier glared, for a Dogra is of other caste than a Sikh, and the banker tittered.

"They are all one to me," said the Amritzar girl.

"That we believe," snorted the cultivator's wife malignantly.

"Nay, but all who serve the Sirkar with weapons in their hands are, as it were, one brotherhood. There is one brotherhood of the caste, but beyond that again" – she looked round timidly – "the bond of the *pulton* – the regiment – eh?"

"My brother is in a Jat regiment," said the cultivator. "Dogras be good men."

"*Thy* Sikhs at least were of that opinion," said the soldier, with a scowl at the placid old man in the corner. "*Thy* Sikhs thought so when our two companies came to help them at the Pirzai Kotal in the face of eight Afridi standards on the ridge not three months gone."

He told the story of a border action in which the Dogra companies of the Ludhiana Sikhs had acquitted themselves well. The Amritzar girl smiled; for she knew the tale was to win her approval.

"Alas!" said the cultivator's wife at the end. "So their villages were burnt and their little children made homeless?"

"They had marked our dead. They paid a great payment after we of the Sikhs had schooled them. So it was. Is this Amritzar?"

"Ay, and here they cut our tickets," said the banker, fumbling at his belt.

The lamps were paling in the dawn when the half-caste guard came round. Ticket-collecting is a slow business in the East, where people secrete their tickets in all sorts of curious places. Kim produced his and was told to get out.

"But I go to Umballa," he protested. "I go with this holy man."

"Thou canst go to Jehannum for aught I care. This ticket is only to Amritzar. Out!"

Kim burst into a flood of tears, protesting that the lama was his father and his mother, that he was the prop of the lama's declining years, and that the lama would die without his care. All the carriage bade the guard be merciful – the banker was specially eloquent here – but the guard hauled Kim on to the platform. The lama blinked – he could not overtake the situation – and Kim lifted up his voice and wept outside the carriage window.

"I am very poor. My father is dead – my mother is dead. O charitable ones, if I am left here, who shall tend that old man?"

"What – what is this?" the lama repeated. "He must go to Benares. He must come with me. He is my *chela*. If there is money to be paid –"

"Oh, be silent," whispered Kim; "are we rajahs to throw away good silver when the world is so charitable?"

The Amritzar girl stepped out with her bundles and it was on her that Kim kept his watchful eye. Ladies of that persuasion, he knew, were generous.

"A ticket – a little *tikkut* to Umballa – O Breaker of Hearts!" She laughed. "Hast thou no charity?"

"Does the holy man come from the north?"

"From far and far in the north he comes," cried Kim. "From among the hills."

"There is snow among the pine-trees in the north – in the hills there is snow. My mother was from Kulu. Get thee a ticket. Ask him for a blessing."

"Ten thousand blessings," shrilled Kim. "O Holy One, a woman has given us in charity so that I can come with thee – a woman with a golden heart. I run for the *tikkut*."

The girl looked up at the lama, who had mechanically followed Kim to the platform. He bowed his head that he might not see her, and muttered in Tibetan as she passed on with the crowd.

"Light come – light go," said the cultivator's wife viciously.

"She has acquired merit," returned the lama. "Beyond doubt it was a nun."

"There be ten thousand such nuns in Amritzar alone. Return, old man, or the *te-rain* may depart without thee," cried the banker.

"Not only was it sufficient for the ticket, but for a little food also," said Kim, leaping to his place. "Now eat, Holy One. Look. Day comes!"

Golden, rose, saffron, and pink, the morning mists smoked away across the flat green levels. All the rich Punjab lay out in the splendour of the keen sun. The lama flinched a little as the telegraph-posts swung by.

"Great is the speed of the *te-rain*," said the banker, with a patronizing grin. "We have gone farther since Lahore than thou couldst walk in two days: at even, we shall enter Umballa."

"And that is still far from Benares," said the lama wearily, mumbling over the cakes that Kim offered. They all unloosed their bundles and made their morning meal. Then the banker, the cultivator, and the soldier prepared their pipes and wrapped the compartment in choking, acrid smoke, spitting and coughing and enjoying themselves. The Sikh and the cultivator's wife chewed *pan;* the lama took snuff and told his beads, while Kim, cross-legged, smiled over the comfort of a full stomach.

"What rivers have ye by Benares?" said the lama of a sudden to the carriage at large.

"We have Gunga," returned the banker, when the little titter had subsided.

"What others?"

"What other than Gunga?"

"Nay, but in my mind was the thought of a certain River of healing."

"That is Gunga. Who bathes in her is made clean and goes to the Gods. Thrice have I made pilgrimage to Gunga." He looked round proudly.

"There was need," said the young sepoy drily, and the travellers" laugh turned against the banker.

"Clean – to return again to the Gods," the lama muttered. "And to go forth on the round of lives anew – still tied to the Wheel." He shook his head testily. "But maybe there is a mistake. Who, then, made Gunga in the beginning?"

"The Gods. Of what known faith art thou?" the banker said, appalled.

"I follow the Law – the Most Excellent Law. So it was the Gods that made Gunga. What like of Gods were they?"

The carriage looked at him in amazement. It was inconceivable that any one should be ignorant of Gunga.

"What – what is thy God?" said the moneylender at last.

"Hear!" said the lama, shifting the rosary to his hand. "Hear: for I speak of him now! O people of Hind, listen!"

He began in Urdu the tale of the Lord Buddha, but, borne by his own thoughts, slid into Tibetan and long-droned texts from a Chinese book of the Buddha's life. The gentle, tolerant folk looked on reverently. All India is full of holy men stammering gospels in strange tongues; shaken and consumed in the fires of their own zeal; dreamers, babblers, and visionaries: as it has been from the beginning and will continue to the end.

"Um!" said the soldier of the Ludhiana Sikhs. "There was a Muhammadan regiment lay next to us at the Pirzai Kotal, and a priest of theirs – he was, as I remember, a *naik* – when the fit was on him, spake prophecies. But the mad all are in God's keeping. His officers overlooked much in that man."

The lama fell back on Urdu, remembering that he was in a strange land. "Hear the tale of the Arrow which our Lord loosed from the bow," he said.

This was much more to their taste, and they listened curiously while he told it. "Now, O people of Hind, I go to seek that River. Know ye aught that may guide me, for we be all men and women in evil case."

"There is Gunga – and Gunga alone – who washes away sin," ran the murmur round the carriage.

"Though past question we have good Gods Jullundur way," said the cultivator's wife, looking out of the window. "See how they have blessed the crops."

"To search every river in the Punjab is no small matter," said her husband. "For me, a stream that leaves good silt on my land suffices, and I thank Bhumia, the God of the Homestead." He shrugged one knotted, bronzed shoulder.

"Think you our Lord came so far north?" said the lama turning to Kim.

"It may be," Kim replied soothingly, as he spat red *pan* juice on the floor.

"The last of the Great Ones," said the Sikh with authority, "was Sikander Julkarn [Alexander the Great]. He paved the streets of Jullundur and built a great tank near Umballa. That pavement holds to this day; and the tank is there also. I never heard of thy God."

"Let thy hair grow long and talk Punjabi," said the young soldier jestingly to Kim, quoting a northern proverb. "That is all that makes a Sikh." But he did not say this very loud.

The lama sighed and shrank into himself, a dingy, shapeless mass. In the pauses of their talk they could hear the low droning – "*Om mane pudme hum! Om mane pudme hum!*" – and the thick click of the wooden rosary beads.

"It irks me," he said at last. "The speed and the clatter irk me. Moreover, my *chela*, I think that maybe we have overpassed that River."

"Peace, peace," said Kim. "Was not the River near Benares? We are yet far from the place."

"But – if our Lord came north, it may be any one of these little ones that we have run across."

"I do not know."

"But thou wast sent to me – wast thou sent to me? – for the merit I had acquired over yonder at Such-zen. From beside the cannon didst thou come – bearing two faces – and two garbs."

"Peace. One must not speak of these things here," whispered Kim. "There was but one of me. Think again and thou wilt remember. A boy – a Hindu boy – by the great green cannon."

"But was there not also an Englishman with a white beard – holy among images – who himself made more sure my assurance of the River of the Arrow?"

"He – we – went to the Ajaib-Gher in Lahore to pray before the Gods there," Kim explained to the openly listening company. "And the sahib of the Wonder House talked to him – yes, this is truth – as a brother. He is a very holy man, from far beyond the Hills. Rest, thou. In time we come to Umballa."

"But my River – the River of my healing?"

"And then, if it please thee, we will go hunting for that River on foot. So that we miss nothing – not even a little rivulet in a field-side."

"But thou hast a Search of thine own?" The lama – very pleased that he remembered so well – sat bolt upright.

"Ay," said Kim, humouring him. The boy was entirely happy to be out chewing *pan* and seeing new people in the great good-tempered world.

"It was a bull – a Red Bull that shall come and help thee – and carry thee – whither? I have forgotten. A Red Bull on a green field, was it not?"

"Nay, it will carry me nowhere," said Kim. "It is but a tale I told thee."

"What is this?" The cultivator's wife leaned forward, her bracelets clinking on her arm. "Do ye both dream dreams? A Red Bull on a green field, that shall carry thee to the heavens – or what? Was it a vision? Did one make a prophecy? *We* have a Red Bull in our village behind Jullundur city, and he grazes by choice in the very greenest of our fields!"

"Give a woman an old wife's tale and a weaver bird a leaf and a thread, they will weave wonderful things," said the Sikh. "All holy men dream dreams, and by following holy men their disciples attain that power."

"A Red Bull on a green field, was it?" the lama repeated. "In a former life it may be thou hast acquired merit, and the Bull will come to reward thee."

"Nay – nay – it was but a tale one told to me – for a jest belike. But I will seek the Bull about Umballa, and thou canst look for thy River and rest from the clatter of the train."

"It may be that the Bull knows – that he is sent to guide us both," said the lama, hopefully as a child. Then to the company, indicating Kim: "This one was sent to me but yesterday. He is not, I think, of this world."

"Beggars a plenty have I met, and holy men to boot, but never such a yogi nor such a disciple," said the woman.

Her husband touched his forehead lightly with one finger and smiled. But the next time the lama would eat they took care to give him of their best.

And at last – tired, sleepy, and dusty – they reached Umballa city station.

"We abide here upon a lawsuit," said the cultivator's wife to Kim. "We lodge with my man's cousin's younger brother. There is room also in the courtyard for thy yogi and for thee. Will – will he give me a blessing?"

"O holy man! A woman with a heart of gold gives us lodging for the night. It is a kindly land, this land of the south. See how we have been helped since the dawn!"

369

The lama bowed his head in benediction.

"To fill my cousin's younger brother's house with wastrels –" the husband began, as he shouldered his heavy bamboo staff.

"Thy cousin's younger brother owes my father's cousin something yet on his daughter's marriage-feast," said the woman crisply. "Let him put their food to that account. The yogi will beg, I doubt not."

"Ay, I beg for him," said Kim, anxious only to get the lama under shelter for the night, that he might seek Mahbub Ali's Englishman and deliver himself of the white stallion's pedigree.

"Now," said he, when the lama had come to an anchor in the inner courtyard of a decent Hindu house behind the cantonments, "I go away for a while – to – to buy us victual in the bazaar. Do not stray abroad till I return."

"Thou wilt return? Thou wilt surely return?" The old man caught at his wrist. "And thou wilt return in this very same shape? Is it too late to look tonight for the River?"

"Too late and too dark. Be comforted. Think how far thou art on the road – an hundred miles from Lahore already."

"Yea – and farther from my monastery. Alas! It is a great and terrible world."

Kim stole out and away, as unremarkable a figure as ever carried his own and a few score thousand other folk's fate slung round his neck. Mahbub Ali's directions left him little doubt of the house in which his Englishman lived; and a groom, bringing a dog-cart home from the club, made him quite sure. It remained only to identify his man, and Kim slipped through the garden hedge and hid in a clump of plumed grass close to the veranda. The house blazed with lights, and servants moved about tables dressed with flowers, glass and silver. Presently forth came an Englishman, dressed in black and white, humming a tune. It was too dark to see his face, so Kim, beggarwise, tried an old experiment.

"Protector of the Poor!"

The man backed towards the voice. "Mahbub Ali says –"

"Hah! What says Mahbub Ali?" He made no attempt to look for the speaker, and that showed Kim that he knew.

"The pedigree of the white stallion is fully established."

"What proof is there?" The Englishman switched at the rose hedge in the side of the drive.

"Mahbub Ali has given me this proof." Kim flipped the wad of folded paper into the air, and it fell on the path beside the man, who put his foot on it as a gardener came round the corner. When the servant passed he picked it up, dropped a rupee – Kim could hear the clink – and strode into the house, never turning round. Swiftly Kim took up the money; but, for all his training, he was Irish enough by birth to reckon silver the least part of any game. What he desired was the visible effect of action; so, instead of slinking away, he lay close in the grass and wormed nearer to the house.

He saw – Indian bungalows are open through and through – the Englishman return to a small dressing-room, in a corner of the veranda, that was half office, littered with papers and despatch-boxes, and sit down to study Mahbub Ali's message. His face, by the full ray of the kerosene lamp, changed and darkened, and Kim, used as every beggar must be to watching countenances, took good note.

"Will! Will, dear!" called a woman's voice. "You ought to be in the drawing-room. They'll be here in a minute."

The man still read intently.

"Will!" said the voice, five minutes later. "*He's* come. I can hear the troopers in the drive."

The man dashed out bareheaded as a big landau with four native troopers behind it halted at the veranda, and a tall, black-haired man, erect as an arrow, swung out, preceded by a young officer who laughed pleasantly.

Flat on his belly lay Kim, almost touching the high wheels. His man and the black stranger exchanged two sentences.

"Certainly, sir," said the young officer promptly. "Everything waits while a horse is concerned."

"We shan't be more than twenty minutes," said Kim's man. "You can do the honours – keep 'em amused, and all that."

"Tell one of the troopers to wait," said the tall man, and they both passed into the dressing-room together as the landau rolled away. Kim saw their heads bent over Mahbub Ali's message, and heard the voices – one low and deferential, the other sharp and decisive.

"It isn't a question of weeks. It is a question of days – hours almost," said the elder. "I'd been expecting it for some time, but this" – he tapped Mahbub Ali's paper – "clinches it. Grogan's dining here tonight, isn't he?"

"Yes, sir, and Macklin too."

"Very good. I'll speak to them myself. The matter will be referred to the Council, of course, but this is a case where one is justified in assuming that we take action at once. Warn the Pindi and Peshawar brigades. It will disorganize all the summer reliefs, but we can't help that. This comes of not smashing them thoroughly the first time. Eight thousand should be enough."

"What about artillery, sir?"

"I must consult Macklin."

"Then it means war?"

"No. Punishment. When a man is bound by the action of his predecessor –"

"But C25 may have lied."

"He bears out the other's information. Practically, they showed their hand six months back. But Devenish would have it there was a chance of peace. Of course they used it to make themselves stronger. Send off those telegrams at once – the new code, not the old – mine and Wharton's. I don't think we need keep the ladies waiting any longer. We can settle the rest over the cigars. I thought it was coming. It's punishment – not war."

As the trooper cantered off, Kim crawled round to the back of the house, where, going on his Lahore experiences, he judged there would be food – and information. The kitchen was crowded with excited scullions, one of whom kicked him.

"Aie," said Kim, feigning tears. "I came only to wash dishes in return for a bellyful."

"All Umballa is on the same errand. Get hence. They go in now with the soup. Think you that we who serve Creighton Sahib need strange scullions to help us through a big dinner?"

"It is a very big dinner," said Kim, looking at the plates.

"Small wonder. The guest of honour is none other than the Jang-i-Lat-Sahib [the Commander-in-Chief]."

"Ho!" said Kim, with the correct guttural note of wonder. He had learned what he wanted, and when the scullion turned he was gone.

"And all that trouble," said he to himself, thinking as usual in Hindustani, "for a horse's pedigree! Mahbub Ali should have come to me to learn a little lying. Every time before that I have borne a message it concerned a woman. Now it is men. Better. The tall man said that they will loose a great army to punish some one – somewhere – the news goes to Pindi and Peshawar. There are also guns. Would I had crept nearer. It is big news!"

He returned to find the cultivator's cousin's younger brother discussing the family lawsuit in all its bearings with the cultivator and his wife and a few friends, while the lama dozed. After the evening meal some one passed him a water-pipe; and Kim felt very much of a man as he pulled at the smooth coconut-shell, his legs spread abroad in the moonlight, his tongue clicking in remarks from time to time. His hosts were most polite; for the cultivator's wife had told them of his vision of the Red Bull, and of his probable descent from another world. Moreover, the lama was a great and venerable curiosity. The family priest, an old, tolerant Sarsut Brahmin, dropped in later, and naturally started a theological argument to impress the family. By creed, of course, they were all on their priest's side, but the lama was the guest and the novelty. His gentle kindliness, and his impressive Chinese quotations, that sounded like spells, delighted them hugely; and in this sympathetic, simple air, he expanded like the Bodhisat's own lotus, speaking of his life in the great hills of Such-zen, before, as he said, "I rose up to seek enlightenment."

Then it came out that in those worldly days he had been a master-hand at casting horoscopes and nativities; and the family priest led him on to describe his methods; each giving the planets names that the others could not understand, and pointing upwards as the big stars sailed across the dark. The children of the house tugged un-rebuked at his rosary; and he clean forgot the Rule which forbids looking at women as he talked of enduring snows, landslips, blocked passes, the remote cliffs where men find sapphires and turquoise, and that wonderful upland road that leads at last into Great China itself.

"How thinkest thou of this one?" said the cultivator aside to the priest.

"A holy man – a holy man indeed. His Gods are not the Gods, but his feet are upon the Way," was the answer. "And his methods of nativities, though that is beyond thee, are wise and sure."

"Tell me," said Kim lazily, "whether I find my Red Bull on a green field, as was promised me."

"What knowledge hast thou of thy birth hour?" the priest asked, swelling with importance.

"Between first and second cockcrow of the first night in May."

"Of what year?"

"I do not know; but upon the hour that I cried first fell the great earthquake in Srinagar which is in Kashmir." This Kim had from the woman who took care of him, and she again from Kimball O'Hara. The earthquake had been felt in India, and for long stood a leading date in the Punjab.

"Ai!" said a woman excitedly. This seemed to make Kim's supernatural origin more certain. "Was not such an one's daughter born then –"

"And her mother bore her husband four sons in four years – all likely boys," cried the cultivator's wife, sitting outside the circle in the shadow.

"None reared in the knowledge," said the family priest, "forget how the planets stood in their houses upon that night." He began to draw in the dust of the courtyard. "At least thou hast good claim to a half of the House of the Bull. How runs thy prophecy?"

"Upon a day," said Kim, delighted at the sensation he was creating, "I shall be made great by means of a Red Bull on a green field, but first there will enter two men making all things ready."

"Yes: thus ever at the opening of a vision. A thick darkness that clears slowly; anon one enters with a broom making ready the place. Then begins the Sight. Two men – thou sayest? Ay, ay. The sun, leaving the House of the Bull, enters that of the Twins. Hence the two men of the prophecy. Let us now consider. Fetch me a twig, little one."

He knitted his brows, scratched, smoothed out, and scratched again in the dust mysterious signs – to the wonder of all save the lama, who, with fine instinct, forbore to interfere.

At the end of half an hour, he tossed the twig from him with a grunt.

"Hm! Thus say the stars. Within three days come the two men to make all things ready. After them follows the Bull; but the sign over against him is the sign of war and armed men."

"There was indeed a man of the Ludhiana Sikhs in the carriage from Lahore," said the cultivator's wife hopefully.

"Tck! Armed men – many hundreds. What concern hast thou with war?" said the priest to Kim. "Thine is a red and angry sign of war to be loosed very soon."

"None – none," said the lama earnestly. "We seek only peace and our River."

Kim smiled, remembering what he had overheard in the dressing-room. Decidedly he was a favourite of the stars.

The priest brushed his foot over the rude horoscope. "More than this I cannot see. In three days comes the Bull to thee, boy."

"And my River, my River," pleaded the lama. "I had hoped his Bull would lead us both to the River."

"Alas, for that wondrous River, my brother," the priest replied. "Such things are not common."

Next morning, though they were pressed to stay, the lama insisted on departure. They gave Kim a large bundle of good food and nearly three annas in copper money for the needs of the road, and with many blessings watched the two go southward in the dawn.

"Pity it is that these and such as these could not be freed from the Wheel of Things," said the lama.

"Nay, then would only evil people be left on the earth, and who would give us meat and shelter?" quoth Kim, stepping merrily under his burden.

"Yonder is a small stream. Let us look," said the lama, and he led from the white road across the fields; walking into a very hornets'-nest of pariah dogs.

Chapter 3

Yea, voice of every Soul that clung
To Life that strove from rung to rung
When Devadatta's rule was young,
The warm wind brings Kamakura.
                    Buddha at Kamakura

Behind them an angry farmer brandished a bamboo pole. He was a market-gardener, Arain by caste, growing vegetables and flowers for Umballa city, and well Kim knew the breed.

"Such an one," said the lama, disregarding the dogs, "is impolite to strangers, intemperate of speech and uncharitable. Be warned by his demeanour, my disciple."

"Ho, shameless beggars!" shouted the farmer. "Begone! Get hence!"

"We go," the lama returned, with quiet dignity. "We go from these unblessed fields."

"Ah," said Kim, sucking in his breath. "If the next crops fail, thou canst only blame thine own tongue."

The man shuffled uneasily in his slippers. "The land is full of beggars," he began, half apologetically.

"And by what sign didst thou know that we would beg from thee, O Mali?" said Kim tartly, using the name that a market-gardener least likes. "All we sought was to look at that river beyond the field there."

"River, forsooth!" the man snorted. "What city do ye hail from not to know a canal-cut? It runs as straight as an arrow, and I pay for the water as though it were molten silver. There is a branch of a river beyond. But if ye need water I can give that – and milk."

"Nay, we will go to the river," said the lama, striding out.

"Milk and a meal," the man stammered, as he looked at the strange tall figure. "I – I would not draw evil upon myself – or my crops. But beggars are so many in these hard days."

"Take notice." The lama turned to Kim. "He was led to speak harshly by the red mist of anger. That clearing from his eyes, he becomes courteous and of an affable heart. May his fields be blessed! Beware not to judge men too hastily, O farmer."

"I have met holy ones who would have cursed thee from hearthstone to byre," said Kim to the abashed man. "Is he not wise and holy? I am his disciple."

He cocked his nose in the air loftily and stepped across the narrow field borders with great dignity.

"There is no pride," said the lama, after a pause, "there is no pride among such as follow the Middle Way."

"But thou hast said he was low-caste and discourteous."

"Low-caste I did not say, for how can that be which is not? Afterwards he amended his discourtesy, and I forgot the offence. Moreover, he is as we are, bound upon the Wheel of Things; but he does not tread the way of deliverance." He halted at a little runlet among the fields, and considered the hoof-pitted bank.

"Now, how wilt thou know thy River?" said Kim, squatting in the shade of some tall sugarcane.

"When I find it, an enlightenment will surely be given. This, I feel, is not the place. O littlest among the waters, if only thou couldst tell me where runs my River! But be thou blessed to make the fields bear!"

"Look! Look!" Kim sprang to his side and dragged him back. A yellow-and-brown streak glided from the purple rustling stems to the bank, stretched its neck to the water, drank, and lay still – a big cobra with fixed, lidless eyes.

"I have no stick – I have no stick," said Kim. "I will get me one and break his back."

"Why? He is upon the Wheel as we are – a life ascending or descending – very far from deliverance. Great evil must the soul have done that is cast into this shape."

"I hate all snakes," said Kim. No native training can quench the white man's horror of the serpent.

"Let him live out his life." The coiled thing hissed and half opened its hood. "May thy release come soon, brother!" the lama continued placidly. "Hast *thou* knowledge, by chance, of my River?"

"Never have I seen such a man as thou art," Kim whispered, overwhelmed. "Do the very snakes understand thy talk?"

"Who knows?" He passed within a foot of the cobra's poised head. It flattened itself among the dusty coils.

"Come, thou!" he called over his shoulder.

"Not I," said Kim. "I go round."

"Come. He does no hurt."

Kim hesitated for a moment. The lama backed his order by some droned Chinese quotation which Kim took for a charm. He obeyed and bounded across the rivulet, and the snake, indeed, made no sign.

"Never have I seen such a man." Kim wiped the sweat from his forehead. "And now, whither go we?"

"That is for thee to say. I am old, and a stranger – far from my own place. But that the *rêl*-carriage fills my head with noises of devil drums I would go in it to Benares now… Yet by so going we may miss the River. Let us find another river."

Where the hard-worked soil gives three and even four crops a year – through patches of sugarcane, tobacco, long white radishes, and nol-kol, all that day they strolled on, turning aside to every glimpse of water; rousing village dogs and sleeping villages at noonday; the lama replying to the volleyed questions with an unswerving simplicity. They sought a River – a River of miraculous healing. Had any one knowledge of such a stream? Sometimes men laughed, but more often heard the story out to the end and offered them a place in the shade, a drink of milk, and a meal. The women were always kind, and the little children as children are the world over, alternately shy and venturesome. Evening found them at rest under the village tree of a mud-walled, mud-roofed hamlet, talking to the headman as the cattle came in from the grazing grounds and the women prepared the day's last meal. They had passed beyond the belt of market-gardens round hungry Umballa, and were among the mile-wide green of the staple crops.

*A yellow-and-brown streak glided from the purple rustling stems
to the bank.*

He was a white-bearded and affable elder, used to entertaining strangers. He dragged out a string bed-stead for the lama, set warm cooked food before him, prepared him a pipe, and, the evening ceremonies being finished in the village temple, sent for the village priest.

Kim told the older children tales of the size and beauty of Lahore, of railway travel, and such-like city things, while the men talked, slowly as their cattle chew the cud.

"I cannot fathom it," said the headman at last to the priest. "How readest thou this talk?" The lama, his tale told, was silently telling his beads.

"He is a Seeker," the priest answered. "The land is full of such. Remember him who came only last month – the *fakir* with the tortoise?"

"Ay, but that man had right and reason, for Krishna himself appeared in a vision promising him Paradise without the burning-pyre if he journeyed to Prayag. This man seeks no god who is within my knowledge."

"Peace, he is old: he comes from far off, and he is mad," the smooth-shaven priest replied. "Hear me." He turned to the lama. "Three *koss* [six miles] to the westward runs the great road to Calcutta."

"But I would go to Benares – to Benares."

"And to Benares also. It crosses all streams on this side of Hind. Now my word to thee, Holy One, is rest here till tomorrow. Then take the road" (it was the Grand Trunk Road he meant) "and test each stream that it overpasses; for, as I understand, the virtue of thy River lies neither in one pool nor place, but throughout its length. Then, if thy Gods will, be assured that thou wilt come upon thy freedom."

"That is well said." The lama was much impressed by the plan. "We will begin tomorrow, and a blessing on thee for showing old feet such a near road." A deep, singsong Chinese half-chant closed the sentence. Even the priest was impressed, and the headman feared an evil spell: but none could look at the lama's simple, eager face and doubt him long.

"Seest thou my *chela?*" he said, diving into his snuff-gourd with an important sniff. It was his duty to repay courtesy with courtesy.

"I see – and hear." The headman rolled his eye where Kim was chatting to a girl in blue as she laid crackling thorns on a fire.

"He also has a Search of his own. No river, but a Bull. Yea, a Red Bull on a green field will some day raise him to honour. He is, I think, not altogether of this world. He was sent of a sudden to aid me in this search, and his name is Friend of all the World."

The priest smiled. "Ho, there, Friend of all the World," he cried across the sharp-smelling smoke, "what art thou?"

"This Holy One's disciple," said Kim. "He says thou art a *būt* [a spirit]."

"Can *būts* eat?" said Kim, with a twinkle. "For I am hungry."

"It is no jest," cried the lama. "A certain astrologer of that city whose name I have forgotten –"

"That is no more than the city of Umballa where we slept last night," Kim whispered to the priest.

"Ay, Umballa was it? He cast a horoscope and declared that my *chela* should find his desire within two days. But what said he of the meaning of the stars, Friend of all the World?"

Kim cleared his throat and looked around at the village greybeards.

"The meaning of my star is war," he replied pompously.

Somebody laughed at the little tattered figure strutting on the brickwork plinth under the great tree. Where a native would have lain down, Kim's white blood set him upon his feet.

"Ay, war," he answered.

"That is a sure prophecy," rumbled a deep voice. "For there is always war along the border – as I know."

It was an old, withered man, who had served the government in the days of the Mutiny as a native officer in a newly raised cavalry regiment. The government had given him a good holding in the village, and though the demands of his sons, now grey-bearded officers on their own account, had impoverished him, he was still a person of consequence. English officials – deputy commissioners even – turned aside from the main road to visit him, and on those occasions he dressed himself in the uniform of ancient days, and stood up like a ramrod.

"But this shall be a great war- a war of eight thousand." Kim's voice shrilled across the quick-gathering crowd, astonishing himself.

"Redcoats or our own regiments?" the old man snapped, as though he were asking an equal. His tone made men respect Kim.

"Redcoats," said Kim at a venture. "Redcoats and guns."

"But – but the astrologer said no word of this," cried the lama, snuffing prodigiously in his excitement.

"But I know. The word has come to me, who am this Holy One's disciple. There will rise a war – a war of eight thousand redcoats. From Pindi and Peshawar they will be drawn. This is sure."

"The boy has heard bazaar-talk," said the priest.

"But he was always by my side," said the lama. "How should he know? *I* did not know."

"He will make a clever juggler when the old man is dead," muttered the priest to the headman. "What new trick is this?"

"A sign. Give me a sign," thundered the old soldier suddenly. "If there were war my sons would have told me."

"When all is ready, thy sons, doubt not, will be told. But it is a long road from thy sons to the man in whose hands these things lie." Kim warmed to the game, for it reminded him of experiences in the letter-carrying line, when, for the sake of a few pice, he pretended to know more than he knew. But now he was playing for larger things – the sheer excitement and the sense of power. He drew a new breath and went on.

"Old man, give *me* a sign. Do underlings order the goings of eight thousand redcoats – with guns?"

"No." Still the old man answered as though Kim were an equal.

"Dost thou know who he is, then, that gives the order?"

"I have seen him."

"To know again?"

"I have known him since he was a lieutenant *top-khana* [the artillery]."

"A tall man. A tall man with black hair, walking thus?" Kim took a few paces in a stiff, wooden style.

"Ay. But that any one may have seen." The crowd were breathless-still through all this talk.

"That is true," said Kim. "But I will say more. Look now. First the great man walks thus. Then he thinks thus." (Kim drew a forefinger over his forehead and downwards till it came to rest by the angle of the jaw.) "Anon he twitches his fingers thus. Anon he thrusts his hat under his left armpit." Kim illustrated the motion and stood like a stork.

The old man groaned, inarticulate with amazement; and the crowd shivered.

"So – so – so. But what does he when he is about to give an order?"

"He rubs the skin at the back of his neck – thus. Then falls one finger on the table and he makes a small sniffing noise through his nose. Then he speaks, saying: 'Loose such and such a regiment. Call out such guns.'"

The old man rose stiffly and saluted.

"'For'" – Kim translated into the vernacular the clinching sentences he had heard in the dressing-room at Umballa – "'For,' says he, 'we should have done this long ago. It is not war – it is a chastisement. Snff!'"

"Enough. I believe. I have seen him thus in the smoke of battles. Seen and heard. It is he!"

"I saw no smoke" – Kim's voice shifted to the rapt sing-song of the wayside fortune-teller. "I saw this in darkness. First came a man to make things clear. Then came horsemen. Then came he, standing in a ring of light. The rest followed as I have said. Old man, have I spoken truth?"

"It is he. Past all doubt it is he."

The crowd drew a long, quavering breath, staring alternately at the old man, still at attention, and ragged Kim against the purple twilight.

"Said I not – said I not he was from the other world?" cried the lama proudly. "He is the Friend of all the World. He is the Friend of the Stars!"

"At least it does not concern us," a man cried. "O thou young soothsayer, if the gift abides with thee at all seasons, I have a red-spotted cow. She may be sister to thy Bull for aught I know –"

"Or I care," said Kim. "My stars do not concern themselves with thy cattle."

"Nay, but she is very sick," a woman struck in. "My man is a buffalo, or he would have chosen his words better. Tell me if she recover?"

Had Kim been at all an ordinary boy, he would have carried on the play; but one does not know Lahore city, and least of all the *fakirs* by the Taksali Gate, for thirteen years without also knowing human nature.

The priest looked at him sideways, something bitterly – a dry and blighting smile.

"Is there no priest, then, in the village? I thought I had seen a great one even now," cried Kim.

"Ay – but –" the woman began.

"But thou and thy husband hoped to get the cow cured for a handful of thanks." The shot told: they were notoriously the closest-fisted couple in the village. "It is not well to cheat the temples. Give a young calf to thine own priest, and, unless thy Gods are angry past recall, she will give milk within a month."

"A master-beggar art thou," purred the priest approvingly. "Not the cunning of forty years could have done better. Surely thou hast made the old man rich?"

"A little flour, a little butter and a mouthful of cardamoms." Kim retorted, flushed with the praise, but still cautious – "Does one grow rich on that? And, as thou canst see, he is mad. But it serves me while I learn the road at least."

He knew what the *fakirs* of the Taksali Gate were like when they talked among themselves, and copied the very inflection of their lewd disciples.

"Is his Search, then, truth or a cloak to other ends? It may be treasure."

"He is mad – many times mad. There is nothing else."

Here the old soldier hobbled up and asked if Kim would accept his hospitality for the night. The priest recommended him to do so, but insisted that the honour of entertaining the lama belonged to the temple – at which the lama smiled guilelessly. Kim glanced from one face to the other, and drew his own conclusions.

"Where is the money?" he whispered, beckoning the old man off into the darkness.

"In my bosom. Where else?"

"Give it me. Quietly and swiftly give it me."

"But why? Here is no ticket to buy."

"Am I thy *chela*, or am I not? Do I not safeguard thy old feet about the ways? Give me the money and at dawn I will return it." He slipped his hand above the lama's girdle and brought away the purse.

"Be it so – be it so." The old man nodded his head. "This is a great and terrible world. I never knew there were so many men alive in it."

Next morning the priest was in a very bad temper, but the lama was quite happy; and Kim had enjoyed a most interesting evening with the old man, who brought out his cavalry sabre and, balancing it on his dry knees, told tales of the Mutiny and young captains thirty years in their graves, till Kim dropped off to sleep.

"Certainly the air of this country is good," said the lama. "I sleep lightly, as do all old men; but last night I slept unwaking till broad day. Even now I am heavy."

"Drink a draught of hot milk," said Kim, who had carried not a few such remedies to opium-smokers of his acquaintance. "It is time to take the Road again."

"The long Road that overpasses all the rivers of Hind," said the lama gaily. "Let us go. But how thinkest thou, *chela*, to recompense these people, and especially the priest, for their great kindness? Truly they are *būts-parast*, but in other lives, maybe, they will receive enlightenment. A rupee to the temple? The thing which is no more than stone and red paint, but the heart of man we must acknowledge when and where it is good."

"Holy One, hast thou ever taken the Road alone?" Kim looked up sharply, like the Indian crows so busy about the fields.

"Surely, child: from Kulu to Pathânkot – from Kulu, where my first *chela* died. When men were kind to us we made offerings, and all men were well-disposed throughout all the Hills."

"It is otherwise in Hind," said Kim drily. "Their Gods are many-armed and malignant. Let them alone."

"I would set thee on thy road for a little, Friend of all the World – thou and thy yellow man." The old soldier ambled up the village street, all shadowy in the dawn, on a gaunt, scissor-hocked pony. "Last night broke up the fountains of remembrance in my so-dried heart, and it was as a blessing to me. Truly there is war abroad in the air. I smell it. See! I have brought my sword."

He sat long-legged on the little beast, with the big sword at his side – hand dropped on the pommel – staring fiercely over the flat lands towards the north. "Tell me again how he showed in thy vision. Come up and sit behind me. The beast will carry two."

"I am this Holy One's disciple," said Kim, as they cleared the village-gate. The villagers seemed almost sorry to be rid of them, but the priest's farewell was cold and distant. He had wasted some opium on a man who carried no money.

"That is well spoken. I am not much used to holy men, but respect is always good. There is no respect in these days – not even when a commissioner sahib comes to see me. But why should one whose star leads him to war follow a holy man?"

"But he *is* a holy man," said Kim earnestly. "In truth, and in talk and in act, holy. He is not like the others. I have never seen such an one. We be not fortune-tellers, or jugglers, or beggars."

"*Thou* art not. That I can see. But I do not know that other. He marches well, though."

The first freshness of the day carried the lama forward with long, easy, camel-like strides. He was deep in meditation, mechanically clicking his rosary.

They followed the rutted and worn country road that wound across the flat between the great dark-green mango groves, the line of the snow-capped Himalayas faint to the eastward. All India was at work in the fields, to the creaking of well wheels, the shouting of ploughmen behind their cattle, and the clamour of the crows. Even the pony felt the good influence and almost broke into a trot as Kim laid a hand on the stirrup-leather.

"It repents me that I did not give a rupee to the shrine," said the lama on the last bead of his eighty-one.

The old soldier growled in his beard, so that the lama for the first time was aware of him.

"Seekest thou the River also?" said he, turning.

"The day is new," was the reply. "What need of a river save to water at before sundown? I come to show thee a short lane to the Big Road."

"That is a courtesy to be remembered, O man of good will. But why the sword?"

The old soldier looked as abashed as a child interrupted in his game of make-believe.

"The sword," he said, fumbling it. "Oh, that was a fancy of mine – an old man's fancy. Truly the police orders are that no man must bear weapons throughout Hind, but" – he cheered up and slapped the hilt – "all the constabeels hereabout know me."

"It is not a good fancy," said the lama. "What profit to kill men?"

"Very little – as I know; but if evil men were not now and then slain it would not be a good world for weaponless dreamers. I do not speak without knowledge who have seen the land from Delhi south awash with blood."

"What madness was that, then?"

"The Gods, who sent it for a plague, alone know. A madness ate into all the army, and they turned against their officers. That was the first evil, but not past remedy if they had then held their hands. But they chose to kill the sahib's wives and children. Then came the sahibs from over the sea and called them to most strict account."

"Some such rumour, I believe, reached me once long ago. They called it the Black Year, as I remember."

"What manner of life hast thou led, not to know the Year? A rumour indeed! All earth knew, and trembled."

"Our earth never shook but once – upon the day that the Excellent One received Enlightenment."

"Umph! I saw Delhi shake at least; and Delhi is the navel of the world."

"So they turned against women and children? That was a bad deed, for which the punishment cannot be avoided."

"Many strove to do so, but with very small profit. I was then in a regiment of cavalry. It broke. Of six hundred and eighty sabres stood fast to their salt – how many, think you? Three. Of whom I was one."

"The greater merit."

"Merit! We did not consider it merit in those days. My people, my friends, my brothers fell from me. They said: 'The time of the English is accomplished. Let each strike out a little holding for himself.' But I had talked with the men of Sobraon, of Chilianwallah, of Moodkee and Ferozeshah. I said: 'Abide a little and the wind turns. There is no blessing in this work.' In those days I rode seventy miles with an English memsahib and her babe on my saddle-bow. (Wow! That was a horse fit for a man!) I placed them in safety, and back came I to my officer – the one that was not killed of our five. 'Give me work,' said I, 'for I am an outcast among my own kin, and my cousin's blood is wet on my sabre.' 'Be content,' said he. 'There is great work forward. When this madness is over there is a recompense.'"

"Ay, there is a recompense when the madness is over, surely?" the lama muttered half to himself.

"They did not hang medals in those days on all who by accident had heard a gun fired. No! In nineteen pitched battles was I; in six-and-forty skirmishes of horse; and in small affairs without number. Nine wounds I bear; a medal and four clasps and the medal of an Order, for my captains, who are now generals, remembered me when the Kaisar-i-Hind had accomplished fifty years of her reign, and all the land rejoiced. They said: 'Give him the Order of Berittish India.' I carry it upon my neck now. I have also my *jaghir* [holding] from the hands of the state a free gift to me and mine. The men of the old days – they are now commissioners – come riding to me through the crops – high upon horses so that all the village sees – and we talk out the old skirmishes, one dead man's name leading to another."

"And after?" said the lama.

"Oh, afterwards they go away, but not before my village has seen."

"And at the last what wilt thou do?"

"At the last I shall die."

"And after?"

"Let the Gods order it. I have never pestered them with prayers. I do not think they will pester me. Look you, I have noticed in my long life that those who eternally break in upon those above with complaints and reports and bellowings and weepings are presently sent for in haste, as our colonel used to send for slack-jawed down-country men who talked too much. No, I have never wearied the Gods. They will remember this, and give me a quiet place where I can drive my lance in the shade, and wait to welcome my sons: I have no less than three Rissaldar-majors all – in the regiments."

"And they likewise, bound upon the Wheel, go forth from life to life – from despair to despair," said the lama below his breath, "hot, uneasy, snatching."

"Ay," the old soldier chuckled. "Three Rissaldar-majors in three regiments. Gamblers a little, but so am I. They must be well mounted; and one cannot take the horses as in the old days one took women. Well, well, my holding can pay for all. How thinkest thou? It is a well-watered strip, but my men cheat me. I do not know how to ask save at the lance's point. Ugh! I grow angry and I curse them, and they feign penitence, but behind my back I know they call me a toothless old ape."

"Hast thou never desired any other thing?"

"Yes – yes – a thousand times! A straight back and a close-clinging knee once more; a quick wrist and a keen eye; and the marrow that makes a man. Oh, the old days – the good days of my strength!"

"That strength is weakness."

"It has turned so; but fifty years since I could have proved it otherwise," the old soldier retorted, driving his stirrup-edge into the pony's lean flank.

"But I know a River of great healing."

"I have drunk Gunga-water to the edge of dropsy. All she gave me was a flux, and no sort of strength."

"It is not Gunga. The River that I know washes from all taint of sin. Ascending the far bank one is assured of Freedom. I do not know thy life, but thy face is the face of the honourable and courteous. Thou has clung to thy Way, rendering fidelity when it was hard to give, in that Black Year of which I now remember other tales. Enter now upon the Middle Way, which is the path to Freedom. Hear the Most Excellent Law, and do not follow dreams."

"Speak, then, old man," the soldier smiled, half saluting. "We be all babblers at our age."

The lama squatted under the shade of a mango, whose shadow played checkerwise over his face; the soldier sat stiffly on the pony; and Kim, making sure that there were no snakes, lay down in the crotch of the twisted roots.

There was a drowsy buzz of small life in hot sunshine, a cooing of doves, and a sleepy drone of well wheels across the fields. Slowly and impressively the lama began. At the end of ten minutes the old soldier slid from his pony, to hear better as he said, and sat with the reins round his wrist. The lama's voice faltered – the periods lengthened. Kim was busy watching a grey squirrel. When the little scolding bunch of fur, close pressed to the branch, disappeared, preacher and audience were fast asleep, the old officer's strong-cut head pillowed on his arm, the lama's thrown back against the tree bole, where it showed like yellow ivory. A naked child toddled up, stared, and, moved by some quick impulse of reverence, made a solemn little obeisance before the lama – only the child was so short and fat that it toppled over sideways, and Kim laughed at the sprawling, chubby legs. The child, scared and indignant, yelled aloud.

"Hai! Hai!" said the soldier, leaping to his feet. "What is it? What orders?…
It is… a child! I dreamed it was an alarm. Little one – little one – do not
cry. Have I slept? That was discourteous indeed!"

"I fear! I am afraid!" roared the child.

"What is it to fear? Two old men and a boy? How wilt thou ever make
a soldier, Princeling?"

The lama had waked too, but, taking no direct notice of the child, clicked
his rosary.

"What is that?" said the child, stopping a yell midway. "I have never seen
such things. Give them me."

"Aha," said the lama, smiling, and trailing a loop of it on the grass:

> "This is a handful of cardamoms,
>   This is a lump of *ghee:*
> This is millet and chillies and rice,
>   A supper for thee and me!"

The child shrieked with joy, and snatched at the dark, glancing beads.

"Oho!" said the old soldier. "Whence hadst thou that song, despiser of
this world?"

"I learned it in Pathânkot – sitting on a doorstep," said the lama shyly.
"It is good to be kind to babes."

"As I remember, before the sleep came on us, thou hadst told me that
marriage and bearing were darkeners of the true light, stumbling-blocks
upon the Way. Do children drop from Heaven in thy country? Is it the Way
to sing them songs?"

"No man is all perfect," said the lama gravely, re-coiling the rosary. "Run
now to thy mother, little one."

"Hear him!" said the soldier to Kim. "He is ashamed for that he has
made a child happy. There was a very good householder lost in thee, my
brother. Hai, child!" He threw it a pice. "Sweetmeats are always sweet." And
as the little figure capered away into the sunshine: "They grow up and
become men. Holy One, I grieve that I slept in the midst of thy preaching.
Forgive me."

"We be two old men," said the lama. "The fault is mine. I listened to thy
talk of the world and its madness, and one fault led to the next."

"Hear him! What harm do thy Gods suffer from play with a babe? And that song was very well sung. Let us go on and I will sing thee the song of Nikal Seyn before Delhi – the old song."

And they fared out from the gloom of the mango tope, the old man's high, shrill voice ringing across the field, as wail by long-drawn wail he unfolded the story of Nikal Seyn [Nicholson] – the song that men sing in the Punjab to this day. Kim was delighted, and the lama listened with deep interest.

"'Ahi! Nikal Seyn is dead – he died before Delhi! Lances of the North, take vengeance for Nikal Seyn.'" He quavered it out to the end, marking the trills with the flat of his sword on the pony's rump.

"And now we come to the Big Road," said he, after receiving the compliments of Kim; for the lama was markedly silent. "It is long since I have ridden this way, but thy boy's talk stirred me. See, Holy One – the Great Road which is the backbone of all Hind. For the most part it is shaded, as here, with four lines of trees; the middle road – all hard – takes the quick traffic. In the days before rail-carriages, the sahibs travelled up and down here in hundreds. Now there are only country-carts and such like. Left and right is the rougher road for the heavy carts – grain and cotton and timber, fodder, lime and hides. A man goes in safety here – for at every few *koss* is a police-station. The police are thieves and extortioners (I myself would patrol it with cavalry – young recruits under a strong captain), but at least they do not suffer any rivals. All castes and kinds of men move here. Look! Brahmins and chumars, bankers and tinkers, barbers and bunnias, pilgrims and potters – all the world going and coming. It is to me as a river from which I am withdrawn like a log after a flood."

And truly the Grand Trunk Road is a wonderful spectacle. It runs straight, bearing without crowding India's traffic for fifteen hundred miles – such a river of life as nowhere else exists in the world. They looked at the green-arched, shade-flecked length of it, the white breadth speckled with slow-pacing folk; and the two-roomed police-station opposite.

"Who bears arms against the law?" a constable called out laughingly, as he caught sight of the soldier's sword. "Are not the police enough to destroy evil-doers?"

"It was because of the police I bought it," was the answer. "Does all go well in Hind?"

"Rissaldar Sahib, all goes well."

"I am like an old tortoise, look you, who puts his head out from the bank and draws it in again. Ay, this is the Road of Hindustan. All men come by this way…"

"Son of a swine, is the soft part of the road meant for thee to scratch thy back upon? Father of all the daughters of shame and husband of ten thousand virtueless ones, thy mother was devoted to a devil, being led thereto by her mother. Thy aunts have never had a nose for seven generations! Thy sister – What owl's folly told thee to draw thy carts across the road? A broken wheel? Then take a broken head and put the two together at leisure!"

The voice and a venomous whip-cracking came out of a pillar of dust fifty yards away, where a cart had broken down. A thin, high Kathiawar mare, with eyes and nostrils aflame, rocketed out of the jam, snorting and wincing as her rider bent her across the road in chase of a shouting man. He was tall and grey-bearded, sitting the almost mad beast as a piece of her, and scientifically lashing his victim between plunges.

The old man's face lit with pride. "My child!" said he briefly, and strove to rein the pony's neck to a fitting arch.

"Am I to be beaten before the police?" cried the carter. "Justice! I will have Justice –"

"Am I to be blocked by a shouting ape who upsets ten thousand sacks under a young horse's nose? That is the way to ruin a mare."

"He speaks truth. He speaks truth. But she follows her man close," said the old man. The carter ran under the wheels of his cart and thence threatened all sorts of vengeance.

"They are strong men, thy sons," said the policeman serenely, picking his teeth.

The horseman delivered one last vicious cut with his whip and came on at a canter.

"My father!" He reined back ten yards and dismounted.

The old man was off his pony in an instant, and they embraced as do father and son in the East.

Chapter 4

Good Luck, she is never a lady,
But the cursedest quean alive,
Tricksy, wincing, and jady –
Kittle to lead or drive.
Greet her – she's hailing a stranger!
Meet her – she's busking to leave!
Let her alone for a shrew to the bone
And the hussy comes plucking your sleeve!
    Largesse! Largesse, O Fortune!
    Give or hold at your will.
    If I've no care for Fortune,
    Fortune must follow me still!
                            The Wishing-Caps

Then, lowering their voices, they spoke together. Kim came to rest under a tree, but the lama tugged impatiently at his elbow.

"Let us go on. The River is not here."

"*Hai mai!* Have we not walked enough for a little? Our River will not run away. Patience, and he will give us a dole."

"This," said the old soldier suddenly, "is the Friend of the Stars. He brought me the news yesterday. Having seen the very man himself, in a vision, giving orders for the war."

"Hm!" said his son, all deep in his broad chest. "He came by a bazaar rumour and made profit of it."

His father laughed. "At least he did not ride to me begging for a new charger, and the Gods know how many rupees. Are thy brothers' regiments also under orders?"

"I do not know. I took leave and came swiftly to thee in case –"

"In case they ran before thee to beg. O gamblers and spendthrifts all! But thou hast never yet ridden in a charge. A good horse is needed there, truly. A good follower and a good pony also for the marching. Let us see – let us see." He thrummed on the pommel.

"This is no place to cast accounts in, my father. Let us go to thy house."

"At least pay the boy, then: I have no pice with me, and he brought auspicious news. Ho! Friend of all the World, a war is toward as thou hast said."

"Nay, as I know, *the* war," returned Kim composedly.

"Eh?" said the lama, fingering his beads, all eager for the road.

"My master does not trouble the stars for hire. We brought the news – bear witness, we brought the news, and now we go." Kim half crooked his hand at his side.

The son tossed a silver coin through the sunlight, grumbling something about beggars and jugglers. It was a four-anna piece, and would feed them well for some days. The lama, seeing the flash of the metal, droned a blessing.

"Go thy way, Friend of all the World," piped the old soldier, wheeling his scrawny mount. "For once in all my days I have met a true prophet – who was not in the army."

Father and son swung round together: the old man sitting as erect as the younger.

A Punjabi constable in yellow linen trousers slouched across the road. He had seen the money pass.

"Halt!" he cried in impressive English. "Know ye not that there is a *takkus* of two annas a head, which is four annas, on those who enter the Road from this side-road. It is the order of the Sirkar, and the money is spent for the planting of trees and the beautification of the ways."

"And the bellies of the police," said Kim, skipping out of arm's reach. "Consider for a while, man with a mud head. Think you we came from the nearest pond like the frog, thy father-in-law. Hast thou ever heard the name of thy brother?"

"And who was he? Leave the boy alone," cried a senior constable, immensely delighted, as he squatted down to smoke his pipe in the veranda.

"He took a label from a bottle of *belaitee-pani* [soda-water], and affixing it to a bridge, collected taxes for a month from those who passed, saying that it was the Sirkar's order. Then came an Englishman and broke his head. Ah, brother, I am a town crow, not a village crow!"

The policeman drew back abashed, and Kim hooted at him all down the road.

"Was there ever such a disciple as I?" he cried merrily to the lama. "All earth would have picked thy bones within ten mile of Lahore city if I had not guarded thee."

"I consider in my own mind whether thou art a spirit, sometimes, or sometimes an evil imp," said the lama, smiling slowly.

"I am thy *chela*." Kim dropped into step at his side – that indescribable gait of the long-distance tramp all the world over.

"Now let us walk," muttered the lama, and to the click of his rosary they walked in silence mile upon mile. The lama, as usual, was deep in meditation, but Kim's bright eyes were open wide. This broad, smiling river of life, he considered, was a vast improvement on the cramped and crowded Lahore streets. There were new people and new sights at every stride – castes he knew and castes that were altogether out of his experience.

They met a troop of long-haired, strong-scented Sansis with baskets of lizards and other unclean food on their backs, their lean dogs sniffing at their heels. These people kept their own side of the road, moving at a quick, furtive jog-trot, and all other castes gave them ample room; for the Sansi is deep pollution. Behind them, walking wide and stiffly across the strong shadows, the memory of his leg-irons still on him, strode one newly released from the jail; his full stomach and shiny skin to prove that the government fed its prisoners better than most honest men could feed themselves. Kim knew that walk well, and made broad jest of it as they passed. Then an Akali, a wild-eyed, wild-haired Sikh devotee in the blue-checked clothes of his faith, with polished steel quoits glistening on the cone of his tall blue turban, stalked past, returning from a visit to one of the independent Sikh states, where he had been singing the ancient glories of the Khalsa to college-trained princelings in top-boots and white-cord breeches. Kim was careful

Here and there they met or were overtaken by the gaily dressed crowds
of whole villages turning out to some local fair.

not to irritate that man; for the Akali's temper is short and his arm quick. Here and there they met or were overtaken by the gaily dressed crowds of whole villages turning out to some local fair; the women, with their babes on their hips, walking behind the men, the older boys prancing on sticks of sugarcane, dragging rude brass models of locomotives such as they sell for a halfpenny, or flashing the sun into the eyes of their betters from cheap toy mirrors. One could see at a glance what each had bought; and if there were any doubt it needed only to watch the wives comparing, brown arm against brown arm, the newly purchased dull glass bracelets that come from the north-west. These merry-makers stepped slowly, calling one to the other and stopping to haggle with sweetmeat-sellers, or to make a prayer before one of the wayside shrines – sometimes Hindu, sometimes Mussulman – which the low-caste of both creeds share with beautiful impartiality. A solid line of blue, rising and falling like the back of a caterpillar in haste, would swing up through the quivering dust and trot past to a chorus of quick cackling. That was a gang of *changars* – the women who have taken all the embankments of all the northern railways under their charge – a flat-footed, big-bosomed, strong-limbed, blue-petticoated clan of earth-carriers, hurrying north on news of a job, and wasting no time by the road. They belong to the caste whose men do not count, and they walked with squared elbows, swinging hips, and heads on high, as suits women who carry heavy weights. A little later a marriage procession would strike into the Grand Trunk with music and shoutings, and a smell of marigold and jasmine stronger even than the reek of the dust. One could see the bride's litter, a blur of red and tinsel, staggering through the haze, while the bridegroom's bewreathed pony turned aside to snatch a mouthful from a passing fodder-cart. Then Kim would join the Kentish-fire of good wishes and bad jokes, wishing the couple a hundred sons and no daughters, as the saying is. Still more interesting and more to be shouted over it was when a strolling juggler with some half-trained monkeys, or a panting, feeble bear, or a woman who tied goat's horns to her feet, and with these danced on a slack-rope, set the horses to shying and the women to shrill, long-drawn quavers of amazement.

The lama never raised his eyes. He did not note the moneylender on his goose-rumped pony, hastening along to collect the cruel interest; or the long-shouting, deep-voiced little mob – still in military formation – of native soldiers on leave, rejoicing to be rid of their breeches and puttees, and saying the most outrageous things to the most respectable women in sight. Even the seller of Ganges water he did not see, and Kim expected that he would at least buy a bottle of that precious stuff. He looked steadily at the ground, and strode as steadily hour after hour, his soul busied elsewhere. But Kim was in the seventh heaven of joy. The Grand Trunk at this point was built on an embankment to guard against winter floods from the foothills, so that one walked, as it were, a little above the country, along a stately corridor, seeing all India spread out to left and right. It was beautiful to behold the many-yoked grain and cotton wagons crawling over the country roads: one could hear their axles, complaining a mile away, coming nearer, till with shouts and yells and bad words they climbed up the steep incline and plunged on to the hard main road, carter reviling carter. It was equally beautiful to watch the people, little clumps of red and blue and pink and white and saffron, turning aside to go to their own villages, dispersing and growing small by twos and threes across the level plain. Kim felt these things, though he could not give tongue to his feelings, and so contented himself with buying peeled sugarcane and spitting the pith generously about his path. From time to time the lama took snuff, and at last Kim could endure the silence no longer.

"This is a good land – the land of the south!" said he. "The air is good; the water is good. Eh?"

"And they are all bound upon the Wheel," said the lama. "Bound from life after life. To none of these has the Way been shown." He shook himself back to this world.

"And now we have walked a weary way," said Kim. "Surely we shall soon come to a *parao* [a resting-place]. Shall we stay there? Look, the sun is sloping."

"Who will receive us this evening?"

"That is all one. The country is full of good folk. Besides," – he sunk his voice beneath a whisper – "we have money."

The crowd thickened as they neared the resting-place which marked the end of their day's journey. A line of stalls selling very simple food and tobacco, a stack of firewood, a police-station, a well, a horse-trough, a few trees, and, under them, some trampled ground dotted with the black ashes of old fires, are all that mark a *parao* on the Grand Trunk; if you except the beggars and the crows – both hungry.

By this time the sun was driving broad golden spokes through the lower branches of the mango trees; the parakeets and doves were coming home in their hundreds; the chattering, grey-backed Seven Sisters, talking over the day's adventures, walked back and forth in twos and threes almost under the feet of the travellers; and shufflings and scufflings in the branches showed that the bats were ready to go out on the night picket. Swiftly the light gathered itself together, painted for an instant the faces and the cart-wheels and the bullocks' horns as red as blood. Then the night fell, changing the touch of the air, drawing a low, even haze, like a gossamer veil of blue, across the face of the country and bringing out, keen and distinct, the smell of wood-smoke and cattle and the good scent of wheaten cakes cooked on ashes. The evening patrol hurried out of the police-station with important coughings and reiterated orders; and a live charcoal ball in the cup of a wayside carter's hookah glowed red while Kim's eye mechanically watched the last flicker of the sun on the brass tweezers.

The life of the *parao* was very like that of the Kashmir Serai on a small scale. Kim dived into the happy Asiatic disorder which, if you only allow time, will bring you everything that a simple man needs.

His wants were few, because, since the lama had no caste scruples, cooked food from the nearest stall would serve; but, for luxury's sake, Kim bought a handful of dung-cakes to build a fire. All about, coming and going round the little flames, men cried for oil, or grain, or sweetmeats, or tobacco, jostling one another while they waited their turn at the well; and under the men's voices you heard from halted, shuttered carts the high squeals and giggles of women whose faces should not be seen in public.

Nowadays, well-educated natives are of opinion that when their women-folk travel – and they visit a good deal – it is better to take them quickly by rail in a properly screened compartment; and that custom is spreading. But there are always those of the old rock who hold by the use of their forefathers; and, above all, there are always the old women – more conservative than the men – who towards the end of their days go a pilgrimage. They, being withered and undesirable, do not, under certain circumstances, object to unveiling. After their long seclusion, during which they have always been in business touch with a thousand outside interests, they love the bustle and stir of the open road, the gatherings at the shrines, and the infinite possibilities of gossip with like-minded dowagers. Very often it suits a long-suffering family that a strong-tongued, iron-willed old lady should disport herself about India in this fashion; for certainly pilgrimage is grateful to the Gods. So all about India, in the most remote places as in the most public, you find some knot of grizzled servitors in nominal charge of an old lady who is more or less curtained and hid away in a bullock-cart. Such men are staid and discreet, and when a European or a high-caste native is near will net their charge with most elaborate precautions; but in the ordinary haphazard chances of pilgrimage the precautions are not taken. The old lady is, after all, intensely human, and lives to look upon life.

Kim marked down a gaily ornamented *ruth* or family bullock-cart, with a broidered canopy of two domes, like a double-humped camel, which had just been drawn into the *parao*. Eight men made its retinue, and two of the eight were armed with rusty sabres – sure signs that they followed a person of distinction, for the common folk do not bear arms. An increasing cackle of complaints, orders, and jests, and what to a European would have been bad language, came from behind the curtains. Here was evidently a woman used to command.

Kim looked over the retinue critically. Half of them were thin-legged, grey-bearded Ooryas from down country. The other half were duffle-clad, felt-hatted hill-men of the north; and that mixture told its own tale, even if he had not overheard the incessant sparring between the two divisions. The old lady was going south on a visit – probably to a rich relative, most probably to a son-in-law, who had sent up an escort as a mark of respect. The hillmen would be of her own people – Kulu or Kangra folk. It was quite clear that she was not taking her daughter down to be wedded, or the curtains would have been laced home and the guard would have allowed no one near the car. A merry and a high-spirited dame, thought Kim, balancing the dung-cake in one hand, the cooked food in the other, and piloting the lama with a nudging shoulder. Something might be made out of the meeting. The lama would give no help, but, as a conscientious *chela*, Kim was delighted to beg for two.

He built his fire as close to the cart as he dared, waiting for one of the escort to order him away. The lama dropped wearily to the ground, much as a heavy fruit-eating bat cowers, and returned to his rosary.

"Stand farther off, beggar!" The order was shouted in broken Hindustani by one of the hillmen.

"Huh! It is only a *pahari* [a hillman]," said Kim over his shoulder. "Since when have the hill-asses owned all Hindustan?"

The retort was a swift and brilliant sketch of Kim's pedigree for three generations.

"Ah!" Kim's voice was sweeter than ever, as he broke the dung-cake into fit pieces. "In *my* country we call that the beginning of love-talk."

A harsh, thin cackle behind the curtains put the hill-man on his mettle for a second shot.

"Not so bad – not so bad," said Kim with calm. "But have a care, my brother, lest we – *we*, I say – be minded to give a curse or so in return. And our curses have the knack of biting home."

The Ooryas laughed; the hillman sprang forward threateningly. The lama suddenly raised his head, bringing his huge tam-o'-shanter hat into the full light of Kim's new-started fire.

"What is it?" said he.

The man halted as though struck to stone. "I – I – am saved from a great sin," he stammered.

"The foreigner has found him a priest at last," whispered one of the Ooryas.

"*Hai!* Why is that beggar-brat not well beaten?" the old woman cried.

The hillman drew back to the cart and whispered something to the curtain. There was dead silence, then a muttering.

"This goes well," thought Kim, pretending neither to see nor hear.

"When – when – he has eaten" – the hillman fawned on Kim – "it – it is requested that the Holy One will do the honour to talk to one who would speak to him."

"After he has eaten he will sleep," Kim returned loftily. He could not quite see what new turn the game had taken, but stood resolute to profit by it. "Now I will get him his food." The last sentence, spoken loudly, ended with a sigh as of faintness.

"I – I myself and the others of my people will look to that – if it is permitted."

"It is permitted," said Kim, more loftily than ever. "Holy One, these people will bring us food."

"The land is good. All the country of the south is good – a great and a terrible world," mumbled the lama drowsily.

"Let him sleep," said Kim, "but look to it that we are well fed when he wakes. He is a very holy man."

Again one of the Ooryas said something contemptuously.

"He is not a *fakir*. He is not a down-country beggar," Kim went on severely, addressing the stars. "He is the most holy of holy men. He is above all castes. I am his *chela*."

"Come here!" said the flat thin voice behind the curtain; and Kim came, conscious that eyes he could not see were staring at him. One skinny brown finger heavy with rings lay on the edge of the cart, and the talk went this way:

"Who is that one?"

"An exceedingly holy one. He comes from far off. He comes from Tibet."

"Where in Tibet?"

"From behind the snows – from a very far place. He knows the stars; he makes horoscopes; he reads nativities. But he does not do this for money. He does it for kindness and great charity. I am his disciple. I am called also the Friend of the Stars."

"Thou art no hillman."

"Ask him. He will tell thee I was sent to him from the stars to show him an end to his pilgrimage."

"Humph! Consider, brat, that I am an old woman and not altogether a fool. Lamas I know, and to these I give reverence, but thou art no more a lawful *chela* than this my finger is the pole of this wagon. Thou art a caste-less Hindu – a bold and unblushing beggar, attached, belike, to the Holy One for the sake of gain."

"Do we not all work for gain?" Kim changed his tone promptly to match that altered voice. "I have heard" – this was a bow drawn at a venture – "I have heard –"

"What hast thou heard?" she snapped, rapping with the finger.

"Nothing that I well remember, but some talk in the bazaars, which is doubtless a lie, that even rajahs – small hill rajahs –"

"But none the less of good Rajput blood."

"Assuredly of good blood. That these even sell the more comely of their womenfolk for gain. Down south they sell them – to zemindars and such-all of Oudh."

If there be one thing in the world that the small hill rajahs deny it is just this charge; but it happens to be one thing that the bazaars believe, when they discuss the mysterious slave traffics of India. The old lady explained to Kim, in a tense, indignant whisper, precisely what manner and fashion of malignant liar he was. Had Kim hinted this when she was a girl, he would have been pommelled to death that same evening by an elephant. This was perfectly true.

"*Ahai!* I am only a beggar's brat, as the Eye of Beauty has said," he wailed in extravagant terror.

"Eye of Beauty, forsooth! Who am I that thou shouldst fling beggar endearments at me?" And yet she laughed at the long-forgotten word. "Forty years ago that might have been said, and not without truth. Ay, thirty years ago. But it is the fault of this gadding up and down Hind that a king's widow must jostle all the scum of the land, and be made a mock by beggars."

"Great Queen," said Kim promptly, for he heard her shaking with indignation, "I am even what the Great Queen says I am; but none the less is my master holy. He has not yet heard the Great Queen's order that –"

"Order? I order a Holy One – a Teacher of the Law – to come and speak to a woman? Never!"

"Pity my stupidity. I thought it was given as an order –"

"It was not. It was a petition. Does this make all clear?"

A silver coin clicked on the edge of the cart. Kim took it and salaamed profoundly. The old lady recognized that, as the eyes and the ears of the lama, he was to be propitiated.

"I am but the Holy One's disciple. When he has eaten perhaps he will come."

"Oh, villain and shameless rogue!" The jewelled forefinger shook itself at him reprovingly; but he could hear the old lady's chuckle.

403

"Nay, what is it?" he said, dropping into his most caressing and confidential tone – the one, he well knew, that few could resist. "Is – is there any need of a son in thy family? Speak freely, for we priests –" That last was a direct plagiarism from a *fakir* by the Taksali Gate.

"We priests! Thou art not yet old enough to –" She checked the joke with another laugh. "Believe me, now and again, we women, O priest, think of other matters than sons. Moreover, my daughter has borne her man-child."

"Two arrows in the quiver are better than one; and three are better still." Kim quoted the proverb with a meditative cough, looking discreetly earthward.

"True – oh, true. But perhaps that will come. Certainly those down-country Brahmins are utterly useless. I sent gifts and monies and gifts again to them, and they prophesied."

"Ah," drawled Kim, with infinite contempt, "they prophesied!" A professional could have done no better.

"And it was not until I remembered my own Gods that my prayers were heard. I chose an auspicious hour, and – perhaps the Holy One has heard of the Abbot of the Lung-Cho lamassery. It was to him I put the matter, and behold in the due time all came about as I desired. The Brahmin in the house of the father of my daughter's son has since said that it was through *his* prayers – which is a little error that I will explain to him when we reach our journey's end. And so afterwards I go to Buddh Gaya, to make *shraddha* for the father of my children."

"Thither go we."

"Doubly auspicious," chirruped the old lady. "A second son at least!"

"O Friend of all the World!" The lama had waked, and, simply as a child bewildered in a strange bed, called for Kim.

"I come! I come, Holy One!" He dashed to the fire, where he found the lama already surrounded by dishes of food, the hillmen visibly adoring him and the southerners looking sourly.

"Go back! Withdraw!" Kim cried. "Do we eat publicly like dogs?" They finished the meal in silence, each turned a little from the other, and Kim topped it with a native-made cigarette.

"Have I not said an hundred times that the south is a good land? Here is a virtuous and high-born widow of a hill rajah on pilgrimage, she says, to Buddh Gaya. She it is sends us those dishes; and when thou art well rested she would speak to thee."

"Is this also thy work?" The lama dipped deep into his snuff-gourd.

"Who else watched over thee since our wonderful journey began?" Kim's eyes danced in his head as he blew the rank smoke through his nostrils and stretched him on the dusty ground. "Have I failed to oversee thy comforts, Holy One?"

"A blessing on thee." The lama inclined his solemn head. "I have known many men in my so long life, and disciples not a few. But to none among men, if so be thou art woman-born, has my heart gone out as it has to thee – thoughtful, wise, and courteous; but something of a small imp."

"And I have never seen such a priest as thou." Kim considered the benevolent yellow face wrinkle by wrinkle. "It is less than three days since we took the road together, and it is as though it were a hundred years."

"Perhaps in a former life it was permitted that I should have rendered thee some service. Maybe" – he smiled – "I freed thee from a trap; or, having caught thee on a hook in the days when I was not enlightened, cast thee back into the river."

"Maybe," said Kim quietly. He had heard this sort of speculation again and again, from the mouths of many whom the English would not consider imaginative. "Now, as regards that woman in the bullock-cart, *I* think she needs a second son for her daughter."

"That is no part of the Way," sighed the lama. "But at least she is from the Hills. Ah, the Hills, and the snow of the Hills!"

He rose and stalked to the cart. Kim would have given his ears to come too, but the lama did not invite him; and the few words he caught were in an unknown tongue, for they spoke some common speech of the mountains. The woman seemed to ask questions which the lama turned over in his mind before answering. Now and again he heard the singsong cadence of a Chinese quotation. It was a strange picture that Kim watched between drooped eyelids. The lama, very straight and erect, the deep folds of his yellow clothing slashed with black in the light of the *parao* fires precisely as a knotted tree-trunk is slashed with the shadows of the low sun, addressed a tinsel and lacquered *ruth* which burned like a many-coloured jewel in the same uncertain light. The patterns on the gold-worked curtains ran up and down, melting and re-forming as the folds shook and quivered to the night wind; and when the talk grew more earnest the jewelled forefinger snapped out little sparks of light between the embroideries. Behind the cart was a wall of uncertain darkness speckled with little flames and alive with half-caught forms and faces and shadows. The voices of early evening had settled down to one soothing hum whose deepest note was the steady chumping of the bullocks above their chopped straw, and whose highest was the tinkle of a Bengali dancing-girl's *sitar*. Most men had eaten and pulled deep at their gurgling, grunting hookahs, which in full blast sound like bull-frogs.

At last the lama returned. A hillman walked behind him with a wadded cotton quilt and spread it carefully by the fire.

"She deserves ten thousand grandchildren," thought Kim. "None the less, but for me, these gifts would not have come."

"A virtuous woman – and a wise one." The lama slackened off, joint by joint, like a slow camel. "The world is full of charity to those who follow the Way." He flung a fair half of the quilt over Kim.

"And what said she?" Kim rolled up in his share of it.

"She asked me many questions and propounded many problems – the most of which were idle tales which she had heard from devil-serving priests who pretend to follow the Way. Some I answered, and some I said were foolish. Many wear the Robe, but few keep the Way."

"True. That is true." Kim used the thoughtful, conciliatory tone of those who wish to draw confidences.

"But by her lights she is most right-minded. She desires greatly that we should go with her to Buddh Gaya; her road being ours, as I understand, for many days' journey to the southward."

"And?"

"Patience a little. To this I said that my Search came before all things. She had heard many foolish legends, but this great truth of my River she had never heard. Such are the priests of the lower hills! She knew the Abbot of Lung-Cho, but she did not know of my River – nor the tale of the Arrow."

"And?"

"I spoke therefore of the Search, and of the Way, and of matters that were profitable; she desiring only that I should accompany her and make prayer for a second son."

"Aha! 'We women' do *not* think of anything save children," said Kim sleepily.

"Now, since our roads run together for a while, I do not see that we in any way depart from our Search if so be we accompany her – at least as far as – I have forgotten the name of the city."

"*Ohé!*" said Kim, turning and speaking in a sharp whisper to one of the Ooryas a few yards away. "Where is your master's house?"

"A little behind Saharunpore, among the fruit gardens." He named the village.

"That was the place," said the lama. "So far, at least, we can go with her."

"Flies go to carrion," said the Oorya, in an abstracted voice.

"For the sick cow a crow; for the sick man a Brahmin." Kim breathed the proverb impersonally to the shadow-tops of the trees overhead.

The Oorya grunted and held his peace. "So then we go with her, Holy One?"

"Is there any reason against? I can still step aside and try all the rivers that the road overpasses. She desires that I should come. She very greatly desires it."

Kim stifled a laugh in the quilt. When once that imperious old lady had recovered from her natural awe of a lama he thought it probable that she would be worth listening to.

He was nearly asleep when the lama suddenly quoted a proverb: "The husbands of the talkative have a great reward hereafter." Then Kim heard him snuff thrice, and dozed off, still laughing.

The diamond-bright dawn woke men and crows and bullocks together. Kim sat up and yawned, shook himself, and thrilled with delight. This was seeing the world in real truth; this was life as he would have it – bustling and shouting, the buckling of belts, and beating of bullocks and creaking of wheels, lighting of fires and cooking of food, and new sights at every turn of the approving eye. The morning mist swept off in a whorl of silver, the parrots shot away to some distant river in shrieking green hosts: all the well wheels within earshot went to work. India was awake, and Kim was in the middle of it, more awake and more excited than any one, chewing on a twig that he would presently use as a toothbrush; for he borrowed right- and left-handedly from all the customs of the country he knew and loved. There was no need to worry about food – no need to spend a cowrie at the crowded stalls. He was the disciple of a holy man annexed by a strong-willed old lady. All things would be prepared for them, and when they were respectfully invited so to do they would sit and eat. For the rest – Kim giggled here as he cleaned his teeth – his hostess would rather heighten the enjoyment of the road. He inspected her bullocks critically, as they came up grunting and blowing under the yokes. If they went too fast – it was not likely – there would be a pleasant seat for himself along the pole; the lama would sit beside the driver. The escort, of course, would walk. The old lady, equally of course, would talk a great deal, and by what he had heard that conversation would not lack salt. She was already ordering, haranguing, rebuking, and, it must be said, cursing her servants for delays.

"Get her her pipe. In the name of the Gods, get her her pipe and stop her ill-omened mouth," cried an Oorya, tying up his shapeless bundles of bedding. "She and the parrots are alike. They screech in the dawn."

"The lead bullocks! *Hai!* Look to the lead bullocks!" They were backing and wheeling as a grain-cart's axle caught them by the horns. "Son of an owl, where dost thou go?" This to the grinning carter.

"*Ai! Yai! Yai!* That within there is the Queen of Delhi going to pray for a son," the man called back over his high load. "Room for the Queen of Delhi and her Prime Minister the grey monkey climbing up his own sword!" Another cart loaded with bark for a down-country tannery followed close behind, and its driver added a few compliments as the *ruth*-bullocks backed and backed again.

From behind the shaking curtains came one volley of invective. It did not last long, but in kind and quality, in blistering, biting appropriateness, it was beyond anything that even Kim had heard. He could see the carter's bare chest collapse with amazement, as the man salaamed reverently to the voice, leaped from the pole, and helped the escort haul their volcano on to the main road. Here the voice told him truthfully what sort of wife he had wedded, and what she was doing in his absence.

"Oh, *shabash!*" murmured Kim, unable to contain himself, as the man slunk away.

"Well done, indeed? It is a shame and a scandal that a poor woman may not go to make prayer to her Gods except she be jostled and insulted by all the refuse of Hindustan – that she must eat *gâli* [abuse] as men eat ghee. But I have yet a wag left to my tongue – a word or two well spoken that serves the occasion. And *still* am I with§out my tobacco! Who is the one-eyed and luckless son of shame that has not yet prepared my pipe?"

It was hastily thrust in by a hillman, and a trickle of thick smoke from each corner of the curtains showed that peace was restored.

If Kim had walked proudly the day before, disciple of a holy man, today he paced with tenfold pride in the train of a semi-royal procession, with a recognized place under the patronage of an old lady of charming manners and infinite resource. The escort, their heads tied up native-fashion, fell in on either side the cart, shuffling enormous clouds of dust.

The lama and Kim walked a little to one side; Kim chewing his stick of sugarcane, and making way for no one under the status of a priest. They could hear the old lady's tongue clack as steadily as a rice husker. She bade the escort tell her what was going on on the road; and so soon as they were clear of the *parao* she flung back the curtains and peered out, her veil a third across her face. Her men did not eye her directly when she addressed them, and thus the proprieties were more or less observed.

A dark, sallowish District Superintendent of Police, faultlessly uniformed, an Englishman, trotted by on a tired horse, and, seeing from her retinue what manner of person she was, chaffed her.

"O mother," he cried, "do they do this in the zenanas? Suppose an Englishman came by and saw that thou hadst no nose?"

"What?" she shrilled back. "Thine own mother has no nose? Why say so, then, on the open road?"

It was a fair counter. The Englishman threw up his hand with the gesture of a man hit at swordplay. She laughed and nodded.

"Is this a face to tempt virtue aside?" She withdrew all her veil and stared at him.

It was by no means lovely, but as the man gathered up his reins he called it a Moon of Paradise, a Disturber of Integrity, and a few other fantastic epithets which doubled her up with mirth.

"That is a *nut-cut* [rogue]," she said. "All police-constables are *nut-cuts*; but the police-wallahs are the worst. *Hai*, my son, thou hast never learned all that since thou camest from *Belait* [Europe]. Who suckled thee?"

"A *pahareen* – a hillwoman of Dalhousie, my mother. Keep thy beauty under a shade – O Dispenser of Delights," and he was gone.

"These be the sort" – she took a fine judicial tone, and stuffed her mouth with *pan* – "These be the sort to oversee justice. They know the land and the customs of the land. The others, all new from Europe, suckled by white women and learning our tongues from books, are worse than the pestilence. They do harm to kings." Then she told a long, long tale to the world at large, of an ignorant young policeman who had disturbed some small hill rajah, a ninth cousin of her own, in the matter of a trivial land-case, winding up with a quotation from a work by no means devotional.

Then her mood changed, and she bade one of the escort ask whether the lama would walk alongside and discuss matters of religion. So Kim dropped back into the dust and returned to his sugarcane. For an hour or more the lama's tam-o'-shanter showed like a moon through the haze; and, from all he heard, Kim gathered that the old woman wept. One of the Ooryas half apologized for his rudeness overnight, saying that he had never known his mistress of so bland a temper and he ascribed it to the presence of the strange priest. Personally, he believed in Brahmins, though, like all natives, he was acutely aware of their cunning and their greed. Still, when Brahmins but irritated with begging demands the mother of his master's wife, and when she sent them away so angry that they cursed the whole retinue (which was the real reason of the second offside bullock going lame, and of the pole breaking the night before), he was prepared to accept any priest of any other denomination in or out of India. To this Kim assented with wise nods, and bade the Oorya observe that the lama took no money, and that the cost of his and Kim's food would be repaid a hundred times in the good luck that would attend the caravan henceforward. He also told stories of Lahore city, and sang a song or two which made the escort laugh. As a town-mouse well acquainted with the latest songs by the most fashionable composers – they are women for the most part – Kim had a distinct advantage over men from a little fruit village behind Saharunpore, but he let that advantage be inferred.

At noon they turned aside to eat, and the meal was good, plentiful, and well-served on plates of clean leaves, in decency, out of drift of the dust. They gave the scraps to certain beggars, that all requirements might be fulfilled, and sat down to a long, luxurious smoke. The old lady had retreated behind her curtains, but mixed most freely in the talk, her servants arguing with and contradicting her as servants do throughout the East. She compared the cool and the pines of the Kangra and Kulu hills with the dust and the mangoes of the south; she told a tale of some old local Gods at the edge of her husband's territory; she roundly abused the tobacco which she was then smoking, reviled all Brahmins, and speculated without reserve on the coming of many grandsons.

Chapter 5

Here come I to my own again –
Fed, forgiven, and known again –
Claimed by bone of my bone again,
  And sib to flesh of my flesh!
The fatted calf is dressed for me,
But the husks have greater zest for me...
I think my pigs will be best for me,
  So I'm off to the styes afresh.

The Prodigal Son

Once more the lazy, string-tied, shuffling procession got under way, and she slept till they reached the next halting-stage. It was a very short march, and time lacked an hour to sundown, so Kim cast about for means of amusement.

"But why not sit and rest?" said one of the escort. "Only the devils and the English walk to and fro without reason."

"Never make friends with the Devil, a monkey, or a boy. No man knows what they will do next," said his fellow.

Kim turned a scornful back – he did not want to hear the old story how the Devil played with the boys and repented of it – and walked idly across country.

The lama strode after him. All that day, whenever they passed a stream, he had turned aside to look at it, but in no case had he received any warning that he had found his River. Insensibly, too, the comfort of speaking to some one in a reasonable tongue, and of being properly considered and

KIM

respected as her spiritual adviser by a well-born woman, had weaned his thoughts a little from the Search. And further, he was prepared to spend serene years in his quest; having nothing of the white man's impatience, but a great faith.

"Where goest thou?" he called after Kim.

"Nowhither – it was a small march, and all this" – Kim waved his hands abroad – "is new to me."

"She is beyond question a wise and a discerning woman. But it is hard to meditate when –"

"All women are thus." Kim spoke as might have Solomon.

"Before the lamassery was a broad platform," the lama muttered, looping up the well-worn rosary, "of stone. On that. I have left the marks of my feet – pacing to and fro with these."

He clicked the beads, and began the "*Om mane pudme hum's* of his devotion; grateful for the cool, the quiet, and the absence of dust.

One thing after another drew Kim's idle eye across the plain. There was no purpose in his wanderings, except that the build of the huts near by seemed new, and he wished to investigate.

They came out on a broad tract of grazing ground, brown and purple in the afternoon light, with a heavy clump of mangoes in the centre. It struck Kim as curious that no shrine stood in so eligible a spot: the boy was observing as any priest for these things. Far across the plain walked side by side four men, made small by the distance. He looked intently under his curved palms and caught the sheen of brass.

"Soldiers. White soldiers!" said he. "Let us see."

"It is always soldiers when thou and I go out alone together. But I have never seen the white soldiers."

"They do no harm except when they are drunk. Keep behind this tree."

They stepped behind the thick trunks in the cool dark of the mango tope. Two little figures halted; the other two came forward uncertainly. They were the advance-party of a regiment on the march, sent out, as usual, to mark the camp. They bore five-foot sticks with fluttering flags, and called to each other as they spread over the flat earth.

At last they entered the mango grove, walking heavily.

413

'What do they prepare?' said the lama, wonderstruck.

"It's here or hereabouts – officers' tents under the trees, I take it, an' the rest of us can stay outside. Have they marked out for the baggage-waggons behind?"

They cried again to their comrades in the distance, and the rough answer came back faint and mellowed.

"Shove the flag in here, then," said one.

"What do they prepare?" said the lama, wonderstruck. "This is a great and a terrible world. What is the device on the flag?"

A soldier thrust a stave within a few feet of them, grunted discontentedly, pulled it up again, conferred with his companion, who looked up and down the shaded cave of greenery, and returned it.

Kim stared with all his eyes, his breath coming short! and sharp between his teeth. The soldiers stamped off into the sunshine.

"O Holy One!" he gasped. "My horoscope! The drawing in the dust by the priest at Umballa! Remember what he said. First come two – *ferashes* – to make all things ready – in a dark place, as it is always at the beginning of a vision."

"But this is not vision," said the lama. "It is the world's illusion, and no more."

"And after them comes the Bull – the Red Bull on the green field. Look! It is he!"

He pointed to the flag that was snap-snapping in the evening breeze not ten feet away. It was no more than an ordinary camp marking-flag; but the regiment, always punctilious in matters of millinery, had charged it with the regimental device, the Red Bull, which is the crest of the Mavericks – the great Red Bull on a background of Irish green.

"I see, and now I remember," said the lama. "Certainly it is thy Bull. Certainly, also, the two men came to make all ready."

"They are soldiers – white soldiers. What said the priest? 'The sign over against the Bull is the sign of war and armed men.' Holy One, this thing touches my Search."

"True. It is true." The lama stared fixedly at the device that flamed like a ruby in the dusk. "The priest at Umballa said that thine was the sign of war."

"What is to do now?"

"Wait. Let us wait."

"Even now the darkness clears," said Kim. It was only natural that the descending sun should at last strike through the tree-trunks, across the grove, filling it with mealy gold light for a few minutes; but to Kim it was crown of the Umballa Brahmin's prophecy.

"Hark!" said the lama. "One beats a drum – far off!"

At first the sound, carrying diluted through the still air, resembled the beating of an artery in the head. Soon a sharpness was added.

"Ah! The music," Kim explained. He knew the sound of a regimental band, but it amazed the lama.

At the far end of the plain a heavy, dusty column crawled in sight. Then the wind brought the tune:

> We crave your condescension
> To tell you what we know
> Of marching in the Mulligan Guards
> To Sligo Port below!

Here broke in the shrill-tongued fifes:

> We shouldered arms,
> We marched – we marched away.
> From Phoenix Park
> We marched to Dublin Bay.
> The drums and the fifes,
> Oh, sweetly they did play,
> As we marched – marched – marched – with the
> Mulligan Guards!

It was the band of the Mavericks playing the regiment to camp; for the men were route-marching with their baggage. The rippling column swung into the level carts behind it – divided left and right, ran about like an ant-hill, and...

"But this is sorcery!" said the lama.

The plain dotted itself with tents that seemed to rise, all spread, from the carts. Another rush of men invaded the grove, pitched a huge tent in silence, ran up yet eight or nine more by the side of it, unearthed cooking-pots, pans, and bundles, which were taken possession of by a crowd of native servants; and behold the mango tope turned into an orderly town as they watched!

"Let us go," said the lama, sinking back afraid, as the fires twinkled and white officers with jingling swords stalked into the mess-tent.

"Stand back in the shadow. No one can see beyond the light of the fire," said Kim, his eyes still on the flag. He had never before watched the routine of a seasoned regiment pitching camp in thirty minutes.

"Look! look! look!" clucked the lama. "Yonder comes a priest."

It was Bennett, the Church of England Chaplain of the regiment, limping in dusty black. One of his flock had made some rude remarks about the Chaplain's mettle; and to abash him Bennett had marched step by step with the men that day. The black dress, gold cross on the watch-chain, the hairless face, and the soft, black wideawake hat would have marked him as a holy man anywhere in all India. He dropped into a camp-chair by the door of the mess-tent and slid off his boots. Three or four officers gathered round him, laughing and joking over his exploit.

"The talk of white men is wholly lacking in dignity," said the lama, who judged only by tone. "But I have considered the countenance of that priest, and I think he is learned. Is it likely that he will understand our talk? I would talk to him of my Search."

"Never speak to a white man till he is fed," said Kim, quoting a well-known proverb. "They will eat now, and – and I do not think they are good to beg from. Let us go back to the resting-place. After we have eaten we will come again. It certainly was a Red Bull – *my* Red Bull."

They were both noticeably absent-minded when the old lady's retinue set their meal before them; so none broke their reserve, for it is not lucky to annoy guests.

"Now," said Kim, picking his teeth, "we will return to that place; but thou, O Holy One, must wait a little way off, because thy feet are heavier than mine and I am anxious to see more of that Red Bull."

"But how canst thou understand the talk? Walk slowly. The road is dark," the lama replied uneasily.

Kim put the question aside. "I marked a place near to the trees," said he, "where thou canst sit till I call. Nay," as the lama made some sort of protest, "remember this is *my* Search – the Search for my Red Bull. The sign in the stars was not for thee. I know a little of the customs of white soldiers, and I always desire to see some new things."

"What dost thou not know of this world?" The lama squatted obediently in a little hollow of the ground not a hundred yards from the hump of the mango trees dark against the star-powdered sky.

"Stay till I call." Kim flitted into the dusk. He knew that in all probability there would be sentries round the camp, and smiled to himself as he heard the thick boots of one. A boy who can dodge over the roofs of Lahore city on a moonlight night, using every little patch and corner of darkness to discomfit his pursuer, is not likely to be checked by a line of well-trained soldiers. He paid them the compliment of crawling between a couple, and, running and halting, crouching and dropping flat, worked his way toward the lighted mess-tent where, close pressed behind the mango tree, he waited till some chance word should give him a returnable lead.

The one thing now in his mind was further information as to the Red Bull. For aught he knew, and Kim's limitations were as curious and sudden as his expansions, the men, the nine hundred thorough devils of his father's prophecy, might pray to the beast after dark, as Hindus pray to the Holy Cow. That at least would be entirely right and logical, and the padre with the gold cross would be therefore the man to consult in the matter. On the other hand, remembering sober-faced padres whom he had avoided in Lahore city, the priest might be an inquisitive nuisance who would bid him learn. But had it not been proven at Umballa that his sign in the high heavens portended war and armed men? Was he not the Friend of the Stars as well as of all the World, crammed to the teeth with dreadful secrets? Lastly – and firstly as the undercurrent of all his quick thoughts – this adventure, though he did not know the English word, was a stupendous lark – a delightful continuation of his old flights across the house-tops, as well as the fulfilment of sublime prophecy. He lay belly-flat and wriggled towards the mess-tent door, a hand on the amulet round his neck.

It was as he suspected. The sahibs prayed to their God; for in the centre of the mess-table – its sole ornament when they were on the line of march – stood a golden bull fashioned from old-time loot of the Summer Palace at Peking – a red-gold bull with lowered head, ramping upon a field of Irish green. To him the sahibs held out their glasses and cried aloud confusedly.

Now the Reverend Arthur Bennett always left mess after that toast, and being rather tired by his march his movements were more abrupt than usual. Kim, with slightly raised head, was still staring at his totem on the table, when the Chaplain stepped on his right shoulder-blade. Kim flinched under the leather, and, rolling sideways, brought down the Chaplain, who, ever a man of action, caught him by the throat and nearly choked the life out of him. Kim then kicked him desperately in the stomach. Mr Bennett gasped and doubled up, but without relaxing his grip, rolled over again, and silently hauled Kim to his own tent. The Mavericks were incurable practical jokers; and it occurred to the Englishman that silence was best till he had made complete inquiry.

"Why, it's a boy!" he said, as he drew his prize under the light of the tent-pole lantern, then shaking him severely cried: "What were you doing? You're a thief. *Choor? Mallum?*" His Hindustani was very limited, and the ruffled and disgusted Kim intended to keep to the character laid down for him. As he recovered his breath he was inventing a beautifully plausible tale of his relations to some scullion, and at the same time keeping a keen eye on and a little under the Chaplain's left arm-pit. The chance came; he ducked for the doorway, but a long arm shot out and clutched at his neck, snapping the amulet string and closing on the amulet.

"Give it me. Oh, give it me. Is it lost? Give me the papers."

The words were in English – the tinny, saw-cut English of the native-bred, and the Chaplain jumped.

"A scapular," said he, opening his hand. "No, some sort of heathen charm. Why – why, do you speak English? Little boys who steal are beaten. You know that?"

"I do not – I did not steal." Kim danced in agony like a terrier at a lifted stick. "Oh, give it me. It is my charm. Do not thieve it from me."

The Chaplain took no heed, but, going to the tent door, called aloud. A fattish, clean-shaven man appeared.

"I want your advice, Father Victor," said Bennett. "I found this boy in the dark outside the mess-tent. Ordinarily, I should have chastized him and let him go, because I believe him to be a thief. But it seems he talks English, and he attaches some sort of value to a charm round his neck. I thought perhaps you might help me."

Between himself and the Roman Catholic Chaplain of the Irish contingent lay, as Bennett believed, an unbridgeable gulf, but it was noticeable that whenever the Church of England dealt with a human problem she was very likely to call in the Church of Rome. Bennett's official abhorrence of the Scarlet Woman and all her ways was only equalled by his private respect for Father Victor.

"A thief talking English, is it? Let's look at his charm. No, it's not a scapular, Bennett." He held out his hand.

"But have we any right to open it? A sound whipping –"

"I did *not* thieve," protested Kim. "You have hit me kicks all over my body. Now give me my charm and I will go away."

"Not quite so fast. We'll look first," said Father Victor, leisurely rolling out poor Kimball O'Hara's "*ne varietur*" parchment, his clearance-certificate, and Kim's baptismal certificate. On this last O'Hara – with some confused idea that he was doing wonders for his son – had scrawled scores of times: "Look after the boy. Please look after the boy" – signing his name and regimental number in full.

"Powers of Darkness below!" said Father Victor, passing all over to Mr Bennett. "Do you know what these things are?"

"Yes," said Kim. "They are mine, and I want to go away."

"I do not quite understand," said Mr Bennett. "He probably brought them on purpose. It may be a begging trick of some kind."

"I never saw a beggar less anxious to stay with his company, then. There's the makings of a gay mystery here. Ye believe in Providence, Bennett?"

"I hope so."

"Well, I believe in miracles, so it comes to the same thing. Powers of Darkness! Kimball O'Hara! And his son! But then he's a native, and I saw Kimball married myself to Annie Shott. How long have you had these things, boy?"

"Ever since I was a little baby."

Father Victor stepped forward quickly and opened the front of Kim's upper garment. "You see, Bennett, he's not very black. What's your name?"

"Kim."

"Or Kimball?"

"Perhaps. Will you let me go away?"

"What else?"

"They call me Kim Rishti ke. That is Kim of the Rishti."

"What is that – 'Rishti'?"

"*Eyĕ*-rishti – that was the regiment – my father's."

"Irish – oh, I see."

"Yess. That was how my father told me. My father, he has lived."

"Has lived where?"

"Has lived. Of *course* he is dead – gone out."

"Oh! That's your abrupt way of putting it, is it?"

Bennett interrupted. "It is possible I have done the boy an injustice. He is certainly white, though evidently neglected. I am sure I must have bruised him. I do not think spirits –"

"Get him a glass of sherry, then, and let him squat on the cot. Now, Kim," continued Father Victor, "no one is going to hurt you. Drink that down and tell us about yourself. The truth, if you've no objection."

Kim coughed a little as he put down the empty glass, and considered. This seemed a time for caution and fancy. Small boys who prowl about camps are generally turned out after a whipping. But he had received no stripes; the amulet was evidently working in his favour, and it looked as though the Umballa horoscope and the few words that he could remember of his father's maunderings fitted in most miraculously. Else why did the fat padre seem so impressed, and why the glass of hot yellow drink from the lean one?

"My father, he is dead in Lahore city since I was very little. The woman, she kept *kabarri* shop near where the hire-carriages are." Kim began with a plunge, not quite sure how far the truth would serve him.

"Your mother?"

"*No!*" – with a gesture of disgust. "She went out when I was born. My father, he got these papers from the Jadoo-Gher – what do you call that?" (Bennett nodded) "because he was in – good standing. What do you call that?" (again Bennett nodded). "My father told me that. He said, too, and also the Brahmin who made the drawing in the dust at Umballa two days ago, *he* said, that I shall find a Red Bull on a green field and that the Bull shall help me."

"A phenomenal little liar," muttered Bennett.

"Powers of Darkness below, what a country!" murmured Father Victor. "Go on, Kim."

"I did *not* thieve. Besides, I am just now disciple of a very holy man. He is sitting outside. We saw two men come with flags, making the place ready. That is *always* so in a dream, or on account of a – a – prophecy. So I knew it was come true. I saw the Red Bull on the green field, and my father he said: 'Nine hundred *pukka* devils and the Colonel riding on a horse will look after you when you find the Red Bull!' I did not know what to do when I saw the Bull, but I went away and I came again when it was dark. I wanted to see the Bull again, and I saw the Bull again with the – the sahibs praying to it. I think the Bull shall help me. The holy man said so too. He is sitting outside. Will you hurt him, if I call him a shout now? He is very holy. He can witness to all the things I say, and he knows I am not a thief."

"'Sahibs praying to a bull!' What in the world do you make of that?" said Bennett. "'Disciple of a holy man!' Is the boy mad?"

"It's O'Hara's boy, sure enough. O'Hara's boy leagued with all the Powers of Darkness. It's very much what his father would have done – if he was drunk. We'd better invite the holy man. He may know something."

"He does not know anything," said Kim. "I will show you him if you come. He is my master. Then afterwards we can go."

"Powers of Darkness!" was all that Father Victor could say, as Bennett marched off, with a firm hand on Kim's shoulder.

They found the lama where he had dropped.

"The Search is at an end for me," shouted Kim in the vernacular. "I have found the Bull, but God knows what comes next. They will not hurt you. Come to the fat priest's tent with this thin man and see the end. It is all new, and they cannot talk Hindi. They are only uncurried donkeys."

"Then it is not well to make a jest of their ignorance," the lama returned. "I am glad if thou art rejoiced, *chela*."

Dignified and unsuspicious, he strode into the little tent, saluted the Churches as a churchman, and sat down by the open charcoal brazier. The yellow lining of the tent reflected in the lamplight made his face red-gold.

Bennett looked at him with the triple-ringed uninterest of the creed that lumps nine-tenths of the world under the title of "heathen".

"And what was the end of the Search? What gift has the Red Bull brought?" The lama addressed himself to Kim.

"He says, 'What are you going to do?'" Bennett was staring uneasily at Father Victor, and Kim, for his own ends, took upon himself the office of interpreter.

"I do not see what concern this *fakir* has with the boy, who is probably his dupe or his confederate," Bennett began. "We cannot allow an English boy – Assuming that he is the son of a Mason, the sooner he goes to the Masonic Orphanage the better."

"Ah! That's your opinion as secretary to the regimental lodge," said Father Victor; "but we might as well tell the old man what we are going to do. He doesn't look like a villain."

"My experience is that one can never fathom the oriental mind. Now, Kimball, I wish you to tell this man what I say – word for word."

Kim gathered the import of the next few sentences and began thus:

"Holy One, the thin fool who looks like a camel says that I am the son of a sahib."

"But how?"

"Oh, it is true. I knew it since my birth, but *he* could only find it out by rending the amulet from my neck and reading all the papers. He thinks that once a sahib is always a sahib, and between the two of them they purpose to keep me in this regiment or to send me to a *madrissah* [a school]. It has happened before. I have always avoided it. The fat fool is of one mind and the camel-like one of another. But that is no odds. I may spend one night here and perhaps the next. It has happened before. Then I will run away and return to thee."

"But tell them that thou art my *chela*. Tell them how thou didst come to me when I was faint and bewildered. Tell them of our Search, and they will surely let thee go now."

"I have already told them. They laugh, and they talk of the police."

"What are you saying?" asked Mr Bennett.

"Oah. He only says that if you do not let me go it will stop him in his business – his ur-gent private af-fairs." This last was a reminiscence of some talk with a Eurasian clerk in the Canal Department, but it only drew a smile, which nettled him. "And if you *did* know what his business was you would not be in such a beastly hurry to interfere."

"What is it then?" said Father Victor, not without feeling, as he watched the lama's face.

"There is a River in this country which he wishes to find so veree much. It was put out by an Arrow which –" Kim tapped his foot impatiently as he translated in his own mind from the vernacular to the clumsy English. "Oah, it was made by our Lord God Buddha, you know, and if you wash there you are washed away from all your sins and made as white as cotton wool." (Kim had heard mission-talk in his time.) "I am his disciple, and we *must* find that River. It is so veree valuable to us."

"Say that again," said Bennett. Kim obeyed, with amplifications.

"But this is gross blasphemy!" cried the Church of England.

"Tck! Tck!" said Father Victor sympathetically. "I'd give a good deal to be able to talk the vernacular. A river that washes away sin! And how long have you two been looking for it?"

"Oh, many days. Now we wish to go away and look for it again. It is not here, you see."

"I see," said Father Victor gravely. "But he can't go on in that old man's company. It would be different, Kim, if you were not a soldier's son. Tell him that the Regiment will take care of you and make you as good a man as your – as good a man as can be. Tell him that if he believes in miracles he must believe that –"

"There is no need to play on his credulity," Bennett interrupted.

"I'm doing no such thing. He must believe that the boy's coming here – to his own regiment – in search of his Red Bull is in the nature of a miracle. Consider the chances against it, Bennett. This one boy in all India, and our regiment of all others on the line o' march for him to meet with! It's predestined on the face of it. Yes, tell him it's *Kismet. Kismet, mallum?* [Do you understand?]"

He turned towards the lama, to whom he might as well have talked of Mesopotamia.

"They say," – the old man's eye lighted at Kim's speech – "they say that

the meaning of my horoscope is now accomplished, and that being led back
– though as thou knowest I went out of curiosity – to these people and
their Red Bull I must needs go to a *madrissah* and be turned into a sahib.
Now I make pretence of agreement, for at the worst it will be but a few
meals eaten away from thee. Then I will slip away and follow down the
road to Saharunpore. Therefore, Holy One, keep with that Kulu woman
– on no account stray far from her cart till I come again. Past question, my
sign is of war and of armed men. See how they have given me wine to drink
and set me upon a bed of honour! My father must have been some great
person. So if they raise me to honour among them, good. If not, good again.
However it goes, I will run back to thee when I am tired. But stay with the
Rajputni, or I shall miss thy feet… Oah yess," said the boy, "I have told
him everything you tell me to say."

"And I cannot see any need why he should wait," said Bennett, feeling
in his trouser pocket. "We can investigate the details later – and I will give
him a ru –"

"Give him time. Maybe he's fond of the lad," said Father Victor, half
arresting the clergyman's motion.

The lama dragged forth his rosary and pulled his huge hat-brim over
his eyes.

"What can he want now?"

"He says" – Kim put up one hand. "He says: Be quiett. He wants to
speak to me by himself. You see, you do not know one little word of what
he says, and I think if you talk he will perhaps give you very bad curses.
When he takes those beads like that, you see, he always wants to be
quiett."

The two Englishmen sat overwhelmed, but there was a look in Bennett's
eye that promised ill for Kim when he should be relaxed to the religious
arm.

"A sahib and the son of a sahib –" The lama's voice was harsh with pain.
"But no white man knows the land and the customs of the land as thou
knowest. How comes it this is true?"

"What matter, Holy One? – but remember it is only for a night or two.
Remember, I can change swiftly. It will all be as it was when I first spoke
to thee under Zam-Zammah the great gun –"

"As a boy in the dress of white men – when I first went to the Wonder House. And a second time thou wast a Hindu. What shall the third incarnation be?" He chuckled drearily. "Ah, *chela*, thou hast done a wrong to an old man because my heart went out to thee."

"And mine to thee. But how could I know that the Red Bull would bring me to this business?"

The lama covered his face afresh, and nervously rattled the rosary. Kim squatted beside him and laid hold upon a fold of his clothing.

"Now it is understood that the boy is a sahib?" he went on in a muffled tone. "Such a sahib as was he who kept the images in the Wonder House." The lama's experience of white men was limited. He seemed to be repeating a lesson. "So then it is not seemly that he should do other than as the sahibs do. He must go back to his own people."

"For a day and a night and a day," Kim pleaded.

"No, ye don't!" Father Victor saw Kim edging towards the door, and interposed a strong leg.

"I do not understand the customs of white men. The Priest of the Images in the Wonder House in Lahore was more courteous than the thin one here. This boy will be taken from me. They will make a sahib of my disciple? Woe to me! How shall I find my River? Have *they* no disciples? Ask."

"He says he is very sorree that he cannot find the River now any more. He says, Why have you no disciples, and stop bothering him? He wants to be washed of his sins."

Neither Bennett nor Father Victor found any answer ready.

Said Kim in English, distressed for the lama's agony: "I think if you will let me go now we will walk away quietly and not steal. We will look for that River like before I was caught. I wish I did not come here to find the Red Bull and all that sort of thing. I do not want it."

"It's the very best day's work you ever did for yourself, young man," said Bennett.

"Good heavens, I don't know how to console him," said Father Victor, watching the lama intently. "He can't take the boy away with him, and yet he's a good man – I'm sure he's a good man. Bennett, if you give him that rupee he'll curse you root and branch!"

They listened to each other's breathing – three – five full minutes. Then the lama raised his head, and looked forth across them into space and emptiness.

"And I am a Follower of the Way," he said bitterly. "The sin is mine and the punishment is mine. I made believe to myself – for now I see it was but make-believe – that thou wast sent to me to aid in the Search. So my heart went out to thee for thy charity and thy courtesy and the wisdom of thy little years. But those who follow the Way must permit not the fire of any desire or attachment, for that is all illusion. As says..." He quoted an old, old Chinese text, backed it with another, and reinforced these with a third. "I stepped aside from the Way, my *chela*. It was no fault of thine. I delighted in the sight of life, the new people upon the roads, and in thy joy at seeing these things. I was pleased with thee who should have considered my Search and my Search alone. Now I am sorrowful because thou art taken away and my River is far from me. It is the Law which I have broken!"

"Powers of Darkness below!" said Father Victor, who, wise in the confessional, heard the pain in every sentence.

"I can see now that the sign of the Red Bull was a sign for me as well as for thee. All desire is red – and evil. I will do penance and find my River alone."

"At least go back to the Kulu woman," said Kim, "otherwise thou wilt be lost upon the roads. She will feed thee till I run back to thee."

The lama waved a hand to show that the matter was finally settled in his mind.

"Now," – his tone altered as he turned to Kim – "what will they do with thee? At least I may, acquiring merit, wipe out past ill."

"Make me a sahib – so they think. The day after tomorrow I return. Do not grieve."

"Of what sort? Such an one as this or that man?" He pointed to Father Victor. "Such an one as those I saw this evening – men wearing swords and stamping heavily?"

"Maybe."

"That is not well. These men follow desire and come to emptiness. Thou must not be of their sort."

"The Umballa priest said that my star was war," Kim interjected. "I will ask these fools – but there is truly no need. I will run away this night, for all I wanted to see the new things."

Kim put two or three questions in English to Father Victor, translating the replies to the lama.

Then: "He says, 'You take him from me and you cannot say what you will make him.' He says, 'Tell me before I go, for it is not a small thing to make a child.'"

"You will be sent to a school. Later on, we shall see. Kimball, I suppose you'd like to be a soldier?"

"*Gorah-log* [white-folk]. No-ah! No-ah!" Kim shook his head violently. There was nothing in his composition to which drill and routine appealed. "I will *not* be a soldier."

"You will be what you're told to be," said Bennett; "and you should be grateful that we're going to help you."

Kim smiled compassionately. If these men lay under the delusion that he would do anything that he did not fancy, so much the better.

Another long silence followed. Bennett fidgeted with impatience, and suggested calling a sentry to evict the *fakir*.

"Do they give or sell learning among the sahibs? Ask them," said the lama, and Kim interpreted.

"They say that money is paid to the teacher – but that money the Regiment will give... What need? It is only for a night."

"And – the more money is paid the better learning is given?" The lama disregarded Kim's plans for an early flight. "It is no wrong to pay for learning. To help the ignorant to wisdom is always a merit." The rosary clicked furiously as an abacus. Then he faced his oppressors.

"Ask them for how much money do they give a wise and suitable teaching? And in what city is that teaching given?"

"Well," said Father Victor in English, when Kim had translated, "that depends. The Regiment would pay for you all the time you are at the Military Orphanage; or you might go on the Punjab Masonic Orphanage's list (not that he or you "ud understand what that means): but the best schooling a boy can get in India is, of course, at St Xavier's in Partibus at Lucknow." This took some time to interpret, for Bennett wished to cut it short.

"He wants to know how much?" said Kim placidly.

"Two or three hundred rupees a year." Father Victor was long past any sense of amazement. Bennett, impatient, did not understand.

"He says: "Write that name and the money upon a paper and give it him." And he says you must write your name below, because he is going to write a letter in some days to you. He says you are a good man. He says the other man is a fool. He is going away."

The lama rose suddenly. "I follow my Search," he cried, and was gone.

"He'll run slap into the sentries," cried Father Victor, jumping up as the lama stalked out; "but I can't leave the boy." Kim made swift motion to follow, but checked himself. There was no sound of challenge outside. The lama had disappeared.

Kim settled himself composedly on the Chaplain's cot. At least the lama had promised that he would stay with the Rajput woman from Kulu, and the rest was of the smallest importance. It pleased him that the two padres were so evidently excited. They talked long in undertones, Father Victor urging some scheme on Mr Bennett, who seemed incredulous. All this was very new and fascinating, but Kim felt sleepy. They called men into the tent – one of them certainly was the Colonel, as his father had prophesied – and they asked him an infinity of questions, chiefly about the woman who looked after him, all of which Kim answered truthfully. They did not seem to think the woman a good guardian.

After all, this was the newest of his experiences. Sooner or later, if he chose, he could escape into great, grey, formless India, beyond tents and padres and colonels. Meantime, if the sahibs were to be impressed, he would do his best to impress them. He too was a white man.

After much talk that he could not comprehend, they handed him over to a sergeant, who had strict instructions not to let him escape. The Regiment would go on to Umballa, and Kim would be sent up, partly at the expense of the Lodge and in part by subscription, to a place called Sanawar.

"It's miraculous past all whooping, Colonel," said Father Victor, when he had talked without a break for ten minutes. "His Buddhist friend has levanted after taking my name and address. I can't quite make out whether he'll pay for the boy's education or whether he is preparing some sort of witchcraft on his own account." Then to Kim: "You'll live to be grateful to your friend the Red Bull yet. We'll make a man of you at Sanawar – even at the price o' making you a Protestant."

"Certainly – most certainly," said Bennett.

"But you will not go to Sanawar," said Kim.

"But we *will* go to Sanawar, little man. That's the order of the Commander-in-Chief, who's a trifle more important than O'Hara's son."

"You will not go to Sanawar. You will go to thee War."

There was a shout of laughter from the full tent.

"When you know your own regiment a trifle better you won't confuse the line of march with line of battle, Kim. We hope to go to 'thee War' sometime."

"Oah, I know all thatt." Kim drew his bow again at a venture. If they were not going to the war, at least they did not know what he knew of the talk in the veranda at Umballa.

"I know you are not at thee war now; but I tell *you* that as soon as you get to Umballa you will be sent to the war – the new war. It is a war of eight thousand men, besides the guns."

"That's explicit. D'you add prophecy to your other gifts? Take him along, sergeant. Take up a suit for him from the Drums, an' take care he doesn't slip through your fingers. Who says the age of miracles is gone by? I think I'll go to bed. My poor mind's weakening."

At the far end of the camp, silent as a wild animal, an hour later sat Kim, newly washed all over, in a horrible stuff suit that rasped his arms and legs.

"A most amazin' young bird," said the sergeant. "He turns up in charge of a yellow-headed buck-Brahmin priest, with his father's Lodge certificates round his neck, talkin' God knows what all of a red bull. The buck-Brahmin evaporates without explanations, an' the bhoy sets cross-legged on the Chaplain's bed prophesyin' bloody war to the men at large. Injia's a wild land for a God-fearin' man. I'll just tie his leg to the tent-pole in case he'll go through the roof. What did ye say about the war?"

"Eight thousand men, besides guns," said Kim. "Very soon you will see."

"You're a consolin' little imp. Lie down between the Drums an' go to bye-bye. Those two boys will watch your slumbers."

Chapter 6

Now I remember comrades –
  Old playmates on new seas –
Whenas we traded orpiment
  Among the savages.
Ten thousand leagues to southward,
  And thirty years removed –
They knew not noble Valdez,
  But me they knew and loved.
                    Song of Diego Valdez

Very early in the morning the white tents came down and disappeared as the Mavericks took a side-road to Umballa. It did not skirt the resting-place, and Kim, trudging beside a baggage-cart under fire of comments from soldiers' wives, was not so confident as overnight. He discovered that he was closely watched – Father Victor on the one side, and Mr Bennett on the other.

In the forenoon the column checked. A camel orderly handed the Colonel a letter. He read it, and spoke to a major. Half a mile in the rear, Kim heard a hoarse and joyful clamour rolling down on him through the thick dust. Then some one beat him on the back, crying: "Tell us how ye knew, ye little limb of Satan? Father dear, see if ye can make him tell."

A pony ranged alongside, and he was hauled on to the priest's saddle-bow.

"Now, my son, your prophecy of last night has come true. Our orders are to entrain at Umballa for the Front tomorrow."

431

"What is thatt?" said Kim, for "*front*" and "*entrain*" were newish words to him.

"We are going to 'thee War', as you called it."

"Of course you are going to thee War. I said last night."

"Ye did; but, Powers o' Darkness, how did ye know?"

Kim's eyes sparkled. He shut his lips, nodded his head and looked unspeakable things. The Chaplain moved on through the dust, and privates, sergeants, and subalterns called one another's attention to the boy. The Colonel, at the head of the column, stared at him curiously. "It was probably some bazaar rumour," he said; "but even then –" He referred to the paper in his hand. "Hang it all, the thing was only decided within the last forty-eight hours."

"Are there many more like you in India?" said Father Victor, "or are you by way o' being a *lusus naturae?*"

"Now I have told you," said the boy, "will you let me go back to my old man? If he has not stayed with that woman from Kulu, I am afraid he will die."

"By what I saw of him he's as well able to take care of himself as you. No. Ye've brought us luck, an' we're goin' to make a man of you. I'll take ye back to your baggage-cart and ye'll come to me this evening."

For the rest of the day Kim found himself an object of distinguished consideration among a few hundred white men. The story of his appearance in camp, the discovery of his parentage, and his prophecy, had lost nothing in the telling. A big, shapeless white woman on a pile of bedding asked him mysteriously whether she thought her husband would come back from the war. Kim reflected gravely, and said that he would, and the woman gave him food. In many respects, this big procession that played music at intervals – this crowd that talked and laughed so easily – resembled a festival in Lahore city. So far, there was no sign of hard work, and he resolved to lend the spectacle his patronage. At evening there came out to meet them bands of music, and played the Mavericks into camp near Umballa railway station. That was an interesting night. Men of other regiments came to visit the Mavericks. The Mavericks went visiting on their own account. Their pickets hurried forth to bring them back, met pickets of strange regiments on the same duty; and, after a while, the bugles blew madly for more pickets with officers to control the tumult. The Mavericks had a reputation for liveliness to live up to. But they fell in on the platform next morning in perfect shape and condition; and Kim, left behind with the sick, women, and boys, found himself shouting farewells excitedly as the trains drew away. Life as a sahib was amusing so far; but he touched it with a cautious hand. Then they marched him back in charge of a drummer-boy to empty, lime-washed barracks, whose floors were covered with rubbish and string and paper, and whose ceilings gave back his lonely footfall. Native-fashion, he curled himself up on a stripped cot and went to sleep. An angry man stumped down the veranda, woke him up, and said he was a schoolmaster. This was enough for Kim, and he retired into his shell. He could just puzzle out the various English police notices in Lahore city, because they affected his comfort; and among the many guests of the woman who looked after him had been a queer German who painted scenery for the Parsee travelling theatre. He told Kim that he had been "on the barricades in Forty-eight", and therefore – at least that was how it struck Kim – he would teach the boy to write in return for food. Kim had been kicked as far as single letters, but did not think well of them.

"I do not know anything. Go away!" said Kim, scenting evil. Hereupon the man caught him by the ear, dragged him to a room in a far-off wing where a dozen drummer-boys were sitting on forms, and told him to be still if he could do nothing else. This he managed very successfully. The man explained something or other with white lines on a black board for at least half an hour, and Kim continued his interrupted nap. He much disapproved of the present aspect of affairs, for this was the very school and discipline he had spent two thirds of his young life in avoiding. Suddenly a beautiful idea occurred to him, and he wondered that he had not thought of it before.

The man dismissed them, and first to spring through the veranda into the open sunshine was Kim.

"'Ere, you! 'Alt! Stop!" said a high voice at his heels. "I've got to look after you. My orders are not to let you out of my sight. Where are you goin'?"

It was the drummer-boy who had been hanging round him all the fore-noon – a fat and freckled person of about fourteen, and Kim loathed him from the soles of his boots to his cap ribbons.

"To the bazaar – to get sweets – for you," said Kim, after thought.

"Well, the bazaar's out o' bounds. If we go there we'll get a dressing-down. You come back."

"How near can we go?" Kim did not know what bounds meant, but he wished to be polite – for the present.

"'Ow near? 'Ow far, you mean! We can go as far as that tree down the road."

"Then I will go there."

"All right. I ain't goin'. It's too 'ot. I can watch you from 'ere. It's no good runnin' away. If you did, they'd spot you by your clothes. That's regimental stuff you're wearing. There ain't a picket in Umballa wouldn't 'ead you back quicker than you started out."

This did not impress Kim as much as the knowledge that his raiment would tire him out if he tried to run. He slouched to the tree at the corner of a bare road leading towards the bazaar, and eyed the natives passing. Most of them were barrack servants of the lowest caste. Kim hailed a sweeper, who promptly retorted with a piece of unnecessary insolence, in the natural belief that the European boy could not follow it. The low, quick answer undeceived him. Kim put his fettered soul into it, thankful for the late chance to abuse somebody in the tongue he knew best. "And now, go to the nearest letter-writer in the bazaar and tell him to come here. I would write a letter."

"But – but what manner of white man's son art thou to need a bazaar letter-writer? Is there not a schoolmaster in the barracks?"

"Ay; and Hell is full of the same sort. Do my order, you – you Od! Thy mother was married under a basket! Servant of Lal Beg" (Kim knew the God of the sweepers), "run on my business or we will talk again."

The sweeper shuffled off in haste. "There is a white boy by the barracks waiting under a tree who is not a white boy," he stammered to the first bazaar letter-writer he came across. "He needs thee."

"Will he pay?" said that spruce scribe, gathering up his desk and pens and sealing-wax all in order.

"I do not know. He is not like other boys. Go and see. It is well worth."

Kim danced with impatience when the slim young Kayeth hove in sight. As soon as his voice could carry he cursed him volubly.

"Wonder on wonder," murmured the letter-writer.

"First I will take my pay," the letter-writer said. "Bad words have made the price higher. But who art thou, dressed in that fashion, to speak in this fashion?"

"Aha! That is in the letter which thou shalt write. Never was such a tale. But I am in no haste. Another writer will serve me. Umballa city is full of them as is Lahore."

"Four annas," said the writer, sitting down and spreading his cloth in the shade of a deserted barrack wing.

Mechanically Kim squatted beside him – squatted as only the natives can – in spite of the abominable clinging trousers.

The writer regarded him sideways.

"That is the price to ask of sahibs," said Kim. "Now fix me a true one."

"An anna and a half. How do I know, having written the letter, that thou wilt not run away?"

"I must not go beyond this tree, and there is also the stamp to be considered."

"I get no commission on the price of the stamp. Once more, what manner of white boy art thou?"

"That shall be said in the letter, which is to Mahbub All, the horse-dealer in the Kashmir Serai, at Lahore. He is my friend."

"Wonder on wonder!" murmured the letter-writer, dipping a reed in the inkstand. "To be written in Hindi?"

"Assuredly. To Mahbub Ali then. Begin! 'I have come down with the old man as far as Umballa in the train. At Umballa I carried the news of the bay mare's pedigree.'" After what he had seen in the garden, he was not going to write of white stallions.

"Slower a little. What has a bay mare to do… Is it Mahbub Ali, the great dealer?"

"Who else? I have been in his service. Take more ink. Again. 'As the order was, so I did it. We then went on foot towards Benares, but on the third day we found a certain regiment.' Is that down?"

"Ay, *pulton*," murmured the writer all ears.

"'I went into their camp and was caught, and by means of the charm about my neck, which thou knowest, it was established that I was the son of some man in the regiment: according to the prophecy of the Red Bull,

436

which thou knowest was common talk of our bazaar.'" Kim waited for this shaft to sink into the letter-writer's heart, cleared his throat, and continued: "'A priest clothed me and gave me a new name... One priest, however, was a fool. The clothes are very heavy, but I am a sahib and my heart is heavy too. They send me to a school and beat me. I do not like the air and water here. Come then and help me, Mahbub Ali, or send me some money, for I have not sufficient to pay the writer who writes this.'"

"'Who writes this.' It is my own fault that I was tricked. Thou art as clever as Husain Bux that forged the Treasury stamps at Nucklao. But what a tale! What a tale! Is it true by any chance?"

"It does not profit to tell lies to Mahbub Ali. It is better to help his friends by lending them a stamp. When the money comes I will repay."

The writer grunted doubtfully, but took a stamp out of his desk, sealed the letter, handed it over to Kim, and departed. Mahbub Ali's was a name of power in Umballa.

"That is the way to win a good account with the Gods," Kim shouted after him.

"Pay me twice over when the money comes," the man cried over his shoulder.

"What was you bukkin' to that nigger about?" said the drummer-boy when Kim returned to the veranda. "I was watchin' you."

"I was only talkin' to him."

"You talk the same as a nigger, don't you?"

"No-ah! No-ah! I onlee speak a little. What shall we do now?"

"The bugles'll go for dinner in arf a minute. My Gawd! I wish I'd gone up to the Front with the Regiment. It's awful doin' nothin' but school down 'ere. Don't you 'ate it?"

"Oah yess!"

"I'd run away if I knew where to go to, but, as the men say, in this bloomin' Injia you're only a prisoner at large. You can't desert without bein' took back at once. I'm fair sick of it."

"You have been in *Be* – England?"

"W'y, I only come out last troopin' season with my mother. I should think I *'ave* been in England. What a ignorant little beggar you are! You was brought up in the gutter, wasn't you?"

"Oah yess. Tell me something about England. My father he came from there."

Though he would not say so, Kim of course disbelieved every word the drummer-boy spoke about the Liverpool suburb which was his England. It passed the heavy time till dinner – a most unappetizing meal served to the boys and a few invalids in a corner of a barrack-room. But that he had written to Mahbub Ali, Kim would have been almost depressed. The indifference of native crowds he was used to; but this strong loneliness among white men preyed on him. He was grateful when, in the course of the afternoon, a big soldier took him over to Father Victor, who lived in another wing across another dusty parade-ground. The priest was reading an English letter written in purple ink. He looked at Kim more curiously than ever.

"An' how do you like it, my son, as far as you've gone? Not much, eh? It must be hard – very hard on a wild animal. Listen now. I've an amazin' epistle from your friend."

"Where is he? Is he well? Oah! If he knows to write me letters, it is all right."

"You're fond of him, then?"

"*Of* course I am fond of him. He was fond of me."

"It seems so by the look of this. He can't write English, can he?"

"Oah no. Not that I know, but *of* course he found a letter-writer who can write English veree well, and so he wrote. I *do* hope you understand."

"That accounts for it. D'you know anything about his money affairs?" Kim's face showed that he did not.

"How can I tell?"

"That's what I'm askin'. Now listen if you can make head or tail o' this. We'll skip the first part... It's written from Jagadhir Road... 'Sitting on wayside in grave meditation, trusting to be favoured with your Honour's applause of present step, which recommend your Honour to execute for Almighty God's sake. Education is greatest blessing if of best sorts. Otherwise no earthly use.' Faith, the old man's hit the bull's-eye that time! 'If your Honour condescending giving my boy best educations Xavier' (I suppose that's St Xavier's in Partibus) 'in terms of our conversation dated in your tent 15th instant' (a business-like touch there!) 'then Almighty God

blessing your Honour's succeedings to third an' fourth generation and' –
now listen! – 'confide in your Honour's humble servant for adequate
remuneration per hoondi per annum three hundred rupees a year to one
expensive education St Xavier, Lucknow, and allow small time to forward
same per hoondi sent to any part of India as your Honour shall address
yourself. This servant of your Honour has presently no place to lay crown
of his head, but going to Benares by train on account of persecution of old
woman talking so much and unanxious residing Saharunpore in any domes-
tic capacity.' Now what in the world does that mean?"

"She has asked him to be her *puro* – her clergyman – at Saharunpore,
I think. He would not do that on account of his River. She *did* talk."

"It's clear to you, is it? It beats me altogether. 'So going to Benares, where
will find address and forward rupees for boy who is apple of eye, and for
Almighty God's sake execute this education, and your petitioner as in duty
bound shall ever awfully pray. Written by Sobrao Satai, Failed Entrance
Allahabad University, for Venerable Teshoo Lama the priest of Such-zen
looking for a River, address care of Tirthankars' Temple, Benares. P.M. –
Please note boy is apple of eye, and rupees shall be sent per hoondi three
hundred per annum. For God Almighty's sake.' Now, is that ravin' lunacy
or a business proposition? I ask you, because I am fairly at my wit's end."

"He says he will give me three hundred rupees a year? So he will give
me them."

"Oh, that's the way you look at it, is it?"

"*Of* course. If he says so!"

The priest whistled; then he addressed Kim as an equal.

"I don't believe it; but we'll see. You were goin' off today to the Military
Orphanage at Sanawar, where the Regiment would keep you till you were
old enough to enlist. Ye'd be brought up to the Church of England. Bennett
arranged for that. On the other hand, if ye go to St Xavier's ye'll get a better
education an' – an' can have the religion. D'ye see my dilemma?"

Kim saw nothing save a vision of the lama going south in a train with
none to beg for him.

"Like most people, I'm going to temporize. If your friend sends the
money from Benares – Powers of Darkness below, where's a street-beggar
to raise three hundred rupees? – ye'll go down to Lucknow and I'll pay

your fare, because I can't touch the subscription-money if I intend, as I do, to make ye a Catholic. If he doesn't, ye'll go to the Military Orphanage at the Regiment's expense. I'll allow him three days' grace, though I don't believe it at all. Even then, if he fails in his payments later on... but it's beyond me. We can only walk one step at a time in this world, praise God! An' they sent Bennett to the Front an' left me behind. Bennett can't expect everything."

"Oah yess," said Kim vaguely.

The priest leaned forward. "I'd give a month's pay to find what's goin' on inside that little round head of yours."

"There is nothing," said Kim, and scratched it. He was wondering whether Mahbub Ali would send him as much as a whole rupee. Then he could pay the letter-writer and write letters to the lama at Benares. Perhaps Mahbub Ali would visit him next time he came south with horses. Surely he must know that Kim's delivery of the letter to the officer at Umballa had caused the great war which the men and boys had discussed so loudly over the barrack dinner-tables. But if Mahbub Ali did not know this, it would be very unsafe to tell him so. Mahbub Ali was hard upon boys who knew, or thought they knew, too much.

"Well, till I get further news." – Father Victor's voice interrupted the reverie. "Ye can run along now and play with the other boys. They'll teach ye something – but I don't think ye'll like it."

The day dragged to its weary end. When he wished to sleep he was instructed how to fold up his clothes and set out his boots; the other boys deriding. Bugles waked him in the dawn; the schoolmaster caught him after breakfast, thrust a page of meaningless characters under his nose, gave them senseless names, and whacked him without reason. Kim meditated poisoning him with opium borrowed from a barrack sweeper, but reflected that, as they all ate at one table in public (this was particularly revolting to Kim, who preferred to turn his back on the world at meals), the stroke might be dangerous. Then he attempted running off to the village where the priest had tried to drug the lama – the village where the old soldier lived. But far-seeing sentries at every exit headed back the little scarlet figure. Trousers and jacket crippled body and mind alike, so he abandoned the project and fell back, oriental-fashion, on time and chance. Three days of torment passed in the big, echoing white rooms. He walked out of afternoons under escort of the drummer-boy, and all he heard from his companion were the few useless words which seemed to make two thirds of the white man's abuse. Kim knew and despised them all long ago. The boy resented his silence and lack of interest by beating him, as was only natural. He did not care for any of the bazaars which were in bounds. He styled all natives "niggers"; yet servants and sweepers called him abominable names to his face, and, misled by their deferential attitude, he never understood. This somewhat consoled Kim for the beatings.

On the morning of the fourth day a judgement overtook that drummer. They had gone out together towards Umballa racecourse. He returned alone, weeping, with news that young O'Hara, to whom he had been doing nothing in particular, had hailed a scarlet-bearded nigger on horseback; that the nigger had then and there laid into him with a peculiarly adhesive quirt, picked up young O'Hara, and borne him off at full gallop. These tidings came to Father Victor and he drew down his long upper lip. He was already sufficiently startled by a letter from the Temple of the Tirthankars at Benares, enclosing a native banker's note of hand for three hundred rupees, and an amazing prayer to "Almighty God". The lama would have been more annoyed than the priest had he known how the bazaar letter-writer had translated his phrase "to acquire merit".

"Powers of Darkness below!" Father Victor fumbled with the note. "An' now he's off with another of his peep-o'-day friends. I don't know whether it will be a greater relief to me to get him back or to have him lost. He's beyond my comprehension. How the Divil – yes, *he's* the man I mean – can a street-beggar raise money to educate white boys?"

Three miles off, on Umballa racecourse, Mahbub Ali, reining a grey Kabuli stallion with Kim in front of him, was saying:

"But, Little Friend of all the World, there is *my* honour and reputation to be considered. All the officer-sahibs in all the regiments, and all Umballa, know Mahbub Ali. Men saw me pick thee up and chastise that boy. We are seen now from far across this plain. How can I take thee away, or account for thy disappearing if I set thee down and let thee run off into the crops? They would put me in jail. Be patient. Once a sahib, always a sahib. When thou art a man – who knows? – thou wilt be grateful to Mahbub Ali."

"Take me beyond their sentries where I can change this red. Give me money and I will go to Benares and be with my lama again. I do not want to be a sahib, and remember I *did* deliver that message."

The stallion bounded wildly. Mahbub Ali had incautiously driven home the sharp-edged stirrup. (He was not the new sort of fluent horse-dealer who wears English boots and spurs.) Kim drew his own conclusions from that betrayal.

"That was a small matter. It lay on the straight road to Benares. I and the sahib have by this time forgotten it. I send so many letters and messages to men who ask questions about horses, I cannot well remember one from the other. Was it some matter of a bay mare that Peters Sahib wished the pedigree of?"

Kim saw the trap at once. If he had said "bay mare" Mahbub would have known by his very readiness to fall in with the amendment that the boy suspected something. Kim replied therefore:

"Bay mare. No. *I* do not forget my messages thus. It was a white stallion."

"Ay, so it was. A white Arab stallion. But thou didst write 'bay mare' to me."

"Who cares to tell truth to a letter-writer?" Kim answered, feeling Mahbub's palm on his heart.

"Hi! Mahbub, you old villain, pull up!" cried a voice, and an Englishman raced alongside on a little polo-pony. "I've been chasing you half over the country. That Kabuli of yours can go. For sale, I suppose?"

"I have some young stuff coming on made by Heaven for the delicate and difficult polo-game. He has no equal. He –"

"Plays polo and waits at table. Yes. We know all that. What the deuce have you got there?"

"A boy," said Mahbub gravely. "He was being beaten by another boy. His father was once a white soldier in the big war. The boy was a child in Lahore city. He played with my horses when he was a babe. Now I think they will make him a soldier. He has been newly caught by his father's regiment that went up to the war last week. But I do not think he wants to be a soldier. I take him for a ride. Tell me where thy barracks are and I will set thee there."

"Let me go. I can find the barracks alone."

"And if thou runnest away who will say it is not my fault?"

"He'll run back to his dinner. Where has he to run to?" the Englishman asked.

"He was born in the land. He has friends. He goes where he chooses. He is a *chabuk sawai* [a sharp chap]. It needs only to change his clothing, and in a twinkling he would be a low-caste Hindu boy."

"The deuce he would!" The Englishman looked critically at the boy as Mahbub headed towards the barracks. Kim ground his teeth. Mahbub was mocking him, as faithless Afghans will; for he went on:

"They will send him to a school and put heavy boots on his feet and swaddle him in these clothes. Then he will forget all he knows. Now, which of the barracks is thine?"

Kim pointed – he could not speak – to Father Victor's wing, all staring white near by.

"Perhaps he will make a good soldier," said Mahbub reflectively. "He will make a good orderly at least. I sent him to deliver a message once from Lahore. A message concerning the pedigree of a white stallion."

Here was deadly insult on deadlier injury – and the sahib to whom he had so craftily given that war-waking letter heard it all. Kim beheld Mahbub Ali frying in flame for his treachery, but for himself he saw one long grey vista of barracks, schools, and barracks again. He gazed imploringly at the clear-cut face in which there was no glimmer of recognition; but even at this extremity it never occurred to him to throw himself on the white man's mercy or to denounce the Afghan. And Mahbub stared deliberately at the Englishman, who stared as deliberately at Kim, quivering and tongue-tied.

"My horse is well trained," said the dealer. "Others would have kicked, Sahib."

"Ah," said the Englishman at last, rubbing his pony's damp withers with his whip-butt. "Who makes the boy a soldier?"

"He says the Regiment that found him, and especially the Padre-sahib of the regiment."

"There is the Padre!" Kim choked as bare-headed Father Victor sailed down upon them from the veranda.

"Powers o' Darkness below, O'Hara! How many more mixed friends do you keep in Asia?" he cried, as Kim slid down and stood helplessly before him.

"Good morning, Padre," the Englishman said cheerily. "I know you by reputation well enough. Meant to have come over and called before this. I'm Creighton."

"Of the Ethnological Survey?" said Father Victor. The Englishman nodded. "Faith, I'm glad to meet you then; an' I owe you thanks for bringing back the boy."

"No thanks to me, Padre. Besides, the boy wasn't going away. You don't know old Mahbub Ali." The horse-dealer sat impassive in the sunlight. "You will when you have been in the station a month. He sells us all our crocks. That boy is rather a curiosity. Can you tell me anything about him?"

"Can I tell you?" puffed Father Victor. "You'll be the one man that could help me in my quandaries. Tell you! Powers o' Darkness, I'm bursting to tell some one who knows something o' the native!"

A groom came round the corner. Colonel Creighton raised his voice, speaking in Urdu. "Very good, Mahbub Ali, but what is the use of telling me all those stories about the pony? Not one pie more than three hundred and fifty rupees will I give."

"The Sahib is a little hot and angry after riding," the horse-dealer returned, with a leer of a privileged jester. "Presently, he will see my horse's points more clearly. I will wait till he has finished his talk with the Padre. I will wait under that tree."

"Confound you!" The Colonel laughed. "That comes of looking at one of Mahbub's horses. He's a regular old leech, Padre. Wait, then, if thou hast so much time to spare, Mahbub. Now I'm at your service, Padre. Where is the boy? Oh, he's gone off to collogue with Mahbub. Queer sort of boy. Might I ask you to send my mare round under cover?"

He dropped into a chair which commanded a clear view of Kim and Mahbub Ali in conference beneath the tree. The Padre went indoors for cheroots.

Creighton heard Kim say bitterly: "Trust a Brahmin before a snake, and a snake before an harlot, and an harlot before a Pathan, Mahbub Ali."

"That is all one." The great red beard wagged solemnly. "Children should not see a carpet on the loom till the pattern is made plain. Believe

444

me, Friend of all the World, I do thee great service. They will not make a soldier of thee."

"You crafty old sinner!" thought Creighton. "But you're not far wrong. That boy mustn't be wasted if he is as advertised."

"Excuse me half a minute," cried the Padre from within, "but I'm getting the documents in the case."

"If through me the favour of this bold and wise Colonel Sahib comes to thee, and thou art raised to honour, what thanks wilt thou give Mahbub Ali when thou art a man?"

"Nay, nay! I begged thee to let me take the Road again, where I should have been safe; and thou hast sold me back to the English. What will they give thee for blood-money?"

"A cheerful young demon!" The Colonel bit his cigar, and turned politely to Father Victor.

"What are the letters that the fat priest is waving before the Colonel? Stand behind the stallion as though looking at my bridle!" said Mahbub Ali.

"A letter from my lama which he wrote from Jagadhir Road, saying that he will pay three hundred rupees by the year for my schooling."

"Oho! Is old Red Hat of that sort? At which school?"

"God knows. I think in Nucklao."

"Yes. There is a big school there for the sons of sahibs – and half-sahibs. I have seen it when I sell horses there. So the lama also loved the Friend of all the World?"

"Ay; and *he* did not tell lies, or return me to captivity."

"Small wonder the Padre does not know how to unravel the thread. How fast he talks to the Colonel Sahib!" Mahbub Ali chuckled. "By Allah!" – the keen eyes swept the veranda for an instant – "thy lama has sent what to me looks like a note of hand. I have had some few dealings in *hoondis*. The Colonel Sahib is looking at it."

"What good is all this to me?" said Kim wearily. "Thou wilt go away, and they will return me to those empty rooms where there is no good place to sleep and where the boys beat me."

"I do not think that. Have patience, child. All Pathans are not faithless – except in horse-flesh."

Five – ten – fifteen minutes passed, Father Victor talking energetically or asking questions which the Colonel answered.

"Now I've told you everything that I know about the boy from beginnin' to end; and it's a blessed relief to me. Did ye ever hear the like?"

"At any rate, the old man has sent the money. Gobind Sahai's notes of hand are good from here to China," said the Colonel. "The more one knows about natives the less can one say what they will or won't do."

"That's consolin' – from the head of the Ethnological Survey. It's this mixture of Red Bulls and Rivers of Healing (poor heathen, God help him!) an' notes of hand and Masonic certificates. Are you a Mason, by any chance?"

"By Jove, I am, now I come to think of it. That's an additional reason," said the Colonel absently.

"I'm glad ye see a reason in it. But as I said, it's the mixture o' things that's beyond me. An' his prophesyin' to our Colonel, sitting on my bed with his little shimmy torn open showing his white skin; an' the prophecy comin' true! They'll cure all that nonsense at St Xavier's, eh?"

"Sprinkle him with holy water," the Colonel laughed.

"On my word, I fancy I ought to sometimes. But I'm hoping he'll be brought up as a good Catholic. All that troubles me is what'll happen if the old beggar-man –"

"Lama, lama, my dear sir; and some of them are gentlemen in their own country."

"The lama, then, fails to pay next year. He's a fine business head to plan on the spur of the moment, but he's bound to die some day. An' takin' a heathen's money to give a child a Christian education –"

"But he said explicitly what he wanted. As soon as he knew the boy was white he seems to have made his arrangements accordingly. I'd give a month's pay to hear how he explained it all at the Tirthankars' Temple at Benares. Look here, Padre, I don't pretend to know much about natives, but if he says he'll pay, he'll pay – dead or alive. I mean, his heirs will assume the debt. My advice to you is, send the boy down to Lucknow. If your Anglican Chaplain thinks you've stolen a march on him –"

"Bad luck to Bennett! He was sent to the Front instead o' me. Doughty certified me medically unfit. I'll excommunicate Doughty if he comes back alive! Surely Bennett ought to be content with –"

"Glory, leaving you the religion. Quite so! As a matter of fact I don't think Bennett will mind. Put the blame on me. I – er – strongly recommend sending the boy to St Xavier's. He can go down on pass as a soldier's orphan, so the railway fare will be saved. You can buy him an outfit from the regimental subscription. The Lodge will be saved the expense of his education, and that will put the Lodge in a good temper. It's perfectly easy. I've got to go down to Lucknow next week. I'll look after the boy on the way – give him in charge of my servants, and so on."

"You're a good man."

"Not in the least. Don't make that mistake. The lama has sent us money for a definite end. We can't very well return it. We shall have to do as he says. Well, that's settled, isn't it? Shall we say that, Tuesday next, you'll hand him over to me at the night train south?"

"That's only three days. He can't do much harm in three days."

"It's a weight off my mind, but – this thing here?" – he waved the note of hand – "I don't know Gobind Sahai: or his bank, which may be a hole in the wall."

"*You've* never been a subaltern in debt. I'll cash it if you like, and send you the vouchers in proper order."

"But with all your own work too! It's askin' –"

"It's not the least trouble indeed. You see, as an ethnologist, the thing's very interesting to me. I'd like to make a note of it for some government work that I'm doing. The transformation of a regimental badge like your Red Bull into a sort of fetish that the boy follows is very interesting."

"But I can't thank you enough."

"There's one thing you can do. All we ethnological men are as jealous as jackdaws of one another's discoveries. They're of no interest to any one but ourselves, of course, but you know what book-collectors are like. Well, don't say a word, directly or indirectly, about the Asiatic side of the boy's character – his adventures and his prophecy, and so on. I'll worm them out of the boy later on and – you see?"

"I do. Ye'll make a wonderful account of it. Never a word will I say to any one till I see it in print."

"Thank you. That goes straight to an ethnologist's heart. Well, I must be getting back to my breakfast. Good Heavens! Old Mahbub here still?

447

He raised his voice, and the horse-dealer came out from under the shadow of the tree. "Well, what is it?"

"As regards that young horse," said Mahbub, "I say that when a colt is born to be a polo-pony, closely following the ball without teaching – when such a colt knows the game by divination – then I say it is a great wrong to break that colt to a heavy cart, Sahib!"

"So say I also, Mahbub. The colt will be entered for polo only. (These fellows think of nothing in the world but horses, Padre.) I'll see you tomorrow, Mahbub, if you've anything likely for sale."

The dealer saluted, horseman-fashion, with a sweep of the off hand. "Be patient a little, Friend of all the World," he whispered to the agonized Kim. "Thy fortune is made. In a little while thou goest to Nucklao, and – here is something to pay the letter-writer. I shall see thee again, I think, many times," and he cantered off down the road.

"Listen to me," said the Colonel from the veranda, speaking in the vernacular. "In three days thou wilt go with me to Lucknow, seeing and hearing new things all the while. Therefore sit still for three days and do not run away. Thou wilt go to school at Lucknow."

"Shall I meet my Holy One there?" Kim whimpered.

"At least Lucknow is nearer to Benares than Umballa. It may be thou wilt go under my protection. Mahbub Ali knows this, and he will be angry if thou returnest to the Road now. Remember – much has been told me which I do not forget."

"I will wait," said Kim, "but the boys will beat me."

Then the bugles blew for dinner.

Chapter 7

Unto whose use the pregnant suns are poised
   With idiot moons and stars retracting stars?
Creep thou betweene – thy coming's all unnoised.
   Heaven hath her high, as Earth her baser, wars.
Heir to these tumults, this affright, that fraye
(By Adam's fathers', own, sin bound alway);
   Peer up, draw out thy horoscope and say
Which planet mends thy threadbare fate or mars!
                        Sir John Christie

In the afternoon the red-faced schoolmaster told Kim that he had been "struck off the strength," which conveyed no meaning to him till he was ordered to go away and play. Then he ran to the bazaar, and found the young letter-writer to whom he owed a stamp.

"Now I pay," said Kim royally, "and now I need another letter to be written."

"Mahbub Ali is in Umballa," said the writer jauntily. He was, by virtue of his office, a bureau of general misinformation.

"This is not to Mahbub, but to a priest. Take thy pen and write quickly. 'To Teshoo Lama, the Holy One from Bhotiyal seeking for a River, who is now in the Temple of the Tirthankars at Benares.' Take more ink! 'In three days I am to go down to Nucklao to the school at Nucklao. The name of the school is Xavier. I do not know where that school is, but it is at Nucklao.'"

"But I know Nucklao," the writer interrupted. "I know the school."

"Tell him where it is, and I give half an anna."

The reed pen scratched busily. "He cannot mistake." The man lifted his head. "Who watches us across the street?"

Kim looked up hurriedly and saw Colonel Creighton in tennis flannels.

"Oh, that is some sahib who knows the fat priest in the barracks. He is beckoning me."

"What dost thou?" said the Colonel, when Kim trotted up.

"I – I am not running away. I send a letter to my Holy One at Benares."

"I had not thought of that. Hast thou said that I take thee to Lucknow?"

"Nay, I have not. Read the letter, if there be a doubt."

"Then why hast thou left out my name in writing to that Holy One?" The Colonel smiled a queer smile. Kim took his courage in both hands.

"It was said once to me that it is inexpedient to write the names of strangers concerned in any matter, because by the naming of names many good plans are brought to confusion."

"Thou hast been well taught," the Colonel replied, and Kim flushed. "I have left my cheroot-case in the Padre's veranda. Bring it to my house this even."

"Where is the house?" said Kim. His quick wit told him that he was being tested in some fashion or another, and he stood on guard.

"Ask any one in the big bazaar." The Colonel walked on.

"He has forgotten his cheroot-case," said Kim, returning. "I must bring it to him this evening. That is all my letter except, thrice over, 'Come to me! Come to me! Come to me!' Now I will pay for a stamp and put it in the post." He rose to go, and as an afterthought asked: "Who is that angry-faced sahib who lost the cheroot-case?"

"Oh, he is only Creighton Sahib – a very foolish sahib, who is a colonel sahib without a regiment."

"What is his business?"

"God knows. He is always buying horses which he cannot ride, and asking riddles about the works of God – such as plants and stones and the customs of the people. The dealers call him the father of fools, because he is so easily cheated about a horse. Mahbub Ali says he is madder than most other sahibs."

"Oh!" said Kim, and departed. His training had given him some small knowledge of character, and he argued that fools are not given information which leads to calling out eight thousand men besides guns. The Commander-in-Chief of all India does not talk, as Kim had heard him talk, to fools. Nor would Mahbub Ali's tone have changed, as it did every time he mentioned the Colonel's name, if the Colonel had been a fool. Consequently – and this set Kim to skipping – there was a mystery somewhere, and Mahbub Ali probably spied for the Colonel much as Kim had spied for Mahbub. And, like the horse-dealer, the Colonel evidently respected people who did not show themselves to be too clever.

He rejoiced that he had not betrayed his knowledge of the Colonel's house; and when, on his return to barracks, he discovered that no cheroot-case had been left behind, he beamed with delight. Here was a man after his own heart – a tortuous and indirect person playing a hidden game. Well, if he could be a fool, so could Kim.

He showed nothing of his mind when Father Victor, for three long mornings, discoursed to him of an entirely new set of Gods and Godlings – notably of a Goddess called Mary, who, he gathered, was one with Bibi Miriam of Mahbub Ali's theology. He betrayed no emotion when, after the lecture, Father Victor dragged him from shop to shop buying articles of outfit, nor when envious drummer-boys kicked him because he was going to a superior school did he complain, but awaited the play of circumstances with an interested soul. Father Victor, good man, took him to the station, put him into an empty second-class next to Colonel Creighton's first, and bade him farewell with genuine feeling.

"They'll make a man o' you, O'Hara, at St Xavier's – a white man, an' I hope, a good man. They know all about your comin', an' the Colonel will see that ye're not lost or mislaid anywhere on the road. I've given you a notion of religious matters – at least I hope so – and you'll remember, when they ask you your religion, that you're a Cath'lic. Better say Roman Cath'lic, tho' I'm not fond of the word."

Kim lit a rank cigarette – he had been careful to buy a stock in the bazaar – and lay down to think. This solitary passage was very different

"They'll make a man of you, O'Hara, at St Xavier's."

from that joyful down-journey in the third-class with the lama. "Sahibs get little pleasure of travel," he reflected. "*Hai mai!* I go from one place to another as it might be a kick-ball. It is my *Kismet*. No man can escape his *Kismet*. But I am to pray to Bibi Miriam, and I am a sahib." He looked at his boots ruefully. "No; I am Kim. This is the great world, and I am only Kim. Who is Kim?" He considered his own identity, a thing he had never done before, till his head swam. He was one insignificant person in all this roaring whirl of India, going southward to he knew not what fate.

Presently the Colonel sent for him, and talked for a long time. So far as Kim could gather, he was to be diligent and enter the Survey of India as a chain-man. If he were very good, and passed the proper examinations, he would be earning thirty rupees a month at seventeen years old, and Colonel Creighton would see that he found suitable employment.

Kim pretended at first to understand perhaps one word in three of this talk. Then the Colonel, seeing his mistake, turned to fluent and picturesque Urdu and Kim was contented. No man could be a fool who knew the language so intimately, who moved so gently and silently, and whose eyes were so different from the dull fat eyes of other sahibs.

"Yes, and thou must learn how to make pictures of roads and mountains and rivers – to carry these pictures in thine eye till a suitable time comes to set them down upon paper. Perhaps some day, when thou art a chain-man, I may say to thee when we are working together: 'Go across those hills and see what lies beyond.' Then one will say: 'There are bad people living in those hills who will slay the chain-man if he be seen to look like a sahib.' What then?"

Kim thought. Would it be safe to return the Colonel's lead?

"I would tell what that other man had said."

"But if I answered: 'I will give thee a hundred rupees for knowledge of what is behind those hills – for a picture of a river and a little news of what the people say in the villages there'?"

"How can I tell? I am only a boy. Wait till I am a man." Then, seeing the Colonel's brow clouded, he went on: "But I think I should in a few days earn the hundred rupees."

"By what road?"

Kim shook his head resolutely. "If I said how I would earn them, another man might hear and forestall me. It is not good to sell knowledge for nothing."

"Tell now." The Colonel held up a rupee. Kim's hand half reached towards it, and dropped.

"Nay, Sahib; nay. I know the price that will be paid for the answer, but I do not know why the question is asked."

"Take it for a gift, then," said Creighton, tossing it over. "There is a good spirit in thee. Do not let it be blunted at St Xavier's. There are many boys there who despise the black men."

"Their mothers were bazaar-women," said Kim. He knew well there is no hatred like that of the half-caste for his brother-in-law.

"True; but thou art a sahib and the son of a sahib. Therefore, do not at any time be led to contemn the black men. I have known boys newly entered into the service of the government who feigned not to understand the talk or the customs of black men. Their pay was cut for ignorance. There is no sin so great as ignorance. Remember this."

Several times in the course of the long twenty-four hours' run south did the Colonel send for Kim, always developing this latter text.

"We be all on one lead-rope, then," said Kim at last, "the Colonel, Mahbub Ali, and I – when I become a chain-man. He will use me as Mahbub Ali employed me, I think. That is good, if it allows me to return to the Road again. This clothing grows no easier by wear."

When they came to the crowded Lucknow station there was no sign of the lama. He swallowed his disappointment, while the Colonel bundled him into a *ticca-gharri* with his neat belongings and despatched him alone to St Xavier's.

"I do not say farewell, because we shall meet again," he cried. "Again, and many times, if thou art one of good spirit. But thou·art not yet tried."

"Not when I brought thee" – Kim actually dared to use the *tum* of equals – "a white stallion's pedigree that night?"

"Much is gained by forgetting, little brother," said the Colonel, with a look that pierced through Kim's shoulder-blades as he scuttled into the carriage.

It took him nearly five minutes to recover. Then he sniffed the new air appreciatively. "A rich city," he said. "Richer than Lahore. How good the bazaars must be! Coachman, drive me a little through the bazaars here."

"My order is to take thee to the school." The driver used the "thou", which is rudeness when applied to a white man. In the clearest and most fluent vernacular Kim pointed out his error, climbed on to the box-seat, and, perfect understanding established, drove for a couple of hours up and down, estimating, comparing, and enjoying. There is no city – except Bombay, the queen of all – more beautiful in her garish style than Lucknow, whether you see her from the bridge over the river, or from the top of the Imambara looking down on the gilt umbrellas of the Chutter Munzil, and the trees in which the town is bedded. Kings have adorned her with fantastic buildings, endowed her with charities, crammed her with pensioners, and drenched her with blood. She is the centre of all idleness, intrigue, and luxury, and shares with Delhi the claim to talk the only pure Urdu.

"A fair city – a beautiful city." The driver, as a Lucknow man, was pleased with the compliment, and told Kim many astounding things where an English guide would have talked of the Mutiny.

"Now we will go to the school," said Kim at last. The great old school of St Xavier's in Partibus, block on block of low white buildings, stands in vast grounds over against the Gumti River, at some distance from the city.

"What like of folk are they within?" said Kim.

"Young sahibs – all devils. But to speak truth, and I drive many of them to and fro from the railway station, I have never seen one that had in him the making of a more perfect devil than thou – this young sahib whom I am now driving."

Naturally, for he was never trained to consider them in any way improper, Kim had passed the time of day with one or two frivolous ladies at upper windows in a certain street, and naturally, in the exchange of compliments, had acquitted himself well. He was about to acknowledge the driver's last insolence, when his eye – it was growing dusk – caught a figure in the long sweep of wall.

"Stop!" he cried. "Stay here. I do not go to the school at once."

"But what is to pay me for this coming and recoming?" said the driver petulantly. "Is the boy mad? Last time it was a dancing-girl. This time it is a priest."

Kim was in the road headlong, patting the dusty feet beneath the yellow robe.

"I have waited here a day and a half," the lama's level voice began. "Nay, I had a disciple with me. He that was my friend at the Temple of the Tirthankars gave me a guide for this journey. I came from Benares in the *te-rain*, when thy letter was given me. Yes, I am well fed. I need nothing."

"But why didst thou not stay with the Kulu woman, O Holy One? In what way didst thou get to Benares? My heart has been heavy since we parted."

"The woman wearied me by constant flux of talk and requiring charms for children. I separated myself from that company, permitting her to acquire merit by gifts. She is at least a woman of open hands, and I made a promise to return to her house if need arose. Then, perceiving myself alone in this great and terrible world, I bethought me of the *te-rain* to Benares, where I knew one abode in the Tirthankars' Temple who was a Seeker, even as I."

"Ah! Thy River," said Kim. "I had forgotten the River."

"So soon, my *chela*? I have never forgotten it. But when I had left thee it seemed better that I should go to the Temple and take counsel, for, look you, India is very large, and it may be that wise men before us, some two or three, have left a record of the place of our River. There is debate in the Temple of the Tirthankars on this matter; some saying one thing, and some another. They are courteous folk."

"So be it; but what dost thou do now?"

"I acquire merit in that I help thee, my *chela*, to wisdom. The priest of that body of men who serve the Red Bull wrote me that all should be as I desired for thee. I sent the money to suffice for one year, and then I came, as thou seest me, to watch for thee going up into the Gates of Learning. A day and a half have I waited – not because I was led by any affection towards thee – that is no part of the Way – but, as they said at the Tirthankars' Temple, because, money having been paid for learning, it was right that I should oversee the end of the matter. They resolved my doubts most clearly. I had a fear that, perhaps, I came because I wished to see thee – misguided by the Red Mist of affection. It is not so... Moreover, I am troubled by a dream."

"But surely, Holy One, thou hast not forgotten the Road and all that befell on it. Surely it was a little to see me that thou didst come?"

"The horses are cold, and it is past their feeding-time," whined the driver.

"Go to Jehannum and abide there with thy reputationless aunt!" Kim snarled over his shoulder. "I am all alone in this land; I know not where I go nor what shall befall me. My heart was in that letter I sent thee. Except for Mahbub Ali, and he is a Pathan, I have no friend save thee, Holy One. Do not altogether go away."

"I have considered that also," the lama replied, in a shaking voice. "It is manifest that from time to time I shall acquire merit – if before that I have not found my River – by assuring myself that thy feet are set on wisdom. What they will teach thee I do not know, but the priest wrote me that no son of a sahib in all India will be better taught than thou. So from time to time, therefore, I will come again. Maybe thou wilt be such a sahib as he who gave me those spectacles" – the lama wiped them elaborately – "in the Wonder House at Lahore. That is my hope, for he was a Fountain of Wisdom – wiser than many abbots... Again, maybe thou wilt forget me and our meetings."

"If I eat thy bread," cried Kim passionately, "how shall I ever forget thee?"

"No – no." He put the boy aside. "I must go back to Benares. From time to time, now that I know the customs of letter-writers in this land, I will send thee a letter, and from time to time I will come and see thee."

"But whither shall I send my letters?" wailed Kim, clutching at the robe, all forgetful that he was a sahib:

"To the Temple of the Tirthankars at Benares. That is the place I have chosen till I find my River. Do not weep; for, look you, all desire is illusion and a new binding upon the Wheel. Go up to the Gates of Learning. Let me see thee go... Dost thou love me? Then go, or my heart cracks... I will come again. Surely I will come again."

The lama watched the *ticca-gharri* rumble into the compound, and strode off, snuffing between each long stride.

"The Gates of Learning" shut with a clang.

*

457

The country-born and -bred boy has his own manners and customs, which do not resemble those of any other land; and his teachers approach him by roads which an English master would not understand. Therefore you would scarcely be interested in Kim's experiences as a St Xavier's boy among two or three hundred precocious youths, most of whom had never seen the sea. He suffered the usual penalties for breaking out of bounds when there was cholera in the city. This was before he had learned to write fair English, and so was obliged to find a bazaar letter-writer. He was, of course, indicted for smoking and for the use of abuse more full-flavoured than even St Xavier's had ever heard. He learned to wash himself with the Levitical scrupulosity of the native-born, who in his heart considers the Englishman rather dirty. He played the usual tricks on the patient coolies pulling the punkahs in the sleeping-rooms where the boys threshed through the hot nights telling tales till the dawn; and quietly he measured himself against his self-reliant mates.

They were sons of subordinate officials in the railway, telegraph, and canal services; of warrant-officers, sometimes retired and sometimes acting as commanders-in-chief to a feudatory rajah's army; of captains of the Indian Marine, government pensioners, planters, presidency shopkeepers, and missionaries. A few were cadets of the old Eurasian houses that have taken strong root in Dhurrumtollah – Pereiras, De Souzas, and D'Silvas. Their parents could well have educated them in England, but they loved the school that had served their own youth, and generation followed sallow-hued generation at St Xavier's. Their homes ranged from Howrah of the railway people to abandoned cantonments like Monghyr and Chunar; lost tea-gardens Shillong way; villages where their fathers were large landholders in Oudh or the Deccan; mission-stations a week from the nearest railway line; seaports a thousand miles south, facing the brazen Indian surf; and cinchona planta-tions south of all. The mere story of their adventures, which to them were no adventures, on their road to and from school would have crisped a West-ern boy's hair. They were used to jogging off alone through a hundred miles of jungle, where there was always the delightful chance of being delayed by tigers; but they would no more have bathed in the English Channel in an English August than their brothers across the world would have lain still while a leopard snuffed at their palanquin. There were boys of fifteen who had spent a day and a half on an islet in the middle of a flooded river, taking charge, as by right, of a camp of frantic pilgrims returning from a shrine. There were seniors who had requisitioned a chance-met rajah's elephant in the name of St Francis Xavier, when the rains once blotted out the cart-track that led to their father's estate, and had all but lost the huge beast in a quicksand. There was a boy, who, he said, and none doubted, had helped his father to beat off with rifles from the veranda a rush of Akas in the days when those head-hunters were bold against lonely plantations.

And every tale was told in the even, passionless voice of the native-born, mixed with quaint reflections, borrowed unconsciously from native foster-mothers, and turns of speech that showed they had been that instant translated from the vernacular. Kim watched, listened, and approved. This was not insipid, single-word talk of drummer-boys. It dealt with a life he knew and in part understood. The atmosphere suited him, and he throve by inches. They gave him a white drill suit as the weather warmed, and he rejoiced in the new-found bodily comforts as he rejoiced to use his sharpened mind over the tasks they set him. His quickness would have delighted an English master; but at St Xavier's they know the first rush of minds developed by sun and surroundings, as they know the half-collapse that sets in at twenty-two or twenty-three.

None the less he remembered to hold himself lowly. When tales were told of hot nights, Kim did not sweep the board with his reminiscences; for St Xavier's looks down on boys who "go native altogether". One must never forget that one is a sahib, and that some day, when examinations are passed, one will command natives. Kim made a note of this, for he began to understand where examinations led.

Then came the holidays from August to October – the long holidays imposed by the heat and the rains. Kim was informed that he would go north to some station in the hills behind Umballa, where Father Victor would arrange for him.

"A barrack-school?" said Kim, who had asked many questions and thought more.

"Yes, I suppose so," said the master. "It will not do you any harm to keep you out of mischief. You can go up with young De Castro as far as Delhi."

Kim considered it in every possible light. He had been diligent, even as the Colonel advised. A boy's holiday was his own property – of so much the talk of his companions had advised him – and a barrack-school would be torment after St Xavier's. Moreover – this was magic worth anything else – he could write. In three months he had discovered how men can speak to each other without a third party, at the cost of half an anna and a little knowledge. No word had come from the lama, but there remained the Road. Kim yearned for the caress of soft mud squishing up between the toes, as his mouth watered for mutton stewed with butter and cabbages, for rice speckled with strong-scented cardamoms, for the saffron-tinted rice, garlic and onions, and the forbidden greasy sweetmeats of the bazaars. They would feed him raw beef on a platter at the barrack-school, and he must smoke by stealth. But again, he was a sahib and was at St Xavier's, and that pig Mahbub Ali... No, he would not test Mahbub's hospitality – and yet... He thought it out alone in the dormitory, and came to the conclusion he had been unjust to Mahbub.

The school was empty; nearly all the masters had gone away; Colonel Creighton's railway pass lay in his hand, and Kim puffed himself that he had not spent Colonel Creighton's or Mahbub's money in riotous living. He was still lord of two rupees seven annas. His new bullock-trunk, marked "K. O'H.", and bedding-roll lay in the empty sleeping-room. "Sahibs are always tied to their baggage," said Kim, nodding at them. "You will stay here." He went out into the warm rain, smiling sinfully, and sought a certain house whose outside he had noted down some time before...

"*Arré!* Dost thou know what manner of women we be in this quarter? Oh, shame!"

"Was I born yesterday?" Kim squatted native-fashion on the cushions of that upper room. "A little dye-stuff and three yards of cloth to help out a jest. Is it too much to ask?"

"Who is *she*? Thou art full young, as sahibs go, for this devilry."

"Oh, she? She is the daughter of a certain schoolmaster of a regiment in the cantonments. He has beaten me twice because I went over their wall in these clothes. Now I would go as a gardener's boy. Old men are very jealous."

"That is true. Hold thy face still while I dab on the juice."

"Not too black, *Naikan*. I would not appear to her as a *hubshi* [nigger]."

"Oh, love makes nought of these things. And how old is she?"

"Twelve years, I think," said the shameless Kim. "Spread it also on the breast. It may be her father will tear my clothes off me, and if I am piebald–" he laughed.

The girl worked busily, dabbing a twist of cloth into a little saucer of brown dye that holds longer than any walnut juice.

"Now send out and get me a cloth for the turban. Woe is me, my head is all unshaved! And he will surely knock off my turban."

"I am not a barber, but I will make shift. Thou was born to be a breaker of hearts! All this disguise for one evening? Remember, the stuff does not wash away." She shook with laughter till her bracelets and anklets jingled. "But who is to pay me for this? Huneefa herself could not have given thee better stuff."

"Trust in the Gods, my sister," said Kim gravely, screwing his face round as the stain dried. "Besides, hast thou ever helped to paint a sahib thus before?"

"Never indeed. But a jest is not money."

"It is worth much more."

"Child, thou art beyond all dispute the most shameless son of Shaitan that I have ever known to take up a poor girl's time with this play, and then to say: 'Is not the jest enough?' Thou wilt go very far in this world." She gave him the dancing-girls' salutation in mockery.

"All one. Make haste and rough-cut my head." Kim shifted from foot to foot, his eyes ablaze with mirth as he thought of the fat days before him. He gave the girl four annas, and ran down the stairs in the likeness of a low-caste Hindu boy – perfect in every detail. A cook-shop was his next point of call, where he feasted in extravagance and greasy luxury.

On Lucknow station platform he watched young De Castro, all covered with prickly-heat, get into a second-class compartment. Kim patronized a third, and was the life and soul of it. He explained to the company that he was assistant to a juggler who had left him behind sick with fever, and that he would pick up his master at Umballa. As the occupants of the carriage changed, he varied this tale, or adorned it with all the shoots of a budding

461

fancy, the more rampant for being held off native speech so long. In all India that night was no human being so joyful as Kim. At Umballa he got out and headed eastward, plashing over the sodden fields to the village where the old soldier lived.

About this time Colonel Creighton at Simla was advised from Lucknow by wire that young O'Hara had disappeared. Mahbub Ali was in town selling horses, and to him the Colonel confided the affair one morning cantering round Annandale racecourse.

"Oh, that is nothing," said the horse-dealer. "Men are like horses. At certain times they need salt, and if that salt is not in the mangers they will lick it up from the earth. He has gone back to the Road again for a while. The *madrissah* wearied him. I knew it would. Another time, I will take him upon the Road myself. Do not be troubled, Creighton Sahib. It is as though a polo-pony, breaking loose, ran out to learn the game alone."

"Then he is not dead, think you?"

"Fever might kill him. I do not fear for the boy otherwise. A monkey does not fall among trees."

Next morning, on the same course, Mahbub's stallion ranged alongside the Colonel.

"It is as I had thought," said the horse-dealer. "He has come through Umballa at least, and there he has written a letter to me, having learned in the bazaar that I was here."

"Read," said the Colonel, with a sigh of relief. It was absurd that a man of his position should take an interest in a little country-bred vagabond; but the Colonel remembered the conversation in the train, and often in the past few months had caught himself thinking of the queer, silent, self-possessed boy. His evasion, of course, was the height of insolence, but it argued some resource and nerve.

Mahbub's eyes twinkled as he reined out into the centre of the cramped little plain, where none could come near unseen.

"'The Friend of the Stars, who is the Friend of all the World–'"

"What is this?"

"A name we give him in Lahore city. 'The Friend of all the World takes leave to go his own places. He will come back upon the appointed day. Let the box and the bedding-roll be sent for; and if there has been a fault let the Hand of Friendship turn aside the Whip of Calamity.' There is yet a little more, but –"

"No matter, read."

"'Certain things are not known to those who eat with forks. It is better to eat with both hands for a while. Speak soft words to those who do not understand this that the return may be propitious.' Now the manner in which that was cast is, of course, the work of the letter-writer, but see how wisely the boy has devised the matter of it so that no hint is given except to those who know!"

"Is this the Hand of Friendship to avert the Whip of Calamity?" laughed the Colonel.

"See how wise is the boy. He would go back to the Road again, as I said. Not knowing yet thy trade –"

"I am not at all sure of that," the Colonel muttered.

"He turns to me to make a peace between you. Is he not wise? He says he will return. He is but perfecting his knowledge. Think, Sahib! He has been three months at the school. And he is not mouthed to that bit. For my part, I rejoice. The pony learns the game."

"Ay, but another time he must not go alone."

"Why? He went alone before he came under the Colonel Sahib's protection. When he comes to the Great Game he must go alone – alone, and at peril of his head. *Then*, if he spits, or sneezes, or sits down other than as the people do whom he watches, he may be slain. Why hinder him now? Remember how the Persians say: The jackal that lives in the wilds of Mazanderan can only be caught by the hounds of Mazanderan."

"True. It is true, Mahbub Ali. And if he comes to no harm, I do not desire anything better. But it is great insolence on his part."

"He does not tell me, even, whither he goes," said Mahbub. "He is no fool. When his time is accomplished he will come to me. It is time the healer of pearls took him in hand. He ripens too quickly – as sahibs reckon."

This prophecy was fulfilled to the letter a month later. Mahbub had gone down to Umballa to bring up a fresh consignment of horses, and Kim met him on the Kalka road at dusk riding alone, begged an alms of him, was sworn at, and replied in English. There was nobody within earshot to hear Mahbub's gasp of amazement.

"Oho! And where hast thou been?"

"Up and down – down and up."

"Come under a tree, out of the wet, and tell."

"I stayed for a while with an old man near Umballa; anon with a household of my acquaintance in Umballa. With one of these I went as far as Delhi to the southward. That is a wondrous city. Then I drove a bullock for a *teli* [an oilman] coming north; but I heard of a great feast forward in Patiala, and thither went I in the company of a firework-maker. It was a great feast" (Kim rubbed his stomach). "I saw rajahs, and elephants with gold and silver trappings; and they lit all the fireworks at once, whereby eleven men were killed, my firework-maker among them, and I was blown across a tent but took no harm. Then I came back to the *rêl* with a Sikh horseman, to whom I was groom for my bread; and so here."

"*Shabash!*" said Mahbub Ali.

"But what does the Colonel Sahib say? I do not wish to be beaten."

"The Hand of Friendship has averted the Whip of Calamity; but another time, when thou takest the Road it will be with me. This is too early."

"Late enough for me. I have learned to read and to write English a little at the *madrissah*. I shall soon be altogether a sahib."

"Hear him!" laughed Mahbub, looking at the little drenched figure dancing in the wet. "Salaam – Sahib," and he saluted ironically. "Well, art tired of the Road, or wilt thou come on to Umballa with me and work back with the horses?"

"I will come with thee, Mahbub Ali."

Chapter 8

Something I owe to the soil that grew –
    More to the life that fed –
But most to Allah Who gave me two
    Separate sides to my head.

I would go without shirts or shoes,
    Friends, tobacco or bread
Sooner than for an instant lose
    Either side of my head.

                 The Two-Sided Man

"Then in God's name take blue for red," said Mahbub, alluding to the Hindu colour of Kim's disreputable turban.

Kim countered with the old proverb, "I will change my faith and my bedding, but *thou* must pay for it."

The dealer laughed till he nearly fell from his horse. At a shop on the outskirts of the city the change was made, and Kim stood up, externally at least, a Muhammadan.

Mahbub hired a room over against the railway station, sent for a cooked meal of the finest with almond-curd sweetmeats [*balushai* we call it] and fine-chopped Lucknow tobacco.

"This is better than some other meat that I ate with the Sikh," said Kim, grinning as he squatted, "and assuredly they give no such victuals at my *madrissah*."

"I have a desire to hear of that same *madrissah*." Mahbub stuffed himself with great boluses of spiced mutton fried in fat with cabbage and golden-brown onions. "But tell me first, altogether and truthfully, the manner of thy escape. For, O Friend of all the World," – he loosed his cracking belt – "I do not think it is often that a sahib and the son of a sahib runs away from there."

"How should they? They do not know the land. It was nothing," said Kim, and began his tale. When he came to the disguisement and the interview with the girl in the bazaar, Mahbub Ali's gravity went from him. He laughed aloud and beat his hand on his thigh.

"*Shabash! Shabash!* Oh, well done, little one! What will the healer of turquoises say to this? Now, slowly, let us hear what befell afterwards – step by step, omitting nothing."

Step by step then, Kim told his adventures between coughs as the full-flavoured tobacco caught his lungs.

"I said," growled Mahbub Ali to himself, "I *said* it was the pony break-ing out to play polo. The fruit is ripe already – except that he must learn his distances and his pacings, and his rods and his compasses. Listen now. I have turned aside the Colonel's whip from thy skin, and that is no small service."

"True." Kim puffed serenely. "That is all true."

"But it is not to be thought that this running out and in is any way good."

"It was my holiday, Hajji. I was a slave for many weeks. Why should I not run away when the school was shut? Look, too, how I, living upon my friends or working for my bread, as I did with the Sikh, have saved the Colonel Sahib a great expense."

Mahbub's lips twitched under his well-pruned Muhammadan moustache.

"What are a few rupees" – the Pathan threw out his open hand care-lessly– "to the Colonel Sahib? He spends them for a purpose, not in any way for love of thee."

"That," said Kim slowly, "I knew a very long time ago."

"Who told?"

"The Colonel Sahib himself. Not in those many words, but plainly enough for one who is not altogether a mud-head. Yea, he told me in the *te-rain* when we went down to Lucknow."

"Be it so. Then I will tell thee more, Friend of all the World, though in the telling I lend thee my head."

"It was forfeit to me," said Kim, with deep relish, "in Umballa, when thou didst pick me up on the horse after the drummer-boy beat me."

"Speak a little plainer. All the world may tell lies save thou and I. For equally is thy life forfeit to me if I chose to raise my finger here."

"And this is known to me also," said Kim, readjusting the live charcoal-ball on the weed. "It is a very sure tie between us. Indeed, thy hold is surer even than mine; for who would miss a boy beaten to death, or, it may be, thrown into a well by the roadside? Many people here and in Simla and across the passes behind the Hills would, on the other hand, say: 'What has come to Mahbub Ali?' if he were found dead among his horses. Surely, too, the Colonel Sahib would make inquiries. But again" – Kim's face puckered with cunning – "he would not make overlong inquiry, lest people should ask, 'What has this Colonel Sahib to do with that horse-dealer?' But I – if I lived –"

"As thou wouldst surely die –"

"Maybe; but I say, *if* I lived, I, and I alone, would know that one had come by night, as a common thief perhaps, to Mahbub Ali's bulkhead in the serai, and there had slain him, either before or after that thief had made a full search into his saddlebags and between the soles of his slippers. Is that news to tell to the Colonel, or would he say to me – (I have not forgotten when he sent me back for a cigar-case that he had *not* left behind him) – 'What is Mahbub Ali to me'?"

Up went a gout of heavy smoke. There was a long pause: then Mahbub Ali spoke in admiration: "And with these things on thy mind, dost thou lie down and rise again among all the sahibs' little sons at the *madrissah* and meekly take instruction from thy teachers?"

"It is an order," said Kim blandly. "Who am I to dispute an order?"

"A most finished Son of Eblis," said Mahbub Ali. "But what is this tale of the thief and the search?"

"That which I saw," said Kim, "the night that my lama and I lay next thy place in the Kashmir Serai. The door was left unlocked, which I think is not thy custom, Mahbub. He came in as one assured that thou wouldst not soon return. My eye was against a knot-hole in the plank. He searched as it were for something – not a rug, not stirrups, nor a bridle, nor brass pots – something little and most carefully hid. Else why did he prick with an iron between the soles of thy slippers?"

"Ha!" Mahbub Ali smiled gently. "And seeing these things, what tale didst thou fashion to thyself, Well of the Truth?"

"None. I put my hand upon my amulet, which lies always next to my skin, and, remembering the pedigree of a white stallion that I had bitten out of a piece of Mussulmani bread, I went away to Umballa perceiving that a heavy trust was laid upon me. At that hour, had I chosen, thy head was forfeit. It needed only to say to that man, 'I have here a paper concerning a horse which I cannot read.' And then?" Kim peered at Mahbub under his eyebrows.

"Then thou wouldst have drunk water twice – perhaps thrice, afterwards. I do not think more than thrice," said Mahbub simply.

"It is true. I thought of that a little, but most I thought that I loved thee, Mahbub. Therefore I went to Umballa, as thou knowest, but (and this thou dost not know) I lay hid in the garden grass to see what Colonel Creighton Sahib might do upon reading the white stallion's pedigree."

"And what did he?" for Kim had bitten off the conversation.

"Dost *thou* give news for love, or dost thou sell it?" Kim asked.

"I sell and – I buy." Mahbub took a four-anna piece out of his belt and held it up.

"Eight!" said Kim, mechanically following the huckster instinct of the East.

Mahbub laughed, and put away the coin. "It is too easy to deal in that market, Friend of all the World. Tell me for love. Our lives lie in each other's hand."

"Very good. I saw the Jang-i-Lat Sahib [the Commander-in-Chief] come to a big dinner. I saw him in Creighton Sahib's office. I saw the two read the white stallion's pedigree. I heard the very orders given for the opening of a great war."

"Hah!" Mahbub nodded with deepest eyes afire. "The game is well played. That war is done now, and the evil, we hope, nipped before the flower – thanks to me – and thee. What didst thou later?"

"I made the news as it were a hook to catch me victual and honour among the villagers in a village whose priest drugged my lama. But I bore away the old man's purse, and the Brahmin found nothing. So next morning he was angry. Ho! Ho! And I also used the news when I fell into the hands of that white regiment with their Bull!"

"That was foolishness." Mahbub scowled. "News is not meant to be thrown about like dung-cakes, but used sparingly – like *bhang*."

"So I think now, and moreover, it did me no sort of good. But that was very long ago" – he made as to brush it all away with a thin brown hand – "and since then, and especially in the nights under the punkah at the *madrissah*, I have thought very greatly."

"Is it permitted to ask whither the Heaven-born's thought might have led?" said Mahbub, with an elaborate sarcasm, smoothing his scarlet beard.

"It is permitted," said Kim, and threw back the very tone. "They say at Nucklao that no sahib must tell a black man that he has made a fault."

Mahbub's hand shot into his bosom, for to call a Pathan a "black man" [*kala admi*] is a blood-insult. Then he remembered and laughed. "Speak, Sahib. Thy black man hears."

"But," said Kim, "I am *not* a sahib, and I say I made a fault to curse thee, Mahbub Ali, on that day at Umballa when I thought I was betrayed by a Pathan. I was senseless; for I was but newly caught, and I wished to kill that low-caste drummer-boy. I say now, Hajji, that it was well done; and I see my road all clear before me to a good service. I will stay in the *madrissah* till I am ripe."

"Well said. Especially are distances and numbers and the manner of using compasses to be learned in that game. One waits in the Hills above to show thee."

"I will learn their teaching upon a condition – that my time is given to me without question when the *madrissah* is shut. Ask that for me of the Colonel."

"But why not ask the Colonel in the sahibs' tongue?"

"The Colonel is the servant of the government. He is sent hither and yon at a word, and must consider his own advancement. (See how much I have already learned at Nucklao!) Moreover, the Colonel I know since three months only. I have known one Mahbub Ali for six years. So! To the *madrissah*

I will go. At the *madrissah* I will learn. In the *madrissah* I will be a sahib. But when the *madrissah* is shut, then must I be free and go among my people. Otherwise I die!"

"And who are thy people, Friend of all the World?"

"This great and beautiful land," said Kim, waving his paw round the little clay-walled room where the oil-lamp in its niche burned heavily through the tobacco smoke. "And, further, I would see my lama again. And, further, I need money."

"That is the need of every one," said Mahbub ruefully. "I will give thee eight annas, for much money is not picked out of horses' hooves, and it must suffice for many days. As to all the rest, I am well pleased, and no further talk is needed. Make haste to learn, and in three years, or it may be less, thou wilt be an aid – even to me."

"Have I been such a hindrance till now?" said Kim, with a boy's giggle.

"Do not give answers," Mahbub grunted. "Thou art my new horse-boy. Go and bed among my men. They are near the north end of the station, with the horses."

"They will beat me to the south end of the station if I come without authority."

Mahbub felt in his belt, wetted his thumb on a cake of Chinese ink, and dabbed the impression on a piece of soft native paper. From Balkh to Bombay men know that rough-ridged print with the old scar running diagonally across it.

"That is enough to show my headman. I come in the morning."

"By which road?" said Kim.

"By the road from the city. There is but one, and then we return to Creighton Sahib. I have saved thee a beating."

"Allah! What is a beating when the very head is loose on the shoulders?"

Kim slid out quietly into the night, walked half round the house, keeping close to the walls, and headed away from the station for a mile or so. Then, fetching a wide compass, he worked back at leisure, for he needed time to invent a story if any of Mahbub's retainers asked questions.

They were camped on a piece of waste ground beside the railway, and, being natives, had not, of course, unloaded the two trucks in which Mahbub's animals stood among a consignment of country-breds bought by the Bombay tram-company. The headman, a broken-down, consumptive-looking Muhammadan, promptly challenged Kim, but was pacified at sight of Mahbub's sign-manual.

"The Hajji has of his favour given me service," said Kim testily. "If this be doubted, wait till he comes in the morning. Meantime, a place by the fire."

Followed the usual aimless babble that every low-caste native must raise on every occasion. It died down, and Kim lay out behind the little knot of Mahbub's followers, almost under the wheels of a horse-truck, a borrowed blanket for covering. Now a bed among brickbats and ballast-refuse on a damp night, between overcrowded horses and unwashen Baltis, would not appeal to many white boys; but Kim was utterly happy. Change of scene, service, and surroundings were the breath of his little nostrils, and thinking of the neat white cots of St Xavier's all arow under the punkah gave him joy as keen as the repetition of the multiplication-table in English.

"I am very old," he thought sleepily. "Every month I become a year more old. I was very young, and a fool to boot, when I took Mahbub's message to Umballa. Even when I was with that white regiment I was very young and small and had no wisdom. But now I learn every day, and in three years the Colonel will take me out of the *madrissah* and let me go upon the Road with Mahbub hunting for horses' pedigrees, or maybe I shall go by myself; or maybe I shall find the lama and go with him. Yes; that is best. To walk again as a *chela* with my lama when he comes back to Benares." The thoughts came more slowly and disconnectedly. He was plunging into a beautiful dreamland when his ears caught a whisper, thin and sharp, above the monotonous babble round the fire. It came from behind the iron-skinned horse-truck.

"He is not here, then?"

"Where should he be but roystering in the city. Who looks for a rat in a frog-pond? Come away. He is not our man."

"He must not go back beyond the passes a second time. It is the order."

"Hire some woman to drug him. It is a few rupees only, and there is no evidence."

"Except the woman. It must be more certain; and remember the price upon his head."

"Ay, but the police have a long arm, and we are far from the border. If it were in Peshawar, now!"

"Yes – in Peshawar," the second voice sneered. "Peshawar, full of his blood-kin – full of bolt-holes and women behind whose clothes he will hide. Yes, Peshawar or Jehannum would suit us equally well."

"Then what is the plan?"

"O fool, have I not told it a hundred times? Wait till he comes to lie down, and then one sure shot. The trucks are between us and pursuit. We have but to run back over the lines and go our way. They will not see whence the shot came. Wait here at least till the dawn. What manner of *fakir* art thou, to shiver at a little watching?"

"Oho!" thought Kim, behind close-shut eyes. "Once again it is Mahbub. Indeed a white stallion's pedigree is not a good thing to peddle to sahibs! Or maybe Mahbub has been selling other news. Now what is to do, Kim? I know not where Mahbub houses, and if he comes here before the dawn they will shoot him. That would be no profit for thee, Kim. And this is not a matter for the police. That would be no profit for Mahbub; and" – he giggled almost aloud – "I do not remember any lesson at Nucklao which will help me. Allah! Here is Kim and yonder are they. First, then, Kim must wake and go away, so that they shall not suspect. A bad dream wakes a man – thus –"

He threw the blanket off his face, and raised himself suddenly with the terrible, bubbling, meaningless yell of the Asiatic roused by nightmare.

"Urr-urr-urr-urr! Ya-la-la-la-la! *Narain!* The *churel!* The *churel!*"

A *churel* is the peculiarly malignant ghost of a woman who has died in child-bed. She haunts lonely roads, her feet are turned backwards on the ankles, and she leads men to torment.

Louder rose Kim's quavering howl, till at last he leaped to his feet and staggered off sleepily, while the camp cursed him for waking them. Some twenty yards farther up the line he lay down again, taking care that the whisperers should hear his grunts and groans as he recomposed himself. After a few minutes he rolled towards the road and stole away into the thick darkness.

He paddled along swiftly till he came to a culvert, and dropped behind it, his chin on a level with the coping-stone. Here he could command all the night-traffic, himself unseen.

Two or three carts passed, jingling out to the suburbs; a coughing policeman and a hurrying foot-passenger or two who sang to keep off evil spirits.
Then rapped the shod feet of a horse.

"Ah! This is more like Mahbub," thought Kim, as the beast shied at the
little head above the culvert.

"Ohé, Mahbub Ali," he whispered, "have a care!"

The horse was reined back almost on its haunches, and forced towards
the culvert.

"Never again," said Mahbub, "will I take a shod horse for night-work.
They pick up all the bones and nails in the city." He stooped to lift its fore-
foot, and that brought his head within a foot of Kim's. "Down – keep down,"
he muttered. "The night is full of eyes."

"Two men wait thy coming behind the horse-trucks. They will shoot thee
at thy lying down, because there is a price on thy head. I heard, sleeping
near the horses."

"Didst thou see them?… Hold still, Sire of Devils!" This furiously to the
horse.

"No."

"Was one dressed belike as a *fakir?*"

"One said to the other, 'What manner of *fakir* art thou, to shiver at a
little watching?'"

"Good. Go back to the camp and lie down. I do not die tonight."

Mahbub wheeled his horse and vanished. Kim tore back down the ditch
till he reached a point opposite his second resting-place, slipped across the
road like a weasel, and re-coiled himself in the blanket.

"At least Mahbub knows," he thought contentedly. "And certainly he
spoke as one expecting it. I do not think those two men will profit by tonight's
watch."

An hour passed, and, with the best will in the world to keep awake all
night, he slept deeply. Now and again a night train roared along the metals
within twenty feet of him; but he had all the Oriental's indifference to mere
noise, and it did not even weave a dream through his slumber.

Mahbub was anything but asleep. It annoyed him vehemently that people
outside his tribe and unaffected by his casual amours should pursue him for
the life. His first and natural impulse was to cross the line lower down, work

up again, and, catching his wellwishers from behind, summarily slay them. Here, he reflected with sorrow, another branch of the government, totally unconnected with Colonel Creighton, might demand explanations which would be hard to supply; and he knew that south of the border a perfectly ridiculous fuss is made about a corpse or so. He had not been troubled in this way since he sent Kim to Umballa with the message, and hoped that suspicion had been finally diverted.

Then a most brilliant notion struck him.

"The English do eternally tell the truth," he said, "therefore we of this country are eternally made foolish. By Allah, I will tell the truth to an Englishman! Of what use is the government police if a poor Kabuli be robbed of his horses in their very trucks. This is as bad as Peshawar! I should lay a complaint at the station. Better still, some young sahib on the railway! They are zealous, and if they catch thieves it is remembered to their honour."

He tied up his horse outside the station, and strode on to the platform.

"Hullo, Mahbub Ali!" said a young assistant district traffic superintendent who was waiting to go down the line – a tall, tow-haired, horsy youth in dingy white linen. "What are you doing here? Selling weeds – eh?"

"No; I am not troubled for my horses. I come to look for Lutuf Ullah. I have a truck-load up the line. Could any one take them out without the railway's knowledge?"

"Shouldn't think so, Mahbub. You can claim against us if they do."

"I have seen two men crouching under the wheels of one of the trucks nearly all the night. *Fakirs* do not steal horses, so I gave them no more thought. I would find Lutuf Ullah, my partner."

"The deuce you did? And you didn't bother your head about it? 'Pon my word, it's just almost as well that I met you. What were they like, eh?"

"They were only *fakirs*. They will no more than take a little grain, perhaps, from one of the trucks. There are many up the line. The state will never miss the dole. I came here seeking for my partner, Lutuf Ullah –"

"Never mind your partner. Where are your horse-trucks?"

"A little to this side of the farthest place where they make lamps for the trains."

"The signal-box? Yes."

"And upon the rail nearest to the road upon the right-hand side – looking up the line thus. But as regards Lutuf Ullah – a tall man with a broken nose, and a Persian greyhound – Aie!"

The boy had hurried off to wake up a young and enthusiastic policeman; for, as he said, the railway had suffered much from depredations in the goods-yard. Mahbub Ali chuckled in his dyed beard.

"They will walk in their boots, making a noise, and then they will wonder why there are no *fakirs*. They are very clever boys – Barton Sahib and Young Sahib."

He waited idly for a few minutes, expecting to see them hurry up the line girt for action. A light engine slid through the station, and he caught a glimpse of young Barton in the cab.

"I did that child an injustice. He is not altogether a fool," said Mahbub Ali. "To take a fire-carriage for a thief is a new game!"

When Mahbub Ali came to his camp in the dawn, no one thought it worth while to tell him any news of the night. No one, at least, but one small horse-boy, newly advanced to the great man's service, whom Mahbub called to his tiny tent to assist in some packing.

"It is all known to me," whispered Kim, bending above saddlebags. "Two sahibs came up on a *te-rain*. I was running to and fro in the dark on this side of the trucks as the *te-rain* moved up and down slowly. They fell upon two men sitting under this truck – Hajji, what shall I do with this lump of tobacco? Wrap it in paper and put it under the salt-bag? Yes – and struck them down. But one man struck at a sahib with a *fakir's* buck's horn" (Kim meant the conjoined black-buck horns, which are a *fakir's* sole temporal weapon) – "the blood came. So the other sahib, first smiting his own man senseless, smote the stabber with a short gun which had rolled from the first man's hand. They all raged as though mad together."

Mahbub smiled with heavenly resignation. "No! That is not so much *dewanee* [madness, or a case for the civil court – the word can be punned upon both ways] as *nizamut* [a criminal case]. A gun, sayest thou? Ten good years in jail."

"Then they both lay still, but I think they were nearly dead when they were put on the *te-rain*. Their heads moved thus. And there is much blood on the line. Come and see?"

"They all raged as though mad together."

"I have seen blood before. Jail is the sure place – and assuredly they will give false names, and assuredly no man will find them for a long time. They were unfriends of mine. Thy fate and mine seem on one string. What a tale for the healer of pearls! Now swiftly with the saddle-bags and the cooking-platter. We will take out the horses and away to Simla."

Swiftly – as Orientals understand speed – with long explanations, with abuse and windy talk, carelessly, amid a hundred checks for little things forgotten, the untidy camp broke up and led the half-dozen stiff and fretful horses along the Kalka road in the fresh of the rain-swept dawn. Kim, regarded as Mahbub Ali's favourite by all who wished to stand well with the Pathan, was not called upon to work. They strolled on by the easiest of stages, halting every few hours at a wayside shelter. Very many sahibs travel along the Kalka road; and, as Mahbub Ali says, every young sahib must needs esteem himself a judge of a horse, and, though he be over head in debt to the moneylender, must make as if to buy. That was the reason that sahib after sahib, rolling along in a stage-carriage, would stop and open talk. Some would even descend from their vehicles and feel the horses' legs; asking inane questions, or, through sheer ignorance of the vernacular, grossly insulting the imperturbable trader.

"When first I dealt with sahibs, and that was when Colonel Soady Sahib was Governor of Fort Abazai and flooded the Commissioner's camping-ground for spite," Mahbub confided to Kim as the boy filled his pipe under a tree, "I did not know how greatly they were fools, and this made me wroth. As thus –" and he told Kim a tale of an expression, misused in all innocence, that doubled Kim up with mirth. "Now I see, however" – he exhaled smoke slowly – "that it is with them as with all men – in certain matters they are wise, and in others most foolish. Very foolish it is to use the wrong word to a stranger; for though the heart may be clean of offence, how is the stranger to know that? He is more like to search truth with a dagger."

"True. True talk," said Kim solemnly. "Fools speak of a cat when a woman is brought to bed, for instance. I have heard them."

"Therefore, in one situate as thou art, it particularly behoves thee to remember this with both kinds of faces. Among sahibs, never forgetting thou art a sahib; among the folk of Hind, always remembering thou art –" He paused, with a puzzled smile.

"What am I? Mussulman, Hindu, Jain, or Buddhist? That is a hard knot."

"Thou art beyond question an unbeliever, and therefore thou wilt be damned. So says my Law – or I think it does. But thou art also my Little Friend of all the World, and I love thee. So says my heart. This matter of creeds is like horseflesh. The wise man knows horses are good – that there is a profit to be made from all; and for myself – but that I am a good *Sunni* and hate the men of Tirah – I could believe the same of all the Faiths. Now manifestly a Kathiawar mare taken from the sands of her birthplace and removed to the west of Bengal founders – nor is even a Balkh stallion (and there are no better horses than those of Balkh, were they not so heavy in the shoulder) of any account in the great northern deserts beside the snow-camels I have seen. Therefore I say in my heart the Faiths are like the horses. Each has merit in its own country."

"But my lama said altogether a different thing."

"Oh, he is an old dreamer of dreams from Bhotiyal. My heart is a little angry, Friend of all the World, that thou shouldst see such worth in a man so little known."

"It is true, Hajji; but that worth do I see, and to him my heart is drawn."

"And his to thine, I hear. Hearts are like horses. They come and they go against bit or spur. Shout Gul Sher Khan yonder to drive in that bay stallion's pickets more firmly. We do not want a horse fight at every resting-stage, and the dun and the black will be locked in a little... Now hear me. Is it necessary to the comfort of thy heart to see that lama?"

"It is one part of my bond," said Kim. "If I do not see him, and if he is taken from me, I will go out of that *madrissah* in Nucklao and, and – once gone, who is to find me again?"

"It is true. Never was colt held on a lighter heel-rope than thou." Mahbub nodded his head.

"Do not be afraid." Kim spoke as though he could have evanished on the moment. "My lama has said that he will come to see me at the *madrissah –*"

"A beggar and his bowl in the presence of those young sa-'"

"Not all!" Kim cut in with a snort. "Their eyes are blued and their nails are blackened with low-caste blood, many of them. Sons of *mehteranees* – brothers-in-law to the *bhungi* [sweeper]."

KIM

We need not follow the rest of the pedigree; but Kim made his little point clearly and without heat, chewing a piece of sugarcane the while.

"Friend of all the World," said Mahbub, pushing over the pipe for the boy to clean, "I have met many men, women, and boys, and not a few sahibs. I have never in all my days met such an imp as thou art."

"And why? When I always tell thee the truth."

"Perhaps the very reason, for this is a world of danger to honest men." Mahbub Ali hauled himself off the ground, girt in his belt, and went over to the horses.

"Or sell it?"

There was that in the tone that made Mahbub halt and turn. "What new devilry?"

"Eight annas, and I will tell," said Kim, grinning. "It touches thy peace."

"O Shaitan!" Mahbub gave the money.

"Rememberest thou the little business of the thieves in the dark, down yonder at Umballa?"

"Seeing they sought my life, I have not altogether forgotten. Why?"

"Rememberest thou the Kashmir Serai?"

"I will twist thy ears in a moment – Sahib."

"No need – Pathan. Only, the second *fakir*, whom the sahibs beat senseless, was the man who came to search thy bulkhead at Lahore. I saw his face as they helped him on the engine. The very same man."

"Why didst thou not tell before?"

"Oh, he will go to jail, and be safe for some years. There is no need to tell more than is necessary at any one time. Besides, I did not then need money for sweetmeats."

"*Allah kerim!*" said Mahbub Ali. "Wilt thou some day sell my head for a few sweetmeats if the fit takes thee?"

Kim will remember till he dies that long, lazy journey from Umballa, through Kalka and the Pinjore Gardens near by, up to Simla. A sudden spate in the Gugger River swept down one horse (the most valuable, be sure), and nearly drowned Kim among the dancing boulders. Farther up the road the horses were stampeded by a government elephant, and being in high condition of grass food, it cost a day and a half to get them together again. Then

479

they met Sikandar Khan coming down with a few unsaleable screws – remnants of his string – and Mahbub, who has more of horse-coping in his little fingernail than Sikandar Khan in all his tents, must needs buy two of the worst, and that meant eight hours' laborious diplomacy and untold tobacco. But it was all pure delight – the wandering road, climbing, dipping, and sweeping about the growing spurs; the flush of the morning laid along the distant snows; the branched cacti, tier upon tier on the stony hillsides; the voices of a thousand water channels; the chatter of the monkeys; the solemn deodars, climbing one after another with down-drooped branches; the vista of the plains rolled out far beneath them; the incessant twanging of the tonga-horns and the wild rush of the led horses when a tonga swung round a curve; the halts for prayers (Mahbub was very religious in dry-washings and bellowings when time did not press); the evening conferences by the halting-places, when camels and bullocks chewed solemnly together and the stolid drivers told the news of the Road – all these things lifted Kim's heart to song within him.

"But, when the singing and dancing is done," said Mahbub Ali, "comes the Colonel Sahib's, and that is not so sweet."

"A fair land – a most beautiful land is this of Hind – and the land of the Five Rivers is fairer than all," Kim half chanted. "Into it I will go again if Mahbub Ali or the Colonel lift hand or foot against me. Once gone, who shall find me? Look, Hajji, is yonder the city of Simla? Allah, what a city!"

"My father's brother, and he was an old man when Mackerson Sahib's well was new at Peshawar, could recall when there were but two houses in it."

He led the horses below the main road into the lower Simla bazaar – the crowded rabbit-warren that climbs up from the valley to the Town Hall at an angle of forty-five. A man who knows his way there can defy all the police of India's summer capital, so cunningly does veranda communicate with veranda, alley-way with alley-way, and bolt-hole with bolt-hole. Here live those who minister to the wants of the glad city – *jhampanis* who pull the pretty ladies' rickshaws by night and gamble till the dawn; grocers, oil-sellers, curio-vendors, firewood-dealers, priests, pickpockets, and native employees of the government. Here are discussed by courtesans the things which are supposed to be profoundest secrets of the India Council; and here gather all the sub-sub-agents of half the native states. Here, too, Mahbub Ali rented a room, much more securely locked than his bulkhead at Lahore, in the house of a Muhammadan cattle-dealer. It was a place of miracles, too, for there went in at twilight a Muhammadan horse-boy, and there came out an hour later a Eurasian lad – the Lucknow girl's dye was of the best – in badly fitting shop-clothes.

"I have spoken with Creighton Sahib," quoth Mahbub Ali, "and a second time has the Hand of Friendship averted the Whip of Calamity. He says that thou hast altogether wasted sixty days upon the Road, and it is too late, therefore, to send thee to any hill-school."

"I have said that my holidays are my own. I do not go to school twice over. That is one part of my bond."

"The Colonel Sahib is not yet aware of that contract. Thou art to lodge in Lurgan Sahib's house till it is time to go again to Nucklao."

"I had sooner lodge with thee, Mahbub."

"Thou dost not know the honour. Lurgan Sahib himself asked for thee. Thou wilt go up the hill and along the road atop, and there thou must forget for a while that thou hast ever seen or spoken to me, Mahbub Ali, who sells horses to Creighton Sahib, whom thou dost not know. Remember this order."

Kim nodded. "Good," said he, "and who is Lurgan Sahib? Nay" – he caught Mahbub's sword-keen glance – "indeed I have never heard his name. Is he by chance" – he lowered his voice – "one of us?"

"What talk is this of *us*; Sahib?" Mahbub Ali returned, in the tone he used towards Europeans. "I am a Pathan; thou art a sahib and the son of a sahib. Lurgan Sahib has a shop among the European shops. All Simla knows it. Ask there… and, Friend of all the World, he is one to be obeyed to the last wink of his eyelashes. Men say he does magic, but that should not touch thee. Go up the hill and ask. Here begins the Great Game."

Chapter 9

S'doaks was son of Yelth the wise –
    Chief of the Raven clan.
Itswoot the Bear had him in care
    To make him a medicine-man.

He was quick and quicker to learn –
    Bold and bolder to dare:
He danced the dread Kloo-Kwallie Dance
    To tickle Itswoot the Bear!

                           Oregon Legend

Kim flung himself wholeheartedly upon the next turn of the wheel. He would be a sahib again for a while. In that idea, so soon as he had reached the broad road under Simla Town Hall, he cast about for one to impress. A Hindu child, some ten years old, squatted under a lamppost.

"Where is Mr Lurgan's house?" demanded Kim.

"I do not understand English," was the answer, and Kim shifted his speech accordingly.

"I will show."

Together they set off through the mysterious dusk, full of the noises of a city below the hillside, and the breath of a cool wind in deodar-crowned Jakko, shouldering the stars. The house lights, scattered on every level, made, as it were, a double firmament. Some were fixed, others belonged to the rickshaws of the careless, open-spoken English folk, going out to dinner.

"It is here," said Kim's guide, and halted in a veranda flush with the main road. No door stayed them, but a curtain of beaded reeds that split up the lamplight beyond.

"He is come," said the boy, in a voice little louder than a sigh, and vanished. Kim felt sure that the boy had been posted to guide him from the first, but, putting a bold face on it, parted the curtain. A black-bearded man, with a green shade over his eyes, sat at a table, and, one by one, with short, white hands, picked up globules of light from a tray before him, threaded them on a glancing silken string, and hummed to himself the while. Kim was conscious that beyond the circle of light the room was full of things that smelt like all the temples of all the East. A whiff of musk, a puff of sandal-wood, and a breath of sickly jessamine oil caught his opened nostrils.

"I am here," said Kim at last, speaking in the vernacular: the smells made him forget that he was to be a sahib.

"Seventy-nine, eighty, eighty-one," the man counted to himself, stringing pearl after pearl so quickly that Kim could scarcely follow his fingers. He slid off the green shade and looked fixedly at Kim for a full half-minute. The pupils of the eye dilated and closed to pin-pricks, as if at will. There was a *fakir* by the Taksali Gate who had just this gift and made money by it, especially when cursing silly women. Kim stared with interest. His disreputable friend could further twitch his ears, almost like a goat, and Kim was disappointed that this new man could not imitate him.

"Do not be afraid," said Lurgan Sahib suddenly.

"Why should I fear?"

"Thou wilt sleep here tonight, and stay with me till it is time to go again to Nucklao. It is an order."

"It is an order," Kim repeated. "But where shall I sleep?"

"Here, in this room." Lurgan Sahib waved his hand towards the darkness behind him.

"So be it," said Kim composedly. "Now?"

He nodded and held the lamp above his head. As the light swept them, there leaped out from the walls a collection of Tibetan devil-dance masks, hanging above the fiend-embroidered draperies of those ghastly functions – horned masks, scowling masks, and masks of idiotic terror. In a corner, a Japanese warrior, mailed and plumed, menaced him with a halberd, and a score of lances and *khandas* and *kuttars* gave back the unsteady gleam. But what interested Kim more than all these things – he had seen devil-dance masks at the Lahore Museum – was a glimpse of the soft-eyed Hindu child who had left him in the doorway, sitting cross-legged under the table of pearls with a little smile on his scarlet lips.

"I think that Lurgan Sahib wishes to make me afraid. And I am sure that that devil's brat below the table wishes to see me afraid. This place," he said aloud, "is like a Wonder House. Where is my bed?"

Lurgan Sahib pointed to a native quilt in a corner by the loathsome masks, picked up the lamp, and left the room black.

"Was that Lurgan Sahib?" Kim asked as he cuddled down. No answer. He could hear the Hindu boy breathing, however, and, guided by the sound, crawled across the floor, and cuffed into the darkness, crying: "Give answer, devil! Is this the way to lie to a sahib?"

From the darkness he fancied he could hear the echo of a chuckle. It could not be his soft-fleshed companion, because he was weeping. So Kim lifted up his voice and called aloud: "Lurgan Sahib! O Lurgan Sahib! Is it an order that thy servant does not speak to me?"

"It is an order." The voice came from behind him and he started.

"Very good. But remember," he muttered, as he re-sought the quilt, "I will beat thee in the morning. I do not love Hindus."

That was no cheerful night; the room being over-full of voices and music. Kim was waked twice by some one calling his name. The second time he set out in search, and ended by bruising his nose against a box that certainly spoke with a human tongue, but in no sort of human accent. It seemed to end in a tin trumpet and to be joined by wires to a smaller box on the floor – so far, at least, as he could judge by touch. And the voice, very hard and whirring, came out of the trumpet. Kim rubbed his nose and grew furious, thinking, as usual, in Hindi.

"This with a beggar from the bazaar might be good, but – I am a sahib and the son of a sahib and, which is twice as much more beside, a student of Nucklao. Yess" (here he turned to English), "a boy of St Xavier's. Damn Mr Lurgan's eyes! – It is some sort of machinery like a sewing-machine. Oh, it is a *great* cheek of him – we are not frightened that way at Lucknow – No!" Then in Hindi: "But what does *he* gain? He is only a trader – I am in his shop. But Creighton Sahib is a colonel – and I think Creighton Sahib gave orders that it should be done. *How* I will beat that Hindu in the morning! What is this?"

The trumpet-box was pouring out a string of the most elaborate abuse that even Kim had ever heard, in a high uninterested voice, that for a moment lifted the short hairs of his neck. When the vile thing drew breath, Kim was reassured by the soft, sewing-machine-like whirr.

"*Chûp!* [Be still]" he cried, and again he heard a chuckle that decided him. "*Chûp* – or I break your head."

The box took no heed. Kim wrenched at the tin trumpet and something lifted with a click. He had evidently raised a lid. If there were a devil inside, now was its time, for – he sniffed – thus did the sewing-machines of the bazaar smell. He would clean that *shaitan*. He slipped off his jacket, and plunged it into the box's mouth. Something long and round bent under the pressure, there was a whirr and the voice stopped – as voices must if you ram a thrice-doubled coat on to the wax cylinder and into the works of an expensive phonograph. Kim finished his slumbers with a serene mind.

In the morning he was aware of Lurgan Sahib looking down on him.

"Oah!" said Kim, firmly resolved to cling to his sahib-dom. "There was a box in the night that gave me bad talk. So I stopped it. Was it your box?"

The man held out his hand.

"Shake hands, O'Hara," he said. "Yes, it was my box. I keep such things because my friends the rajahs like them. That one is broken, but it was cheap at the price. Yes, my friends, the kings, are very fond of toys – and so am I sometimes."

Kim looked him over out of the corners of his eyes. He was a sahib in that he wore sahib's clothes; the accent of his Urdu, the intonation of his English, showed that he was anything but a sahib. He seemed to understand what moved in Kim's mind ere the boy opened his mouth, and he took no pains to explain himself as did Father Victor or the Lucknow masters. Sweetest of all – he treated Kim as an equal on the Asiatic side.

"I am sorry you cannot beat my boy this morning. He says he will kill you with a knife or poison. He is jealous, so I have put him in the corner and I shall not speak to him today. He has just tried to kill me. You must help me with the breakfast. He is almost too jealous to trust, just now."

Now a genuine imported sahib from England would have made a great to-do over this tale. Lurgan Sahib stated it as simply as Mahbub Ali was used to record his little affairs in the north.

The back veranda of the shop was built out over the sheer hillside, and they looked down into their neighbours' chimney-pots, as is the custom of Simla. But even more than the purely Persian meal cooked by Lurgan Sahib with his own hands, the shop fascinated Kim. The Lahore Museum was larger, but here were more wonders – ghost-daggers and prayer-wheels from Tibet; turquoise and raw amber necklaces; green jade bangles; curiously packed incense-sticks in jars crusted over with raw garnets; the devil-masks of overnight and a wall full of peacock-blue draperies; gilt figures of Buddha, and little portable lacquer altars; Russian samovars with turquoises on the lid; egg-shell china sets in quaint octagonal cane boxes; yellow ivory cruci-fixes – from Japan of all places in the world, so Lurgan Sahib said; carpets in dusty bales, smelling atrociously, pushed back behind torn and rotten screens of geometrical work; Persian water-jugs for the hands after meals; dull copper incense-burners neither Chinese nor Persian, with friezes of fantastic devils running round them; tarnished silver belts that knotted like raw hide; hairpins of jade, ivory, and plasma; arms of all sorts and kinds, and a thousand other oddments were cased, or piled, or merely thrown into the room, leaving a clear space only round the rickety deal table, where Lurgan Sahib worked.

"Those things are nothing," said his host, following Kim's glance. "I buy them because they are pretty, and sometimes I sell – if I like the buyer's look. My work is on the table – some of it."

It blazed in the morning light – all red and blue and green flashes, picked out with the vicious blue-white spurt of a diamond here and there. Kim opened his eyes.

"Oh, they are quite well, those stones. It will not hurt them to take the sun. Besides, they are cheap. But with sick stones it is very different." He piled Kim's plate anew. "There is no one but *me* can doctor a sick pearl and re-blue turquoises. I grant you opals – any fool can cure an opal – but for a sick pearl there is only me. Suppose I were to die! Then there would be no one... Oh no! *You* cannot do anything with jewels. It will be quite enough if you understand a little about the turquoise – some day."

He moved to the end of the veranda to refill the heavy, porous clay water-jug from the filter.

"Do you want drink?"

Kim nodded. Lurgan Sahib, fifteen feet off, laid one hand on the jar. Next instant, it stood at Kim's elbow, full to within half an inch of the brim – the white cloth only showing, by a small wrinkle, where it had slid into place.

"Wah!" said Kim in most utter amazement. "That is magic." Lurgan Sahib's smile showed that the compliment had gone home.

"Throw it back."

"It will break."

"I say, throw it back."

Kim pitched it at random. It fell short and crashed into fifty pieces, while the water dripped through the rough veranda boarding.

"I said it would break."

"All one. Look at it. Look at the largest piece."

That lay with a sparkle of water in its curve, as it were a star on the floor. Kim looked intently. Lurgan Sahib laid one hand gently on the nape of his neck, stroked it twice or thrice, and whispered: "Look! It shall come to life again, piece by piece. First the big piece shall join itself to two others on the right and the left – on the right and the left. Look!"

To save his life, Kim could not have turned his head. The light touch held him as in a vice, and his blood tingled pleasantly through him. There was one large piece of the jar where there had been three, and above them the shadowy outline of the entire vessel. He could see the veranda through it, but it was thickening and darkening with each beat of his pulse. Yet the jar – how slowly the thoughts came! – the jar had been smashed before his eyes. Another wave of prickling fire raced down his neck, as Lurgan Sahib moved his hand.

"Look! It is coming into shape," said Lurgan Sahib.

So far Kim had been thinking in Hindi, but a tremor came on him, and with an effort like that of a swimmer before sharks, who hurls himself half out of the water, his mind leaped up from a darkness that was swallowing it and took refuge in – the multiplication-table in English!

"Look! It is coming into shape," whispered Lurgan Sahib.

The jar had been smashed – yess, smashed – not the native word, he would not think of that – but smashed – into fifty pieces, and twice three was six, and thrice three was nine, and four times three was twelve. He clung desperately to the repetition. The shadow outline of the jar cleared like a mist after rubbing eyes. There were the broken shards; there was the spilt water drying in the sun, and through the cracks of the veranda showed, all ribbed, the white house wall below – and thrice twelve was thirty-six!

"Look! Is it coming into shape?" asked Lurgan Sahib.

"But it *is* smashed – smashed," he gasped – Lurgan Sahib had been muttering softly for the last half-minute. Kim wrenched his head aside. "Look! *Dekho!* It is there as it was there."

"It is there as it was there," said Lurgan, watching Kim closely while the boy rubbed his neck. "But you are the first of a many who has ever seen it so." He wiped his broad forehead.

"Was that more magic?" Kim asked suspiciously. The tingle had gone from his veins; he felt unusually wide awake.

"No, that was not magic. It was only to see if there was – a flaw in a jewel. Sometimes very fine jewels will fly all to pieces if a man holds them in his hand, and knows the proper way. That is why one must be careful before one sets them. Tell me, did you see the shape of the pot?"

"For a little time. It began to grow like a flower from the ground."

"And then what did you do? I mean, how did you think?"

"Oah! I knew it was broken, and so, I think, that was what I thought – and it *was* broken."

"Hm! Has any one ever done that same sort of magic to you before?"

"If it was," said Kim, "do you think I should let it again? I should run away."

"And now you are not afraid – eh?"

"Not now."

Lurgan Sahib looked at him more closely than ever. "I shall ask Mahbub Ali – not now, but some days later," he muttered. "I am pleased with you – yes; and I am pleased with you – no. You are the first that ever saved himself. I wish I knew what it was that… But you are right. You should not tell that – not even to me."

He turned into the dusky gloom of the shop, and sat down at the table, rubbing his hands softly. A small, husky sob came from behind a pile of carpets. It was the Hindu child obediently facing towards the wall. His thin shoulders worked with grief.

"Ah! He is jealous, so jealous. I wonder if he will try to poison me again in my breakfast, and make me cook it twice."

"*Kubbee – kubbee nahin*" [Never – never. No!], came the broken answer.

"And whether he will kill this other boy?"

"*Kubbee – kubbee nahin.*"

"What do *you* think he will do?" He turned suddenly on Kim.

"Oah! I do not know. Let him go, perhaps. Why did he want to poison you?"

"Because he is so fond of me. Suppose you were fond of some one, and you saw some one come, and the man you were fond of was more pleased with him than he was with you, what would you do?"

Kim thought. Lurgan repeated the sentence slowly in the vernacular.

"I should not poison that man," said Kim reflectively, "but I should beat that boy – *if* that boy was fond of my man. But first I would ask that boy if it were true."

"Ah! He thinks every one must be fond of me."

"Then I think he is a fool."

"Hearest thou?" said Lurgan Sahib to the shaking shoulders. "The sahib's son thinks thou art a little fool. Come out, and next time thy heart is troubled, do not try white arsenic quite so openly. Surely the Devil Dasim was lord of our tablecloth that day! It might have made me ill, child, and then a stranger would have guarded the jewels. Come!"

The child, heavy-eyed with much weeping, crept out from behind the bale and flung himself passionately at Lurgan Sahib's feet, with an extravagance of remorse that impressed even Kim.

"I will look into the ink-pools – I will faithfully guard the jewels! Oh, my Father and my Mother, send *him* away!" He indicated Kim with a backward jerk of his bare heel.

"Not yet – not yet. In a little while he will go away again. But now he is at school – at a new *madrissah* – and thou shalt be his teacher. Play the Play of the Jewels against him. I will keep tally."

The child dried his tears at once, and dashed to the back of the shop, whence he returned with a copper tray.

"Give me!" he said to Lurgan Sahib. "Let them come from thy hand, for he may say that I knew them before."

"Gently – gently," the man replied, and from a drawer under the table dealt a half-handful of clattering trifles into the tray.

"Now," said the child, waving an old newspaper. "Look on them as long as thou wilt, stranger. Count and, if need be, handle. One look is enough for *me*." He turned his back proudly.

"But what is the game?"

"When thou hast counted and handled and art sure thou canst remember them all, I cover them with this paper, and thou must tell over the tally to Lurgan Sahib. *I* will write mine."

"Oah!" The instinct of competition waked in his breast. He bent over the tray. There were but fifteen stones on it. "That is easy," he said after a minute. The child slipped the paper over the winking jewels and scribbled in a native account-book.

"There are under that paper five blue stones – one big, one smaller, and three small," said Kim, all in haste. "There are four green stones, and one with a hole in it; there is one yellow stone that I can see through, and one like a pipe-stem. There are two red stones, and – and – I made the count fifteen, but two I have forgotten. No! Give me time. One was of ivory, little and brownish; and – and – give me time…"

"One – two" – Lurgan Sahib counted him out up to ten. Kim shook his head.

"Hear my count!" the child burst in, trilling with laughter. "First, are two flawed sapphires – one of two ruttees and one of four as I should judge. The four-ruttee sapphire is chipped at the edge. There is one Turkestan turquoise, plain with black veins, and there are two inscribed – one with a Name of God in gilt, and the other being cracked across, for it came out of an old ring, I cannot read. We have now all five blue stones. Four flawed emeralds there are, but one is drilled in two places, and one is a little carven –"

"Their weights?" said Lurgan Sahib impassively. "Three – five – five – and four ruttees as I judge it. There is one piece of old greenish pipe amber, and a cut topaz from Europe. There is one ruby of Burma, of two ruttees, without a flaw, and there is a balas-ruby, flawed, of two ruttees. There is a carved ivory from China representing a rat sucking an egg; and there is last – ah ha! – a ball of crystal as big as a bean set on a gold leaf."

He clapped his hands at the close.

"He is thy master," said Lurgan Sahib, smiling.

"Huh! He knew the names of the stones," said Kim, flushing. "Try again! With common things such as he and I both know."

They heaped the tray again with odds and ends gathered from the shop, and even the kitchen, and every time the child won, till Kim marvelled.

"Bind my eyes – let me feel once with my fingers, and even *then* I will leave thee open-eyed behind," he challenged.

Kim stamped with vexation when the lad made his boast good.

"If it were men – or horses," he said, "I could do better. This playing with tweezers and knives and scissors is too little."

"Learn first – teach later," said Lurgan Sahib. "Is he thy master?"

"Truly. But how is it done?"

"By doing it many times over till it is done perfectly – for it is worth doing."

The Hindu boy, in highest feather, actually patted Kim on the back.

"Do not despair," he said. "I myself will teach thee."

"And I will see that thou art well taught," said Lurgan Sahib, still speaking in the vernacular, "for except my boy here – it was foolish of him to buy so much white arsenic when, if he had asked, I could have given it – except my boy here I have not in a long time met with one better worth teaching. And there are ten days more ere thou canst return to Nucklao where they teach nothing at the long price. We shall, I think, be friends."

They were a most mad ten days, but Kim enjoyed himself too much to reflect on their craziness. In the morning they played the Jewel Game – sometimes with veritable stones, sometimes with piles of swords and daggers, sometimes with photographs of natives. Through the afternoons he and the Hindu boy would mount guard in the shop, sitting dumb behind a carpet-bale or a screen and watching Mr Lurgan's many and very curious visitors. There were small rajahs, escorts coughing in the veranda, who came to buy curiosities – such as phonographs and mechanical toys. There were ladies in search of necklaces, and men, it seemed to Kim – but his mind may have been vitiated by early training – in search of the ladies; natives from independent and feudatory courts whose ostensible business was the repair of broken necklaces – rivers of light poured out upon the table – but whose true end seemed to be to raise money for angry maharanees or young rajahs. There were babus to whom Lurgan Sahib talked with austerity and authority, but at the end of each interview he gave them money in coined silver and currency and currency notes. There were occasional gatherings of long-coated theatrical natives who discussed metaphysics in English and Bengali, to Mr Lurgan's great edification. He was always interested in religions. At the end of the day, Kim and the Hindu boy – whose name varied at Lurgan's pleasure – were expected to give a detailed account of all that they had seen and heard – their view of each man's character, as shown in his face, talk, and manner, and their notions of his real errand. After dinner, Lurgan Sahib's fancy turned more to what might be called dressing-up, in which game he took a most informing interest. He could paint faces to a marvel; with a brush dab here and a line there changing them past recognition. The shop was full of all manner of dresses and turbans, and Kim was apparelled variously as a young Muhammadan of good family, an oilman, and once – which was a joyous evening – as the son of an Oudh landholder in the fullest of full dress. Lurgan Sahib had a hawk's eye to detect the least flaw in the make-up; and lying on a worn teak-wood couch, would explain by the half-hour together how such and such a caste talked, or walked, or coughed, or spat, or sneezed, and, since "hows" matter little in this world, the "why" of everything. The Hindu child played this game clumsily. That little mind, keen as an icicle where tally of jewels was concerned, could not temper itself to enter another's soul; but a demon in Kim woke up and sang with joy as he put on the changing dresses, and changed speech and gesture therewith.

Carried away by enthusiasm, he volunteered to show Lurgan Sahib one evening how the disciples of a certain caste of *fakir*, old Lahore acquaintances, begged doles by the roadside; and what sort of language he would use to an Englishman, to a Punjabi farmer going to a fair, and to a woman without a veil. Lurgan Sahib laughed immensely, and begged Kim to stay as he was, immobile for half an hour – cross-legged, ash-smeared, and wild-eyed in the back room. At the end of that time entered a hulking, obese babu whose stockinged legs shook with fat, and Kim opened on him with a shower of wayside chaff. Lurgan Sahib – this annoyed Kim – watched the babu and not the play.

"I think," said the babu heavily, lighting a cigarette, "I am of opeenion that it is most extra-ordinary and effeecient performance. Except that you had told me I should have opined that – that – that you were pulling my legs. How soon can he become approximately effeecient chain-man? Because *then* I shall indent for him."

"That is what he must learn at Lucknow."

"Then order him to be jolly-dam'-quick. Goodnight, Lurgan." The babu swung out with the gait of a bogged cow.

When they were telling over the day's list of visitors, Lurgan Sahib asked Kim who he thought the man might be.

"God knows!" said Kim cheerily. The tone might almost have deceived Mahbub Ali, but it failed entirely with the healer of sick pearls.

"That is true. God, He knows; but I wish to know what you think."

Kim glanced sideways at his companion, whose eye had a way of compelling truth.

"I – I think he will want me when I come from the school, but" – confidentially, as Lurgan Sahib nodded approval – "I do not understand how *he* can wear many dresses and talk many tongues."

"Thou wilt understand many things later. He is a writer of tales for a certain colonel. His honour is great only in Simla, and it is noticeable that he has no name, but only a number and a letter – that is a custom among us."

"And is there a price upon his head too – as upon Mah – all the others?"

"Not yet; but if a boy rose up who is now sitting here and went – look, the door is open! – as far as a certain house with a red-painted veranda, behind that which was the old theatre in the Lower Bazaar, and whispered through the shutters: 'Hurree Chunder Mookerjee bore the bad news of last month', that boy might take away a belt full of rupees."

"How many?" said Kim promptly.

"Five hundred – a thousand – as many as he might ask for."

"Good. And for how long might such a boy live after the news was told?" He smiled merrily at Lurgan Sahib's very beard.

"Ah! That is to be well thought of. Perhaps if he were very clever, he might live out the day – but not the night. By no means the night."

"Then what is the babu's pay if so much is put upon his head?"

"Eighty – perhaps a hundred – perhaps a hundred and fifty rupees; but the pay is the least part of the work. From time to time, God causes men to be born – and thou art one of them – who have a lust to go abroad at the risk of their lives and discover news – today it may be of far-off things, tomorrow of some hidden mountain, and the next day of some nearby men who have done a foolishness against the state. These souls are very few; and of these few, not more than ten are of the best. Among these ten I count the babu, and that is curious. How great, therefore, and desirable must be a business that brazens the heart of a Bengali!"

"True. But the days go slowly for me. I am yet a boy, and it is only within two months I learned to write Angrezi. Even now I cannot read it well. And there are yet years and years and long years before I can be even a chain-man."

"Have patience, Friend of all the World" – Kim started at the title. "Would I had a few of the years that so irk thee. I have proved thee in several small ways. This will not be forgotten when I make my report to the Colonel Sahib." Then, changing suddenly into English with a deep laugh:

"By Jove! O'Hara, I think there is a great deal in you; but you must not become proud and you must not talk. You must go back to Lucknow and be a good little boy and mind your book, as the English say, and perhaps, next holidays if you care, you can come back to me!" Kim's face fell. "Oh, I mean *if* you like. I know where you want to go."

Four days later a seat was booked for Kim and his small trunk at the rear of a Kalka tonga. His companion was the whale-like babu, who, with a fringed shawl wrapped round his head, and his fat openwork-stockinged left leg tucked under him, shivered and grunted in the morning chill.

"How comes it that this man is one of *us*?" thought Kim, considering the jelly back as they jolted down the road; and the reflection threw him into most pleasant daydreams. Lurgan Sahib had given him five rupees – a splendid sum – as well as the assurance of his protection if he worked.

Unlike Mahbub, Lurgan Sahib had spoken most explicitly of the reward that would follow obedience, and Kim was content. If only, like the babu, he could enjoy the dignity of a letter and a number – and a price upon his head! Some day he would be all that and more. Some day he might be almost as great as Mahbub Ali! The house-tops of his search should be half India; he would follow kings and ministers, as in the old days he had followed *vakils* and lawyers' touts across Lahore city for Mahbub Ali's sake. Meantime, there was the present, and not at all unpleasant, fact of St Xavier's immediately before him. There would be new boys to condescend to, and there would be tales of holiday adventures to hear. Young Martin, son of the tea-planter at Manipur, had boasted that he would go to war, with a rifle, against the head-hunters. That might be, but it was certain young Martin had not been blown half across the forecourt of a Patiala palace by an explosion of fireworks; nor had he... Kim fell to telling himself the story of his own adventures through the last three months. He could paralyse St Xavier's – even the biggest boys who shaved – with the recital, were that permitted. But it was, of course, out of the question. There would be a price upon his head in good time, as Lurgan Sahib had assured him; and if he talked foolishly now, not only would that price never be set, but Colonel Creighton would cast him off – and he would be left to the wrath of Lurgan Sahib and Mahbub Ali – for the short space of life that would remain to him.

"So I should lose Delhi for the sake of a fish," was his proverbial philosophy. It behoved him to forget his holidays (there would always remain the fun of inventing imaginary adventures) and, as Lurgan Sahib had said, to work.

Of all the boys hurrying back to St Xavier's, from Sukkur in the sands to Galle beneath the palms, none was so filled with virtue as Kimball O'Hara, jiggeting down to Umballa behind Hurree Chunder Mookerjee, whose name on the books of one section of the Ethnological Survey was R17.

And if additional spur were needed, the babu supplied it. After a huge meal at Kalka, he spoke uninterruptedly. Was Kim going to school? Then he, an MA of Calcutta University, would explain the advantages of education. There were marks to be gained by due attention to Latin and Wordsworth's *Excursion* (all this was Greek to Kim). French, too, was vital, and the best was to be picked up in Chandernagore, a few miles from Calcutta. Also a man might go far, as he himself had done, by strict attention to plays called *Lear* and *Julius Caesar*, both much in demand by examiners. *Lear* was not so full of historical allusions as *Julius Caesar*; the book cost four annas, but could be bought second-hand in Bow Bazaar for two. Still more important than Wordsworth, or the eminent authors, Burke and Hare, was the art and science of mensuration. A boy who had passed his examination in these branches – for which, by the way, there were no cram books – could, by merely marching over a country with a compass and a level and a straight eye, carry away a picture of that country which might be sold for large sums in coined silver. But as it was occasionally inexpedient to carry about measuring-chains, a boy would do well to know the precise length of his own foot-pace, so that when he was deprived of what Hurree Chunder called "adventitious aids" he might still tread his distances. To keep count of thousands of paces, Hurree Chunder's experience had shown him nothing more valuable than a rosary of eighty-one or a hundred and eight beads, for "it was divisible and sub-divisible into many multiples and submultiples". Through the volleying drifts of English, Kim caught the general trend of the talk, and it interested him very much. Here was a new craft that a man could tuck away in his head; and by the look of the large wide world unfolding itself before him, it seemed that the more a man knew the better for him.

Said the babu when he had talked for an hour and a half, "I hope some day to enjoy your offeecial acquaintance. *Ad interim*, if I may be pardoned that expression, I shall give you this betel-box, which is highly valuable article and cost me two rupees only four years ago." It was a cheap, heart-shaped thing with three compartments for carrying the eternal betel-nut, lime and *pan*-leaf; but it was filled with little tabloid-bottles. "That is reward of merit for your performance in character of that holy man. You see, you are so young you think you will last for ever and not take care of your body. It is great nuisance to go sick in the middle of business. I am fond of drugs myself, and they are handy to cure poor people too. These are good departmental drugs – quinine and so on. I give it you for souvenir. Now goodbye. I have urgent private business here by the roadside."

He slipped out noiselessly as a cat, on the Umballa road, hailed a passing cart and jingled away, while Kim, tongue-tied, twiddled the brass betel-box in his hands.

The record of a boy's education interests few save his parents, and, as you know, Kim was an orphan. It is written in the books of St Xavier's in Parti-bus that a report of Kim's progress was forwarded at the end of each term to Colonel Creighton and to Father Victor, from whose hands duly came the money for his schooling. It is further recorded in the same books that he showed a great aptitude for mathematical studies as well as map-making, and carried away a prize *(The Life of Lord Lawrence*, tree-calf, two vols, nine rupees, eight annas) for proficiency therein; and the same term played in St Xavier's eleven against the Alighur Muhammadan College, his age being fourteen years and ten months. He was also re-vaccinated (from which we may assume that there had been another epidemic of smallpox at Lucknow) about the same time. Pencil notes on the edge of an old muster-roll record that he was punished several times for "conversing with improper persons", and it seems that he was once sentenced to heavy pains for "absenting himself for a day in the company of a street beggar". That was when he got over the gate and pleaded with the lama through a whole day down the banks of the Gumti to accompany him on the Road next holidays – for one month – for a little week; and the lama set his face as a flint against it, averring that the time had not yet come. Kim's business, said the old man as they ate cakes together, was to get all the wisdom of the sahibs and then he would see. The Hand of Friendship must in some way have averted the Whip of Calamity, for six weeks later Kim seems to have passed an examination in elementary surveying "with great credit", his age being fifteen years and eight months. From this date the record is silent. His name does not appear in the year's batch of those who entered for the subordinate Survey of India, but against it stand the words "removed on appointment".

Several times in those three years, cast up at the Temple of the Tirthankars in Benares the lama, a little thinner and a shade yellower, if that were possible, but gentle and untainted as ever. Sometimes it was from the south that he came – from south of Tuticorin, whence the wonderful fire-boats go to Ceylon where are priests who know Pali; sometimes it was from the wet green west and the thousand cotton-factory chimneys that ring Bombay; and once from the north, where he had doubled back eight hundred miles to talk for a day with the Keeper of the Images in the Wonder House. He would stride to his cell in the cool, cut marble – the priests of the Temple were good to the old man – wash off the dust of travel, make prayer, and depart for Lucknow, well accustomed now to the ways of the rail, in a third-class carriage. Returning, it was noticeable, as his friend the Seeker pointed out to the head-priest, that he ceased for a while to mourn the loss of his River, or to draw wondrous pictures of the Wheel of Life, but preferred to talk of the beauty and wisdom of a certain mysterious *chela* whom no man of the Temple had ever seen. Yes, he had followed the traces of the Blessed Feet throughout all India. (The Curator has still in his possession a most marvellous account of his wanderings and meditations.) There remained nothing more in life but to find the River of the Arrow. Yet it was shown to him in his dreams that it was a matter not to be undertaken with any hope of success unless that seeker had with him the one *chela* appointed to bring the event to a happy issue, and versed in great wisdom – such wisdom as white-haired Keepers of Images possess. For example, (here came out the snuff-gourd, and the kindly Jain priests made haste to be silent):

"Long and long ago, when Devadatta was King of Benares – let all listen to the *Jâtaka!* – an elephant was captured for a time by the king's hunters and, ere he broke free, beringed with a grievous leg-iron. This he strove to remove with hate and frenzy in his heart, and hurrying up and down the forests, besought his brother-elephants to wrench it asunder. One by one, with their strong trunks, they tried and failed. At the last they gave it as their opinion that the ring was not to be broken by any bestial power. And in a thicket, new-born, wet with the moisture of birth, lay a day-old calf of the herd whose mother had died. The fettered elephant, forgetting his own agony, said: 'If I do not help this suckling it will perish under our feet.' So he stood above the young thing, making his legs buttresses against the uneasily moving herd; and he begged milk of a virtuous cow, and the calf throve, and the ringed elephant was the calf's guide and defence. Now the days of an elephant – let all listen to the *Jâtaka!* – are thirty-five years to his full strength, and through thirty-five rains the ringed elephant befriended the younger, and all the while the fetter ate into the flesh.

"Then one day the young elephant saw the half-buried iron, and turning to the elder said: 'What is this?' 'It is even my sorrow,' said he who had befriended him. Then that other put out his trunk and in the twinkling of an eyelash abolished the ring, saying: 'The appointed time has come.' So the virtuous elephant who had waited temperately and done kind acts was relieved, at the appointed time, by the very calf whom he had turned aside to cherish – let all listen to the *Jataka!* – for the Elephant was Ananda, and the Calf that broke the ring was none other than the Lord himself…"

Then he would shake his head benignly, and over the ever-clicking rosary point out how free that elephant-calf was from the sin of pride. He was as humble as a *chela* who, seeing his master sitting in the dust outside the Gates of Learning, overleapt the gates (though they were locked) and took his master to his heart in the presence of the proud-stomached city. Rich would be the reward of such a master and such a *chela* when the time came for them to seek freedom together!

So did the lama speak, coming and going across India as softly as a bat. A sharp-tongued old woman in a house among the fruit trees behind Saharunpore honoured him as the woman honoured the prophet, but his chamber was by no means upon the wall. In an apartment of the forecourt overlooked by cooing doves he would sit, while she laid aside her useless veil and chattered of spirits and fiends of Kulu, of grandchildren unborn, and of the free-tongued brat who had talked to her in the resting-place. Once, too, he strayed alone from the Grand Trunk Road below Umballa to the very village whose priest had tried to drug him; but the kind Heaven that guards lamas sent him at twilight through the crops, absorbed and unsuspicious, to the Rissaldar's door. Here was like to have been a grave misunderstanding, for the old soldier asked him why the Friend of the Stars had gone that way only six days before.

"That may not be," said the lama. "He has gone back to his own people."

"He sat in that corner telling a hundred merry tales five nights ago," his host insisted. "True, he vanished somewhat suddenly in the dawn after foolish talk with my granddaughter. He grows apace, but he is the same Friend of the Stars as brought me true word of the war. Have ye parted?"

"Yes – and no," the lama replied. "We – we have not altogether parted, but the time is not ripe that we should take the Road together. He acquires wisdom in another place. We must wait."

"All one – but if it were not the boy, how did he come to speak so continually of thee?"

"And what said he?" asked the lama eagerly.

"Sweet words – an hundred thousand – that thou art his father and mother and such all. Pity that he does not take the Queen's service. He is fearless."

This news amazed the lama, who did not then know how religiously Kim kept to the contract made with Mahbub Ali and perforce ratified by Colonel Creighton...

"There is no holding the young pony from the game," said the horse-dealer when the Colonel pointed out that vagabonding over India in holiday time was absurd. "If permission be refused to go and come as he chooses, he will make light of the refusal. Then who is to catch him? Colonel Sahib, only once in a thousand years is a horse born so well fitted for the game as this our colt. And we need men."

Chapter 10

Your tiercel's too long at hack, Sire. He's no eyass
But a passage-hawk that footed ere we caught him,
Dangerously free o' the air. Faith! were he mine
(As mine's the glove he binds to for his tirings)
I'd fly him with a make-hawk. He's in yarak
Plumed to the very point – so manned, so
  weathered...
Give him the firmament God made him for,
And what shall take the air of him?

Gow's Watch

Lurgan Sahib did not use as direct speech, but his advice tallied with Mahbub's; and the upshot was good for Kim. He knew better now than to leave Lucknow city in native garb, and if Mahbub were anywhere within reach of a letter, it was to Mahbub's camp he headed, and made his change under the Pathan's wary eye. Could the little Survey paintbox that he used for map-tinting in term-time have found a tongue to tell of holiday doings, he might have been expelled. Once Mahbub and he went together as far as the beautiful city of Bombay, with three truck-loads of tram-horses, and Mahbub nearly melted when Kim proposed a sail in a dhow across the Indian Ocean to buy Gulf Arabs, which, he understood from a hanger-on of the dealer Abdul Rahman, fetched better prices than mere Kabulis.

He dipped his hand into the dish with that great trader when Mahbub and a few co-religionists were invited to a big Haj dinner. They came back by way of Karachi by sea, when Kim took his first experience of sea-sickness on the fore-hatch of a coasting-steamer, well persuaded he had been poisoned. The babu's famous drug-box proved useless, though Kim had restocked it at Bombay. Mahbub had business at Quetta, and there Kim, as Mahbub admitted, earned his keep, and perhaps a little over, by spending four curious days as scullion in the house of a fat Commissariat sergeant, from whose office-box, in an auspicious moment, he removed a little vellum ledger which he copied out – it seemed to deal entirely with cattle and camel sales – by moon-light, lying behind an outhouse, all through one hot night. Then he returned the ledger to its place, and, at Mahbub's word, left that service unpaid, rejoining him six miles down the road, the clean copy in his bosom.

"That soldier is a small fish," Mahbub Ali explained, "but in time we shall catch the larger one. He only sells oxen at two prices – one for himself and one for the government – which I do not think is a sin."

"Why could not I take away the little book and be done with it?"

"Then he would have been frightened, and he would have told his master. Then we should miss, perhaps, a great number of new rifles which seek their way up from Quetta to the north. The Game is so large that one sees but a little at a time."

"Oho!" said Kim, and held his tongue. That was in the monsoon holidays, after he had taken the prize for mathematics. The Christmas holidays he spent – deducting ten days for private amusements – with Lurgan Sahib, where he sat for the most part in front of a roaring wood-fire – Jakko road was four feet deep in snow that year – and – the small Hindu had gone away to be married – helped Lurgan to thread pearls. He made Kim learn whole chapters of the Koran by heart, till he could deliver them with the very roll and cadence of a mullah. Moreover, he told Kim the names and properties of many native drugs, as well as the runes proper to recite when you administer them. And in the evenings he wrote charms on parchment – elaborate pentagrams crowned with the names of devils – Murra, and Awan the Companion of Kings – all fantastically written in the corners. More to the point, he advised Kim as to the care of his own body, the cure of fever-fits, and simple remedies of the Road. A week before it was time to go down, Colonel Creighton Sahib – this was unfair – sent Kim a written examination-paper that concerned itself solely with rods and chains and links and angles.

Next holidays he was out with Mahbub, and here, by the way, he nearly died of thirst, plodding through the sand on a camel to the mysterious city of Bikanir, where the wells are four hundred feet deep, and lined throughout with camel-bone. It was not an amusing trip from Kim's point of view, because – in defiance of the contract – the Colonel ordered him to make a map of that wild, walled city; and since Muhammadan horse-boys and pipe-tenders are not expected to drag survey-chains round the capital of an independent native state, Kim was forced to pace all his distances by means of a bead rosary. He used the compass for bearings as occasion served – after dark chiefly, when the camels had been fed – and by the help of his little Survey paintbox of six colour-cakes and three brushes, he achieved something not remotely unlike the city of Jeysulmir. Mahbub laughed a great deal, and advised him to make up a written report as well; and in the back of the big account-book that lay under the flap of Mahbub's pet saddle Kim fell to work.

"It must hold everything that thou hast seen or touched or considered. Write as though the Jang-i-Lat Sahib himself had come by stealth with a vast army outsetting to war."

"How great an army?"

"Oh, half a lakh of men."

"Folly! Remember how few and bad were the wells in the sand. Not a thousand thirsty men could come near by here."

"Then write that down – also all the old breaches in the walls – and whence the firewood is cut – and what is the temper and disposition of the king. I stay here till all my horses are sold. I will hire a room by the gateway, and thou shalt be my accountant. There is a good lock to the door."

The report in its unmistakable St Xavier's running script, and the brown, yellow and lake-daubed map, was on hand a few years ago (a careless clerk filed it with the rough notes of E23's second Seistan survey), but by now the pencil characters must be almost illegible. Kim translated it, sweating under the light of an oil-lamp, to Mahbub, the second day of their return-journey. The Pathan rose and stooped over his dappled saddlebags.

"I knew it would be worthy a dress of honour, and so I made one ready," he said smiling. "Were I Amir of Afghanistan (and some day we may see him), I would fill thy mouth with gold." He laid the garments formally at

Kim's feet. There was a gold-embroidered Peshawar turban-cap, rising to a cone, and a big turban-cloth ending in a fringe of gold. There was a Delhi embroidered waistcoat to slip over a milky white shirt, fastening to the right, ample and flowing; green pyjamas with twisted silk waist-string; and that nothing might be lacking russia-leather slippers, smelling divinely, with arrogantly curled tips.

"Upon a Wednesday, and in the morning, to put on new clothes is auspicious," said Mahbub solemnly. "But we must not forget the wicked folk in the world. So!"

He capped all the splendour, that was taking Kim's delighted breath away, with a mother-of-pearl, nickel-plated, self-extracting .450 revolver.

"I had thought of a smaller bore, but reflected that this takes government bullets. A man can always come by those – especially across the border. Stand up and let me look." He clapped Kim on the shoulder. "May you never be tired, Pathan! Oh, the hearts to be broken! Oh, the eyes under the eyelashes, looking sideways!"

Kim turned about, pointed his toes, stretched, and felt mechanically for the moustache that was just beginning. Then he stooped towards Mahbub's feet to make proper acknowledgement with fluttering, quick-patting hands; his heart too full for words. Mahbub forestalled and embraced him.

"My son," said he, "what need of words between us? But is not the little gun a delight? All six cartridges come out at one twist. It is borne in the bosom next the skin, which, as it were, keeps it oiled. Never put it elsewhere, and please God, thou shalt some day kill a man with it."

"*Hai mai!*" said Kim ruefully. "If a sahib kills a man he is hanged in the jail."

"True: but one pace beyond the border, men are wiser. Put it away; but fill it first. Of what use is a gun unfed?"

"When I go back to the *madrissah* I must return it. They do not allow little guns. Thou wilt keep it for me?"

"Son, I am wearied of that *madrissah*, where they take the best years of a man to teach him what he can only learn upon the Road. The folly of the sahibs has neither top nor bottom. No matter. Maybe thy written report shall save thee further bondage; and God he knows we need men more and more in the Game."

He capped all the splendour, that was taking Kim's delighted breath away, with a mother-of-pearl, nickel-plated, self-extracting .450 revolver.

They marched, jaw-bound against blowing sand, across the salt desert to Jodhpur, where Mahbub and his handsome nephew Habib Ullah did much trading; and then sorrowfully, in European clothes, which he was fast outgrowing, Kim went second-class to St Xavier's. Three weeks later, Colonel Creighton, pricing Tibetan ghost-daggers at Lurgan's shop, faced Mahbub Ali openly mutinous. Lurgan Sahib operated as support in reserve.

"The pony is made – finished – mouthed and paced, Sahib! From now on, day by'day, he will lose his manners if he is kept at tricks. Drop the rein on his back and let go," said the horse-dealer. "We need him."

"But he is so young, Mahbub – not more than sixteen – is he?"

"When I was fifteen, I had shot my man and begot my man, Sahib."

"You impenitent old heathen!" Creighton turned to Lurgan. The black beard nodded assent to the wisdom of the Afghan's dyed scarlet.

"*I* should have used him long ago," said Lurgan. "The younger the better. That is why I always have my really valuable jewels watched by a child. You sent him to me to try. I tried him in every way: he is the only boy I could not make to see things."

"In the crystal – in the ink-pool?" demanded Mahbub. "No. Under my hand, as I told you. That has never happened before. It means that he is strong enough – but you think it skittles, Colonel Creighton – to make any one do anything he wants. And that is three years ago. I have taught him a good deal since, Colonel Creighton. I think you waste him now."

"Hmm! Maybe you're right. But, as you know, there is no Survey work for him at present."

"Let him out – let him go," Mahbub interrupted. "Who expects any colt to carry heavy weight at first? Let him run with the caravans – like our white camel-colts – for luck. I would take him myself, but –"

"There is a little business where he would be most useful – in the south," said Lurgan, with peculiar suavity, dropping his heavy blued eyelids.

"E23 has that in hand," said Creighton quickly. "He must not go down there. Besides, he knows no Turki."

"Only tell him the shape and the smell of the letters we want and he will bring them back," Lurgan insisted.

"No. That is a man's job," said Creighton.

It was a wry-necked matter of unauthorized and incendiary correspondence between a person who claimed to be the ultimate authority in all
matters of the Muhammadan religion throughout the world, and a younger
member of a royal house who had been brought to book for kidnapping
women within British territory. The Muslim Archbishop had been emphatic
and over-arrogant; the young prince was merely sulky at the curtailment
of his privileges, but there was no need he should continue a correspondence
which might some day compromise him. One letter indeed had been procured,
but the finder was later found dead by the roadside in the habit of an Arab
trader, as E23, taking up the work, duly reported.

These facts, and a few others not to be published, made both Mahbub
and Creighton shake their heads.

"Let him go out with his Red Lama," said the horse-dealer with visible
effort. "He is fond of the old man. He can learn his paces by the rosary at
least."

"I have had some dealings with the old man – by letter," said Colonel
Creighton, smiling to himself. "Whither goes he?"

"Up and down the land, as he has these three years. He seeks a River
of Healing. God's curse upon all –" Mahbub checked himself. "He beds
down at the Temple of the Tirthankars or at Buddh Gaya when he is in
from the Road. Then he goes to see the boy at the *madrissah*, as we know,
for the boy was punished for it twice or thrice. He is quite mad, but a
peaceful man. I have met him. The babu also has had dealings with him.
We have watched him for three years. Red Lamas, are not so common in
Hind that one loses track."

"Babus are very curious," said Lurgan meditatively. "Do you know what
Hurree Babu really wants? He wants to be made a member of the Royal
Society by taking ethnological notes. I tell you, I tell him about the lama
everything which Mahbub and the boy have told me. Hurree Babu goes
down to Benares – at his own expense, I think."

"I don't," said Creighton briefly. He had paid Hurree's travelling expenses,
out of a most lively curiosity to learn what the lama might be.

"And he applies to the lama for information on lamaism, and devil-
dances, and spells and charms, several times in these few years. Holy Virgin!
I could have told him all that yee-ars ago. I think Hurree Babu is getting

too old for the Road. He likes better to collect manners and customs information. Yes, he wants to be an FRS."

"Hurree thinks well of the boy, doesn't he?"

"Oh, very indeed – we have had some pleasant evenings at my little place – but I think it would be waste to throw him away with Hurree on the ethnological side."

"Not for a first experience. How does that strike you, Mahbub? Let the boy run with the lama for six months. After that we can see. He will get experience."

"He has it already, Sahib – as a fish controls the water he swims in. But for every reason it will be well to loose him from the school."

"Very good, then," said Creighton, half to himself. "He can go with the lama, and if Hurree Babu cares to keep an eye on them so much the better. He won't lead the boy into any danger as Mahbub would. Curious – his wish to be an FRS. Very human, too. He *is* best on the ethnological side – Hurree."

No money and no preferment would have drawn Creighton from his work on the Indian Survey, but deep in his heart also lay the ambition to write "FRS" after his name. Honours of a sort he knew could be obtained by ingenuity and the help of friends, but, to the best of his belief, nothing save work – papers representing a life of it – took a man into the Society which he had bombarded for years with monographs on strange Asiatic cults and unknown customs. Nine men out of ten would flee from a Royal Society soiree in extremity of boredom; but Creighton was the tenth, and at times his soul yearned for the crowded rooms in easy London where silver-haired, bald-headed gentlemen who know nothing of the army move among spectroscopic experiments, the lesser plants of the frozen tundras, electric flight-measuring machines, and apparatus for slicing into fractional millimetres the left eye of the female mosquito. By all right and reason, it was the Royal Geographical that should have appealed to him, but men are as chancy as children in their choice of playthings. So Creighton smiled, and thought the better of Hurree Babu, moved by like desire.

He dropped the ghost-dagger and looked up at Mahbub.

"How soon can we get the colt from the stable?" said the horse-dealer, reading his eyes.

"Hmm! If I withdraw him by order now – what will he do, think you? I have never before assisted at the teaching of such an one."

"He will come to me," said Mahbub promptly. "Lurgan Sahib and I will prepare him for the Road."

"So be it, then. For six months he shall run at his choice. But who will be his sponsor?"

Lurgan slightly inclined his head. "He will not tell anything, if that is what you are afraid of, Colonel Creighton."

"It's only a boy, after all."

"Ye-es; but first, he has nothing to tell; and secondly, he knows what would happen. Also, he is very fond of Mahbub, and of me a little."

"Will he draw pay?" demanded the practical horse-dealer.

"Food and water allowance only. Twenty rupees a month."

One advantage of the Secret Service is that it has no worrying audit. That Service is ludicrously starved, of course, but the funds are administered by a few men who do not call for vouchers or present itemized accounts. Mahbub's eyes lighted with almost a Sikh's love of money. Even Lurgan's impassive face changed. He considered the years to come when Kim would have been entered and made to the Great Game that never ceases day and night, throughout India. He foresaw honour and credit in the mouths of a chosen few, coming to him from his pupil. Lurgan Sahib had made E23 what E23 was, out of a bewildered, impertinent, lying little North-West Province man.

But the joy of these masters was pale and smoky beside the joy of Kim when St Xavier's head called him aside, with word that Colonel Creighton had sent for him.

"I understand, O'Hara, that he has found you a place as an assistant chain-man in the Canal Department: that comes of taking up mathematics. It is great luck for you, for you are only sixteen; but of course you understand that you do not become *pukka* [permanent] till you have passed the autumn examination. So you must not think you are going out into the world to enjoy yourself, or that your fortune is made. There is a great deal of hard work before you. Only, if you succeed in becoming *pukka*, you can rise, you know, to four hundred and fifty a month." Whereat the Principal gave him much good advice as to his conduct, and his manners, and his morals; and others, his elders, who had not been wafted into billets, talked as only Anglo-Indian lads can, of favouritism and corruption. Indeed, young Cazalet, whose father was a pensioner at Chunar, hinted very broadly that Colonel Creighton's interest in Kim was directly paternal; and Kim, instead of retaliating, did not even use language. He was thinking of the immense fun to come, of Mahbub's letter of the day before, all neatly written in English, making appointment for that afternoon in a house the very name of which would have crisped the Principal's hair with horror...

Said Kim to Mahbub in Lucknow railway station that evening, above the luggage-scales: "I feared lest, at the last, the roof would fall upon me and cheat me. Is it indeed all finished, O my father?"

Mahbub snapped his fingers to show the utterness of that end, and his eyes blazed like red coals.

"Then where is the pistol that I may wear it?"

"Softly! A half-year, to run without heel-ropes. I begged that much from Colonel Creighton Sahib. At twenty rupees a month. Old Red Hat knows that thou art coming."

"I will pay thee *dustoorie* (commission) on my pay for three months," said Kim gravely. "Yea, two rupees a month. But first we must get rid of these." He plucked his thin linen trousers and dragged at his collar. "I have brought with me all that I need on the Road. My trunk has gone up to Lurgan Sahib's."

"Who sends his salaams to thee – Sahib."

"Lurgan Sahib is a very clever man. But what dost thou do?"

"I go north again, upon the Great Game. What else? Is thy mind still set on following old Red Hat?"

"Do not forget he made me that I am – though he did not know it. Year by year, he sent the money that taught me."

"I would have done as much – had it struck my thick head," Mahbub growled. "Come away. The lamps are lit now, and none will mark thee in the bazaar. We go to Huneefa's house."

On the way thither, Mahbub gave him much the same sort of advice as his mother gave to Lemuel, and curiously enough, Mahbub was exact to point out how Huneefa and her likes destroyed kings.

"And I remember," he quoted maliciously, "one who said, 'Trust a snake before an harlot, and an harlot before a Pathan, Mahbub Ali.' Now, excepting as to Pathans, of whom I am one, all that is true. Most true is it in the Great Game, for it is by means of women that all plans come to ruin and we lie out in the dawning with our throats cut. So it happened to such a one." He gave the reddest particulars.

"Then why –?" Kim paused before a filthy staircase that climbed to the warm darkness of an upper chamber, in the ward that is behind Azim Ullah's tobacco-shop. Those who know it call it the Bird-cage – it is so full of whisperings and whistlings and chirrupings.

The room, with its dirty cushions and half-smoked hookahs, smelt abominably of stale tobacco. In one corner lay a huge and shapeless woman clad in greenish gauzes, and decked, brow, nose, ear, neck, wrist, arm, waist and ankle, with heavy native jewellery. When she turned it was like the clashing of copper pots. A lean cat in the balcony outside the window mewed hungrily. Kim checked, bewildered, at the door-curtain.

"Is that the new stuff, Mahbub?" said Huneefa lazily, scarce troubling to remove the mouthpiece from her lips. "O Buktanoos!" – like most of her kind, she swore by the djinns – "O Buktanoos! He is very good to look upon."

"That is part of the selling of the horse," Mahbub explained to Kim, who laughed.

"I have heard that talk since my Sixth Day," he replied, squatting by the light. "Whither does it lead?"

"To protection. Tonight we change thy colour. This sleeping under roofs has blanched thee like an almond. But Huneefa has the secret of a colour that catches. No painting of a day or two. Also, we fortify thee against the chances of the Road. That is *my* gift to thee, my son. Take out all metals on thee and lay them here. Make ready, Huneefa."

Kim dragged forth his compass, Survey paintbox, and the new-filled medicine-box. They had all accompanied his travels, and boy-like he valued them immensely.

The woman rose slowly and moved with her hands a little spread before her. Then Kim saw that she was blind. "No, no," she muttered, "the Pathan speaks truth – my colour does not go in a week or a month, and those whom I protect are under strong guard."

"When one is far off and alone, it would not be well to grow blotched and leprous of a sudden," said Mahbub. "When thou wast with me I could oversee the matter. Besides, a Pathan is a fair-skin. Strip to the waist now and look how thou art whitened." Huneefa felt her way back from an inner room. "It is no matter, she cannot see." He took a pewter bowl from her ringed hand.

The dye-stuff showed blue and gummy. Kim experimented on the back of his wrist, with a dab of cotton wool; but Huneefa heard him.

"No, no," she cried, "the thing is not done thus, but with the proper ceremonies. The colouring is the least part. I give thee the full protection of the Road."

"*Jadoo* [magic]?" said Kim, with a half start. He did not like the white, sightless eyes. Mahbub's hand on his neck bowed him to the floor, nose within an inch of the boards.

"Be still. No harm comes to thee, my son. I am thy sacrifice!"

He could not see what the woman was about, but heard the clish-clash of her jewellery for many minutes. A match lit up the darkness; he caught the well-known purr and fizzle of grains of incense. Then the room filled with smoke – heavy, aromatic, and stupefying. Through growing drowse he heard the names of devils – of Zulbazan, Son of Eblis, who lives in bazaars and *paraos*, making all the sudden lewd wickedness of wayside halts; of Dulhan, invisible about mosques, the dweller among the slippers of the Faithful, who hinders folk from their prayers; and Musboot, Lord of lies and panic. Huneefa, now whispering in his ear, now talking as from an immense distance, touched him with horrible soft fingers, but Mahbub's grip never shifted from his neck till, relaxing with a sigh, the boy lost his senses.

"Allah! How he fought! We should never have done it but for the drugs. That was his white blood, I take it," said Mahbub testily. "Go on with the *dawut* [invocation]. Give him full protection."

"*O Hearer! Thou that hearest with ears, be present. Listen, O Hearer!*" Huneefa moaned, her dead eyes turned to the west. The dark room filled with moanings and snortings.

From the outer balcony, a ponderous figure raised a round bullet head and coughed nervously.

"Do not interrupt this ventriloquial necromanciss, my friend," it said in English. "I opine that it is very disturbing to you, but no enlightened observer is jolly-well upset."

"... *I will lay a plot for their ruin! O Prophet, bear with the unbelievers. Let them alone awhile!*" Huneefa's face, turned to the northward, worked horribly, and it was as though voices from the ceiling answered her.

Hurree Babu returned to his notebook, balanced on the windowsill, but his hand shook. Huneefa, in some sort of drugged ecstasy, wrenched herself to and fro as she sat crosslegged by Kim's still head, and called upon devil after devil, in the ancient order of the ritual, binding them to avoid the boy's every action.

"*With Him are the keys of the Secret Things! None knoweth them beside Himself. He knoweth that which is in the dry land and in the sea!*" Again broke out the unearthly whistling responses.

"I – I apprehend it is not at all malignant in its operation?" said the babu, watching the throat muscles quiver and jerk as Huneefa spoke with tongues. "It – it is not likely that she has killed the boy? If so, I decline to be witness at the trial... What was the last hypothetical devil mentioned?"

"Babuji," said Mahbub in the vernacular. "I have no regard for the devils of Hind, but the Sons of Eblis are far otherwise, and whether they be *jumalee* [well-affected] or *jullalee* [terrible] they love not Kafirs."

"Then you think I had better go?" said Hurree Babu, half rising. "They are, of course, dematerialized phenomena. Spencer says –"

Huneefa's crisis passed, as these things must, in a paroxysm of howling, with a touch of froth at the lips. She lay spent and motionless beside Kim, and the crazy voices ceased.

"Wah! That work is done. May the boy be better for it; and Huneefa is surely a mistress of *dawut*. Help haul her aside, Babu. Do not be afraid."

"How am I to fear the absolutely non-existent?" said Hurree Babu, talking English to reassure himself. It is an awful thing still to dread the magic that you contemptuously investigate – to collect folklore for the Royal Society with a lively belief in all Powers of Darkness.

Mahbub chuckled. He had been out with Hurree on the Road ere now. "Let us finish the colouring," said he. "The boy is well protected if – if the

513

Lords of the Air have ears to hear. I am a Sufi [free-thinker], but when one can get blind-sides of a woman, a stallion, or a devil, why go round to invite a kick? Set him upon the way, Babu, and see that old Red Hat does not lead him beyond our reach. I must get back to my horses."

"All raight," said Hurree Babu. "He is at present curious spectacle."

About third cockcrow, Kim woke after a sleep of thousands of years. Huneefa, in her corner, snored heavily, but Mahbub was gone.

"I hope you were not frightened," said an oily voice at his elbow. "I superintended entire operation, which was most interesting from ethnological point of view. It was high-class *dawut*."

"Huh!" said Kim, recognizing Hurree Babu, who smiled ingratiatingly.

"And also I had honour to bring down from Lurgan your present costume. I am not in the habit offeecially of carrying such gauds to subordinates, but" – he giggled – "your case is noted as exceptional on the books. I hope Mr Lurgan will note my action."

Kim yawned and stretched himself. It was good to turn and twist within loose clothes once again.

"What is this?" He looked curiously at the heavy duffle-stuff loaded with the scents of the far north.

"Oho! That is inconspicuous dress of *chela* attached to service of lamaistic lama. Complete in every particular," said Hurree Babu, rolling into the balcony to clean his teeth at a goglet. "I am of opeenion it is not your old gentleman's precise releegion, but rather sub-variant of same. I have contributed rejected notes to *Asiatic Quarterly Review* on these subjects. Now it is curious that the old gentleman himself is totally devoid of releegiosity. He is not a dam' particular."

"Do you know him?"

Hurree Babu held up his hand to show he was engaged in the prescribed rites that accompany tooth-cleaning and such things among decently bred Bengalis. Then he recited in English an Arya-Somaj prayer of a theistical nature, and stuffed his mouth with *pan* and betel.

"Oah yes. I have met him several times at Benares, and also at Buddh Gaya, to interrogate him on releegious points and devil-worship. He is pure agnostic – same as me."

Huneefa stirred in her sleep, and Hurree Babu jumped nervously to the copper incense-burner, all black and discoloured in morning-light, rubbed a finger in the accumulated lampblack, and drew it diagonally across his face.

"Who has died in thy house?" asked Kim in the vernacular.

"None. But she may have the Evil Eye – that sorceress," the babu replied.

"What dost thou do now, then?"

"I will set thee on thy way to Benares, if thou goest thither, and tell thee what must be known by Us."

"I go. At what hour runs the *te-rain*?" He rose to his feet, looked round the desolate chamber and at the yellow-wax face of Huneefa as the low sun stole across the floor. "Is there money to be paid that witch?"

"No. She has charmed thee against all devils and all dangers – in the name of her devils. It was Mahbub's desire." In English: "He is highly obsolete, I think, to indulge in such supersteetion. Why, it is all ventri*lo*quy. Belly-speak – eh?"

Kim snapped his fingers mechanically to avert whatever evil – Mahbub, he knew, meditated none – might have crept in through Huneefa's ministrations; and Hurree giggled once more. But as he crossed the room he was careful not to step in Huneefa's blotched, squat shadow on the boards. Witches – when their time is on them – can lay hold of the heels of a man's soul if he does that.

"Now you must well listen," said the babu when they were in the fresh air. "Part of these ceremonies which we witnessed they include supply of effeecient amulet to those of our Department. If you feel in your neck you will find one small silver amulet, verree cheap. That is *ours*. Do you understand?"

"Oah yes, *hawa-dilli* [a heart-lifter]," said Kim, feeling at his neck.

"Huneefa she makes them for two rupees twelve annas with – oh, all sorts of exorcisms. They are quite common, except they are partially black enamel, and there is a paper inside each one full of names of local saints and such things. *Thatt* is Huneefa's lookout, you see? Huneefa makes them onlee for us, but in case she does not, when we get them we put in, before issue, one small piece of turquoise. Mr Lurgan he gives them. There is no other source of supply; but it was me invented all this. It is strictly unoffeecial of course, but convenient for subordinates. Colonel Creighton he does not know. He is European. The turquoise is wrapped in the paper... Yes, that is road to railway station... Now suppose you go with the lama, or with me, I hope, some day, or with Mahbub. Suppose we get into a dam'-tight place. I am a fearful man – most fearful – but I tell you I have been in dam'-tight places more than hairs on my head. You say: 'I am Son of the Charm.' Verree good."

"I do not understand quite. We must not be heard talking English here."

"That is all raight. I am only babu showing off my English to you. All we babus talk English to show off," said Hurree, flinging his shoulder-cloth jauntily. "As I was about to say, 'Son of the Charm' means that you may be member of the *Sat Bhai* – the Seven Brothers, which is Hindi *and* Tantric. It is popularly supposed to be extinct Society, but I have written notes to show it is still extant. You see, it is all my invention. Verree good. *Sat Bhai* has many members, and perhaps before they jolly-well-cut-your-throat they may give you just a chance for life. That is useful, anyhow. And moreover, these foolish natives – if they are not too excited – they always stop to think before they kill a man who says he belongs to any speecific organization. You see? You say then when you are in tight place, 'I am Son of the Charm,' and you get – perhaps – ah – your second wind. That is only in extreme instances, or to open negotiations with a stranger. Can you quite see? Verree good. But suppose now, I, or any one of the Department, come to you dressed quite different. You would not know me at all unless I choose, I bet you. Some day I will prove it. I come as Ladakhi trader – oh, anything – and I say to you: 'You want to buy precious stones?' You say: 'Do I look like a man who buys precious stones?' Then I say: 'Even verree poor man can buy a turquoise or *tarkeean*.'"

"That is *kichree* – vegetable curry," said Kim.

"Of course it is. You say: 'Let me see the *tarkeean*.' Then I say: 'It was cooked by a woman, and perhaps it is bad for your caste.' Then you say: 'There is no caste when men go to – look for *tarkeean*.' You stop a little between those words, 'to – look'. That is thee whole secret. The little stop before the words."

Kim repeated the test sentence.

"That is all right. Then I will show you my turquoise if there is time, and then you know who I am, and then we exchange views and documents and those-all things. And so it is with any other man of us. We talk sometimes about turquoises and sometimes about *tarkeean*, but always with that little stop in the words. It is verree easy. First, 'Son of the Charm', if you are in a tight place. Perhaps that may help you – perhaps not. Then what I have told you about the *tarkeean*, if you want to transact offeecial business with a strange man. Of course, at present, you have no offeecial business. You are – ah ha! – super-numerary on probation. Quite unique specimen. If you were Asiatic of birth you might be employed right off; but this half-year of leave is to make you de-Englishized, you see? The lama he expects you, because I have demi-offeecially informed him you have passed all your examinations, and will soon obtain government appointment. Oh ho! You are on acting-allowance, you see: so if you are called upon to help Sons of the Charm mind you jolly-well try. Now I shall say goodbye, my dear fellow, and I hope you – ah – will come out top-side allraight."

Hurree Babu stepped back a pace or two into the crowd at the entrance of Lucknow station and – was gone. Kim drew a deep breath and hugged himself all over. The nickel-plated revolver he could feel in the bosom of his sad-coloured robe, the amulet was on his neck; begging-gourd, rosary, and ghost-dagger (Mr Lurgan had forgotten nothing) were all to hand, with medicine, paintbox, and compass, and in a worn old purse-belt embroidered with porcupine-quill patterns lay a month's pay. Kings could be no richer. He bought sweetmeats in a leaf-cup from a Hindu trader, and ate them with glad rapture till a policeman ordered him off the steps.

Chapter 11

Give the man who is not made
  To his trade
Swords to fling and catch again,
Coins to ring and snatch again,
Men to harm and cure again,
Snakes to charm and lure again –
He'll be hurt by his own blade,
By his serpents disobeyed,
By his clumsiness bewrayed,
By the people mocked to scorn –
  So 'tis not with juggler born!
Pinch of dust or withered flower,
  Chance-flung fruit or borrowed staff,
Serve his need and shore his power,
  Bind the spell, or loose the laugh!
             But a man who, etc.
        The Juggler's Song, Op. 15

Followed a sudden natural reaction.

"Now am I alone – all alone," he thought. "In all India is no one so alone as I! If I die today, who shall bring the news – and to whom? If I live and God is good, there will be a price upon my head, for I am a Son of the Charm – I, Kim."

A very few white people, but many Asiatics, can throw themselves into amazement as it were by repeating their own names over and over again

518

to themselves, letting the mind go free upon speculation as to what is called personal identity. When one grows older, the power, usually, departs, but while it lasts it may descend upon a man at any moment.

"Who is Kim – Kim – Kim?"

He squatted in a corner of the clanging waiting-room, rapt from all other thoughts; hands folded in lap, and pupils contracted to pin-points. In a minute – in another half-second – he felt he would arrive at the solution of the tremendous puzzle; but here, as always happens, his mind dropped away from those heights with the rush of a wounded bird, and passing his hand before his eyes, he shook his head.

A long-haired Hindu *bairagi* [holy man], who had just bought a ticket, halted before him at that moment and stared intently.

"I also have lost it," he said sadly. "It is one of the Gates to the Way, but for me it has been shut many years."

"What is the talk?" said Kim, abashed.

"Thou wast wondering there in thy spirit what manner of thing thy soul might be. The seizure came of a sudden. I know. Who should know but I? Whither goest thou?"

"Toward Kashi [Benares]."

"There are no Gods there. I have proved them. I go to Prayag [Allahabad] for the fifth time – seeking the Road to Enlightenment. Of what faith art thou?"

"I too am a Seeker," said Kim, using one of the lama's pet words. "Though" – he forgot his northern dress for the moment – "though Allah alone knoweth what I seek."

The old fellow slipped the *bairagi's* crutch under his armpit and sat down on a patch of ruddy leopard's skin as Kim rose at the call for the Benares train.

"Go in hope, little brother," he said. "It is a long road to the feet of the One; but thither do we all travel."

Kim did not feel so lonely after this, and ere he had sat out twenty miles in the crowded compartment, was cheering his neighbours with a string of most wonderful yarns about his own and his master's magical gifts.

Benares struck him as a peculiarly filthy city, though it was pleasant to find how his cloth was respected. At least one third of the population prays eternally to some group or other of the many million deities, and so reveres every sort of holy man. Kim was guided to the Temple of the Tirthankars, about a mile outside the city, near Sarnath, by a chance-met Punjabi farmer – a Kamboh from Jullundur way who had appealed in vain to every God of his homestead to cure his small son, and was trying Benares as a last resort.

"Thou art from the north?" he asked, shouldering through the press of the narrow, stinking streets much like his own pet bull at home.

"Ay, I know the Punjab. My mother was a *pahareen*, but my father came from Amritzar – by Jandiala," said Kim, oiling his ready tongue for the needs of the Road.

"Jandiala – Jullundur? Oho! Then we be neighbours in some sort, as it were." He nodded tenderly to the wailing child in his arms. "Whom dost thou serve?"

"A most holy man at the Temple of the Tirthankars."

"They are all most holy and – most greedy," said the Jat with bitterness. "I have walked the pillars and trodden the temples till my feet are flayed, and the child is no whit better. And the mother being sick too... Hush, then, little one... We changed his name when the fever came. We put him into girl's clothes. There was nothing we did not do, except – I said to his mother when she bundled me off to Benares – she should have come with me – I *said* Sakhi Sarwar Sultan would serve us best. We know His generosity, but these down-country Gods are strangers."

The child turned on the cushion of the huge corded arms and looked at Kim through heavy eyelids.

"And was it all worthless?" Kim asked, with easy interest.

"All worthless – all worthless," said the child, lips cracking with fever.

"The Gods have given him a good mind, at least," said the father proudly. "To think he should have listened so cleverly. Yonder is thy Temple. Now I am a poor man – many priests have dealt with me – but my son is my son, and if a gift to thy master can cure him – I am at my very wits' end."

Kim considered for a while, tingling with pride. Three years ago he would have made prompt profit on the situation and gone his way without a thought; but now, the very respect the Jat paid him proved that he was a man. Moreover, he had tasted fever once or twice already, and knew enough to recognize starvation when he saw it.

KIM

"Call him forth and I will give him a bond on my best yoke, so that the child is cured."

Kim halted at the carved outer door of the temple. A white-clad Oswal banker from Ajmir, his sins of usury new wiped out, asked him what he did.

"I am *chela* to Teshoo Lama, an Holy One from Bhotiyal – within there. He bade me come. I wait. Tell him."

"Do not forget the child," cried the importunate Jat over his shoulder, and then bellowed in Punjabi: "O Holy One – O disciple of the Holy One – O Gods above all the Worlds – behold affliction sitting at the gate!" That cry is so common in Benares that the passers never turned their heads.

The Oswal, at peace with mankind, carried the message into the darkness behind him, and the easy, uncounted Eastern minutes slid by; for the lama was asleep in his cell, and no priest would wake him. When the click of his rosary again broke the hush of the inner court where the calm images of the Arhats stand, a novice whispered, "Thy *chela* is here," and the old man strode forth, forgetting the end of that prayer.

Hardly had the tall figure shown in the doorway than the Jat ran before him, and, lifting up the child, cried: "Look upon this, Holy One; and if the Gods will, he lives – he lives!"

He fumbled in his waist-belt and drew out a small silver coin.

"What is now?" The lama's eyes turned to Kim. It was noticeable he spoke far clearer Urdu than long ago, under Zam-Zammah; but the father would allow no private talk.

"It is no more than a fever," said Kim. "The child is not well fed."

"He sickens at everything, and his mother is not here."

"If it be permitted, I may cure, Holy One."

"What! Have they made thee a healer? Wait here," said the lama, and he sat down by the Jat upon the lowest step of the temple, while Kim, looking out of the corner of his eyes, slowly opened the little betel-box. He had dreamed dreams at school of returning to the lama as a sahib – of chaffing the old man before he revealed himself – boy's dreams all. There was more drama in this abstracted, brow-puckered search through the tabloid-bottles, with a pause here and there for thought and a muttered invocation between whiles. Quinine he had in tablets, and dark brown meat-lozenges – beef

521

"Look upon this, Holy One; and if the Gods will, he lives – he lives."

most probably, but that was not *his* business. The little thing would not eat, but it sucked at a lozenge greedily, and said it liked the salt taste.

"Take then these six." Kim handed them to the man. "Praise the Gods, and boil three in milk; other three in water. After he has drunk the milk give him this" (it was the half of a quinine pill), "and wrap him warm. Give him the water of the other three, and the other half of this white pill when he wakes. Meantime, here is another brown medicine that he may suck at on the way home."

"Gods, what wisdom!" said the Kamboh, snatching.

It was as much as Kim could remember of his own treatment in a bout of autumn malaria – if you except the patter that he added to impress the lama.

"Now go! Come again in the morning."

"But the price – the price," said the Jat, and threw back his sturdy shoulders. "My son is my son. Now that he will be whole again, how shall I go back to his mother and say I took help by the wayside and did not even give a bowl of curds in return?"

"They are alike, these Jats," said Kim softly. "The Jat stood on his dung-hill and the king's elephants went by. 'O driver,' said he, 'what will you sell those little donkeys for?'"

The Jat burst into a roar of laughter, stifled with apologies to the lama. "It is the saying of my own country – the very talk of it. So are we Jats all. I will come tomorrow with the child; and the blessing of the Gods of the Homesteads – who are good little Gods – be on you both... Now, son, we grow strong again. Do not spit it out, little Princeling! King of my Heart, do not spit it out, and we shall be strong men, wrestlers and club-wielders, by morning."

He moved away, crooning and mumbling. The lama turned to Kim, and all the loving old soul of him looked out through his narrow eyes.

"To heal the sick is to acquire merit; but first one gets knowledge. That was wisely done, O Friend of all the World."

"I was made wise by thee, Holy One," said Kim, forgetting the little play just ended; forgetting St Xavier's; forgetting his white blood; forgetting even the Great Game as he stooped, Muhammadan-fashion, to touch his master's feet in the dust of the Jain temple. "My teaching I owe to thee. I have eaten thy bread three years. My time is finished. I am loosed from the schools. I come to thee."

"Herein is my reward. Enter! Enter! And is all well?" They passed to the inner court, where the afternoon sun sloped golden across. "Stand that I may see. So!" He peered critically. "It is no longer a child, but a man, ripened in wisdom, walking as a physician. I did well – I did well when I gave thee up to the armed men on that black night. Dost thou remember our first day under Zam-Zammah?"

"Ay," said Kim. "Dost thou remember when I leapt off the carriage the first day I went to –"

"The Gates of Learning? Truly. And the day that we ate the cakes together at the back of the river by Nucklao. Aha! Many times hast thou begged for me, but that day I begged for thee."

"Good reason," quoth Kim. "I was then a scholar in the Gates of Learning, and attired as a sahib. Do not forget, Holy One," he went on playfully, "I am still a sahib – by thy favour."

"True. And a sahib in most high esteem. Come to my cell, *chela*."

"How is that known to thee?"

The lama smiled. "First by means of letters from the kindly priest whom we met in the camp of armed men; but he is now gone to his own country, and I sent the money to his brother." Colonel Creighton, who had succeeded to the trusteeship when Father Victor went to England with the Mavericks, was hardly the Chaplain's brother. "But I do not well understand sahibs' letters. They must be interpreted to me. I chose a surer way. Many times when I returned from my Search to this Temple, which has always been a nest to me, there came one seeking Enlightenment – a man from Leh – that had been, he said, a Hindu, but wearied of all those Gods." The lama pointed to the Arhats.

"A fat man?" said Kim, a twinkle in his eye.

"Very fat; but I perceived in a little his mind was wholly given up to useless things – such as devils and charms and the form and fashion of our tea-drinkings in the monasteries, and by what road we initiated the novices. A man abounding in questions; but he was a friend of thine, *chela*. He told me that thou wast on the road to much honour as a scribe. And I see thou art a physician."

"Yes, that am I – a scribe, when I am a sahib, but it is set aside when I come as thy disciple. I have accomplished the years appointed for a sahib."

"As it were a novice?" said the lama, nodding his head. "Art thou freed from the schools? I would not have thee unripe."

"I am all free. In due time I take service under the government as a scribe –"

"Not as a warrior. That is well."

"But first I come to wander – with thee. Therefore I am here. Who begs for thee, these days?" he went on quickly. The ice was thin.

"Very often I beg myself; but, as thou knowest, I am seldom here, except when I come to look again at my disciple. From one end to another of Hind have I travelled afoot and in the *te-rain*. A great and a wonderful land! But here, when I put in, is as though I were in my own Bhotiyal."

He looked round the little clean cell complacently. A low cushion gave him a seat, on which he had disposed himself in the cross-legged attitude of the Bodhisat emerging from meditation; a black teak-wood table, not twenty inches high, set with copper tea-cups, was before him. In one corner stood a tiny altar, also of heavily carved teak, bearing a copper-gilt image of the seated Buddha and fronted by a lamp, an incense-holder, and a pair of copper flower-pots.

"The Keeper of the Images in the Wonder House acquired merit by giving me these a year since," he said, following Kim's eye. "When one is far from one's own land such things carry remembrance; and we must reverence the Lord for that he showed the Way. See!" He pointed to a curiously built mound of coloured rice crowned with a fantastic metal ornament. "When I was abbot in my own place – before I came to better knowledge – I made that offering daily. It is the Sacrifice of the Universe to the Lord. Thus do we of Bhotiyal offer all the world daily to the Excellent Law. And I do it even now, though I know that the Excellent One is beyond all pinchings and pattings." He snuffed from his gourd.

"It is well done, Holy One," Kim murmured, sinking at ease on the cushions, very happy and rather tired.

"And also," the old man chuckled, "I write pictures of the Wheel of Life. Three days to a picture. I was busied on it – or it may be I shut my eyes a little – when they brought word of thee. It is good to have thee here: I will show thee my art – not for pride's sake, but because thou must learn. The sahibs have not *all* this world's wisdom."

He drew from under the table a sheet of strangely scented yellow Chinese paper, the brushes, and slab of Indian ink. In cleanest, severest outline he had traced the Great Wheel with its six spokes, whose centre is the conjoined Hog, Snake, and Dove (Ignorance, Anger, and Lust), and whose compartments are all the Heavens and Hells, and all the chances of human life. Men say that the Bodhisat himself first drew it with grains of rice upon dust, to teach his disciples the cause of things. Many ages have crystallized it into a most wonderful convention crowded with hundreds of little figures whose every line carries a meaning. Few can translate the picture-parable; there are not twenty in all the world who can draw it surely without a copy: of those who can both draw and expound are but three.

"I have a little learned to draw," said Kim. "But this is a marvel beyond marvels."

"I have written it for many years," said the lama. "Time was when I could write it all between one lamp-lighting and the next. I will teach thee the art – after due preparation; and I will show thee the meaning of the Wheel."

"We take the Road, then?"

"The Road and our Search. I was but waiting for thee. It was made plain to me in a hundred dreams – notably one that came upon the night of the day that the Gates of Learning first shut – that without thee I should never find my River. Again and again, as thou knowest, I put this from me, fearing an illusion. Therefore I would not take thee with me that day at Lucknow, when we ate the cakes. I would not take thee till the time was ripe and auspicious. From the hills to the sea, from the sea to the hills have I gone, but it was vain. Then I remembered the *Jâtaka*."

He told Kim the story of the elephant with the leg-iron, as he had told it so often to the Jain priests.

"Further testimony is not needed," he ended serenely. "Thou wast sent for an aid. That aid removed, my Search came to naught. Therefore we will go out again together, and our Search is sure."

"Whither go we?"

"What matters, Friend of all the World? The Search, I say, is sure. If need be, the River will break from the ground before us. I acquired merit when I sent thee to the Gates of Learning, and gave thee the jewel that is Wisdom. Thou didst return, I saw even now, a follower of Sakyamuni, the Physician, whose altars are many in Bhotiyal. It is sufficient. We are together, and all things are as they were – Friend of all the World – Friend of the Stars – my *chela!*"

Then they talked of matters secular; but it was noticeable that the lama never demanded any details of life at St Xavier's, nor showed the faintest curiosity as to the manners and customs of sahibs. His mind moved all in the past, and he revived every step of their wonderful first journey together, rubbing his hands and chuckling, till it pleased him to curl himself up into the sudden sleep of old age.

Kim watched the last dusty sunshine fade out of the court, and played with his ghost-dagger and rosary. The clamour of Benares, oldest of all earth's cities awake before the Gods, day and night, beat round the walls as the sea's roar round a breakwater. Now and again, a Jain priest crossed the court, with some small offering to the images, and swept the path about him lest by chance he should take the life of a living thing. A lamp twinkled, and there followed the sound of a prayer. Kim watched the stars as they rose one after another in the still, sticky dark, till he fell asleep at the foot of the altar. That night he dreamed in Hindustani, with never an English word…

"Holy One, there is the child to whom we gave the medicine," he said, about three o'clock in the morning, when the lama, also waking from dreams, would have fared forth on pilgrimage. "The Jat will be here at the light."

"I am well answered. In my haste I would have done a wrong." He sat down on the cushions and returned to his rosary. "Surely old folk are as children," he said pathetically. "They desire a matter – behold, it must be done at once, or they fret and weep! Many times when I was upon the Road I have been ready to stamp with my feet at the hindrance of an ox-cart in the way, or a mere cloud of dust. It was not so when I was a man – a long time ago. None the less it is wrongful – '

"But thou art indeed old, Holy One."

"The thing was done. A Cause was put out into the world, and, old or young, sick or sound, knowing or unknowing, who can rein in the effect of that Cause? Does the Wheel hang still if a child spin it – or a drunkard? *Chela*, this is a great and a terrible world."

"I think it good," Kim yawned. "What is there to eat? I have not eaten since yesterday even."

"I had forgotten thy need. Yonder is good Bhotiyal tea and cold rice."

"We cannot walk far on such stuff." Kim felt all the European's lust for flesh-meat, which is not accessible in a Jain temple. Yet, instead of going out at once with the begging-bowl, he stayed his stomach on slabs of cold rice till the full dawn. It brought the farmer, voluble, stuttering with gratitude.

"In the night the fever broke and the sweat came," he cried. "Feel here – his skin is fresh and new! He esteemed the salt lozenges, and took milk with greed." He drew the cloth from the child's face, and it smiled sleepily at Kim. A little knot of Jain priests, silent but all-observant, gathered by the temple door. They knew, and Kim knew that they knew, how the old lama had met his disciple. Being courteous folk, they had not obtruded themselves overnight by presence, word, or gesture. Wherefore Kim repaid them as the sun rose.

"Thank the Gods of the Jains, brother," he said, not knowing how those gods were named. "The fever is indeed broken."

"Look! See!" The lama beamed in the background upon his hosts of three years. "Was there ever such a *chela*? He follows our Lord the Healer."

Now the Jains officially recognize all the gods of the Hindu creed, as well as the Lingam and the Snake. They wear the Brahminical thread; they adhere to every claim of Hindu caste-law. But, because they knew and loved the lama, because he was an old man, because he sought the Way, because he was their guest, and because he collogued long of nights with the head-priest – as free-thinking a metaphysician as ever split one hair into seventy – they murmured assent.

"Remember," – Kim bent over the child – "this trouble may come again."

"Not if thou hast the proper spell," said the father.

"But in a little while we go away."

"True," said the lama to all the Jains. "We go now together upon the Search whereof I have often spoken. I waited till my *chela* was ripe. Behold him! We go north. Never again shall I look upon this place of my rest, O people of good will."

"But I am not a beggar." The cultivator rose to his feet, clutching the child.

"Be still. Do not trouble the Holy One," a priest cried.

"Go," Kim whispered. "Meet us again under the big railway bridge, and for the sake of all the Gods of our Punjab, bring food – curry, pulse, cakes fried in fat, and sweetmeats. Specially sweetmeats. Be swift!"

The pallor of hunger suited Kim very well as he stood, tall and slim, in his sad-coloured, sweeping robes, one hand on his rosary and the other in the attitude of benediction, faithfully copied from the lama. An English observer might have said that he looked rather like the young saint of a stained-glass window, whereas he was but a growing lad faint with emptiness.

Long and formal were the farewells, thrice ended and thrice renewed. The Seeker – he who had invited the lama to that haven from far-away Tibet, a silver-faced hairless ascetic – took no part in it, but meditated, as always, alone among the images. The others were very human; pressing small comforts upon the old man – a betel-box, a fine new iron pen-case, a food-bag, and such-like – warning him against the dangers of the world without, and prophesying a happy end to the Search. Meantime Kim, lonelier than ever, squatted on the steps, and swore to himself in the language of St Xavier's.

"But it is my own fault," he concluded. "With Mahbub, I ate Mahbub's bread, or Lurgan Sahib's. At St Xavier's, three meals a day. Here I must jolly-well look out for myself. Besides, I am not in good training. *How* I could eat a plate of beef now!... Is it finished, Holy One?"

The lama, both hands raised, intoned a final blessing in ornate Chinese. "I must lean on thy shoulder," said he, as the temple gates closed. "We grow stiff, I think."

The weight of a six-foot man is not light to steady through miles of crowded streets, and Kim, loaded down with bundles and packages for the way, was glad to reach the shadow of the railway bridge.

"Here we eat," he said resolutely, as the Kamboh, blue-robed and smiling, hove in sight, a basket in one hand and the child on the other.

"Fall to, Holy Ones!" he cried from fifty yards. (They were by the shoal under the first bridge-span, out of sight of hungry priests.) "Rice and good curry, cakes all warm and well scented with *hing* [asafoetida], curds and sugar. King of my fields," – this to the small son – "let us show these holy men that we Jats of Jullundur can pay a service... I had heard the Jains would eat nothing that they had not cooked, but truly" – he looked away politely over the broad river – "where there is no eye there is no caste."

"And we," said Kim, turning his back and heaping a leaf-platter for the lama, "are beyond all castes."

They gorged themselves on the good food in silence. Nor till he had licked the last of the sticky sweetstuff from his little finger did Kim note that the Kamboh too was girt for travel.

"If our roads lie together," he said roughly, "I go with thee. One does not often find a worker of miracles, and the child is still weak. But *I* am not altogether a reed." He picked up his *lathi* – a five-foot male-bamboo ringed with bands of polished iron – and flourished it in the air. "The Jats are called quarrelsome, but that is not true. Except when we are crossed, we are like our own buffaloes."

"So be it," said Kim. "A good stick is a good reason."

The lama gazed placidly upstream, where in long, smudged perspective the ceaseless columns of smoke go up from the burning-ghats by the river. Now and again, despite all municipal regulations, the fragment of a half-burned body bobbed by on the full current.

"But for thee," said the Kamboh to Kim, drawing the child into his hairy breast, "I might today have gone thither – with this one. The priests tell us that Benares is holy – which none doubt – and desirable to die in. But I do not know their Gods, and they ask for money; and when one has done one worship a shaved-head vows it is of none effect except one do another. Wash here! Wash there! Pour, drink, lave, and scatter flowers – but always pay the priests. No, the Punjab for me, and the soil of the Jullundur-*doab* for the best soil in it."

"I have said many times – in the Temple, I think – that if need be, the River will open at our feet. We will therefore go north," said the lama, rising. "I remember a pleasant place, set about with fruit trees, where one can walk in meditation – and the air is cooler there. It comes from the Hills and the snow of the Hills."

"What is the name?" said Kim.

"How should I know? Didst thou not – no, that was after the army rose out of the earth and took thee away. I abode there in meditation in a room against the dovecot – except when she talked eternally."

"Oho! the woman from Kulu. That is by Saharunpore." Kim laughed.

"How does the spirit move thy master? Does he go afoot, for the sake of past sins?" the Jat demanded cautiously. "It is a far cry to Delhi."

"No," said Kim. "I will beg a *tikkut* for the *te-rain*." One does not own to the possession of money in India.

"Then, in the name of the Gods, let us take the fire-carriage. My son is best in his mother's arms. The government has brought on us many taxes, but it gives us one good thing – the *te-rain* that joins friends and unites the anxious. A wonderful matter is the *te-rain*."

They all piled into it a couple of hours later, and slept through the heat of the day. The Kamboh plied Kim with ten thousand questions as to the lama's walk and work in life, and received some curious answers. Kim was content to be where he was, to look out upon the flat north-western land-scape, and to talk to the changing mob of fellow-passengers. Even today, tickets and ticket-clipping are dark oppression to Indian rustics. They do not understand why, when they have paid for a magic piece of paper, strangers should punch great pieces out of the charm. So, long and furious are the debates between travellers and Eurasian ticket-collectors. Kim assisted at two or three with grave advice, meant to darken counsel and to show off his wisdom before the lama and the admiring Kamboh. But at Somna Road the Fates sent him a matter to think upon. There tumbled into the compartment, as the train was moving off, a mean, lean little person – a Mahratta, so far as Kim could judge by the cock of the tight turban. His face was cut, his muslin upper garment was badly torn, and one leg was bandaged. He told them that a country-cart had upset and nearly slain him: he was going to Delhi, where his son lived. Kim watched him closely. If, as he asserted, he had been rolled over and over on the earth, there should have been signs of gravel-rash on the skin. But all his injuries seemed clean cuts, and a mere fall from a cart could not cast a man into such extremity of terror. As, with shaking fingers, he knotted up the torn cloth about his neck he laid bare an amulet of the kind called a keeper-up of the heart. Now, amulets are common enough, but they are not generally strung on square-plaited copper wire, and still fewer amulets bear black enamel on silver. There were none except the Kamboh and the lama in the compartment, which luckily was of an old type with solid ends. Kim made as to scratch in his bosom, and thereby lifted his own amulet. The Mahratta's face changed altogether at the sight, and he disposed the amulet fairly on his breast.

"Yes," he went on to the Kamboh, "I was in haste, and the cart, driven by a bastard, bound its wheel in a water-cut, and besides the harm done to me there was lost a full dish of *tarkeean*. I was not a Son of the Charm [a lucky man] that day."

"That was a great loss," said the Kamboh, withdrawing interest. His experience of Benares had made him suspicious.

"Who cooked it?" said Kim.

"A woman." The Mahratta raised his eyes.

"But all women can cook *tarkeean*," said the Kamboh. "It is a good curry, as I know."

"Oh yes, it is a good curry," said the Mahratta.

"And cheap," said Kim. "But what about caste?"

"Oh, there is no caste where men go to – look for *tarkeean*," the Mahratta replied, in the prescribed cadence. "Of whose service art thou?"

"Of the service of this Holy One." Kim pointed to the happy, drowsy lama, who woke with a jerk at the well-loved word.

"Ah, he was sent from Heaven to aid me. He is called the Friend of all the World. He is also called the Friend of the Stars. He walks as a physician – his time being ripe. Great is his wisdom."

"And a Son of the Charm," said Kim under his breath, as the Kamboh made haste to prepare a pipe lest the Mahratta should beg.

"And who is *that*?" the Mahratta asked, glancing sideways nervously.

"One whose child I – we have cured, who lies under great debt to us – Sit by the window, man from Jullundur. Here is a sick one."

"Humph! *I* have no desire to mix with chance-met wastrels. *My* ears are not long. *I* am not a woman wishing to overhear secrets." The Jat slid himself heavily into a far corner.

"Art thou anything of a healer? I am ten leagues deep in calamity," cried the Mahratta, picking up the cue.

"This man is cut and bruised all over. I go about to cure him," Kim retorted. "None interfered between thy babe and me."

"I am rebuked," said the Kamboh meekly. "I am thy debtor for the life of my son. Thou art a miracle-worker – I know it."

"Show me the cuts." Kim bent over the Mahratta's neck, his heart nearly choking him; for this was the Great Game with a vengeance. "Now, tell thy tale swiftly, brother, while I say a charm."

"I came from the south, where my work lay. One of us they slew by the roadside. Hast thou heard?" Kim shook his head. He, of course, knew nothing of E23's predecessor, slain down south in the habit of an Arab trader. "Having found a certain letter which I was sent to seek, I came away. I escaped from the city and ran to Mhow. So sure was I that none knew, I did not change my face. At Mhow a woman brought charge against me of theft of jewellery in that city which I had left. Then I saw the cry was out against me. I ran from Mhow by night, bribing the police, who had been bribed to hand me over without question to my enemies in the south. Then I lay in old Chitor city a week, a penitent in a temple, but I could not get rid of the letter which was my charge. I buried it under the Queen's Stone, at Chitor, in the place known to us all."

Kim did not know, but not for worlds would he have broken the thread.

"At Chitor, look you, I was all in kings' country; for Kotah to the east is beyond the Queen's law, and east again lie Jaipur and Gwalior. Neither love spies, and there is no justice. I was hunted like a wet jackal; but I broke through at Bandakui, where I heard there was a charge against me of murder in the city I had left – of the murder of a boy. They have both the corpse and the witnesses waiting."

"But cannot the government protect?"

"We of the Game are beyond protection. If we die, we die. Our names are blotted from the book. That is all. At Bandakui, where lives one of us, I thought to slip the scent by changing my face, and so made me a Mahratta.

Then I came to Agra, and would have turned back to Chitor to recover the letter. So sure I was I had slipped them. Therefore I did not send a *tar* [telegram] to any one saying where the letter lay. I wished the credit of it all."

Kim nodded. He understood that feeling well.

"But at Agra, walking in the streets, a man cried a debt against me, and approaching with many witnesses, would hale me to the courts then and there. Oh, they are clever in the south! He recognized me as his agent for cotton. May he burn in Hell for it!"

"And wast thou?"

"O fool! I was the man they sought for the matter of the letter! I ran into the Fleshers' Ward and came out by the House of the Jew, who feared a riot and pushed me forth. I came afoot to Somna Road – I had only money for my *tikkut* to Delhi – and there, while I lay in a ditch with a fever, one sprang out of the bushes and beat me and cut me and searched me from head to foot. Within earshot of the *te-rain* it was!"

"Why did he not slay thee out of hand?"

"They are not so foolish. If I am taken in Delhi at the instance of lawyers, upon a proven charge of murder, my body is handed over to the state that desires it. I go back guarded, and then – I die slowly for an example to the rest of us. The south is not my country. I run in circles – like a goat with one eye. I have not eaten for two days. I am marked" – he touched the filthy bandage on his leg – "so that they will know me at Delhi."

"Thou art safe in the *te-rain*, at least."

"Live a year at the Great Game and tell me that again! The wires will be out against me at Delhi, describing every tear and rag upon me. Twenty – a hundred, if need be – will have seen me slay that boy. And thou art useless!"

Kim knew enough of native methods of attack not to doubt that the case would be deadly complete – even to the corpse. The Mahratta twitched his fingers with pain from time to time. The Kamboh in his corner glared sullenly; the lama was busy over his beads; and Kim, fumbling doctor-fashion at the man's neck, thought out his plan between invocations.

"Hast thou a charm to change my shape? Else I am dead. Five – ten minutes alone, if I had not been so pressed, and I might –"

"Is he cured yet, miracle-worker?" said the Kamboh jealously. "Thou hast chanted long enough."

"Nay. There is no cure for his hurts, as I see, except he sit for three days in the habit of a *bairagi*." This is a common penance, often imposed on a fat trader by his spiritual teacher.

"One priest always goes about to make another priest," was the retort. Like most grossly superstitious folk, the Kamboh could not keep his tongue from deriding his Church.

"Will thy son be a priest, then? It is time he took more of my quinine."

"We Jats are all buffaloes," said the Kamboh, softening anew.

Kim rubbed a fingertip of bitterness on the child's trusting little lips. "I have asked for nothing," he said sternly to the father, "except food. Dost thou grudge me that? I go to heal another man. Have I thy leave – Prince?"

Up flew the man's huge paws in supplication. "Nay – nay. Do not mock me thus."

"It pleases me to cure this sick one. Thou shalt acquire merit by aiding. What colour ash is there in thy pipe-bowl? White. That is auspicious. Was there raw turmeric among thy foodstuffs?"

"I – I –"

"Open thy bundle!"

It was the usual collection of small oddments: bits of cloth, quack medicines, cheap fairings, a clothful of *atta* – greyish, rough-ground native flour – twists of down-country tobacco, tawdry pipe-stems, and a packet of curry-stuff, all wrapped in a quilt. Kim turned it over with the air of a wise warlock, muttering a Muhammadan invocation.

"This is wisdom I learned from the sahibs," he whispered to the lama; and here, when one thinks of his training at Lurgan's, he spoke no more than the truth. "There is a great evil in this man's fortune, as shown by the Stars, which – which troubles him. Shall I take it away?"

"Friend of the Stars, thou hast done well in all things. Let it be at thy pleasure. Is it another healing?"

"Quick! Be quick!" gasped the Mahratta. "The train may stop."

"A healing against the shadow of death," said Kim, mixing the Kamboh's flour with the mingled charcoal and tobacco ash in the red-earth bowl of

"We must make thee a yellow Saddhu all over."

the pipe. E23, without a word, slipped off his turban and shook down his long black hair.

"That is my food – priest," the Jat growled.

"A buffalo in the temple! Hast thou dared to look even thus far?" said Kim. "I must do mysteries before fools; but have a care for thine eyes. Is there a film before them already? I save the babe, and for return thou – oh, shameless!" The man flinched at the direct gaze, for Kim was wholly in earnest. "Shall I curse thee, or shall I –" He picked up the outer cloth of the bundle and threw it over the bowed head. "Dare so much as to think a wish to see, and – and – even I cannot save thee. Sit! Be dumb!"

"I am blind – dumb. Forbear to curse! Co – come, child; we will play a game of hiding. Do not, for my sake, look from under the cloth."

"I see hope," said E23. "What is thy scheme?"

"This comes next," said Kim, plucking the thin body-shirt. E23 hesitated, with all a north-west man's dislike of baring his body.

"What is caste to a cut-throat?" said Kim, rending it to the waist. "We must make thee a yellow Saddhu all over. Strip – strip swiftly, and shake thy hair over thine eyes while I scatter the ash. Now, a caste-mark on thy forehead." He drew from his bosom the little Survey paintbox and a cake of crimson lake.

"Art thou only a beginner?" said E23, labouring literally for the dear life, as he slid out of his body-wrappings and stood clear in the loincloth while Kim splashed in a noble caste-mark on the ash-smeared brow.

"But two days entered to the Game, brother," Kim replied. "Smear more ash on the bosom."

"Hast thou met – a physician of sick pearls?" He switched out his long, tight-rolled turban-cloth and, with swiftest hands, rolled it over and under about his loins into the intricate devices of a Saddhu's cincture.

"Hah! Dost thou know his touch, then? He was my teacher for a while. We must bar thy legs. Ash cures wounds. Smear it again."

"I was his pride once, but thou art almost better. The Gods are kind to us! Give me *that*."

It was a tin box of opium pills among the rubbish of the Jat's bundle. E23 gulped down a half handful. "They are good against hunger, fear, and chill. And they make the eyes red too," he explained. "Now I shall have heart to play the Game. We lack only a Saddhu's tongs. What of the old clothes?"

Kim rolled them small, and stuffed them into the slack folds of his tunic. With a yellow-ochre paint cake he smeared the legs and the breast, great streaks against the background of flour, ash, and turmeric.

"The blood on them is enough to hang thee, brother."

"Maybe; but no need to throw them out of the window... It is finished." His voice thrilled with a boy's pure delight in the Game. "Turn and look, O Jat!"

"The Gods protect us," said the hooded Kamboh, emerging like a buffalo from the reeds. "But – whither went the Mahratta? What hast thou done?"

Kim had been trained by Lurgan Sahib; and E23, by virtue of his business, was no bad actor. In place of the tremulous, shrinking trader there lolled against the corner an all but naked, ash-smeared, ochre-barred, dusty-haired Saddhu, his swollen eyes – opium takes quick effect on an empty stomach – luminous with insolence and bestial lust, his legs crossed under him, Kim's brown rosary round his neck, and a scant yard of worn, flowered chintz on his shoulders. The child buried his face in his amazed father's arms.

"Look up, Princeling! We travel with warlocks, but they will not hurt thee. Oh, do not cry... What is the sense of curing a child one day and killing him with fright the next?"

"The child will be fortunate all his life. He has seen a great healing. When I was a child I made clay men and horses."

"I have made them too. Sir Banás, he comes in the night and makes them all alive at the back of our kitchen-midden," piped the child.

"And so thou art not frightened at anything. Eh, Prince?"

"I was frightened because my father was frightened. I felt his arms shake."

"Oh, chicken-man!" said Kim, and even the abashed Jat laughed. "I have done a healing on this poor trader. He must forsake his gains and his account-books, and sit by the wayside three nights to overcome the malignity of his enemies. The stars are against him."

"The fewer moneylenders the better, say I; but, Saddhu or no Saddhu, he should pay for my stuff on his shoulders."

"So? But that is thy child on thy shoulder – given over to the burning-ghat not two days ago. There remains one thing more. I did this charm in thy presence because need was great. I changed his shape and his soul. None the less, if, by any chance, O man from Jullundur, thou rememberest what thou hast seen, either among the elders sitting under the village tree, or in thine own house, or in company of thy priest when he blesses thy cattle, a murrain will come among the buffaloes, and a fire in thy thatch, and rats in thy corn-bin, and the curse of our Gods upon thy fields that they may be barren before thy feet and after thy ploughshare." This was part of an old curse picked up from a *fakir* by the Taksali Gate in the days of Kim's innocence. It lost nothing by repetition.

"Cease, Holy One! In mercy, cease!" cried the Jat. "Do not curse the household. I saw nothing! I heard nothing! I am thy cow!" and he made to grab at Kim's bare foot beating rhythmically on the carriage floor.

"But since thou hast been permitted to aid me in the matter of a pinch of flour and a little opium and such trifles as I have honoured by using in my art, so will the Gods return a blessing," and he gave it at length, to the man's immense relief. It was one that he had learned from Lurgan Sahib.

The lama stared through his spectacles as he had not stared at the business of disguisement.

"Friend of the Stars," he said at last, "thou hast acquired great wisdom. Beware that it does not give birth to pride. No man having the Law before his eyes speaks hastily of any matter which he has seen or encountered."

"No – no – no, indeed," cried the farmer, fearful lest the master should be minded to improve on the pupil. E23, with relaxed mouth, gave himself up to the opium that is meat, tobacco, and medicine to the spent Asiatic.

So, in a silence of awe and great miscomprehension, they slid into Delhi about lamp-lighting time.

Chapter 12

Who hath desired the Sea – the sight of salt-water unbounded?
The heave and the halt and the hurl and the crash of the comber
    wind-hounded?
The sleek-barrelled swell before storm – grey, foamless, enormous,
    and growing?
Stark calm on the lap of the Line – or the crazy-eyed hurricane
    blowing?
His Sea in no showing the same – his Sea and the same 'neath all
    showing –
      His Sea that his being fulfils?
So and no otherwise – so and no otherwise hill-men desire their Hills!

                        The Sea and the Hills

"I have found my heart again," said E23, under cover of the platform's tumult. "Hunger and fear make men dazed, or I might have thought of this escape before. I was right. They come to hunt for me. Thou hast saved my head."

A group of yellow-trousered Punjab policemen, headed by a hot and perspiring young Englishman, parted the crowd about the carriages. Behind them, inconspicuous as a cat, ambled a small fat person who looked like a lawyer's tout.

"See the young sahib reading from a paper. My description is in his hand," said E23. "They go carriage by carriage, like fisher-folk netting a pool."

When the procession reached their compartment, E23 was counting his beads with a steady jerk of the wrist; while Kim jeered at him for being so

drugged as to have lost the ringed fire-tongs which are the Saddhu's distin-
guishing mark. The lama, deep in meditation, stared straight before him;
and the farmer, glancing furtively, gathered up his belongings.

"Nothing here but a parcel of holy-bolies," said the Englishman aloud,
and passed on amid a ripple of uneasiness; for native police mean extortion
to the native all India over.

"The trouble now," whispered E23, "lies in sending a wire as to the place
where I hid that letter I was sent to find. I cannot go to the *tar*-office in this
guise."

"Is it not enough I have saved thy neck?"

"Not if the work be left unfinished. Did never the healer of sick pearls
tell thee so? Comes another sahib! Ah!"

This was a tallish, sallowish District Superintendent of Police – belt,
helmet, polished spurs and all – strutting and twirling his dark moustache.

"What fools are these police sahibs!" said Kim genially.

E23 glanced up under his eyelids. "It is well said," he muttered in a
changed voice. "I go to drink water. Keep my place."

He blundered out almost into the Englishman's arms, and was bad-
worded in clumsy Urdu.

"*Tum mut?* You drunk? You mustn't bang about as though Delhi station
belonged to you, my friend."

E23, not moving a muscle of his countenance, answered with a stream
of the filthiest abuse, at which Kim naturally rejoiced. It reminded him of
the drummer-boys and the barrack-sweepers at Umballa in the terrible time
of his first schooling.

"My good fool," the Englishman drawled. "*Nickle-jao!* Go back to your
carriage."

Step by step, withdrawing deferentially, and dropping his voice, the
yellow Saddhu clomb back to the carriage, cursing the DSP to remotest
posterity by – here Kim almost jumped – by the curse of the Queen's Stone,
by the writing under the Queen's Stone and by an assortment of Gods with
wholly new names.

"I don't know what you're saying" – the Englishman flushed angrily –
"but it's some piece of blasted impertinence. Come out of that!"

E23, affecting to misunderstand, gravely produced his ticket, which the Englishman wrenched angrily from his hand.

"Oh, *zoolum!* What oppression!" growled the Jat from his corner. "All for the sake of a jest too." He had been grinning at the freedom of the Saddhu's tongue. "Thy charms do not work well today, Holy One!"

The Saddhu followed the policeman, fawning and supplicating. The ruck of passengers, busy with their babies and their bundles, had not noticed the affair. Kim slipped out behind him; for it flashed through his head that he had heard this angry, stupid sahib discoursing loud personalities to an old lady near Umballa three years ago.

"It is well," the Saddhu whispered, jammed in the calling, shouting, bewildered press – a Persian greyhound between his feet and a cageful of yelling hawks under charge of a Rajput falconer in the small of his back. "He has gone now to send word of the letter which I hid. They told me he was in Peshawar. I might have known that he is like the crocodile – always at the other ford. He has saved me from present calamity, but I owe my life to thee."

"Is he also one of us?" Kim ducked under a Mewar camel-driver's greasy armpit and cannoned off a covey of jabbering Sikh matrons.

"Not less than the greatest. We are both fortunate! I will make report to him of what thou hast done. I am safe under his protection."

He bored through the edge of the crowd besieging the carriages, and squatted by the bench near the telegraph-office.

"Return, or they take thy place! Have no fear for the work, brother – or my life. Thou hast given me a breathing-space, and Strickland Sahib has pulled me to land. We may work together at the Game yet. Farewell!"

Kim hurried to his carriage: elated, bewildered, but a little nettled in that he had no key to the secrets about him.

"I am only a beginner at the Game, that is sure. *I* could not have leaped into safety as did the Saddhu. He knew it was darkest under the lamp. *I* could not have thought to tell news under pretence of cursing... and how clever was the sahib! No matter, I saved the life of one... Where is the Kamboh gone, Holy One?" he whispered, as he took his seat in the now crowded compartment.

"A fear gripped him," the lama replied, with a touch of tender malice. "He saw thee change the Mahratta to a Saddhu in the twinkling of an eye, as a protection against evil. That shook him. Then he saw the Saddhu fall sheer into the hands of the *polis* – all the effect of thy art. Then he gathered up his son and fled; for he said that thou didst change a quiet trader into an impudent bandier of words with sahibs, and he feared a like fate. Where is the Saddhu?"

"With the *polis*," said Kim… "Yet I saved the Kamboh's child."

The lama snuffed blandly.

"Ah, *chela*, see how thou art overtaken! Thou didst cure the Kamboh's child solely to acquire merit. But thou didst put a spell on the Mahratta with prideful workings – I watched thee – and with sidelong glances to bewilder an old old man and a foolish farmer: whence calamity and suspicion."

Kim controlled himself with an effort beyond his years. Not more than any other youngster did he like to eat dirt or to be misjudged, but he saw himself in a cleft stick. The train rolled out of Delhi into the night.

"It is true," he murmured. "Where I have offended thee I have done wrong."

"It is more, *chela*. Thou hast loosed an act upon the world, and as a stone thrown into a pool so spread the consequences thou canst not tell how far."

This ignorance was well both for Kim's vanity and for the lama's peace of mind, when we think that there was then being handed in at Simla a code-wire reporting the arrival of E23 at Delhi, and, more important, the whereabouts of a letter he had been commissioned to – abstract. Incidentally, an over-zealous policeman had arrested, on charge of murder done in a far southern state, a horribly indignant Ajmir cotton-broker, who was explaining himself to a Mr Strickland on Delhi platform, while E23 was paddling through byways into the locked heart of Delhi city. In two hours several telegrams had reached the angry minister of a southern state reporting that all trace of a somewhat bruised Mahratta had been lost; and by the time the leisurely train halted at Saharunpore the last ripple of the stone Kim had helped to heave was lapping against the steps of a mosque in far-away Roum – where it disturbed a pious man at prayers.

The lama made his in ample form near the dewy bougainvillea trellis near the platform, cheered by the clear sunshine and the presence of his disciple. "We will put these things behind us," he said, indicating the brazen engine and the gleaming track. "The jolting of the *te-rain* – though a wonderful thing – has turned my bones to water. We will use clean air henceforward."

"Let us go to the Kulu woman's house" said Kim, and stepped forth cheerily under the bundles. Early morning Saharunpore way is clean and well scented. He thought of the other mornings at St Xavier's, and it topped his already thrice-heaped contentment.

"Where is this new haste born from? Wise men do not run about like chickens in the sun. We have come hundreds upon hundreds of *koss* already, and, till now, I have scarcely been alone with thee an instant. How canst thou receive instruction all jostled of crowds? How can I, whelmed by a flux of talk, meditate upon the Way?"

"Her tongue grows no shorter with the years, then?" The disciple smiled.

"Nor her desire for charms. I remember once when I spoke of the Wheel of Life" – the lama fumbled in his bosom for his latest copy – "she was only curious about the devils that besiege children. She shall acquire merit by entertaining us – in a little while – at an after-occasion – softly, softly. Now we will wander loose-foot, waiting upon the Chain of Things. The Search is sure."

So they travelled very easily across and among the broad bloomful fruit-gardens – by way of Aminabad, Sahaigunge, Akrola of the Ford, and little Phulesa – the line of the Siwaliks always to the north, and behind them again the snows. After long, sweet sleep under the dry stars came the lordly, leisurely passage through a waking village – begging-bowl held forth in silence, but eyes roving in defiance of the Law from sky's edge to sky's edge. Then would Kim return soft-footed through the dust to his master under the shadow of a mango tree or the thinner shade of a white Doon *siris*, to eat and drink at ease. At midday, after talk and a little wayfaring, they slept; meeting the world refreshed when the air was cooler. Night found them adventuring into new territory – some chosen village spied three hours before across the fat land, and much discussed upon the road.

There they told their tale – a new one each evening so far as Kim was concerned – and there were they made welcome, either by priest or head-man, after the custom of the kindly East.

When the shadows shortened and the lama leaned more heavily upon Kim, there was always the Wheel of Life to draw forth, to hold flat under wiped stones, and with a long straw to expound cycle by cycle. Here sat the Gods on high – and they were dreams of dreams. Here was our Heaven and the world of the demi-Gods – horsemen fighting among the hills. Here were the agonies done upon the beasts, souls ascending or descending the ladder and therefore not to be interfered with. Here were the Hells, hot and cold, and the abodes of tormented ghosts. Let the *chela* study the troubles that come from overeating – bloated stomach and burning bowels. Obediently, then, with bowed head and brown finger alert to follow the pointer, did the *chela* study; but when they came to the Human World, busy and profitless, that is just above the Hells, his mind was distracted; for by the roadside trundled the very Wheel itself, eating, drinking, trading, marrying, and quarrelling – all warmly alive. Often the lama made the living pictures the matter of his text, bidding Kim – too ready – note how the flesh takes a thousand thousand shapes, desirable or detestable as men reckon, but in truth of no account either way; and how the stupid spirit, bond-slave to the Hog, the Dove, and the Serpent – lusting after betel-nut, a new yoke of oxen, women, or the favour of kings – is bound to follow the body through all the Heavens and all the Hells, and strictly round again. Sometimes a woman or a poor man, watching the ritual – it was nothing else – when the great yellow chart was unfolded, would throw a few flowers or a handful of cowries upon its edge. It sufficed these humble ones that they had met a Holy One who might be moved to remember them in his prayers.

"Cure them if they are sick," said the lama, when Kim's sporting instincts woke. "Cure them if they have fever, but by no means work charms. Remember what befell the Mahratta."

"Then all doing is evil?" Kim replied, lying out under a big tree at the fork of the Doon road, watching the little ants run over his hand.

"To abstain from action is well – except to acquire merit."

"At the Gates of Learning we were taught that to abstain from action was unbefitting a sahib. And I am a sahib."

"Friend of all the World," – the lama looked directly at Kim – "I am an old man – pleased with shows as are children. To those who follow the

Way there is neither black nor white, Hind nor Bhotiyal. We be all souls seeking escape. No matter what thy wisdom learned among sahibs, when we come to my River thou wilt be freed from all illusion – at my side. *Hai!* my bones ache for that River, as they ached in the *te-rain;* but my spirit sits above my bones, waiting. The Search is sure!"

"I am answered. Is it permitted to ask a question?"

The lama inclined his stately head.

"I ate thy bread for three years – as thou knowest. Holy One, whence came –?"

"There is much wealth, as men count it, in Bhotiyal," the lama returned with composure. "In my own place I have the illusion of honour. I ask for that I need. I am not concerned with the account. That is for my monastery. *Ai!* The black high seats in the monastery, and the novices all in order!"

And he told stories, tracing with a finger in the dust, of the immense and sumptuous ritual of avalanche-guarded cathedrals; of processions and devil-dances; of the changing of monks and nuns into swine; of holy cities fifteen thousand feet in the air; of intrigue between monastery and monastery; of voices among the hills, and of that mysterious mirage that dances on dry snow. He spoke even of Lhasa and of the Dalai Lama, whom he had seen and adored.

Each long, perfect day rose behind Kim for a barrier to cut him off from his race and his mother-tongue. He slipped back to thinking and dreaming in the vernacular, and mechanically followed the lama's ceremonial observances at eating, drinking, and the like. The old man's mind turned more and more to his monastery as his eyes turned to the steadfast snows. His River troubled him nothing. Now and again, indeed, he would gaze long and long at a tuft or a twig, expecting, he said, the earth to cleave and deliver its blessing; but he was content to be with his disciple, at ease in the temperate wind that comes down from the Doon. This was not Ceylon, nor Buddh Gaya, nor Bombay, nor some grass-tangled ruins that he seemed to have stumbled upon two years ago. He spoke of those places as a scholar removed from vanity, as a Seeker walking in humility, as an old man, wise and temperate, illumining knowledge with brilliant insight. Bit by bit, disconnectedly, each tale called up by some wayside thing, he spoke of all his wanderings up and down Hind; till Kim, who had loved him without reason, now loved him for fifty good reasons. So they enjoyed themselves in high felicity, abstaining, as the Rule demands, from evil words, covetous desires; not overeating, not lying on high beds, nor wearing rich clothes. Their stomachs told them the time, and the people brought them their food, as the saying is. They were lords of the villages of Aminabad, Sahaigunge, Akrola of the Ford, and little Phulesa, where Kim gave the soulless woman a blessing.

But news travels fast in India, and too soon shuffled across the crop-land, bearing a basket of fruits with a box of Kabul grapes and gilt oranges, a white-whiskered servitor – a lean, dry Oorya – begging them to bring the honour of their presence to his mistress, distressed in her mind that the lama had neglected her so long.

"Now do I remember" – the lama spoke as though it were a wholly new proposition. "She is virtuous, but an inordinate talker."

Kim was sitting on the edge of a cow's manger, telling stories to a village smith's children.

"She will only ask for another son for her daughter. I have not forgotten her," he said. "Let her acquire merit. Send word that we will come."

They covered eleven miles through the fields in two days, and were overwhelmed with attentions at the end; for the old lady held a fine tradition of hospitality, to which she forced her son-in-law, who was under the thumb of his women-folk and bought peace by borrowing of the money-lender. Age had not weakened her tongue or her memory, and from a discreetly barred upper window, in the hearing of not less than a dozen servants, she paid Kim compliments that would have flung European audiences into unclean dismay.

"But thou art still the shameless beggar-brat of the *parao*," she shrilled. "I have not forgotten thee. Wash ye and eat. The father of my daughter's son is gone away awhile. So we poor women are dumb and useless."

For proof, she harangued the entire household unsparingly till food and drink were brought; and in the evening – the smoke-scented evening, copper-dun and turquoise across the fields – it pleased her to order her palanquin to be set down in the untidy forecourt by smoky torchlight; and there, behind not too closely drawn curtains, she gossiped.

"Had the Holy One come alone, I should have received him otherwise; but with this rogue, who can be too careful?"

"Maharanee," said Kim, choosing as always the amplest title, "is it my fault that none other than a sahib – a *polis*-sahib – called the Maharanee whose face he–"

"Chutt! That was on the pilgrimage. When we travel – thou knowest the proverb."

"Called the Maharanee a Breaker of Hearts and a Dispenser of Delights?"

"To remember that! It was true. So he did. That was in the time of the bloom of my beauty." She chuckled like a contented parrot above the sugar lump. "Now tell me of thy goings and comings – as much as may be without shame. How many maids, and whose wives, hang upon thine eyelashes? Ye hail from Benares? I would have gone there again this year, but my daughter – we have only two sons. Phaii! Such is the effect of these low plains. Now in Kulu men are elephants. But I would ask thy Holy One – stand aside, rogue – a charm against most lamentable windy colics that in mango-time overtake my daughter's eldest. Two years back he gave me a powerful spell."

"Oh, Holy One!" said Kim, bubbling with mirth at the lama's rueful face.

"It is true. I gave her one against wind."

"Teeth – teeth – teeth," snapped the old woman.

"'Cure them if they are sick,'" Kim quoted relishingly, "'but by no means work charms. Remember what befell the Mahratta.'"

"That was two rains ago; she wearied me with her continual importunity." The lama groaned as the Unjust Judge had groaned before him. "Thus it comes – take note, my *chela* – that even those who would follow the Way are thrust aside by idle women. Three days through, when the child was sick, she talked to me."

"*Arré!* and to whom else should I talk? The boy's mother knew nothing, and the father – in the nights of the cold weather it was – 'Pray to the Gods,' said he, forsooth, and turning over, snored!"

"I gave her the charm. What is an old man to do?"

"'To abstain from action is well – except to acquire merit.'"

"Ah, *chela*, if thou desertest me, I am all alone."

"He found his milk-teeth easily at any rate," said the old lady. "But all priests are alike."

Kim coughed severely. Being young, he did not approve of her flippancy. "To importune the wise out of season is to invite calamity."

"There is a talking mynah" – the thrust came back with the well-remembered snap of the jewelled forefinger – "over the stables which has picked up the very tone of the family priest. Maybe I forget honour to my guests, but if ye had seen *him* double his fists into his belly, which was like a half-grown gourd, and cry: 'Here is the pain!' ye would forgive. I am half minded to take the *hakim's* medicine. He sells it cheap, and certainly it makes him as fat as Shiv's own bull. *He* does not deny remedies, but I doubted for the child because of the inauspicious colour of the bottles."

The lama, under cover of the monologue, had faded out into the darkness towards the room prepared.

"Thou hast angered him, belike," said Kim.

"Not he. He is wearied, and I forgot, being a grandmother. (None but a grandmother should ever oversee a child. Mothers are only fit for bearing.) Tomorrow, when he sees how my daughter's son is grown, he will write the charm. Then, too, he can judge of the new *hakim's* drugs."

"Who is the *hakim*, Maharanee?"

"A wanderer, as thou art, but a most sober Bengali from Dacca – a master of medicine. He relieved me of an oppression after meat by means of a small pill that wrought like a devil unchained. He travels about now, vending preparations of great value. He has even papers, printed in Angrezi, telling what things he has done for weak-backed men and slack women. He has been here four days; but hearing ye were coming (*hakims* and priests are snake and tiger the world over) he has, as I take it, gone to cover."

While she drew breath after this volley, the ancient servant, sitting unrebuked on the edge of the torchlight, muttered: "This house is a cattle-pound, as it were, for all charlatans and – priests. Let the boy stop eating mangoes... but who can argue with a grandmother?" He raised his voice respectfully: "Sahiba, the *hakim* sleeps after his meat. He is in the quarters behind the dovecot."

Kim bristled like an expectant terrier. To outface and down-talk a Calcutta-taught Bengali, a voluble Dacca drug-vendor, would be a good game. It was not seemly that the lama, and incidentally himself, should be thrown aside for such an one. He knew those curious bastard English advertisements at the backs of native newspapers. St Xavier's boys sometimes brought them in by stealth to snigger over among their mates; for the language of the grateful patient recounting his symptoms is most simple and revealing. The Oorya, not unanxious to play off one parasite against the other, slunk away towards the dovecot.

"Yes," said Kim, with measured scorn. "Their stock-in-trade is a little coloured water and a very great shamelessness. Their prey are broken-down kings and overfed Bengalis. Their profit is in children – who are not yet born."

The old lady chuckled. "Do not be envious. Charms are better, eh? *I* never gainsaid it. See that thy Holy One writes me a good amulet by the morning."

"None but the ignorant deny" – a thick, heavy voice boomed through the darkness, as a figure came to rest squatting – "None but the ignorant deny the value of charms. None but the ignorant deny the value of medicines."

"A rat found a piece of turmeric. Said he: 'I will open a grocer's shop,'" Kim retorted.

Battle was fairly joined now, and they heard the old lady stiffen to attention.

"The priest's son knows the names of his nurse and three Gods. Says he: 'Hear me, or I will curse you by the three million Great Ones.'" Decidedly this invisible had an arrow or two in his quiver. He went on: "I am but a teacher of the alphabet. I have learned all the wisdom of the sahibs."

"The sahibs never grow old. They dance and they play like children when they are grandfathers. A strong-backed breed," piped the voice inside the palanquin.

"I have, too, our drugs which loosen humours of the head in hot and angry men. *Sinà* well compounded when the moon stands in the proper House; yellow earths I have – *arplan* from China that makes a man renew his youth and astonish his household; saffron from Kashmir, and the best salep of Kabul. Many people have died before –"

"That I surely believe," said Kim.

"They knew the value of my drugs. I do not give *my* sick the mere ink in which a charm is written, but hot and rending drugs which descend and wrestle with the evil."

"Very mightily they do so," sighed the old lady.

The voice launched into an immense tale of misfortune and bankruptcy, studded with plentiful petitions to the government. "But for my fate, which overrules all, I had been now in government employ. I bear a degree from the great school at Calcutta – whither, maybe, the son of this house shall go."

"He shall indeed. If our neighbour's brat can in a few years be made an FA" (First Arts – she used the English word, of which she had heard so often), "how much more shall children clever as somé that I know bear away prizes at rich Calcutta."

"Never," said the voice, "have I seen such a child! Born in an auspicious hour, and – but for that colic which, alas! turning into black cholers, may carry him off like a pigeon – destined to many years, he is enviable."

"*Hai mai!*" said the old lady. "To praise children is inauspicious, or I could listen to this talk. But the back of the house is unguarded, and even in this soft air men think themselves to be men, and women we know… The child's father is away too, and I must be *chowkedar* [watchman] in my old age. Up! Up! Take up the palanquin. Let the *hakim* and the young priest settle between them whether charms or medicine most avail. Ho! worthless people, fetch tobacco for the guests, and – round the homestead go I!"

The palanquin reeled off, followed by straggling torches and a horde of dogs. Twenty villages knew the Sahiba – her failings, her tongue, and her large charity. Twenty villages cheated her after immemorial custom, but no man would have stolen or robbed within her jurisdiction for any gift under heaven. None the less, she made great parade of her formal inspections, the riot of which could be heard half-way to Mussoorie.

Kim relaxed, as one augur must when he meets another. The *hakim*, still squatting, slid over his hookah with a friendly foot, and Kim pulled at the good weed. The hangers-on expected grave professional debate, and perhaps a little free doctoring.

"To discuss medicine before the ignorant is of one piece with teaching the peacock to sing," said the *hakim*.

"True courtesy," Kim echoed, "is very often in-attention."

These, be it understood, were company-manners, designed to impress.

"Hi! I have an ulcer on my leg," cried a scullion. "Look at it!"

"Get hence! Remove!" said the *hakim*. "Is it the habit of the place to pester honoured guests? Ye crowd in like buffaloes."

"If the Sahiba knew –" Kim began.

"*Ai! Ai!* Come away. They are meat for our mistress. When her young Shaitan's colics are cured perhaps we poor people may be suffered to –"

"The mistress fed thy wife when thou wast in jail for breaking the moneylender's head. Who speaks against her?" The old servitor curled his white moustaches savagely in the young moonlight. "*I* am responsible for the honour of this house. Go!" and he drove the underlings before him.

Said the *hakim*, hardly more than shaping the words with his lips: "How do you do, Mister O'Hara? I am jolly glad to see you again."

Kim's hand clenched about the pipe-stem. Anywhere on the open road, perhaps, he would not have been astonished; but here, in this quiet backwater of life, he was not prepared for Hurree Babu. It annoyed him, too, that he had been hoodwinked.

"Ah ha! I told you at Lucknow – *resurgam* – I shall rise again and you shall not know me. How much did you bet –eh?"

He chewed leisurely upon a few cardamom seeds, but he breathed uneasily.

"But why come here, Babuji?"

"Ah! *Thatt* is the question, as Shakespeare hath it. I come to congratulate you on your extraordinary effeecient performance at Delhi. Oah! I tell you we are all proud of you. It was verree neat and handy. Our mutual friend, he is old friend of mine. He has been in some dam" tight places. Now he will be in some more. He told me; I tell Mr Lurgan; and he is pleased you graduate so nicely. All the Department is pleased."

For the first time in his life, Kim thrilled to the clean pride (it can be a deadly pitfall, none the less) of departmental praise – ensnaring praise from an equal of work appreciated by fellow-workers. Earth has nothing on the same plane to compare with it. But, cried the Oriental in him, babus do not travel far to retail compliments.

"Tell thy tale, Babu," he said authoritatively.

"Oah, it is nothing. Onlee I was at Simla when the wire came in about what our mutual friend said he had hidden, and old Creighton –" He looked to see how Kim would take this piece of audacity.

"The Colonel Sahib," the boy from St Xavier's corrected.

"*Of* course. He found me at a loose string, and I had to go down to Chitor to find that beastly letter. I do not like the south – too much railway travel; but I drew good travelling allowance. Ha! Ha! I meet our mutual at Delhi on the way back. He lies quiett just now, and says Saddhu disguise suits him to the ground. Well, there I hear what you have done so well, so quickly, upon the instantaneous spur of the moment. I tell our mutual you take the bally bun, by Jove! It was splendid. I come to tell you so."

"Umm!"

The frogs were busy in the ditches, and the moon slid to her setting. Some happy servant had gone out to commune with the night and to beat upon a drum. Kim's next sentence was in the vernacular.

"How didst thou follow us?"

"Oah. Thatt was nothing. I know from our mutual friend you go to Saharunpore. So I come on. Red Lamas are not inconspicuous persons. I buy myself my drug-box, and I am very good doctor really. I go to Akrola of the Ford, and hear all about you and I talk here and talk there. All the common people know what you do. I knew when the hospitable old lady sent the *dooli*. They have great recollections of the old lama's visits here. I know old ladies cannot keep their hands from medicines. So I am a doctor, and – you hear my talk? *I* think it is verree good. My word, Mister O'Hara, they know about you and the lama for fifty miles – the common people. So I come. Do you mind?"

"Babuji," said Kim, looking up at the broad, grinning face, "I am a sahib."

"My dear Mister O'Hara –"

"And I hope to play the Great Game."

"You are subordinate to me departmentally at present."

"Then why talk like an ape in a tree? Men do not come after one from Simla and change their dress, for the sake of a few sweet words. I am not a child. Talk Hindi and let us get to the yolk of the egg. Thou art here – speaking not one word of truth in ten. Why art thou here? Give a straight answer."

"That is so verree disconcerting of the Europeans, Mister O'Hara. *You* should know a heap better at your time of life."

"But I want to know," said Kim, laughing. "If it is the Game, I may help. How can I do anything if you *bukh* [babble] all round the shop?"

Hurree Babu reached for the pipe, and sucked it till it guggled again.

"Now I will speak vernacular. You sit tight, Mister O'Hara… It concerns the pedigree of a white stallion."

"Still? That was finished long ago."

"When every one is dead the Great Game is finished. Not before. Listen to me till the end. There were five kings who prepared a sudden war three years ago, when thou wast given the stallion's pedigree by Mahbub Ali. Upon them, because of that news, and ere they were ready, fell our army."

"Ay – eight thousand men with guns. I remember that night."

"But the war was not pushed. That is the government custom. The troops were recalled because the government believed the five kings were cowed; and it is not cheap to feed men among the high passes. Hilás and Bunár – rajahs with guns – undertook for a price to guard the passes against all coming from the north. They protested both fear and friendship." He broke off with a giggle into English: "Of course, I tell you this unoffeecially to elucidate political situation, Mister O'Hara. Offeecially, I am debarred from criticizing any action of superiors. Now I go on – This pleased the government, anxious to avoid expense, and a bond was made for so many rupees a month that Hilás and Bunár should guard the passes as soon as the state's troops were withdrawn. At that time – it was after we two met – I, who had been selling tea in Leh, became a clerk of accounts in the army. When the troops were withdrawn, I was left behind to pay the coolies who made new roads in the Hills. This road-making was part of the bond between Bunár, Hilás, and the government."

"So? And then?"

"I tell you, it was jolly-beastly cold up there too, after summer," said Hurree Babu confidentially. "I was afraid these Bunár men would cut my throat every night for thee pay-chest. My native sepoy-guard, they laughed at me! By Jove! I was such a fearful man. Nevar mind thatt. I go on colloquially… I send word many times that these two kings were sold to the north; and Mahbub Ali, who was yet farther north, amply confirmed it. Nothing was done. Only my feet were frozen, and a toe dropped off. I sent word that the roads for which I was paying money to the diggers were being made for the feet of strangers and enemies."

"For?"

"For the Russians. The thing was an open jest among the coolies. Then I was called down to tell what I knew by speech of tongue. Mahbub came south too. See the end! Over the passes this year after snow-melting" – he shivered afresh – "come two strangers under cover of shooting wild goats. They bear guns, but they bear also chains and levels and compasses."

"Oho! The things get clearer."

"They are well received by Hilás and Bunár. They make great promises; they speak as the mouthpiece of a kaisar with gifts. Up the valleys, down the valleys go they, saying, 'Here is a place to build a breastwork; here can ye pitch a fort. Here can ye hold the road against an army' – the very roads for which I paid out the rupees monthly. The government knows, but does nothing. The three other kings, who were *not* paid for guarding the passes, tell them by runner of the bad faith of Bunár and Hilás. When all the evil is done, look you – when those two strangers with the levels and the compasses make the five kings to believe that a great army will sweep the passes tomorrow or the next day – hill-people are all fools – comes the order to me, Hurree Babu, 'Go north and see what those strangers do.' I say to Creighton Sahib, 'This is not a lawsuit, that we go about to collect eyidence.'" Hurree returned to his English with a jerk: "'By Jove,' I said, 'why the dooce do you not issue demi-offeecial orders to some brave man to poison them, for an example? It is, if you permit the observation, most reprehensible laxity on your part.' And Colonel Creighton, he laughed at me! It is all your beastly English pride. You think no one dare conspire! That is all tommy-rott."

Kim smoked slowly, revolving the business, so far as he understood it, in his quick mind.

"Then thou goest forth to follow the strangers?"

"No. To meet them. They are coming in to Simla to send their horns and heads to be dressed at Calcutta. They are exclusively sporting gentlemen, and they are allowed special faceelities by the government. Of course, we always do that. It is our British pride."

"Then what is to fear from them?"

"By Jove, they are not black people. I can do all sorts of things with black people, of course. They are Russians, and highly unscrupulous people. I – I do not want to consort with them without a witness."

"Will they kill thee?"

"Oah, thatt is nothing. I am good enough Herbert Spencerian, I trust, to meet little thing like death, which is all in my fate, you know. But – but they may beat me."

"Why?"

Hurree Babu snapped his fingers with irritation. "Of *course* I shall affee-liate myself to their camp in supernumerary capacity as perhaps interpreter, or person mentally impotent and hungree, or some such thing. And then I must pick up what I can, I suppose. That is as easy for me as playing Mister Doctor to the old lady. Onlee – onlee – you see, Mister O'Hara, I am unfortunately Asiatic, which is serious detriment in some respects. And *all-so* I am Bengali – a fearful man."

"God made the Hare and the Bengali. What shame?" said Kim, quoting the proverb.

"It was process of Evolution, *I* think, from Primal Necessity, but the fact remains in all the *cui bono*. I am, oh, awfully fearful! – I remember once they wanted to cut off my head on the road to Lhasa. (No, I have never reached to Lhasa.) I sat down and cried, Mister O'Hara, anticipating Chinese tortures. I do not suppose these two gentlemen will torture me, but I like to provide for possible contingency with European assistance in emergency." He coughed and spat out the cardamoms. "It is purely unoffeecial indent, to which you can say 'No, Babu.' If you have no pressing engagement with your old man – perhaps you might divert him; perhaps I can seduce his fancies – I should like you to keep in departmental touch with me till I find those sporting coves. I have great opeenion of you since I met my friend at Delhi. And also I will embody your name in my offeecial report when matter is finally adjudicated. It will be a great feather in your cap. That is why I come really."

"Humph! The end of the tale, I think, is true; but what of the fore-part?"

"About the five kings? Oah! there is ever so much truth in it. A lots more than you would suppose," said Hurree earnestly. "You come – eh? I go from here straight into the Doon. It is verree verdant and painted meads. I shall go to Mussoorie – to good old Munsoorie Pahar, as the gentlemen and ladies say. Then by Rampur into Chini. That is the only way they can come. I do not like waiting in the cold, but we must wait for them. I want to walk with them to Simla. You see, one Russian is a Frenchman, and I know my French pretty well. I have friends in Chandernagore."

"*He* would certainly rejoice to see the Hills again," said Kim meditatively. "All his speech these ten days past has been of little else. If we go together –"

"Oah! We can be quite strangers on the road, if your lama prefers. I shall just be four or five miles ahead. There is no hurry for Hurree – thatt is an Europe pun, ha! ha! – and you come after. There is plenty of time; they will plot and survey and map, of course. I shall go tomorrow, and you the next day, if you choose. Eh? You go think on it till morning. By Jove, it is near morning now." He yawned ponderously, and with never a civil word lumbered off to his sleeping-place. But Kim slept little, and his thoughts ran in Hindustani:

"Well is the Game called great! I was four days a scullion at Quetta, waiting on the wife of the man whose book I stole. And that was part of the Great Game! From the south – God knows how far – came up the Mahratta, playing the Great Game in fear of his life. Now I shall go far and far into the north playing the Great Game. Truly, it runs like a shuttle throughout all Hind. And my share and my joy" – he smiled to the darkness – "I owe to the lama here. Also to Mahbub Ali – also to Creighton Sahib, but chiefly to the Holy One. He is right – a great and a wonderful world – and I am Kim – Kim – Kim – alone – one person – in the middle of it all. But I will see these strangers with their levels and chains..."

"What was the upshot of last night's babble?" said the lama after his orisons.

"There came a strolling seller of drugs – a hanger-on of the Sahiba's. Him I abolished by arguments and prayers, proving that our charms are worthier than his coloured waters."

"Alas, my charms! Is the virtuous woman still bent upon a new one?"

"Very strictly."

"Then it must be written, or she will deafen me with her clamour." He fumbled at his pen-case.

"In the Plains," said Kim, "are always too many people. In the Hills, as I understand, there are fewer."

"Oh! the Hills, and the snows upon the Hills." The lama tore off a tiny square of paper fit to go in an amulet. "But what dost thou know of the Hills?"

"They are very close." Kim thrust open the door and looked at the long, peaceful line of the Himalayas flushed in morning-gold. "Except in the dress of a sahib, I have never set foot among them."

The lama snuffed the wind wistfully.

"If we go north," – Kim put the question to the waking sunrise – "would not much midday heat be avoided by walking among the lower hills at least?… Is the charm made, Holy One?"

"I have written the names of seven silly devils – not one of whom is worth a grain of dust in the eye. Thus do foolish women drag us from the Way!"

Hurree Babu came out from behind the dovecot, washing his teeth with ostentatious ritual. Full-fleshed, heavy-haunched, bull-necked, and deep-voiced, he did not look like a "fearful man". Kim signed almost imperceptibly that matters were in good train, and when the morning toilet was over, Hurree Babu, in flowery speech, came to do honour to the lama. They ate, of course, apart, and afterwards the old lady, more or less veiled behind a window, returned to the vital business of green-mango colics in the young. The lama's knowledge of medicine was, of course, sympathetic only. He believed that the dung of a black horse, mixed with sulphur, and carried in a snake-skin, was a sound remedy for cholera; but the symbolism interested him far more than the science. Hurree Babu deferred to these views with enchanting politeness, so that the lama called him a courteous physician. Hurree Babu replied that he was no more than an inexpert dabbler in the mysteries; but at least – he thanked the Gods therefore – he knew when he sat in the presence of a master. He himself had been taught by the sahibs, who do not consider expense, in the lordly halls of Calcutta; but, as he was ever first to acknowledge, there lay a wisdom behind earthly wisdom – the high and lonely lore of meditation. Kim looked on with envy. The Hurree Babu of his knowledge – oily, effusive, and nervous – was gone; gone, too, was the brazen drug-vendor of overnight. There remained – polished, polite, attentive – a sober, learned son of experience and adversity, gathering wisdom from the lama's lips. The old lady confided to Kim that these rare levels were beyond her. She liked charms with plenty of ink that one could wash off in water, swallow, and be done with. Else what was the use of the Gods? She liked men and women, and she spoke of them – of kinglets she had known in the past; of her own youth and beauty; of the depredations of leopards and the eccentricities of love Asiatic; of the inci- dence of taxation, rack-renting, funeral ceremonies, her son-in-law (this by allusion, easy to be followed), the care of the young, and the age's lack of decency. And Kim, as interested in the life of this world as she soon to leave it, squatted with his feet under the hem of his robe, drinking all in, while the lama demolished one after another every theory of body-curing put forward by Hurree Babu.

At noon the Babu strapped up his brass-bound drug-box, took his patent-leather shoes of ceremony in one hand, a gay blue-and-white umbrella in the other, and set off northwards to the Doon, where, he said, he was in demand among the lesser kings of those parts.

"We will go in the cool of the evening, *chela*," said the lama. "That doctor, learned in physic and courtesy, affirms that the people among these lower hills are devout, generous, and much in need of a teacher. In a very short time – so says the *hakim* – we come to cool air and the smell of pines."

"Ye go to the Hills? And by Kulu road? Oh, thrice happy!" shrilled the old lady. "But that I am a little pressed with the care of the homestead I would take palanquin... but that would be shameless, and my reputation would be cracked. Ho! Ho! I know the road – every march of the road I know. Ye will find charity throughout – it is not denied to the well-looking. I will give orders for provision. A servant to set you forth upon your jour-ney? No... Then I will at least cook ye good food."

"What a woman is the Sahiba!" said the white-bearded Oorya, when a tumult rose by the kitchen quarters. "She has never forgotten a friend: she has never forgotten an enemy in all her years. And her cookery – wah!" He rubbed his slim stomach.

There were cakes, there were sweetmeats, there was cold fowl stewed to rags with rice and prunes – enough to burden Kim like a mule.

"I am old and useless," she said. "None now love me – and none respect – but there are few to compare with me when I call on the Gods and squat to my cooking-pots. Come again, O people of good will. Holy One and disciple, come again. The room is always prepared; the welcome is always ready... See the women do not follow thy *chela* too openly. *I* know the women of Kulu. Take heed, *chela*, lest he run away when he smells his Hills again... *Hai!* Do not tilt the rice bag upside down... Bless the household, Holy One, and forgive thy servant her stupidities."

She wiped her red old eyes on a corner of her veil, and clucked throatily.

"Women talk," said the lama at last, "but that is a woman's infirmity. I gave her a charm. She is upon the Wheel and wholly given over to the shows of this life, but none the less, *chela*, she is virtuous, kindly, hospitable of a whole and zealous heart. Who shall say she does not acquire merit?"

"Not I, Holy One," said Kim, reslinging the bountiful provision on his shoulders. "In my mind – behind my eyes – I have tried to picture such an one altogether freed from the Wheel – desiring nothing, causing nothing – a nun, as it were."

"And, O imp?" The lama almost laughed aloud.

"I cannot make the picture."

"Nor I. But there are many, many millions of lives before her. She will get wisdom a little it may be, in each one."

"And will she forget how to make stews with saffron upon that road?"

"Thy mind is set on things unworthy. But she has skill. I am refreshed all over. When we reach the lower hills I shall be yet stronger. The *hakim* spoke truly to me this morn when he said a breath from the snows blows away twenty years from the life of a man. We will go up into the Hills – the high hills – up to the sound of snow-waters and the sound of the trees – for a little while. The *hakim* said that at any time we may return to the Plains, for we do no more than skirt the pleasant places. The *hakim* is full of learning; but he is in no way proud. I spoke to him – when thou wast talking to the Sahiba – of a certain dizziness that lays hold upon the back of my neck in the night, and he said it rose from excessive heat – to be cured by cool air. Upon consideration, I marvelled that I had not thought of such a simple remedy."

"Didst thou tell him of thy Search?" said Kim, a little jealously. He preferred to sway the lama by his own speech – not through the wiles of Hurree Babu.

"Assuredly. I told him of my dream, and of the manner by which I had acquired merit by causing thee to be taught wisdom."

"Thou didst not say I was a sahib?"

"What need? I have told thee many times we be but two souls seeking escape. He said – and he is just herein – that the River of Healing will break forth even as I dreamed – at my feet, if need be. Having found the Way, seest thou, that shall free me from the Wheel, need I trouble to find a way about the mere fields of the earth – which are illusion? That were senseless. I have my dreams, night upon night repeated; I have the *Jâtaka*; and I have thee, Friend of all the World. It was written in thy horoscope that a Red Bull on a green field – I have not forgotten – should bring thee to honour. Who but I saw that prophecy accomplished? Indeed, I was the instrument. Thou shalt find me my River, being in return the instrument. The Search is sure!"

He set his ivory-yellow face, serene and untroubled, towards the beckoning Hills; his shadow shouldering far before him in the dust.

Chapter 13

Who hath desired the Sea – the immense and contemptuous surges?
The shudder, the stumble, the swerve ere the star-stabbing
 bowsprit emerges –
The orderly clouds of the Trades and the ridged roaring sapphire
 thereunder –
Unheralded cliff-lurking flaws and the head-sails'
 low-volleying thunder?
His Sea in no wonder the same – his Sea and the same in each
 wonder –
     His Sea that his being fulfils?
So and no otherwise – so and no otherwise hill-men desire their Hills!
                                        The Sea and the Hills

"Who goes to the Hills goes to his mother." They had crossed the Siwaliks and the half-tropical Doon, left Mussoorie behind them, and headed north along the narrow hill roads. Day after day they struck deeper into the huddled mountains, and day after day Kim watched the lama return to a man's strength. Among the terraces of the Doon he had leaned on the boy's shoulder, ready to profit by wayside halts. Under the great ramp to Mussoorie he drew himself together as an old hunter faces a well-remembered bank, and where he should have sunk exhausted swung his long draperies about him, drew a deep double lungful of the diamond air, and walked as only a hillman can. Kim, plains-bred and plains-fed, sweated and panted astonished. "This is *my* country," said the lama. "Beside Such-zen, this is flatter than a rice field"; and with steady, driving strokes

562

from the loins he strode upwards. But it was on the steep downhill marches, three thousand feet in three hours, that he went utterly away from Kim, whose back ached with holding back, and whose big toe was nigh cut off by his grass sandal-string. Through the speckled shadow of the great deodar forests; through oak feathered and plumed with ferns; birch, ilex, rhododendron, and pine, out on to the bare hillsides' slippery sunburnt grass, and back into the woodlands' coolth again, till oak gave way to bamboo and palm of the valley, the lama swung untiring.

Glancing back in the twilight at the huge ridges behind him and the faint, thin line of the road whereby they had come, he would lay out, with a hillman's generous breadth of vision, fresh marches for the morrow; or, halting in the neck of some uplifted pass that gave on Spiti and Kulu, would stretch out his hands yearningly towards the high snows of the horizon. In the dawns they flared windy-red above stark blue, as Kedarnath and Badrinath – kings of that wilderness – took the first sunlight. All day long they lay like molten silver under the sun, and at evening put on their jewels again. At first they breathed temperately upon the travellers, winds good to meet when one crawled over some gigantic hog's back; but in a few days, at a height of nine or ten thousand feet, those breezes bit; and Kim kindly allowed a village of hillmen to acquire merit by giving him a rough blanket-coat. The lama was mildly surprised that any one should object to the knife-edged breezes which had cut the years off his shoulders.

"These are but the lower hills, *chela*. There is no cold till we come to the true Hills."

"Air and water are good, and the people are devout enough, but the food is very bad," Kim growled; "and we walk as though we were mad – or English. It freezes at night, too."

"A little, maybe; but only enough to make old bones rejoice in the sun. We must not always delight in soft beds and rich food."

"We might at the least keep to the road."

Kim had all a plainsman's affection for the well-trodden track, not six feet wide, that snaked among the mountains; but the lama, being Tibetan, could not refrain from short cuts over spurs and the rims of gravel-strewn slopes. As he explained to his limping disciple, a man bred among mountains can prophesy the course of a mountain road, and though low-lying clouds

Day after day they struck deeper into the huddled mountains.

might be a hindrance to a short-cutting stranger, they made no earthly difference to a thoughtful man. Thus, after long hours of what would be reckoned very fair mountaineering in civilized countries, they would pant over a saddleback, sidle past a few landslips, and drop through forest at an angle of forty-five on to the road again. Along their track lay the villages of the hill-folk – mud and earth huts, timbers now and then rudely carved with an axe – clinging like swallows' nests against the steeps, huddled on tiny flats half-way down a three-thousand-foot glissade; jammed into a corner between cliffs that funnelled and focused every wandering blast; or, for the sake of summer pasture, cowering down on a neck that in winter would be ten feet deep in snow. And the people – the sallow, greasy, duffle-clad people, with short bare legs and faces almost Esquimo – would flock out and adore. The Plains – kindly and gentle – had treated the lama as a holy man among holy men. But the Hills worshipped him as one in the confidence of all their devils. Theirs was an almost obliterated Buddhism, overlaid with a nature-worship fantastic as their own landscapes, elaborate as the terracing of their tiny fields; but they recognized the big hat, the clicking rosary, and the rare Chinese texts for great authority; and they respected the man beneath the hat.

"We saw thee come down over the black Breasts of Eua," said a Betah who gave them cheese, sour milk, and stone-hard bread one evening. "We do not use that often – except when calving cows stray in summer. There is a sudden wind among those stones that casts men down on the stillest day. But what should such folk care for the Devil of Eua!"

Then did Kim, aching in every fibre, dizzy with looking down, footsore with cramping desperate toes into inadequate crannies, take joy in the day's march – such joy as a boy of St Xavier's who had won the quarter-mile on the flat might take in the praises of his friends. The hills sweated the ghee and sugar suet off his bones; the dry air, taken sobbingly at the head of cruel passes, firmed and built out his upper ribs; and the tilted levels put new hard muscles into calf and thigh.

They meditated often on the Wheel of Life – the more so since, as the lama said, they were freed from its visible temptations. Except the grey eagle and an occasional far-seen bear grubbing and rooting on the hillside; a vision of a furious painted leopard met at dawn in a still valley devouring a goat; and now and again a bright-coloured bird, they were alone with the winds and the grass singing under the wind. The women of the smoky huts over whose roofs the two walked as they descended the mountains, were unlovely and unclean, wives of many husbands, and afflicted with goitre. The men were woodcutters when they were not farmers – meek, and of an incredible simplicity. But that suitable discourse might not fail, Fate sent them, overtaking and overtaken upon the road, the courteous Dacca physician, who paid for his food in ointments good for goitre and counsels that restore peace between men and women. He seemed to know these hills as well as he knew the hill dialects, and gave the lama the lie of the land towards Ladakh and Tibet. He said they could return to the Plains at any moment. Meantime, for such as loved mountains, yonder road might amuse. This was not all revealed in a breath, but at evening encounters on the stone threshing-floors, when, patients disposed of, the doctor would smoke and the lama snuff, while Kim watched the wee cows grazing on the house-tops, or threw his soul after his eye across the deep blue gulfs between range and range. And there were talks apart in the dark woods, when the doctor would seek herbs, and Kim, as budding physician, must accompany him.

"You see, Mister O'Hara, I do not know what the deuce-an'-all I shall do when I find our sporting friends; but if you will kindly keep within sight of my umbrella, which is fine fixed point for cadastral survey, I shall feel much better."

Kim looked out across the jungle of peaks. "This is not my country, *hakim*. Easier, I think, to find one louse in a bearskin."

"Oah, thatt is my strong points. There is no hurry for Hurree. They were at Leh not so long ago. They said they had come down from the Karakorum with their heads and horns and all. I am onlee afraid they will have sent back all their letters and compromising things from Leh into Russian terri-toree. Of course they will walk away as far to the east as possible – just to show that they were never among the western states. You do not know the Hills?" He scratched with a twig on the earth. "Look! They should have come in by Srinagar or Abbottabad. *Thatt* is their short road – down the river by Bunji and Astor. But they have made mischief in the west. So" – he drew a furrow from left to right – "they march and they march away east to Leh (ah! it is cold there), and down the Indus to Han-lé (I know that road), and then down, you see, to Bushahr and Chini valley. That is ascertained by process of elimination, and also by asking questions from people that I cure so well. Our friends have been a long time playing about and producing impressions. So they are well known from far off. You will see me catch them somewhere in Chini valley. Please keep your eye on the umbrella."

It nodded like a wind-blown harebell down the valleys and round the mountain sides, and in due time the lama and Kim, who steered by compass, would overhaul it, vending ointments and powders at eventide. "We came by such and such a way!" The lama would throw a careless finger backward at the ridges, and the umbrella would expend itself in compliments.

They crossed a snowy pass in cold moonlight, when the lama, mildly chaffing Kim, went through up to his knees, like a bactrian camel – the snow-bred, shag-haired sort that come into the Kashmir Serai. They dipped across beds of light snow and snow-powdered shale, where they took refuge from a gale in a camp of Tibetans hurrying down tiny sheep, each laden with a bag of borax. They came out upon grassy shoulders still snow-speckled, and through forest, to grass anew. For all their marchings, Kedarnath and Badrinath were not impressed; and it was only after days of travel that Kim, uplifted upon some insignificant ten-thousand-foot hummock, could see that a shoulder-knot or horn of the two great lords had – ever so slightly – changed outline.

At last they entered a world within a world – a valley of leagues where the high hills were fashioned of the mere rubble and refuse from off the knees of the mountains. Here one day's march carried them no farther, it seemed, than a dreamer's clogged pace bears him in a nightmare. They skirted a shoulder painfully for hours, and, behold, it was but an outlying boss in an outlying buttress of the main pile! A rounded meadow revealed itself, when they had reached it, for a vast tableland running far into the valley. Three days later, it was a dim fold in the earth to the southward.

"Surely the Gods live here!" said Kim, beaten down by the silence and the appalling sweep and dispersal of the cloud-shadows after rain. "This is no place for men!"

"Long and long ago," said the lama, as to himself, "it was asked of the Lord whether the world were everlasting. To this the Excellent One returned no answer... When I was in Ceylon, a wise Seeker confirmed that from the Gospel which is written in Pali. Certainly, since we know the way to Freedom, the question were unprofitable, but – look, and know illusion, *chela*! These are the true Hills! They are like my hills by Such-zen. Never were such hills!"

Above them, still enormously above them, earth towered away towards the snow-line, where from east to west across hundreds of miles, ruled as with a ruler, the last of the bold birches stopped. Above that, in scarps and blocks upheaved, the rocks strove to fight their heads above the white smother. Above these again, changeless since the world's beginning, but changing to every mood of sun and cloud, lay out the eternal snow. They could see blots and blurs on its face where storm and wandering wullie-wa got up to dance. Below them, as they stood, the forest slid away in a sheet of blue-green for mile upon mile; below the forest was a village in its sprinkle of terraced fields and steep grazing grounds. Below the village they knew, though a thunderstorm worried and growled there for the moment, a pitch of twelve or fifteen hundred feet gave to the moist valley where the streams gather that are the mothers of young Sutluj.

As usual, the lama had led Kim by cow-track and by-road, far from the main route along which Hurree Babu, that "fearful man", had bucketed three days before through a storm to which nine Englishmen out of ten would have given full right of way. Hurree was no game-shot – the snick of a trigger made him change colour – but, as he himself would have said, he was "fairly effeecient stalker", and he had raked the huge valley with a pair of cheap binoculars to some purpose. Moreover, the white of worn canvas tents against green carries far. Hurree Babu had seen all he wanted to see when he sat on the threshing-floor of Ziglaur, twenty miles away as the eagle flies, and forty by road – that is to say, two small dots which one day were just below the snow-line, and the next had moved downward perhaps six inches on the hillside. Once cleaned out and set to the work, his fat bare legs could cover a surprising amount of ground, and this was the reason why, while Kim and the lama lay in a leaky hut at Ziglaur till the storm should be overpast, an oily, wet, but always smiling Bengali, talking the best of English with the vilest of phrases, was ingratiating himself with two sodden and rather rheumatic foreigners. He had arrived, revolving many wild schemes, on the heels of a thunderstorm which had split a pine over against their camp, and so convinced a dozen or two forcibly impressed baggage-coolies the day was inauspicious for farther travel that with one accord they had thrown down their loads and jibbed. They were subjects of a hill rajah who farmed out their services, as is the custom, for his private gain; and, to add to their personal distresses, the strange sahibs had already threatened them with rifles. The most of them knew rifles and sahibs of old: they were trackers and *shikarris* of the northern valleys, keen after bear and wild goat; but they had never been thus treated in their lives. So the forest took them to her bosom, and, for all oaths and clamour, refused to restore. There was no need to feign madness or – the babu had thought of another means of securing a welcome. He wrung out his wet clothes, slipped on his patent-leather shoes, opened the blue-and-white umbrella, and with mincing gait and a heart beating against his tonsils appeared as "agent for His Royal Highness the Rajah of Rampur, gentlemen. What can I do for you, please?"

The gentlemen were delighted. One was visibly French, the other Russian, but they spoke English not much inferior to the babu's. They begged his kind offices. Their native servants had gone sick at Leh. They had hurried on because they were anxious to bring the spoils of the chase to Simla ere the skins grew moth-eaten. They bore a general letter of introduction (the babu salaamed to it orientally) to all government officials. No, they had not met any other shooting-parties *en route*. They did for themselves. They had plenty of supplies, They only wished to push on as soon as might be. At this he waylaid a cowering hillman among the trees, and after three minutes' talk and a little silver (one cannot be economical upon state service, though Hurree's heart bled at the waste) the eleven coolies and the three hangers-on reappeared. At least the babu would be a witness to their oppression.

"My royal master, he will be much annoyed, but these people are onlee common people and grossly ignorant. If your honours will kindly overlook unfortunate affair, I shall be much pleased. In a little while rain will stop and we can then proceed. You have been shooting, eh? That is fine performance!"

He skipped nimbly from one *kilta* to the next, making pretence to adjust each conical basket. The Englishman is not, as a rule, familiar with the

Asiatic, but he would not strike across the wrist a kindly babu who had accidentally upset a *kilta* with a red oilskin top. On the other hand, he would not press drink upon a babu were he never so friendly, nor would he invite him to meat. The strangers did all these things, and asked many questions – about women mostly – to which Hurree returned gay and unstudied answers. They gave him a glass of whitish fluid like to gin, and then more; and in a little time his gravity departed from him. He became thickly treasonous, and spoke in terms of sweeping indecency of a government which had forced upon him a white man's education and neglected to supply him with a white man's salary. He babbled tales of oppression and wrong till the tears ran down his cheeks for the miseries of his land. Then he staggered off, singing love-songs of Lower Bengal, and collapsed upon a wet tree-trunk. Never was so unfortunate a product of English rule in India more unhappily thrust upon aliens.

"They are all just of that pattern," said one sportsman to the other in French. "When we get into India proper thou wilt see. I should like to visit his rajah. One might speak the good word there. It is possible that he has heard of us and wishes to signify his goodwill."

"We have not time. We must get into Simla as soon as may be," his companion replied. "For my own part, I wish our reports had been sent back from Hilás, or even Leh."

"The English post is better and safer. Remember we are given all facilities – and Name of God! – they gave them to us too! Is it unbelievable stupidity?"

"It is pride – pride that deserves and will receive punishment."

"Yes! To fight a fellow-continental in our game is something. There is a risk attached, but these people – bah! It is too easy."

"Pride – all pride, my friend."

"Now what the deuce is good of Chandernagore being so close to Calcutta and all," said Hurree, snoring open-mouthed on the sodden moss, "if I cannot understand their French? They talk so particularly fast! It would have been much better to cut their beastly throats."

When he presented himself again he was racked with a headache – penitent, and volubly afraid that in his drunkenness he might have been indiscreet. He loved the British government – it was the source of all prosperity and honour, and his master at Rampur held the very same opinion. Upon this the men began to deride him and to quote past words, till step by step, with deprecating smirks, oily grins, and leers of infinite cunning, the poor babu was beaten out of his defences and forced to speak – truth. When Lurgan was told the tale later, he mourned aloud that he could not have been in the place of the stubborn, inattentive coolies, who with grass mats over their heads and the raindrops puddling in their footprints, waited on the weather. All the sahibs of their acquaintance – rough-clad men joyously returning year after year to their chosen gullies – had servants and cooks and orderlies, very often hillmen. These sahibs travelled without any retinue. Therefore they were poor sahibs, and ignorant; for no sahib in his senses would follow a Bengali's advice. But the Bengali, appearing from somewhere, had given them money, and could make shift with their dialect. Used to comprehensive ill-treatment from their own colour, they suspected a trap somewhere, and stood by to run if occasion offered.

Then through the new-washed air, steaming with delicious earth-smells, the babu led the way down the slopes – walking ahead of the coolies in pride; walking behind the foreigners in humility. His thoughts were many and various. The least of them would have interested his companions beyond words. But he was an agreeable guide, ever keen to point out the beauties of his royal master's domain. He peopled the hills with anything they had a mind to slay – thar, ibex, or markhor, and bear by Elisha's allowance. He discoursed of botany and ethnology with unimpeachable inaccuracy, and his store of local legends – he had been a trusted agent of the state for fifteen years, remember – was inexhaustible.

"Decidedly this fellow is an original," said the taller of the two foreigners. "He is like the nightmare of a Viennese courier."

"He represents in little India in transition – the monstrous hybridism of East and West," the Russian replied. "It is *we* who can deal with Orientals."

"He has lost his own country and has not acquired any other. But he has a most complete hatred of his conquerors. Listen. He confided to me last night," said the other.

Under the striped umbrella Hurree Babu was straining ear and brain to follow the quick-poured French, and keeping both eyes on a *kilta* full of maps and documents – an extra-large one with a double red oilskin cover.

He did not wish to steal anything. He only desired to know what to steal, and, incidentally, how to get away when he had stolen it. He thanked all the Gods of Hindustan, and Herbert Spencer, that there remained some valuables to steal.

On the second day the road rose steeply to a grass spur above the forest; and it was here, about sunset, that they came across an aged lama – but they called him a bonze – sitting cross-legged above a mysterious chart held down by stones, which he was explaining to a young man, evidently a neophyte, of singular, though unwashen, beauty. The striped umbrella had been sighted half a march away, and Kim had suggested a halt till it came up to them.

"Ha!" said Hurree Babu, resourceful as Puss-in-Boots. "That is eminent local holy man. Probably subject of my royal master."

"What is he doing? It is very curious."

"He is expounding holy picture – *all* hand-worked."

The two men stood bareheaded in the wash of the afternoon sunlight low across the gold-coloured grass. The sullen coolies, glad of the check, halted and slid down their loads.

"Look!" said the Frenchman. "It is like a picture for the birth of a religion – the first teacher and the first disciple. Is he a Buddhist?"

"Of some debased kind," the other answered. "There are no true Buddhists among the Hills. But look at the folds of the drapery. Look at his eyes – how insolent! Why does this make one feel that we are so young a people?" The speaker struck passionately at a tall weed. "We have nowhere left our mark yet. Nowhere! *That*, do you understand, is what disquiets me." He scowled at the placid face, and the monumental calm of the pose.

"Have patience. We shall make your mark together – we and you young people. Meantime, draw his picture."

The babu advanced loftily; his back out of all keeping with his deferential speech, or his wink towards Kim.

"Holy One, these be sahibs. My medicines cured one of a flux, and I go into Simla to oversee his recovery. They wish to see thy picture –"

"To heal the sick is always good. This is the Wheel of Life," said the lama, "the same I showed thee in the hut at Ziglaur when the rain fell."

"And to hear thee expound it."

The lama's eyes lighted at the prospect of new listeners. "To expound the Most Excellent Way is good. Have they any knowledge of Hindi, such as had the Keeper of Images?"

"A little, maybe."

Hereat, simply as a child engrossed with a new game, the lama threw back his head and began the full-throated invocation of the Doctor of Divinity ere he opens the full doctrine. The strangers leaned on their alpenstocks and listened. Kim, squatting humbly, watched the red sunlight on their faces, and the blend and parting of their long shadows. They wore un-English leggings and curious girt-in belts that reminded him hazily of the pictures in a book in St Xavier's library: *The Adventures of a Young Naturalist in Mexico* was its name. Yes, they looked very like the wonderful M. Sumichrast of that tale, and very unlike the "highly unscrupulous folk" of Hurree Babu's imagining. The coolies, earth-coloured and mute, crouched reverently some twenty or thirty yards away, and the babu, the slack of his thin gear snapping like a marking-flag in the chill breeze, stood by with an air of happy proprietorship.

"These are the men," Hurree whispered, as the ritual went on and the two whites followed the grass-blade sweeping from Hell to Heaven and back again. "All their books are in the large *kilta* with the reddish top – books and reports and maps – and I have seen a king's letter that either Hilás or Bunár has written. They guard it most carefully. They have sent nothing back from Hilás or Leh. That is sure."

"Who is with them?"

"Only the *beegar*-coolies. They have no servants. They are so close they cook their own food."

"But what am I to do?"

"Wait and see. Only if any chance comes to me thou wilt know where to seek for the papers."

"This were better in Mahbub Ali's hands than a Bengali's," said Kim scornfully.

"There are more ways of getting to a sweetheart than butting down a wall."

"See here the Hell appointed for avarice and greed. Flanked upon the one side by Desire and on the other by Weariness." The lama warmed to his work, and one of the strangers sketched him in the quick-fading light.

"That is enough," the man said at last brusquely. "I cannot understand him, but I want that picture. He is a better artist than I. Ask him if he will sell it."

"He says 'No, sar,'" the babu replied. The lama, of course, would no more have parted with his chart to a casual wayfarer than an archbishop would pawn the holy vessels of the cathedral. All Tibet is full of cheap reproductions of the Wheel; but the lama was an artist, as well as a wealthy abbot in his own place.

"Perhaps in three days, or four, or ten, if I perceive that the sahib is a Seeker and of good understanding, I may myself draw him another. But *this* was used for the initiation of a novice. Tell him so, *hakim*."

"He wishes it now – for money."

The lama shook his head slowly and began to fold up the Wheel. The Russian, on his side, saw no more than an unclean old man haggling over a dirty piece of paper. He drew out a handful of rupees, and snatched half-jestingly at the chart, which tore in the lama's grip. A low murmur of horror went up from the coolies – some of whom were Spiti men and, by their lights, good Buddhists. The lama rose at the insult; his hand went to the heavy iron pen-case that is the priest's weapon, and the babu danced in agony.

"Now you see – you see why I wanted witnesses. They are highly unscrupulous people. Oh, sar! sar! You must *not* hit holy man!"

"*Chela!* He has defiled the Written Word!"

It was too late. Before Kim could ward him off, the Russian struck the old man full on the face. Next instant he was rolling over and over downhill with Kim at his throat. The blow had waked every unknown Irish devil in the boy's blood, and the sudden fall of his enemy did the rest. The lama dropped to his knees, half-stunned; the coolies under their loads fled up the hill as fast as plainsmen run across the level. They had seen sacrilege unspeakable, and it behoved them to get away before the Gods and devils of the hills took vengeance. The Frenchman ran towards the lama, fumbling at his revolver with some notion of making him a hostage for his companion. A shower of cutting stones – hillmen are very straight shots – drove him away, and a coolie from Ao-chung snatched the lama

Next instant he was rolling over and over downhill with Kim at his throat.

into the stampede. All came about as swiftly as the sudden mountain darkness.

"They have taken the baggage and all the guns," yelled the Frenchman, firing blindly into the twilight.

"All right, sar! All right! Don't shoot. I go to rescue," and Hurree, pounding down the slope, cast himself bodily upon the delighted and astonished Kim, who was banging his breathless foe's head against a boulder.

"Go back to the coolies," whispered the babu in his ear. "They have the baggage. The papers are in the *kilta* with the red top, but look through all. Take their papers, and specially the *murasla* [king's letter]. Go! The other man comes!"

Kim tore uphill. A revolver bullet rang on a rock by his side, and he cowered partridge-wise.

"If you shoot," shouted Hurree, "they will descend and annihilate us. I have rescued the gentleman, sar. This is particularly dangerous."

"By Jove!" Kim was thinking hard in English. "This is dam'-tight place, but *I* think it is self-defence." He felt in his bosom for Mahbub's gift, and uncertainly – save for a few practice shots in the Bikanir desert, he had never used the little gun – pulled trigger.

"What did I say, sar!" The babu seemed to be in tears. "Come down here and assist to resuscitate. We are all up a tree, I tell you."

The shots ceased. There was a sound of stumbling feet, and Kim hurried upward through the gloom, swearing like a cat – or a country-bred.

"Did they wound thee, *chela*?" called the lama above him.

"No. And thou?" He dived into a clump of stunted firs.

"Unhurt. Come away. We go with these folk to Shamlegh-under-the-Snow."

"But not before we have done justice," a voice cried. "I have got the sahibs' guns – all four. Let us go down."

"He struck the Holy One – we saw it! Our cattle will be barren – our wives will cease to bear! The snows will slide upon us as we go home... Atop of all other oppression too!"

The little fir clump filled with clamouring coolies – panic-stricken, and in their terror capable of anything. The man from Ao-chung clicked the breech-bolt of his gun impatiently, and made as to go downhill.

"Wait a little, Holy One; they cannot go far. Wait till I return," said he.

"It is this person who has suffered wrong," said the lama, his hand over his brow.

"For that very reason," was the reply.

"If this person overlooks it, your hands are clean. Moreover, ye acquire merit by obedience."

"Wait, and we will all go to Shamlegh together," the man insisted.

For a moment, for just so long as it needs to stuff a cartridge into a breech-loader, the lama hesitated. Then he rose to his feet, and laid a finger on the man's shoulder.

"Hast thou heard? I say there shall be no killing – I who was Abbot of Such-zen. Is it any lust of thine to be re-born as a rat, or a snake under the eaves – a worm in the belly of the most mean beast? Is it thy wish to –"

The man from Ao-chung fell to his knees, for the voice boomed like a Tibetan devil-gong.

"Ai! ai!" cried the Spiti men. "Do not curse us – do not curse him. It was but his zeal, Holy One!... Put down the rifle, fool!"

"Anger on anger! Evil on evil! There will be no killing. Let the priest-beaters go in bondage to their own acts. Just and sure is the Wheel, swerving not a hair! They will be born many times – in torment." His head drooped, and he leaned heavily on Kim's shoulder.

"I have come near to great evil, *chela*," he whispered in that dead hush under the pines. "I was tempted to loose the bullet; and truly, in Tibet there would have been a heavy and a slow death for them... He struck me across the face... upon the flesh..." He slid to the ground, breathing heavily, and Kim could hear the over-driven heart bump and check.

"Have they hurt him to the death?" said the Ao-chung man, while the others stood mute.

Kim knelt over the body in deadly fear. "Nay," he cried passionately, "this is only a weakness." Then he remembered that he was a white man, with a white man's camp-fittings at his service. "Open the *kiltas*! The sahibs may have a medicine."

"Oho! Then I know it," said the Ao-chung man with a laugh. "Not for five years was I Yankling Sahib's *shikarri* without knowing that medicine. I too have tasted it. Behold!"

577

He drew from his breast a bottle of cheap whisky – such as is sold to explorers at Leh – and cleverly forced a little between the lama's teeth.

"So I did when Yankling Sahib twisted his foot beyond Astor. Aha! I have already looked into their baskets – but we will make fair division at Shamlegh. Give him a little more. It is good medicine. Feel! His heart goes better now. Lay his head down and rub a little on his chest. If he had waited quietly while I accounted for the sahibs this would never have come. But perhaps the sahibs may chase us here. Then it would not be wrong to shoot them with their own guns, heh?"

"One is paid, I think, already," said Kim between his teeth. "I kicked him in the groin as we went downhill. Would I had killed him!"

"It is well to be brave when one does not live in Rampur," said one whose hut lay within a few miles of the rajah's rickety palace. "If we get a bad name among the sahibs, none will employ us as *shikarris* any more."

"Oh, but these are not Angrezi sahibs – not merry-minded men like Fostum Sahib or Yankling Sahib. They are foreigners – they cannot speak Angrezi as do sahibs."

Here the lama coughed and sat up, groping for the rosary.

"There shall be no killing," he murmured. "Just is the Wheel! Evil on evil –"

"Nay, Holy One. We are all here." The Ao-chung man timidly patted his feet. "Except by thy order, no one shall be slain. Rest awhile. We will make a little camp here, and later, as the moon rises, we go to Shamlegh-under-the-Snow."

"After a blow," said a Spiti man sententiously, "it is best to sleep."

"There is, as it were, a dizziness at the back of my neck, and a pinching in it. Let me lay my head on thy lap, *chela*. I am an old man, but not free from passion… We must think of the Cause of Things."

"Give him a blanket. We dare not light a fire lest the sahibs see."

"Better get away to Shamlegh. None will follow us to Shamlegh."

This was the nervous Rampur man.

"I have been Fostum Sahib's *shikarri*, and I am Yankling Sahib's *shikarri*. I should have been with Yankling Sahib now but for this cursed *beegar* [the *corvée*]. Let two men watch below with the guns lest the sahibs do more foolishness. *I* shall not leave this Holy One."

They sat down a little apart from the lama, and, after listening awhile, passed round a water-pipe whose receiver was an old Day and Martin blacking-bottle. The glow of the red charcoal as it went from hand to hand lit up the narrow, blinking eyes, the high Chinese cheekbones, and the bull throats that melted away into the dark duffle folds round the shoulders. They looked like kobolds from some magic mine – gnomes of the hills in conclave. And while they talked, the voices of the snow-waters round them diminished one by one as the night-frost choked and clogged the runnels.

"How he stood up against us!" said a Spiti man admiring. "I remember an old ibex, out Ladakh way, that Dupont Sahib missed on a shoulder-shot, seven seasons back, standing up just like him. Dupont Sahib was a good *shikarri*."

"Not as good as Yankling Sahib." The Ao-chung man took a pull at the whisky bottle and passed it over. "Now hear me – unless any other man thinks he knows more."

The challenge was not taken up.

"We go to Shamlegh when the moon rises. There we will fairly divide the baggage between us. I am content with this new little rifle and all its cartridges."

"Are the bears only bad on thy holding?" said a mate, sucking at his pipe.

"No; but musk-pods are worth six rupees apiece now, and thy women can have the canvas of the tents and some of the cooking-gear. We will do all that at Shamlegh before dawn. Then we all go our ways, remembering that we have never seen or taken service with these sahibs, who may, indeed, say that we have stolen their baggage."

"That is well for thee, but what will our rajah say?"

"Who is to tell him? Those sahibs, who cannot speak our talk, or the babu, who for his own ends gave us money? Will *he* lead an army against us? What evidence will remain? That we do not need we shall throw on Shamlegh-midden, where no man has yet set foot."

"Who is at Shamlegh this summer?" The place was only a grazing centre of three or four huts.

"The Woman of Shamlegh. *She* has no love for sahibs, as we know. The

others can be pleased with little presents; and here is enough for us all."
He patted the fat sides of the nearest basket.

"But – but –"

"I have said they are not true sahibs. *All* their skins and heads were bought in the bazaar at Leh. I know the marks. I showed them to ye last march."

"True. They were all bought skins and heads. Some had even the moth in them."

That was a shrewd argument, and the Ao-chung man knew his fellows.

"If the worst comes to the worst, I shall tell Yankling Sahib, who is a man of a merry mind, and he will laugh. We are not doing any wrong to any sahibs whom we know. *They* are priest-beaters. They frightened us. We fled! Who knows where we dropped the baggage? Do ye think Yankling Sahib will permit down-country police to wander all over the hills, disturbing his game? It is a far cry from Simla to Chini, and farther from Shamlegh to Shamlegh-midden."

"So be it, but I carry the big *kilta*. The basket with the red top that the sahibs pack themselves every morning."

"Thus it is proved," said the Shamlegh man adroitly, "that they are sahibs of no account. Who ever heard of Fostum Sahib, or Yankling Sahib, or even the little Peel Sahib that sits up at nights to shoot serow – I say, who ever heard of these sahibs coming into the hills without a down-country cook, and a bearer, and – and all manner of well-paid, high-handed and oppressive folk in their tail? How can *they* make trouble? What of the *kilta*?"

"Nothing, but that it is full of the Written Word – books and papers in which they wrote, and strange instruments, as of worship."

"Shamlegh-midden will take them all."

"True! But how if we insult the sahibs' Gods thereby? I do not like to handle the Written Word in that fashion. And their brass idols are beyond my comprehension. It is no plunder for simple hill-folk."

"The old man still sleeps. Hst! We will ask his *chela*." The Ao-chung man refreshed himself, and swelled with pride of leadership.

"We have here," he whispered, "a *kilta* whose nature we do not know."

"But I do," said Kim cautiously. The lama drew breath in natural, easy sleep, and Kim had been thinking of Hurree's last words. As a player of the Great Game, he was disposed just then to reverence the babu. "It is a *kilta* with a red top full of very wonderful things, not to be handled by fools."

"I said it; I said it," cried the bearer of that burden. "Thinkest thou it will betray us?"

"Not if it be given to me. I can draw out its magic. Otherwise it will do great harm."

"A priest always takes his share." Whisky was demoralizing the Ao-chung man.

"It is no matter to me." Kim answered, with the craft of his mother-country. "Share it among you, and see what comes!"

"Not I. I was only jesting. Give the order. There is more than enough for us all. We go our way from Shamlegh in the dawn."

They arranged and rearranged their artless little plans for another hour, while Kim shivered with cold and pride. The humour of the situation tickled the Irish and the Oriental in his soul. Here were the emissaries of the dread Power of the North, very possibly as great in their own land as Mahbub or Colonel Creighton, suddenly smitten helpless. One of them, he privately knew, would be lame for a time. They had made promises to kings. Tonight they lay out somewhere below him, chartless, foodless, tentless, gunless – except for Hurree Babu, guideless. And this collapse of their Great Game (Kim wondered to whom they would report it), this panicky bolt into the night, had come about through no craft of Hurree's or contrivance of Kim's, but simply, beautifully, and inevitably as the capture of Mahbub's *fakir* friends by the zealous young policeman at Umballa.

"They are there – with nothing; and, by Jove, it is cold! I am here with all their things. Oh, they will be angry! I am sorry for Hurree Babu."

Kim might have saved his pity, for though at that moment the Bengali suffered acutely in the flesh, his soul was puffed and lofty. A mile down the hill, on the edge of the pine forest, two half-frozen men – one powerfully sick at intervals – were varying mutual recriminations with the most poignant abuse of the babu, who seemed distraught with terror. They demanded a plan of action. He explained that they were very lucky to be alive; that their coolies, if not then stalking them, had passed beyond-recall; that the rajah, his master, was ninety miles away, and, so far from lending them money and a retinue for the Simla journey, would surely cast them into prison if he heard that they had hit a priest. He enlarged on this sin and its consequences till they bade him change the subject. Their one hope, said he, was unostentatious flight from village to village till they reached civilization; and, for the hundredth time dissolved in tears, he demanded of the high stars why the sahibs "had beaten holy man".

Ten steps would have taken Hurree into the creaking gloom utterly beyond their reach – to the shelter and food of the nearest village, where glib-tongued doctors were scarce. But he preferred to endure cold, belly-pinch, bad words, and occasional blows in the company of his honoured employers. Crouched against a tree-trunk, he sniffed dolefully.

"And have you thought," said the uninjured man hotly, "what sort of spectacle we shall present wandering through these hills among these aborigines?"

Hurree Babu had thought of little else for some hours, but the remark was not to his address.

"We cannot wander! I can hardly walk," groaned Kim's victim.

"Perhaps the holy man will be merciful in loving-kindness, sar, otherwise –"

"I promise myself a peculiar pleasure in emptying my revolver into that young bonze when next we meet," was the unchristian answer.

"Revolvers! Vengeance! Bonzes!" Hurree crouched lower. The war was breaking out afresh. "Have you no consideration for our loss? The baggage! The baggage!" He could hear the speaker literally dancing on the grass. "Everything we bore! Everything we have secured! Our gains! Eight months' work! Do you know what that means? 'Decidedly it is we who can deal with Orientals!' Oh, you have done well."

They fell to it in several tongues, and Hurree smiled. Kim was with the *kiltas*, and in the *kiltas* lay eight months of good diplomacy. There was no means of communicating with the boy, but he could be trusted. For the rest, Hurree could so stage-manage the journey through the hills that Hilás, Bunár, and four hundred miles of hill roads should tell the tale for a generation. Men who cannot control their own coolies are little respected in the Hills, and the hillman has a very keen sense of humour.

"If I had done it myself," thought Hurree, "it would not have been better; and, by Jove, now I think of it, of course I arranged it myself. How quick I have been! Just when I ran downhill I thought it! Thee outrage was accidental, but onlee me could have worked it – ah – for all it was dam'-well worth. Consider the moral effect upon these ignorant peoples! No treaties – no papers – no written documents at all – and *me* to interpret for them. How I shall laugh with the Colonel! I wish I had their papers also: but you cannot occupy two places in space simultaneously. Thatt is axiomatic."

Chapter 14

My brother kneels (so saith Kabir)
  To stone and brass in heathen wise,
But in my brother's voice I hear
  My own unanswered agonies.
His God is as his Fates assign –
His prayer is all the world's – and mine.

                                    The Prayer

A t moonrise the cautious coolies got under way. The lama, refreshed by
his sleep and the spirit, needed no more than Kim's shoulder to bear
him along – a silent, swift-striding man. They held the shale-sprinkled grass
for an hour, swept round the shoulder of an immortal cliff, and climbed
into a new country entirely blocked off from all sight of Chini valley. A
huge pasture-ground ran up fan-shaped to the living snow. At its base was
perhaps half an acre of flat land, on which stood a few soil and timber huts.
Behind them – for, hill-fashion, they were perched on the edge of all things
– the ground fell sheer two thousand feet to Shamlegh-midden, where never
yet man has set foot.

The men made no motion to divide the plunder till they had seen the
lama bedded down in the best room of the place, with Kim shampooing
his feet, Muhammadan-fashion.

"We will send food," said the Ao-chung man, "and the red-topped *kilta*.
By dawn there will be none to give evidence, one way or the other. If anything
is not needed in the *kilta* – see here!"

He pointed through the window – opening into space that was filled

584

with moonlight reflected from the snow – and threw out an empty whisky bottle.

"No need to listen for the fall. This is the world's end," he said, and went out. The lama looked forth, a hand on either sill, with eyes that shone like yellow opals. From the enormous pit before him white peaks lifted themselves yearning to the moonlight. The rest was as the darkness of interstellar space.

"These," he said slowly, "are indeed my Hills. Thus should a man abide, perched above the world, separated from delights, considering vast matters."

"Yes; if he has a *chela* to prepare tea for him, and to fold a blanket for his head, and to chase out calving cows."

A smoky lamp burned in a niche, but the full moonlight beat it down; and by the mixed light, stooping above the food cups and bags, Kim moved like a tall ghost.

"*Ai!* But now I have let the blood cool, my head still beats and drums, and there is a cord round the back of my neck."

"No wonder. It was a strong blow. May he who dealt it –"

"But for my own passions there would have been no evil."

"What evil? Thou hast saved the sahibs from the death they deserved a hundred times."

"The lesson is not well learnt, *chela*." The lama came to rest on a folded blanket, as Kim went forward with his evening routine. "The blow was but a shadow upon a shadow. Evil in itself – my legs weary apace these latter days! – it met evil in me – anger, rage, and a lust to return evil. These wrought in my blood, woke tumult in my stomach, and dazzled my ears." Here he drank scalding block-tea ceremonially, taking the hot cup from Kim's hand. "Had I been passionless, the evil blow would have done only bodily evil – a scar, or a bruise – which is illusion. But my mind was *not* abstracted, for rushed in straightway a lust to let the Spiti men kill. In fighting that lust, my soul was torn and wrenched beyond a thousand blows. Not till I had repeated the Blessings" (he meant the Buddhist Beatitudes) "did I achieve calm. But the evil planted in me by that moment's carelessness works out to its end. Just is the Wheel, swerving not a hair! Learn the lesson, *chela*."

"It is too high for me," Kim muttered. "I am still all shaken. I am glad I hurt the man."

"I felt that, sleeping upon thy knees, in the wood below. It disquieted me in my dreams – the evil in thy soul working through to mine. Yet on the other hand" – he loosed his rosary – "I have acquired merit by saving two lives – the lives of those that wronged me. Now I must see into the Cause of Things. The boat of my soul staggers."

"Sleep, and be strong. That is wisest."

"I meditate. There is a need greater than thou knowest."

Till the dawn, hour after hour, as the moonlight paled on the high peaks, and that which had been belted blackness on the sides of the far hills showed as tender green forest, the lama stared fixedly at the wall. From time to time he groaned. Outside the barred door, where discomfited kine came to ask for their old stable, Shamlegh and the coolies gave itself up to plunder and riotous living. The Ao-chung man was their leader, and once they had opened the sahibs' tinned foods and found that they were very good they dared not turn back. Shamlegh kitchen-midden took the dunnage.

When Kim, after a night of bad dreams, stole forth to brush his teeth in the morning chill, a fair-coloured woman with turquoise-studded headgear drew him aside.

"The others have gone. They left thee this *kilta* as the promise was. I do not love sahibs, but thou wilt make us a charm in return for it: We do not wish little Shamlegh to get a bad name on account of the – accident. I am the Woman of Shamlegh." She looked him over with bold, bright eyes, unlike the usual furtive glance of hillwomen.

"Assuredly. But it must be done in secret."

She raised the heavy *kilta* like a toy and slung it into her own hut.

"Out and bar the door! Let none come near till it is finished," said Kim.

"But afterwards – we may talk?"

Kim tilted the *kilta* on the floor – a cascade of survey-instruments, books, diaries, letters, maps, and queerly scented native correspondence. At the very bottom was an embroidered bag covering a sealed, gilded, and illuminated document such as one king sends to another. Kim caught his breath with delight, and reviewed the situation from a sahib's point of view.

"The books I do not want. Besides, they are logarithms – survey, I suppose." He laid them aside. "The letters I do not understand, but Colonel Creighton will. They must all be kept. The maps – they draw better maps than me – *of* course. All the native letters – oho! – and particularly the *murasla*." He sniffed the embroidered bag. "That must be from Hilás or Bunár, and Hurree Babu spoke truth. By Jove! It is a fine haul. I wish Hurree could know... The rest must go out of the window." He fingered a superb prismatic compass and the shiny top of a theodolite. But after all, a sahib cannot very well steal, and the things might be inconvenient evidence later. He sorted out every scrap of manuscript, every map, and the native letters. They made one softish slab. The three locked ferril-backed books, with five worn pocket-books, he put aside.

"The letters and the *murasla* I must carry inside my coat and under my belt, and the handwritten books I must put into the food-bag. It will be very heavy. No. I do not think there is anything more. If there is, the coolies have thrown it down the *khud*, so *thatt* is all right. Now you go too." He repacked the *kilta* with all he meant to lose, and hove it up on to the windowsill. A thousand feet below lay a long, lazy, round-shouldered bank of mist, as yet untouched by the morning sun. A thousand feet below that was a hundred-year-old pine-forest. He could see the green tops looking like a bed of moss when a wind eddy thinned the cloud.

"No! I don't think any one will go after *you*!"

The wheeling basket vomited its contents as it dropped. The theodolite hit a jutting cliff ledge and exploded like a shell; the books, inkstands, paintboxes, compasses, and rulers showed for a few seconds like a swarm of bees. Then they vanished; and, though Kim, hanging half out of the window, strained his young ears, never a sound came up from the gulf.

"Five hundred – a thousand rupees could not buy them," he thought sorrowfully. "It was verree wasteful, but I have all their other stuff – everything they did – I hope. Now how the deuce am I to tell Hurree Babu, and *whatt* the deuce am I to do? And my old man is sick. I must tie up the letters in oilskin. That is something to do first – else they will get all sweated... And I am all alone!" He bound them into a neat packet, swedging down the stiff, sticky oilskin at the corners, for his roving life had made him as methodical as an old hunter in matters of the road.

Then with double care he packed away the books at the bottom of the food-bag.

The woman rapped at the door.

"But thou hast made no charm," she said, looking about.

"There is no need." Kim had completely overlooked the necessity for a little patter-talk. The woman laughed at his confusion irreverently.

"None – for thee. Thou canst cast a spell by the mere winking of an eye. But think of us poor people when thou art gone! They were all too drunk last night to hear a woman. Thou art not drunk?"

"I am a priest." Kim had recovered himself, and, the woman being aught but unlovely, thought best to stand on his office.

"I warned them that the sahibs will be angry and will make an inquisition and a report to the rajah. There is also the babu with them. Clerks have long tongues."

"Is that all thy trouble?" The plan rose fully formed in Kim's mind, and he smiled ravishingly.

"Not all," quoth the woman, putting out a hard brown hand all covered with turquoises set in silver.

"I can finish that in a breath," he went on quickly. "The babu is the very *hakim* (thou hast heard of him?) who was wandering among the hills by Ziglaur. I know him."

"He will tell for the sake of a reward. Sahibs cannot distinguish one hillman from another, but babus have eyes for men – and women."

"Carry a word to him from me."

"There is nothing I would not do for thee."

He accepted the compliment calmly, as men must in lands where women make the love, tore a leaf from a notebook, and with a patent indelible pencil wrote in gross Shikast – the script that bad little boys use when they write dirt on walls: "I have everything that they have written: their pictures of the country, and many letters. Especially the *murasla*. Tell me what to do. I am at Shamlegh-under-the-Snow. The old man is sick."

"Take this to him. It will altogether shut his mouth. He cannot have gone far."

"Indeed no. They are still in the forest across the spur. Our children went to watch them when the light came, and have cried the news as they moved."

Kim looked his astonishment; but from the edge of the sheep-pasture floated a shrill, kite-like trill. A child tending cattle had picked it up from a brother or sister on the far side of the slope that commanded Chini valley.

"My husbands are also out there gathering wood." She drew a handful of walnuts from her bosom, split one neatly, and began to eat. Kim affected blank ignorance.

"Dost thou not know the meaning of the walnut – priest?" she said coyly, and handed him the half-shells.

"Well thought of." He slipped the piece of paper between them quickly. "Hast thou a little wax to close them on this letter?"

The woman sighed aloud, and Kim relented.

"There is no payment till service has been rendered. Carry this to the babu, and say it was sent by the Son of the Charm."

"*Ai!* Truly! Truly! By a magician – who is like a sahib."

"Nay, a Son of the Charm: and ask if there be any answer."

"But if he offer a rudeness? I – I am afraid."

Kim laughed. "He is, I have no doubt, very tired and very hungry. The Hills make cold bedfellows. *Hai*, my" – it was on the tip of his tongue to say Mother, but he turned it to Sister – "though art a wise and witty woman. By this time all the villages know what has befallen the sahibs – eh?"

"True. News was at Ziglaur by midnight, and by tomorrow should be at Kotgarh. The villages are both afraid and angry."

"No need. Tell the villages to feed the sahibs and pass them on, in peace. We must get them quietly away from our valleys. To steal is one thing – to kill another. The babu will understand, and there will be no after-complaints. Be swift. I must tend my master when he wakes."

"So be it. After service – thou hast said? – comes the reward. I am the Woman of Shamlegh, and I hold from the rajah. I am no common bearer of babes. Shamlegh is thine: hoof and horn and hide, milk and butter. Take or leave."

She turned resolutely uphill, her silver necklaces clicking on her broad breast, to meet the morning sun fifteen hundred feet above them. This time

Kim thought in the vernacular as he waxed down the oilskin edges of the packets.

"How can a man follow the Way or the Great Game when he is so-always pestered by women? There was the girl at Akrola of the Ford: and there was the scullion's wife behind the dovecot – not counting the others – and now comes this one! When I was a child it was well enough, but now I am a man and they will not regard me as a man. Walnuts, indeed! Ho! ho! It is almonds in the plains!"

He went out to levy on the village – not with a begging-bowl, which might do for down-country, but in the manner of a prince. Shamlegh's summer population is only three families – four women and eight or nine men. They were all full of tinned meats and mixed drinks, from ammoniated quinine to white vodka, for they had taken their full share in the overnight loot. The neat continental tents had been cut up and shared long ago, and there were patent aluminium saucepans abroad.

But they considered the lama's presence a perfect safeguard against all consequences, and impenitently brought Kim of their best – even to a drink of *chang* – the barley-beer that comes from Ladakh way. Then they thawed out in the sun, and sat with their legs hanging over infinite abysses, chattering, laughing, and smoking. They judged India and its government solely from their experience of wandering sahibs who had employed them or their friends as *shikarris*. Kim heard tales of shots missed upon ibex, serow, or markhor, by sahibs twenty years in their graves – every detail lighted from behind like twigs on tree-tops seen against lightning. They told him of their little diseases, and, more important, the diseases of their tiny, sure-footed cattle; of trips as far as Kotgarh, where the strange missionaries live, and beyond even to marvellous Simla, where the streets are paved with silver, and any one, look you, can get service with the sahibs, who ride about in two-wheeled carts and spend money with a spade. Presently, grave and aloof, walking very heavily, the lama joined himself to the chatter under the eaves, and they gave him great room. The thin air refreshed him, and he sat on the edge of precipices with the best of them, and, when talk languished, flung pebbles into the void. Thirty miles away, as the eagle flies, lay the next range, seamed and channelled and pitted with little patches of brush – forests, each a day's dark march. Behind the village, Shamlegh hill itself cut off all view to southward. It was like sitting in a swallow's nest under the eaves of the roof of the world.

From time to time the lama stretched out his hand, and with a little low-voiced prompting would point out the road to Spiti and north across the Parungla.

"Beyond, where the hills lie thickest, lies De-ch'en" (he meant Han-lé), "the great monastery. s'Tag-stan-ras-ch'en built it, and of him there runs this tale." Whereupon he told it: a fantastic piled narrative of bewitchment and miracles that set Shamlegh a-gasping. Turning west a little, he speered for the green hills of Kulu, and sought Kailung under the glaciers. "For thither came I in the old, old day. From Leh I came, over the Baralachi."

"Yes, yes; we know it," said the far-faring people of Shamlegh.

"And I slept two nights with the priests of Kailung. These are the Hills of my delight! Shadows blessed above all other shadows! There my eyes opened on this world; there my eyes were opened to this world; there I found Enlightenment; and there I girt my loins for my Search. Out of the Hills I came – the high Hills and the strong winds. Oh, just is the Wheel!" He blessed them in detail – the great glaciers, the naked rocks, the piled moraines and tumbled shale; dry upland, hidden salt-lake, age-old timber and fruitful water-shot valley one after the other, as a dying man blesses his folk; and Kim marvelled at his passion.

"Yes – yes. There is no place like our Hills," said the people of Shamlegh. And they fell to wondering how a man could live in the hot terrible plains where the cattle run as big as elephants, unfit to plough on a hillside; where village touches village, they had heard, for a hundred miles; where folk went about stealing in gangs, and what the robbers spared the police carried utterly away.

So the still forenoon wore through, and at the end of it Kim's messenger dropped from the steep pasture as unbreathed as when she had set out.

"I sent a word to the *hakim*," Kim explained, while she made reverence.

"He joined himself to the idolaters? Nay, I remember he did a healing upon one of them. He has acquired merit, though the healed employed his strength for evil. Just is the Wheel! What of the *hakim*?"

"I feared that thou hadst been bruised and – and I knew he was wise."

Kim took the waxed walnut-shell and read in English on the back of his note: "Your favour received. Cannot get away from present company at present, but shall take them into Simla. After which, hope to rejoin you. Inexpedient to follow angry gentlemen. Return by same road you came, and will overtake. Highly gratified about correspondence due to my fore-thought." "He says, Holy One, that he will escape from the idolaters, and will return to us. Shall we wait awhile at Shamlegh, then?"

The lama looked long and lovingly upon the hills and shook his head.

"That may not be, *chela*. From my bones outward I do desire it, but it is forbidden. I have seen the Cause of Things."

"Why? When the Hills give thee back thy strength day by day? Remember we were weak and fainting down below there in the Doon."

"I became strong to do evil and to forget. A brawler and a swashbuckler upon the hillsides was I." Kim bit back a smile. "Just and perfect is the Wheel, swerving not a hair. When I was a man – a long time ago – I did pilgrimage to Guru Ch'wan among the poplars" (he pointed Bhotan-wards), "where they keep the Sacred Horse."

"Quiet, be quiet!" said Shamlegh, all arow. "He speaks of Jam-lin-nin-k'or, the Horse That Can Go round the World in a Day."

"I speak to my *chela* only," said the lama, in gentle reproof, and they scattered like frost on south eaves of a morning. "I did not seek truth in those days, but the talk of doctrine. All illusion! I drank the beer and ate the bread of Guru Ch'wan. Next day one said: 'We go out to fight Sangor Gutok down the valley to discover' (mark again how lust is tied to anger!) 'which abbot shall bear rule in the valley and take the profit of the prayers they print at Sangor Gutok.' I went, and we fought a day."

"But how, Holy One?"

"With our long pen-cases as I could have shown... I say, we fought under the poplars, both abbots and all the monks, and one laid open my forehead to the bone. See!" He tilted back his cap and showed a puckered silvery scar. "Just and perfect is the Wheel! Yesterday the scar itched, and after fifty years I recalled how it was dealt and the face of him who dealt it; dwelling a little in illusion. Followed that which thou didst see – strife and stupidity. Just is the Wheel! The idolater's blow fell upon the scar. Then I was shaken in my soul: my soul was darkened, and the boat of my soul rocked upon the waters of illusion. Not till I came to Shamlegh could I meditate upon the Cause of Things, or trace the running grass roots of Evil. I strove all the long night."

"But, Holy One, thou art innocent of all evil. May I be thy sacrifice!"

Kim was genuinely distressed at the old man's sorrow, and Mahbub Ali's phrase slipped out unawares.

"In the dawn," the lama went on more gravely, ready rosary clicking between the slow sentences, "came enlightenment. It is here... I am an old man... hill-bred, hill-fed, never to sit down among my Hills. Three years I travelled through Hind, but – can earth be stronger than Mother Earth? My stupid body yearned to the Hills and the snows of the Hills, from below there. I said, and it is true, my Search is sure. So, at the Kulu woman's house I turned hillward, over-persuaded by myself. There is no blame to the *hakim*. He – following Desire – foretold that the Hills would make me strong. They strengthened me to do evil, to forget my Search. I delighted in life and the lust of life. I desired strong slopes to climb. I cast about to find them. I measured the strength of my body, which is evil, against the high Hills. I made a mock of thee when thy breath came short under Jamnotri. I jested when thou wouldst not face the snow of the pass."

"But what harm? I *was* afraid. It was just. I am not a hillman; and I loved thee for thy new strength."

"More than once I remember" – he rested his cheek dolefully on his hand – "I sought thy praise and the *hakim's* for the mere strength of my legs. Thus evil followed evil till the cup was full. Just is the Wheel! All Hind for three years did me all honour. From the Fountain of Wisdom in the Wonder House to" – he smiled – "a little child playing by a big gun – the world prepared my road. And why?"

"Because we loved thee. It is only the fever of the blow. I myself am still sick and shaken."

"No! It was because I was upon the Way – tuned as are *si-nen* [cymbals] to the purpose of the Law. I departed from that ordinance. The tune was broken: followed the punishment. In my own Hills, on the edge of my own country, in the very place of my evil desire, comes the buffet – here!" (He touched his brow.) "As a novice is beaten when he misplaces the cups, so am I beaten, who was Abbot of Such-zen. No word, look you, but a blow, *chela.*"

"But the sahibs did not know thee, Holy One?"

"We were well matched. Ignorance and Lust met Ignorance and Lust upon the road, and they begat Anger. The blow was a sign to me, who am no better than a strayed yak, that my place is not here. Who can read the Cause of an act is half-way to Freedom! 'Back to the path,' says the Blow. 'The Hills are not for thee. Thou canst not choose Freedom and go in bondage to the delight of life.'"

"Would we had never met that cursed Russian!"

"Our Lord himself cannot make the Wheel swing backward. And for my merit that I had acquired I gain yet another sign." He put his hand in his bosom, and drew forth the Wheel of Life. "Look! I considered this after I had meditated. There remains untorn by the idolater no more than the breadth of my finger-nail."

"I see."

"So much, then, is the span of my life in this body. I have served the Wheel all my days. Now the Wheel serves me. But for the merit I have acquired in guiding thee upon the Way, there would have been added to me yet another life ere I had found my River. Is it plain, *chela*?"

Kim stared at the brutally disfigured chart. From left to right diagonally the rent ran – from the Eleventh House where Desire gives birth to the Child (as it is drawn by Tibetans) – across the human and animal worlds, to the Fifth House – the empty House of the Senses. The logic was unanswerable.

"Before our Lord won Enlightenment" – the lama folded all away with reverence – "he was tempted. I too have been tempted, but it is finished. The Arrow fell in the Plains – not in the Hills. Therefore, what make we here?"

"Shall we at least wait for the *hakim*?"

"I know how long I shall live in this body. What can a *hakim* do?"

"But thou art all sick and shaken. Thou canst not walk."

"How can I be sick if I see Freedom?" He rose unsteadily to his feet.

"Then I must get food from the village. Oh, the weary Road!" Kim felt that he too needed rest.

"That is lawful. Let us eat and go. The Arrow fell in the Plains... but I yielded to Desire. Make ready, *chela*."

Kim turned to the woman with the turquoise headgear who had been idly pitching pebbles over the cliff. She smiled very kindly.

"I found him like a strayed buffalo in a cornfield – the babu; snorting and sneezing with cold. He was so hungry that he forgot his dignity and gave me sweet words. The sahibs have nothing." She flung out an empty palm. "One is very sick about the stomach. Thy work?"

Kim nodded, with a bright eye.

"I spoke to the Bengali first – and to the people of a nearby village after. The sahibs will be given food as they need it – nor will the people ask money. The plunder is already distributed. The babu makes lying speeches to the sahibs. Why does he not leave them?"

"Out of the greatness of his heart."

"Was never a Bengali yet had one bigger than a dried walnut. But it is no matter... Now as to walnuts. After service comes reward. I have said the village is thine."

"It is my loss," Kim began. "Even now I had planned desirable things in my heart which" – there is no need to go through the compliments proper to these occasions. He sighed deeply... "But my master, led by a vision –"

"Huh! What can old eyes see except a full begging-bowl?"

"– turns from this village to the Plains again."

"Bid him stay."

Kim shook his head. "I know my Holy One, and his rage if he be crossed," he replied impressively. "His curses shake the Hills."

"Pity they did not save him from a broken head! I heard that thou wast the tiger-hearted one who smote the sahib. Let him dream a little longer. Stay!"

"Hillwoman," said Kim, with austerity that could not harden the outlines of his young oval face, "these matters are too high for thee."

"The Gods be good to us! Since when have men and women been other than men and women?"

"A priest is a priest. He says he will go upon this hour. I am his *chela*, and I go with him. We need food for the road. He is an honoured guest in all the villages, but" – he broke into a pure boy's grin – "the food here is good. Give me some."

"What if I do not give it thee? I am the woman of this village."

"Then I curse thee – a little – not greatly, but enough to remember." He could not help smiling.

"Thou hast cursed me already by the down-dropped eyelash and the uplifted chin. Curses? What should I care for mere words?" She clenched her hands upon her bosom... "But I would not have thee to go in anger, thinking hardly of me – a gatherer of cow-dung and grass at Shamlegh, but still a woman of substance."

"I think nothing," said Kim, "but that I am grieved to go, for I am very weary; and that we need food. Here is the bag."

The woman snatched it angrily. "I was foolish," said she. "Who is thy woman in the Plains? Fair or black? I was fair once. Laughest thou? Once, long ago, if thou canst believe, a sahib looked on me with favour. Once, long ago, I wore European clothes at the mission-house yonder." She pointed towards Kotgarh. "Once, long ago, I was Ker-lis-ti-an and spoke English – as the sahibs speak it. Yes. My sahib said he would return and wed me – yes, wed me. He went away – I had nursed him when he was sick – but he never returned. Then I saw that the Gods of the Kerlistians lied, and I went back to my own people... I have never set eyes on a sahib since. (Do not laugh at me. The fit is past, little priestling.) Thy face and thy walk and thy fashion of speech put me in mind of my sahib, though thou art only a wandering mendicant to whom I give a dole. Curse me? Thou canst neither curse nor bless!" She set her hands on her hips and laughed bitterly. "Thy Gods are lies; thy works are lies; thy words are lies. There are no Gods under all the Heavens. I know it... But for a while I thought it was my sahib come back, and he was my God. Yes, once I made music on a *pianno* in the mission-house at Kotgarh. Now I give alms to priests who are *heatthen*." She wound up with the English word, and tied the mouth of the brimming bag.

"I wait for thee, *chela*," said the lama, leaning against the door-post.

The woman swept the tall figure with her eyes. "He walk! He cannot cover half a mile. Whither would old bones go?"

At this Kim, already perplexed by the lama's collapse and foreseeing the weight of the bag, fairly lost his temper.

"What is it to thee, woman of ill-omen, where he goes?"

"Nothing – but something to thee, priest with a sahib's face. Wilt thou carry him on thy shoulders?"

"I go to the Plains. None must hinder my return. I have wrestled with my soul till I am strengthless. The stupid body is spent and we are far from the Plains."

"Behold!" she said simply, and drew aside to let Kim see his own utter helplessness. "Curse me. Maybe it will give him strength. Make a charm! Call on thy great God. Thou art a priest." She turned away.

The lama had squatted limply, still holding by the door-post. One cannot strike down an old man that he recovers again like a boy in a night. Weakness bowed him to the earth, but his eyes that hung on Kim were alive and imploring.

"It is all well," said Kim. "It is the thin air that weakens thee. In a little while we go! It is the mountain-sickness. I too am a little sick at stomach,"… and he knelt and comforted with such poor words as came first to his lips. Then the woman returned, more erect than ever.

"Thy Gods useless, heh? Try mine. *I* am the Woman of Shamlegh." She hailed hoarsely, and there came out of a cow-pen her two husbands and three others with a *dooli*, the rude native litter of the Hills, that they use for carrying the sick and for visits of state. "These cattle" – she did not condescend to look at them – "are thine for so long as thou shalt need."

"But we will not go Simla way. We will not go near the sahibs," cried the first husband.

"They will not run away as the others did, nor will they steal baggage. Two I know for weaklings. Stand to the rear-pole, Sonoo and Taree." They obeyed swiftly. "Lower now, and lift in that holy man. I will see to the village and your virtuous wives till ye return."

"When will that be?"

"Ask the priests. Do not pester me. Lay the food-bag at the foot, it balances better so."

"Oh, Holy One, thy Hills are kinder than our Plains!" cried Kim, relieved, as the lama tottered to the litter. "It is a very king's bed – a place of honour and ease. And we owe it to –"

"Lower now, and lift in that holy man."

"A woman of ill-omen. I need thy blessings as much as I do thy curses. It is *my* order and none of thine. Lift and away! Here! Hast thou money for the road?"

She beckoned Kim to her hut, and stooped above a battered English cash-box under her cot.

"I do not need anything," said Kim, angered where he should have been grateful. "I am already rudely loaded with favours."

She looked up with a curious smile and laid a hand on his shoulder. "At least, thank me. I am foul-faced and a hillwoman, but, as thy talk goes, I have acquired merit. Shall I show thee how the sahibs render thanks?" and her hard eyes softened.

"I am but a wandering priest," said Kim, his eyes lighting in answer. "Thou needest neither my blessings nor my curses."

"Nay. But for one little moment – thou canst overtake the *dooli* in ten strides – *if* thou wast a sahib, shall I show thee what thou wouldst do?"

"How if I guess, though?" said Kim, and putting his arm round her waist, he kissed her on the cheek, adding in English: "Thank you verree much, my dear."

Kissing is practically unknown among Asiatics, which may have been the reason that she leaned back with wide-open eyes and a face of panic.

"Next time," Kim went on, "you must not be so sure of your heatthen priests. Now I say goodbye." He held out his hand English-fashion. She took it mechanically. "Goodbye, my dear."

"Goodbye, and – and" – she was remembering her English words one by one – "you will come back again? Goodbye, and – thee God bless you."

Half an hour later, as the creaking litter jolted up the hill path that leads south-easterly from Shamlegh, Kim saw a tiny figure at the hut door waving a white rag.

"She has acquired merit beyond all others," said the lama. "For to set a man upon the way to Freedom is half as great as though she herself had found it."

"Umm," said Kim thoughtfully, considering the past. "It may be that I have acquired merit also... At least she did not treat me like a child." He hitched the front of his robe, where lay the slab of documents and maps, re-stowed the precious food-bag at the lama's feet, laid his hand on the litter's edge, and buckled down to the slow pace of the grunting husbands.

"These also acquire merit," said the lama, after three miles.

"More than that, they shall be paid in silver," quoth Kim. The Woman of Shamlegh had given it to him; and it was only fair, he argued, that her men should earn it back again.

Chapter 15

I'd not give room for an Emperor –
    I'd hold my road for a King.
To the Triple Crown I'd not bow down –
    But this is a different thing!
I'll not fight with the Powers of Air –
    Sentry, pass him through!
Drawbridge let fall – He's the Lord of us all –
    The Dreamer whose dream came true!
              The Siege of the Fairies

Two hundred miles north of Chini, on the blue shale of Ladakh, lies Yankling Sahib, the merry-minded man, spy-glassing wrathfully across the ridges for some sign of his pet tracker – a man from Ao-chung. But that renegade, with a new Männlicher rifle and two hundred cartridges, is elsewhere, shooting musk-deer for the market, and Yankling Sahib will learn next season how very ill he has been.

Up the valleys of Bushahr – the far-beholding eagles of the Himalayas swerve at his new blue-and-white gored umbrella – hurries a Bengali, once fat and well-looking, now lean and weather-worn. He has received the thanks of two foreigners of distinction, piloted not unskilfully to Mashobra tunnel, which leads to the great and gay capital of India. It was not his fault that, blanketed by wet mists, he conveyed them past the telegraph-station and European colony of Kotgarh. It was not his fault, but that of the Gods, of whom he discoursed so engagingly, that he led them into the borders of Nahan, where the rajah of that state mistook them for deserting British

soldiery. Hurree Babu explained the greatness and glory, in their own country, of his companions, till the drowsy kinglet smiled. He explained it to
every one who asked – many times – aloud – variously. He begged food,
arranged accommodation, proved a skilful leech for an injury of the groin
– such a blow as one may receive rolling down a rock-covered hillside in
the dark – and in all things indispensable. The reason of his friendliness did
him credit. With millions of fellow-serfs, he had learned to look upon Russia
as the great deliverer from the north. He was a fearful man. He had been
afraid that he could not save his illustrious employers from the anger of an
excited peasantry. He himself would just as lief hit a holy man as not, but…
He was deeply grateful and sincerely rejoiced that he had done his "little
possible" towards bringing their venture to – barring the lost baggage – a
successful issue. He had forgotten the blows; denied that any blows had
been dealt that unseemly first night under the pines. He asked neither pension
nor retaining fee, but, if they deemed him worthy, would they write him a
testimonial? It might be useful to him later, if others, their friends, came
over the passes. He begged them to remember him in their future great-
nesses, for he "opined subtly" that he, even he, Mohendro Lal Dutt, MA
of Calcutta, had "done the state some service".

They gave him a certificate praising his courtesy, helpfulness, and unerr-
ing skill as a guide. He put it in his waist-belt and sobbed with emotion;
they had endured so many dangers together. He led them at high noon
along crowded Simla Mall to the Alliance Bank of Simla, where they wished
to establish their identity. Thence he vanished like a dawn-cloud on
Jakko.

Behold him, too fine-drawn to sweat, too pressed to vaunt the drugs in
his little brass-bound box, ascending Shamlegh slope, a just man made
perfect. Watch him, all babudom laid aside, smoking at noon on a cot, while
a woman with turquoise-studded headgear points southeasterly across the
bare grass. Litters, she says, do not travel as fast as single men, but his birds
should now be in the Plains. The holy man would not stay though Lispeth
pressed him. The babu groans heavily, girds up his huge loins, and is off
again. He does not care to travel after dusk; but his days' marches – there
is none to enter them in a book – would astonish folk who mock at his
race. Kindly villagers, remembering the Dacca drug-vendor of two months

ago, give him shelter against evil spirits of the wood. He dreams of Bengali gods, university textbooks of education, and the Royal Society, London, England. Next dawn the bobbing blue-and-white umbrella goes forward.

On the edge of the Doon, Mussoorie well behind them and the Plains spread out in golden dust before, rests a worn litter in which – all the Hills know it – lies a sick lama who seeks a River for his healing. Villages have almost come to blows over the honour of bearing it, for not only has the lama given them blessings, but his disciple good money – full one-third sahibs' prices. Twelve miles a day has the *dooli* travelled, as the greasy, rubbed pole-ends show, and by roads that few sahibs use. Over the Nilang Pass in storm when the driven snow-dust filled every fold of the impassive lama's drapery; between the black horns of Raieng where they heard the whistle of the wild goats through the clouds; pitching and strained on the shale below; hard-held between shoulder and clenched jaw when they rounded the hideous curves of the Cut Road under Bhagirati; swinging and creaking to the steady jog-trot of the descent into the Valley of the Waters; pressed along the steamy levels of that locked valley; up, up and out again, to meet the roaring gusts off Kedarnath; set down of middays in the dun gloom of kindly oak forests; passed from village to village in dawn chill, when even devotees may be forgiven for swearing at impatient holy men; or by torchlight, when the least fearful think of ghosts – the *dooli* has reached her last stage. The little hill-folk sweat in the modified heat of the lower Siwaliks, and gather round the priests for their blessing and their wage.

"Ye have acquired merit," says the lama. "Merit greater than your knowing. And ye will return to the Hills," he sighs.

"Surely. The high Hills as soon as may be." The bearer rubs his shoulder, drinks water, spits it out again, and readjusts his grass sandal. Kim – his face is drawn and tired – pays very small silver from his belt, heaves out the food-bag, crams an oilskin packet – they are holy writings – into his bosom, and helps the lama to his feet. The peace has come again into the old man's eyes, and he does not look for the hills to fall down and crush him as he did that terrible night when they were delayed by the flooded river.

The men pick up the *dooli* and swing out of sight between the scrub clumps.

The lama raises a hand toward the rampart of the Himalayas. "Not with you, O blessed among all hills, fell the Arrow of Our Lord! And never shall I breathe your airs again!"

"But thou art ten times the stronger man in this good air," says Kim, for to his wearied soul appeal the well-cropped, kindly Plains. "Here, or hereabouts, fell the Arrow, yes. We will go very softly, perhaps a *koss* a day, for the Search is sure. But the bag weighs heavy."

"Ay, our Search is sure. I have come out of great temptation."

It was never more than a couple of miles a day now, and Kim's shoulders bore all the weight of it – the burden of an old man, the burden of the heavy food-bag with the locked books, the load of the writings on his heart, and the details of the daily routine. He begged in the dawn, set blankets for the lama's meditation, held the weary head on his lap through the noonday heats, fanning away the flies till his wrists ached, begged again in the evenings, and rubbed the lama's feet, who rewarded him with promise of Freedom – today, tomorrow, or, at furthest, the next day.

"Never was such a *chela*. I doubt at times whether Ananda more faithfully nursed Our Lord. And thou art a sahib? When I was a man – a long time ago – I forgot that. Now I look upon thee often, and every time I remember that thou art a sahib. It is strange."

"Thou hast said there is neither black nor white. Why plague me with this talk, Holy One? Let me rub the other foot. It vexes me. I am *not* a sahib. I am thy *chela*, and my head is heavy on my shoulders."

"Patience a little! We reach Freedom together. Then thou and I, upon the far bank of the River, will look back upon our lives as in the Hills we saw our days' marches laid out behind us. Perhaps I was once a sahib."

"Was never a sahib like thee, I swear it."

"I am certain the Keeper of the Images in the Wonder House was in past life a very wise abbot. But even his spectacles do not make my eyes see. There fall shadows when I would look steadily. No matter – we know the tricks of the poor stupid carcass – shadow changing to another shadow. I am bound by the illusion of Time and Space. How far came we today in the flesh?"

"Perhaps half a *koss*." (Three quarters of a mile, and it was a weary march.)

"Half a *koss*. Ha! I went ten thousand thousand in the spirit. How we are all lapped and swathed and swaddled in these senseless things." He looked at his thin blue-veined hand that found the beads so heavy. "*Chela*, hast thou never a wish to leave me?"

Kim thought of the oilskin packet and the books in the food-bag. If some one duly authorized would only take delivery of them the Great Game might play itself for aught he then cared. He was tired and hot in his head, and a cough that came from the stomach worried him.

"No," he said almost sternly. "I am not a dog or a snake to bite when I have learned to love."

"Thou art too tender towards me."

"Not that either. I have moved in one matter without consulting thee. I have sent a message to the Kulu woman by that woman who gave us the goat's milk this morn, saying that thou wast a little feeble and wouldst need a litter. I beat myself in my mind that I did not do it when we entered the Doon. We stay in this place till the litter returns."

"I am content. She is a woman with a heart of gold, as thou sayest, but a talker – something of a talker."

"She will not weary thee. I have looked to that also. Holy One, my heart is very heavy for my many carelessnesses towards thee." An hysterical catch rose in his throat. "I have walked thee too far: I have not picked good food always for thee; I have not considered the heat; I have talked to people on the road and left thee alone... I have – I have... *Hai mai!* But I love thee... and it is all too late... I was a child... Oh, why was I not a man?..." Overborne by strain, fatigue, and the weight beyond his years, Kim broke down and sobbed at the lama's feet.

"What a to-do is here!" said the old man gently. "Thou hast never stepped a hair's breadth from the Way of Obedience. Neglect *me*? Child, I have lived on thy strength as an old tree lives on the lime of a new wall. Day by day, since Shamlegh down, I have stolen strength from thee. *There-fore*, not through any sin of thine, art thou weakened. It is the Body – the silly, stupid Body – that speaks now. Not the assured Soul. Be comforted! Know at least the devils that thou fightest. They are earth-born – children of illusion. We will go to the woman from Kulu. She shall acquire merit in housing us, and specially in tending me. Thou shalt run free till strength returns. I had forgotten the stupid Body. If there be any blame, I bear it. But we are too close to the Gates of Deliverance to weigh blame. I could praise thee, but what need? In a little – in a very little – we shall sit beyond all needs."

And so he petted and comforted Kim with wise saws and grave texts on that little-understood beast, our Body, who, being but a delusion, insists on posing as the Soul, to the darkening of the Way, and the immense multiplication of unnecessary devils.

"*Hai! hai!* Let us talk of the woman from Kulu. Think you she will ask for another charm for her grandsons? When I was a young man, a very long time ago, I was plagued with these vapours – and some others – and I went to an abbot – a very holy man and a seeker after truth, though then I knew it not. Sit up and listen, child of my soul! My tale was told. Said he to me, '*Chela*, know this. There are many lies in the world, and not a few liars, but there are no liars like our bodies, except it be the sensations of our bodies.' Considering this I was comforted, and of his great favour he suffered me to drink tea in his presence. Suffer me now to drink tea, for I am thirsty."

With a laugh across his tears, Kim kissed the lama's feet and set about the tea-making.

"Thou leanest on me in the body, Holy One, but I lean on thee for some other things. Dost know it?"

"I have guessed maybe," and the lama's eyes twinkled. "We must change that."

So, when with scufflings and scrapings and a hot air of importance, paddled up nothing less than the Sahiba's pet palanquin sent twenty miles, with that same grizzled old Oorya servant in charge, and when they reached the disorderly order of the long white rambling house behind Saharunpore, the lama took his own measures.

Said the Sahiba cheerily from an upper window, after compliments: "What is the good of an old woman's advice to an old man? I told thee – I *told* thee, Holy One, to keep an eye upon the *chela*. How didst thou do it? Never answer me! *I* know. He has been running among the women. Look at his eyes – hollow and sunk – and the Betraying Line from the nose down! He has been sifted out! Fie! Fie! And a priest, too!"

Kim looked up, over-weary to smile, shaking his head in denial.

"Do not jest," said the lama. "That time is done. We are here upon great matters. A sickness of soul took me in the Hills, and him a sickness of the body. Since then I have lived upon his strength – eating him."

"Children together – young and old," she sniffed, but forbore to make any new jokes. "May this present hospitality restore ye! Hold awhile and I will come to gossip of the high good Hills."

At evening time – her son-in-law was returned, so she did not need to go on inspection round the farm – she won to the meat of the matter, explained low-voicedly by the lama. The two old heads nodded wisely together. Kim had reeled to a room with a cot in it, and was dozing soddenly. The lama had forbidden him to set blankets or get food.

"I know – I know. Who but I?" she cackled. "We who go down to the burning-ghats clutch at the hands of those coming up from the River of Life with full water-jars – yes, brimming water-jars. I did the boy wrong. He lent thee his strength? It is true that the old eat the young daily. Stands now we must restore him."

"Thou hast many times acquired merit –"

"*My* merit. What is it? Old bag of bones making curries for men who do not ask 'Who cooked this?' Now if it were stored up for my grandson –"

"He that had the belly-pain?"

"To think the Holy One remembers *that!* I must tell his mother. It is most singular honour! 'He that had the belly-pain' – straightway the Holy One remembered. She will be proud."

"My *chela* is to me as is a son to the unenlightened."

"Say grandson, rather. Mothers have not the wisdom of our years. If a child cries they say the heavens are falling. Now a grandmother is far enough separated from the pain of bearing and the pleasure of giving the breast to consider whether a cry is wickedness pure or the wind. And since thou speakest once again of wind, when last the Holy One was here, maybe I offended in pressing for charms."

"Sister," said the lama, using that form of address a Buddhist monk may sometimes employ towards a nun, "if charms comfort thee –"

"They are better than ten thousand doctors."

"I say, if they comfort thee, I who was Abbot of Such-zen, will make as many as thou mayest desire. I have never seen thy face –"

"*That* even the monkeys who steal our loquats count for a gain. Hee! hee!"

"But as he who sleeps there said," – he nodded at the shut door of the guest-chamber across the forecourt – 'thou hast a heart of gold… And he is in the spirit my very 'grandson' to me."

"Good! I am the Holy One's cow." This was pure Hinduism, but the lama never heeded. "I am old. I have borne sons in the body. Oh, once I could please men! Now I can cure them." He heard her armlets tinkle as though she bared arms for action. "I will take over the boy and dose him, and stuff him, and make him all whole. *Hai! hai!* We old people know something yet."

Wherefore when Kim, aching in every bone, opened his eyes, and would go to the cook-house to get his master's food, he found strong coercion about him, and a veiled old figure at the door, flanked by the grizzled manservant, who told him very precisely the things that he was on no account to do.

"Thou must have? Thou shalt have nothing. What? A locked box in which to keep holy books? Oh, that is another matter. Heavens forbid I should come between a priest and his prayers! It shall be brought, and thou shalt keep the key."

They pushed the coffer under his cot, and Kim shut away Mahbub's pistol, the oilskin packet of letters, and the locked books and diaries, with a groan of relief. For some absurd reason their weight on his shoulders was nothing to their weight on his poor mind. His neck ached under it of nights.

"Thine is a sickness uncommon in youth these days: since young folk have given up tending their betters. The remedy is sleep, and certain drugs," said the Sahiba; and he was glad to give himself up to the blankness that half menaced and half soothed him.

She brewed drinks, in some mysterious Asiatic equivalent to the still-room – drenches that smelt pestilently and tasted worse. She stood over Kim till they went down, and inquired exhaustively after they had come up. She laid a taboo upon the forecourt, and enforced it by means of an armed man. It is true he was seventy odd, that his scabbarded sword ceased at the hilt; but he represented the authority of the Sahiba, and loaded wains, chattering servants, calves, dogs, hens, and the like; fetched a wide compass by those parts. Best of all, when the body was cleared, she cut out from the mass of poor relations that crowded the back of the buildings – household dogs, we name them – a cousin's widow, skilled in what Europeans, who know nothing about it, call massage. And the two of them, laying him east and west, that the mysterious earth-currents which thrill the clay of our bodies might help and not hinder, took him to pieces all one long afternoon – bone by bone, muscle by muscle, ligament by ligament, and lastly, nerve by nerve. Kneaded to irresponsible pulp, half hypnotized by the perpetual flick and readjustment of the uneasy *chudders* that veiled their eyes, Kim slid ten thousand miles into slumber – thirty-six hours of it – sleep that soaked like rain after drought.

Then she fed him, and the house spun to her clamour. She caused fowls to be slain; she sent for vegetables, and the sober, slow-thinking gardener, nigh as old as she, sweated for it; she took spices, and milk, and onion, with little fish from the brooks – anon limes for sherbets, fat quails from the pits, then chicken livers upon a skewer, with sliced ginger between.

"I have seen something of the world," she said over the crowded trays, "and there are but two sorts of women in it – those who take the strength out of a man and those who put it back. Once I was that one, and now I am this. Nay – do not play the priestling with me. Mine was but a jest. If it does not hold good now, it will when thou takest the road again. Cousin," – this to the poor relation, never wearied of extolling her patroness's charity – "he is getting a bloom on the skin of a new-curried horse. Our work is like polishing jewels to be thrown to a dance-girl – eh?"

Kim sat up and smiled. The terrible weakness had dropped from him like an old shoe. His tongue itched for free speech again, and but a week back the lightest word clogged it like ashes. The pain in his neck (he must have caught it from the lama) had gone with the heavy dengue-aches and the evil taste in the mouth. The two old women, a little, but not much, more careful about their veils now, clucked as merrily as the hens that had entered pecking through the open door.

"Where is my Holy One?" he demanded.

"Hear him! Thy Holy One is well," she snapped viciously. "Though that is none of *his* merit. Knew I a charm to make him wise, I'd sell my jewels and buy it. To refuse good food that I cooked myself – and go roving into the fields for two nights on an empty belly – and to tumble into a brook at the end of it – call you *that* holiness? Then, when he has nearly broken what thou hast left of my heart with anxiety, he tells me that he has acquired merit. Oh, how like are all men! No, that was not it – he tells me that he is freed from all sin. *I* could have told him that before he wetted himself all over. He is well now – this happened a week ago – but burn me such holiness! A babe of three would do better. Do not fret thyself for the Holy One. He keeps both eyes on thee when he is not wading our brooks."

"I do not remember to have seen him. I remember that the days and nights passed like bars of white and black, opening and shutting. I was not sick: I was but tired."

"A lethargy that comes by right some few score years later. But it is done now."

"Maharanee," Kim began, but led by the look in her eye, changed it to the title of plain love – "Mother, I owe my life to thee. How shall I make thanks? Ten thousand blessings upon thy house and –"

"The house be unblessed!" (It is impossible to give exactly the old lady's word.) "Thank the Gods as a priest if thou wilt, but thank me, if thou carest, as a son. Heavens above! Have I shifted thee and lifted thee and slapped and twisted thy ten toes to find texts flung at my head? Somewhere a mother must have borne thee to break her heart. What used thou to her – son?"

"I had no mother, my mother," said Kim. "She died, they tell me, when I was young."

"*Hai mai!* Then none can say I have robbed her of any right if – when thou takest the road again and this house is but one of a thousand used for shelter and forgotten, after an easy-flung blessing. No matter. I need no blessings, but – but –" She stamped her foot at the poor relation. "Take up the trays to the house. What is the good of stale food in the room, O woman of ill-omen?"

"I ha – have borne a son in my time too, but he died," whimpered the bowed sister-figure behind the *chudder*. "Thou knowest he died! I only waited for the order to take away the tray."

"It is I that am the woman of ill-omen," cried the old lady penitently. "We that go down to the *chattris* [the big umbrellas above the burning-ghats where the priests take their last dues] clutch hard at the bearers of the *chattis* [water-jars – young folk full of the pride of life, she meant; but the pun is clumsy]. When one cannot dance in the festival one must e'en look out of the window, and grandmothering takes all a woman's time. Thy master gives me all the charms I now desire for my daughter's eldest, by reason – is it? – that he is wholly free from sin. The *hakim* is brought very low these days. He goes about poisoning my servants for lack of their betters."

"What *hakim*, mother?"

"That very Dacca man who gave me the pill which rent me in three pieces. He cast up like a strayed camel a week ago, vowing that he and thou had been blood-brothers together up Kulu way, and feigning great anxiety for thy health. He was very thin and hungry, so I gave orders to have him stuffed too – him and his anxiety!"

"I would see him if he is here."

"He eats five times a day, and lances boils for my hinds to save himself from an apoplexy. He is so full of anxiety for thy health that he sticks to the cookhouse door and stays himself with scraps. He will keep. We shall never get rid of him."

"Send him here, mother" – the twinkle returned to Kim's eye for a flash – "and I will try."

"I'll send him, but to chase him off is an ill turn. At least he had the sense to fish the Holy One out of the brook; thus, as the Holy One did *not* say, acquiring merit."

"He is a very wise *hakim*. Send him, mother."

"Priest praising priest? A miracle! If he is any friend of thine (ye squabbled at your last meeting) I'll hale him here with horse-ropes and – and give him a caste-dinner afterwards, my son... Get up and see the world! This lying abed is the mother of seventy devils... my son! my son!"

She trotted forth to raise a typhoon off the cookhouse, and almost on her shadow rolled in the babu, robed as to the shoulders like a Roman emperor, jowled like Titus, bare-headed, with new patent-leather shoes, in highest condition of fat, exuding joy and salutations.

"By Jove, Mister O'Hara, but I *am* jolly-glad to see you. I will kindly shut the door. It is a pity you are sick. Are you very sick?"

"The papers – the papers from the *kilta*. The maps and the *murasla*!" He held out the key impatiently; for the present need on his soul was to get rid of the loot.

"You are quite right. That is correct departmental view to take. You have got everything?"

"All that was handwritten in the *kilta* I took. The rest I threw down the hill." He could hear the key's grate in the lock, the sticky pull of the slow-rending oilskin, and a quick shuffling of papers. He had been annoyed out of all reason by the knowledge that they lay below him through the sick idle days – a burden incommunicable. For that reason the blood tingled through his body, when Hurree, skipping elephantinely, shook hands again.

"This is fine! This is finest! Mister O'Hara! You have – ha! ha! – swiped the whole bag of tricks – locks, stocks, and barrels. They told me it was eight months' work gone up the spouts! By Jove, how they beat me!... Look, here is the letter from Hilás!" He intoned a line or two of Court Persian, which is the language of authorized and unauthorized diplomacy. "Mister Rajah Sahib has just about put his foot in the holes. He will have to explain offeecially how the deuce-an' – all he is writing love-letters to the Tsar. And they are very clever maps... and there is three or four prime ministers of these parts implicated by the correspondence. By Gad, sar! The British government will change the succession in Hilás and Bunár, and nominate new heirs to the throne. 'Trea-son most base'... but you do not understand? Eh?"

"Are they in thy hands?" said Kim. It was all he cared for.

"Just you jolly-well bet yourself they are." He stowed the entire trove about his body, as only Orientals can. "They are going up to the office too. The old lady thinks I am a permanent fixture here, but I shall go away with these straight off – immediately. Mr Lurgan will be proud man. You are offeecially subordinate to me, but I shall embody your name in my verbal report. It is a pity we are not allowed written reports. We

Bengalis excel in thee exact science." He tossed back the key and showed the box empty.

"Good. That is good. I was very tired. My Holy One was sick, too. And did he fall into –"

"Oah yess. I am his good friend, I tell you. He was behaving very strange when I came down after you, and I thought perhaps he might have the papers. I followed him on his meditations, and to discuss ethnological points also. You see, I am verree small person here nowadays, in comparison with all his charms. By Jove, O'Hara, do you know, he is afflicted with infirmity of fits. Yess, I tell you. Cataleptic, too, if not also epileptic. I found him in such a state under a tree *in articulo mortem*, and he jumped up and walked into a brook and he was nearly drowned but for me. I pulled him out."

"Because I was not there!" said Kim. "He might have died."

"Yes, he might have died, but he is dry now, and asserts he has undergone transfiguration." The babu tapped his forehead knowingly. "I took notes of his statements for Royal Society – *in posse*. You must make haste and be quite well and come back to Simla, and I will tell you all my tale at Lurgan's. It was splendid. The bottoms of their trousers were *quite* torn, and old Nahan Rajah, he thought they were European soldiers deserting."

"Oh, the Russians? How long were they with thee?"

"One was a Frenchman. Oh, days and days and days! Now all the hill-people believe all Russians are all beggars. By Jove! they had not one dam'-thing that I did not get them. And I told the common people – oah, *such* tales and anecdotes! I will tell you at old Lurgan's when you come up. We will have – ah – a night out! It is feather in both our caps! Yess, and they gave me a certificate. That is creaming joke. You should have seen them at the Alliance Bank identifying themselves! And thank Almighty God you got their papers so well! You do not laugh verree much, but you shall laugh when you are well. Now I will go straight to the railway and get out. You shall have all sorts of credits for your game. When do you come along? We are very proud of you though you gave us great frights. And especially Mahbub."

"Ay, Mahbub. And where is he?"

"Selling horses in this vi-cinity, of course."

"Here! Why? Speak slowly. There is a thickness in my head still."

The babu looked shyly down his nose. "Well, you see, I am a fearful man, and I do not like responsibility. You were sick, you see, and I did not know where deuce-an'-all the papers were, and if so, how many. So when I had come down here I slipped in private wire to Mahbub – he was at Meerut for races – and I tell him how case stands. He comes up with his men and he consorts with the lama, and then he calls me a fool, and is very rude –"

"But wherefore – wherefore?"

"That is what *I* ask. I only suggest that if any one steals the papers I should like some good strong, brave men to rob them back again. You see, they are vitally important, and Mahbub Ali he did not know where you were."

"Mahbub Ali to rob the Sahiba's house? Thou art mad, Babu," said Kim with indignation.

"I wanted the papers. Suppose she had stole them? It was only practical suggestion, *I* think. You are not pleased, eh?"

A native proverb – unquotable – showed the blackness of Kim's disapproval.

"Well," – Hurree shrugged his shoulders – "there is no accounting for thee taste. Mahbub was angry too. He has sold horses all about here, and he says old lady is *pukka* [thorough] old lady and would not condescend to such ungentlemanly things. *I* do not care. I have got the papers, and I was very glad of moral support from Mahbub. I tell you, I am fearful man, but, somehow or other, the more fearful I am the more dam'-tight places I get into. So I was glad you came with me to Chini, and I am glad Mahbub was close by. The old lady she is sometimes very rude to me and my beautiful pills."

"Allah be merciful!" said Kim on his elbow, rejoicing. "What a beast of wonder is a babu! And that man walked alone – if he did walk – with robbed and angry foreigners!"

"Oah, thatt was nothing, after they had done beating me; but if I lost the papers it was pretty-jolly serious. Mahbub he nearly beat me too, and he went and consorted with the lama no end. I shall stick to ethnological investigations henceforwards. Now goodbye, Mister O'Hara. I can catch 4.25 p.m. to Umballa if I am quick. It will be good times when we all tell thee tale up at Mr Lurgan's. I shall report you offeecially better. Goodbye, my dear fallow, and when next you are under thee emotions please do not use the Muhammadan terms with the Tibetan dress."

He shook hands twice – a babu to his boot-heels – and opened the door. With the fall of the sunlight upon his still triumphant face he returned to the humble Dacca quack.

"He robbed them," thought Kim, forgetting his own share in the game. "He tricked them. He lied to them like a Bengali. They gave him a *chit* [a testimonial]. He makes them a mock at the risk of his life – *I* never would have gone down to them after the pistol shots – and then he says he is a fearful man... And he *is* a fearful man. I must get into the world again."

At first his legs bent like bad pipe-stems, and the flood and rush of the sunlit air dazzled him. He squatted by the white wall, the mind rummaging among the incidents of the long *dooli* journey, the lama's weaknesses, and, now that the stimulus of talk was removed, his own self-pity, of which, like the sick, he had great store. The unnerved brain edged away from all the outside, as a raw horse, once rowelled, sidles from the spur. It was enough, amply enough, that the spoil of the *kilta* was away – off his hands – out of his possession. He tried to think of the lama – to wonder why he had stumbled into a brook – but the bigness of the world, seen between the forecourt gates, swept linked thought aside. Then he looked upon the trees and the broad fields, with the thatched huts hidden among crops – looked with strange eyes unable to take up the size and proportion and use of things – stared for a still half-hour. All that while he felt, though he could not put it into words, that his soul was out of gear with its surroundings – a cog-wheel unconnected with any machinery, just like the idle cog-wheel of a cheap Beheea sugar-crusher laid by in a corner. The breezes fanned over him, the parrots shrieked at him, the noises of the populated house behind – squabbles, orders, and reproofs – hit on dead ears.

"I am Kim. I am Kim. And what is Kim?" His soul repeated it again and again.

He did not want to cry – had never felt less like crying in his life – but of a sudden easy, stupid tears trickled down his nose, and with an almost audible click he felt the wheels of his being lock up anew on the world without. Things that rode meaningless on the eyeball an instant before slid into proper proportion. Roads were meant to be walked upon, houses to be lived in, cattle to be driven, fields to be tilled, and men and women to be talked to. They were all real and true – solidly planted upon the feet – perfectly comprehensible – clay of his clay, neither more nor less. He shook himself like a dog with a flea in his ear, and rambled out of the gate. Said the Sahiba, to whom watchful eyes reported this move: "Let him go. I have done my share. Mother Earth must do the rest. When the Holy One comes back from meditation, tell him."

There stood an empty bullock-cart on a little knoll half a mile away, with a young banyan tree behind – a lookout, as it were, above some new-ploughed levels; and his eyelids, bathed in soft air, grew heavy as he neared it. The ground was good clean dust – no new herbage that, living, is half-way to death already, but the hopeful dust that holds the seeds of all life. He felt it between his toes, patted it with his palms, and joint by joint, sighing luxuriously, laid him down full length along in the shadow of the wooden-pinned cart. And Mother Earth was as faithful as the Sahiba. She breathed through him to restore the poise he had lost lying so long on a cot cut off from her good currents. His head lay powerless upon her breast, and his opened hands surrendered to her strength. The many-rooted tree above him, and even the dead manhandled wood beside, knew what he sought, as he himself did not know. Hour upon hour he lay deeper than sleep.

Towards evening, when the dust of returning kine made all the horizons smoke, came the lama and Mahbub Ali, both afoot, walking cautiously, for the house had told them where he had gone.

"Allah! What a fool's trick to play in open country!" muttered the horse-dealer. "He could be shot a hundred times – but this is not the border."

"And," said the lama, repeating a many-times-told tale, "never was such a *chela*. Temperate, kindly, wise, of ungrudging disposition, a merry heart upon the road, never forgetting, learned, truthful, courteous. Great is his reward!"

"I know the boy – as I have said."

"And he was all of those things?"

"Some of them – but I have not yet found a Red Hat's charm for making him overly truthful. He has certainly been well nursed."

"The Sahiba is a heart of gold," said the lama earnestly. "She looks upon him as her son."

"Hmph! Half Hind seems that way disposed. I only wished to see that the boy had come to no harm and was a free agent. As thou knowest, he and I were old friends in the first days of your pilgrimage together."

"That is a bond between us." The lama sat down. "We are at the end of the pilgrimage."

"No thanks to thee thine was not cut off for good and all a week back. I heard what the Sahiba said to thee when we bore thee up on the cot." Mahbub laughed, and tugged his newly dyed beard.

"I was meditating upon other matters that tide. It was the *hakim* from Dacca broke my meditations."

"Otherwise" – this was in Pushtu for decency's sake – "thou wouldst have ended thy meditations upon the sultry side of Hell – being an unbeliever and an idolater for all thy child's simplicity. But now, Red Hat, what is to be done?"

"This very night," – the words came slowly, vibrating with triumph – "this very night he will be as free as I am from all taint of sin – assured as I am, when he quits this body, of Freedom from the Wheel of Things. I have a sign" – he laid his hand above the torn chart in his bosom – "that my time is short; but I shall have safeguarded him throughout the years. Remember, I have reached Knowledge, as I told thee only three nights back."

"It must be true, as the Tirah priest said when I stole his cousin's wife, that I am a Sufi [a free-thinker]; for here I sit," said Mahbub to himself, "drinking in blasphemy unthinkable… I remember the tale. On that, then, he goes to *Jannatu l'Adn* [the Gardens of Eden]. But how? Wilt thou slay him or drown him in that wonderful river from which the babu dragged thee?"

"I was dragged from no river," said the lama simply. "Thou hast forgotten what befell. I found it by Knowledge."

"Oh, ay. True," stammered Mahbub, divided between high indignation and enormous mirth. "I had forgotten the exact run of what happened. Thou didst find it knowingly."

"And to say that I would take life is – not a sin, but a madness simple. My *chela* aided me to the River. It is his right to be cleansed from sin – with me."

"Ay, he needs cleansing. But afterwards, old man – afterwards?"

"What matter under all the Heavens? He is sure of Nibban – enlightened – as I am."

"Well said. I had a fear he might mount Muhammad's Horse and fly away."

"Nay – he must go forth as a teacher."

"Aha! Now I see! That is the right gait for the colt. Certainly he must go forth as a teacher. He is somewhat urgently needed as a scribe by the state, for instance."

"To that end he was prepared. I acquired merit in that I gave alms for his sake. A good deed does not die. He aided me in my Search. I aided him in his. Just is the Wheel, O horse-seller from the North. Let him be a teacher; let him be a scribe – what matter? He will have attained Freedom at the end. The rest is illusion."

"What matter? When I must have him with me beyond Balkh in six months! I come up with ten lame horses and three strong-backed men – thanks to that chicken of a babu – to break a sick boy by force out of an old trot's house. It seems that I stand by while a young sahib is hoisted into Allah knows what of an idolater's Heaven by means of old Red Hat. And I am reckoned something of a player of the Game myself! But the madman is fond of the boy; and I must be very reasonably mad too."

"What is the prayer?" said the lama, as the rough Pushtu rumbled into the red beard.

"No matter at all; but now I understand that the boy, sure of Paradise, can yet enter government service, my mind is easier. I must get to my horses. It grows dark. Do not wake him. I have no wish to hear him call thee master."

"But he *is* my disciple. What else?"

"He has told me." Mahbub choked down his touch of spleen and rose laughing. "I am not altogether of thy faith, Red Hat – if so small a matter concern thee."

"It is nothing," said the lama.

"I thought not. Therefore it will not move thee, sinless, new-washed and three parts drowned to boot, when I call thee a good man – a very good man. We have talked together some four or five evenings now, and for all I am a horse-coper I can still, as the saying is, see holiness beyond the legs of a horse. Yea, can see, too, how our Friend of all the World put his hand in thine at the first. Use him well, and suffer him to return to the world as a teacher, when thou hast – bathed his legs, if that be the proper medicine for the colt."

"Why not follow the Way thyself, and so accompany the boy?"

Mahbub stared stupefied at the magnificent insolence of the demand, which across the border he would have paid with more than a blow. Then the humour of it touched his worldly soul.

"Softly – softly – one foot at a time, as the lame gelding went over the Umballa jumps. I may come to Paradise later – I have workings that way – great motions – and I owe them to thy simplicity. Thou hast never lied?"

"What need?"

"O Allah, hear him! 'What need' in this thy world! Nor ever harmed a man?"

"Once – with a pen-case – before I was wise."

"So? I think the better of thee. Thy teachings are good. Thou hast turned one man that I know from the path of strife." He laughed immensely. "He came here open-minded to commit a *dacoity* [a house-robbery with violence]. Yes, to cut, rob, kill, and carry off what he desired."

"A great foolishness!"

"Oh! black shame too. So he thought after he had seen thee – and a few others, male and female. So he abandoned it; and now he goes to beat a big fat babu man."

"I do not understand."

"Allah forbid it! Some men are strong in knowledge, Red Hat. Thy strength is stronger still. Keep it – I think thou wilt. If the boy be not a good servant, pull his ears off."

With a hitch of his broad Bokhariot belt the Pathan swaggered off into the gloaming, and the lama came down from his clouds so far as to look at the broad back.

"That person lacks courtesy, and is deceived by the shadow of appearances. But he spoke well of my *chela*, who now enters upon his reward. Let me make the prayer!... Wake, O fortunate above all born of women. Wake! It is found!"

Kim came up from those deep wells, and the lama attended his yawning pleasure; duly snapping fingers to head off evil spirits.

"I have slept a hundred years. Where –? Holy One, hast *thou* been here long? I went out to look for thee, but" – he laughed drowsily – "I slept by the way. I am all well now. Hast thou eaten? Let us go to the house. It is many days since I tended thee. And the Sahiba fed thee well? Who shampooed thy legs? What of the weaknesses – the belly and the neck, and the beating in the ears?"

"Gone – all gone. Dost thou not know?"

"I know nothing, but that I have not seen thee in a monkey's age. Know what?"

"Strange the knowledge did not reach out to thee, when all my thoughts were theeward."

"I cannot see the face, but the voice is like a gong. Has the Sahiba made a young man of thee by her cookery?"

He peered at the cross-legged figure, outlined jet-black against the lemon-coloured drift of light. So does the stone Bodhisat sit who looks down upon the patent self-registering turnstiles of the Lahore Museum.

The lama held his peace. Except for the click of the rosary and a faint *clop-clop* of Mahbub's retreating feet, the soft, smoky silence of evening in India wrapped them close.

"Hear me! I bring news."

"But let us –"

Out shot the long yellow hand compelling silence. Kim tucked his feet under his robe-edge obediently.

"Hear me! I bring news! The Search is finished. Comes now the Reward... Thus. When we were among the Hills, I lived on thy strength till the young branch bowed and nigh broke. When we came out of the Hills, I was troubled for thee and for other matters which I held in my heart. The boat of my soul lacked direction; I could not see into the Cause of Things. So I gave thee over to the virtuous woman altogether. I took no food. I drank no water. Still I saw not the Way. They pressed food upon me and cried at my shut door. So I removed myself to a hollow under a tree. I took no food. I took no water. I sat in meditation two days and two nights, abstracting my mind; inbreathing and outbreathing in the required manner... Upon the

"… the hakim from Dacca bore up my head in the waters of the River."

621

second night – so great was my reward – the wise Soul loosed itself from the silly Body and went free. This I have never before attained, though I have stood on the threshold of it. Consider, for it is a marvel!"

"A marvel indeed. Two days and two nights without food! Where was the Sahiba?" said Kim under his breath.

"Yea, my Soul went free, and, wheeling like an eagle, saw indeed that there was no Teshoo Lama nor any other soul. As a drop draws to water, so my Soul drew near to the Great Soul which is beyond all things. At that point, exalted in contemplation, I saw all Hind, from Ceylon in the sea to the Hills, and my own Painted Rocks at Such-zen; I saw every camp and village, to the least, where we have ever rested. I saw them at one time and in one place; for they were within the Soul. By this I knew the Soul had passed beyond the illusion of Time and Space and of Things. By this I knew that I was free. I saw thee lying in thy cot, and I saw thee falling downhill under the idolater – at one time, in one place, in my Soul, which, as I say, had touched the Great Soul. Also I saw the stupid body of Teshoo Lama lying down, and the *hakim* from Dacca kneeled beside, shouting in its ear. Then my Soul was all alone, and I saw nothing, for I was all things, having reached the Great Soul. And I meditated a thousand thousand years, passionless, well aware of the Causes of all Things. Then a voice cried: 'What shall come to the boy if thou art dead?' and I was shaken back and forth in myself with pity for thee; and I said: 'I will return to my *chela*, lest he miss the Way.' Upon this my Soul, which is the Soul of Teshoo Lama, withdrew itself from the Great Soul with strivings and yearnings and retchings and agonies not to be told. As the egg from the fish, as the fish from the water, as the water from the cloud, as the cloud from the thick air, so put forth, so leaped out, so drew away, so fumed up the Soul of Teshoo Lama from the Great Soul. Then a voice cried: 'The River! Take heed to the River!' and I looked down upon all the world, which was as I had seen it before – one in time, one in place – and I saw plainly the River of the Arrow at my feet. At that hour my Soul was hampered by some evil or other whereof I was not wholly cleansed, and it lay upon my arms and coiled round my waist; but I put it aside, and I cast forth as an eagle in my flight for the very place of the River. I pushed aside world upon world for thy sake. I saw the River below me – the River of the Arrow – and, descending, the waters of it closed over me; and behold I was again in the body of Teshoo Lama, but free from sin, and the *hakim* from Dacca bore up my head in the waters of the River. It is here! It is behind the mango tope here – even here!"

"*Allah kerim!* Oh, well that the babu was by! Wast thou very wet?"

"Why should I regard? I remember the *hakim* was concerned for the body of Teshoo Lama. He haled it out of the holy water in his hands, and there came afterwards thy horse-seller from the north with a cot and men, and they put the body on the cot and bore it up to the Sahiba's house."

"What said the Sahiba?"

"I was meditating in that body, and did not hear. So thus the Search is ended. For the merit that I have acquired, the River of the Arrow is here. It broke forth at our feet, as I have said. I have found it. Son of my Soul, I have wrenched my Soul back from the Threshold of Freedom to free thee from all sin – as I am free, and sinless! Just is the Wheel! Certain is our deliverance! Come!"

He crossed his hands on his lap and smiled, as a man may who has won salvation for himself and his beloved.